CIRCLE OF BLOOD:

BOOKS 1 - 3

Other books by R. A. Steffan

The Horse Mistress: Book 1
The Horse Mistress: Book 2
The Horse Mistress: Book 3
The Horse Mistress: Book 4
The Complete Horse Mistress Collection

The Lion Mistress: Book 1
The Lion Mistress: Book 2
The Lion Mistress: Book 3
The Complete Lion Mistress Collection

Antidote: Love and War, Book 1

The Queen's Musketeers: Book 1
The Queen's Musketeers: Book 2
The Queen's Musketeers: Book 3
The D'Artagnan Collection: Books 1-3
The Queen's Musketeers: Book 4

Sherlock Holmes & The Case of the Magnate's Son

Diamond Bar Apha Ranch
Diamond Bar Alpha 2: Angel & Vic
(with Jaelynn Woolf)

CIRCLE OF BLOOD:

BOOKS 1 - 3

R. A. STEFFAN & JAELYNN WOOLF

Circle of Blood: Books 1 - 3

For information, contact the author at
http://www.rasteffan.com/contact/

First Edition: March 2018

INTRODUCTION

This series contains graphic violence and explicit sexual content. It is intended for a mature audience. While Books 1-3 are part of a series with an over-arching plot, they can be read as standalones with "happy ever after" endings for the three couples, and a satisfying resolution of the storylines. If you don't intend to continue the series, you may wish to avoid the Book Three epilogue.

TABLE OF CONTENTS

CIRCLE OF BLOOD, BOOK ONE:

LOVER'S REBIRTH

R. A. STEFFAN & JAELYNN WOOLF

ONE

Human blood always tasted sweetest when the world was falling apart around you. That indisputable fact was one of the great ironies of vampirism, Tré reflected. It was a bone-deep truth that spoke to the bottomless well of darkness within his soul—if he could still lay claim to having such a human thing as a soul, at any rate.

Once, he had been Vladimir Illych Romanov III, a man of importance, respected by all. Now, he was merely Tré, a shadow hidden among shadows, lost in the night.

What was left of Tré's soul was little more than a tattered flag planted on a barren, muddy hill where the battle had already been lost, and the war had moved on to richer, more fertile fields. A remnant. An overlooked scrap too unimportant to bother tearing down and burning.

Yes, that was his soul in a nutshell. His soul, and the souls of his fellow vampires.

The unremarkable blond-haired, hazel-eyed young human currently slumped in Tré's strong grip shifted restlessly, a low moan slipping free from his throat. Tré could feel the vibration beneath his lips, through his sensitive fangs.

Reluctantly, he disengaged. Around him, the shadowed corridor at the back of the seedy New Orleans nightclub slipped back into focus, the sound of jazz replacing the low, steady *shush-shush, shush-shush* of a human heart pumping blood through veins and arteries.

A few drops of that sweet, sweet blood dribbled from the neat bite mark over the kid's jugular before the healing power of Tré's saliva sealed the two small, circular wounds. Tré swiped the trickle of red with his thumb and licked it clean.

Destroying the evidence.

His victim that night was a typical Midwest frat boy, drawn to the Big Easy by the siren call of plentiful alcohol and loose morals in the run-up to Mardi Gras. He'd made the drunken mistake of wandering off on his own after his friends decided to head back to their hotel, and now he'd become lunch for an apex predator.

Fortunately for him, however, the days of Tré's uncontrollable bloodlust and hunger were long past. This particular plain-faced prey animal would live to enjoy his hangover in the morning, with nothing more than an additional bit of weakness and dizziness to encourage him to make better life choices in the future.

As if the phrase *better life choices* had been some sort of mental summons, Xander chose that moment to stick his head around the corner.

He took in the scene and raised an eyebrow. "Oy, fearless leader—stop playing with your food, and let's get a move on. Sun'll be up soon, and even the rioters over in the Lower Ninth Ward are probably ready to call it a night at this point."

The broad vowels of Old London were out of place amongst the rich Creole drawl of the city's natives. Other than that, however, Xander fit right in with his tailored trousers, leather shoes polished to a high shine, and black silk shirt open at the neck—a shameless hedonist to the core.

Xander's pupils were blown wide and dark. Tré wondered if he'd managed to find a heroin addict to drink from tonight.

Again.

The blond frat boy grunted and scrubbed a shaky hand over his face. "Oh, wow," he said. The voice of middle America. The wholesome boy next door. "Sorry I checked out on you like that, bro." He reeled a bit, and Tré steadied him. "Not sure what happened there. Maybe I had... had a bit too much to drink?" He laughed awkwardly. "So... um, right. Sorry. What were we talking about, again?"

"It's not important," Tré told him. "You have your phone?"

The boy fumbled in his pocket and nodded, still dazed.

"Call a cab," Tré ordered, making eye contact and placing a bit of will behind the words.

The frat kid nodded. "Yeah, I'll... uh... I'll just call a cab now, I think. Anyway, it was good hangin' with you, man—"

Tré didn't bother to reply, already turning away to join Xander as they headed for the back door of the club.

"You seen Duchess?" Xander asked, as they exited into the humid winter chill of the Louisiana predawn.

The lazy energy of the city at night prickled against Tré's skin, sharper than usual and with a heavy air of anticipation that he didn't much like.

"Not since she disappeared into one of the back rooms earlier, with a couple of boy toys in tow," he said, unconcerned.

"In her element, then," Xander observed. The words were wry. "Guess she'll make her way back in her own time. Or not, as the case may be." He took a deep breath, as if scenting the air. "Something's off today. S'like a storm coming. But not an *actual* storm, you know? Can't say I'm too broken up about it. It's getting boring just waiting around for something new to happen. You can feel it too, right?"

"Yes," Tré said. "I can feel it, too."

Xander drew the night air into his lungs again, and rolled his neck from side to side, the vertebrae popping one after the other. "Damn. That was some *really* good smack, Tré. Even second-hand. We should totally go clubbing more often."

Around them, the city held its breath. Waiting.

-o-o-o-

These days, Delaney LeBlanc dreamed in riddles.

A swirl of hazy, nonsensical images. The touch of a hand, rough calluses dragging against the soft skin of her cheek as she smiled and pressed into the contact. Whispered words in a half forgotten language. Children's laughter. The purr of a cat and the excited yip of a dog. The chatter of voices speaking words that seemed both strange and strikingly familiar. If she listened just a bit more closely, she'd be able to understand them, she was sure —

Della woke with a start, dizzy from the series of disconnected scenes that had haunted her sleep. Rolling onto an elbow, she glanced at the glowing red numbers of the clock on her bedside table and groaned.

"*Argh*! It's *four-thirty in the morning*. What the hell, brain?" she rasped, the plaintive question disappearing into the silent room around her. The darkness did not reply.

Her long honey-colored hair, insane from restless sleep, was plastered against her face, a tangled mess on top of her head. Flipping it back, she sat up in bed and started to comb her fingers through it, attempting to soothe her raw nerves with the mindless, repetitive motion. As the tangles came free, she closed her eyes, carding her fingers slowly through the heavy length. Feeling her heartbeat gradually slow.

The dream had made no sense, but it had still felt *so real*. Della couldn't quite shake the feeling that she'd had the same dream before, many times, always culminating in waking up early with this disconcerting feeling of loss and need. It was almost as though she were seeing images from someone else's life. Someone she had long forgotten, like a childhood friend.

Of course, that was absurd. She had grown up in suburban New Jersey. None of her usual playmates had spoken a different language. And that part of the dream was *very* clear in her mind. What perplexed her most, however, was that she felt she should have no trouble understanding the voices of the happy children who chattered away in — what language could it be?

She had no idea. It didn't sound like French, or Spanish, or German, or any language she'd heard people speak in the real world.

Probably something I've made up, which is why I feel like I should be able to understand it, Della thought with a yawn. *Dreams are weird. It's just my subconscious blowing off steam. I hope.*

Della decided that her subconscious must be really messed up, given how bizarre her nighttime visions had grown of late. Sometimes, she felt like she was going honest-to-god insane, a feeling heightened by the stress and anxiety she had been under recently.

Not wanting to start her thoughts down that particular path this early in the morning, Della threw her legs over the side of her bed and stood up, toes digging into the deep shag of the carpet. With the ease of long practice, she flipped on the lamp beside her bed without looking and straightened, reaching for the ceiling, as high as her arms would go.

She stretched her short, five-foot frame as far as she could, feeling her joints pop and crack in protest. Wriggling her toes, Della concentrated on the sensations under her feet and throughout her body, dragging her attention away from the dream images and into the present. Where it belonged.

Focus, girl, she coached herself, trying to shake the disturbing remnants of her subconscious delusions. *Life goes a lot smoother when you pay attention to the real world, not an imaginary one.*

When she felt awake and more or less calm, she padded across the bedroom and slipped out into the main room of her dark apartment. The gloom this morning felt oppressive. Not at all like the cozy, sleepy stillness that had greeted her early morning habits in years past. This darkness felt malicious and full of intent.

She suppressed a shudder and fumbled for the light switch. With her living room bathed in the harsh yellow light of cheap, compact fluorescent light bulbs, Della blinked and glanced around, checking for an intruder. She felt like she was being watched from the shadows, yet she was completely alone in her apartment.

She sighed, suddenly weary.

Jesus. I'm getting paranoid. Maybe I need to go to the doctor for something to help me sleep better, because this is getting ridiculous. If I don't get at least a few uninterrupted of hours of rest tonight, I'm going to start hallucinating pink elephants instead of imaginary burglars.

Della stifled an ugly snort of laughter at the irony. She already felt like she was losing her mind without adding sleep deprivation on top of everything else.

"Coffee," she muttered aloud, heading into the kitchen to brew a pot. Maybe she would go into the office early today and get a few reports done. Might as well be a productive insomniac.

When she was growing up, Della had never once fantasized about being the receptionist for a small insurance company in New Orleans. Yet, despite all her good intentions, here she was, stuck in a dead end job and with no prospect of changing that fact or moving on to better things.

Life had been going okay until just a few years ago. For a given definition of *okay*, at any rate. Her family was kind of a train wreck, admittedly. Her older sister had been killed in a car crash when Della was ten, and the strain of the tragedy had eventually driven her parents apart. Her mom eventually remarried, to a guy Della could barely stand. Her dad had pulled away, to the point that her only contact with him was an occasional stilted email on her birthday or Christmas, when he didn't forget. With her grandparents dead and no real contact with her far-flung aunts and uncles, she was essentially alone.

That was all right, though. She loved her parents, of course, but it was a remote, intellectual sort of love. The kind that was better served by distance. When she'd headed off to college, rather than homesickness, she'd felt... *relief*. She'd graduated four years later with a degree in graphic design and started working for a greeting card company, putting together cover samples to be vetted by a panel of marketing analysts.

The job was great, the money was decent, and she lived comfortably in an apartment about two miles from work. On beautiful days, she had been able to walk there with a friend. Even though it seemed like everything was going perfectly, Della had struggled with feeling out of step with the world around her. It was a feeling of waiting for the other shoe to drop. Like the calm before a thunderstorm.

Maybe that was why she had a lot of trouble understanding—or sympathizing with—her peers' petty concerns about boyfriends, hair, drama, celebrities, and fashion. Oh, she would smile politely and tell them she loved their new outfits and would exclaim in horror when her friends complained that their most recent dates never responded to their text messages, but on the inside, Della had a deep longing for something more. Something *real*. Something that had meaning beyond the shallow, two-dimensional lives the others around her seemed to be leading.

Be careful what you wish for, right?

She'd had a couple of good years at the greeting card company before the market plummeted suddenly and they had been forced to downsize. Della's job was eliminated and she was laid off with a modest severance package.

The memory still brought the ridiculous burn of tears to her eyes. She swiped a hand across her face and shoveled spoonful after spoonful of coffee grounds into the white filter. She needed something strong this morning to combat her sleepless night.

"Coffee should put hair on your chest," her late grandmother used to say, while making a brew so bitter that Della's jaw hurt while she drank it.

The memory brought a wistful smile to her lips as she started the brewing cycle. Soon, the smell of fresh coffee wafted through her kitchen, waking her more effectively than anything else could have.

If there was one thing that defined Della, it was her ability to survive. She had taken some hard knocks in life, but she prided herself on her ability to come up swinging every time. After being let go from her job in Hoboken, Della decided that it was the perfect opportunity for her to pursue a secret dream she had long harbored in the back of her mind.

Della's father's family had originally come up from New Orleans in the early 1900s. She had never been able to visit the city as a child, but after learning about her family's history, she became fascinated by the rich culture and vibrant soul that seemed to explode from the seams of the city, as if it could not be contained.

Even though she had no connections there, she had packed up all of her possessions in one small moving truck and driven southwest until she reached Louisiana. Within a few days, she found a relatively inexpensive apartment a few blocks away from A.L. Davis Park, and applied for several jobs in the design field.

It quickly became apparent, however, that she needed to set her sights lower. She settled for a receptionist position with Lighthouse Insurance Company, telling herself it was only until she landed something better. That had been more than a year ago. And, although she was fond enough of her coworkers and her boss, the pay was barely sufficient to keep her afloat in the small one-bedroom apartment she rented.

The benefits are very competitive, I think you'll find. She could practically hear the weary hopefulness in the owner's voice as he'd conducted her second interview — hoping that she'd accept the position; hoping that he wouldn't have to go through the hiring process again a month from now.

And so, there she remained. Too loyal to leave the company for another dead-end job outside of her field. Too poor to look for a different place to live. Feeling like she was way past her expiration date. Her life was boring and quiet, yet not the quiet of peace. It was the quiet of vague, half-hearted desperation, struggling beneath a thick layer of inertia. Della knew she was just waiting for something big and inevitable to happen, even if she had no idea when it would occur or what form it would take.

How long can I keep doing this? It was the constant mantra in her life. *What happens when I can't any more?*

Of course, it wasn't as if she thought she was the only one. No, Della knew that it wasn't just her life that seemed to be teetering on the edge of some precipice. She could barely turn on the television without hearing horrific stories of rapes, kidnappings, stabbings, mass shootings, bombings, and natural disasters that claimed the lives of innocent people going about their day-to-day business. The growing wave of fear and violence was like an infection, spreading across the world, into every town and every city.

New Orleans was no different. In fact, it seemed like in the last few months, things here had gone from bad to worse. There was rioting and violence in the city almost every night now, occurring at rates that baffled FBI crime statisticians and forensic psychologists. No one could explain why everything seemed to be going wrong all at once.

"It's like living in a freaking war zone," one of her coworkers had said in frustration, after being mugged outside a restaurant the evening before. "All we need now is for another hurricane to hit us. That would just be icing on the cake."

Della could only nod sympathetically and murmur vague agreement. Things really were out of control, as if more and more people were losing their minds and turning into wild animals, preying on the weak.

Well, at least she wasn't alone in the *losing her mind* department.

These depressing early morning thoughts swirled around her brain, not helping with the fuzziness caused by lack of sleep. She sighed and rubbed gritty eyes. Since her damn coffee wasn't ready yet, she'd have to take more direct action to shake the fretful worries still clinging to her like shadows.

"I need a shower," she told her goldfish, Jewel, who was swimming sedately around her fishbowl. Della wasn't allowed to have pets other than fish in her apartment, so she talked to the little creature like it was a dog or a cat. It felt good knowing she had something to come home to, even if it *was* just a stupid fish.

Fifteen minutes later, she was slumped forehead-first against the cool plastic liner of the walk-in shower. Hot water pounded against her back, relaxing tense muscles that felt like they had been knotted for weeks. Afterward, as Della flicked water off her skin with a towel, she caught a whiff of coffee coming under the door of her small bathroom.

Wrapping up in a fuzzy robe, she walked out into the kitchen and poured a much needed cup. Despite the scalding temperature, she took several deep gulps, feeling her eyes water from the heat.

Thank God for coffee. Now I'm finally ready to face this day.

I hope.

-o-o-o-

At five minutes to seven, Della unlocked the office door and slid inside with a sigh of relief. She hated walking alone through her neighborhood in the early morning darkness to get to her tram stop, but thankfully most of the crazies seemed to have either gone home or passed out in the gutter by the time she ventured forth today.

The streetcar operator looked about as frazzled and red-eyed as she felt, but he'd at least spared her a strained smile when he glanced at her phone to check her thirty-one-day RTA pass as she boarded at Third Street, in the Garden District. The tram was nearly deserted. She huddled in a seat near the back, cardigan wrapped around her body to hold the late February chill at bay.

One transfer to the Canal Street line, followed by another ten-minute walk, brought her to the unprepossessing brick and concrete building that housed the insurance agency. There was a musty smell in the air as she flipped on all the lights. The carpet was old and as the humidity started to rise in the mornings, the smell would begin to rise as well.

Her desk was neat and comfortingly familiar, with the picture of her family—before a drunk driver had taken Jaymie away from them—set in a modest frame near the back edge. Her area was situated near the front door where she could greet any visitors, but could also assist the insurance agents with anything they needed, back in their offices. Besides her direct boss, Rich, there were three other women, two agents and an office manager, along with two other men who worked at Lighthouse.

It wouldn't be long before her coworkers would begin arriving, she knew. She was looking forward to the hustle and bustle of people around her. The noise would be welcome after feeling as though the silence around her was pressing on her, like someone trying to suffocate her with a pillow.

To dispel the image and the unnatural quiet, Della flipped on the small radio she kept on her desk. She always turned the station to the oldies, because they rarely played any current news reports. She was beyond tired of hearing about all the death and violence around her. She didn't need a reminder of it every hour of every day.

The sound of the music relaxed her. It helped to keep some of her jitters at bay. Even so, she was really happy when Ryan and Sean showed up an hour and fifteen minutes later.

"Good morning," Della said, knowing her smile must look forced and unconvincing.

They both murmured good morning, Ryan yawning widely behind his hand.

"You're here early," Sean observed.

"Yeah, couldn't sleep. Thought I might as well be productive."

"That's mighty enterprising of you," Ryan answered in a deep southern drawl. His kind brown eyes twinkled at her as he made his way towards his office.

Della turned back towards her computer screen and started sorting through emails. She flagged a few on her to-do list, and decided that she could get started on this month's expense reports.

The day passed without serious incident, although after the first couple of hours, the familiar tedium seemed to bore into Della in a way that nearly drove her crazy. By lunchtime, she wished she could go home, but then she remembered that she was likely to face another lonely and restless night of disturbing dreams.

I just can't win, no matter what I do, she thought miserably. She really was starting to feel like she was losing her mind. *Maybe I do need to go see a doctor or something. This can't be right — I don't think normal people feel this way all the time. I just need to sleep. That would make everything a hell of a lot easier.*

"Hey, Earth to Della. Can you hear me?" The voice was mere inches from her ear, and startled her into a flinch.

"Huh? Oh, sorry Alice." Della stared up at her co-worker's face like a deer in the headlights. Alice stared back, looking distinctly concerned.

"Della, are you okay, honey? You seem really out of it today," Alice asked, her brow furrowed.

Della wondered how long she'd sat there staring into space. The look of worry seemed out of place on Alice's thin face — her friend was usually upbeat to the point of being annoying.

"Yeah, sorry," she said quickly. "I, uh, just haven't been sleeping that well in the last few weeks."

Alice frowned in earnest. "Uh-oh, why's that?"

Della sighed. "I wish I knew, to be honest."

"Well, if you need anything, don't hesitate to call me, okay?"

"Yeah, okay."

Alice smiled at her and turned towards her office. Della watched her go, thankful for the presence of at least some friendly faces in her life. Even if they seldom socialized outside of work, it was about the only thing she had going for her these days.

By the time six o'clock rolled around and everyone had cleared out to head home, Della was completely exhausted. She could barely keep her eyes open as she turned off all the computers, locked the doors, and walked towards the first of the two trams that would take her back to the nearest stop to her apartment. It was an unseasonably cold evening in February, and Della shivered against the chilly gusts of wind blustering against her back.

As she was walking toward Canal Street through the deepening dusk, she followed a group of commuters, most of whom were clutching their bags and jackets to themselves, trying to stay out of the wind.

"I haven't felt this cold here in years," one woman commented, turning up her coat collar.

"Well, it's definitely not a record low," her companion answered, "but I'm ready for our typical balmy weather to come back. This is gonna be hell on the new palm trees Jim and I just had planted in the back yard."

Della felt like she was two minutes away from falling asleep on her feet, which probably explained why she reacted so slowly to what came next.

A group of people dressed in black with masks pulled down over their faces barged onto the street from a side alley. They were all clutching handguns, and one was holding what looked like an assault rifle, cradled against his chest like a baby.

Several gasps and cries broke out as the crowd stuttered to a stop, pressing together like a squeezed accordion. The gunman standing at the front raised his weapon in the air and screamed, firing two shots into the sky. His eyes were crazed, and unhinged laughter spilled out from the blank mouth opening of the dark balaclava.

Pandemonium broke out around Della, who was standing frozen with shock, her eyes glued to the gunmen. The crowd that she had been following scattered in all directions, screaming and pushing and shoving against each other as they ran. The sharp retort of gunfire shattered the evening.

Above Della's head a window shattered, raining glass down on her. A large, burly man with a bushy beard slammed into her in his attempt to get away. She staggered as his huge frame plowed into her and she began to fall. Miraculously, he paused long enough to grab her arm and keep her from hitting the ground. With his help, she was able to steady herself on her feet. Before she could wrap her stunned brain around the idea of thanking him, however, he fled down the sidewalk towards the corner.

Della took a few stumbling steps after him, still dazed. Her breath was ragged in her lungs, which burned with pain as she tried to pull cold air through her mouth.

This can't be happening, this can't be happening, this can't be happening.

Her brain was stuck on an endless loop, unable to jerk free from the terror spilling onto the street around her. Her vision was tunneling and she couldn't focus on the figures rushing past her and out into the street. Car horns blared, tires shrieking as several vehicles crashed into each other, trying to avoid the panicking people now flooding into traffic.

Della knew she needed to get away, but it felt like her legs were mired in quicksand. She couldn't run and she felt an enormous pressure constricting around her chest, as if she were being suffocated.

Oh, God. I'm going to die right here on this sidewalk.

The thought ripped through her mind like a lightning bolt. The adrenaline burst that accompanied the terrifying realization propelled her forward so quickly, she almost fell to her knees again. Still mindlessly following the man that had stopped her from falling, Della tried to make it to the corner.

An explosion of sound seemed to fill Della's awareness, and the man with the beard crumpled to the ground ahead of her. At first, she didn't connect the two things — not until she saw the bright red splotchy patch blossoming over his gray jacket.

Della was moving, but she felt like her arms and legs were made of lead. She stumbled towards him, completely horrified at what she was seeing. The man was face down, gagging and gasping for air on the sidewalk, his breaths coming in terrible, wet rattles. Della knelt down beside him, the spreading puddle of his blood soaking into her dress pants and she placed a hand on his back.

Before she could even begin to help him, she felt him shudder and go completely still.

Della's heart was pounding so hard and fast, she felt like it was going to leap out of her chest, yet the thumping in her ears was sluggish, and everything around her seemed to be moving in slow motion. The gunmen were making their way in her direction. More explosions of noise echoed against the facades of the tall buildings around her. More bodies were falling to the ground. Terrified shrieks seemed to reach her ears as if she were underwater, muffled and distant. Yet Della remained on her knees, unable to leave the still body under her shaking hand. Sudden, crippling grief poured out of her for the man who had helped her — however briefly — at the cost of his own life.

Fuck this, Della thought savagely, anger surging behind the sorrow. She'd heard on the news that experts now recommended fighting and throwing things at gunmen in a mass shooting situation, rather than trying to flee or hide.

The man's messenger bag was lying on the ground next to her, as well as a small, decorative metal trashcan that must have been knocked over when people stampeded through the outdoor seating area of the café nearby. With fumbling fingers, Della reached for the strap in one hand and the trashcan in the other. She stood in one swift movement, bracing herself for a fight to the death, adrenaline lending her muscles a sudden, unexpected strength.

One of the gunmen was just behind her; she could hear his excited breathing and then the press of cold metal against her back.

"Are you ready to die, little kitty?" he sneered in her ear.

Her answer was to plant her feet and swing the bag and trashcan around so fast that the gunman, who was clearly not expecting her to fight back, didn't have time to duck or get out of the way.

As she spun, Della felt her makeshift weapons make contact with the man's shoulder and side. He let out a loud *oof* as the air was forced out of his lungs. The impact caused him to take one heavy step to the side, but he didn't fall and he didn't drop his weapon. Della dropped the bag but clung to the trashcan, raising it in both hands like a bat.

The gunman swore at her and pointed the gun straight at Della's face.

Completely terrified, she threw the trashcan at him as hard as she could, which caused him to lower the gun so he could knock it aside before it hit him.

"You're going to regret that, bitch!" he growled, lunging for her. Della stumbled backwards, trying to get away, but he grabbed her shoulder and spun her around, wrapping his arm around her and pressing the cold barrel of the gun against her temple.

TWO

Della held her breath and gripped the meaty forearm that was wrapped around her chest with clawed hands, trying desperately to pull the man's arm away. Even if she had managed to rip herself free, though, she knew that the minute she made a move to get away, the gunman would blow her head off. She simply held on, fingernails digging into the heavy black material of his shirt, feeling the seconds tick by one at a time, like dripping molasses.

With the gunman behind her, she could see the chaos on the street again. At least ten bodies lay in pools of blood. The dark red puddles seemed to shimmer under the streetlights. It was as though a heat haze had descended on the block, making everything waver in her vision. Her eyes flickered around, going in and out of focus, searching for any sign of the police or a SWAT team. Praying for help.

There was no one. She was alone with the dead, and the deadly. The other gunmen were chasing stragglers down the block and shooting bullets into fallen bodies. They blasted out windows of shops, including the one she and her captor were standing in front of, which caused him to yell in anger at his comrade.

"What are you doing, you stupid fuck! Trying to get me killed? Point that damn thing somewhere else!"

Della gasped aloud, despite trying valiantly to remain silent. She could hear a dull whine developing in her mind, an all-pervasive buzzing noise that drowned out any thought of defending herself. Panic was flooding her, followed by shock, preventing her from formulating any sort of coherent thought.

"Now, time to deal with you, pretty kitty," the man said, jerking Della from behind so that her feet slipped out from underneath her. He dragged her backwards towards the building as she scrambled to find her footing.

"Let me go," she pleaded.

"Not until you've fucking paid for that little trick with the trash can, whore," he said, spinning her around to face him. His breath was hot and smelly on her face. She gagged and fought to get away from him, desperate for fresh air.

He slammed her down on the ground, and her head hit the pavement with a sharp crack. She sprawled there for a moment, stunned by the blow. Lights popped in front of her eyes and Della lay completely still, forgetting where she was or what was going on around her.

The sound of gunfire above her jerked her back to reality. The man standing over her had shot at a car that had driven by, blowing out the windshield and passenger-side window.

Della clapped her hands around her head and curled into a ball, her ears ringing from the repeated blasts so close to her.

Suddenly the man was back, kneeling over her and yanking her arms away from her body. She fought back furiously, swinging and clawing at every square inch of him she could reach. He used his body weight to pin her legs down and pressed the gun against her cheek.

"Lie still," he commanded.

Della struggled for a moment more, but went limp when he pressed the barrel harder against her face.

She looked up into the face of pure evil, seeing his cold, blank eyes gazing back at her. There was only dark mirth and chilly indifference to be found there. She knew with complete certainty that she was going to die any moment now.

Out of nowhere, a mist descended around the site of carnage, swirling as if caught in a high breeze, even though everything in the night had gone completely still. It wrapped itself around the man crouched over her, flowing across his face. He jerked his head to the side, completely bewildered, and tried to swipe at the fog. His fingers passed straight through it, but the mist blew on towards the middle of the street, drawing his gaze. By the way the other gunmen were staggering around and waving their arms, Della guessed that something similar had happened to them.

The mist seemed to solidify in a dense patch in the middle of the blocked street, coalescing to reveal five dark figures. A strange aura of power radiated from them. Several of the gunmen backed away, raising their weapons.

"What the fuck, Benson?" one yelled in confusion in the direction of Della's attacker.

The man called Benson grabbed Della by the hair and dragged her to her feet. She shrieked in pain, clamping her hands around his and scrambling desperately for purchase, trying to find her feet and support her weight.

"Don't just stand there! Kill them!" Benson roared, making Della flinch in fright.

All at once, the shadowy figures burst into motion. Their speed was inhuman, Della realized with a jolt. No one could run that fast, not even if they were being pushed by a huge dump of adrenaline. They were moving *unnaturally* fast, almost as if they were flying towards the cluster of gunmen.

Della watched in open-mouthed awe as two women in the group launched themselves at the man carrying the assault rifle. He stumbled back in shock and fired off several rounds, all of which missed the newcomers and buried themselves in a building across the street with an explosion of brick dust. One of the women used a powerful blow to turn the barrel of the rifle towards the ground and slammed her fist into the man's face. His nose erupted in a gush of blood. He fell back onto the ground and both women landed on top of him.

The man who appeared to be in charge of the group of newcomers surveyed the scene with startling light gray eyes that seemed to glow silver in the low light. He effortlessly swiped the legs out from underneath the gunman standing closest to him before his pale gaze fell on Della and her captor. Benson growled and raised his gun, pointing it at the man with a shaking hand.

"Help the woman," the silver-eyed newcomer said, apparently unconcerned by the threat. His tone was deep and rich. Crushed velvet over tempered steel.

Somewhere in the back of Della's overwrought brain, she realized that he had the most amazing voice she had ever heard. She would have probably gone weak at the knees if she weren't already shaking like a leaf in a high wind.

Della heard a rushing sound and blinked. When she opened her eyes, a large man was standing in front of her, looking at her attacker with the intense green eyes of a hunting tiger. He took a calculated step forward, fists clenched as if he were about to strike. Benson stepped backwards, pulling her with him, and Della could feel him trembling against her. He fired off another deafening round from his handgun, and her would-be rescuer jerked to the side as it hit him in the chest, under the clavicle.

To Della's utter surprise, the man did not crumple to the ground. Instead, the wound only seemed to make him angrier. He surged forward, grabbing Benson by the head with both hands. Benson dropped Della, who fell to the ground as her tormenter began to scream and struggle wildly, waving the gun around. She rolled quickly out from between the two and watched, horrified, as the newcomer lifted Benson from the ground by his head and threw him into the nearest wall, face first. He crumpled to the ground — a discarded rag doll, lying in a heap on the dirty pavement, obviously unconscious. The man with the gunshot wound in his chest walked over and stomped his heel down on Benson's face, assuring that he would not be getting up again.

Ever.

The crunch of his skull smashing made Della's stomach churn. She felt bile rising in her mouth and coughed, trying not to vomit. She crawled backwards on her elbows, using her feet to propel her, trying to get away from the grisly tableau.

The movement seemed to catch her rescuer's attention. He walked forward slowly, his hands raised in a peace token, and dropped to one knee next to her.

"Hey, now. Easy, there. Are you all right?" His tone was soothing, and very, very British. Della could still feel the aura of raw power radiating from him, which terrified her just as much as the armed man who had taken her hostage. Yet, she could not help but be captivated by his eyes, which seemed almost to glow in the low light. They were mesmerizing, and she realized that she was staring at him like a fool, silent and slack-jawed.

She shook her head, trying to clear it, and raised a hand to her pounding temple.

"Y-yeah, I think so," she answered in a shaking voice.

He knelt next to her.

"It's okay. Take a moment. You've had quite a scare," he said, his voice calm and collected. Della's eyes strayed to the gaping hole under his collarbone, oozing blood that looked almost black in the low light.

"Ah. Yes. Sorry about the gore," he said, noticing her gaze. "It's really unfortunate, that. Smarts like hell, actually, now that I think about it." He winced, lifting a hand to prod at the wound and craning his neck to try to look at it. "Son of a bitch, that's gonna leave a mark. I do *not* get paid enough to deal with this shit while I'm sober…"

Della's mouth was still hanging open, but she couldn't speak. She looked around wildly, wanting nothing more than to just go home and pretend that none of this had ever happened. She felt a bone-deep weariness underneath her pounding heart, and she was still fighting down nausea that threatened to overcome her willpower.

She could see the other figures walking towards her through the darkening evening, all converging on them.

The gray-eyed leader walked over to her rescuer and looked down at the wound on his chest, a crease of worry forming on his forehead. His hair was dark, falling tousled above a serious brow, sharp cheekbones, and full, sensuous lips.

"Xander, you obviously neglected to duck again," he said in that deep velvet voice. "We've talked about this before, have we not?"

Della felt her heart skip a beat despite her terror.

The man called Xander had a hand clamped over the wound now, trying to stem the bleeding. "That we have. And I believe I made it perfectly clear that we need to keep a flask or two of the good stuff on us when dealing with this kind of crap. If I'm going to get shot through the lung by some redneck shithead with crooked teeth and halitosis, I'd prefer to be considerably more intoxicated than this, beforehand."

Ignoring the litany of complaints, the leader knelt and reached out a hand to steady Xander, who had started to sway.

"Well, fuck," Xander said matter-of-factly, and half-collapsed into his friend's supporting grip. Trying to keep both of them upright, the leader set his hand down hard on the ground for balance. His fingers grazed the skin on Della's wrist — the barest of brushes.

It was like touching a live wire. An electric jolt shot through Della's entire body. She felt as though she had been punched in the stomach. Air was forced through her mouth in a sound of shock that was echoed by the leader's surprised grunt. He jerked his hand away and leapt gracefully to his feet with his injured friend held securely in his grip, staring down at Della on the ground as if he had never seen anything like her.

Their eyes met, and she saw something like dismay flicker behind his silver-gray eyes. His lips parted, as if he wanted to say something to her, but no sound escaped his mouth. They stared at each other for several moments, the wounded man next to him flicking his eyes back and forth between the two. His eyebrows furrowed in confusion.

"Tré?" he asked.

The gray-eyed man did not respond, just continued to stare into Della's face. She thought she saw *recognition* flash behind his eyes.

But that was impossible. How could he recognize her? They had never met before. She would have remembered if they had, she was sure.

"*Tré*," The wounded man said, more insistent this time. "Police approaching. Time to leave. Unless you'd like to try answering their questions while I bleed out in the back of a human ambulance?"

This seemed to startle the leader out of his reverie, and he broke eye contact with Della.

"Oksana," he commanded in a hoarse tone. "Wipe her memory."

"Wait. Wipe my *what*?" Della demanded, jerking into a sitting position. She tried valiantly to scramble away from the female figure descending upon her. "No. *No*! Stay away from me."

"It's all right, sweetheart," the woman said in a soothing voice. "Hey, look at me. Relax. That's it."

Della felt all the tightness in her muscles start to drain away. She shook her head, trying to clear it, but a dreamy veil seemed to fall in front of her eyes, making everything foggy.

"No... wait," she said in a weak voice, feeling everything around her grow dim. Grayness seemed to swirl around the edges of her vision and she tried to shake her head again, feeling it flop back and forth in slow motion.

The glare of the streetlights and the chill of the rough pavement beneath her slipped away, sending her into warm, soft darkness.

-o-o-o-

"Ma'am? Ma'am, are you all right?"

Della's eyes jerked open, rolling drunkenly in their sockets, unable to focus on anything. *"Wait..."*

"Ma'am? Are you injured?"

Della's vision gradually cleared. She realized that she was being pulled into a sitting position by a police officer who looked deeply shaken. "Ma'am?"

"I—I don't know," Della answered in a hoarse voice. "What just happened?"

"You were involved in a shooting. Please, we need to get you to the paramedics. Can you stand?" he asked.

"I think so," Della said, and the police officer helped pull her to her feet. She swayed as all the blood in her head rushed toward her feet.

"Easy, now," the police officer said, wrapping an arm around her shoulders. "Take it easy."

Moving slowly, he led her around the corner to where a barricade was set up. Behind the line of police— all pointing weaponry in their direction—Della could see the flashing lights of ambulances.

"Ma'am, did you see what happened to the gunmen?"

Della stumbled, leaning against the cop heavily. "I don't know. I don't remember anything."

She wracked her brain, trying to remember the shooting, but only feeling terror threaten to paralyze her on the spot. No mental images formed in her mind. She couldn't even remember how she got onto the street. The whole day seemed hazy and distant. She looked around, trying to orient herself, the flashing lights and wail of sirens dominating her immediate surroundings.

Where am I? How did I get here?

"It's okay," the officer said, his tone soothing as he patted her arm.

"Why can't I remember?" Della breathed, feeling as if something inside her was falling away. Darkness swirled around in her mind, making her stomach churn uncomfortably. "Why — *Jesus.* Why can't I *remember* anything?"

-o-o-o-

"Of course they had to have assault rifles. *Assault rifles,* seriously? God, I hate this country. Have I mentioned that lately? And here I am, sober as a fucking *nun* after a damn bullet punched a hole through my chest. This shit is evil, I tell you. Pure evil. And they call *us* the demons…" Xander complained, the strength behind his words fading as he slowly bled out.

Tré ignored him, exercising all of his self-control merely to keep his friend propped upright between him and Eris. If he allowed himself to think about what had just happened, he'd lose his shit completely. And they couldn't afford that right now.

Of all the insane, astounding, unexpected things to happen, he never would have foreseen this. It was *impossible.* How could *she* be here? Now? All of these centuries later?

"I've just decided," Xander slurred. "I hate bullets. Do you hate bullets, Tré? Because I do. *Hate* 'em."

"I hadn't realized it was possible for a vampire to become delirious after an injury," Eris said conversationally. "I thought that was just a human thing."

Tré allowed himself a bitter snort. "Trust Xander to break the mold."

"I'm one of a kind, you know," Xander protested. His feet dragged as sudden exhaustion seemed to overwhelm him.

"You'd better stay with us, in that case," Tré said dryly. "Since you'd be impossible to replace." He turned his attention back to their footing as they stumbled across the rickety bridge leading up to the abandoned plantation house they'd been using as a base of operations.

They had discovered the place, deep in the Louisiana bayou, several months ago. Since then, they'd hidden themselves here, fixing it up enough to be marginally habitable, and venturing into New Orleans only as necessary.

Tré had sent the others ahead to prepare, knowing that time would be of the essence once he and Eris arrived with Xander.

The air was thick with humidity, mist rising around them as Tré and Eris stomped through mud and sludge, making their way up the hill to dry land.

"You know what?" Xander said suddenly, his voice somewhat clearer. "Walking sucks. Why do humans do this all the time? I wouldn't bother."

Eris and Tré's eyes met over the top of their friend's drooping head. "You're the one who morphed back into solid form half a mile shy of our destination," Eris pointed out, a look of consternation crossing his handsome Mediterranean features.

It was true that they would normally have traveled as mist, or in the form of owls. But Xander's owl would have manifested the same horrific injury he now sported in vampire form. And by the time Oksana had wiped the human woman's memory, Xander had lost enough blood and life force that he couldn't maintain his transformation into mist all the way back to the plantation house. Tré supposed they were lucky he'd made it as far as he did.

But… *the woman.*

Tré's mind wandered back to her. He felt a complex tangle of emotion surge through him as he recalled exactly how her skin felt as it brushed against his. It was a touch so old — yet so familiar — that he had momentarily been paralyzed by the unexpected warmth of life flowing through his cold limbs.

His thoughts carried him all the way to the door of the old house. Oksana opened it for them, looking deeply concerned as the trio slipped quickly through the entrance.

"Tré," she called after them. "We've put some clean linens down in Xander's room."

"Thank you," he responded. "With luck, he's lost enough blood by this point that he won't end up bleeding all over them."

"You're a terrible friend," Xander muttered. "You know that, right? Because I feel it's important for me to drive this point home."

Eris snorted in dark amusement as they trudged up the stairs to the second floor, listening with some trepidation to the creak of ancient wood under their feet. Thankfully, the old boards supported their combined weight without cracking, and they passed awkwardly around the bend in the steps, reaching the landing without mishap. The second door on the right, Xander's room, stood ajar and they shuffled him across the threshold in an awkward three-way dance.

After lowering the wounded vampire's limp frame onto the bed, Eris nodded silently to Tré and slipped out of the room, shutting the door behind him with a quiet click.

Tré propped Xander's feet up on a stack of pillows and removed his boots.

"I don't care to make a habit of this," he told the other vampire, who seemed more aware of his surroundings now that he was fully reclined. "Particularly not when you are, as you have repeatedly pointed out, completely sober."

Xander's flat gaze was unimpressed. "I assure you, this was not how I intended to spend my evening."

After freeing the buttons, Tré pulled Xander's sticky, blood-soaked shirt back, and examined the wound under his collarbone.

"That will take some time to heal," he murmured, using his fingers to press the skin back down around the gaping hole. If they were lucky, it would heal correctly and not leave a substantial mark on Xander's marble skin. "Still, I suppose it could be worse. You have lost much of your life force, though. I can feel it weakening."

"Don't fuss. I'll recover," Xander said. He sounded confident, yet Tré noticed that his eyes had drifted shut. He looked as comfortable as he could be, under the circumstances, so Tré pulled up a chair next to him.

"Here. You need to feed," Tré said, offering his wrist.

Despite his earlier protestations, Xander barely hesitated. Like a child, he opened his mouth gratefully, revealing sharp fangs that sank into Tré's skin.

Tré felt his flesh pierced, but he did not flinch as Xander suckled weakly at the blood dripping into his mouth. Knowing that he was in for a long night, Tré adjusted his position in the chair to a more comfortable one, and rested his elbow on the bed next to Xander. After several quiet moments, color seeped back into his friend's pale skin, and Tré could feel the steady throb of

Xander's power growing stronger. The blood he had shared was already beginning to do its job.

"How do you feel now?" he asked when Xander paused in his feeding.

"Like shit... but better than I did earlier," Xander admitted. He sounded tired, but more aware and centered than during his ramblings on the journey back to the house.

"Good. Rest for a while. Then you will need to feed again. Every few hours throughout the night, I'd expect."

Xander nodded and blinked several times before meeting Tré's eyes directly and holding them.

"What happened to you back there, Tré?" he asked quietly.

Tré frowned. "What do you mean?"

Xander refused to be put off. "With the woman we saved? I felt something strange happen when you touched her, and you looked like you'd seen a ghost, afterward."

"It was nothing, just stirred up some old memories. Nothing for you to be worried about right now."

"But—"

He shook his head. "Xander. You need to rest and focus on healing. Here, please feed some more. I'm strong enough, and it will help knit the wound back together more quickly."

Xander looked as if he wanted to argue, but instead he sighed and latched on to Tré's proffered wrist again.

While his friend drank more forcefully, Tré allowed his mind to drift again towards the woman. He could not seem to banish her from his thoughts, as much as he tried to.

He had touched her skin and for a moment, his power had nearly exploded out of the bounds of his body. He'd felt the absolute, overwhelming certainty that he knew her. This was no casual acquaintance from days past, however. No, he had recognized her as his long lost Irina. The only woman he had ever loved.

But that was truly impossible. She had died, centuries ago, a horrific death, wrought by his own blood-soaked hands. The same hands that were supposed to protect her and shield her from all suffering.

Memories flooded Tré's mind, very much against his will. He had been haunted by these memories every single day of his endless, immortal life, stuck in a brooding cycle of guilt and self-loathing that would never cease. Not for all eternity.

Tré had been turned from a mortal man into a vampire at the hands of the most evil power the world had ever known — the demonic spirit, Bael. Among other horrific abilities, Bael had the power to tear a soul into two pieces and cast the Light side into the depths of hell, leaving only the Dark behind.

According to the doddering old village priest, Tré had been marked by evil from the time he was a small child. Yet Bael did not succeed in capturing him until he was a young man, barely twenty-three years of age when it finally happened.

The demon had come upon him in the dead of night, surrounding him like a suffocating cloud that burned his skin and eyes and tore the air from his lungs. Tré could remember how he thrashed and struggled, trying to fight off the force of darkness that felt like it was permeating his entire being. He had been dragged down into a hole — a grave designed for the living — and at the bottom of the pit, the torture had truly begun. He'd fought with everything in him — with the crazed frenzy of a cornered animal, all his strength pouring out to no effect.

He could not escape the demon's clutches. The agony of having his soul torn into two pieces, the Light and the Dark, was a torment he would never forget, despite the hundreds of years that had passed since that time. But something had happened. Something had gone wrong.

Instead of submitting to the rape and defilement of all the good in him, Tré had managed to claw his way out of the pit that Bael had cast him into. He still remembered Bael's unearthly shriek of fury upon seeing that his victim had escaped. But Tré had cared nothing for the demon's dismay.

A burning thirst seemed to ignite in his gut, spreading up into his throat and his mouth until he felt he must surely die from the craving. He could feel his body shuddering, changing, and strength he had never known flooded through his limbs.

It was at that moment that his life changed forever. With his soul torn in two, he had left the mortal world and stepped into the night as a vampire. He was crazed, desperate, and panicked by the lust for blood that made his head spin and his canines lengthen into fangs.

He had crawled along the ground, pulling himself forward by his fingernails, an inch at a time, dirt and ashes filling his mouth. At that moment, he had looked up through the haze of pain and rage and seen a graceful figure making its way towards him. Tré blinked rapidly, averting his eyes. It seemed as though a dazzling light was pouring from her, shining against his burning skin. Shining into his very soul.

It was his beloved, Irina. They had been betrothed for nearly a year, and Tré loved her with a passion that seemed terrifying at times. They were soulmates, destined for each other and no one else.

He snarled, drawing his arms and legs up underneath him, ready to spring towards the source of life, light, and blood that he could smell radiating from her. He needed her to quench his bone-deep thirst. Nothing else would do. Nothing else could stop his agony.

Irina had seen him, covered in dirt and mud, a broken specter of the man that she loved. She had rushed forward, drawing her hood back and revealing her distraught face, tragically beautiful in the moonlight.

"Vlad!" she cried, falling to her knees in front of him. He sprang at her, feeling a burst of strength he had never experienced before, propelling him forward through the air.

He crashed into her delicate frame, pinning her to the ground beneath him. She screamed, terrified by his twisted features, his burning eyes. He bared his fangs with a feral growl and —

Tré shook his head violently, trying to free himself from the memories that had assaulted him, seemingly out of nowhere. He could not afford to think about that terrible night. He needed to focus. He needed to maintain discipline.

There was work to be done, and many things to be considered. Bael was behind everything dark, all the evil in the world. Tré had sensed his presence during the shooting today, even if the demon had not shown himself directly during the attack.

He and his fellow vampires had vowed to spend eternity fighting against Bael, to seek revenge for all of the mortal lives that had been lost, including their own. They were the products of Bael's failure, as each of them had somehow managed to escape his clutches before being turned into lifeless, animated puppets, capable of only evil. Their miraculous escapes, however, had come at a cost that could never be repaid.

The last flicker of Light inside them had only been shielded by the willing sacrifice of a true love, which formed a fragile bond between the two broken halves of their souls. In Tré's case, the sacrifice had come from Irina, who had cowered on the ground, rolling over and covering Tré's body with her own protectively as Bael had descended upon them.

The memory of that terrible moment threatened to shatter Tré's divided soul into a million shards and scatter them into the wind. He trembled as he sat next to Xander, whose eyes were open, studying him closely and with no small amount of concern.

Tré broke eye contact and forced his mind back to the ever-growing problem before them. It did no good to revisit old memories of Irina's sacrifice. Such indulgence was a weakness.

It was clear to all of them that Bael's power was growing, and the tides of the long war between Light and Darkness were turning in the demon's favor. This perplexed Tré. Why now? What had changed? How many more lives would be lost or destroyed before Bael could be forever defeated?

Could he be defeated?

Eris — the scholar among them — had done a vast amount of studying over the centuries. He'd discovered that a handful of ancient texts predicted the downfall of Bael at the hands of thirteen failed undead, a council of immortals who would join together and cast the demon into his own hell, forever condemned to the same mutilations he had inflicted on the world.

He and Tré had scoured the globe, discovering four more vampires in turn, but never finding any more than that despite their ongoing search. It appeared that only six of them had survived the turning with their sanity intact... though that assessment might be a bit optimistic in Snag's case. The oldest of the vampires, a sad skeleton of a creature that had been turned long before Tré, long before Eris, was hardly what you would consider *sane*.

At any rate, Eris had told them the ancient texts pointed towards that very love, which had saved them from Bael in the first place, being the uniting force that would ultimately be the demon's demise. This, in Tré's opinion, was errant nonsense. Laughable, even. There was no love left in him, only cold bitterness. With the possible exceptions of Eris and Oksana, they were all a bunch of ancient, bitter ghouls who probably should have been staked centuries ago.

So why—*why*—had the touch of that woman awoken such feelings of peace and belonging within him? It made no sense. Perhaps, he thought, she was some distant relative of his long lost love? But that would be impossible. Irina had died before she had borne any children. How could there be any connection?

Xander's voice broke into his morbid musings. "Tré, no offense, but your blood tastes like some punk emo kid angsting over his latest existential crisis. Are you absolutely sure you don't want to share your thoughts with the class?"

Tré frowned at him. To his private relief, Xander looked almost completely normal again, after the healing blood he had provided. "Not really. It's merely a ghost from the past."

Xander gave him a look that was almost pitying, but to Tré's eternal relief, he didn't press the issue.

"Right. Whatever you say. Thanks for the top-up, anyway. Though, you know—if you really loved me, you'd've downed a bottle or three of Glenmorangie beforehand to help take the edge off." He stretched carefully. "Now, go brood somewhere else for awhile and let me sleep. I'll let you know if I need you."

Without a word, Tré pushed the chair back against the wall and left the room, his thoughts still swirling around the honey-haired, hazel-eyed woman who seemed to somehow possess Irina's long dead spirit.

THREE

"Okay, try to stay calm." The blonde police offi-cer—whose nametag identified her as Sgt. Diane Sheffield—spoke in a soft voice, rubbing Della's shoulder. Della wished she would stop.

She was sitting on the tailgate of an ambulance, wrapped in a reflective, crinkly blanket, unable to do more than huddle there and shake. Her fingers trembled violently as she tried to wrap the blanket more tightly around herself.

"I—I can't remember much," Della said for the dozenth time, feeling her teeth rattle together from the force of her tremors.

"That's okay. Just try to tell me what you do know. What happened after the gunman knocked you down and you hit your head?"

She strained her memory, attempting to focus on the hazy images. "I lay there for a minute, but I was too scared to really move because he was still pointing the gun at me."

"What did the gun look like?"

Della furrowed her eyebrows, trying so hard to re-member. "Black handle, but it was made of silver metal."

"Was it an automatic or revolver?"

Della blinked in confusion at the police officer. "What?"

"Sorry," Diane said. "Did it have a circular chamber that spun when he fired? Like out of one of those old west movies? Or did he have to cock it like this?"

With her hands, she made a sliding motion back and forth.

Della shut her eyes, trying to remember. It was all so dim and jumbled together. The paramedics had assured her that it was normal for the mind to short circuit like that during a traumatic situation, but it didn't make the experience of memory loss any less terrifying.

"It's like your brain tries to take in too much information and your fear makes things spill back out. You may never get these memories back, and that's perfectly normal," one of the EMTs had told her, while shining a bright light in her eyes.

Della believed him, but there was still something about the whole thing that felt... *wrong*. She felt like there was something on the edge of her mind, obscured by the haze. She was *sure* it was important. Drastically important. Life changing, even. Yet, she could not draw it forward into her conscious mind, no matter how hard she tried.

It wasn't all that surprising, she supposed. Her heart was still thudding out of control and she could feel her pulse pounding in her eyes and face. She knew that she was fighting shock at this point, which was why the paramedics had insisted that she speak with police while wrapped up. They were trying to keep her body temperature from falling.

"Miss LeBlanc?" The police officer said.

Della realized that she had been silent for several long moments, lost in thought. She had completely forgotten that the officer was waiting for an answer.

"What? Oh, the gun. Sorry. Um, I don't think anything on the gun spun, but I can't be sure," she said, staring at her knees.

"That's okay, we just want to make sure that we haven't missed any weapons that may have been dropped in the street."

"What do you mean?"

"The gunmen were still holding their weapons when—" The officer's voice trailed away and she shook her head. "Well. Never mind about that part. We just want to make sure we haven't missed anything."

Della nodded, wiping cold sweat from her face with the edge of the blanket. She could feel the adrenaline that had been coursing through her body for what felt like hours draining away. She was left feeling weak, shaky, and nauseated. As her stomach gurgled uncomfortably, she leaned against the side of the ambulance and looked up into the officer's face.

"Can I go home now? Please?"

Sgt. Sheffield gazed sadly at Della, who knew she must look completely weak and defeated.

"Of course," said the officer. "We'll have someone take you home in a few minutes. And, Della?"

"Hmm?" Della answered, not looking at the woman.

"Please make sure that you follow up with someone—a therapist, or a doctor, or a pastor, or *someone* about this. We may also need to call you in for more information, but not for the next couple of days, probably. Are you willing to help us?"

"Of course," Della answered, clearing her throat. She slid unsteadily to her feet, feeling Sgt. Sheffield grip her arm above her elbow to support her.

Della let herself be guided towards a police car and another officer, who drove her home.

Along the way, Della stared mutely out of the window, unable to see much through the heavy blanket of darkness. It was as if the streetlights weren't penetrating through the gloom as well as they usually did, or maybe her eyes weren't working properly.

She couldn't even muster up enough energy to rub at them to try to bring everything into focus.

"Are you going to be all right, there?" The officer asked. She jerked in surprise and looked over at him.

She had barely paid attention to who was sliding into the car next to her, so she was surprised to see an attractive young cop with sandy blonde hair glancing back and forth between her and the street ahead. On a normal day, she might have thought he was kind of cute. Today, she would be happy never to see him again.

"Yeah," Della answered in a dull tone. "Thanks."

When she finally made it home, the officer walked her to her apartment, tipped his hat to her, and left as she slipped inside. With her back against the door, she locked the handle, deadbolt, and the chain above her head before standing stock still, hugging herself.

Everything felt unreal. Della looked down at her hands, amazed to see fingers attached. She rubbed them together, but couldn't feel the slide of skin against skin. She was completely numb, only aware of a vague tingling that was passing over her entire body.

Knowing that she desperately needed sleep, Della tossed her handbag onto the ground right next to the door, not even bothering to grab her cell phone out of it first. She supposed she was lucky that one of the officers had retrieved it from where she must have dropped it, and returned it to her. She stepped out of her shoes and stumbled into the bathroom.

After washing her face and brushing her teeth with rote movements, Della fell into bed, feeling ever so slightly more human after the splash of warm water on her face.

Sleep seemed to be waiting for her, dragging her down into her squishy mattress the second her head hit the pillow.

I should at least turn the light off, Della thought vaguely. Her eyes cracked open and she blinked at the offending lamp on the bedside table. Even though it was only a few inches away, she couldn't summon the energy to reach up and turn it off. The weariness in her arms and legs was so absolute, she felt like she weighed five hundred pounds.

At last, sleep overcame her, pulling her down into dark, fitful dreams.

-o-o-o-

She was standing on the edge of a small, quaint town, like one of those fake villages they dragged you to in grade school so you could see how people lived hundreds of years ago. Only here, there were no little hints of the modern world hidden around — no extension cords bundled along the base of a wall; no plastic water bottles stuffed hastily behind an olde-tymey market stall. By the indistinct light pouring out through the windows of the little cottages around her, Della could see that fires were lit inside. The sweet, rich smell of wood smoke lingered in the air around her.

A sense of urgency overcame her. She whirled and took off running, out of the village and into the trees, somehow knowing exactly where she needed to go. As she ran, she realized that she was wearing a simple dress of brown, woven cloth. The heavy skirts swished around her feet, which were bare.

She was traveling along a dirt trail, feeling her feet sinking into the wet earth. Mud squished between her toes.

Suddenly, through the darkness, she became aware of a creeping presence coming closer, ever closer. A chill ran up her spine and she recoiled, a suffocating sense of evil surrounding her. Looking ahead, she saw a dark figure writhing on the ground. Something was terribly familiar about it — the strong line of the man's back and shoulders, maybe. Or perhaps the timbre of the tortured cries floating towards her through the mist.

A swirling dark cloud exploded out of a pit and surrounded the figure, who shrieked in agony as it enveloped him.

Della felt a stab of shock as the man turned over, his limbs flopping like a broken doll's. Merciful God. She recog-

nized his face – but where had she seen it before? The sense of familiarity she'd felt solidified into blank horror.

"Vlad!" she heard her dream-self scream. Tears were streaming down her face. She was terrified, but her heart propelled her forward through the fear. She stumbled over a tree root before righting herself and staggering the last few steps toward the man she... loved? She threw herself down onto her hands and knees at his side, mud splattering everywhere.

Her mind merged with that of her dream-self like double vision coming into diamond-sharp focus. Her betrothed panted on the ground, twisting and clawing at himself like a wounded animal. When he opened his eyes, Della saw a fire burning behind them that she had never seen before. They had always been a calm gray, like the sea on a cloudy morning. Now, they shone silver, glowing from within. She choked back another scream at the unnatural sight. His face and neck were covered in terrible scorch marks, and he barely seemed to recognize her.

But, no – something flickered in his eyes when he looked up into her face. Before she could draw breath, he moved faster than anyone she had ever seen. A heavy weight plowed into her and she was thrown backwards, sinking into the mud. A strong body, familiar but changed, crouched over her, caging her with arms and legs.

She could feel the black cloud of evil surrounding her, burning her skin, sucking the air from her lungs and leaving her gasping. She struggled under the suffocating, intangible weight of it, to no avail. Her heart pounded as if trying to escape the prison of her chest.

The blackness had done this, somehow. This strange, evil force had attacked her beloved, and changed him into a tortured beast.

"No! Stop! Leave him alone!" she croaked, each word a searing pain in her throat.

A dark, malicious voice echoed with laughter inside her mind. It came, she felt sure, from the black cloud swirling around them as Vlad pressed her down to the ground. Her *lover's hand came up and gripped her arm. Words swirled across her flickering awareness, confusing and dark. They did not come from her beloved.*

"What will you give me in return?"

The voice was cold, yet sounded darkly amused by its own offer. Della felt the hair on her arms and neck stand on end as she realized that she was hearing a voice from the depths of hell itself. The pressure holding her down vanished as Vlad crumpled with a primal scream, landing next to her and convulsing in pain.

"I will give my life for his," she cried, throwing her body over her fiancé's as if she could somehow protect him physically from the forces of Satan.

Vlad struggled and groaned beneath her. To Della's shock, he pressed his mouth against her throat as if in a kiss. An instant later, Della felt a sharp stabbing pain. She shrieked and tried to tear herself away, but strong hands grabbed her like claws, holding her in place.

"Your love cannot save him," the voice purred in her ear. "He has already been turned. Your lover has forgotten you. You are nothing but meat to him now, and he will destroy you in your insolence."

"My life for his, then," Della ground out, feeling razor-sharp fangs sink deeper into her flesh.

More laughter, the sound making her skin crawl as if insects were scurrying over her body. The fangs pulled out and she was flipped over – tossed on her back again. The dark figure that had once been her true love loomed over her, salivating with bloodlust. Feeling the inevitability of what was about to happen, Della bared her bleeding neck to him, trying to keep his eyes locked on hers.

"Take what you need, my love," she whispered, forcing the words past the ruin of her throat. "I... give it... freely..."

With a flash, the beast that had once been Vlad sank his teeth into her neck as she let out a choked cry.

He did not answer, but continued to draw from her neck, a feral snarl escaping from his chest. The pain grew distant, but she felt terribly cold. The darkness of the moonlit forest seemed to be deepening to pitch black. Her hand slipped from Vlad's shoulder, flopping down into the mud as her awareness narrowed to a hazy tunnel.

-o-o-o-

Della struggled wildly, her legs tangling in the sheets and blankets. As she jerked awake, gasping for air, a black whisper rustled at the edge of her hearing.

"Oh yes, child. I do remember you."

Della blinked into awareness and found that she was on the floor, lying in a heap next to her bed. She must have tried to leap to her feet and ended up pulling all of her bedclothes with her onto the floor. She was panting as if she had run a marathon, covered in sweat. As she woke more fully, shaking the last vestiges of the dream from her head, she felt that terrible looming presence retreat and fade.

Clutching a hand over her heart, which was thudding loudly in her chest, Della tried to slow her breathing to a normal rate before she hyperventilated.

"I am *losing my goddamned mind*," she said to the empty room.

She stumbled to her feet, clutching the bed frame until her shaking knees stopped threatening to send her right back down to the floor. When she was steady enough, she grabbed her robe and slipped it around her shoulders, feeling the warmth soothing her tense muscles as she padded quietly through her apartment and out into the courtyard behind her building, still barefoot. She left her sliding glass door open to allow the fresh air to filter into the living room, and sat down on the lichen-encrusted bench.

The unusual cold snap had abated while she slept, leaving the night cool against her overheated skin, but not freezing. The dew had fallen and she stared into the sky, trying to see the stars past the bright city lights. Somewhere off in the distance, she could hear sirens wailing. She shivered at the noise, wondering what horrors were occurring beyond the confines of her little sanctuary.

A moment later, the faint rustle of wings caught her attention.

There was a live oak tree standing in the center of the courtyard. It had grown tall and broad over the decades, casting the apartments around her into shadow despite the bright moonlight that painted her bench pale gray. On one of the lower branches, she spotted a large owl perched silently, its round, silvery eyes gazing down on her. The huge bird ruffled its wings again before folding them neatly against its body.

She felt herself relax and exhaled the breath she hadn't been aware she was holding. The owl blinked slowly at her and then swiveled his head around, as if checking for other visitors. An unexpected sense of serenity settled over Della, making her eyelids droop as exhaustion caught up with her. A soft breeze caressed her face. She sat still and silent, listening to the sounds of the restless city around her.

Della tried not to think about the horrible events from the previous day, knowing that doing so would destroy the momentary calm that she seemed to have found, sitting here in the moonlight. In a way, she was grateful that she had few memories of what had happened. Even though it made the events seem disturbingly distant and unreal, she knew that she was less likely to be traumatized by memories that she did not truly possess anymore.

These thoughts passed through her mind, but she remained relaxed in the courtyard, untroubled by fear or memory. Right now, she felt like she could sleep peacefully for a week. Not wanting to waste the moment, she stood.

"Thanks for the nighttime company, owl," she said, and stumbled back to her bed. She was already half asleep when her head hit the pillow.

This time, Della didn't have any frightening nighttime visions. Instead, she drifted into a deep slumber, imagining a gentle touch running over her skin—the hand of a lover. She felt protected and safe, wrapped in a cocoon of sheets, peace and security warming her.

As the early morning hours slipped by, the imagined caress grew more intimate, rousing her blood without piercing the aura of drowsy contentment that draped over her dreams like the softest of blankets. When she awoke, she was covered in a light sheen of sweat, liquid heat pooling between her legs.

-o-o-o-

"Are you going to be all right now, Xander?" Tré asked, eyeing his fellow vampire with misgiving.

His injured friend had stumbled down from his room after a short nap, and was currently lounging on a dusty sofa that looked original to the early 1900s, a slow grin spreading over his handsome face. He was grasping a bottle of what Xander presumed was spiked blood, and he pointed his finger drunkenly at Tré with the same hand that gripped his drink.

"You," he slurred, "worry too much. You need to learn to let this shit *go*, Tré."

Tré scowled, skeptical. "We can't all drown our woes in drink. Also, do I even want to know where you got that bottle? Or how?"

"Almost certainly not," Xander mumbled, taking another drink and wiping away the trickle of deep red that escaped the corner of his mouth to drip down his chin. "Still, you should try it sometime as an alternative to your incessant brooding."

"Don't worry, Tré," a dry female voice said from behind him. "I'll keep an eye on him."

Tré turned, meeting Duchess' eyes with a raised eyebrow. Her blue gaze was as cold and depthless as the water at the bottom of a well. Her blond hair was draped elegantly over her left shoulder, falling in wavy curls far too perfectly formed to be random. Tré nodded his thanks and let his eyes slide back to Xander.

"Don't let him have another bottle," he said. Tré knew that Duchess was more than a match for Xander, especially when he was this drunk. She would manage to keep him under control by fair means or foul.

"You're the boss," she replied with a shrug, tossing her hair over her other shoulder and walking past Tré into the room.

"Behave," Tré commanded, looking at Xander, who lifted his eyebrows in response and made an innocent *who, me?* gesture with his free hand.

"I resent your implication," Xander said, forming the words with careful precision. "You should be more concerned with our resident man-eater's behavior than with little old me."

"I was speaking to both of you, actually," Tré clarified, and left the room without a backward glance.

Tonight, he had other concerns.

The woman. He had to see her. He had to know the truth. Tré's thoughts had been running along a single narrow path ever since returning from the battle where Xander had been wounded. He needed to find out the truth about the mysterious girl who—to all appearances—possessed the same gentle, loving soul as his long-lost Irina.

Stepping out of the front door, Tré took a deep breath, bringing all of his power into a central focus beneath his heart and lungs. Letting it flow once more through his limbs on a slow breath, he transformed into the shape of a huge gray owl. He spread his powerful wings wide and took flight, reveling in the way the ground fell away as he was borne aloft on silent feathers.

He could see much better in the darkness as an owl, and flicked his gaze back and forth as he flew low over the trees surrounding the old plantation house. Rodents scurried for cover as he flew overhead, but he ignored them. He was not on the hunt tonight. He headed toward the glowing lights of the city, a beacon in the moonlit night despite the lateness of the hour.

Less than half an hour later, Tré glided down to perch on the roof of a building, surveying the bustling crime scene below. Police, fire crews, and medical examiners walked back and forth between the dead bodies, talking to each other in low voices and comparing notes. Tré saw no sign of the woman. Knowing it hadn't been that long since the attack, Tré assumed that she would still be nearby—tied up in red tape, waiting for medical attention, speaking with police. He turned his head past ninety degrees to his left and saw that a mass of people were huddled around the corner and down the street.

He took flight again and settled on the eaves of another building, just in time to see the woman being led to a police car. A female officer with blond hair helped guide her into the seat and shut the door behind her, while another male officer stepped into the driver's seat.

Tré felt an unbidden stab of jealousy and possessiveness. He ruthlessly tamped it down.

Irrational. Ridiculous. This is not the time or the place, he scolded himself.

He followed the police cruiser all the way back to the woman's apartment building and watched as the officer escorted her inside. He flew low over the building, searching for a window that he could see through, only to find that shades or blinds blocked every one of them.

In frustration, he landed on a low branch of the tree in the small courtyard.

Even if I can't see her, he thought, *I just need to be near her. Just for a while, until all this starts to make sense.*

Perhaps if he stayed close by, he would be able to sense her life force. To discover if it was just a coincidence, a distant relation, maybe, or if it was truly his beloved Irina, reborn. Yet, how could such a thing be? How could Irina — brave, tragic Irina — *possibly* be here, of all places? It made no sense.

Tré grew lost in thought, turning the night's events over and over in his mind. He could not shake the impression that Bael was nearby, and centuries-old revulsion coursed through him. It was as corrosive as acid, this gut-deep hatred. It ate at the small reserve of Light that was still trapped inside him, for all that it was no longer unified with his soul.

And that was both the terrible power and the terrible failure of Bael. The demon had intended to rip the Light from Tré's soul and cast it into the pit of hell, but Irina had saved him. Her selfless, loving sacrifice had bound the Light inside him, turning him into a vampire rather than an undead puppet of his evil creator, filled with nothing but destruction and evil. A mere vessel for Bael's twisted desires.

According to Eris, ancient prophecy foretold that Bael could only be defeated in the coming War between Light and Darkness by a council composed of thirteen of his failures. Tré interpreted that to mean thirteen vampires, like himself. Thirteen people who had been saved by the sacrifices of true love, and transformed into powerful creatures who walked the empty spaces between the Light and the Dark.

But there weren't thirteen vampires roaming the earth. There were six.

Maybe Bael's cruelty and malice wasn't finished? Perhaps he simply hadn't created the other seven yet?

You'd think he'd learn from six mistakes, and stop trying, Tré thought bitterly.

His musings were interrupted by the sound of a sliding glass door being pulled back just below him. To his complete surprise, the woman from the mass shooting stumbled outside, wrapped in a robe and looking distraught. She dropped onto a bench near her door, leaving it open wide to the chilly night air, and scrubbed her face with her hands.

She was obviously troubled, despite Oksana's removal of her memories.

Tré wondered if she had been able to sleep at all, or if the events of the previous evening — those that she still remembered — were haunting her. Keeping her awake. Tré shook himself, ruffling feathers. He needed to keep his heart out of this matter. He was here purely for observation, to figure out what was going on. Not to satisfy the pangs of aching loneliness and desire he felt when looking at her.

He rustled his wings again, trying to shake free of the trance he had fallen into when she stepped outside.

The movement seemed to draw her attention and for a moment they stared at each other. Again, Tré felt a strong sense of recognition in his heart. It was as though someone had ignited a fire in his tattered soul, burning through him as he stared at the woman. He had never met her before that day, yet somehow, he knew her as well as he knew himself. He was drawn to her with an intensity that nearly knocked him right out of the tree.

Feeling an overwhelming need to protect her, Tré swiveled his head around, searching for any sign of danger that might disrupt the fragile sanctuary she seemed to have found here in the courtyard. He could feel Bael hovering over the city, but the demon did not seem to be focused on this place. Tré's wary tension eased somewhat, and he looked back toward the woman.

He could hear her breathing, which was slow and tranquil now. At that, he felt a strange sensation somewhere between a deep ache, and the promise of peace that he had never known in the endless years since his turning. All this, wrapped up within one tiny woman huddled on a cold bench. He could hardly bear the sensation, which seemed to resonate between the two halves of his broken soul like a struck tuning fork.

Suddenly, the woman stood.

"Thanks for the nighttime company, owl," she said in a low, lyrical voice. A moment later, she yawned and turned back toward the sliding door. Tré could tell by her heartbeat that sleep was stealing up on her. He watched as she shuffled inside on unsteady feet and slid the door shut behind her. He could clearly hear the satisfying sound of a clicking lock, and then a thud as she rolled a heavy length of wood into the track of the door.

She will be safe tonight, he thought with satisfaction.

Still, it was difficult to leave. With the beat of mighty wings, Tré finally took flight and headed towards home, feeling as though he were leaving part of his heart behind.

FOUR

Tré's return to the abandoned plantation house did not go unnoticed, but the other vampires wisely decided not to ask him for details of where he'd been. Instead, he sensed them silently retreating further into the house. Staying out of his way.

With the dawn approaching, they would soon go their separate ways to sleep and recuperate from the events of the night. Indeed, when Tré walked into the dusty, moldering parlor, it was to find Xander looking pale, worn, and far too sober as he headed for the stairs.

"So, you didn't drink yourself into oblivion after all?" Tré asked without emotion.

"Your guard dog wouldn't let me," Xander said, with a yawn and a stretch. "I feel like shit, though—thanks for asking. I'm going to bed."

"Call me if you need to feed again," Tré reminded him as he watched Xander laboriously climb the stairs, his shoulders drooping with exhaustion. A careless wave of one hand was the only answer he received.

With a shake of his head, Tré continued through the house to the kitchen. The space was rarely used, except when Oksana decided to go on one of her human junk food binges. For some reason, that eccentric trait had never faded during the decades that he'd known her. With every passing year, it seemed that she would discover some new culinary abomination with which to drown her sorrows.

Personally, Tré didn't understand how she could swallow the stuff without choking. None of the other vampires retained any vestige of liking for human food, subsisting instead on a strict diet of blood.

Well. Make that *blood, alcohol, and psychoactive drugs,* in Xander's case.

Yet, Oksana could often be found stashing away bags of greasy chips and sickly sweet confections in crinkling plastic wrappers, the mere smell of which turned Tré's stomach. Her current obsession was something called *no-bake cookies*, which she insisted were the best thing that she had ever eaten.

Still, who was he to judge? As coping mechanisms went, it wasn't the worst he'd seen over the years. Case in point... *Xander.*

Tré pushed his way through the creaking kitchen door and found several of the others seated around a large table in the center of the echoing room. Snag, Tré noticed, was not present. Not that he had expected the ancient vampire to be here. The oldest of their group, Snag spent the vast majority of his time sitting in the back bedroom in total silence, his cold, mournful eyes staring unblinking at anyone who dared enter his sterile domain. Tré hadn't heard him utter a sound in a little over a century, and often wondered if he'd lost the ability to speak.

For all intents and purposes, the old vampire was barely alive, even by their standards. He was rail-thin, and his skin hung off him like wax paper—parched and colorless. He was covered, head to toe, in scars that looked like they came from burns and claw marks, but Tré had never asked for details of what had happened to him after his turning, millennia ago. He was reasonably certain he didn't want to know.

Mostly, Snag would sit alone, sometimes staring out of the window, sometimes staring at nothing. He refused to feed on humans. As far as Tré could tell, only Eris' careful tending kept him from slipping into the petrified, coma-like state that seemed to be as close as vampires could come to the release of death in the normal course of things.

Eris alone seemed able to break through to Snag. To a degree, anyway. All the others harbored the belief that the ancient vampire was deranged, and would eventually lose his mind completely. Not Eris, however. From time to time, Eris could convince Snag to feed from him. He had been known to sit and talk to the old vampire for hours, even if he never received an answer.

He claimed the two of them played chess sometimes. Though, to Tré's knowledge, there had been no independent confirmation of such a thing. And he, at least, found it very hard to picture.

"Hello again, Tré. You certainly look like shit this morning," Duchess observed, her eyes raking up and down Tré's body. She, of course, had already touched up her makeup and hair sometime following the battle. Her bright red lipstick almost seemed to glow from her perfect, cupid's bow lips.

Eris gave her a quelling look. "It's been a rough night, Duchess," he said, no real ire behind the words. "You need to lay off."

"No," Tré said with a sigh as he sat on an empty bar stool. "It's fine. Though I imagine Xander is still going to win the *looking like shit* award for today."

The others nodded with varying degrees of sympathy.

"Thanks for keeping him from getting completely plastered, Duchess, by the way," Tré added.

"I have no more desire to listen to him snoring like a freight train and talking to himself all day than you do," Duchess said.

Oksana drew a quick breath, as if she were about to speak, only to pause and chew her lip with a thoughtful expression. Finally, she said, "You know, it just seems odd to me that so many of these terrible things have been happening here in New Orleans over the past few months."

"Well, New Orleans *is* a city that stays up late and parties hard," Eris pointed out. "It always has been."

"Yes," she agreed, "I know that. But it still seems like everything is getting worse here. Like it's becoming some sort of... I don't know. *Locus.*"

"Things are bad everywhere, but you do have a point about the area feeling like a sort of focal point," Tré said. He leaned wearily against the edge of the table. "Eris, have you run across anything like this in any of the ancient texts about Bael?"

"What? Specifically about a surge of violence in one place, you mean?" Eris asked.

"Yes, exactly."

"Not really, no."

Tré swallowed his disappointment. He'd never placed too much stock in what was predicted in dusty old prophecies. Even so, he would have appreciated a little insight from any source at all, if the lore masters could have been bothered to come up with something that would actually *help* them.

"It feels to me as if things here are getting more organized," Oksana said quietly. "Take the gunmen last night. That wasn't an act of a random violence, like a riot, or someone snapping and killing his family, or a drive-by shooting. It took planning, preparation, and careful execution of a coordinated attack. I don't think the perps were gang members, either. And while I don't doubt that the authorities will play the Islamic terrorist card, I didn't get that vibe from them at all."

The other members of the group nodded agreement. Duchess ran her fingers through her long hair, ruffling it and tossing it casually over her shoulder.

"I think you're right that it's all related somehow to the growing pattern of violence we've seen in the city in the past few weeks, *ma chère*," she said eventually.

"There seems to be no question that the attacks are growing in scale and organization."

"Agreed," Tré said.

Oksana yawned behind her hand and cast a longing eye towards a plate of cookies she'd left on the counter. Everyone was still and thoughtful except Eris. Eris looked troubled.

"Does... anyone else get the feeling that darkness is being *drawn* here, to New Orleans? Like we're standing at the center of a vortex?" he asked.

"Yes," Tré answered, the words striking a chord within him. "That's it, precisely. In fact, I was thinking about that on the way back. But... why *here*? Why now?"

"New Orleans does have one thing that the rest of the world lacks," Eris said, appearing decidedly disconcerted now. "It has the six of us."

"Why would that matter?" Oksana argued, frowning at Eris. "It's not like *we're* behind the attacks."

"No," Eris said with a shrug, "but it does seem like an odd coincidence that the only six vampires in the world would be residing in the city that's currently going to hell in a handbasket."

"But we're really only here in the first place because we *followed* the trail of destruction and violence," Duchess reminded Eris.

He nodded, but did not seem entirely convinced. Tré knew that Eris would spend hours—if not days—mulling over the theory. No doubt he would immerse himself the vast file of notes he kept on an old laptop, copied from the ancient texts that fascinated him so. Looking for some explanation, some *meaning* for what they had observed.

"There's something *different* about this place," Eris said in a quiet voice. "And it's new. I didn't feel it the last time I was here, a few years ago. It's also worth noting that, if the theory of darkness being somehow drawn to New Orleans is correct, it might explain why *we* were drawn here, as well. Vampires are, after all, dark creatures."

The words seemed to spark a connection in Tré's mind, and he frowned.

His mind wandered back over the last several weeks since they had arrived, following the reports of violence and unrest in hopes that it would somehow lead them to Bael. It was true that the incidents were getting deadlier and more public as time went on. It used to be that they could often manage small flare-ups with only one or two of them. Now, as the previous night had shown, it sometimes required all of them combining their strengths to stop the loss of life.

Yet, at the same time, they were utterly helpless to eradicate or eliminate the underlying source—the evil that seemed to possess some of the humans who acted as catalysts for the violence. On an almost nightly basis, there were riots across the city. The individuals involved did not appear to have any political or social aims. They simply seemed to enjoy getting into large groups, burning cars and buildings as they moved along the streets, sometimes even managing to force the police back with hails of rocks and Molotov cocktails.

Law enforcement presence didn't faze the rioters, who seemed almost impervious to normal crowd control and pain compliance techniques. The New Orleans Police Department was at a loss regarding how to proceed, and simply attempted to manage the situation to prevent the spread of the rioting to residential parts of the city. Already, there had been calls for National Guard troops to be brought in to help support local departments. But, of course, New Orleans was not the only fire needing to be put out in the U.S. these days—it was merely the one burning the hottest, right now.

To Tré, it seemed bizarre that mass panic had not yet taken root among the populace. And yet, he knew that humans were notorious for their ability to rationalize things. No doubt, someone reading the newspaper over breakfast would tut at the headlines, marvel at the state of the world today, then shake it off with a muttered hope that none of it would come close enough to affect their little slice of the world.

It seemed likely, however, that a tipping point would come — a point after which everything would descend into total chaos. That, Tré knew, would be when the real nightmare began for humanity.

Eris was right. It didn't make sense, without some sort of catalyst. Why New Orleans? Why now? What was different about this city, compared to all the other cities in the world? Obviously, the Big Easy had always hidden a dark side, rife with tension between the *haves* and the *have-nots*. Every large city did, though in New Orleans, the divide between the rich and the poor had been exacerbated over the decades by natural disasters and economic hardship.

But that could not explain everything they were seeing. There was something else.

Tré's thoughts turned inexorably back to the woman who both was and was not Irina. A terrible suspicion entered his mind. Eris had pointed out that New Orleans was different because *they* were there. Yet, the six of them had moved from place to place for years, now. Decades. *Centuries.*

But *they* were not the only ones in the city. A ghost from the past was here with them, as well.

Tré took a deep, troubled breath and tried to clear his thoughts. He was jumping to conclusions. It was ridiculous to believe that a single human woman had anything to do with the violence that was spiraling out of control in New Orleans. It was just a strange coincidence, which happened to have popped up at a time when Tré was distracted by old memories and not on his best game.

Oksana yawned so widely that it looked like her jaw might break, and insisted that they all go to bed and prepare for another night of whatever insanity might come. He nodded agreement and wished the others a good day's rest, in a tone that was admittedly somewhat distant.

A few minutes later, Tré slipped gratefully in between the sheets of the grand four-poster bed in the room he'd claimed as his own. He'd left his door slightly ajar so he could listen for Xander, who was right across the hall, and hear him if he needed help during the day.

With a last, troubled sigh, Tré turned over and allowed his eyes to close, drifting into an uneasy sleep as the sun rose over the eastern horizon beyond the protection provided by the heavy crimson drapes.

-o-o-o-

Della stumbled into the office in a rush. She was nearly twenty minutes late for work—unheard of, for her. Her coworkers stared at her in consternation as she half-collapsed into the chair behind her desk, muttering hasty apologies as she did so.

Sean walked over to her, his blue eyes wide with concern. She could hardly blame him for being worried, Della had never been so much as one minute late to work since she'd been hired. She hadn't even realized any of her coworkers had a copy of the key so they could open the building without her.

"Della, you all right, there?" Sean asked in a low voice, leaning over her desk to get a closer look at her.

His concern threatened to stir up the deep well of shock and horror that was trapped behind her ribcage. But she couldn't… she could *not* afford to lose it at work. This job was the last marginally sane thing in her life. She *couldn't* screw it up.

To avoid having to speak, she nodded, the movement jerky. Sean raised his eyebrows at her and she looked back, trying to plaster a normal expression on her face. What did a normal expression even look like? She wasn't at all sure she'd pulled it off, but after a moment, he gave a quiet sigh and walked back towards his office.

Della let out the breath she'd been holding, not feeling as though she could come up with the strength and energy it would take to tell everyone that she'd been right in the middle of the mass shooting the previous evening.

She tried valiantly to power her way through the pile of reports clogging her inbox, but her mind kept straying back, replaying horrible loops of memories from the previous night. By mid-morning, Della was covered in clammy sweat and felt like she was on the verge of tears.

She hurried into the bathroom, locked the door, and tried to absorb the moisture from her eyes with dry, scratchy paper toweling from the dispenser. In the end, she achieved nothing more than making the whites of her eyes look even more blood shot.

When she returned to her desk, Alice wandered over, carrying an iPad in her right hand.

"Can you believe this?" she demanded, practically thrusting the little tablet under Della nose.

"Hmm?" Della replied, barely glancing up. The last thing she needed right now was for Alice to notice her tears.

"The shooting last night! Haven't you heard?" Alice said, her voice rising with emotion. "It happened not far from here and a whole bunch of people *died*."

Della didn't know what to say. Other than the police at the scene who helped her, she had told no one about what happened the previous day. She didn't feel like she could even *begin* to explain it to the righteously angry woman currently leaning against the edge of Della's desk.

"I just can't believe all the terrible things that are happening right now," Alice continued. "It really seems like things are getting worse, you know? I wonder if it's terrorists... I just can't understand why the politicians won't *act* — what the hell do they think we voted them in for?"

She continued ranting along these lines, the droning complaints failing to hold Della's fractured attention for more than a minute or two. The office went hazy around her, and she felt her heart pounding. In her mind's eye, she was again staring at the barrel of a gun as it swung upward and pointed directly into her face.

"...released the name of one of the men who was killed. Did you see that? Della?"

Della only caught the end of Alice's statement. She had become so lost in memory that Alice's words were drowned out by the rushing sound of panic in her ears.

"I'm sorry, what?" she asked, clearing her throat and trying to shake herself free of the flashback before she had a full-on meltdown right here at her desk.

Alice looked at her curiously and repeated, "I said, the police released some information about one the men who was killed. Did you see the news?"

"No."

"It's just so senseless and tragic! They say he was a single dad with twin girls. I guess they're orphans now. Apparently his wife died a few years ago from cancer. Who would *do* that to someone with children?"

Alice held up the iPad again. The screen showed a picture of a smiling, bearded man with two identical toddlers held in his arms. To Della's horror, she recognized him as the guy who had stopped her falling during the mass panic as the gunmen poured onto the street. She had knelt by his side, her hand pressed against his back, as he breathed his last.

Two girls? He had children? Oh, God…

Della felt like she was falling. She sat back against her chair and tipped her chin forward, trying to breathe through the dizziness and nausea that was threatening to overwhelm her. If it hadn't been for her, standing there frozen with shock, he might have made it around the corner. If it hadn't been for her, he might still be alive.

Something terrible was clawing up from deep inside her stomach and she tasted bile in her mouth. Her eyes began to water and she started to pant, distraught by the news that Alice had unknowingly shared. Della felt as if her whole stupid, meaningless life was crashing down around her.

It was her fault he was dead. *Her fault.*

"Della?" Alice was saying, and Della knew it wasn't the first time she'd repeated it. "Della, honey? What is it? Are you all right?"

Della clamped her eyes shut. She couldn't speak—not while she was concentrating on swallowing around the bile that was trying to rise in her throat.

"*Della.* Hey, now. You're scaring me," Alice said, coming around the desk and putting a manicured hand on Della's shoulder. She gave it a gentle shake, as if trying to rouse Della from sleep. "Seriously. Are you okay?"

Della let her eyes open slowly and glanced into Alice's pinched, worried face.

"No," Della murmured, the word coming out hoarse. She had successfully forced her stomach to subside—for the moment at least—but she felt like her tenuous control over her emotions and rebelling gut would not last for very long. "I'm just… not feeling very well."

"Yeah. No kidding, honey. You look terrible," Alice said, and frowned. "Maybe you should go home?"

Della sat silently for a moment. The idea of taking the day off was appealing, but on the other hand, the idea of being alone with her thoughts was not. Still, the last thing she needed was for her coworkers to see her like this.

"I think you're right," Della decided, rising to her feet and gathering her stuff.

-o-o-o-

Several hours later, Della was installed in a quiet corner of the public library. She had not gone home after leaving work. Instead, she'd decided to try losing herself between the pages of a book, something she'd often done as a child when she was upset. As she'd walked towards the public library at the corner of Tulane and Loyola, Della tried to distract herself by picking apart pieces of her nightmare. She had the strangest feeling that she'd dreamed the dream many times before. It was so familiar to her. Even the brush of coarse fabric against her skin had seemed like something she knew intimately.

But how could that be? She had no particular knowledge about medieval Europe or the type of clothing people wore at that time. Hell, it was even a mystery to her how she could tell for certain that the setting of the dream *was* medieval Europe. There was no way she could know that from the handful of scattered images she could remember, and yet she was as sure of it as she was of anything in her life.

With a stack of books in front of her, Della systematically flipped through pages, reading here and there and examining pictures of old tapestries and woodcuts. She never got a sense of familiarity from any of the books, though. Certainly not like she had from her dream.

Della rubbed tired, aching eyes as she pulled a book closer. She could smell the faintly musty scent of old paper as she carefully turned the pages of the well-used history tome.

Without warning, a shout shattered the quiet peace of the library. Della gasped and looked up, ducking down behind her stack of books in instinctive fear. She peered cautiously at the gap between two large pillars near the front of the library. A man, dressed in the tattered clothing of a homeless person, was screaming obscenities at the staff, all of whom were standing like statues behind the desk. His hand waved through the air as he gestured. As it passed through a ray of sunlight, something glinted silver. He had a knife clutched in his fist.

Fresh fear jolted through her. Was there no escape from the madness that seemed to be closing in around her? She scrambled back and hid behind a row of shelves, peeking through the spaces at the scene unfolding in front of her.

As she watched, feeling her pulse thundering in her ears, two security guards lunged forward and muscled the man to the floor. He continued to scream, his voice muffled as his face was pressed into the ugly, gray-brown carpet. Della could see the library staff huddling close together, looking shocked and frightened. She couldn't blame them — this was a *library*. Stuff like this wasn't supposed to happen in *libraries*.

Della returned to her table when it became clear that the situation was under control. She sat slowly, feeling her body going numb again and her eyes drifting out of focus. A fog seemed to be pressing down on her, weighing her down. Darkness passed in front of her eyes, and she blinked rapidly, trying to clear it.

There were no coherent thoughts in her mind, only a sense of dread and isolation. She felt suddenly alone, completely cut off from the world around her as the darkness and the damp chill swirled through her. Vertigo overcame her, and she realized that she was holding her breath and had been for some time.

Something is coming.

Della's thoughts ground back to life and, with a struggle, she was able to jerk herself back to reality. There was a presence here with her, like a breath of evil and decay on the back of her neck. Della whipped her head around. There was no one near her. And yet, she could not shake the sensation that malicious eyes were watching her.

She could feel icy prickling on her shoulders and head, as if an invisible spotlight had found her and was shining down on her with light so cold it burned. Della tried to focus mentally and banish the irrational, unsettling feeling. Glancing around, she found that the library was almost empty. The light coming in through the windows was a dim, golden glow.

"Shit!" Della exclaimed in shock. She had sat in the library all afternoon, and now it was evening. Had she… fallen asleep or something? Was the sense of evil just some crazy dream? Or had she really spaced out for that entire time, staring at nothing?

What was *happening* to her? She had to get out of there before dark. She suddenly wanted, more than anything, to be locked up safely in her apartment, with her stupid goldfish and her television and her pile of overdue bills.

She jumped up and gathered her possessions, shoving them in the small bag that she had slung over her shoulder.

"Oh yeah, this is just great," Della muttered as she hurried out onto the street. Already, the streetlights were coming on.

The tram stop was right outside, and she waited nervously for the next one to come along. When it did, she boarded gratefully and sat in her customary place near the back. It was about half full, but the other passengers seemed edgy, glancing at her and looking away quickly.

Della gripped the hard wooden back of the seat in front of her, feeling the edge dig into her palm. She counted ten stops, trying to push a vague sense of unease to the back of her mind. She got off at Martin Luther King and Lasalle, relieved when a handful of other people did as well. The small group headed downriver, in the general direction of A.L. Davis Park.

No one seemed in a mood to talk, only in a mood to get where they were going. Della ducked her chin and followed a woman wearing a long raincoat down the street. The uneven sidewalks, missing random bricks and heaving up wherever tree roots grew underneath them, were usually part of the city's strange, down-at-heel charm. Right now, though, they were yet another irritation, slowing her progress, threatening a stumble or a twisted ankle if her attention wandered.

Maybe I'll get lucky, Della thought with a hint of bitterness, *and just make it home without any problems tonight.*

The woman in front of her turned into a convenience store on the corner of the street. Della kept walking. Soon, the sound of other footsteps died away as her fellow commuters turned onto side roads, one by one. Feeling unaccountably nervous now as she hurried down the familiar streets, Della gripped her bag against her side with cold hands.

The dark, hovering presence that had seemed to dog her steps since the library persisted. She felt as if her footsteps were slowing—like she was wading through water or sand towards her shabby little apartment in the unfashionable part of town. Gritting her teeth, she pressed onward, desperate to reach the perceived safety of her building's front door.

Through the deepening darkness around her, Della could hear a low, evil laugh ring out. It sounded very far away, as if it were being projected through a long, echoing cave. Again, the sense of malevolent eyes on her back raised the fine hair on her neck.

Della spun, ready to face whomever was following her head on. To her surprise, however, the street behind her was completely deserted. The laughter continued as she whipped her head back and forth, trying to determine which direction the sound was coming from. Nothing was visible in the failing light. Indeed, nothing on the street was moving *at all*. The gentle breeze that had lifted her hair as she walked out of the library had completely died, leaving things still.

Dead.

A choking feeling threatened to rise up from Della's chest as she turned back towards her home, now only a few blocks away. Breaking into a fast, jerky walk, Della tried to hold her chin up and look confident, even as she fought not to succumb to the treacherous, uneven sidewalk and the sensation of wading through invisible, icy water that dragged at her feet. In reality, she was shaking so badly that she felt lightheaded.

I just need to get home. Home, where it's safe. Then, I can eat something, go to sleep, and try to relax so I can forget this whole, horrendous week.

The buildings along this stretch of road were mostly two stories tall, set close together with dark alleys in between, stinking of garbage and cat piss. Old businesses, many of them empty and boarded up for years now. *Looming*, in the dark. The silence around her seemed to press against her skin. Suddenly, she heard the noise she had been straining—and dreading—to hear. The soft scuff of footsteps behind her met her ears. Della gripped the strap of her handbag more tightly and pushed forward, even though she felt that terrible weight again, trying to hold her back.

With her peripheral vision, Della saw two large figures coming up to flank her on either side. Before she even had a chance to consider her options, she heard two more swing in behind her. Almost despite herself, she turned her head enough to look at them.

They were walking alongside her, staring with leering mouths and flat, cold eyes. Della reached into her bag and yanked out the canister of pepper spray nestled there. She ran forward and whirled around, so that she was facing her pursuers.

She held the pepper spray straight out in front of her, but she could see her hand trembling with fear. Gripping the cylinder tighter, Della sucked in a huge breath and yelled at the top of her lungs. "Stay back! *Get away from me!*"

The four men laughed as if she had said something terribly funny. The sound made her skin crawl, but it was not the same laugh that had pierced the night only a few moments previously. This sound was higher-pitched, more human, although the same flat, lifeless anger was audible behind it. Della shuddered, and started to hurry backwards, never taking her eyes off the men in front of her.

They exchanged glances, and one at the back crossed his arms with a shake of his head and a cold grin.

A foul odor hit Della in the face, reminding her of the rotting corpse of a dead raccoon she had come across while walking one day, as a teenager. She gagged and held her breath.

Who *were* these people? God, they smelled *awful*. Were they more crazy homeless people, like the guy at the library earlier?

For a moment, Della's attention was distracted the terrible stench forming an aura around the men. They were surrounding her again, and she reminded herself forcefully that she needed to stop worrying about body odor and focus on not getting killed.

"I'm warning you," she said in a loud voice. Anger was coming to her defense now, but underneath she could hear the hint of fear and vulnerability in her tone. The telltale signs of the cornered prey animal. It was seriously beginning to look like Della was cursed to die at the hands of one fucking nut-job or another, given the events of the last twenty-four hours.

"You're mine now, girlie," the man on her right hissed, as he grabbed her arm and wrenched her towards him.

Della's finger closed over the pepper spray canister and a cloud of *oleoresin capsicum* erupted between them, making her eyes burn and a cough try to choke its way free of her chest.

Her attacker blinked once, as if confused by her action. His eyes grew bright red, but he shook it off and continued forward as if she had merely sprayed water in his face.

Terror gripped Della, and she took two stumbling steps backwards over the uneven bricks beneath her feet, yanking against his grip on her arm.

She had deployed her only defense, and it had been completely useless. She was at the mercy of four men twice her size, and God only knew what they were going to do to her now.

FIVE

Della maintained her grip on the can of pepper spray, hoping that maybe the contents would have more effect on the other men who were now closing in around her.

The attacker on her right had only tightened his grip on her arm after she sprayed him in the face, and Della felt a sharp ache from the bruises she'd gotten the previous night — painful leftovers from her *last* life-or-death experience.

She tried again to pull away, feeling — if it was possible — even *more* afraid of these men than she had been of the shooters who had slaughtered innocent bystanders right in front of her. It was their eyes, she thought. They were just... *wrong*. Completely flat and empty, with no life behind them. The vice-like grip around her bicep was cold and clammy, like a steak left to thaw too long on the counter.

Everything in her screamed that they could not possibly be human. And this time, she wasn't just some random passerby caught up in something larger. Their attention was focused squarely on *her*.

Her attacker dragged her into an alleyway, the others following along behind. All four men only leered at her as she screamed. She felt her vocal chords straining and was sure that she was tearing her throat as she shrieked for help. In her heart, though, she knew she was completely alone. No one was coming to her rescue. Her cries of terror and rage at the unfairness of it all echoed off the walls of the stinking alley, sounding strangely flat.

Silence was her only answer. There was nothing around her but rubbish. No one nearby to hear her cries.

"Pretty little piece of meat. You're about to regret the day you were born," one of the men rasped at her.

Della opened her mouth to scream again, but only a whimper emerged. She could only imagine what was about to happen. She had no cash or expensive jewelry that they could possibly want to steal. That left *her*. They wanted *her*. What could four men with no souls do to one defenseless woman, with no witnesses around to stop them or hold them back?

In desperation, she lifted the pepper spray again, but a large hand effortlessly batted it from her grasp. She heard it clatter against the pavement. Her captor shoved her to the ground. She stumbled on the way down, striking her head against the brick wall behind her. Bright lights went off in front of her eyes like flashbulbs as she lay on her side in a dazed, crumpled heap.

Rough hands turned her over onto her back, and she blinked up at the four men, trying to clear the haze in her head. As if in slow motion, she saw one raise his open palm to strike her across the face.

It was odd. She could feel the distant, stinging pain and taste blood from her split lip, but it was as if her mind could not take in any more information. Like she had already gone through too much, and her awareness was simply shutting down. She hadn't truly registered being hit. Maybe she was concussed or something— slipping in and out of consciousness.

Her arms and legs were completely limp, and she felt herself being dragged to the middle of the alley, bits of broken glass and gravel cutting into her back where her shirt had pulled up. One of the men was pawing at her exposed stomach, trying to pull down her waistband. Della felt herself retch weakly at the clammy, raw meat feel of his skin against hers.

From out of nowhere, a dark shape slammed into the man who was pinning her down. The impact knocked him away from her, further into the shadowed alley. Della's head was pounding, but she tried to crane around to see what had happened. The sickening sound of bones cracking met her ears, followed by the fleshy *thump* of a limp body falling to the ground.

The three other men were scrambling to their feet around her, balling up their fists as if preparing for a fight. The dark figure rushed at them, taking the feet out from one of Della's assailants with an almost casual sweep. He pounced on the fallen man, tearing at him like an animal. Blood sprayed across the alley.

Della could smell the coppery tang of it, and tried in vain to claw herself into an upright position. She wanted to flee like a frightened rabbit, but her legs were made of rubber and she couldn't even feel her hands or feet after the blow to her head. She tripped and felt the rough brick scrape skin from her forearms as she scrabbled for purchase.

Finally giving up, she curled against the base of the alley wall and clamped her hands over her ears, trying to block out the screams of agony coming from men who were being killed right in front of her. She squeezed her eyes shut, but no amount of sensory deprivation could block out the impression of bodies being torn apart, their discarded limbs hurled across the alley to lie in pools of dark, congealing blood.

Please, I just want to go home. Please, let me go home. Della rocked forward and back, curling into a ball and hiding her face. She could not even crawl away on her hands and knees, so great was her distress.

Barely parting her eyelids, Della peered out from behind her arms like a child peeking at a scary TV show. Her defender stood in a pale chink of illumination from one of the streetlights on the far side of the main road. He was rail thin and gaunt, with a shaved head. There was something exotic about his features, like an ancient stone statue, worn down to harsh angles by the passage of time. Despite his nearly skeletal aspect, something about his high cheek bones and straight nose seemed to recall a face of royalty. His eyes glowed with a fierce inner light as he lunged at the last of the men who had attacked Della.

She felt a thrill of combined terror and satisfaction as she watched her attacker drop all pretence and attempt to run. He turned and sprinted towards the street. Just as he was about to reach the corner, the man with the shaved head reached out with a movement that seemed almost lazy and caught the collar of his shirt. They both tumbled to the ground in a tangle.

With a snarl, her attacker rolled onto his back and attempted to punch the skeletal man in the face. He managed to land two blows that snapped his shaved head first to one side, and then the other, but the heavy impacts didn't appear to faze the newcomer in the least. In fact, he looked a bit bored as he stood and placed his foot in the center of the other man's chest.

The man on the ground bellowed in rage, the sound cut off abruptly when her defender pressed down hard with his foot. A sickening *crack* and several splintering noises threatened to make Della lose the minimal contents of her stomach as he smashed the man's chest, breaking every rib and crushing the organs inside.

With one last twitch, he lay completely still, obviously dead.

Relief poured through Della for a bare instant before it was swallowed again by terror. The gaunt man was turning toward her now, examining Della on the ground in a cold, distant sort of way. The same way a butterfly collector might survey a particularly interesting moth, right before pinning it to a board and sticking it inside a glass case.

She opened her mouth, intending to yell at him to stay back. But apparently she'd used all the air available to her, back when the attack had started. She couldn't even produce a squeak. She mouthed at him in silent terror for a moment before edging herself backwards along the wall, trying to get away from him as he advanced towards her, step by step.

There was no flicker of empathy, friendliness, or concern in his eyes, which were chilly and distant. Not *flat*, like those of the four men that were now scattered in pieces all over the alley, though. Rather, this man looked almost as haunted as Della felt. As if he had lived a million years of misery, and simply wished that everything would end.

As he passed through the illumination filtering in from the street again, Della could see that his skin was scarred and marked by what appeared to be claws. She stared, open-mouthed, as he came closer, wondering what could have happened to him to cause such injuries, when he was obviously so powerful and strong.

"*Please,*" Della forced out, the word a hoarse, barely audible whisper. Fear of the man now walking steadily towards her pinned her in place. Perhaps it was her imagination, but it seemed that his movements were almost predatory in nature. He stalked silently forward, never taking his cold, glowing eyes off of her.

Darkness was gathering at the edges of her mind as the events of the past few minutes caught up with her. Fighting to stay conscious, Della pushed herself into more of a sitting position, but doing so only caused her head to spin and spots to erupt in front of her eyes. She felt sick and giddy.

She put her hand up, trying to motion for him to stop, but it seemed to waver in front of her, as if growing alternately close and far away.

Huh, that's odd, she thought numbly.

When the man was within arm's reach of her, the last of Della's strength seemed to evaporate. Blackness washed in around her like floodwater, and she slumped to the ground in a dead faint.

-o-o-o-

Tré's eyes flew open. It was as if someone had shouted in his ear, jerking him out of a fitful sleep. He sat bolt upright in his bed, the sheets and blankets bunching up around his waist.

He didn't know what had caused his abrupt return to consciousness, so he listened intently to the sounds inside the house. He could hear the even breathing of sleep coming from several of the others' rooms as his housemates slumbered peacefully on, untroubled by whatever had awoken him. Tré could also detect the soft sounds of Duchess one floor below in the sitting room, idly turning the pages of a book. He could tell that she wasn't really reading it that closely, since she often flipped back and forth, as if skimming for some bit of information.

He cocked his head while scanning the house more closely, searching for Snag. The last member of their clan appeared to be... *absent*.

Certain that he had simply missed the muted sounds of life from the half-dead vampire, Tré reached out with his mind to touch the life forces present. He could tell that Xander was starting to wake, roused by the brush against his mind. Oksana and Eris slept peacefully, lost in dreams of the past. Duchess raised an eyebrow when she felt Tré poking around. He could feel her flare of mild indignation at the fact that he was probing her thoughts. He searched through the rest of the house and found it empty.

"*Damn*. Where is he?" he muttered, rolling to his feet and fumbling for clothing.

Tré had been concerned for some time now that the oldest, most damaged of their group would eventually lose his reason and disappear into the night without warning. He had done everything he could to keep Snag safe and calm, a goal helped along significantly by Eris' inexplicable bond with the ancient creature.

From the time they moved into the abandoned plantation house, Tré was quite certain that Snag had never left. He never hunted, sustained only by the generous offer of blood that Eris provided him whenever he could be tempted into feeding. His absence struck Tré as very ominous, indeed.

He had always harbored a half-formed idea that Snag might snap someday, and Tré would end up having to protect the other vampires from him—or worse, some random, innocent human bystanders. Such protection would, quite possibly, come at the cost of his own life, since Tré wasn't at all sure he could best the powerful, ancient vampire in a fight.

He hoped that today was not going to be the day he found out—if nothing else, Eris would be devastated. Tré hurried downstairs and into the sitting room, where Duchess was still reading. Her back was to him, but he knew she was aware of his presence.

Sure enough, she spoke as soon as he came around the corner. "Looking for something in particular, oh fearless leader?" she asked in a dark tone.

Tré didn't mince words. "Where's Snag?"

Duchess went still in the act of turning a page. He could tell that she was listening hard, just as he had done moments before.

"He's not here," she murmured, turning a worried expression towards Tré. "How strange."

"That's what I thought," Tré replied.

Her earlier irritation vanished instantly in the face of the unexpected revelation. "You should go wake Eris."

Tré mulled that over for a bare instant before nodding agreement. He jogged back up the stairs and knocked on Eris' door.

A moment later, Eris pulled the door open, looking a little groggy and a lot confused. He was bare-chested, a pair of soft pajama bottoms slung low on his hips. "Tré?" he asked. "What is it?"

"Snag is missing."

"*What?*" Eris asked. Tré saw his gaze turn inward, searching.

"He's not here, or nearby," Tré said. "It looks like he's wandered off."

Eris raked his hand through his hair. "Okay. Right. Just let me put some clothes on."

Tré leaned against the doorframe while Eris disappeared back into the bedroom, a sense of foreboding settling in his stomach as he waited for the other vampire to get ready. He could hear Eris splashing water on his face from the ewer on the dresser, and changing clothes. When he emerged, he looked both alert and determined.

"Come on. Let's go find him," Eris said.

From nowhere, a terrified scream tore through Tré's mind, making him stagger as if from a powerful blow to the head. Eris reached out and steadied him on his feet, gripping his shoulders with strong hands.

"Talk to me. What just happened?" he demanded. "I felt something, but I think it was just the backwash from you."

Tré's heart was pounding out of control, as if he had just received an electric shock.

"*Irina.*"

Tré knew that cry of anguished pain and fear anywhere. It was the same cry that had reverberated through his mind in a dark forest in fifteenth-century Moldavia, the night he had been turned by Bael. Usually, when his thoughts strayed down that dark road, he felt a surge of hatred toward Bael so powerful that he was barely able to control himself. This time, however, he felt nothing other than cold dread that something terrible was happening to his beloved *right now*.

It was the woman from the shooting the previous day. The woman he had followed and stood guard over during the night. It had to be.

She was in trouble, and this time, Tré was damn well going to save her, or die trying.

"'Irina'?" Eris echoed, looking completely bewildered.

"The woman," he breathed. "The one we saved from the shooters. Her life is in danger."

Without another word, Tré drew all of his power into a tight knot in his chest and changed himself into mist, hurtling out of the open window near Eris' bed and flying towards New Orleans.

The woman's cries reverberated in his mind, a beacon as bright as a lighthouse, drawing him to her side. Behind him, he could sense Eris following. He reached out with his mind to touch the other vampire's consciousness.

Where are we going, Tré? Eris thought. *You're following something, but I can only sense it reflected through you.*

It's Irina. The woman. I can hear her screams.

Tré could practically taste Eris' confusion.

But... how?

I've heard those same screams for hundreds of years. I know them better than I know myself. Only now, the veil of death no longer hangs over them.

Eris pulled back from the connection, lapsing into mental silence. Tré could hardly blame him for being taken aback. It was unprecedented that any one of them would have such a strong telepathic connection to a human.

Tré and the others were mentally connected because they had fed from one another many times over the years. If one of them became sick or hurt, the life-blood of their fellows would strengthen them and speed the healing process. It bound the six of them together in fellowship. An unbreakable circle of blood. They were united as one in the face of Bael, and that unity extended to their thoughts as well as their bodies.

This fact was what made Snag's absence all the more startling. He would have to be very far away—or else purposely shielding—in order for Tré, whose mental capacity was incredibly strong and far reaching, not to be able to sense him. And what reason would he have to shield his thoughts?

A gripping fear and nausea that was not his own dragged Tré's attention back to the here-and-now. He could tell that the woman was injured, and it only made him press forward more quickly, hurtling toward the source of the terror. He followed her presence like a searchlight in the pitch darkness, guiding him to her, compelling him to her side.

A few moments later, Tré felt that beacon flicker and go out. The sensation very nearly sent him crashing back to earth in solid form. Eris swirled next to him, their forms mixing, as if Eris was lifting Tré up and keeping him moving forward.

Tré might have lost his mental grip on the woman, but it did not matter. They were close enough now that he could smell her.

He and Eris materialized at the mouth of an alley, stumbling to a halt as they took in the bloodbath around them. A powerful smell of dead flesh met his nose and he reeled, realizing that there were body parts all around him. Was Irina—?

"Bael's minions," Eris said succinctly, looking at the corpses scattered in pieces on the ground. "But how — ?"

His words trailed off as their eyes fell on the woman, huddled against the alley wall. A lone, skeletal figure loomed over her, reaching down to lift her limp form. Her head lolled, like a broken doll's.

Tré's breath caught. *Snag.*

The ancient vampire lowered his hand towards the woman's mouth, wiping a trail of blood away with apparent curiosity. He licked his thumb, tasting it, and pulled her closer to him.

Unthinking rage flooded Tré's body in an instant, and he stepped forward with a growl.

SIX

"Put. Her. *Down*." Tré demanded in a deadly voice. Snag froze, his mouth halfway to the woman's neck, and glanced back at the two newcomers with an arrested look on his face. He did not release the woman, and Tré's tenuous control snapped.

He sprang forward towards Snag, ready to tear him to pieces for daring to lay a hand on Irina. On his *mate*. The knowledge that Snag was a powerful vampire who could almost certainly best him in a fight fell away, unimportant. The understanding that, for their safety, the six of them needed to band together was as distant as the moon above them.

Tré forgot *everything* in the blind rage that poured through his body, eliminating all other thought and feeling. He snarled as he launched himself forward but was brought back sharply to reality when a strong grip jerked him around by the shoulder, halting his momentum.

The sharp pain as his back hit the alley wall cleared his head, at least partially, and he glared at Eris' face, inches from his own. His companion had grabbed him and slammed him against the wall, pinning him in place. Tré sometimes forgot that, despite his generally mild, bookish demeanor, Eris, too, was a vampire of great age and power. Older, in fact, than Tré. Older than *all* of them, with the exception of Snag.

But if he thought that would be enough to keep Tré from getting to Irina, he was sorely mistaken.

"Get off me!" he hissed at Eris, still furious. Tré shoved against his hold, still angry and determined to get to Snag.

"Tré, get a grip on yourself and *look around*!" Eris demanded. He gestured at the alley with a jerk of his chin, leading Tré's gaze toward the piles of body parts. "*Use your nose*, for fuck's sake!"

Tré finally shook Eris off and pushed away from the wall, brushing dirt from his jacket. With his angry gaze still locked on Snag, who had not moved, he took a deep breath through his nose and tried to separate the overpowering tangle of scents into something useful.

He could smell the woman. She was alive, but unconscious, and her sweet scent seemed to roll over him. Yet a putrid reek was rising as well, coming from the bodies lying all around them.

It was the scent of the undead.

Shock at this revelation pinned Tré to the spot, replaced by the cold realization of what Eris had already sensed, and tried to communicate to him earlier.

It was Bael.

Bael was behind this attack on his mate. Not Snag.

He took several deep breaths, forcing himself to return to a state of calm, and nodded brusquely at Eris, who had kept a hand on Tré's shoulder in case he made another attempt to attack Snag.

Throughout the entire thing, Snag had not moved or spoken. He remained crouched on the ground, supporting the woman's upper body in a loose grip.

Eris, seeing that Tré was in control again, squeezed his shoulder once and dropped his hand back to his side.

Tré moved forward and squatted in front of the pair on the ground. He avoided Snag's eyes, and stared down into the face of the woman he had both loved and destroyed. Her head had rolled to one side, resting against Snag's wiry bicep.

Tré could hear her heart beating. It seemed to be much faster and threadier than he thought it should have been. Dark shadows were smeared under her eyes. She looked ghostly pale under the glare of the distant streetlight.

He stretched out a hand as if to brush her soft hair out of her face. Just before he made contact, he jerked it back, misgivings flooding his mind.

What if she wasn't really Irina? What if he had been deluding himself? Perhaps he should have been worrying less about Snag's sanity, and more about his own. Nervousness bubbled up in his stomach—unusual, for him. He prided himself in being self-assured and confident; neither bold to the point of foolishness, nor timid to the point of paralysis. However, an unfamiliar chill was settling over him as this new fear awoke in his heart.

Tré was terrified that if he touched her, he would not feel that same bright spark of recognition. This woman had turned his entire world upside down and shaken the very foundation underneath him. He was captivated by her. But if it turned out she was not Irina, Tré was quite sure that the sense of grief and betrayal to the memory of his lost soul mate would tear the last, threadbare fibers of his soul apart.

Paradoxically, he was nearly as afraid that he would feel the same sensation he did the last time he touched her skin. He had mourned the loss of his beloved Irina. Had known that it was his fault she was irretrievably dead and gone. The burden of guilt lay heavily on him, only partially assuaged by his furious desire for revenge and his eternal battle against Bael.

That loss… that guilt… had defined him for centuries now. If Irina was *here*, lying in front of him, what would he do?

Tré felt Eris' mind brush against his softly, as if his friend had rested a gentle hand on his shoulder.

He looked back at Eris, who was standing a couple of steps behind him.

"Just trying to figure out what's going on with you, my friend," Eris said, watching him closely. "You've been staring at her for several minutes without moving or speaking, you realize."

Tré let his breath out slowly, and turned back to the woman in Snag's arms. "Just... thinking."

"I'm a huge proponent of thinking," Eris said, scratching the back of his head and looking around. "Unfortunately, we're standing in an alley full of undead body parts, so time is not really our ally at the moment. Did she see you?"

The question was clearly meant for Snag. Tré glanced up at him, still feeling self-conscious over his misjudgment of the ancient creature's motives. The older vampire merely stared back at both of them, his mouth a thin line. After a few moments, he gave a single, curt nod, barely perceptible through the gloom.

Eris swore quietly under his breath in Greek, his bright eyes searching the alley and the street beyond. "Well, I don't think we have much of a choice, in that case."

"What do you mean?" Tré asked, his sluggish mind struggling to keep up with the night's events.

Eris frowned at him. "I doubt a memory wipe will work on her while she's unconscious. I know I wouldn't be able to delve into her mind and find the correct memories to pull without risking significant damage to her cognitive abilities. She might wind up being a vegetable, and judging by your earlier reaction, I'm assuming you wouldn't approve."

Tré felt a flicker of annoyance at Eris' insouciant attitude, but did not comment on it. Instead, he nodded and rose to his feet. "We'll take her back to the house, then."

Eris gave him an appraising glance and raised his eyebrows. Tré knew exactly what he was thinking.

Of the six of them, Snag was the only one powerful enough to transform a human into mist with him, and travel great distances with speed. The knowledge stabbed at him as he watched Snag rise, pulling the woman more securely into his arms.

Tré approached the pair, giving Snag a burning look as he stepped up, face to face. For the briefest of moments, Tré thought that Snag was about to speak. His dry lips parted and he drew breath, but then at the last moment he seemed to change his mind. He sighed and brushed Tré's mind with his own, the contact so light that it was barely perceptible. There were no clear thoughts or words, just a sense of assurance and peace.

Tré relaxed his aggressive stance with effort. He knew he needed to trust Snag to get this woman back to the plantation house safely so he could care for her. His raging protectiveness was only getting in the way. Eris clapped a hand on his back, startling him out of his reverie.

"Come on," he said in a low voice, "let's just get out of here before the humans find this mess and start panicking."

Snag shut his eyes and straightened his spine. Tré watched as a mist swirled around him and the unconscious woman in his arms. A cool breeze wafted through the thick miasma of death and fear that had settled over the dark alley, and the mist blew away.

Tré pulled all of his life force inward. His body dissolved, and he sped after Snag and the woman, with Eris close behind. As he flew towards the abandoned house, he sank into the deepest parts of his consciousness, trying to contain the crazed emotions that were cracking his control and resolve.

Get yourself together, he thought, knowing that the next few hours would be nothing short of exhausting. *You can't afford to go to pieces now.*

As they flew, the last faint glow that had been illuminating the western horizon faded as total dark fell around them. The trees rustled as they passed and Tré poured everything into speeding towards the old plantation—his sole focus on the mysterious woman Snag was carrying.

He and Eris landed side-by-side at the front door, where Snag was already waiting for them. Tré immediately turned towards the older vampire. He was grateful for the power that had given the injured woman safe passage out of New Orleans, but now he felt an overwhelming need to have her in his embrace.

Snag relinquished his hold on her tiny, limp frame, transferring her into Tré's arms as Eris pushed the door open. To Tré's relief, he was able to hold her against his chest without their skin touching directly.

Coward.

Without a word or a glance, Snag walked into the manor house and headed towards his cold, barren room at the back. Tré paused, one foot on the top step of the of the porch stairs as he watched the other vampire go.

"Thank you," he murmured. He knew that Snag had heard him, and, indeed, the ancient vampire paused for a bare instant before passing out of sight.

After Eris shut the door behind them, Tré walked quickly up the stairs, cradling the unconscious body in his arms. As he stepped sideways through the doorway into his bedroom, he could hear her heart beating. To his relief, it sounded stronger than it had in the alley. Tré wondered if that meant she had passed from shock and unconsciousness into regular sleep. He placed her gently on his bed, hoping that was the case. Once she was settled, he strode quickly to the door and shut it, desperate for some quiet and privacy.

After listening intently for a moment, he could discern all five vampires in the house, present and accounted for. With a quiet sigh, he returned to the bed, and the enigma lying in it.

Tré stared down at the beautiful woman nestled against his pillows, barely resisting the urge to brush a wisp of honey-colored hair out of her face. It felt like his heart was swelling beyond the confines of his ribcage, threatening to burst free of his body.

What was *happening* to him?

Her beauty was like a song, calling to his soul, whispering to a place in his heart he had thought long dead. A great cloud of energy seemed to flow through his body, bringing warmth to his cold flesh and making his nerves tingle.

With trembling fingers, he reached out and touched the woman's arm.

Just as suddenly as last time, Tré felt a rush of shock — of *knowing* — pulse through his body. It was a bit more muted this time, and he wondered if that was because she was unconscious. Yet, there was no doubt in his mind that this was his soulmate. His beloved Irina.

He didn't know how she had come to be here, or how her soul could be in the possession of the sleeping woman in front of him. It was a complete mystery to him, but at the moment he felt no urgency to uncover the truth. He was blissfully happy just to be in her presence again, even if he dreaded the moment when she would wake up.

Unable to stop himself, Tré licked his fingers and reached out, wiping the dried blood away from her split lip with a gentle movement. He could smell its coppery scent on his hand. It intoxicated him, making his head spin.

How was he supposed to explain this to her? Where could he even begin?

In his mind, Tré rehearsed how the conversation might go. *"Hello, my name is Vladimir Illych Romanov III, but you can call me Tré. I'm a vampire, and you appear to be the reincarnation of my soulmate who has been dead for centuries, ever since I killed her and drained her dry in a frenzy of bloodlust after a demon turned me into an undead monster. Weird, huh? Let's be friends."*

Hysterical amusement tried to rise in his chest, and he pushed it down. She'd be screaming for the men with white coats and butterfly nets before he got the last word out. With a growing sense of doom, he pulled a chair closer to the bed and settled in, waiting for her to awaken.

-o-o-o-

A tangle of voices and the memory of rushing wind in her ears ushered Della back to awareness. She didn't immediately open her eyes, still feeling terribly confused and disoriented.

It felt like she was lying flat on her back, propped against a pile of soft, fluffy pillows and covered with a warm blanket. Rubbing her fingers back and forth with tiny movements, Della could feel soft sheets under her hands. They were much nicer than anything she had ever owned. Suddenly, she wanted nothing more than to nestle deeper under the covers and drop off into peaceful unconsciousness again.

She allowed herself to drift, wondering idly where she was and how she had gotten here. It seemed like there was something she had forgotten, something very important that was buzzing for attention at the edges of her mind. Yet somehow, she couldn't bring herself to be troubled by it. The memories were out of her reach, so instead, she let herself bask in the peaceful feeling that was wrapping her in a warm cocoon, whispering to her of sleep.

Knowing she would regret an extended slumber later, Della reluctantly tried to rouse herself.

With a sigh, she opened her eyes. It felt like it took longer than it should have before she was able to bring everything into focus. She blinked rapidly. When she was finally able to distinguish details, she saw that she was lying in a magnificent four-poster bed, with a gauzy canopy and beautiful deep red hangings pulled back around the posts. With what seemed like a great effort, she pushed herself into a sitting position. Her gaze fell on a man, sitting quietly by her bedside.

He was... holy *shit*. He was the most gorgeous thing she had ever seen. How was it even possible that this work of art was human? Good lord above. His cheekbones alone could probably cut glass, and his *eyes* —

She had to fight to keep her jaw from dropping open as she gawped at him like some kind of mental case. He leaned forward in his chair, regarding her in turn. Relief colored his beautifully sculpted features, but so did worry. She swallowed hard and blinked again, not wanting to look like a ridiculous schoolgirl in addition to her messy hair and crumpled clothes.

She couldn't help it, though—she continued to stare, wide-eyed, at the man.

He met her gaze with pale, intense eyes. The pupils were such a light, piercing gray that they appeared almost silver. Della felt her skin heat up as those eyes raked over her, looking at her like a starving man staring at a feast for the first time in years. She felt an inexplicable sense of familiarity with that hot gaze. A sense of *rightness*, as if she had met him years before, but had somehow forgotten.

Could she have known him when she was a child? He was about the same age she was, at a guess. Or... maybe a bit older than that? Perhaps in his late twenties. There was something timeless about those silver eyes —

The moment stretched, but neither one of them spoke. Burning curiosity pulled Della's attention away from his face, moving lower to take in the muscular frame hidden under finely tailored clothing that suited him, but also gave him something of a dark, mysterious air. She could sense a sort of... *chill*... emanating from him. A coldness, despite his hot gaze. It was a bit eerie, but she immediately shook it off, dismissing it as part of her growing paranoia after the past couple of days.

She sucked in a breath. *The past couple of days.*

Memory dawned, sweeping away any further frivolous thoughts she might have had about the inhumanly handsome man sitting next to her. *Jesus.* The alley. The men. They'd been about to—

Half-remembered images of unimaginable violence rose, murky and unclear. Something had happened, but then she'd lost consciousness, and now it was all one big muddle. She lifted a hand to the back of her head and winced when her fingers brushed a lump the size of an egg that throbbed and ached when she touched it.

The reality of her situation finally penetrated the haze surrounding her wits, and her heart began to race.

"Where am I?" she whispered. She clenched the comforter and blanket with white knuckles, feeling a flicker of growing fear as she searched the bedroom for any indication of where she was or how she got there. Would she never be free of the madness that seemed to be surrounding her life these days?

"You're in an abandoned plantation house, not far from the city limits. You're safe now. We rescued you from your attackers." The man's voice was velvet over steel—deep and dark, with a hint of an accent she didn't recognize. Della felt her heart slow down and her panic ebb, though she could not have said why.

"What happened to my attackers?" she asked cautiously.

The man's eyes lingered on her face for a moment before he spoke. "You don't remember?"

Once again, she concentrated on the memories, trying to sort through the muddle.

Clammy hands grabbing her. The horrible reek from the bodies pressed close around her. Leering smiles and flat, lifeless eyes. Pepper spray. The alley. Then... a shadowy figure. And blood. Blood everywhere.

She gasped and scrabbled back against the headboard, one hand coming up to clutch at her chest. She looked at the man sitting next to her in horror.

"How-? *Who*—?"

He frowned, as if choosing his words carefully. "I heard you screaming. An... acquaintance of mine arrived first, and defended you until I got there, accompanied by another friend of mine. You were injured, so we brought you here to this house so you could recover in safety. We didn't feel it wise to take you to a hospital. You might still have been in danger there."

Della struggled to grasp what he was saying. "Your *acquaintance* defended me?" She stared at him in disbelief. "From what I remember, it was more like he *massacred* four huge men without taking more than a couple of hits himself. *How*? What he did was not humanly possible!"

Before he could answer, there was a soft knock at the door. A moment later, it opened partway and a brown-haired, green-eyed man stuck his head into the room.

"Tré?" asked the newcomer.

So, her incredibly attractive rescuer and/or kidnapper was apparently called *Tré*. Before she could turn that new piece of the puzzle over in her mind, he turned to the newcomer and snarled, "*Get out.*" His full lips curled in anger, revealing pointed fangs.

The man who had just entered looked affronted, and parted his lips to snarl back. With another wave of shock, Della realized that his teeth, too, were long and sharply pointed.

It was too much. Della's mouth worked silently for a moment before she was able to drag in a ragged breath.

"*No!*" The word was a hoarse scream. Panicked, she scrambled backward toward the opposite side the bed, trying to get as far away as possible from the... *creatures* in front of her.

The sudden commotion seemed to startle both men. They turned and looked at her in concern, their growling match apparently forgotten.

"Stay the hell away from me, both of you!" Della shouted, holding out a hand to ward them off. She licked her dry lips, and found the copper taste of blood on them from where she had been struck in the face.

"Sorry," the green-eyed man said with a marked British accent, slinking back out of the room, his hands raised in gesture of peace. "Look, I'm sorry about that, Tré. I'll go."

Tré made a frustrated sound and turned back towards Della, who flung a pillow at him in her terror.

"Oh, *hell*, no!" she yelled, anger coming to her defense now. "I am *done* with this shit! You get back; don't come near me!"

"Irina... *please*," he said, lifting a hand toward her.

Della scrambled further away, very nearly catapulting herself right off the edge of the bed. She kicked at the heavy covers, trying to free her legs. She knew, deep down, that there was no escape from the madness that seemed intent on destroying her, but at this point, she was ready to die trying.

Before she could completely untangle her legs, though, she felt a heavy weight pressing down on her mind. The world seemed to be descending into a thick, gray cloud. Dizziness engulfed her. She clapped a hand to her head, trying in vain to fight the sensation. Her eyelids grew heavy.

"Not again," she slurred, exhaustion dragging at her.

Cool hands gripped her, drawing her back towards the center of the bed, settling her carefully against the stack of pillows. Her eyes fell closed, and she sank into darkness. The last thing she felt — or *thought* she felt, was a fleeting touch of trembling fingers, brushing her hair away from her face and tucking it behind her ear.

"Oh, *Irina*," whispered a deep velvet voice. "*What have I done?*"

SEVEN

When Della next gained awareness, it was not with the same slow transition back into wakefulness. Instead, she jerked awake with a cry.

Panting and sweating, she looked around with wild eyes.

"Do try your best to remain calm, if you wouldn't mind," said a bored female voice from next to the bed. "I find human hysteria dreadfully tedious."

Della's gaze flew to her immediate right, where she found a beautiful woman sitting in the chair next to the bed. Gaping at her, Della took in the woman's striking, porcelain-doll features.

Pale blond hair fell in graceful waves over the woman's elegant shoulders. Her bright blue eyes were accented by high, rounded cheekbones, finely arched eyebrows, and the blood red of her lipstick. Her expression was schooled into a haughty, disdainful look.

It took a moment for her words to register.

"Stay *calm*? *Seriously*?" Della asked, incredulous. She could have just as soon have detached her right leg and eaten it.

The woman shifted her position from where she had her feet propped up on the edge of the bed. She was wearing tight jeans, a black silk blouse, and high heels that matched the color of her lipstick. In a moment of completely inappropriate and shallow frivolity, Della realized that the shoes alone probably cost more than her last paycheck. A bubble of hysterical laughter tried to force its way up her throat, and she choked it back down.

Seeming supremely unconcerned with Della's emotional outburst, the other woman merely examined her perfect fingernails while Della attempted to regain control of her breathing.

"You're completely safe here, you know," she said, still sounding as though she found the whole situation hopelessly tiresome. "You can call me Duchess, by the way. I've been tasked with babysitting you while you slept."

When Della only stared at her, Duchess raised a sculpted eyebrow. "I'll take your generous expression of thanks as a given, then, shall I?"

Resuming her examination of her nails, the woman settled back in her chair.

Della's memories weren't working right. There were several things that she knew must be very important, but she was having trouble untangling the strands into a narrative that made sense.

"The men. The ones in the alley," she began, remembering that part well enough. "What happened to the men that attacked me?"

"One of my housemates found you, and managed to fight them off before they could do anything serious to you. Though you do seem to have hit your head. You've been in and out of consciousness for some time now. It's about three o' clock in the morning, in case you're wondering."

Della looked at the large picture window across the room. The heavy curtains were drawn back, and pale moonlight illuminated the skeletal branches of a tree outside.

"I'm surprised you remember it at all, to be honest," Duchess said, drawing Della's attention back towards her.

Della glanced into the perfect features that, despite their owner's dismissive tone, appeared focused and observant—as if she was feeling Della out for her responses.

Oh, I am so *not playing games with you right now, woman*, Della thought, as more memories surfaced—shocking, but far too clear and intense to have been a dream.

"And the two vampires that were in here earlier?" she asked pointedly. "Are you going to try to tell me I dreamt that?"

The two women stared at each other for several moments. Della was sure that Duchess was sizing her up. Measuring her.

"That depends. Are you going to faint again if I answer honestly?" Duchess asked.

Della felt her temper flare and she sat up in bed. "I've just been attacked and nearly killed twice in two days. Now, as near as I can tell, I've been kidnapped by a group of unemployed Calvin Klein models with extreme dental abnormalities. So, I'm not about to sit here and listen to—"

Without warning, Duchess grinned, showing her own pointed teeth, and set her feet down on the floor with a sharp clack of stiletto heels. She stood in a single, fluid motion and strode towards the door, ignoring Della's startled flinch.

"Tré," Duchess called, as she opened the door. "You might as well stop hovering and get in here. She knows."

The one called Tré stood in the doorway, looking strangely apprehensive as Duchess brushed past him and turned down the hall.

Della's gaze followed her departure before looking back to the man—*vampire?*—in the doorway. Their eyes met and held for a long, drawn out moment. Della felt her mouth growing dry as he shifted his weight, stepping fully into the bedroom and shutting the door behind him.

A million questions swirled around her mind, and she tried to form words with lips made numb by the complicated tangle of fear and fascination swirling around inside her.

"Who are you?" she finally whispered.

"My name is Vladimir Illych Romanov III. Though it is far simpler for you to call me Tré, as everybody else does these days," he said.

Despite the situation, a shiver of wholly inappropriate warmth slithered up Della's spine at the sound of his low voice. She tried valiantly to ignore it.

"What is this place?" she asked, not daring to tear her eyes away from Tré, who was leaning against the wall next to the door, with his hands shoved deep into the pockets of his dark, tailored trousers.

"This is my home. For now, at least. It's an abandoned plantation house, located a few miles south of New Orleans. My... housemates and I are restoring it and living here at the same time."

"And you're a vampire?"

Tré hesitated before replying. He looked unnerved, and licked his lips once.

"Yes," he said eventually.

Della felt a swooping sense of realization, as the obvious answer occurred to her.

"Oh, God. It's finally happened, hasn't it?" she asked, resigned.

Tré frowned. "Excuse me?"

She dragged a hand over her face, scrubbing at the cobwebs. Her answer was matter-of-fact. "I've lost my mind. Gone completely crazy. Certifiably batshit."

To her surprise, Tré smiled, his features relaxing for a moment before he sobered again. He crossed the few steps separating them and sank into the chair that Duchess had just vacated, his movements smooth as a hunting cat's.

"No," he said. "You most definitely haven't lost your mind. No more than the rest of us, at any rate."

Her eyebrows drew together in consternation. "Sure about that, are you?"

"Quite."

"But this is impossible!" Della insisted, her hands falling to lie limply in her lap. "Vampires don't exist! And those men... those *things* that attacked me? They stunk like rotting meat. I pepper sprayed one of them directly in the face, and he just laughed at me. They weren't... *human*." The mere memory raised a shudder of horror.

"No, they weren't human," Tré answered with a shrug. "Not anymore. There's a lot of that going around these days, unfortunately."

"Oh, terrific," Della answered, fighting the urge to roll her eyes. "You realize how all this sounds, surely."

Tré smiled again—a strangely sad expression—and gazed at Della's face as if drinking her in. It unnerved her, as she could find no basis for the look of affection and desire she saw in him. The sum total of their acquaintance consisted of him sitting by her bedside and— what? Perving on her while she slept? Then flashing his fangs at her, at which point she'd basically screamed in his face and fainted like the heroine in a bad Victorian romance novel.

He's not the only one who's been perving, now, is he, said the little voice that often seemed to whisper uncomfortable truths in her ear. Still, as the basis for a relationship went, calling it *flimsy* was an understatement.

"Yes. I realize how it all sounds," he said, replying to her earlier statement. "You must admit, though, as cover stories go, it's not the sort of thing you'd make up, now, is it?"

Almost despite herself, she smiled back at him for an instant before another question rose in her mind, turning her expression thoughtful as she struggled to recall details. "What did you call me earlier? Iris, or something like that?"

Tré's handsome face clouded. "Irina."

"Yes, that was it," Della said, remembering now. "Why did you call me that? My name is Della."

Silence stretched, until she thought perhaps he wouldn't answer at all.

"It's… very complicated," Tré said eventually. His face had grown drawn and distant, as if he was remembering something painful.

"I'm willing to listen," Della said.

"It's quite a long story, I'm afraid, and not a very nice one," Tré replied. "I have a question for you, first."

"Erm… okay?"

Tré leaned forward, stretching out a hand towards hers. He moved slowly, keeping his face calm and smooth, as if to assure her that he meant no harm. Della felt a flicker of fear, quickly subsumed by curiosity. She could not explain it to herself, but she wanted his touch. *Needed* it, as much as he seemed to.

Yes, it was true that he was the most beautiful man she'd ever laid eyes on, but that wasn't it. Not completely. There was something else, hovering in the air between them like the electric charge in the air before a thunderstorm.

In the infinitesimal slice of time before their hands touched, Della felt a thrill of foreboding, as if she was on the verge of remembering something huge and important.

Before she could make sense of the feeling, however, Tré slipped his fingers through hers. As soon as their skin touched, Della felt as if a wire had come alive from her hand straight down into her soul. She gasped and jumped, but did not release Tré's hand. Instead, she gripped tighter.

"You feel it, then?" Tré asked, staring at her intently.

For a moment, his eyes lit with a fierce sort of joy — an intensity that took her breath away.

"Yes, I--," she started to say, only to cut herself off. She shook her head, as if to clear it. "What *is* that?"

Tré hesitated, as if he did not want to speak his thought aloud. "I'm not entirely sure. I think it's a sign that the two of us are... *connected*... in some way."

From the reluctance in his voice, Della thought that he wasn't being entirely truthful. Or perhaps he was withholding something from her. But she did not press the matter as Tré spoke again.

"I need you to understand, Della, that there are dark forces gathering around you." He swallowed. "I don't know why, and I don't know yet how to stop them. But I am making a vow to you right now that I will protect you from them, this time."

This time?

Before Della could even open her mouth to give voice to the many questions that were wheeling and circling in her mind like a flock of birds, Tré stretched forward and brushed her split lip with his thumb. All of her thoughts and worries froze and crashed to the ground at her body's unexpected reaction to the touch.

"You're hurt," he breathed. "Let me help."

Her mouth opened and closed several times before she whispered, "How?"

He smiled again — with the same sad expression that did not touch the pain in his eyes. Rather than answer in words, he cradled her jaw with his fingertips and used the light touch to guide her toward him, stretching forward to meet her halfway.

She could have pulled back. Flinched away. She probably *should* have pulled back. Maybe she would have, if this were any kind of a sane situation. But, instead, she breathed in, the tiny gasp cut off when smooth, dry lips slid over hers. A sharp throb of pain made her flinch as the movement jostled the injury where her attacker had hit her, but it was all mixed up with a shock of pleasure spreading warmth along her overstretched nerves.

She couldn't help it — she moaned into the kiss, her heart racing with something other than fear for the first time in what felt like *ages*. Without even realizing she was doing it, her free hand came up to grasp the back of Tré's neck, holding him in place. She felt him smile against her mouth for a moment before he obligingly deepened the kiss.

He licked along the seam of her lips and pulled her injured lower lip between his teeth, lapping at the dried blood there. She shivered — *vampire* — and the pain flared for a brief moment before fading away to nothing. Goosebumps erupted on her arms as the nagging ache of swollen, split flesh gave way to the unadulterated pleasure of being kissed, and she practically melted beneath his sure touch.

There was no telling what she would have done — what she would have let *him* do — had they continued. Della was no innocent virgin, but she had never before been kissed like this. She could feel her blood rushing through her body like a drug. She wondered if he could feel it, too.

The thought was enough to bring her back to herself, at least a bit. As if sensing it, Tré pulled away a fraction, resting their foreheads together. He stretched up, brushing a kiss to her temple, and another to the top of her head. The fingers cradling her jaw slid back, urging her to bow her head as his slick, wet lips pressed against the bruise and cut where her head had hit the wall in the alley. Again, the dull pain of the injury faded.

Her eyes slipped closed, only to fly open when she felt him retreat.

Tré pulled back, gazing uncertainly into her eyes.

"What did you do?" Della asked, barely recognizing her own voice.

"More than I probably should have," Tré answered, and rose to leave without another word.

Della sat still on the bed, staring after him, still lost in the sensations coursing through her body — too intent on bringing the spinning room back to stillness to feel particularly annoyed by Tré's abrupt departure.

She ran her tongue along her lips, feeling for the coppery split where she'd been injured. She could still taste the faint tang of dried blood, but the swelling was completely gone. The wound was healed, as if it had never been.

Confused and flustered, Della looked around as the quiet click of footsteps returned through the door. She was somewhat disappointed to see that it was Duchess, having hoped in vain that Tré would return to answer her questions.

And, y'know, maybe to kiss her again. That would be good, too.

"Where did Tré go?" Della asked, pushing the blankets completely off.

Duchess shrugged, unconcerned. "Not my day to keep track of our fearless coven leader's whereabouts, I'm afraid."

Della narrowed her eyes at the woman's flippancy. "Coven?"

Duchess stared at her. "That's what we are-- a coven of vampires."

She took a moment to digest that. "Oh. And... Tré is your leader?"

Duchess smirked. "It's a dirty job, but somebody has to do it. And no one else wants to."

"Right," Della said hesitantly. To her embarrassment, her stomach chose that moment to rumble audibly. "Okay. Look, I hate to ask, but... I'm actually starving right now. Do you have any food here? I honestly can't remember the last time I ate or drank anything, and, unlike some people, I'm a mere mortal."

"Ugh. Sounds dreadful. But never mind. Oksana can probably help you out," Duchess said carelessly. "Come on, we'll go find her."

Della rose cautiously from the bed, pleased when her knees didn't wobble. She was stiff, sore, and light-headed, but at least she could walk. A thought occurred to her.

"Is Oksana a vampire, too?" Della asked as they headed out of the bedroom.

Duchess nodded. "Yes. We're all bloodsuckers, here. Present company excepted."

Della was busy concentrating on finding her footing down each of the creaking steps in the once-grand staircase. Despite her earlier relief at being able to walk unaided, hunger and dehydration were making her legs shake, unsteady beneath her. She felt strangely giddy.

"Don't worry, though," Duchess said, humor lending an unexpected lightness to her tone. "Oksana has a surprisingly eclectic palate for a vampire. We won't force you to adhere to our diet."

"Thank goodness for small mercies," Della managed, feeling like a clumsy moose as she plodded after Duchess, whose graceful steps practically seemed to float across the entry way and down a short hallway. The blonde vampire opened the door to a dimly lit kitchen that appeared largely unused.

Della was finally starting to take in the details of the house, as her initial shock faded. The bedroom had been a strange combination of creepy and luxurious, with expensive, high quality furniture and bedding, but cobwebs clinging to the ceilings and chunks of plaster missing from the walls. The staircase and entryway must have been like something from out of *Gone with the Wind* when they were new, but decades of neglect had left them shabby and in need of refurbishing.

The kitchen was ancient, and didn't look as though it had been updated since it was first built. It was lit, she realized, by candles. Thinking back, she realized that she'd seen no sign of electricity. The lighting had all been candles and oil lamps, along with a fire burning in the fireplace in the bedroom, which had beaten back the February chill.

At the table in the middle of the kitchen, a beautiful young woman, presumably Oksana, sat at the table in a pair of loose shorts and a tank-top. Her mocha-colored skin was smooth and clear. Flawless. The only imperfection on her body was an ugly scar just below her knee, disappearing into the sleeve of a high-tech metal prosthetic where her foot should have been.

As the two women walked through the door, she turned dark brown eyes on them and smiled, flashing dazzlingly white teeth. Della caught a brief glimpse of pointed fangs.

Duchess walked around Oksana, sliding her hand across the other vampire's shoulders in a surprisingly companionable gesture as she went.

"Hello, *ma petite*," she said. "Watch the human for me, would you? And feed her some of that garbage you call food, if you wouldn't mind. I need to go out for an hour or two and grab a bite, myself."

Oksana smiled up at her. "Of course, *ma chérie*. Be safe."

Duchess passed out of the back door as Oksana turned to Della. She frowned upon seeing the way Della was gripping the back of a chair for balance as her dizziness grew worse, and rose from her seat. Her gait was slightly uneven as she set her left foot down with a dull thud on the floor, but otherwise she seemed completely unencumbered by her distinctive injury. Della tried hard not to stare.

"Welcome," she said. "In case Duchess didn't tell you, my name is Oksana."

"Hi," Della said, feeling awkward. "I'm Della."

"Well, Della — it's nice to see you. Again," Oksana said cheerfully.

"A-again?" Della stammered, confused. There *was* something vaguely familiar about the lovely woman standing in front of her, but she couldn't place her. Possibly her low blood sugar and recent head injury weren't helping, but surely she would remember — ?

"Yes," Oksana said kindly. "We've met before. Are you hungry? No offense, but you look weak as a kitten right now."

Distracted from her confusion, Della nodded, feeling her stomach clench hard. She hadn't really been up to eating anything the previous day, and she was paying for it now, in spades.

"Food would be... really good right now, thanks," she said.

"Well, lucky for you I'm a junk food addict," Oksana said matter-of-factly. "All the other ghouls around here ever want is human blood. All blood, all the time. I'd go mad."

Della swallowed a wash of queasiness as Oksana bustled around the kitchen. She'd gathered that was what vampires consumed, if all the horror movies were to be believed. Yet, she wasn't really prepared to wrap her mind around the reality of it right now.

Grab a bite, Duchess had said as she left. Della shivered.

After a few moments, Oksana returned from the large closet pantry, her arms full of packages and bags of food. Dumping them unceremoniously on the table, Oksana gestured Della over and said, "Please, eat something. You look dead on your feet."

Della sat down and picked up several bags, examining them. She was startled to see that the food was very ordinary, although the strange assortment suggested that Oksana wasn't used to dining with others. There were bags of Cheetos, Cracker Jacks, and a handful of boxed cookies. As she was perusing the options, Oksana reappeared at her side, handing her a full glass of something red.

"Uhh..." she said, eyeing the crimson liquid with misgivings.

Oksana laughed, a clear, bell-like sound. "Sorry, I wasn't thinking. It's Madeira, from the cellar. A '79, which I'm told was a good year."

"Oh," Della said, surprised. "Thanks."

"Don't mention it. I'd get you a glass of water, but all we have is a hand pump outside right now. I've no idea if the water is safe for humans to drink, so we'd better not risk it. Eris thinks he can teach himself how to run plumbing in here at some point, but... well. We'll see."

"How many of you are there?" Della asked curiously, popping open a bag of Cheetos.

"Six. You've met Duchess and Tré, I take it. The other three are Xander, Eris, and Snag."

"You all have very...unusual names."

Oksana smiled. "It's because we are old; much older than you children walking the Earth right now." She hesitated. "Well... except for Snag. In his case, it's because he won't tell us his real name. Snag's short for *snaggle tooth*. Which will make sense when you get a good look at him."

Despite the smile, Della thought that Oksana sounded sad, and heard her tapping the prosthetic foot rhythmically against the leg of the table.

"But all of you don't like human food?" Della asked, holding up a kernel of popcorn she had just pulled from the Cracker Jack box.

Oksana snickered and pulled the open box towards her, taking out a handful. She leaned back in her chair and tossed some pieces into the air, catching them easily in her mouth. "Nope. Not hardly. That's just me."

"But you *can* eat?"

"Of course!" Oksana said, around another mouthful. "Vampires are much more like humans than the stories would lead you to believe."

"How so?"

"Well, we eat—or we drink, at least. We sleep, just like you do—albeit during the day, rather than at night. We feel, and think, and have the full spectrum of emotions—that sort of thing."

"Do you have reflections?"

Oksana laughed aloud. "Yeah, I'm not really sure where that particular piece of folklore came from, but we joke about it a lot. If we didn't have reflections, do you think that Duchess could put on *that* much makeup every day?"

Della smiled, unable to resist Oksana's infectious good humor. She thought about that for a few moments, trying to dredge up everything she had ever heard about vampires. "There are differences though, right? Aside from the obvious fangs-and-biting-people thing."

A troubled look passed across Oksana's face. "Well—yes, there are many. We can't go out in sunlight. We have what I guess you'd call *special powers*. We do not age or grow, nor can we die a natural death. There are only a few ways we can be killed."

"A stake through the heart, or something like that?"

Oksana raised an eyebrow. "Not planning on doing a spot of vampire hunting, are you?"

Della's eyes went wide as she realized how that must have sounded, and she gave a horrified shake of her head. "No! I didn't mean—"

Oksana only burst into giggles again, though, and clutched Della's arm. Della hid her face in her hand, an answering laugh of relief choking its way free. "Sorry."

"Oh, Della, the look on your face was priceless!" Oksana said. She appeared to be trying to rein herself in and took several deep breaths, wiping tears of mirth from the corners of her eyes.

It was hard not to feel comfortable in Oksana's presence. Something that had been troubling Della spilled out of her mouth without her volition.

"Oksana," Della began, "Tré said that there are dark forces surrounding me, or something like that. Do you know what he meant by that?"

Oksana sobered, looking at her with clear sympathy. "We aren't completely sure," she answered after a moment of silence. "But it does seem like Bael is targeting you, somehow — sending his dark forces after you."

She had never heard the name before, so why did it send a shiver of dread through her?

"Bael?" she asked, not sure she wanted the answer.

A dark look passed across Oksana's face. "Bael is the demon that tore our souls in two, and condemned us to this half-life of vampirism. The six of us have sworn vengeance against him. We have vowed to fight him — for eternity, if necessary — and oppose him at every turn."

Della considered that, as she sat at a candlelit table with a vampire, munching on boxed cookies and sipping hundred-dollar wine.

"This is all so overwhelming. I'm still not completely convinced that I haven't just had a psychotic break or something."

Oksana gave her a sympathetic look and nodded. "If you have, then so have the rest of us. Maybe I should release your memories."

Della frowned and said, "Release my memories? What do you mean?"

Oksana looked oddly sheepish. "Yeah... that's a bit awkward. Sorry. We met a few days ago, but I had to wipe your memories so that we could get away safely."

"Hang on. You can *do* that? You can mess with my mind?" Della demanded, sitting up straighter.

Oksana nodded apologetically, and stretched her hand across the corner of the table to touch Della's knuckles. The beautiful vampire took a deep breath and closed her eyes, turning inward. Della felt a sensation like floodgates opening in her mind. Image after image bubbled up from her memory, leaving her reeling.

The gunmen on Canal Street. Dark figures emerging from swirling mist. Bodies strewn everywhere. Being shielded and protected by a terrifying figure who had just shaken off a bullet through the chest like it was *nothing*. Tré's hand accidentally brushing her skin. An electric shock of familiarity shooting through her.

Della gasped and clutched the table, feeling her heart thundering in her ribs. She felt disoriented, the combination of memory and wine making the world tilt alarmingly for a moment.

"I'm so sorry," Oksana said. "It's an uncomfortable sensation, I know, but I thought you ought to be able to remember the entire story."

"You were there, too! I recognize you now." Della pointed a shaking finger at Oksana.

"Yes. We were there trying to stop the attack. Not that it really helped things much in the long run," Oksana replied in a bitter voice.

"But the guy that freed me was hurt! He was shot in the chest."

"Mm-hmm," Oksana confirmed. "It happens sometimes. That was Xander. Don't worry, though—he's fine now. Or will be shortly, at any rate."

Della gaped at her "How?"

"Well," she said, "that's one of the differences between vampires and humans. We have an amazing ability to heal. Our blood and saliva have healing properties, so Tré just allowed Xander to... um... borrow some of his blood to heal the gunshot wound."

Della felt more than a little nauseous at the idea, but wisely decided not to comment.

Once her stomach had quieted enough to deal with food again, she and Oksana ate in silence for several minutes. Despite everything that had happened in the last two days, Della felt more centered and connected to her surroundings than she had in years. It was almost a disappointment when her thoughts drifted back to mundane matters.

"When can I go home?" she finally asked, her mind turning towards the future. She realized that all of her possessions had been lost when the men had attacked her. "I don't have anything with me. It's all back in that alley, or in a police station somewhere."

A new trickle of disquiet entered Della's mind, despite the aura of serenity that seemed to hover over the old house. She was surrounded by strangers—*vampires*, no less—with no phone, no money, and no way to contact anyone for help. She didn't even know where she was, exactly, or how to get back.

Would anyone even be looking for her? They wouldn't. Not until she failed to show up to work for a couple of days without calling in, anyway.

She was completely on her own.

EIGHT

A door behind Della opened abruptly. She jumped, nearly spilling her glass of wine.

Okay, obviously I don't feel as peaceful as I thought I did.

Tré walked through the door, looking cool and un-ruffled.

"You can't go home," he said in a flat voice.

Della blinked once, sure that he was joking. "What do you mean I *can't go home*?"

"Exactly what I said. You. Can't. Go. Home," he repeated.

Oksana shuffled some empty wrappers and stood up from the table, as if she suddenly wanted nothing more than to vacate the premises before the fireworks started.

"Of course I'm going home!" Della said, glaring at Tré as fiercely as she could manage while Oksana made a quiet escape.

"It's too dangerous," he said. "You need to understand that Bael is clearly after you, and I can't guarantee that we'll be able to swoop in and save you every time he decides to attack. *Think.* What if we had been two minutes later yesterday?"

"I never asked you to come rescue me," Della snapped, ignoring the twinge of discomfort as she remembered the way she'd been silently praying for someone… *anyone*… to save her.

Yes, it was true she'd been terrified and depress-ingly useless at defending herself. But the fact that Tré had played white knight for her twice now didn't automatically give him some kind of... *claim* on her. It didn't automatically give him control over her life.

Tré rubbed his eyes wearily and shook his head. "You didn't have to. I can't *not* come to your rescue."

Della's gaze narrowed as she stared at him.

"I can't just sit back and let it happen once I hear you," he continued, his voice growing quiet enough that she had to strain to make out the words.

"Hear me? How could you have heard me?" she asked, bewildered.

Tré looked like he would rather not answer the question and shifted his weight from one foot to the other. "I can hear you in my mind."

Okay, then. As if this day couldn't get any weirder.

Della blinked and opened her mouth, but no words came out.

Tré sighed and said, "When you screamed, I heard it in my thoughts, and I was compelled to fly to your aid."

She snapped her jaw shut and swallowed. "Is that normal for vampires?"

Tré hesitated before answering. "Not... exactly."

"Then how —?"

"Look, Della It's clear that you and I are connected somehow. I don't really understand it yet, but I will. In the meantime, you must stay here so that we can keep you safe."

"Absolutely not!" Della replied, crossing her arms defensively. "In the last couple of days, I've been shot at, punched, threatened with rape and murder, and had my memories wiped. *I want to go home.* I need to try to find my lost phone and I.D., change my clothes, and call into work to let them know what happened. I can't just hole up here like some frightened rabbit —"

"Here, you will be safe," Tré interjected.

She scoffed. "Yeah, not to be rude or anything, but I'm the only human in a house full of vampires. I think *safe* is kind of a relative term at this point, don't you?"

He was still burning holes in her with his eyes. She took a deep breath, and changed tack.

"Also, if I change how I'm living my life, doesn't it mean that this creature—*Bael*—has won? I'm not willing to let that happen, Tré, and you shouldn't be, either. I need to go home. And if you plan on keeping me prisoner here against my will, what does that make you? You'd be as bad as him."

Tré deliberated silently for long moments.

"Fine," he replied eventually. "*Fine.*"

Della exhaled in relief, relishing the idea of simply being able to go home and take a *shower*. Strange, what seemed important in the midst of chaos.

Tré wasn't finished, though. "But I'll be going with you to protect you while you do whatever it is you need to do. After which, we'll return here."

Della's expression fell. She narrowed her eyes, studying Tré's determined features. Resentful but resigned to the inevitable, Della sighed in frustration before nodding and getting to her feet.

She just needed to get back to the city. To normal people, and familiar surroundings. Then, she could figure out what to do.

"All right, then. So, how are we going to get there from here?" Della asked, following Tré down the hall. She still had no real memories of arriving at the old house, but she felt confident that a bunch of vampires with super mind-controlling powers weren't exactly going to commute back and forth in a Prius.

"I suppose we'll have to be creative," Tré answered in a clipped tone. "Come with me."

He was clearly still irked at her stubbornness, but he led the way out of the front door and down a short flight of steps leading off the porch. Della glanced over her shoulder. The plantation house had once been a grand building, though it had fallen into disrepair. Nature was slowly pulling it back into the swamp, as it tried to do with all human structures in this part of the world. A proliferation of ivy grew over the walls and half of the roof, wrapping itself around the windowsills as though trying to find a way inside.

She shivered. Inside, the place might have been strangely peaceful, but from out here in the dark of night, it was creepy as hell.

She and Tre followed a dirt footpath that wound down a gentle slope and into a clump of trees. In the moonlight, Della could make out an old, run-down barn with shingles that were falling in through gaps in the roof.

"Er... what are we doing out here, exactly?" she asked.

"Nothing remotely as unsavory as what you're probably contemplating," Tré answered in a dry tone. He ushered her toward the old outbuilding with a light touch to her lower back. She almost missed the rest of his sentence, distracted by the warmth that lit up her insides at the simple touch. He continued, "This is where we keep the Jeep—Xander's current obsession. We don't generally have need of it, for obvious reasons. But if we didn't keep something around for him to tinker with when he gets bored, he'd lose his mind. What's left of it, anyway."

"He... works on cars when he's bored?" Della asked, confused.

Tré shrugged, the movement barely visible in the pale moonlight.

Della laughed; she couldn't help it. These vampires were immortal, had magical powers, and were battling a demon that was apparently intent on destroying the world. Yet one had an unhealthy obsession with junk food, and another was a closet mechanic.

Tré shot her a dark look from under his brows as he hauled the door open on rusted hinges. The screech sounded loud against the quiet backdrop of the bayou at night.

"Why cars?" she asked.

Tré grimaced and shrugged. "I've never asked. All I care about is that it keeps him out of trouble. *Mostly*. He has to be doing *something*. Otherwise he'd spend all his spare time hunting drug addicts. As distractions go, this one could be much worse."

"Hunting *drug addicts*?" Della asked, appalled. They entered the old building, which smelled of mildew and engine grease. Something small scrabbled away from them in the darkness, and she jumped.

Tré took in the disturbed look on Della's face, and raised an eyebrow. "No need to look like that. He doesn't kill them. None of us do. We don't have to kill humans to feed. As for Xander, he just happens to appreciate blood that's been, shall we say, *adulterated*. Preferably with extremely strong mind-altering substances."

Della swallowed and nodded, still feeling more than a little queasy at the idea of blood-drinking, whether illegal narcotics were involved or not. Still, it *was* reassuring to learn that the vampires were able to feed without murdering humans. She wondered idly if any of them had fed from her while she was unconscious, and rubbed a nervous hand around her neck.

Tré's glowing silver eyes pinned her in place. "*Please*, Della. I can feel the fear pouring off of you in waves. You're perfectly safe from us, you know. You have my word on that."

"I'm sorry, this is all just so much to take in," Della murmured, and dropped her hand back to her side.

The corners of his mouth turned down. "Then let's get this over with, so we can both relax."

He walked over to a vehicle covered by a brown tarp, and pulled it off. The disturbance sent plumes of dust into the air, and Della sneezed, waving a hand in front of her face. She looked skeptically at the ancient Jeep, wondering if it would even *start*, let alone get them all the way back to New Orleans.

Tré yanked on the passenger side door, which popped open with an ominous creak of metal.

"Ladies first," he said, the words sounding decidedly wry, and gestured for Della to get inside. Despite the hint of self-deprecating humor at the state of their ride, his expression was still set in deep, worried lines.

As she slid into the passenger seat, Della could detect the faint smell of oil and gasoline. She didn't claim to know much about cars, but she thought that this was probably the oldest Jeep she had ever seen. It looked like something straight out of a documentary about World War II.

Tré climbed into the driver's seat and turned the key, which was already in the ignition. After only a brief sputter, the engine roared into life and settled into a steady growl.

"He must be pretty good to keep this thing running," Della commented.

Tré snorted. "Please don't ever tell him that, unless you want to be subjected to a three-hour lecture on engine maintenance."

Despite her misgivings, she felt a smile tugging at her lips.

It didn't last long, though. The journey to New Orleans was not exactly what you'd call a comfortable one. Having no memory of arriving at the manor house, Della was surprised to find just how remote the place really was. The road that they took back towards the city could hardly be called that. It was more of a track, littered with washouts and potholes that caused the Jeep to lurch and jounce, threatening to bang Della's head on the bottom of the hardtop every couple of minutes.

What seemed like a very long time later, Tré pulled out onto a smooth, paved highway, much to Della's relief. Her head was pounding from clenching her jaw, and she had a vice-like grip on the handle above the door. They had not spoken the entire time, not wanting to shout over the bumping of the car and the loud growl of the engine.

"You might suggest that Xander take a look at the suspension next time he's in a mood to tinker," Della said. "You know. Just saying."

"I'll pass it along," Tré replied, shooting her a sidelong glance.

Della looked out of the window and tried to get her bearings. She still didn't know where they were. The Jeep was traveling along a dark road surrounded by lush trees. She could see no sign of the approaching city.

"What side of New Orleans are we on, anyway?" she asked, trying valiantly to get a conversation going.

"Lakeside," Tré answered, not offering more.

Della watched him with interest. During the walk across the grounds of the plantation house, he had seemed cautious and reserved, but not unfriendly. Now, though, he seemed noticeably tense and watchful. His eyes were completely focused as he stared out of the windshield, maintaining a firm grip on the steering wheel. At frequent intervals, his gaze would flicker up to the rearview mirror, as if he was watching for someone behind them. When Della turned to look, she could see no sign of headlights.

Had she said something that made him withdraw? If so, what? They hadn't exactly been touching on deep topics. After a few more failed attempts at drawing him out, Della gave up and sat staring out the passenger window in silence.

Figures, she thought. *He's the hottest damn thing I've ever laid eyes on. Typical that I would be attracted to someone who isn't even human. 'Emotionally unavailable' probably doesn't even begin to cover it. Seems about on par for my life these days.*

Surreptitiously, Della glanced out of the corner of her eye and studied Tré's features. His dark hair, longer at the top, fell in tousled curls on the left side of his forehead. The rest was cleanly cut above his ears. Della could see strong muscles in Tré's neck and guessed that the same fit physique extended beneath the dark clothing that shrouded him in the blackness of the night.

By the time they reached her apartment, Della was ready for a break from Tré's gloomy presence, regardless of whatever wonders of male musculature might be hidden under those expensive, tailored clothes. It was bad enough being attracted to a vampire, but first he'd kissed her senseless and now he seemed aloof to the point of indifference.

Apparently mixed signals weren't exclusively the purview of human men. Who knew?

As they walked towards the front door of her apartment building, Della noticed the pale glow of predawn lightening the eastern horizon. She paused and glanced at Tré, who had followed her to the front stoop with silent footsteps.

He'll never have time to make it back before dawn, she realized.

She pulled at the door with one hand and paused with it partially open, a warm, humid breeze wafting out from the entryway beyond.

"Look," she said quietly, "it's going to be light out soon. You'd better come inside."

She made the offer before taking time to truly wrap her mind around what she was doing. Something niggled in her memory... something about inviting a vampire into your house. Was that one of the real superstitions, she wondered, or one of the stupid ones, like not having a reflection?

As Tré stepped into the pool of light cast by the lamp above the front door, Della was startled to see how exhausted and worn he looked. There was an edge to his eyes, and dark circles made him look drawn and pale under the orange glow.

Tré pinned his gaze upon her with such intensity that, despite his wan appearance, Della felt herself flush under his regard.

Jesus. He looks like he wants to devour me whole, Della thought with a shiver.

What she felt was not *alarm*, though. Not exactly. It was hotter than that. More primal. Because there was also tenderness in that tightly focused gaze. Tré moved closer to her, an expression of sudden, desperate longing behind his pale gray eyes.

Della felt her knees quiver under her weight, and tightened the muscles in her legs to lock them. The last thing she needed was to embarrass herself further in front of him.

"All right," Tré said. "Thank you."

She was momentarily confused, her higher brain functions once again caught up in the la-la land of raging hormones. She stared at him with parted lips, completely bewildered for the space of two heartbeats before something clunked back into place in her head.

Oh. You invited him inside. Duh. Real smooth, there.

Della turned around and pulled the door open further, leading Tré down a dimly lit hallway, counting the three doors to her apartment.

With fumbling fingers, she pulled her keys out of her pocket and unlocked the door. She'd been relieved to find them there, after losing her cell phone and purse in the assault.

When she pushed open the door, she felt a rush of air drift out, carrying the familiar scent of *home*. Finally, she relaxed. Everything in her apartment was still in place, the sweet smell of honey and lemon from a wax warmer standing on her kitchen counter tickling her nostrils.

With a vague gesture inviting Tré further into her apartment, Della dropped her keys on the table by her door and kicked off her shoes. She walked quietly across the living room before stopping by the fishbowl.

"Hey, Jewel," she said to the little creature inside, which swam around to regard her through the glass, its mouth opening and closing. She smiled. "Yeah, count yourself lucky that you're just a goldfish, and don't have to deal with the kind of excitement I've had over the past couple of days."

Jewel continued to make fish faces at her, and — predictably — did not reply. Della sprinkled a bit of food in the top of the bowl and went into the kitchen. She yanked open the refrigerator, suddenly ravenous despite the snacks Oksana had shared with her earlier.

She pulled out leftovers from a simple meal she had prepared a few days previously. After sniffing suspiciously at them, Della shrugged and dumped the rice, vegetables, and sweet sausage onto a plate. It still smelled all right, and frankly, on the list of things that seemed likely to kill her these days, food poisoning ranked pretty low. She grabbed an apple out of her fruit tray and started munching on it.

"Want some food?" Della asked, turning towards Tré with her mouth full.

He appeared more than a little amused, if the odd quirk of his lips was anything to go by, but he merely shook his head and said, "No. I ate a couple of days ago."

Della shrugged acknowledgement and began pulling out utensils and a glass for water.

A few minutes later, she was sitting at her table with a steaming plate of food in front of her. Without glancing at the silent figure standing motionless in the corner—though she was still viscerally aware of his presence—Della began to eat.

I've got to find a way to get my phone back, she thought. She'd left her laptop sitting on the kitchen table and, between mouthfuls, she pulled it over and started jotting down a list of her missing possessions so she could file a police report. Next, she searched through her emails for a credit card and bank statement so she could freeze her accounts.

Damn. I'm going to need to have all of these account numbers and card numbers changed and reissued. Thank God I at least have a passport, otherwise I'm not sure they'd even let me do it. I'll need to get a new driver's license and buy another cell phone, too.

With her mental list growing, Della felt a crease of worry beginning to form between her eyebrows.

"Jesus. What if someone steals my identity?" she said aloud. She'd only been talking to herself, but Della saw Tré move towards her from where he'd been lounging against her counter. A look of concern clouded his face.

"Sorry," she said quickly, trying to wave it off. "I'm just thinking aloud."

Tré stopped next to her and leaned down until they were at eye level, resting his hands on the table. He captured her gaze and held it with his, effortlessly.

"Della," he said in a low, careful voice. "None of those things matter any more."

"They matter to me," she whispered, even as her body reacted to his nearness.

She could feel herself alternating rapidly between hot and cold, barely able to breathe. She wanted to dismiss his claim that her life had changed irrevocably; that she could never return to her normal day-to-day existence.

Yet, when he focused on her like this, she was also completely captivated by his presence. Not only was he the most amazing thing she had ever laid eyes on—she could also sense the power he held. It was shrouded, yes. Held under strict control. But it was there, and it made her tremble—everything else she'd been thinking about, forgotten in an instant.

In this moment, however, his eyes looked lost, as if he were searching for stable ground amidst a sea of crashing waves. All of the cold distance from earlier had vanished like smoke, replaced by this strange vulnerability. Her hand rose without conscious volition, stretching forward to gently cup his face. As before, the touch of skin on skin was like an electric shock, completing some circuit that flowed between the two of them.

Oh my God, this is so messed up, a voice whispered in the back of her mind. *What are you even thinking, Della?*

Della searched Tré's face, and found unmistakable hunger reflected back at her in his eyes.

She knew, on some level, that she was playing with fire. With elemental forces that she couldn't hope to stand against. He was a *vampire*, for Christ's sake. For all she knew, he had her under some sort of hypnosis or spell. She had already discovered that they could mess with her mind and alter her memories. What if they could take away her free will, as well?

What if what she felt... *wasn't really what she felt?* How would she know?

NINE

"Kiss me again," she commanded, in a fit of what might have been either bravery, or foolishness. "I have to know if what I'm feeling is real."

Tré's eyes darkened, growing hot. Intense. He straightened away from her touch on his cheek, and she thought at first that he was withdrawing from her. He wasn't, though. He circled behind her chair, his movements smooth as a stalking panther's.

He was so close that when he spoke, it sent shivers down her spine, the fine hairs on the back of her neck standing up. "It is real," he said. "It is also very, very dangerous."

She tried her best not to let her voice quaver. It *almost* worked. "A demon who can rip people's souls in half apparently wants me dead, and I live in a city that's trying to tear itself apart. Define *dangerous*."

He gave a low rumble of dark amusement that jolted something low in her belly. Fingers trailed over the line of her shoulder, drawing her heavy mass of curls to the side.

"This, *draga mea*." The unfamiliar words had the feel of an endearment. They tickled at some half-forgotten dream memory in the back of her mind. "*This* is the definition of danger."

His lips closed on the line of muscle his fingertips had just explored, and she gasped. His hand tangled in her messy mane of hair; he used the grip to draw her head to the side, baring the side of her neck to him as well. He kissed his way up her shoulder and the column of her throat, lighting every nerve along the way.

Her eyes slipped close and her mouth fell open as lust slammed into her with a power she had never known in her life. She wasn't a virgin, by any means. She hadn't been for years, despite always being a little too short and a little too chubby. A little too awkward, a little too flaky, and with a stupid little black mole on her right cheek that she'd always hated, but never had the time or money to get removed.

Even so, she'd had boyfriends. She'd had sex, and it had always been okay. She'd liked it. It was nice.

But she'd never gone weak and lightheaded at the touch of a man's lips to the side of her neck. No one had ever gathered her hair into a tight grip and used it to hold her still while he suckled and nipped at her earlobe. No one had ever pulled the neckline of her stretchy top over her shoulder and then used his teeth to drag her bra strap out of the way.

She had never before in her life felt so hot and needy that she was afraid she would *die* if the kisses stopped.

The place between her legs ached and throbbed against the hard seat of the kitchen chair. She wriggled, searching for relief, only to go limp and pliant again as Tré pulled her head back, baring her throat to him completely. He kissed her temple... her cheek... her closed eyelids. His free hand roamed over her, skimming her sensitive breasts before sliding up her vulnerable neck to cradle her jaw—holding her face cupped between his hands like a chalice.

Della's heart pounded, her breath coming in little pants as he slowly lowered his lips to hers. She tried to strain toward him, but she was completely under his control. He teased her for long moments, kissing the sides of her mouth, brushing his lips to hers for only an instant, backing off between butterfly touches.

She was undone already... dizzy... unraveled... too far gone even to beg for what she needed. *What was he doing to her?*

When he finally took pity on her and sealed their lips together, plundering her with a hunger that matched her own, her sex clenched and clenched as if she might come from nothing more than the touch of his lips on hers, his strong hands holding her helplessly in place as he ravished her mouth.

When he let her up, she gasped for air like a drowning woman, immediately straining upward again, trying to chase him. Again, he prevented her, the hand tangled in her thick hair and the hand cupping her jaw keeping her effortlessly in place as he returned to teasing. The tip of his tongue outlined her swollen lower lip, and dipped inside to tease at her own tongue. Dueling with her. Playing with her. All of her senses honed with laser focus onto that tiny point of slick, teasing contact.

"*Please*," she begged, when his hand slid back down to cup her breast and he returned to kissing his way along her shoulder and the nape of her neck. "Please, please, I need you, I *need* this. Don't stop..."

She should have been humiliated. Appalled. Embarrassed beyond all thought at the idea of begging for sex like a cheap hooker, from a man she barely knew. Her scalp tingled as he rolled her head back again for another brief, fierce kiss.

"I couldn't stop now if I tried, *draga*," he said, the words low and hoarse. "May God have mercy on whatever's left of my soul for it."

She moaned and reached for him blindly, tearing at buttons until she could touch the flawless marble skin underneath. No, not flawless—a complicated pattern of tattoos was visible over his right shoulder as she pushed the tailored black shirt back, disappearing down into the sleeve.

He gave her lip a final nip and released her hair in favor of pulling her top over her head. She knew she was dirty, sweaty, and smelly after the events of the previous night, but it was the bruising over her ribcage and upper arms that made him suck in a breath and draw back.

She reached for him, needy and pathetic, and hating herself just a tiny bit for it. "No, please," she said, "don't pull away. They're... they're not important—"

"They *are* important," he replied, "but I have no intention of pulling away. Come."

He guided her to shaky feet and tucked her under his arm, pressing kisses to her hair as he led her with halting steps down the hallway. It took them longer than it should have to reach the apartment's uninspiring three-quarter bath with its pedestal sink and molded plastic walk-in shower—probably because she kept shoving him against the wall along the way to mouth at his exposed collarbone and run her hands over his hard chest.

"No bathtub?" he asked, looking around the cramped space in confusion for a moment before returning his attention to her. "Ah, well. No matter. Someday I will fill a huge claw-foot tub at the plantation house with steaming water and rose petals for you. And I will lay you down in it and pleasure you until water sloshes out onto the floor under the force of your ecstasy."

The noise she made sounded like it had been punched from her, and she probably would have blushed scarlet if she'd had any blood left above the waist.

"Now, though," he continued, "let me take care of you, beloved. Let me live here inside this beautiful dream with you for a little while longer."

"Anything," she breathed. "Anything, Tré... *please.*"

He examined the shower for a moment and turned on the flow of water, letting it warm up while he turned back to her and tenderly removed the rest of her clothing, kissing the newly exposed skin as he went.

"So beautiful," he said, running his large hands over hips that were too fat, a waist that wasn't flat enough, thighs that rubbed together when she walked. "So beautiful, *draga mea*, in any lifetime."

She wasn't. She *knew* she wasn't. But… maybe, here and now, it would be all right to pretend that she was? A lump rose in her throat, and she returned to pulling at his clothing, wanting to see more. "Off," she said. "Get it all *off*."

He was the beautiful one, and if some inexplicable moment of insanity meant that she got to experience that beauty for a bit, she was damn well going to relish every moment.

He chuckled and helped her shed the rest of his clothing. The tattoo wrapped around his right arm like a sleeve, vaguely tribal. His chest was smooth and hairless, but a line of dark hair trailed down from his navel to the thick patch framing his erect cock.

He was perfect. Mouth-watering. She wanted to devour him. Without conscious thought, she started to go down to her knees in front of him, but he caught her by the shoulders and lifted her back up.

"No, *draga*," he said. "Not this time, at least. I won't last, and there's only one place I want to be right now."

She was already wet between her thighs, but the words made her even wetter. Christ, she could *smell* herself. There was no question that he could, too. Again, the thought should have horrified her — but it only made her hotter.

"In," he said, and guided her into the shower, following her and closing the door behind them, enclosing them in the warm, wet, intimate space.

Warm water flowed down her body as he positioned her under the spray. It soothed her aches and bruises, but did *nothing* to soothe her need. He soaped up a washcloth and washed her, the movements slow and achingly tender. The nubby texture of the terrycloth swiped over her face and neck, her shoulders and arms, her collarbone.

She gasped and clutched at his shoulder for balance as it rubbed over first one tender breast and then the other, her nipples going hard and sensitive under the attention. He soaped her stomach and pulled her forward to rest against him so he could wash her back. His hard length nestled in the crease of her thigh and she rolled her hips, wanting to feel more.

He hissed out a breath and buried his face in her hair for a moment before pushing her back to lean against the shower wall.

"Still so impatient, after all this time," he said, though the words made no sense.

He returned to washing her, running the cloth down first one leg and then the other, lifting her feet one at a time and setting them back down carefully. Finally... *finally*... he threw the washcloth into the corner and slid his bare hand up the inside of her leg.

Della bit her lip and let her head fall back against the cool plastic of the shower stall. When he reached his destination, she was wet and dripping for him in a way that had nothing whatsoever to do with the spray of water playing over them. He *growled*, cupping her and letting his fingertips delve into her heat.

Della panted, balanced once more on the cusp of orgasm, dizzy with need. "Tré, *please...*"

Thankfully for her tattered sanity, he didn't make her wait any longer. Instead, inhumanly strong hands gripped the meat of her thighs and lifted her, still with her back pressed against the wall of the cramped shower stall. She clutched at his shoulders and wrapped her legs around his hips, feeling deliciously open and vulnerable as the tip of his hard cock slid against her folds, seeking her entrance.

She shivered and angled her hips to position him, relishing the groan that was dragged from his lips. The connection between them flared to new heights as she sank down on his length, impaling herself, her mouth open in a soundless '*oh*' of pleasure.

It was like slotting the last piece of a puzzle into place, only to find that the picture revealed was far more beautiful than you ever thought it could be. Warmth spread from her core outward, driving away the icy chill that had settled in her soul over the past few horrible, harrowing days. He flexed his hips, and she nearly sobbed with how perfect it all was.

She buried her face against his shoulder, heat surrounding her from within and without as water from the shower flowed over their bodies.

"So perfect," he murmured into her hair, echoing her thoughts. "*Draga mea...*"

She was helpless to do more than wriggle, held as she was in his sure, inhumanly strong grip. So she wriggled, circling her hips to feel him move inside her. He groaned and used those perfect, long-fingered hands to lift her and let her slide back down his length, over and over, each slow, deep thrust sending her higher and higher until she cried out, clenching hard around him as her ecstasy spilled over like wine poured from a jug.

He held her through all the little fluttering aftershocks, cradled against his muscular form, every last bit of tension flowing from her spent body for the first time in what felt like *years*. The feeling of complete and utter serenity was so divine—so *unexpected*—that a low moan slipped from her lips.

He was still hard inside her, but he merely murmured, "Rest, beloved. I have you." He held her like that for long minutes, pressing kisses to her temple and the wet mass of her hair, before carefully lifting her off of his hard length and helping her steady herself on her feet, still leaning against the wall.

She was beyond speech, beyond anything except gratitude as he turned off the shower and guided her out into the steamy bathroom. He rubbed a towel over her pliant body and led her, naked, to her small bedroom. The bed was still unmade after her frantic late-morning rush after oversleeping her alarm—had it really only been a day ago?

He pulled back the tangle of sheets and blankets, laying her down on her back in the center of the bed, following her to settle in the cradle of her thighs. Still drugged and mindless with pleasure, Della wrapped her legs around him and used the grip to pull him back inside her. He came willingly.

They rocked together for an endless, perfect stretch of time, the sky beyond the curtains growing gradually lighter as night released its grip on the world. Della's thoughts slowly reassembled themselves in the aftermath of the shattering climax she'd experienced, only to come apart again as Tré altered the angle of his hips and brushed against a new place inside her that sent her flying.

She wrapped her arms around him, stroking up and down his back, feeling the play of muscles under her hands. Feeling wild and wanton, she stretched down to splay her fingers over the perfect swell of his buttocks, using the grip to encourage him to go faster. Deeper.

He groaned low and latched onto her shoulder with his lips, his thrusts growing sloppy. She arched as the sensation pushed her over another peak. As she came back to Earth, panting and sweat-damp, it was to the sight of Tré tearing his lips away from her and rearing up, his fangs bared and his eyes glowing silver as he toppled over the edge, shuddering and pulsing into her.

A jolt of real fear punctured Della's haze of pleasure, and she caught her breath. The small noise seemed to penetrate Tré's awareness, and a look of horror creased his features. He disengaged and pulled away clumsily, staggering out of the bed and across the room, putting space between them. Obviously fighting for control.

Della gaped at him for a moment before scrabbling to pull a sheet over herself, as if that would make any difference to what had just happened. And... what *had* just happened?

"Tré?" she asked uncertainly.

"Don't—" he began, only to cut himself off with a shake of the head. His face was haunted. He angled it away from her and closed his glowing eyes. "Just... give me a minute."

She stayed very still and silent, caught between the flood of happy hormones from the *best freaking sex of her life,* and the realization of what he had—apparently— almost done to her.

He took a deep breath and let it out slowly. When he opened his eyes again, they were no longer shining with that eerie silver light.

"I should leave," he said in a hoarse voice.

She glanced at the muted light visible through the curtains with a look of consternation, and then back at him. "Don't be stupid," she said. "It's almost daylight out there."

He only shook his head. "You're not safe with me here."

Della took a moment to consciously relax her body and release her grip on the sheet. "Well, I'm over here, and you're way over there looking like you're about to jump out of your own skin, so..."

He still wasn't looking at her. "I almost—"

"But you didn't," Della said gently, sitting up and letting the sheet fall away from her breasts, unashamed.

He hadn't, and right now he looked like he'd rather chew off his own arm than let his fangs get within two feet of her neck.

"Della," he said. "*I'm not safe for you.*"

She frowned. "I think we've had this conversation already. *I'm not safe*, period. A demon is trying to kill me. I thought you were the one who was going to protect me. Wasn't that why you came here in the first place?"

It was a low blow, she knew. And, indeed, she couldn't help the stab of guilt she felt at the expression of agonized uncertainty that flickered over his features before he could hide it.

She made a conscious effort to soften her tone. "Are you all right now? Your eyes aren't glowing any more."

She saw the bob of his Adam's apple as he swallowed. "I'm in control again."

"Then come back to bed." He drew breath to refuse, but she cut him off. "No, let me finish. It was the sex, right? So... no sex. Just come back to bed so we can hold each other. I trust you, Tré."

It was true. Ironically, it was the very fact that he'd freaked out on her and fled the bed when he'd felt himself start to lose control that had sealed her trust. If he hadn't allowed himself to harm her in the throes of passion, he would never allow himself to harm her, no matter what.

She had many things to fear these days, it seemed, but he was not one of them.

Tré appeared to be struggling with himself. Finally, he looked up and met her eyes. "You are foolish to trust me, *draga*. But I am also weak. I could never resist you. And you always knew it."

Again, he was talking as if they'd known each other before, somehow. But he approached the bed with cautious steps and climbed into it when she held the covers aside for him. When he was situated, she shuffled over and curled against his body, resting her head on his shoulder—eager to reclaim the sense of security she'd felt in his embrace. After a moment's hesitation, his arm curled around her shoulders, and she let out a sigh of contentment.

"That's the ticket," she murmured, happiness once more flooding her, making her feel warm and sheltered. "I'll take this over *safe*, any day of the week."

Tré shook his head, disregarding her words. "I lost myself. I must be better than that."

"'Better than that?'" Della craned up so she could look down at him, a wicked expression sliding across her face. "What... you mean you were holding out on me earlier? I find that difficult to credit..."

Tré gave her a despairing look, but eventually he softened—unable, as he had confessed earlier, to resist her. The knowledge made her feel even warmer inside.

"No," he finally murmured, scooting closer to her and pulling her back down so he could kiss her hair. "I would never have the strength to do such a thing, with you naked and wanting me. But I promised myself a long time ago that I would always, always remain in control of my instincts. I will never again be a blood-thirsty beast controlled by hunger and rage."

At first, Della did not know what to say. She reached out and traced her fingers along his shoulder, down finely chiseled muscles and across planes of soft, smooth skin.

"What does that mean?" she finally asked.

Tré went as still as stone, and Della looked up at him, worried. He was regarding her with a closed expression, as if debating something.

Finally, he took a deep breath and said, "Remember what you asked me earlier today? Back at the manor house?"

Della thought back. Everything from the last two days had seemed like such a blur that she struggled to place her finger on one specific conversation.

"Oh," she said, finally. "Yes. I asked you why you called me Irina."

TEN

"Do you still want to know?"
"More than ever," she said, meaning it.
"Are you certain of that?"

Della looked curiously at him. He seemed tortured again, his eyes flashing with old pain, as if from memories that should have been long forgotten.

"Why wouldn't I be?" Della asked.

"It will change what you think about me," Tré told her in a flat, dead voice.

Della scoffed. "I sincerely doubt that."

Tré shrugged as if resigned, pain still buried under his voice as he began, "I was born to a nobleman's family centuries ago, in a small village in what was then Moldavia—in Eastern Europe. At that time, relationships between a young man and a young woman were strictly forbidden outside of a betrothal."

Della listened silently. Tré's gaze wandered past her shoulder and into the middle distance, as if he were seeing things that she could not.

"I respected the laws that my father upheld, until the day I fell in love."

His softened in memory, as if warm sunlight were flooding across his pale skin.

"Her name was Irina and she was the most beautiful woman I had ever seen. She was the daughter of a local *voivode*, an administrative official. We spoke one day at a gathering both our families had been asked to attend. We fell in love that night, talking together in the moonlight beside a window. I will never forget how her hair shone in the pale light. How her eyes seemed to sparkle with life.

"I spoke with my father the next day and our families agreed to our union. That was the happiest day of my life. Not only was I getting a beautiful, perfect woman, but I would also be responsible for allying two powerful families."

Della lifted her eyebrows and gave him a wry smile. "You old romantic," she quipped.

"It wasn't the power that attracted me to her," Tré said, as if wanting to dispel the idea immediately, "but her beauty, her kindness, and her mind. She was perfect in every way."

Silence fell for several moments, and Della made no move to break it. It seemed to her that Tré was struggling with the memories. He shut his eyes and his face twitched as if in pain.

"The region was already on the brink of war. In the evenings you could feel it hanging heavy in the air, like electricity from a gathering storm. It was making everyone else uneasy, but not me. I defied the darkness because I was so happy and at peace."

Tré shook his head as if in disgust. "So young. So naïve. My disregard for the evil around me did not shield me from the coming violence. Instead, it drew the evil right to me."

Della looked at Tré in confusion, completely baffled by what he was saying.

"Bael," Tré responded to her unspoken question. "The demon of the underworld, ever present on this earth. He came for me one night."

"I thought demons were only a fantasy," Della said quietly, "or, you know, some kind of religious metaphor for humanity's dark side."

Tré smiled, but it was a sad expression. "You probably thought vampires weren't real up until today, too."

"That is very true," Della said. "So, this demon came and found you?"

"Yes," Tré breathed. "He could see the power I was gaining in my homeland. He wanted to enslave me, and take it for himself."

"How?" Della asked.

"The same way he created the undead men who attacked you. He would have done the same thing to me, or worse."

"But… *how*?" she said again, needing to understand.

Tré was quiet for a moment, considering her. He looked as if he did not want to say what was in his mind. Finally, he spoke again, the words emerging slowly.

"Bael has a terrible power—to rend the soul from the body. He surrounds his victims in blackness and tears the Light from their soul. Then, he casts it into the very pits of hell, leaving nothing but Darkness behind. They are not dead, but they are not truly alive, either."

"He did that to your soul?" Della asked, her eyes wide. The shape and magnitude of the danger in which she found herself was finally sinking in. She shivered. Tré drew her closer to him. If this was the danger she was facing, she understood now why he had been so on edge when they were traveling.

"Yes," he continued, "every person has both Light and Dark in their souls. Some people have more of one or the other, but typically the Light balances the Dark. What Bael does is to… tear those fragments apart and cast the Light into hell. All you are left with is the darkest parts of yourself, and he is free to exert his will over you."

Tears sprang into Della's eyes, unbidden. She laid her hand on Tré's chest, as if trying to sense his soul hidden within. "But you're not an undead puppet."

At this, Tre looked anguished. "No. I'm not."

He squeezed his eyes shut, as if the pain inside him had taken on a physical manifestation. Della wrapped herself around him, trying to ease his obvious distress.

His words were barely audible. "Bael lured me into the forest on the outskirts of my village, in the depths of night. I couldn't resist him; it was like a beacon that I was compelled to follow. I walked along the familiar paths in a sort of…trance. When I reached the end, Bael cast me into a pit. I was covered in mud and filth, and the blackness of his evil spirit settled over me."

Della ran a comforting hand over Tré's chest, feeling it heave beneath her touch. She wondered if he had ever spoken about this to anyone, or if he had carried the heavy weight of these memories around for centuries, with no outlet.

"The pain was unbearable. I remember screaming for death, begging Bael to just… *end my life* rather than tear my soul into pieces. We are supposed to be whole. What Bael does is a violation against nature."

"What saved you?" Della asked, although something was stirring in her memory. There was something familiar about Tré's words. She could not understand how or why, but she could almost see the place in her mind. It was like watching a video playing in a loop in her head, as Della saw him covered in mud and thrashing on the ground amidst a dark cloud.

"Irina saved me," Tré murmured, turning to look at her. "Her love saved me. I don't know how she knew to come, but she suddenly appeared through the trees, calling for me."

In Della's mind, she could feel herself running, branches scratching her arms, stumbling a little along a dirt path.

"I clawed my way out of the pit," he continued. "The surprise of it stopped Bael from tearing my soul out of me, although it was now in two pieces. It was like a knife had ripped me open while fire was consuming my flesh."

In her mind, Della could see Tré screaming, his hands tearing at his hair as he flailed around on the ground.

"I could feel burning in my throat, like the worst thirst I had ever experienced. All of my senses were heightened. I could hear ants crawling along the bark of the tree nearby. The veins of all the creatures in the forest around me were pulsing with blood, and the sound of it drove me mad with bloodlust. Then, suddenly, Irina was there."

The images in Della's mind were so strong that they blocked out her room and Tré's face. She could see herself falling to her knees, her hands trying to soothe the shuddering body in front of her.

"She smelled like the most delicious feast I had ever attended, and I could feel saliva welling up in my mouth. Instinct commanded me to bite, but I was too weak to move at first."

The smell of mud and stagnant water nearby choked her. An icy breeze bit at her exposed neck. She grasped her beloved's shoulders, trying to shake life back into him. His crazed eyes rolled wildly, burning silver from within.

"Sometimes I wish that I had done it," Tré whispered. Della could see that he was teetering on the edge of emotional control.

"Done what?" she asked, trying to follow his words despite the visions swimming in front of her eyes.

Tré closed his eyes and grimaced. "Killed her while she begged for mercy. That would have been the final death knell for my soul. Bael could have had it, and there would have been nothing left of me."

Horror flooded her. As Tré was speaking, memories were pouring into her—memories she had long forgotten, or never even knew she possessed. "But you didn't?"

A flash of brilliantly white fangs.

"No," Tré continued, shaking his head. He didn't speak for some time, but lay next to Della, breathing deeply, still trying to maintain control. "Bael surrounded us, laughing. He glories in destruction and desolation. He delights in ruining lives and ripping families and loved ones apart. It's almost as though he gains power from it."

Della could hear the horrible cackle echoing in the back of her mind, as if it reverberated across the centuries. Feeling sick, she asked, "Then what happened?"

"The bloodlust and thirst threw me into a feeding frenzy. I was out of my mind, and the longer I laid there in her arms, the stronger I became, as Bael's bitter venom poured through me. I think Irina knew what was happening. I remember hearing her yelling into the night, trying to fight off Bael, but I was already sinking into the Darkness in my mind."

"No! Stop! Leave him alone!"

Della could hear herself shrieking. She closed her eyes and she could see herself turning to face the Darkness, defiant.

"He will destroy you," a voice crooned in her ear. "Your childish insolence will not save you; then your soul will be mine forever."

"No," she replied, in the calmest voice she could muster. "You are a thing of evil, a damned spirit of the underworld. I will not bow to your darkness or violence. You will spare his life."

"Who are you to command me?" The voice answered, simultaneously like ice and fire. "What will you give me in return?"

"I will give my life for his."

The evil spirit seemed to consider this, swirling and taking shape around her. Finally, a face loomed at her through the mist, bodiless as it floated along, ever closer. To her astonishment, she saw that she was speaking with an ancient and wrinkled toad. All around her there was the sound of skittering legs, and she felt as if bugs were crawling up her skin as he moved closer and closer.

"Your love cannot save him. He's been turned and has already forgotten. He will destroy you in your insolence. And yet, you will give me your pathetic life?"

"For his," she said again.

"Then you will suffer for all eternity, knowing that it was your beloved who drained every last drop of your life blood."

Tré's voice seemed to shatter the darkness of Della's mental images.

"Irina bared her throat to me. All I remember is sinking my fangs deep into her jugular and drinking as if my life depended on it. In her last breath, she told me that we would see each other again. That our souls could not be kept apart."

Della couldn't help herself, she recoiled in horror. Tré, intent upon recounting his memories, seemed to hardly notice.

"When I came to, I was... myself again. Bael was gone and Irina was dead at my feet. Before I could even fully take in what I had done, there was a noise in the trees nearby. I could see men crashing about, torches in their hands. I ran. I ran and I wept tears of blood for my lost love. I did not understand at first what had happened to me, that I had been changed into a creature of the night, forever condemned. I have wandered the world all these long years, trying to offer penance for my actions. I have long considered Irina's dying words to me. I thought that she meant in the afterlife, but upon meeting you I realized I was wrong. She meant we would see each other again in the mortal world."

Shock rooted Della to the spot. The full meaning of Tré's words finally hit her. She realized, now, that when

Tré looked at her, he wasn't seeing her at all. He was seeing the reincarnated spirit of his lost love.

But how was that possible? Della was *Della*, not some woman from medieval Europe. This *Irina* person was dead, and had been for centuries.

She opened her mouth, but found no words to speak.

And yet, she had these memories. Was it possible that she *had* been reincarnated? Could she truly be Irina, reborn?

"It was not mere chance that we met each other a few days ago," Tré said, looking into Della's eyes intently. "It is my belief that Bael has tracked you here and that he is surrounding you with violence as... a sort of *punishment* for his failure."

"But—" Della stammered. "But that can't be possible! How could I be her? And why would Bael hunt me down? *I haven't done anything!*"

"You represent one of his greatest failures, and his greatest weakness."

"Weakness?" Della demanded, sitting up in bed. Fear and anger were burning in her stomach, making her head spin. "How is an evil spirit with the power to tear apart souls concerned about me being his weakness? That's ludicrous."

Tré shook his head. "We aren't completely sure, I'm sorry to say. It's possible that..."

His voice trailed off. Della turned and looked at him, willing him to continue. She needed to know the worst.

"*What?*" she finally asked, as Tré continued to stare into space. "It's possible that... *what?*"

"There was a prophecy that one of us located, saying that a Council of Thirteen would convene, and that it would mean the destruction of Bael. These thirteen, so the prophecy goes, would be his greatest failures."

Seeing Della's bewildered look, Tré continued, "Vampires are Bael's greatest failures."

Della struggled to picture the vampires she'd met or been told about when she was at the old plantation house. "But... there are only six of you. Are you saying I'm the seventh?"

"I don't know," Tré answered. He looked deeply unnerved as he considered her.

Great, she thought, with more than a touch of hysteria. *I just fell into bed with a powerful supernatural creature who thinks I'm the reincarnation of his lost love, destined to join him in an eternal battle against evil. Suddenly, that psychotic break is looking way more attractive than it did a few hours ago.*

Tré and his friends had saved her life twice now. But it wasn't really *her* they were saving. It was the memory of a dead woman from centuries ago.

She'd fallen into bed with Tré, a powerful, immortal creature. But he hadn't fallen into bed with Della, the insurance agency receptionist who loved jazz and kept a pet goldfish.

No. He'd fallen into bed with Irina, a ghost from the distant past.

-o-o-o-

Tré felt Della go still next to him. He could hear her heart rate speeding up. The expression on her rapidly paling face was growing distant. Cold, almost. He could smell her sudden disquiet, pungent in the small bedroom.

Why the hell had he blurted out those things in the way that he had? Tré mentally cursed himself, already regretting his decision to be completely honest with the woman next to him. Why had he told her about the prophecy? If it wasn't alarming enough to discover that there are vampires in the world, he had to essentially outline centuries' worth of a bitter war that had nearly torn the heavens and earth apart forever.

All he had succeeded in doing was to terrify her before she even had a chance to process everything. He reached out a hand, desperate to soothe away Irina's —

No, not Irina. Irina was still dead, as much as he might delude himself otherwise. This was Della, and he owed it to her to remember that. He tried to soothe away Della's growing horror, palpable around them. To his dismay, she pulled away from him and rolled onto her back.

"It's just so much to take in," she whispered quietly, still looking deeply troubled.

"I know. I apologize for springing all this on you at once, but I feel compelled to be honest with you."

Della smirked at the ceiling. It was not a pleasant expression. She scrubbed a hand over her eyes and said, "Yeah, not that it matters anyway, right? You could simply wipe my mind blank, like before."

Tré sighed. "Della, you have to understand —"

But she interrupted him with a harsh laugh. "Don't worry, Tré, I understand just fine. I was an inconvenience to you at that point. Oksana explained everything. You needed a quick getaway and I had already seen too much to attribute it to shock or trauma."

Tré remained silent. She was completely correct, of course. Yet, Della could have no idea of the mental anguish he had gone through in the moment that he recognized her spirit. Not only had his body responded to her presence, as though he had touched a live wire. His tattered soul had started calling to her, as well, desperate for recognition. He wanted to be known and to know her, learn everything about her again.

He would never grow tired of seeking out the deepest parts of her soul.

Della lay silently next to him, not speaking. Her eyes were closed, but Tré could see the tension in her shoulders. Despite his centuries of experience, he was at a complete loss on how to respond.

"Della, what Oksana did to you is… not a practice that we use often," he said in a low voice.

She snorted derisively.

"It's true," he continued.

"So I guess I was just lucky, then?" Della asked. Her eyes were burning with a fire that Tré recognized. It was the same intense look that Irina would use when he was being particularly pig-headed about something.

Her expression was so endearingly familiar that he almost smiled. *Almost*. But…

"No," he said. "You are, by far, the unluckiest soul I've ever met. Even centuries ago when we fell in love. You managed to find the one man within an entire continent that was being hunted by a spirit of the underworld."

His attempt at levity seemed to go completely unnoticed, as Della didn't even crack a smile.

"So, this *Bael*. He's like the devil or something?" Della asked.

"That's a good question," Tré replied, growing thoughtful. "On the whole, I would say not."

"You keep answering in riddles. What does that even *mean*?"

Tré shook his head. "What you have to understand, Della, is that we have spent years studying Bael. Decades. *Centuries*. Eris, in particular, has been most studious, and has sought a deeper understanding of the spiritual realm present on Earth. He is one of the most renowned—though unknown—scholars of his age, yet even he doesn't fully understand Bael."

"It all sounds like some crazy religion," Della observed. "Or maybe a cult."

"Where do you think your various religions came from?" Tré asked, raising an eyebrow at her. "They are all inspired by the truth, it's just that different humans from different areas during different times have given their gods different names, and put different interpretations on events."

Della looked interested almost in spite of herself. "It's all the same?"

"Yes, of course. There are aspects of it that all the major religions have correct. And, no doubt, aspects that they have wrong."

"So, this *master religion*. Does it start with 'In the Beginning, God created the heavens and the earth...'" Della asked, somewhat sardonically.

Tré snorted a laugh. "I suppose you could say that. Untold aeons ago, the Light and the Dark lived in balance with one another. One never overpowered the other until something happened to offset that balance."

"Something?" Della asked curiously.

"That's one of the things that Eris is unclear about."

"How convenient," Della retorted with an eye roll.

Tré frowned at her, but continued, "When the balance was thrown off, there was a disturbance throughout time and space. The Void, which is where the Light and the Dark had existed mutually, began to coalesce in a ball of energy as the Light and Dark pulled apart. Then it exploded, forming the universe which is still expanding to this day, propelled outward by the force of the explosion."

Della remained silent, taking everything in.

"Our reality," Tré continued, "is literally driving apart the Light and the Dark."

He had struck a chord in her. He could tell.

She frowned. "But... that's *horrible*. Can the two halves ever be reunited?"

Tré shrugged, thoughtful. "Maybe one day, at the end of time."

Her frown deepened.

"Well, that all sounds dead depressing to me," she said. The idea that her world would end in a fusion of the Light and the Dark seemed to really bother her, but she tried visibly to shake it off. "So, where does Bael come into this picture?"

"The Light and the Dark are made up of a multitude of beings—humans included. Bael was once an archangel, of sorts. He helped bridge the gap between the two forces. He became fascinated by the Dark, though, and soon fell into corruption. When the Void was destroyed, he was hurled from his place of neutrality into the clutches of the Dark. Instead of fighting back, however, he fully surrendered and allowed himself to be transformed into a thing of base evil. Stripped of all the good that had helped balance his soul, he grew in power in the Dark. Like a parasite, I suppose, growing fat on power not his own."

Della wrinkled her nose and looked away, as if disgusted by the mental picture. "Sounds like he deserved what he got."

Tré felt anger possess him at the memory of all that Bael had done to him, and to the others. He clasped his hands together, the knuckles growing white. "Yes, he deserves everything he has gotten… and more."

"Were there others like him?"

"Other archangels, you mean?" he asked.

"Yes."

"Of course. Eris believes that the Biblical figure of the Archangel Michael is based on Israfael, for instance."

"Who?"

"She was the balance to Bael. The other half of the bridge. When the Light and the Dark were ripped apart, she was weakened in the great battle that ensued. Israfael is the Bringer of Light. I believe you are filled with her spirit and her goodness."

Della looked taken aback. "Me? You're kidding, right?"

"Not at all," Tré answered calmly. "How else would you have been able to use your love to bind the fragments of my soul together? Israfael can cast out evil from within and without. She has the power to heal any wound, physical, mental, or spiritual. Or, at least, she had that power once. Now she's a shell of what she was. Our greatest hope is that the Council of Thirteen will, as the prophecy suggests, restore Israfael to full power and cast Bael into the pit of Darkness forever."

Della remained silent for long moments. Tré looked at her, apprehensive—still not at all sure that he should have been completely honest with her. Yet, he could find no real regret in his heart.

She needed to know. Even if she didn't truly understand, she was Irina reborn, and she was cursed to be hunted by Bael until the end of her life.

The thought chilled Tré to the bone. He was sickened by the idea that he would lose her again. Though it was perhaps foolish of him to do so, he vowed to prevent it this time.

Somehow.

He had the ability to control himself now, at least. He had spent centuries developing the discipline not to take human life when he was forced to feed. He no longer fell victim to the terrible bloodlust that possessed his mind. He no longer let his vampiric instincts control him, turning him into a beast.

Not even, he finally acknowledged to himself, when he had been sorely tempted by passion and lust earlier. He had stopped himself before he'd tasted Della's blood, though it had been a close-run thing.

Tré lay completely still, watching Della silently. He knew that he had frightened her badly with talk of the spiritual war in which she had inadvertently become embroiled. He could practically hear the confused thoughts whirling around inside her head.

"I do have bad luck," she murmured after a moment.

"Yes," Tré breathed.

"And now he — Bael — is after me?"

"So it would seem."

"And the only way to bring back this good angel, Israfael, or whatever, is to unite thirteen vampires together? That will somehow give her back her power?"

Tré grimaced. "Much of this is conjecture. But... that is what Eris has been able to gather from the prophecies."

There was another long stretch of silence.

"I need a shower before work," Della said, rolling out of bed. Tré blinked in confusion at her abrupt departure.

ELEVEN

Della walked out of the bedroom without another word. Tré followed her with burning eyes, but did not attempt to stop her from entering the bathroom and shutting the door with a solid click. His heightened senses allowed him to hear her quietly slide the lock closed on the door and knew that she needed privacy more than anything at that moment.

And who wouldn't? It was a lot to take in. Especially all at once.

Outside of the questionable sanctuary of Della's apartment, Tré knew that the sun was rising above the horizon. He could feel the heat on his skin, even through the walls. As long as they were under shelter, the warmth was not unpleasant or too intense.

Yet, despite long centuries of practice, he had never quite adjusted to the inability to step into direct sunlight. When he had been mortal, one of his favorite sensations had been the sun on his face and a cool breeze in his hair. Now, though, he would scorch as if being lit on fire. He could survive direct sunlight, and had—but it was intense agony every time.

Bael was surely aware that the sun was rising, too. As a creature of the dark, his power would wane in the sunlight and wax by the moonlight.

It was clear to Tré that Della intended to return to work. He scowled, knowing that it would be very difficult for him to follow her. And, of course, if she knew, she would try to prevent him regardless. He did not need to read her thoughts to know that she was pulling away, trying to distance herself from the horrors he had laid at her feet.

Tré sighed and stared at the ceiling, imagining he could see Bael floating above Della's apartment, waiting for her to emerge again. Perhaps he was unwilling to attack while Tré was present. Tré had been completely unnerved when Bael had allowed the two of them to pass through New Orleans without harassment earlier, even though the demon could hardly have been unaware of their travel.

Tré listened to the sounds of Della showering, and tried to decide what to do. He could hear the quiet snap of her shampoo bottle and the sound of water dripping off her beautiful hair. He could feel love and desire swelling inside him. His soul was completely convinced that this woman was Irina, who had managed to find her way back to him despite all odds. He would do everything in his power to protect her, even if it meant sacrificing himself.

He would never forgive himself for betraying her centuries ago. He knew, intellectually, that no mortal could withstand the terrible power of being turned into a vampire, and the insane bloodlust that followed. But still, he could not forgive what he had done.

I will make this right, he thought with quiet determination. *Come what may, this time I will not fail her.*

-o-o-o-

An hour later, Della walked the last stretch of road leading to her office. She'd been set for a fight when she emerged from the shower, armed with an argument Tré couldn't refute. Bael was a creature of darkness, he'd said. Just as he was. Tré couldn't emerge into the daylight. And judging by the fact that most of the craziness these days kicked off after dark, neither could Bael.

But she could. And she would—just long enough to check in at work and let her boss know she was okay, but that she needed some time off. Then she would run a couple of errands, like getting a new phone and ID, and come right back.

She rounded the street corner a block from the agency and stared in horror.

It looked as if a bomb had detonated in the center of the street.

She moved forward with slow steps, staring at the blown out buildings surrounded by police tape, many of which had clearly been burned in vicious fires. Her gaze was drawn toward a car, blackened and empty, little more than a metal shell of its former self.

Hurrying now, Della sped up and found that the insurance agency was still, miraculously, standing.

She picked her way along the sidewalk, stepping over broken glass spread all over the concrete. As she approached the building, she noticed that a maintenance worker was boarding up one of the front windows to the left of the door. She murmured a distracted good morning to him, staring with wide eyes at the destruction. He nodded back solemnly, but did not speak.

When she stepped through the door, she found Rich—her boss—standing in the center of the demolished office, looking around. His arms were hanging limp at his side. His eyes were wide and blank with horror.

Della saw that her desk, which stood several paces straight through the front door, was one of the few that were still standing. All its contents had been strewn on the floor nearby. Filing cabinets were overturned, the manila files full of white paper regurgitated into heaps all over the place. Ugly slash marks marred the top of her desk, and the picture she kept of herself, her parents, and her sister before she'd died was stomped into shreds near her chair, which was on its side.

"Oh, my God... *Rich*. What happened?" Della whispered.

Rich, who appeared to have not heard her enter, looked around at her voice.

"Riot. Last night." They were the only words he appeared able to speak. He covered his eyes with one hand and took several steadying breaths.

A loud exclamation sounded from the doorway, and Della turned to see Alice standing framed against the light. Her expression mirrored the shock and disbelief that seemed to have settled in Della's stomach like a cold, dense ball of lead.

Bael, Della thought savagely, then shook herself. How could she believe that a demon from the underworld had anything to do with this mess? Catastrophes had been happening all over the city for months, there was no reason to suddenly start blaming everything on an evil spirit, just because a vampire had told her a scary story that morning. *Pull yourself together.*

She brushed past Rich and leaned over, placing her hands underneath a small, overturned filing cabinet. Lifting with her legs, Della set it upright with a soft thump that made Rich flinch and come back to himself a bit. His lost expression softened as he watched Della riffling through papers that were hanging out of files and sorting them into stacks.

She looked up at him, where he was watching her without moving.

"*What?*" she asked, more sharply than she intended. "We can't just sit around and let them win. So let's get this office back together and open for business."

Her words were apparently enough to shake Rich out of his reverie. He blinked. "Yes," he said slowly, "you're right, of course. Let's get to work."

Della and Alice set about finding all the scattered documents in the lobby of the office, placing them in piles on Della's desk.

"What happened?" Alice whispered after Rich slunk into his office, looking ill, and closed the door behind him.

"I guess there was a riot down here last night," Della whispered back. They cleared an area on the floor and sat down, sorting through the stacks of creased and trampled papers—organizing them as best they could.

"Do you know what it was about?" Alice asked.

"Who knows," Della murmured back. Suddenly, Della felt a shift in the air around her, almost as if a fluttering wing had rubbed lightly across the back of her neck. With a shiver and a jump, Della looked around, but saw nothing. Distantly, she thought she heard the sound of cold laughter, and a chill ran through her.

"Della?" Alice asked, staring at her friend with concern. "What is it?"

"*Nothing*," she snapped, the word coming out harsh.

Alice frowned. "Are you sure?"

"Yes!" Della said. "I'm… just a little on edge with all these horrible things going on. That's all."

"You and me both, honey," Alice said, and went back to her stack of invoices.

-o-o-o-

Several hours later, Della stood and brushed bits of dirt and lint off of her clothes. She and Alice had worked straight up to lunch and Della, completely famished, decided to walk a few blocks down to a small deli to buy a sandwich.

If the place is still standing, Della thought bitterly. She went to grab her purse, only to realize that it had been lost in the alley the day before. All she had was her apartment key and the pitiful wad of emergency cash she'd pulled out from under her mattress and stuffed in her pocket that morning.

She lifted a hand in a goodbye wave to Alice and Rich, both of whom looked a bit less shell-shocked after the progress they had made cleaning things up over the last few hours. With a final deep breath, Della headed out the door.

After purchasing a cheap turkey sandwich from the thankfully-still-standing deli, Della crossed to the opposite side of the street and started meandering back towards the office by an indirect route. When she was about two blocks away, she noticed a small door to the side of the main entrance of a building. It stood in the shadows, completely sheltered from the sun, set in a dark frame.

A plaque on the front read *Madame Francine's Voodoo Shop* in ancient, scrawling letters. Della rolled her eyes at the blatantly clichéd kitschiness of it—yet another tourist trap where visitors could buy 'authentic New Orleans merchandise' to send home to their families during Mardi Gras.

After a moment of hesitation, however, she felt the strangest compulsion to enter the shop, which suddenly seemed to offer respite from the madness of the outside world. She wondered vaguely what the titular *Madame Francine* might have to say about all the horrible things occurring in her city.

Almost without realizing she was doing it, Della opened the door and stepped inside. The smell of burning incense tickled her nose, threatening to make her sneeze. It was complex and sweet, in sharp opposition to the briny smell that always seemed to hover over this part of New Orleans.

Della's eyes flitted around the profusion of merchandise in the shop, only to fall on one of the oldest women she had ever seen. Madame Francine had coffee-colored skin, soft and deeply wrinkled. Around her head, she wore a beautiful red headscarf with shockingly white hair peeking out from underneath. Her dark eyes were clouded with cataracts, but Della had the distinct impression that Madame Francine could see more of the world than most.

Her very presence eased the tension in Della's shoulders. The old woman was like a deep fountain, overflowing with spring water.

These realizations flashed through Della's mind so quickly that she did not have time to speak. Madame Francine beckoned her with an imperious wave. Obediently, Della shuffled forward, a glass case standing between them.

"You are troubled, my dear," Madame Francine said in a grave voice.

With furrowed eyebrows, Della stared back and nodded silently. She had no idea what to say.

"The deepening darkness is swirling around you, taking shape, coming ever closer. Have you sensed it?"

Della thought back to all the horrible things that had happened to her in the last few days. It did feel as if she were hurtling towards a point, like she was balanced on the brink of a terrible battle for her soul.

"I... don't know what to do about it," Della breathed, feeling her eyes well up with tears. "I've tried to run away from it, but I can't. It's following me."

Was it possible that all the people in New Orleans had suffered because Bael was after her? Had all the bloodshed and destruction somehow been her fault?

"Running away is never the answer, child. Follow me," Madame Francine said, and led Della into a back room. The tiny space was crowded with deep-cushioned furniture and smelled even more strongly of incense than the rest of the shop. Madame Francine settled herself in a chair and gestured Della to take the one opposite from her.

Della sat, feeling a deep sense of unease.

"Tell me your story," Madame Francine said in a voice like warm molasses.

Without conscious volition, Della opened her mouth and the story of the last few days came pouring out, the words practically tumbling over each other. She did not know why she trusted this complete stranger, but something about Madame Francine gave Della the feeling that she held answers to at least some of her questions.

Della described the first shooting; the man that had died in front of her. She told Madame Francine about the frightening people with extraordinary powers that had rescued her, but wiped her memories. She spoke about being attacked in the alley and taken to the manor house where she met the coven of vampires. She told Madame Francine everything, and was only able to stem the flow of words when she got to the part about sleeping with Tré that morning.

She poured out the soul-deep fear that she had barely acknowledged to herself—that she had finally lost her mind and imagined all of it from start to finish.

"It's just so farfetched," Della said, winding down. "How can I be expected to believe that vampires and demons and angels and the mortal struggle between good and evil is taking place around me? Everything in our world says that these things are all fairy tales! How? I can't just change my entire thinking in one day!"

Madame Francine sat back and observed Della over her folded hands. They sat in silence for a long time while the old woman regarded Della, deep in thought.

"I am very old, child," she finally said, "and I have learned to see beyond the physical world. I sense a great struggle in you as the Darkness settles over this city. And I can tell you that humans are not the only beings that inhabit this world. The ones you call vampires are merely another facet of the battle between Light and Dark. Another reflection in the mirror of humanity."

"But they're so..." Della's voice trailed away for a moment as she strained to find the right word to describe her interactions with the vampires. "They are so *scary* in a lot of ways. They give off this cold and calculating vibe, but then they put themselves at great risk to rescue humans from danger. Tré—their leader—told me it was their eternal battle. And yet—being around them makes the hair on my neck stand up at the same time."

Her treacherous memories returned to the morning's events—lips trailing over those fine hairs on the back of her neck, drawing every nerve to attention.

Not helpful, damn it.

"Perhaps you are sensing the damage to their souls—or the threat of a predator?" Madame Francine suggested.

She sighed. "Maybe."

"You have the same awareness of the spiritual world as I do, child. With time and observation, you will be able to open your eyes further and see into their realm. I believe that you will become very powerful in your own way, if you can survive this coming Night. But you are in grave danger now, child."

Della shivered at her words.

"What do I do?" she begged. "How can I survive a war that I have no part of? This isn't my battle—I didn't do anything wrong! I just want to live my life the way I choose!"

"Do you think that we have sole control over our destinies?" Madame Francine asked, pointing a knotted finger at Della. "Do you think it is up to you to decide your fate?"

Della did not respond, terrified that the answer might not be what she wanted it to be.

"You do not have the power to choose your life," Madame Francine said. "You were given these experiences, this path to walk. It is your job to do the best you can with the circumstances before you, but you cannot flee from the coming storm. None of us can. Things will come to a head very soon, and you will have to face the truth—or be destroyed."

"So you're saying I should go back to the vampires?" Della asked after a long moment.

"You should take any help that is offered to you. These creatures are halfway between our realm and the spiritual realm. They are uniquely able to guide you and protect you from harm while you are preparing for the fight ahead, Della."

-o-o-o-

It was only later, as she was hurrying back towards her office, that Della realized she had never actually told Madame Francine her name.

She shivered, not sure if she felt more or less afraid than she did before going into Madame Francine's shop. The old woman's words were alarming in more ways than one, but on the other hand, the advice she gave seemed sound.

At least in theory, Della thought. She wondered about the pronouncement that she supposedly had the ability to sense the spiritual realm. Part of her wanted to reject the idea as absolute nonsense, but another part of her had always known that her awareness was greater than that of most of the people around her.

With time and observation, you will be able to open your eyes further and see into their realm, Madame Francine had said. What did that *mean*? How could she become more powerful? She wasn't a vampire; she was just a human.

Della rounded the corner towards her office and immediately felt a chill skitter down her spine, making her shudder. Della glanced behind her and saw nothing. Then, unable to help herself, she scanned the skies above her, looking for... what?

Perhaps it was her imagination, but she thought that the sky had darkened as the midday winter sun passed its zenith.

Pushing the disturbing thought out of her mind, Della reached for the door handle of the office. As soon as her hand touched the cold metal, it was as though she was being wrapped in a suffocating cocoon. Her skin prickled uncomfortably and her breathing grew labored. She distinctly felt the sensation of ants crawling up her legs. She brushed her ankles against each other, trying to dislodge the feeling, and pulled the doors open.

A terrible scene greeted her. Alice was lying sprawled on the floor in a heap, clearly dead. Her body was limp... broken... like a rag doll tossed away by a child.

As Della inched closer, her mouth falling open in horror, she noticed the slowly expanding pool of blood surrounding her friend. A gaping wound was clearly visible in the middle of her back.

Alice had been shot.

The feeling that ants were crawling up her body intensified. Della clawed at her arms, trying to relieve the terrible sensation even as silent tears coursed down her face.

As if in a trance, she made her way deeper into the office. The door to Rich's office was ajar. Her boss lay slumped over his desk. Blood was dripping steadily off the polished wooden surface, and his skull had been blown apart at the back. Brain matter was flung everywhere on the floor and wall behind him.

Reeling, Della stumbled backwards, tripping over a trashcan. She landed hard on her back and scrambled away from the horrific scene as fast as her arms and legs could carry her.

Bile filled her mouth and she gagged once, feeling her stomach trying to propel its contents upward.

Laughter rang again in her head and she scrambled unsteadily to her feet, barely breathing.

What do I do? What do I do?

Panic flooded her mind. A small part of her knew
that she was supposed to call for help. She was supposed to contact the police and give them a statement,
but that very small voice was quickly silenced by a
crushing presence descending on her mind.

She was like a crazed thing as she flung herself out
the door and landed on her hands and knees on the
sidewalk in front of the building. She heaved several
times, emptying the contents of her stomach onto the
ground in front of her with a sickening splatter. The
smell made her gag again. She tried in vain to draw
breath, desperate for untainted air.

There was none. There was nothing but death and
rotting flesh around her. She could smell it as she
scrambled to her feet again, the bitter taste of bile still
coating her mouth. Della staggered down the road in a
stumbling run, falling over curbs and crashing into
parked cars. The world around her was spinning and
swaying before her eyes. She tripped and fell hard
against a concrete retaining wall at the end of the street.

Dimly, Della was aware of pedestrians staring at
her open-mouthed, hurrying to get out of her way. She
must have looked like a madwoman, stumbling down
the street, her eyes flitting wildly from side to side, fresh
vomit staining the front of her shirt.

A woman cried out in alarm and pulled her small
child closer, shielding him from Della as she stumbled
past. A man cursed at her and darted off the sidewalk to
avoid her. Others crossed to the far side of the street as
they saw her coming.

For well over an hour, Della alternated running,
walking, and crawling her way towards her apartment,
which was more than three miles from her office. At
long last, she collapsed in front of the building, thrash-

ing around on the ground, convinced that spiders were crawling in her hair and clothes.

She dry heaved, having lost the last of her stomach contents long ago. Evil laughter surrounded her, further confusing her. She was almost home, but she could no more have risen to her feet and walked the final few steps to her door than she could have sprouted wings and flown.

The din of cold, hysterical laughter was deafening, and she clasped her hands over her ears. Curling up into the fetal position, she closed her eyes and prayed for help, or for a quick death.

I can't fight anymore, I can't! Oh God, please! Help me. Please, somebody help me. Tré!

TRÉ!

TWELVE

Moments later, Della felt gentle hands touching her face. She cracked open an eyelid, even as she continued to claw at the skin on her arms.

Relief flooded her as she saw Tré standing over her, blocking the bright sunlight from her eyes. He was wearing a black t-shirt and effortlessly slid his arms under Della, pulling her against him.

As she was lifted up, Della struggled wildly, feeling like she was about to fly off the earth and into space because of the tilting motion in her mind.

"Della, be still," Tré said urgently.

His voice was tight, and Della knew, in the corner of her mind that still maintained a tenuous grip on sanity, that something was wrong. There was some reason why he shouldn't have been able to come for her... what was it?

Carrying her as if she weighed nothing, Tré whisked Della up to her apartment building. As soon as they were in the cool shade of the entryway, Tré breathed a sigh of relief, hurrying along the hallway to her unit.

Still cradling Della against his chest, he used her key to open the door and slip inside. Della could sense the familiar surroundings, but the evil presence was still curling through her thoughts, wrapping around them like a serpent and *squeezing*. It was like a toxic substance creeping in her soul, and it made her feel like black oil was pumping through her veins and filling her mouth. She retched again and sobbed into Tré's shirt.

He lowered her onto her bed and brushed tangled hair out of her face. Madame Francine's words came back to her again, as if they were crackling through a badly tuned radio. She remembered that the shop proprietress had said she could gain power against the Darkness.

Pressing her fingers to her head, Della concentrated as she had never done before, trying to imagine the toxic oil being siphoned out of her body. She mentally pushed at it and found that, unlike real oil, it had density that she could grasp, although it cost her a huge amount of energy to do so.

"Yes, that's it," Tré encouraged, covering her hands with his own. "Fight back against him, Della. *Push him out.*"

Della shoved and kicked at the blackness, feeling it recede with each surge of effort. Sweat broke out across her forehead and under her clothes, but Della did not give up. She imagined herself as a powerful angel, able to banish Bael with a simple thought.

Suddenly, a brilliant light shone in her mind, the most intense radiance she had ever experienced. With a jolt of recognition, Della sensed that the expansive spirit was Tré, filling her mind with his, and flooding her with his love. She realized in a daze that she was immersed in the Light side of his spirit, being shielded and protected from the evil that had surrounded and violated her. Mentally, Della reached out to Tré, feeling his warmth like balm creeping through her heart, expanding outward through her body.

She could sense him within her. His emotions were open to her — his thoughts and feelings. She could feel his heart swelling with a depth of love for her that she could never have imagined. There was recognition and honor of Irina's soul within that love, it was true, but there was also delight and enjoyment in *her*. He sensed the connection she shared with his long lost love, but it was *Della* that he saw when he looked at her.

It was *Della* he had acted to save.

This realization was such a profound shock that Della actually jerked in surprise. Her heart swelled, threatening to break free of her ribcage as a surge of love for him in return flooded her spirit. He had come for her. He had fought… *for her.*

With that, Bael's grip on her mind loosened, slipped, and was gone. The emptiness felt strange after sharing her mind with a demon for more than an hour.

Exhausted, Della slumped back onto the bed, turning her face so that it was hidden against Tré's neck. The last vestiges of Bael's dark possession had not yet worn off, and Della still felt as though ants were crawling on her. She flinched, wanting to scratch at them, but she was too weak to do much more than moan.

"Shhh, it will fade, *draga mea.* Just try to rest. You've been through a terrible ordeal today. Breathe deeply and slowly," Tré murmured, kissing her forehead.

Della took a slow, deep breath and nearly gagged as the smell of bile assaulted her senses. "Oh, my God." The words were a bare whisper. "I smell horrible!"

Tré chuckled and held her tighter. "Well, to be fair, I've smelled worse. But, yeah, you definitely stink."

Della made a weak sound, midway between a laugh and a sob, as reaction set in and made her tremble. She let Tré release his grip on her so he could carefully pull the soiled shirt over her head. He threw it onto the floor in the far corner of the room. She breathed more easily, then, relieved to be free of the noxious smell from her clothing.

Tré settled her more securely against him, and she sighed with contentment as he wrapped his arms protectively around her. As he started to rub her back, though, Della's vision cleared enough that she could see angry burns blistering his skin.

"Oh, my God, Tré—is that from the sun?" she exclaimed, trying to sit up.

"It's of no importance," Tré assured her, pulling her back down to lie against him.

She was too weak to resist, but she scowled. "The hell it isn't. You're hurt!"

Tré shrugged with evident indifference and started rubbing gentle circles on her exposed skin. Della, exhausted from her struggle with Bael, felt her eyelids droop despite herself. She leaned more heavily into him, even as she struggled to stay awake and maintain focus.

"I would do it again," Tré said quietly. "A thousand times, if necessary. I made a grave error of judgment today, Della, and I almost lost you."

Della shivered again, despite the warmth of his embrace. "What happened to me?"

Tré did not answer for a moment, prompting Della to glance up at him. His expression was grave. His normally pale face, even paler.

"I thought you would be safe enough, in the daylight. But Bael is growing in strength. You were possessed by him. I'm quite sure he would have destroyed you, given a bit more time."

"He wouldn't have just turned me into a vampire?" Della asked, swallowing hard.

"I… don't believe so. No."

"Why not?"

"Revenge," Tré answered simply.

Della fell quiet, contemplating his words. It all made a twisted sort of sense now—the reason she was continually being tortured for *nothing*. Bael was getting back at her for sins she'd committed against him in another lifetime. For Irina's interruption of the atrocity he'd been attempting to perform on Tré's soul. Her argument with Madame Francine rose in her mind.

"This isn't my war," she said, hearing a plaintive note creep into her voice.

But that was a lie, and she knew it now. It *was* her war. She'd been a player in the battle against Bael for centuries without ever knowing it. Was it possible she'd lived *other* lives since then? Had her soul passed by Tré's before, like two ships in the night, each never knowing that the other was near?

Madame Francine was right. She could not choose which path to walk, but she could choose how she reacted to the demon bent on her destruction. Della pulled Tré closer and trembled against him as her thoughts turned towards Alice and Rich.

"The people at my office…" Della started to say, her voice quivering.

Tré placed a comforting hand on her cheek. "There's nothing you can do for them now, Della. It's over."

"You know what happened?"

"I saw it in your mind when I joined with you to fight Bael."

"Is it my fault?"

"Did you pull the trigger of that gun?" Tré asked.

"Of course not."

"Then how could it be your fault?"

Della looked at him with wide eyes, feeling tears burn behind them. "Bael is attacking this city to get to me. Everyone is suffering because of my presence."

Tré tightened his arms around her. "I won't argue with you that he has his focus here because of you, but Bael's plans are far grander and more ambitious than mere revenge against one soul."

Della made a skeptical noise, but Tré continued, inexorable. "He wants to turn the Earth into his realm, made into darkness in his likeness. It doesn't matter to him where he attacks, just as long as he is consuming souls and creating an army of the undead. If it wasn't here, it would be somewhere else."

"But, it's my fault that Rich—" She swallowed hard, unable to finish the statement.

"No, it's not." Tré insisted. "Della, listen to me. Your employer was not possessed by Bael when he took his life. That's not how Bael works. He would rather have turned the man into a pawn to use against you. I believe that Rich already struggled with the darkness inside himself, and saw no way back to the Light."

Della tried to digest the words. It did not absolve her from her grief and guilt, but it made sense that if Bael wanted to inflict the maximum damage against her, he would have been more likely to turn Rich into one of his puppets. He would have been perfectly positioned, close to Della.

"I never knew," she murmured quietly. "I never knew he was struggling so much."

Tré shrugged again. "Those in most need of help are often least inclined to seek it."

Della stared at the angry skin on Tré's arm, tears trickling down her cheek, lost in thought.

Everyone who gets close to me is in danger, from within and without. When is this going to end? How can we possibly survive this? Is everyone around me going to die? Am I... going to die?

-o-o-o-

Tré was suppressing the pain on his arms, head, and neck with some considerable difficulty. The sun had eaten at his exposed skin from the moment that he had stepped out of the building and run to scoop Della into his arms, until he had whisked her back inside. The depth of his fear for her when he heard her mental cry and realized what was happening meant that he did not feel the scalding pain until afterward.

Now, however, he felt it. Felt it to his very bones. He clenched his jaw in an effort not to show it, feeling the sharp points of his fangs scrape at the inside of his cheeks. Della was still staring at the burns with wide, liquid eyes. The intensity of her gaze made the hair on his scalp prickle.

"You must be in agony. What do we need to do about this?" Della asked.

Tré could tell that she was using worry for him as a distraction from her own pain. Which was fair, he supposed, since he'd been using worry for her as a distraction from his. He mentally shook himself and attempted to concentrate.

"It will heal," he said, which was true as far as it went.

"Do you need medicine?"

"No," he admitted after a pause. "I... need Xander, or one of the others."

Della's finely drawn brows drew together. "Another vampire, you mean?"

Tré nodded, feeling his skin pull and seep fluid onto his shirt. "Yes, I'll be able to heal much more quickly with help."

As much as Tré might want to keep Della to himself, curled together in her bed with the illusion that the outside world was safely held at bay, doing so would be a poor tactical decision on several fronts.

He exhaled quietly and shut his eyes. It was harder to concentrate on sending a mental call when his pain was so acute. After a moment, he felt Xander's mind brush against his, and tasted the concern permeating the response.

He pushed a small part of his pain towards the other vampire to communicate that he was injured and needed help. Immediately he felt Xander spring into action and then disappear from their mental connection.

"Xander is coming," he said, noting that Della still looked worried.

Worry gave way to confusion. "How—?"

"Our minds are connected," he explained. "I just called to him and conveyed that I was injured."

Della looked intrigued. "Okay. That's interesting. Like telepathy?"

Despite his pain, Tré felt the corner of his lips rise in a smile at her obvious curiosity.

"Not quite like what you might read in science fiction, or see in the movies," he said. "We didn't... think words at each other. It's more along the lines of sharing impressions, I suppose. We can communicate in more detail if it becomes necessary, but it requires considerable concentration and energy expenditure. Xander and I are very close, so I'm confident he understood the gist."

"Handy," Della said, lifting a hand to scratch at her scalp through her tangled hair. "So, what is he going to do?"

"Come here, I would assume."

Della looked alarmed and clambered out of bed. He was relieved to see that, although she was a bit shaky still, she seemed to be recovering from the attack.

She rummaged around in the chest of drawers sitting across from the bed. "*Shit*. I need to brush my teeth and clean up. Change clothes —"

"You've got time," Tré assured her, glancing out of the window. Dusk was starting to fall around them, but he knew that Xander would not risk movement during daylight hours while he was still recovering from his own injury. He would have been able to tell through the link that Tré was not in immediate danger.

Della gave him another searching look. "You're sure you'll be okay? There's nothing I can do to help until he gets here?"

Tré's face softened. "I told you, *draga*," he said, the endearment rolling from his tongue in Romanian and leaving a sweet taste in its wake. "It's of no real importance, and it will heal."

Della bit her lower lip uncertainly and nodded. "If you're sure. I'll just be down the hall, though, if you need anything. All right?"

With a final searching look, she turned and disappeared into the bathroom, leaving Tré alone. He heard the shower turn on a moment later, and let out a pained breath of amusement at Della's protectiveness. She had no real conception of how much more fragile she was than he. *She* was the one in need of protection, here.

Tré bit down on his lip to control the pain as he examined the skin on his arms. It was worse than he had thought at first. Without blood from one of the others, it would take a very long time to heal, and would probably scar.

Still, it truly was no matter. Tré leaned back onto Della's pillows and stared at the ceiling. He felt reasonably confident that the attack today had finally convinced Della of the danger she was in. Would it be enough to persuade her to return to the plantation house, though?

Bael would surely think twice about trying to attack her there, with all the vampires united under one roof. They had already proved their ability to stand against his undead forces in the various skirmishes they'd engaged in over recent months.

Though they numbered six and not thirteen, it was clear that Bael was already wary of them. If Della were under their direct protection, would he give up his desire for revenge against the soul she carried?

Deep down, though, the pessimistic part of Tré knew that there would be a final battle over Della's soul—and very soon. But he still hoped to whisk her away to the closest thing he could offer to safe haven before that time came.

His worries must have chased him down into an uneasy doze, because before he knew it, Della was standing over him. She was wrapped in a towel and smelled sweetly of shampoo, along with an intoxicating scent rising from her skin that was all her own.

Despite the pain of his burned flesh, Tré smiled up at the perfect vision hovering above him, and she smiled back.

"How are you feeling?" she asked softly.

"Better, with you standing there looking down at me," Tré replied. "How are you?"

Della paused, as if assessing herself. "Honestly? Shaken. I'm also hungry and a little lightheaded. I really need to get some food in me at some point."

"That's easily remedied," Tré said, glancing at the falling darkness outside. "Xander will be here shortly, I'd imagine."

Della nodded and began to dress. She slipped into a comfortable pair of jeans and a t-shirt that clung to her waist, accentuating her delectable curves. Tré's eyes feasted on her, feeling desire building up inside him again in spite of everything.

At that moment, he heard a soft whoosh in the hallway outside of her apartment, heralding Xander's arrival. He reached out with is mind and found that Eris was with him.

"They're here," he said to Della, who nodded and went to the front door. He remained where he was on the bed, finding it much easier to lie still than try to get up in the state he was in.

He heard her say, "Come in, please—he's in the bedroom." An indistinct murmur of voices followed, and three sets of footsteps approached.

A moment later, Xander and Eris entered the bedroom behind Della, both of them towering over her petite frame. She straightened her spine and turned to look up at them, but Tré could tell she was still intimidated by their presence.

Xander raised an eyebrow at her. "Apparently your mother never warned you about inviting vampires across the threshold?" he asked. Only someone who knew him well would be able to see the hint of amusement playing around his green eyes.

Della swallowed, but glared up at him gamely. "Bit late for that now, or so it would appear," she said.

The amused crinkle around Xander's eyes deepened, and he expanded his gaze to include Tré, sprawled in her bed. "Evidently," he agreed.

"*Xander*. Enough," Tré said, summoning a severe expression.

Perhaps it fell short of the mark, because Eris stopped his curious perusal of Della's apartment and shot him a deeply unimpressed look.

"If we're going to list off tales from vampire lore, perhaps we should start with the part about *not going out in the sun*," he said, raising a dark eyebrow.

Della shifted her feet, looking uncomfortable.

Tré scowled. "Or, for preference, we could fast forward to the part where someone gives me some damned blood before any more of my skin sloughs off."

"Your wish is our command, oh fearless leader," Xander answered with a brief, mocking half-bow. His eyes cut to Eris and back again. "That's actually why I dragged this one along. I'm still a bit weak, and he's already used to acting like a milk cow."

"Yes, *thank you*, Xander," Eris said, clearly past done with the banter. He turned his attention to unbuttoning the cuff of his white shirt and rolling the sleeve up past his elbow, baring the olive-tinted skin of a well-muscled forearm.

"Della," Tré said, "as you've probably gathered, these are Xander and Eris, two more of my fellow vampires. Try not to hold them against vampire-kind in general."

"Uh... nice to meet you both," Della said, seeming a bit taken aback by the interaction.

"Likewise," Eris said, giving her a brief once-over before crossing to Tré. Eris had been tight-lipped after the incident with Snag in the alley, and Tré wondered what their resident scholar made of her.

"It's a pleasure to meet you when I'm not bleeding out from a gaping chest wound," Xander said pleasantly. His expression morphed into a frown. "Or do you not remember that part?"

Della caught her lower lip between her teeth for a moment before letting it slide free. Tré found himself unable to look away from her full, perfect mouth, his pain momentarily forgotten.

"No," she said, looking up at Xander. "I remember it now. Thank you. You... saved my life."

Xander's return smile was charming, for all that it did not touch his eyes. "Oh, it was nothing," he said. "All part of the service, I assure you."

Eris had foregone the extended introductions in favor of looking over Tré's injuries with a practiced eye.

"You've really done a number on yourself," he said with professional interest. "This is going to take some serious transfer of life force to heal properly."

"But, hey—look on the bright side. At least you didn't get shot," Xander told him, flopping down into the room's single chair to watch.

Tré raised an eyebrow at him, covering the flinch at how much doing so hurt his face.

Eris started rolling up his other sleeve, and eyed Della curiously. "So, you are the embodiment of infamous and much-mourned Irina, then? This whole situation is fascinating, I must say."

"So I've been told. But my name is Della," she replied, lifting her chin defiantly.

Rather than being offended by her hard tone, it seemed that her attitude pleased Eris in some way. He nodded with satisfaction and gave her a brief smile. "So it is," he said. "And rightly so. My apologies for the presumption."

To Tré's relief, he finally proffered his wrist, returning his full attention to the reason they were there in the first place.

Tré barely contained a moan of longing as he sank his fangs deep into Eris' arm. With a rumble of satisfaction, he drew the sweet, healing blood from Eris' punctured vein and felt it course through him, adding to his own blood supply. His life force had been pulsing angrily along with the flashes of pain from his skin, but Eris' gift was like a balm that soothed and cooled the angry storm.

He had not realized just how tightly he was holding himself until he relaxed and allowed the breath to flow out of his lungs, taking much of his tension with it.

"That's better," Xander said in encouragement, rising from his borrowed chair to stand over Eris' shoulder while Tré fed. He grasped Tré's hand from where it was clasped around Eris' wrist, and used it to lift his arm so that the light from a lamp nearby illuminated the blistered, peeling skin.

As they watched, the skin grew lighter, the red patches fading to pink and then back to their normal pale coloration. The pain vanished over the course of several minutes while Tré fed from Eris' arm.

As he did so, he felt the bond between them strengthen, and could more clearly sense the other vampire's mind and mood. Tré could discern a deep feeling of concern underneath his facade of calm.

He could even taste the relief seeping through Eris' blood as he continued to drink. The rich taste of it eased the bone-deep thirst that had been growing in him since his injury.

Allowing his eyes to slide away from Eris, Tré's gaze found Della, who was standing in the corner with her arms folded. She looked fascinated by what was taking place in front of her, but the faint tinge of green in her face told Tré that she was also disturbed by what she was seeing.

After he drank his fill and his skin was no longer blistered and throbbing, Tré leaned back with a deep sigh of relief.

"Just rest for a few more minutes," Eris said, his voice emerging raspy. The process of sharing blood with an injured comrade was both draining and intimate. As Xander had said, Eris was more familiar with it than most of them, given his odd, one-sided relationship with Snag. Nevertheless, it was clear that his own strength was sapped after the generous gift he'd offered.

Tré patted him on the arm and ran a hand over his eyes. "Take your own advice, *tovarăş*."

There was a huff, and the mattress dipped as Eris settled on its edge. Meanwhile, Xander returned to his borrowed chair and flopped down in it again, lacing his hands together across his stomach.

"So," he began, "are you going to tell us how this happened, or are we going to have to start guessing?"

When Tré didn't answer, Xander said, "Fine. You can tell me when I get close. Tré, you let Della here out of your sight because you thought it was safe during the daytime. But it wasn't, because our lives are doomed to be fucked five ways from Sunday, and so you ended up getting nearly turned into a pile of ash in a — thankfully successful — attempt to keep her alive."

Tré leveled a hard stare at Xander, who returned it without backing down. It would have been easier to maintain the severe expression if the other vampire hadn't hit on nearly the exact truth with his very first guess.

"It wasn't Tré's fault. It was mine," Della said, looking rather ill.

"Nonsense. The only one at fault is Bael," Tré said into the ensuing silence. He let his head fall back to rest against the headboard, and closed his eyes. "He caught you in a moment of weakness and tried to possess you, Della. I've honestly no idea how you managed to make it back here without succumbing—and on foot, no less."

Della's reply was very quiet. "I had to get back here. I knew, somehow, that I had to get back... to you."

Tré's eyes flew open. He straightened away from the support of the headboard to meet her gaze, an unaccustomed lump rising in his throat even as something large and warm swelled in his chest.

"And so you did," he said after a beat, their eyes locking for a long moment as the others looked on curiously. With an effort of will, he broke away from her to glance at Xander. "Unfortunately, I had to rush out into the sunlight to get her inside. It's... been a bad day for everyone involved."

"It has," Della agreed in a whisper. She cleared her throat. "I got to work this morning, only to discover that a riot had broken out on my street and the rioters had trashed our office. A couple of us were trying to get everything cleaned up. I left for lunch, and when I got back, Bael tried to take over my mind. I'd just discovered that..."

Her voice trailed away and Tré saw her bite her lip.

"You'd just discovered... what?" Eris asked, rousing enough to rejoin the conversation.

Della took a deep, shaky breath. "My boss had a gun. He killed one of my co-workers. She was a friend of mine. He shot her, and then turned the weapon on himself. I... found their bodies, and that's when I felt Bael's presence."

"He used that moment of shock and despair as a way to enter your mind?" Eris clarified, glancing from Della to Tré, who nodded.

"And all this, during daylight?" Xander asked, his face deadly serious. They all knew that Bael's power waned significantly during the daytime hours. It was unusual for him to strike while the sun was high.

"Yes," Tré answered.

"Well, that's certainly ominous," Eris said, his voice deceptively mild. He blinked, returning his full attention to Della. "But you managed to get back here, and against all odds, you fought him off. How?"

Della glanced at Tré, and her face colored. "It was Tré. He... helped me somehow. Lent me his strength, so I was able to push Bael out of my mind."

Eris' dark eyebrows lifted in clear surprise, and he sent Tré a speaking look. "Did he, now?"

Xander was staring at him, too. "You joined mentally," he said, "with a human." The words had the form of a question, but the delivery was flat.

"I didn't even realize that was possible," Eris said, looking at Della with new interest. "And you were aware of this mental joining, at the time? He didn't just tell you about it afterward?"

Della frowned. "Well, of course I was aware of it. It was kind of a hard thing to miss. I could feel what he felt and he added his strength to mine. Why do you both look so surprised? I thought you vampires could muck around in human minds with no problem." She paused. "Which, by the way, is *creepy as hell*, in case no one has ever mentioned that before."

Xander snorted.

"It's not something we do often, or lightly," Eris said. "But the human mind isn't really designed to process such things. It's not so much the fact that Tré gained access to your mind, but rather the fact that you were aware of it and able to make sense of what was happening. That's a vampiric trait."

"Oh," Della said. She looked taken aback.

"Were you aware of it when Oksana wiped your memories, the first time we crossed paths?" Eris continued.

"No," said Della. "I had no idea what was happening. I thought I must be going mad, but the EMTs convinced me it was just a natural reaction to severe trauma."

Eris nodded, still obviously fascinated. "Which lends credence to the idea that you and Tré were able to join in such a way because it was your soul that shielded his, all those years ago when Bael turned him. You saved him, and that connection still persists to this day."

The unexpected mention of that darkest of times sent a sliver of ice through Tré's chest. But Della was staring at Eris, shaking her head.

"I really didn't, you know," she said. "You all keep talking about me being this person... this Irina... but I'm a twenty-six year old receptionist from New Jersey. I didn't do any of these things you think I did."

Tré could understand how hard this must be for her. But her safety rested on her willingness to accept the dark realities life had dealt her.

"Do you deny the connection between us, *draga mea*?" he asked.

She looked so lost and confused for a moment that he longed to chase the others away so he could take her in his arms — but now was not the time. After the space of several heartbeats, though, she seemed to deflate.

"No," she said quietly. "I don't *understand* it — but I don't deny it. I feel it, too. I felt it from the moment your skin first brushed mine. Like an electric shock, straight to the heart."

"Bael will not rest until he has revenge on her, Tré," Xander said. "You have to realize that."

"I concur," Eris echoed.

Tré nodded and closed his eyes for a moment, thinking. He knew that Della possessed a stubborn spirit, identical to Irina's. He hoped she would not fight them on this.

"So what does this mean for me?" she asked into the silence.

"It means," Eris said, "that your life will never be the same again."

She blinked, tears pooling in her eyes, but not spilling over. "I can't stay here, can I? This place has always been my sanctuary from the outside world — but it's not any more, is it?" The words were wistful. Sad.

Tré didn't want her to be sad.

"No," he said, before either of the other two could speak. "At the house in the bayou, you would be under our combined protection. I can't imagine that Bael would dare attempt a full attack on the place, with so many of his own failed creations gathered in one place, and spoiling for a fight with him."

Della let out a slow breath, growing resigned. "I guess I've got no choice, then. God knows, if I'm going to survive this, I need the help. You six are the only option I have."

The ice in Tré's chest stabbed a little deeper. "You *will* survive this, *draga mea*," he said, intense. "I will lay down my life, if necessary, to ensure it."

Rather than look reassured, she clenched her jaw and looked away. Wordlessly, she started walking around her room, gathering a small bag's worth of clothing and personal items with angry, efficient movements.

"I don't want you to lay down your life," she said, still not looking at him. "I just want this... not to be happening, I guess."

She stowed a couple of foil-wrapped energy bars in the bag's front pouch, and slipped on a pair of hiking boots. Pulling her honey-colored hair back off her neck, she tied it up and slung her bag over her shoulder.

"But it is happening," she continued, glancing around the room at the three of them. "So let's move. Tré? Are you strong enough?"

"Yes," Tré said, already rolling off the bed despite the echo of his injuries still draining his vitality. "Of course I am. Let's go."

THIRTEEN

Della took a deep breath and followed the three vampires out of her bedroom.

I should be terrified right now, she thought, remembering the way Eris' deep brown eyes and Xander's cold green ones had studied her intently when she had opened the door, as if sizing up her possibilities. *Voluntarily giving myself over to a coven of vampires, for God's sake. What the hell is wrong with me?*

But she could still feel the security of Tré's arms around her. She could remember the fierce protectiveness of his mind as it swirled together with hers, like water and wine mixed in a glass. Those things could not be faked. They were *real*.

When they reached the front door, Della glanced around her beloved little apartment and wondered if she would ever see it again. She knew that she was fleeing for her life, and there was no time to linger over physical possessions. Yet she still felt tears sting her eyes as she scanned the familiar walls. This place had been her own. Her retreat. Her safe haven. Leaving it now felt like she was leaving a part of herself behind.

Tré must have sensed her turmoil, because he was suddenly *there*, by her side, gently taking her hand in his own.

"Della?" he asked, looking down at her.

Get yourself together, girl,, Della thought savagely. *Now is not the time to show weakness or fear. Bael can get you that way.*

Della didn't know if that was exactly true, but the demon had seemed to slip so easily into her mind when she was distraught over the loss of her coworkers. She squeezed the strong, callused fingers wrapped around hers and tried to wrap herself up in every good feeling of hope and happiness that she could muster, as if doing so would shield her from the threat of an oily, malignant presence in her mind and the sensation of spiders crawling over her body.

Della shivered, but looked steadily back into Tré's pinched, worried face.

"It's okay," she said. "I'm just going to miss this place. That's all."

Tré's expression softened with understanding. "I know. Hopefully it won't be for very long."

Della laughed, though it was not a happy sound. She doubted very much that this battle would be a quick or easy one.

"Yeah. Now, how are we getting back to the plantation house?" Della asked.

Eris had stepped out into the hallway of her apartment complex. He glanced up and down the hallway, clearly checking for anyone who might take note of their presence.

"We'll have to take the Jeep," he responded. "Unfortunately."

"I have a car," Della said quickly, pulling out her keys. "I almost never use it, though. Easier to take the tram to work and errands than try to find parking."

She passed the keys to Xander, who took them from her hands, his eyes lighting with interest.

"What kind of car is it?" he asked.

"Xander," Tré said in exasperation. "Does it really matter?"

Xander gave Tré a withering look. "You really don't get it at all, do you? Of course it *matters*."

Eris cleared his throat. "As charming as this little domestic argument is, I think we should probably stick with the Jeep. The road to the manor house isn't exactly conducive to a small car."

"Agreed," Tré said, and gestured them all forward.

A thought occurred to her, and she started rummaging through her bag.

"Did you forget something?" Tré asked, a furrow forming between his brows. "We need to get moving."

She came up with a little pad of Post-It notes and a pencil stub. "Just a minute. I need to write Mrs. Carpenter down the hall a note. Someone needs to take care of Jewel if I'm not here."

Xander frowned. "You have a jewel? Bring it with you. It might come in handy if we need untraceable money on short notice."

She stared at him. "Jewel is my pet fish. She'll die if no one takes care of her."

She thought she saw a smile tug at Eris' lips in her peripheral vision, but he covered it when she leveled a glare at him.

"Do it quickly, then," Tré said, his eyes scanning their surroundings as if he expected an attack at any moment.

She nodded and jotted a note for her neighbor, who had watched her apartment on several occasions when she'd been out of town. Confident that Jewel wouldn't become an unintended casualty of her bad luck, she hurried back to the others and readjusted the bag on her shoulder as they headed for the main entrance.

Once they were outside, Eris led them around the corner to the little parking lot in the back, where the Jeep was squeezed between two large trucks. Della glanced up at her car, four spaces down, to make sure it was still okay. She usually tried to drive it once a week, just to make sure that the oil and gasoline did not become stale in the engine, but otherwise it was saved for trips back home to see her family. Would she ever drive it again?

"2011 Nissan Sentra," Xander said, walking around the vehicle with an appraising eye. "Standard package?"

Della stared at him and shrugged one shoulder. She had known some of the specifications when she bought it, but at the moment it did not seem very important.

"Just get in the Jeep, Xander," Eris said with a groan, motioning towards their beaten up vehicle. "We've got a long drive ahead of us."

Xander rolled his eyes. "Right. Fine. Tré, give me the damn keys. And before you ask—yes, I'm sober. *Painfully* so."

"Wonders never cease," Tré said, and tossed him the keys. Eris slid in the front seat, leaving Della and Tré to sit in the back.

Xander positioned himself behind the wheel and started the vehicle with a low rumble. "So. I bet that car of yours gets about thirty-two miles to the gallon, am I right?"

"Something like that, I guess," Della answered. She glanced over at Tré in consternation, and he gave her a look in return that clearly said, *humor him.*

They drove through the cramped roads of the Garden District and got on the highway to cross the river before heading southwest, toward Lake Salvador. It seemed incredible to Della that there could be people out here with them, just driving around—going about their daily lives without a care in the world.

In the past few days, everything in Della's life had been upended and turned on its head. She'd seen people die. She'd been attacked. Terrorized. She had no job, and she'd just left her home behind, carrying nothing but a small overnight bag slung over her shoulder. Her future was bleak, with a demon of the ancient underworld hunting her down and a group of eccentric vampires her only hope.

The irony was enough to make her choke.

"Are you all right?" Tré asked, his voice pitched for her ears alone, breaking into Della's musing.

"Yeah," she answered, turning back towards the window on her left. "*Great.*"

He took her hand, which had been resting on the seat next to her, and gently squeezed her fingers. At his touch, Della felt herself relax a bit, reassured by his steady presence, almost despite herself.

They had been driving for nearly thirty minutes when Della — still lost in memories of the life she might never be able to return to — felt the car slowing down. She glanced around and saw that Tré, Eris, and Xander all seemed to be on high alert. The three vampires were leaning forward in their seats, looking out through the front windshield with matching wary expressions.

"What is it? What's going on?" Della asked, her heart starting to race.

"It's a roadblock of some kind," Tré answered without taking his eyes off the line of flashing red and blue lights in front of them.

"Oh," Della answered with considerable relief, "it's probably just the police setting up a DUI checkpoint or something like that."

Tré's gaze swiveled in her direction. "A DUI check-point?"

"Yeah," Della said encouragingly. She felt giddy with relief that it was nothing more frightening. "You know — *driving under the influence.* There's usually one of them somewhere in the city. It keeps drunk driving down when folks know that the police are out looking for them."

"You're quite sure of that?" Tré interrupted, his eyes still staring fixedly at the flashing lights ahead.

Della faltered and glanced back out of the window. "Well, I mean... *yeah.* I—I think so. What else would it be?"

"Roll the windows down a crack, Eris, just to be safe," Tré said quickly. "And Xander, if you're lying about being sober, so help me — "

"*Nice*," Xander said. "Thanks for that."

As soon as the back windows were cracked an inch or two, Tré's nostrils flared, as if scenting for something.

"Look, you three," Della said, trying to put them all at ease, including herself. "Think about all the craziness that's been happening around New Orleans recently. It only makes sense that there would be a greater police presence. They probably just... don't want the violence and problems to spread, or something."

No one answered her. Tré had his head cocked towards the cracked window as the line of cars in front of them proceeded through the checkpoint. Della watched red brake lights fade into the distance, after winding their way through the heavy, plastic barriers.

Xander inched to a stop and rolled his window down completely. A state trooper wearing a blue uniform and one of those vaguely ridiculous Smoky-the-Bear hats sauntered over to them. He held his hand up to shield his eyes from the headlights and Della frowned. He was wearing sunglasses, which seemed rather unusual after nightfall.

The officer stepped up to the side of the car, his hand resting casually on his utility belt.

"License and registration," he said in a flat voice. Something about his lack of inflection made Della's neck prickle.

Xander, never taking his eyes off the officer, dug around in his back pocket for his wallet and slipped an ID into his hand. Eris, who had been rummaging around in the glove compartment, passed over the registration papers.

The officer examined them slowly, a hint of a leer playing around the corners of his mouth.

"That all seems to be in order," he said, passing them back through the window.

He paused, glancing into the backseat. She couldn't tell because of the man's dark shades, but she felt certain that he was staring right at her. Nonplussed, Della shrank back, trying to melt into the shadows of the vehicle. She made herself small, which seemed to stiffen Tré's spine with additional tension. She saw him lean forward and lay a warning hand on Eris' shoulder.

"Anything else we can do for you, officer?" Xander asked, his British accent lending a lazy drawl of challenge to the words.

The state trooper considered Della for a moment longer before his gaze turned back to Xander.

"Yes," he said in the same flat drone, "you can all step out of the vehicle for me, please."

At that moment, he lifted his hand to his sunglasses and pulled the frames off his face. The strobing lights surrounding the traffic stop illuminated his features, and what Della saw made her gasp out loud. His eyes were flat and dead.

Inhaling, she caught the same whiff of decay that had surrounded the undead men who attacked her in the alley near her apartment building. An identical scent surrounded the officer's body like a cloud as his eyes continued to stare blankly at each of them.

At that moment, several things happened at once. Tré gripped her arm so tightly it hurt, Xander swore loudly, Eris jerked back and covered his nose, and the Jeep's tires squealed as Xander stamped on the gas.

Before she could do or say anything, the tires found traction and her body was slammed backwards into the seat behind her as Xander crashed through the flimsy portable barricade. A loud scraping of metal and plastic told them that the plastic barrier had dragged their bumper off as it was flung aside by the vehicle.

"*Shit*," Xander snarled, spinning the steering wheel madly as he tried to avoid a tree on the side of the road.

"What was he?" Della asked loudly as she and Tré were flung to the side of the car. Xander had evidently decided that their best means of escape was an off-road chase through the bayou, and she scrabbled for purchase.

It felt like her heart had frozen inside her chest, and she massaged her ribs with one hand while she tried desperately to cling to the door handle with the other.

"One of the undead," Eris spat back, sounding furious—his mild, bookish demeanor vanishing in the space of a moment.

"One of Bael's puppets," Xander clarified.

Della spun around and saw that red and blue lights were following them. Through the misty darkness, it was impossible to tell how far away their pursuers were.

"So they're after us now?" Della asked, terrified. "How did they find us? How did they even know to *look* for us?"

"A good question, and one for another time," Eris said, his voice low and dangerous.

"Shouldn't we have stayed on the highway?" Tré called to Xander over the roar of engine noise. "We could have driven faster!"

"Those police cruisers would have smoked this old wreck," Xander snapped in reply. "This was the best option at the time."

"*Brilliant.* I imagine you're having second thoughts right now?" Eris countered. Della could practically hear him gritting his teeth. "You know, when I woke up this evening, I really didn't think this was how my night was going to go!"

Della could see that Eris was gripping the handle above his head with white knuckles.

"There seems to be a lot of that going around," Tré shot back. "*Xander*—"

"Would you both just *shut the hell up*?" Xander yelled over the howl of old machinery pushed past its limits. "I'm a bit busy trying not to wreck us!"

Tré and Eris fell silent as Xander reached over and killed the headlights. They were plunged into total darkness as they continued bumping and juddering along, broken only by the flashing red and blue lights behind them, occasionally filtering into the cab of the vehicle.

"Maybe we should stop and talk to them?" Della asked half-heartedly. "We could try to explain what happened. Surely they're not all undead, right?"

"If only that were true," Eris answered her.

"This is insane, though!" Della shouted. "Isn't there a chance that some of them would be normal that could help us? Whereas, this is basically guaranteed to kill us!"

Della gestured to the pitch-blackness in front of them, even though she doubted that Eris could see her.

Xander didn't answer but spun the wheel to one side and then the other, barely missing a large tree that loomed out of nowhere in the darkness.

Della and Tré hung on for dear life, occasionally cracking their heads on the roof of the vehicle when they were pitched upwards by an unseen hole in the trail they were forging through the bayou. Mud and loose dirt slapped against the windows as the tires tore up the boggy ground. All the while, police cruisers followed, slowly but surely gaining on them.

Della could see one cruiser just a few car lengths off the Jeep's left rear bumper, jouncing along just as badly as they were on the uneven track. She imagined, although she could not be sure through the chaos and darkness, that she caught a gleam of dead eyes in the driver's side seat, watching her.

Of all the terrible things that had happened in the last few days, Della was more frightened in this moment, more convinced that she was about to die, than at any other time. She was abruptly certain they were about to crash into a swamp where she would meet an ugly death by drowning or being eaten by alligators. Horrible images of her own neck being snapped as they were propelled head first into a tree filtered across her mind's eye as she fought to remain upright while being tossed around like a rag doll.

"We need a plan," Tré finally barked. "Crashing through the swamp in the dark does not constitute a plan! Our luck is going to run out sooner rather than later!"

Xander laughed, wild and derisive. "Yeah—sorry, boss. I've been trying to think of something in between dodging rocks and huge holes that could swallow this Jeep completely. How about I concentrate on not killing us? Piece of cake, right? Here's an idea, though! Why don't *you two* figure out someth—"

Xander's words were cut off by a scream of metal as the vehicle dropped suddenly, the ground beneath falling away. For the space of one breath, the Jeep was suspended in the air before smashing into the wet earth. Della flew forward, the safety mechanism on the ancient seat belt snapping without slowing her forward momentum.

Tré's arm came out of nowhere, stopping her body before she could smash into the back of the driver's seat. It felt like running into a solid steel guardrail, chest first.

Feeling as though she'd been hit by a bus, Della groaned and clutched at the back of her neck, which was throbbing with pain.

"Are you all right?" Tré's frantic voice cut through the gloom and the sound of sirens as the Jeep came to rest at an angle. "Della!"

Della coughed once, feeling aching ribs protest at the movement. "I think so," she croaked.

They moved around, feeling for each other in the darkness as Tré called to the other two vampires. "Xander? Eris? You're all right?"

In response, they heard the engine grinding as Xander cranked the key in his hand.

"Come on," he growled as he pumped the gas pedal, trying in vain to turn over the engine.

"Even if you get it started," Eris said in a strained voice, "I don't think we're going anywhere. We're stuck in the bottom of a ditch, you clod."

Della felt horror punch her in the stomach, even as Tré's hand closed around her wrist.

They were trapped. The vampires could fly away if they had to. But for her, there would be no escape.

FOURTEEN

"Everybody out, don't let them flank us!" Tré ordered, pulling Della towards the door on his side. The window on her left had smashed as the car landed against the roots of a large tree. The impact to the trunk had caused leaves and sticks to fall from the branches overhead onto the top of the disabled vehicle.

Tré threw his shoulder against the door pulling on the handle at the same time. "Damn it. It's jammed."

He spun easily onto his back and gripped the seats on either side of him. With immense strength, he kicked the door, which popped open partway and stuck again.

Xander and Eris were clambering out of the passenger side as Tré carefully pulled Della through the gap. As soon as she landed in the mud, Della saw flashing lights creeping closer to the edge of the ditch.

"What do we do?" She asked, shrinking against Tré's side and quivering as reaction to the crash set in. For all her talk earlier, she held out no real hope that these officers drawing ever nearer to them were not a part of the undead uprising led by Bael.

"*You* are going to run," Tré told her. With a sound of metal scraping against metal, Tré pulled a wicked looking knife from a hidden sheath at the small of his back. "*We* are going to fight."

Ignoring her open-mouthed stare of disbelief, he pressed the handle of the dagger into the palm of her hand and pushed her forward.

"Go," he commanded, uncompromising.

Della took a single stumbling step and balked, looking up at Tré in consternation. Her gorge rose at the idea of leaving him there, surrounded by the undead they could already see gathering at the edge of the embankment.

"Go!" Tré ordered. "Della, you have to run now. Don't worry—I'll find you. I'll come back for you, I promise." He surged forward and pressed his lips to hers for a bare instant before pushing her away again.

"I—I—" Della stammered, unable to articulate the horror rising in her mind. She was terrified at the idea of leaving Tré behind—it would be like leaving part of herself behind. The bond between them stretched, pulling at her heart. She was damned well not going to allow an army of Bael's servants to destroy that connection.

She would run, but only far enough to get out of the vampires' way as they fought.

"*Go!*" Tré bellowed.

Della stumbled backwards at the unexpected shout and tripped. Flipping onto her knees, she scrambled forward until she was sprinting into the darkness without the slightest idea where she was going.

Once Della made it several yards away, she darted into the trees. She peeked out from behind a trunk to see Tré and the others illuminated by large spotlights wielded by police officers on the track above them.

As she watched, panting for breath, she saw Xander pull a gun out from his waistband and cock it with a practiced movement, holding it securely in his right hand. Eris pulled out two daggers, flipping one to Tre, handle first. He caught it with a sharp nod of thanks. Together, the three men turned towards the large group of cops gathering nearby. The breeze lifted Della's hair off her neck, prickling the skin, and she could detect the smell of rotting flesh in the air. Choking back a gag, Della realized the three of them were about to be overrun by the undead.

-o-o-o-

"We need backup," Xander said as he pulled the 9mm Makarov out of his waistband. "Much as I hate to admit it, having Snag's batshit crazy super-strength here right now would be *really* helpful, assuming he aimed it in the right direction."

"Yeah, I'm on it," Eris muttered as he flipped his extra dagger to Tré.

As the three vampires turned towards the army of undead scurrying around the police cruisers, Tré felt Eris send out a strong call for help to the others back at the plantation house. The power of the summons echoed through the depths of his divided soul.

Would they get the message and respond in time? Were they close enough to sense it? Tré knew that they were still quite a distance from the house. Sometimes mental messages went astray in the heat of a moment, especially across long distances.

"Drop your weapons and put your hands in the air." The flat voice resounded through a bullhorn's speaker. Spotlights from above were blinding them, so they could not see who had spoken.

"Hmm," Xander said philosophically. "He sounds very unfriendly, doesn't he? You'd almost think we were criminals or something."

"You just drove through a police barricade," Eris reminded him. "You *are* a criminal."

"They weren't real police! Besides, you don't have much room to talk. You're an art thief!"

"*Former* art thief, if you please. Don't be crass when we're about to be attacked by undead minions, Xander."

"Shut up, both of you," Tré snapped. "We're in a bit of a spot here, in case it's somehow escaped your attention. They hold the high ground."

"Drop your weapons, now! Get on the ground!" The voice bellowed again.

"So, which is it? Put our hands up or get on the ground? Your instructions seem very unclear to me," Xander called back, making no move to relinquish his gun.

"Are you two ready?" Tré asked, running a quick gaze over his companions.

Eris gave a curt nod, and Xander grinned, showing fangs.

"You kidding, Tré? I told you days ago that I'd been getting bored lately," Xander drawled.

"Then let's do this." Tré closed his eyes and pulled his life force deep into his center. He felt his physical body dissolve into mist, swirling in the night air. He could sense Xander and Eris next to him, their forms mingling with his. Their power united, and they hurtled towards the police cars.

They formed into a dense cloud, flying through and around the crowd of undead, disorienting them and slamming them against their own vehicles. Several yelled and waved their guns around, but with nothing to aim at, they did not fire their weapons.

Tré separated from the other two and materialized behind two sergeants crouched by a large SUV, their weapons pointed into the air. Before they had a chance to turn, Tré slammed his fists into the backs of their heads before pulling himself into a mist again.

Both undead men bashed their faces against the glass of the window and crumpled to the ground for a moment, blood spraying out of their noses as they recovered themselves and staggered to their feet. It looked oily and nearly black in the dim light.

One opened fire, aiming at Tré. He dematerialized, sensing the passage of the bullet through the place where his body had been. He darted through the cracked windows of a patrol vehicle and found Eris on the other side, fighting in his physical form with a very large, burly man.

Eris, a much leaner figure, was losing his advantage over the undead man. A cut above his eye was already starting to swell as he twisted around his attacker. Tré, exploding into physical presence right above the undead man, dropped onto his shoulders and knocked him to the ground, grabbing his neck and twisting with a fierce jerk until the vertebra snapped.

Eris wiped blood out of his face and gave Tré a hand up. They turned to stand back-to-back.

Before either of them had a chance to speak, a blow to the side of Tré's head knocked him to the ground, temporarily stunned. Tré could see people moving around him in the darkness, but their voices sounded far away and dull, as if he were listening to something underwater. The world swam hazily and, for a moment, he wondered where he was and what he was doing. There seemed to be a fight in front of him but he could not remember why.

Then he blinked as the body of an undead man fell on top of him, and everything came rushing back into harsh focus. He scrambled against the man, who had wrapped his putrid hands around Tré's neck and started to squeeze.

Tré brought his left hand up above his head, breaking the grip of the undead, and flipped him over using a defensive roll. Anger boiled inside him as he pummeled Bael's minion into the dirt.

Another dark body crashed against his. As they slammed onto their sides, Tré twisted violently in the man's arms until they were facing one another. The attacker gasped in surprise as the heel of Tré's hand connected with his chin. Tré, using momentum from the blow, launched himself to his feet and stood over the dazed police officer. With a single smooth movement, he stamped a booted foot down, shattering his opponent's face and jaw.

Tré felt a sharp summons echo through his mind and looked up to find Xander. He and Eris had become separated as he battled the last two men. To his dismay, he found his fellows back to back a few yards away, on the far side of the police cruiser, surrounded by twenty or more undead who seemed to have popped up from nowhere. Many were wearing police uniforms, but others were dressed in gray, dirty rags.

The stench from their bodies was overpowering, the reek rising into the night.

Hope flickered and began to die in Tré's heart at the sight. They were surrounded by undead now, badly outnumbered. Della had disappeared into the darkness, but she had not left, as he'd hoped. Her human scent lingered nearby. It would not take this army long to find her, and all three of them had already been wounded in the brief foray.

Something grabbed at Tré's ankle and he stamped down on a hand before even looking at the source. He felt the bones snap and a snarl of fury sounded from the ground. It seemed that one of the corpses had crawled through the darkness, over the bodies of his fellows, and reached Tré's feet while he stood assessing the situation. Both of its legs were missing below the knee.

Another undead corpse sprang at Tré, and he grappled with it, trying to toss it away and get to the others' sides. Although the thing's right arm hung useless, it still landed several hard blows to Tré's ribs with its left.

Pushing forward, Tré used both his hands to gain an advantage on his opponent. Several well-placed strikes to the face caused the thing to stagger and fall into the darkness. A piercing cry startled Tré, and he looked down.

The thing had fallen on another of the corpses, which had been gripping a knife in its lifeless hand. The knife had pierced the man's back, the tip protruding obscenely through its chest. The undead creature struggled for a minute and then fell still.

Tré turned back and saw that even more of the things had surrounded Xander and Eris, who had created a low wall of bodies in front of them in hand-to-hand combat. Yet the group creeping forward grew ever larger.

We can't win, Tré thought. *We won't be able to stop the darkness coming for Della.*

He could sense the endgame approaching, even now. He could feel Bael's presence drawing ever closer, looming over the battle in hopes of a feast. His greatest mistakes, his centuries-old errors, were finally being rectified. Tré wavered, on the verge of ordering the other two to flee. Only the thought of Della held him back.

"Don't be an ass, Tré," Xander called, and he realized that he must not have been shielding his thoughts. "We're not going anywhere."

Shouts and harsh, lifeless laughter rose up from the army as they closed in around his friends.

With a surge of strength, Tré transformed into mist and flew to their sides. They would stand together, in the vain hope that their sacrifice would mean that Della could get away. If there was the slightest chance that she would live, Tré was willing to take it.

Xander looked grim and battered as he raised his gun, shooting fruitlessly into the oncoming hoard. Eris' normally unflappable demeanor was slipping, his face smeared with mud and blood as he hacked at anything within reach of his dagger.

As he took his physical form inside the ring of undead corpses already dispatched by the others, Tré pressed his shoulders against theirs and let them feel his flash of regret at dragging them into this mess.

Xander snorted derisively, and glanced around at the leering faces and flat, bloodthirsty eyes surrounding them. "And where else would we be, Tré? Still, it's one hell of a way to go."

From out of the darkness, the cry of a hunting owl rent the night air. It was echoed by two others. Tré felt Eris catch his breath in surprise. He expanded his awareness to the trees around him and sensed Oksana, Duchess, and Snag, all swooping low to their rescue.

The three huge birds crashed into the crowd of two dozen undead, clawing at faces, and puncturing eyes with their sharp talons. Pandemonium broke all around them as the undead broke ranks, turning to face the new threat.

Eris and Xander sprang forward into the fray, knocking heads together and tearing at limbs. Tré's attention was drawn towards the far left of the battling crowd. He could see two undead men, their heads turned in the direction of the abandoned Jeep, making their way further down into the ditch.

Della! A shock of horror seemed to stop Tré's heart for a beat.

With a cry of rage, Tré leapt forward, bowling over anything that got in his way, hot in pursuit of the two creatures that were hunting his mate. Hurtling after them, he caught up to the closest one and tackled it to the ground. His victim, who had turned at the last minute, only had time to raise a bloody knife in one hand before Tré slammed against him.

As their bodies landed together in the mud, Tré felt his hands sliding against rotting flesh, and the bite of the blade against his chest.

Placing both hands on the sides of the undead's face, Tré wrenched the thing's head to the right, feeling a satisfying snap as its neck broke. Instantly, the struggle went out of it. As always, Bael's power abandoned the animated corpse immediately—the moment it was no longer useful to him.

Tré struggled to draw breath into lungs that felt... *wrong*... and looked around for the second undead. He found his target roughly seven yards away from him, a look of triumph on its pale, ghastly face.

Ignoring the explosion of pain in his chest, Tré planted one foot firmly on the ground and attempted to lunge forward for another tackle. But, for some reason, his body was no longer cooperating. He propelled himself forward by force of will, only to crash back to the muddy ground as violent tremors shook his arms and legs.

Looking down, Tré saw the handle of the knife that his last victim had been holding. The blade disappeared straight into his chest, directly through his heart.

-o-o-o-

Della screamed in denial as Tré attempted to rise and collapsed back to the ground, the hilt of a knife protruding from his chest. "No! *Tré! No!*"

She had not fled when she had the chance. Instead she had observed the arrival of the other vampires from her position behind the tree, transfixed in horror by the brutality of the battle.

As her cries filled the night, she saw Xander look towards her, then follow her gaze to where Tré was lying on the ground, the blade lodged in his chest.

The sound also attracted the attention of the undead man still standing near Tré's body. He spotted Della, who had stumbled forward without thought into the illumination of the spotlights.

Xander swore and wrenched his right arm free of the two undead he was fighting. With one of his precious remaining bullets, he managed to fire off a shot that caught the creature advancing on Della in the thigh.

Della saw the thing lurch at the impact of the bullet, but it continued to shamble forward as if nothing could stop it from achieving its goal. Oily, black blood seeped out from under the man's rags, further staining them along with the filth of centuries. Della gripped the knife that Tré had given her and looked into the thing's face.

His eyes were completely blank, glossed over with a white film. His mouth was pulled wide in a ghastly grimace that showed teeth rotting out of his decomposing skull. Knowing her death was only seconds away, Della's eyes fell onto Tré, still crumpled on the ground in a lifeless heap.

A firestorm of righteous anger flared in Della's chest, and she tightened her hold on the handle of the blade Tré had given her. With a yell like a banshee, she flung herself forward towards the creature. Perhaps she caught it by surprise, if the thing could even feel surprise. Whatever the case, it did not raise its arms in time to fight her off. She plunged the knife deep into the undead's stomach, black blood spurting all over her hands and torso.

The thing let out a loud *oof* noise as putrid air was forced out of its lungs in a rush. Della twisted the handle and the man staggered against her. His momentum propelled them both towards the ground.

Della landed flat on her back in the mud at the bottom of the ditch, still holding the knife tightly in her hands. The heavy body landed on top of her, forcing the knife even deeper into the man's gut. Della continued to snarl and scream in rage, wrestling against the dead weight on top of her.

To her horror, the thing began to move again with a raspy groan, its eyes still lifeless as it pressed itself up, away from the blade.

"You'll have to spill more blood than that to finish me, pretty little piece of meat," it rasped, leaning forward to whisper in her ear. Della shrieked again in rage, trying to wrestle the knife out from between them.

The thing let out a cackle of cold laughter and ground her down further into the mud. It leaned forward to run its cold, slimy tongue up Della's face as she struggled fruitlessly to free herself, and she knew that she going to die now. Bile rose in her throat and tears sprang to her eyes.

Still fighting like a madwoman, she screamed for help one last time and tried to knee the thing in the groin. She twisted and writhed beneath the creature, unable to break free.

Suddenly, Della felt its body fly off her as if jerked away by a puppeteer's strings. She struggled upright and saw Duchess crouched above it in the mud a few feet away, a look of disgust on her beautiful face.

She, too, held a blade in her hands, and she slashed the sharp edge across the thing's throat. With a gurgle, more blood sprayed everywhere and it finally went limp.

Panting heavily, Della dragged her filthy sleeve across her face. She tried in vain to wipe the stench of the man off her skin as she rolled over and clambered onto her knees.

"Thanks," she gasped, unable to say more. Duchess nodded tightly in acknowledgement and stood up, looking around for a moment before rushing back into the fray.

Sounds of the battle filtered through Della's sluggish mind and she pushed herself unsteadily to her feet.

She had to get to Tré.

Her mind seemed stuck in a horrific loop, replaying the moment he fell over and over again. With faltering footsteps, she stumbled towards the body of the man who had loved her for centuries, still lying prone on the ground. The knife remained firmly lodged in his chest.

Tripping over a twisted root protruding from the ground, Della fell, landing in a muddy puddle and sinking up to her wrists. It barely slowed her down, as she yanked her hands free and crawled the remaining distance towards Tré.

"Tré!" she cried, grabbing his shoulder with filthy fingers and shaking it. He did not stir. His eyelids did not so much as flicker. Della lowered her ear towards his mouth, trying in vain to hear the sounds of life coming from his lungs.

A final death shriek from one of the undead police officers filled the night air, and silence fell. Della listened with all her might, but all she could hear was her own pounding heart and the blood in her ears rushing back and forth.

"*Tré*! Come on, wake up!" Della begged, tears spilling over and running down her face as she shook him again.

The splatter of boots in mud made her look up in time to see Xander running toward them. He slid on his knees next to Tré's other side and put a hand on Tré's chest.

With a quick, one-handed motion, he ripped Tré's shirt so they could see the wound exposed under the floodlights that had illuminated the battle.

The blade had clearly pierced his heart.

Della stared at Xander, whose left arm was dangling uselessly at his side, dislocated at the shoulder.

A hand on her upper arm made her jerk in surprise and look around wildly. It was only Eris, lowering himself slowly to his knees next to her, a grave expression on his face. Blood was streaming from a wound on his head, and he seemed to be moving carefully, as if he had broken several ribs.

Oksana and Duchess hurried up, both looked shaken and muddy, but unhurt. Oksana's eyes fell on Della, worry and grief shining from their dark depths.

Della looked up at her, pleading. "He can't die! He's a vampire! That... that means he's immortal, right?"

Oksana's lips flattened to a thin, unhappy line. "We can still be destroyed. It might not be death as you know it, but things can be done to us to end our existence in this realm."

Della thought about Oksana's missing leg and choked down bile.

"We've got to get him back to the house," Xander said in a strained voice, drawing her attention back. He reached forward and jerked the knife out of Tré's chest, examining the dark metal blade. "Iron. *Fuck*. He's going to need a huge infusion of blood and life force to survive this. It would have been worse with a wooden stake, but we've still got to hurry. We have very little time."

"How? How can we get him there?" Della whispered, feeling as though her terror was strangling her. The air around her seemed far too thick and heavy. She choked on it, trying to fill her lungs in spite of the crushing sense of doom that was pressing on her heart.

"*Snag*." Eris said quietly. He stood up and stepped away, pulling Della back with him. She looked up at him, confused, then towards the darkness where the others were looking.

She had not noticed the sixth vampire standing in the shadows, but she could see his outline now, moving slowly towards them. He stepped into the light, blinking sunken, red-rimmed eyes in the glare from the police lamps.

His features were chiseled, unyielding as ancient stone. He looked around the scene with eyes that held a permanently haunted look, as if he had lived through eons of suffering. The aura of barely restrained power around him was truly terrifying, and a chill slithered down Della's sweaty back.

He walked forward towards Tré, his mouth a flat, narrow line.

"What's he going to do?" Della whispered to Eris.

Eris looked at her for a long moment. "Help. I hope," he said.

FIFTEEN

At Della's words, Snag's gaze rested on her. They stared at each other for the stretch of several heartbeats. A jumble of images bubbled up from Della's memory—a powerful, shadowy figure descending like a hurricane on the alley where she was being assaulted, tearing her undead attackers limb from limb, blood spraying the walls. She lifted a hand to her mouth.

Something flickered in the depths of Snag's eyes. Eris, standing behind Della, stirred as though he, too, noticed a change in the old vampire.

Snag lowered himself to the ground in a movement that was oddly graceful. After a brief hesitation, he reached out and drew Tré into his arms. Although the ancient vampire was whipcord thin—almost skeletal—he seemed to possess immense strength. He lifted Tré's heavy form effortlessly into his arms and stood.

"What are you doing?" Della demanded, unsure if he would answer.

He remained silent, staring at her with a depthless expression. Despite her terror for the one she loved... despite the fact that she was exhausted, sore, and had just had the fight of her life... Della felt a wave of peace steal over her. Peace that she could not understand.

"I—" she stammered, but was unable to finish.

Della felt sure that somehow, the ancient vampire was using his power to communicate with her without words. He was tempering her anxiety. She felt a deep sense of reassurance from a source she could not identify. She lifted a hand to her head and blinked rapidly, trying to make sense of the sensations.

"Don't fight him," Duchess advised in a wry tone. "He'll put you in a coma if you don't calm down."

Drawn up short, Della nodded and lifted her hands in a gesture of peace, still staring at the vampire in front of her. "All right. I'm not fighting. Just... help him. *Please*."

Snag gave a silent nod in return, and shut his eyes. Immediately, he and Tré dissolved into mist and swirled away. Movement out of the corner of Della's eyes told her that Eris and Oksana had followed them, floating into the night sky and away from the scene of the battle.

"Can we do that?" Della asked, gesturing towards the now empty space around them.

"No," Xander said with a grimace, as Duchess moved towards him with a determined look in her eyes. "Snag is the only one powerful enough to transport anyone while in the form of mist. We'll have to get back some other way."

Duchess circled him, examining his shoulder from all angles.

"The joint is out of its socket," she said.

Xander lifted an eyebrow. "Gee. You think?"

Duchess raised a brow right back at him. "Don't get smart with the only one here strong enough to put it back in for you," she said. "Now sit down. *Mon Dieu*, you're tiresome when you're sober."

Xander flopped down, clearly exhausted. Duchess sighed and placed a small, elegantly shod foot against his side, dragging his useless arm up into a raised position.

"Do it," Xander commanded through gritted teeth.

With a wet pop that made Della's stomach turn, Duchess jerked his shoulder back into place.

Xander swore creatively in at least three different languages. Duchess straightened and stepped away from him, brushing mud and dirt off her hands as though she performed such tasks on a regular basis. Xander, however, massaged his shoulder with his uninjured hand and gave her an aggrieved look.

"Vicious hellcat. You could have reset it without half that much force," he said in a dark voice. A sheen of sweat was visible across his forehead, and his skin looked clammy.

Duchess gave a short bark of laughter and started towards the Jeep, still wedged against a tree.

"This thing is never going to run again," she said, turning back towards Xander.

Still massaging his shoulder, Xander walked up and looked at the battered vehicle with a mournful expression. Della knew that he had spent many hours working on it.

With a sigh, Xander said, "We'll use one of the police cruisers instead."

In the end, they found an SUV that was more or less undamaged by the battle. The keys were on the ground, clasped in the loose grip of a beheaded undead cop. Xander delicately removed the key ring with a wrinkled nose, clearly disgusted by the pungent smell.

As they drove towards the manor house, Della sat in the back and tried not to imagine Tré's lifeless body with the knife sticking out of it.

How long before Snag reached the manor house? What could the vampires do to heal Tre? Surely he would be dead after a knife pierced his heart? But... *could* vampires even die? Oksana had made it sound like they could...

Disturbing thoughts swirled through Della's mind, yet her body remained still and calm. Even though there was a storm going on inside her, it seemed that her brain was overloaded. She had seen too much violence, blood, and death to take in anymore, and her body simply remained in a state of shock.

When they reached the old house, she slid from the leather seat and landed with a soft thud on the ground. She followed Duchess and Xander up the front steps and inside in a daze. Wearily, she climbed the stairs up to the room in which she had awoken the previous day, though it seemed like a lifetime ago.

Snag was standing in one corner of the room, a silent specter. He appeared calmly unruffled by the scene before him. Oksana was sitting in the chair by the bed, holding her wrist over Tré's parted lips. He was completely still and did not appear to be breathing.

Della watched, not even flinching as Oksana sank her teeth into her own wrist, drawing fresh blood to the surface. She wiped the blood over Tré's lips, pulling his jaw open a little more.

"He won't drink," she said, as the three newcomers walked in, an undertone of desperation coloring the words.

Della saw that Eris was standing next to Oksana, rubbing Tré's neck near his jawline.

"I'm trying to stimulate his feeding instinct," he explained, glancing up at her, "and Oksana has been wiping blood in his mouth. He should be able to sense it and allow his body to take over and drink it."

"He's too far gone to bite down," Oksana said, still visibly upset.

"Is he dead?" Della asked, as tears started rolling down her muddy face.

"Not exactly," Eris said. "I can sense his life force, but it's very weak, flickering in and out. He needs to feed, or we'll lose him."

The others glanced around helplessly.

Oksana stood abruptly and glared at Snag, who had made no move toward the others, or the man on the bed. "Your blood would heal him, Snag."

Snag blinked slowly at her and did not respond. Instead, his eyes moved to Della, who stood paralyzed under the mesmerizing stare. He seemed to be beckoning to her somehow, because Eris looked up at her with a snap of his head.

"*Oh*," he said in surprise, a troubled expression flickering across his handsome face as he looked from her to Snag, and back again.

Xander, Oksana, and Duchess all fell completely silent, turning towards Della in unison.

"There's only one person in this room whose blood can heal Tré's heart," Eris said quietly.

Della glanced around wildly at all the vampires now staring at her. "Wh-what? You mean... me?"

Eris nodded without speaking.

Della stood frozen in place, sure that these vampires had lost their minds. How could her blood save Tré, when she wasn't a vampire? They all had a close bond already from sharing blood, because vampire blood had healing properties. Hadn't that been what Tré had told her?

Doubt flooded her, followed closely by alarm. She barely knew any of these people — these *vampires* — and here she was, trusting them with her life. They had acted to save her, yes — but, what they were asking of her now was...

She swallowed.

"He's going to need a huge infusion of blood and life force to survive this," Xander had said.

They were asking her to sacrifice her life for Tré's, just as Irina had done centuries ago.

"I don't know if I can do this," she said in a tiny voice. "You're asking me to —"

"Della. I know this must be terrifying," Oksana said in a quiet voice. Della glanced at her face and was startled by what she saw reflected in Oksana's eyes. There was no deception there, just empathy, coupled with desperate hope. "But your soul is connected to his in a way the rest of us can never be. You can *save him*. I know you can."

Della's feet carried her closer to the bed as if she was in a trance. She looked down at Tré, who was rapidly losing the last color remaining in his face. Although his features had always been pale, Della thought he looked waxen now, like he'd already departed from his body, and what lay before them was now merely a lifeless corpse.

Are we too late? Della wondered, as grief possessed her heart again. *Can I really save him? Do I have the courage to even try?*

Della remembered how Tré had risked his life to rush to her aid when she was in Bael's clutches, and love surged inside her breast. She remembered his skin blistering and searing under the bright afternoon sun. He had ignored it in the face of her need for him, and not only had he carried her to the safety of her apartment, but he had lent her his strength and power to drive the demon out. A demon that he hated with every fiber of his being—the one who had nearly torn his soul in two.

She could see now what a sacrifice that had been. He had injured his body and put his soul at risk yet again by exposing himself to the same demon that had ripped his life into pieces and destroyed her in her former life.

Tré had flung himself into deadly danger time and time again to rescue her. During their last battle, he had tried to fight off the second undead creature coming after her, even with a jagged knife protruding from his chest. He had been mortally wounded saving her life, and here she was, questioning whether or not she should sacrifice herself for him?

He loved her, and she loved him. There was no doubt in her mind. From the most carefully guarded depths of her being, Della could feel his arms wrapping around her, cradling her as they made love. She had felt like the most precious thing on the planet as his hands had caressed her. Her body sang under his touch, coming to life as if for the first time.

Heart thudding madly, Della exhaled the breath she'd been holding and took a step forward. Without a word, Oksana and Eris stepped away from Tré, making a path towards the bed. Della could feel her blood rushing through her head and ears. It sounded like the ocean. She tried to swallow, but her mouth was completely dry.

Will it hurt to die?

The thought made her feet stumble, but only for a moment. She kept moving forward. It seemed to her that she had always been destined for a horrible end—even when she was Irina, centuries ago. And now, again, as Della, walking calmly towards her own destruction. She was never meant to survive, and all Tré and his fellow vampires had done was to delay the inevitable for a few days.

She breathed slowly, trying to calm the instinctive, animal impulse to flee from the room and never look back. She might be demon-cursed, but she was *better* than that, damn it.

Each step, each thud of her muddy hiking boots on the floor, seemed to take an age to filter into her mind. It was like a death march, playing slowly in the background of her final moments.

Even as everything inside her screamed for survival, the love that had woken in her heart kept her moving forward, towards the man who had sacrificed everything in a doomed attempt to save her from the inevitable.

I will give my life for his. He is my soulmate, the one I was destined for. And... the world needs him more than it needs me. He and the others are all that stand between humanity and chaos.

As she walked past Oksana, their eyes met. Della could see sadness there. The lovely vampire reached out and touched Della's cheek, as if imparting strength to her. Della felt bolstered by the gentle brush of fingers, confident that she was making the correct choice.

She reached the bed and climbed onto the mattress, settling next to Tré, whose eyes flickered at the movement on the bed, a tiny furrow forming on his brow. She caught her breath at the nearly undetectable sign of life.

He opened his silver-gray eyes slowly. They almost slipped shut again several times, as if he was being dragged down by weakness and exhaustion.

Eris was right, his life force was nearly spent.

Tré gazed up at her with a distant, dazed expression. Della wondered if he could even see her, and if he was aware enough of his surroundings to really understand what was happening.

"I love you," she whispered hoarsely. She had to lick her lips with a parched tongue before she could make any sound at all. "Take what you need of me, Tré. I give it freely. Perhaps…"

Della's voice trailed away as tears welled in her eyes. She knew what to say next, even though she could not clearly remember her life as Irina as anything more than a dream. "…perhaps we will meet again in another lifetime."

Tré's unfocused eyes sharpened—a final burst of strength. Air rattled through his damaged chest as he attempted to speak. "I won't… take your life… Della. Not… again. Never… again."

Della smiled through her tears. "You're not taking it, Tré. I'm giving it."

She leaned forward, pressing a kiss to his cool forehead. She could smell the wonderful scent of his hair. She closed her eyes and breathed in, wanting his smell to be the last thing she would ever know.

A sudden thought came to her, though, and her eyes flew open. She looked up, meeting the others' eyes one by one.

"Don't let him punish himself over this. You have to promise me—all of you. And..." she hesitated, suppressing a shiver. "... don't let me become one of those... undead *things*. Burn my body afterward, if that's what it takes. I don't want Bael using me like that."

Oksana made a pained noise and stepped forward, reaching for her. "Della," she said, "*ti cheri*, no! You thought we were asking you to sacrifice your life for his?"

Della blinked in confusion. "What else?" she asked, barely a whisper.

"Snag believes Tré can turn you," Eris said, also appearing taken aback. "Make you one of us."

Della straightened in shock, looking around at the vampires assembled in the bedroom. She thought about her unfulfilling life and how she seemed to have screwed everything up as a mortal.

"Is that even possible?" she asked.

"If Snag thinks it's possible, then he's probably right," Xander answered. "But you should understand what that means first. We thought you already did."

She stared at his green eyes and handsome face, her mind whirling. "Which is what?"

"Your soul is complete right now," he said. "If you surrender to life as a vampire, it would mean that your soul will be ripped into two pieces. You would be a physical shell for both the Light and the Dark, but they will no longer be in balance inside you."

Della frowned, trying to understand. "Well," she said, "given my track record as a human, that doesn't sound so bad right now."

"Also," Duchess said, "It will be the most exquisite agony you have ever experienced."

"Oh," Della said, feeling as if all the air had been punched from her lungs.

"Think carefully before you do this," Xander said. The serious tone of his voice was in stark contrast to his normal shallow demeanor and sarcasm. His pale face was pinched with worry—for her or for Tré, she wasn't sure.

Della felt Tré's fingers brush her wrist, and the now-familiar swoop in her stomach that followed.

"Will it save his life?" Della asked, staring down at Tré, her eyes filling with tears again.

"Yes," said Eris. "At least, Snag seems to think so. And he is seldom wrong about such matters."

She bit her lip. She didn't know what to do, and time was running out. She looked at Eris' brown-eyed, olive-skinned face with its finely sculpted Mediterranean features. She thought of all the undead that he had destroyed to protect her, and the efforts he put into saving her life.

She glanced over at Xander, Tré's closest friend and comrade. She glanced next to Oksana, whose soul-deep kindness surpassed that of most humans she had known. At Duchess, who was brave and beautiful and brilliant and calculating in a way that made Della's heart burn with jealousy.

Finally, her eyes fell on Snag. Ancient, withered, and haunted, he stood silently against the wall behind the group gathered around the bed. Their eyes met, and she felt as if she were falling into that tired, pain-filled gaze.

What do I do? Is this really the right thing? she thought, not sure if he could hear her.

Snag cocked his head in slow motion, as if listening. For a moment, they stood staring at one another in a frozen tableau. Then, without warning, Della felt the same sense of calm steal over her that she had felt after the battle earlier. It felt to her as if Snag was reassuring her that her sacrifice would, in fact, save Tré's life. That it would save both of their lives from Bael's bloodthirsty desire for revenge.

She took a deep breath and nodded her understanding. A moment later, he tipped his chin in acknowledgement—a bare hint of movement.

Della turned back to Xander and the others, new determination flooding her.

"I'll do it," she said, reaching out for Tré's hand as she spoke. She gripped it tightly, even though he could manage no more than a weak twitch of the fingers. "I'll become a vampire. Please, help me save him. Tell me what to do."

"All right, then," Xander said, relief audible in his words. "First, let him bite you."

She shivered, unable to stop herself.

"Okay," she said, and turned back to Tré, her heart pounding. "Okay..."

Their eyes met for the briefest of moments, and she kissed him, a chaste brush of lips. She slid her cheek along his, feeling him press weakly into the contact, burying his face against her neck and shoulder.

She felt the butterfly brush of his eyelashes against her skin, and closed her eyes. Clearly using the last of his strength, Tré surged forward and sank his teeth into her throat.

Della gasped in shock, feeling his fangs slide into her neck. She felt Tré draw on her blood; heard his groan of hunger... of need. Strength seemed to flood back into his limbs. He reached up and gathered her into a tight embrace, holding her to him as he suckled at her neck.

At first, there was no pain, and Della wondered in one tiny corner of her whirling, spinning thoughts if Duchess had been wrong about it hurting. There was only a deep, drawing sensation that seemed almost... *sexual*, pulling at her depths as Tré demanded that she give herself over to him, and something in her responded, surrendering to his need.

Then, an awful tearing sensation began to grow in her chest, as if her heart and lungs were being ripped from her rib cage. She cried out in pain as her eyes flew open, seeing nothing but a swirling fog of red and gray. She could dimly feel Tré continuing to drain blood from her neck, but also felt herself falling into a pit of fire, flames licking across every nerve.

She screamed and flailed, losing track of her surroundings. Everything was confusion—she knew the bed was just beneath her, but she seemed to fall a great distance, burning all the way. With one last agonizing shudder as her soul burst apart at the seams, Della slipped into merciful unconsciousness.

-o-o-o-

With the first infusion of Della's blood, Tré felt his flesh begin knitting itself back together. The pain lessened, and the fog that had clouded his vision lifted.

He drank deeply, instinct taking over as he tasted the sweet nectar of her life force entering his, strengthening him, bolstering his body and spirit. He sat up, cradling Della in his arms as he pulled more of her essence into himself.

She whimpered and cried out in pain, struggling weakly before collapsing against him. Still, he drained more and more blood from her, feeling the worst sense of *déjà vu* he had ever experienced wash over him like a wave.

Outside the sanctuary of the old house full of vampires, Tré could sense storm clouds gathering in the sky as Bael hovered nearby, convinced that his terrible vengeance against Irina's spirit—and Tré's—was imminent.

An evil voice whispered in his mind, full of hate and glee. *She will die at your hands once again, my beautiful abomination. Her soul will be mine forever.*

The words seemed to permeate the room. Tré was aware of the others' reactions as they flinched and set themselves as if for battle. Yet all Tré felt at the threat was a strong surge of defiance.

He would not allow Bael to take his beloved from him. Not again. *Never again.*

The first time he had drained Irina's life to save his own, he had been weak, crazed, mad with pain and horror after his turning at the demon's hands. He'd had no control over his instincts, and had simply latched onto the first living thing that crossed his path, which happened to be Irina.

Waking to find her lifeless shell laying at his feet and his hands covered in her blood had been the worst moment of a lifetime that now spanned centuries.

But he was no longer that crazed and desperate beast.

As the storm raged outside, Tré focused everything on the fragile form in his arms, stretching out all his powers to surround Della, to hold her life force together as her soul split in two. He could sense that the transformation was almost complete. Her blood began to taste less and less like a human's blood, and more like a vampire's. Her smell changed, growing less musky and more coppery.

"Careful, Tré. She's nearly there," Eris said. Tré could feel him standing poised next to the bed next to Xander, both of them prepared to spring at Tré and tear him away bodily before allowing him to take Della's life.

I know. I have control.

The mental message spread through the group, one by one. Possibly, it was undercut by the hint of a growled warning at the idea of anyone trying to pull his mate from him… but even so, he felt them all relax marginally.

"It's not that we don't trust you Tré," Oksana said, worry woven through her sweet voice. "It's just that you were almost… *gone.*"

The way she choked on the last word told Tré clearly that his life force had nearly been spent when Della provided the sacrifice necessary to save him.

He owed this beautiful, amazing woman everything. He owed her the integrity of his soul after her sacrifice when she had been Irina, and now he owed her his very existence. She had given up her humanity to save him, despite her fears. He vowed, then and there, that he would spend the rest of his life protecting her, shielding her from harm.

Tré wrapped his life force around Della's more fully, sheltering her from the wild storm of Bael's rage beyond the walls of the old house. He felt the last vestiges of her soul rip free under the strain of her draining blood. With a bone-deep shudder, Della jerked and seized as the Light and the Dark finally separated inside her. In that instant, Tré released her neck and cradled her securely in his arms like a child.

Oksana stepped forward cautiously and tilted Della's chin back, as the windows rattled in their frames. Tré fought an irrational stab of territorial aggression, unable to stem the protective instincts surging through him.

"Easy, Tré, I'm just trying to help," Oksana reassured, keeping her voice soft and her movements slow.

Tré nodded and clenched his jaw, trying to maintain control over his instincts. He raised his own wrist to his mouth and sank his teeth into the flesh.

Blood spurted around his fangs. He lowered his wrist over Della's slack mouth and rubbed it onto her lips.

"Drink, *draga mea*," he whispered. He could feel her life force flickering feebly and mentally willed her to accept the blood. "Come. You must drink now."

Long seconds ticked by as Della remained seemingly lifeless, unmoving in Tré's arms.

Drawing on all his mental power, he reached for the familiar contours of her mind and thrust a single command into its flickering depths.

Drink!

SIXTEEN

She was nearly gone, and the weakness of her divided spirit chilled him to the core. Outside, the wind grew even wilder, tearing at the trees and dragging loose shingles from the roof.

Icy fingers of doubt assailed him. *Had he made a mistake? A second terrible mistake in his miserable, endless existence? Had he drained too much life from her? Was she too weakened by the events over the past few days to withstand the transformation process?*

After a terrifying moment of mental silence, Della's tongue darted out to capture the blood lingering on her lips. With a feeble groan, she closed her mouth around his proffered wrist and began drawing blood. Tré could feel her gaining strength from him, and relief flooded his body, leaving him shaking.

She would be all right. If she was strong enough to feed, she had survived the change.

Once more becoming aware of the others' presence, Tré looked around at the solemn faces surrounding them. Oksana was still supporting Della's head, holding her in position to help her feed. She stroked Della's hair out of her face tenderly.

"That's it. Keep going, *ti cheri*," she said in a soft voice, the beginnings of a smile playing at the corners of her full lips. "You're both going to be just fine."

Eris looked thoughtful. "A new vampire has just been born—for the first time in over two hundred years."

Something crashed downstairs—a window shattering under the force of the storm, perhaps. They ignored it, secure in the strength of their bond against the creature that had created them.

Duchess frowned. "And is what's been done to her any less horrible than what was done to us? We've condemned her to a half-life spent in darkness."

"She consented," Oksana said, frowning up at her blood-sister. "We didn't."

"And it seemed unlikely that she could have survived Bael's attentions for much longer as a human," Eris said pointedly as something—a tree branch, perhaps—crashed against the outside wall.

A flash of mental pain and a faint *whoosh* of departing mist told Tré that Snag had left the room.

"What's eating him, anyway?" Xander asked, no doubt picking up on the same surge of disquiet from the ancient vampire that Tré had felt. "This was his idea in the first place!"

Della, oblivious, continued to suckle at Tré's wrist like an infant on the breast. Her brow furrowed as if she were concentrating. Oksana relinquished her supporting grip, and Tré tucked her more securely against his body.

"Della?" he asked. "*Della?*"

She didn't answer, but drew harder at his wrist. Her hands came up to grip his arm, and he felt the same spark between them, the same soaring sensation in his heart. The same electric connection with her as he had when his fingers had first accidentally brushed her skin.

Her eyelids flickered open, revealing a golden glow radiating from behind her soulful hazel eyes. At that moment, the house shuddered on its foundation, making the others jump in alarm. Tré was aware of the disturbance, but it was unimportant. He could not take his eyes off the beautiful face before him.

Della released his wrist and blinked slowly up at him, her mouth stained red with his blood. As the storm howled even more loudly around them, Tré lowered his lips to hers and kissed her with all the tenderness he possessed. The sweet smell and taste of her surrounded him, filling the empty places that had languished within him for centuries.

As they pulled apart, the wind that was making the house quake died down, the storm's strength finally spent.

It was over. They had won.

"Tré?" Della asked, sounding sleepy and dazed. "Did it work? Are you okay now?"

Her voice was like music to his ears. Love for her swelled within him until he thought his body would not be able to contain it. "Of course I am, *draga mea*. You are here with me, are you not?"

"And... Bael?" Della asked.

As soon as she had spoken, a distant, unearthly wail sounded over the dying wind. It made the hair stand up on Tré's neck. Duchess drew in an audible breath, while Eris and Xander looked around sharply. Yet the sound was mournful. Defeated.

Bael was fleeing before the immense power held within the old, abandoned house. The power of two united, unconquerable souls, joined at last after centuries apart.

The power of love, in the face of death.

-o-o-o-

Hours later, Della's eyes drifted open. A muted hint of sunlight was filtering in through heavy drapes across the window. Oddly, she could feel it on her skin, even though the dark crimson curtains kept the room itself in shadow—a prickling sensation that, while not precisely unpleasant in and of itself, hinted at danger for the unwary.

She and Tré were alone. She vaguely remembered that the others had been present, at first—all except Snag, who left earlier, smelling of old pain that could not be assuaged. Xander and Eris had offered Tré blood, both to speed his healing and, she presumed, so he would have enough to offer her throughout the first night of her turning.

In the end, though, it had been Oksana and Duchess who had nourished him. Though they were like brothers to him, with his mating instincts roused, Tré had been unwilling to allow the other males close to her. Something about the idea sent a delicious shiver through her, for all that she knew it was a temporary side effect of what the two of them had shared.

She stretched, exploring the changes in her body as she recovered from the turning. She felt... *strong*. Stronger than she had ever felt in her old life, where she had always secretly thought of herself as weak and a bit useless.

Confident. It was as though she had always been meant for a life of immortality. But she could also sense the damage done to her soul. Perhaps it should have bothered her more, but she had seen how the others acted with nobility and love—how they valued honor and the bond of friendship.

The Light and Dark halves of them might have been torn asunder, but they were still present. She would simply chose to draw her life force from the Light, rather than the Dark, she decided.

The sun, too, interested her. She could see the weak rays not blocked by the drapes and even feel heat on her skin through walls of the house. She knew that it would blister and burn if she were to step directly into it, and she felt a strong aversion. This alone troubled her about her new life, as she had always loved the feel of the sun on her skin when she was mortal.

The benefits, however, far outweighed the costs, and a secret smile twitched at her lips. Della stretched again, like a cat, feeling strong new muscles pull across her back.

"Good morning, *draga*," a velvety voice whispered in her ear.

The smile widened, and she turned to Tré, still lying next to her. He was propped up on his elbow, staring down at her as if he had never seen anything like her before in his centuries-long life.

"Good morning," she murmured back, craning up for a kiss.

"How do you feel?"

Della turned inward for a moment, taking stock. "Hungry," she decided.

Tré laughed—a low, rumbling sound that did interesting things to her insides. "Is that so? Don't tell me that you're going to be the next Oksana in the house," he teased.

"Ha. Very funny," Della said, and flicked him on the arm. "I'm going to tell her you said that."

He smirked, the expression far more attractive than it should have been.

"I didn't say it would be a bad thing if you were. But... there will be a lot about this that you'll need to get used to," Tré said, growing serious. "Don't hesitate to ask one of us if you have any questions."

Della chewed on her lip, feeling the unaccustomed prick of pointed fangs pressing hard against the inside of her cheek. "I do have one question now," she said.

"Yes?"

"How do you read each others' minds?"

Tré looked at her with a considering gaze. "That's a rather interesting question, actually. I'm not sure exactly how to answer it. I suppose that it's like... pressing your awareness outside of your body. Like remaining motionless but reaching for something across the room. It takes considerable concentration, but it becomes easier with time. Though some of us are more skilled than others."

Della frowned. "So, just reach out with my mind?"

Tré nodded, still looking at her as if he never wanted to look away. A new flood of warmth suffused her. She closed her eyes and tried to imagine herself with invisible fingers, reaching out for Tré. She concentrated so hard that she felt a prickle of sweat breaking out across her forehead.

"Did I do it?" she finally asked, unsure of what she was supposed to be feeling if she succeeded.

Tré chuckled and shook his head. "No, I'm afraid not. At least, I didn't feel anything. You might've reached for someone else by mistake, though."

That was interesting. "Would I know it if I did?" she asked.

He was obviously still amused. "Yes, it's pretty unmistakable."

Della tried again, closing her eyes. She strained and strained until Tré cupped her face with a callused palm.

"You're trying too hard. It's a matter of *allowing*, not *making*. Don't force it so much. You'll break something important." He tapped the furrow in her forehead lightly. "Or your expression might freeze that way. Didn't your mother ever tell you that?"

"You're making fun of me," she accused with a mock scowl.

The devilish gleam in his pale eyes belied his expression of innocence. "I would never do such a thing."

She tried on a glare, but it collapsed into a sappy smile in short order. She snorted in wry amusement. "Yes, you would."

"Well, perhaps I would," Tré conceded. "But only a little. Now, try again, but relax this time. Allow your mental awareness to expand with your breath."

Della flopped down flat on her back, pushing a rolled-up pillow under her neck. She took several deep breaths and tried to relax, letting her muscles go loose and pliant, one by one.

She concentrated on the life force she felt inside her. It seemed to swirl and undulate within her body, and she imagined for a moment that she could control the rippling waves. Channel them, and bend them to her will. Without warning, it was as if she could see everything in the entire house within her mind's eye.

She could tell that Oksana was wandering around the kitchen, digging into a bag of cookies as she hummed a sad tune. Eris and Duchess were in the living room, talking quietly to one another. Snag was holed up in the back bedroom, his thoughts hidden behind a featureless shield that she could not penetrate. Xander was still asleep down the hall. She looked towards Tré. She could see him clearly, both with her physical eyes and her newly awakened mental awareness.

Murmured thoughts tickled her awareness like whispers against the shell of her ear, and she drew in a breath.

You are so beautiful. So flawless. You were truly made for this immortal life, draga mea. How could I possibly be so lucky that my soul's true mate would find me, all these endless centuries later?

Della blinked in shock, and the awareness faded as quickly as it had come. She was astonished, knowing that she had just seen inside Tré's mind.

"I felt that," he said quietly. "Your mental touch was light as a feather."

She was still breathless. "Was it? I didn't feel like I was touching you."

"No?"

She shook her head. "It was more like… looking at you. Looking *inside* you."

"Interesting," Tré answered, lifting an eyebrow. "I've never heard it described that way. For me it's like reaching out and touching the mind of another person."

"Oh. Was I... doing it wrong? Do you think there's something wrong with my new powers?" Della asked, old fears and insecurities already trying to creep back into her heart.

"You," Tré said in a stern voice, "are absolutely perfect as you are. Remember, Della, there's great diversity in our experiences, even as vampires. Your powers will grow, and you'll be able to control them better very soon. I know it."

Della nestled against his neck, feeling reassured and very much in love. "Thank you."

Tré hummed in contentment, wrapping his arms more securely around her. "Why are you thanking me? I'm only telling you the truth."

Della thought for a moment, unable to put her complicated emotions into words. "You didn't have to save me that first night, you know. You could have let me die in a hail of gunfire along with the others in the street. I was nothing to you—just another faceless victim of the violence spreading over the city. But... you didn't let me die, even though it put your closest friend in harm's way. And from that point forward, you were protecting me."

Tré nodded, but did not speak; he seemed strangely lost for words.

"I don't know what I would have done," she continued. "I'm sure that Bael would have destroyed me without your protection. Now, you've put me beyond his reach forever."

"I wasn't really thinking about it like that," Tré admitted.

Della blinked up at him.

"You make it all sound so... chivalrous," Tré said, "but it was pure selfishness on my part, *draga*, I assure you. I simply *couldn't* leave you alone. It was like a stab of mortal pain, to think about you by yourself. I watched you, you know—even when you didn't know who or what I was."

Something stirred in Della's memory. It was hard to draw the images forward, as though she were wading through murky river water, searching for a single stone.

"Wait a minute," she finally said, sitting up in surprise. "The owl! You were at my apartment! You were sitting in the tree that night, watching over me!"

The realization hit her out of the blue. One of them had told her, early on, that vampires had the power to transform into owls, and she had seen it for herself during the last, awful battle with the undead.

"You were there, protecting me, even then," Della accused, looking down at her fated mate.

Tré gave a small shrug of concession. "You have a fantastic ability to get yourself into trouble, Della. I... needed to be close by, just in case."

Della smiled at him, rueful, but unable to dispute his words. She curled up against his side once more and began to daydream what her owl form would be like. After a moment, Tré gently nudged her with his shoulder.

"Does that not upset you?" he asked.

She craned to look at him. "Why would it upset me?"

"Some random vampire in the form of an owl, sitting outside your window all night watching you?" he asked. "That's not upsetting?"

She laughed—she couldn't help it. "Tré, do you honestly think that's the creepiest thing that has happened to me in the last several days?"

This argument seemed to sway him, and he pressed a kiss to her forehead. "Maybe not."

Della, who felt wide awake and suddenly far more interested in physical pursuits than talking, rolled on top of Tré's broad chest, now thankfully whole and unscarred once more. His silver eyes darkened, and she smiled down at him, feeling playful.

"You know," she reminded him, "I told you awhile ago that I was hungry. Aren't you supposed to be seeing to my needs during my period of transformation?"

A furrow of worry grew between his dark eyebrows. "Forgive me, *draga*," he said. "Do you need more blood? Or should I get Oksana to bring you something from the kitchen—?"

Her smile turned wicked, and she rolled her hips against his, drawing a nearly imperceptible gasp from his lips. "I said I was hungry," she repeated innocently, and repeated the movement just to feel him shiver beneath her. "I didn't say for what."

"Minx," he accused, swiping the pad of his thumb over her lower lip. "You realize that we're both still completely filthy from the swamp."

"Yup," she said, nipping at his thumb and looking down at him intently. "But you know what else I've realized? I'm *alive*, when I didn't really expect to be. And so are you."

"Good answer," Tré said. "Perhaps we could remove some of this dried mud from the bed by removing the clothes it's attached to."

"I *do* like the way you think," Della said. She reared up to straddle Tré's hips so she could pull her t-shirt over her head and toss her bra away, unsure where this new sense of brashness was coming from.

The way his silver eyes darkened made her body tingle, and she decided that maybe brashness was a pretty terrific thing after all. A strong male hand came up to cup her left breast, as if assessing the weight, and her eyelids flickered closed. The hunger she'd teased him about earlier roared to the fore, startling her with its intensity.

"I can feel your need, *draga mea*." The words were a low growl. "Can you feel mine?"

He thrust up against her and, yes, his stiff, hot length told her just how hungry he was for her in turn. "Too many clothes!" she managed on a gasp, though the barrier of fabric between them didn't stop her from grinding back down against him.

He flipped her smoothly off of her perch and shrugged out of the torn remains of his shirt. When that was done, he tugged her legs to the edge of the bed so he could pull off her hiking boots and socks. She hadn't even realized she'd still been wearing them—the others must have been too worried about setting off Tré's protective instincts to dare remove any of her clothing, no matter how innocently.

Della scrabbled at the button and zip of her jeans, lifting her hips to help Tré pull the mud-stiffened denim down and off. Finally, he leaned in and nipped at her inner thigh, sending her heart pounding madly as he slowly tugged her cotton panties off and flicked them away.

Tré rose to a standing position in the space between her parted legs, looking down at her as he deliberately unclasped his belt and let his tailored trousers—ruined, now—slide down his muscular legs. He wasn't wearing anything underneath, and Della's mouth watered at the sight of his bare flesh.

This time, she decided, she would not be denied. No sooner had he kicked his discarded clothing away than she clasped his hips, holding him in place so she could bend forward and lick a stripe up his length. He hissed and wove his fingers through the thick tangle of her hair.

"*My beloved*," he whispered, as she kissed and laved the tip of his cock, reveling in the smell and taste of him. She looked up at him from under her lashes, wanting to see his face as she took him fully into her mouth.

He looked... *undone*... with his lips parted and his pupils blown wide. She wanted to put that look on his face over and over, for the rest of eternity. Della swirled her tongue and sucked, watching and smiling around the thick length in her mouth as his eyes fell closed in ecstasy.

She was no great expert at this, but seeing her effect on him gave her the confidence to experiment. The hand he still had wrapped in her hair seemed, quite honestly, to be more about steadying himself than guiding her. She got the impression that, short of not minding her fangs, there was very little she could do to him that he would not find pleasurable.

It was a heady feeling, that realization.

She continued to play with him, pulling him deeper and sliding back until she could flick her tongue over his tip, over and over, losing herself in the feel of him, grinding her aching sex against the edge of the mattress with small, instinctive movements to ease her own need.

"Enough," he grated eventually, using his hold on her mass of hair to ease her back, despite her mewled protest. She panted up at him, knowing that she must look debauched—lips swollen and wet, eyes dark with desire.

Without a word, he pushed her to lie back on the bed, her bare legs still hanging over the edge. He knelt smoothly between them, dragging her toward him another few inches and resting his head on her belly. His breath came in warm puffs against her cool skin as he collected himself.

"I will have you in every way it is possible for a man to have a woman, Della," he said into the crease of her thigh, and she shuddered with need, writhing under him to try and get him where she wanted him.

He didn't leave her waiting, trailing soft lips down to her inner thigh. From there, he lifted one of her legs over his shoulder and kissed her outer lips before brushing the tip of his nose along the seam, breathing her in.

She moaned—she couldn't help it. The sound turned into a whimper as his tongue parted her folds and dipped inside, tracing complex runes against her sensitive flesh. She wrapped her legs around him to keep him in place, feeling need coil tightly in her belly, growing and growing, ready to explode.

One of her on-again, off-again boyfriends had gone down on her a handful of times—always acting like he was doing her a favor. No one had ever attacked her sex with his tongue as if trying to devour her whole... as if she was water in the desert, and he was dying of thirst.

It only took moments before she was bucking, crying out her release as Tré's strong hands held her in place and made her take everything he could give. Made her feel every last nerve overloading and shorting out in a single, drawn-out wave of euphoria.

"So beautiful," Tré breathed against her, drawing another trembling aftershock from her body.

He slid two fingers inside her, making her keen and twist her hips restlessly.

"*More*," she begged.

She thought she felt him smile against her thigh, and then his clever tongue was teasing the sides of her oversensitive clit, working her toward another peak as he stroked over the front wall of her passage with insistent fingers. He sucked her throbbing nub between his lips and worried at it, sending her flying again.

When she came down, his fingers were still working her, even as her body fluttered around them.

"Tré, *please*," she whispered. "*Please!*"

Before meeting him, Della had never begged for sex in her life. She would have expected to find the idea embarrassing. Pathetic. But as Tré gave her a final kiss and rose gracefully to his feet, saying, "Anything you desire, *draga*—you already have all of me," a new wave of heat washed over her, and somehow *she* felt like the powerful one.

Tré grasped her by the ankles, lifting her legs and curling her body up until her knees nearly touched her shoulders, leaving her dripping sex deliciously exposed to him. She had always been flexible—a memento of a childhood spent in gymnastics classes. Thanks to that flexibility, coupled with the new strength and dexterity bestowed by vampirism, the position was not uncomfortable.

Still, it made her feel as though she was completely at Tré's mercy—under his control—and she instantly loved it. His cock was still rock hard as the tip brushed over her entrance, teasing. She tried to wriggle—to hurry him—but she could barely move. Her sex clenched over and over, trying to grasp at his length as he pressed the tip inside and backed off.

"Are you ready for me, Della?" he asked, sliding in an inch or two and back out again.

She wriggled again, needing him inside with every fiber of her being. "You know I am! You're just being cruel now…"

His thumb rubbed along the tendon of her ankle. "Cruel? To you? Never," he rumbled, and thrust inside her to the hilt.

She gasped his name, her vision whiting out as the most perfect feeling of fullness she had ever experienced flooded over her. Tré rocked into her, effortlessly controlling the pace. Della floated along on the waves of sensation, the angle keeping her riding the edge without *quite* being able to tumble down into another orgasm.

It was divine.

She couldn't have said how much time passed, but eventually, Tré's thrusts slowed until he was merely rolling his hips against hers. She whimpered when he pulled out, but it was only so he could release her legs and reposition her on her back in the center of the bed. When he settled himself in the cradle of her thighs and re-entered her, it was even better than before.

She wrapped her arms and legs around him, pulling him down into a kiss. The taste of him—and of her own juices still clinging to his lips—awakened a new kind of need in her, a hunger every bit as fierce as the one she'd teased him about earlier.

She pulled back, trying to force herself under control as saliva flooded her mouth. Her fangs itched to pierce his flesh. He slid his stubbled cheek along her smooth one, even as he gave a sharp thrust of his hips that drove her lust for him even higher.

"I can feel your hunger," he whispered in her ear, lips brushing. His hips snapped forward again. "Give into it, *draga*. You can't hurt me."

She moaned, powerless to fight it as her instincts propelled her forward the last couple of inches. Her fangs sunk into Tré's jugular, and the coppery taste that had quickly become wrapped up in feelings of *life love safety* poured into her mouth.

Their souls twined together as Tré's blood and life force flowed into her. Della stiffened and came harder than she ever had before, swallowing and swallowing as visions flashed through her mind like vibrant scenes from a film.

She was a boot maker's daughter in Germany, hurrying home from the market with a loaf of bread and some turnips, too worried about being out past dark to notice the handsome stranger walking on the other side of the street.

She was a nun in a Transylvanian abbey, too pious to look up from her prayers when a group of travelers arrived, begging sanctuary from the Mother Superior until nightfall.

She was the youngest sibling in a family of Mexican cattle ranchers...

She was a factory worker in Manchester...

She was a staff leader in the Women's Army Corps during World War II...

The circle of her life turned and turned, until it eventually landed here, in this bed in an old house in the Louisiana bayou.

She pulled away from Tré's neck, shaking, clinging to him, tears running down her cheeks. "So many lives... Tré... I didn't know there could be so *many!*"

Tré cradled her, still joined with her both physically and mentally. "Della," he said. "Della, my beloved. If I had only known to look for you sooner—"

She squeezed him tighter, the truth finally clear in her mind. "It doesn't matter. You're here now. *We're* here. We finally found each other."

He made a sound like the breath had been punched out of him and pressed deeper inside her. His teeth nipped at the side of her throat, the feeling sparking down her spine to the place where they were joined. She rolled her head to the side, baring her neck, *wanting* it, and he obliged—piercing her skin with two sharp pinpricks of sensation. Drawing her essence into himself as he shuddered and came inside her.

She held him, feeling strong and powerful and wise for perhaps the first time in her entire life. *This* was what she had been meant for. She and Tré were two parts of a whole. Without each other, they were incomplete.

But together, they were perfect.

SEVENTEEN

For almost a full day, Della stayed hidden in Tré's bedchamber, feeding from him whenever a new wave of hunger came over her. For some reason, she felt unaccountably nervous about joining the other vampires, and delayed her return into the wider world beyond their cloistered bedroom. Instead, she and Tré had wrapped themselves in a hazy cocoon of passion, and she sensed that he, too, was unwilling to shatter the peace around them after such a chaotic time.

Finally, during a quiet moment as she stood to one side of the large picture window, holding a corner of the drapes to one side so she could stare outside at the setting sun on the horizon, Tré came up behind her and wrapped his arms around her waist.

"Are you ready to go downstairs and talk to the others?" he asked, lifting a hand to play with her hair. She could feel the words rumble through his chest and into her back where their bodies pressed together.

Della hesitated, unsure. "I don't know. I could still turn out to be a horrible vampire, you know."

She felt his unhappy huff of breath tickle the top of her head, and turned to face him, pasting on a sly grin. "Or—who knows? I guess I could turn out to be a better vampire than even you."

Tré traced his fingers down the side of her face and hooked a stray lock of tangled hair behind her ear. "I wouldn't doubt that for a moment. You have always been the better part of me."

A lump rose in Della's throat. She wrapped her arms around him, and felt him press her more tightly against his chest.

"Everything seems so perfect right now," Della murmured.

"Everything *is* perfect right now," Tré corrected. "But I do know what you mean—the feeling that if we leave this room, terrible things will start happening again."

They stood in silence, wrapped up safely in each others' arms for several moments longer before Della eventually stirred.

"There's no use delaying it anymore, is there?" she said. "Let's go see what the others are up to."

Della's t-shirt was completely ruined. Her jeans had dried, stiff with mud, but she scraped it off and shook out as much of the resulting dust as she could before donning them and one of Tré's old button down shirts. It came down to mid-thigh on her, surrounding her in a cloud of his reassuring scent.

Muck from the swamp had soaked into her bra as well, so she went without. The material of the shirt was delightfully soft, and her nipples hardened as they brushed against it.

I will not drag Tré back to the bed and ravish him again, she told herself firmly. *I will act like a grown-up and go talk to the other nice vampires who risked their lives to save me so Tré and I could be together.*

Tré shot her a smoldering look that also managed to convey amusement, as if he knew exactly what she was thinking. Which, to be fair, he may well have done.

I will not drag Tré back to the bed and ravish him... yet, she amended. *I will go talk to the other nice vampires like a grown-up, then drag him back here and ravish him again afterward.*

He was still looking at her, the corners of his eyes crinkling nearly imperceptibly. "You will be the death of me, *draga*, I can tell already. And I will enjoy every single moment of it."

She couldn't help it. She grinned, joy suffusing her like the sunlight she would never feel again.

They walked through the old house together, hand in hand. Della found that, as a vampire, her senses were much sharper, and she could detect very subtle scents on the air. Their footsteps seemed overly loud, even when muffled by the moth-eaten carpet under their feet.

A low murmur of voices down the hallway greeted them. Della could tell immediately that all the vampires were gathered in the kitchen, with the exception of Snag.

When they pushed open the door, four pairs of eyes lifted to greet them.

"Well, now," Xander said, his eyes going wide an innocent in a way that was wholly unconvincing. "We were beginning to think you two would be holed up in Tré's room, going at it like rabbits for the rest of the century."

"Charming as always," Duchess said dryly. "What *would* we do without you, Xander?"

Della blushed, but she couldn't work up any real embarrassment. Perhaps being shameless was another side effect of vampirism.

"Tempting," she said. "But the bed will still be there in an hour. We came to see what the rest of you were up to."

Oksana laughed gaily, and popped open a bottle of wine that had been standing on the table. "Celebrating your turning, of course!"

Della could smell the sickly sweet scent of the wine all the way across the room, and wrinkled her nose at it. "Um, that's great."

Oksana poured herself a glass, not bothering to offer any to the other vampires in the room, and toasted her.

"Wow. Yesterday, I would have joined in with you in a heartbeat. Now, I don't think I could swallow a drop. That's so weird," Della said, looking on with a faint sense of queasiness as Oksana took a large sip.

"We've been telling her that for the last century," Tré said with a shake of his head.

Oksana smiled a bit sheepishly. "What can I say? Everyone needs a hobby. Cheers, eh?"

Looking around at the others, Della noted that the only person who did not seem pleased by the recent turn of events was Eris.

Della watched him surreptitiously for a few moments. He seemed lost in thought. Troubled, even. Thinking now was as good of a time as any for a bit of mental practice, Della concentrated on looking inside Eris with her mind. She had absolutely no illusion that her clumsy attempt would go unnoticed, so she was unsurprised when he looked up at her.

"What is it, Eris?" Tré asked, easily catching Della's concern and tracing its path back to the other vampire.

Eris blinked back to the present. "I've just been thinking."

"Well, that's never good," Xander said, not moving from his relaxed slouch against the far wall.

Eris ignored the jab, studying Della with his dark, intelligent eyes, lit from within by a hint of gold.

"Come now. You might as well spit it out, Eris — whatever it is," Oksana coaxed. "Della is one of us now, after all."

Eris sighed and shook his head, focusing his attention on Della. "I was just reflecting on how we stumbled upon you, Della. It was as though we followed the trail of destruction right to your door."

She sobered, the reality of the last few days puncturing the bubble of happiness that had surrounded her since she woke, safe and whole in Tré's arms, after their ordeal.

"Don't remind me," she said.

Eris gave her an apologetic look. "I am sorry, Della. It wasn't my intention to make you sad during what should be a happy time for the both of you. Honestly, I was just...wondering if that approach could work again for us."

Tré cocked his head, looking curiously at Eris. "Explain."

Eris rustled around under a stack of papers on a table in the corner and pulled out an ancient book with brittle, cracking pages. Della could smell dust and old ink when Eris flipped it open, and she breathed in, entranced.

He brought the book over to the large kitchen table and placed it down carefully, dropping into a chair in front of it.

"I've been rereading passages foretelling the fall of Bael," he said.

The others gathered around, intent. Della scooted closer, trying to read over Eris' shoulder but found that the text was written in an alphabet she did not recognize.

"The prophecy clearly states that the Council of Thirteen will unite, and the power of Bael will be cast from the land into eternal darkness," Eris said, running his finger along a line of strange shapes. Della frowned. Maybe it was Cyrillic?

Tré put a hand on Eris' shoulder. The older vampire leaned back into the contact and scrubbed a hand over his face, looking weary.

"We've been over this many times," Tré said. "There aren't thirteen vampires in the world. We would have found the others, if they existed."

"No. There are not thirteen vampires," Eris agreed, before gesturing towards Della. "There are, however, *seven*, whereas a short time ago, there were only six."

Oksana looked back and forth between the two of them, understanding dawning. "You think that we were the first half of the council, and the other half is out there somewhere, waiting to be turned?"

"I think it's possible," Eris replied, looking towards Della again. "We found you, Della, didn't we? Against all odds..."

The room was silent as they pondered Eris' words.

"So, if there are others out there like me — reincarnated souls of those you've lost — how do we find them?" Della asked quietly.

"We follow Bael, I suppose," Tré answered. He glanced towards Eris, who nodded and shrugged.

"But how did Bael know where I was and who I was?" Della asked, dragging up another chair and sitting down next to Eris. "*I* didn't even know who I was."

"That, Della, I do not know," he answered gravely. "He is a very powerful being, and also a very angry one. Vengeance appears to be one of his driving motivations."

"But why not just come and kill me when I was a kid? Or at any one of the thousands upon thousands of moments in my life when I was completely vulnerable?" Della asked. "Why take out his anger on an entire city?"

"His desire for vengeance is not merely against you," Eris said. "It's against all of us."

"His *failures*," Xander said, and Della was startled by the depth of bitterness behind the words.

"It's as we discussed before," Tré said. "Bael is attempting to change this world into his own. Trying to remake it in his image. He doesn't care how much he destroys in the process. He will not be satisfied until the living are nothing more than meat for the undead, and entertainment for his cruel desires."

Della shuddered, appalled anew by the evil that had located her so easily. She knew on a gut level that she was lucky to be in one piece, and sane. Her life as a human suddenly seemed as fragile as a butterfly's wing.

"You've overlooked one small detail," Duchess said. She had been very quiet during the discussion, leaning against the edge of the marble countertop with her arms crossed. Della could feel defensiveness rolling off her in waves, and wondered at it.

"What's that?" Xander asked. He looked tired. Drawn. She could tell that he, too, found something deeply disturbing about the conversation, and wished that her mental acuity were more developed so she could make sense of the undercurrents swirling throughout the room.

Duchess let out an unhappy breath.

"Let's just say for a second that Eris is right, and we can all locate our reincarnated mates, those who sacrificed themselves so we could survive Bael's turning," she said. "Let's just, for one second, assume that we can follow Bael's trail of destruction to each of them, and save them before they become his victims. The last time I checked, six vampires and six reincarnated mates do not make a Council of Thirteen."

Eris folded his arms and stared back at her.

"Yes, Duchess — I am, in fact, capable of performing basic arithmetic. But I'd still much rather have twelve of us than six if we have to do battle again. Which we almost certainly will. My instincts tell me that Bael will be enraged by his defeat here. It's possible that the next encounter will be far worse."

"And aren't you just a ray of sunshine on a cloudy day?" Xander asked, flashing a brief, brittle smile at Eris that came nowhere near his eyes.

"Pot, kettle," Eris shot back, looking sour.

"It will work out somehow," Tré said firmly, putting an end to the debate. "Whatever may come, we will face it together as we have done for centuries."

He reached over and clasped Della's shoulder, the gentle grip reassuring. Regardless of what lay before her, no matter what furious battle she was facing with Bael in the future, she felt serene, knowing that Tré was at her side.

She would never again have to fight her demons alone.

-o-o-o-

A week and a day after Della left her mortal life behind, she soared and dipped alongside Tré's owl form, feeling the night air ruffle the beautiful white feathers of her wings.

To her delight, her avian form had turned out to be a snowy owl—swift and nimble, with a smattering of black flecks across her wing coverts. She loved flying. It had already become by far her favorite thing about being a vampire. It was like a dream made real, and even better when Tré's large gray form flew silently next to her, the tips of their flight feathers brushing affectionately now and then as they drifted along the air currents rising from the city below.

Tonight, her heightened senses were nearly overwhelmed by the swirl of color and noise below them as Tré led her downriver through New Orleans' Garden District, where the Bacchus parade was in full swing during the run-up to Mardi Gras. Carnival goers packed the streets in droves, celebrating both the traditional festivities and the easing of tension within the city after weeks of violence and rioting.

Tré had been close-mouthed about where, precisely, they were going—only insisting that she wear the extravagant green and gold evening dress he'd bought her the previous day. It was by far the most amazing piece of clothing she'd ever owned, a satin confection obviously meant for Carnival, complete with a two-foot train that Duchess had needed to teach her how to deal with when wearing the high-heeled strap sandals that were part of the outfit.

She was dressed for a Ball to end all Balls. Her long, wavy hair was piled up in a riot of curls on top of her head, twisted through with ribbons of purple and green. A purple and gold half-mask covered the upper part of her face, the edges encrusted with rhinestones. Oksana had insisted on accentuating the little mole at the corner of Della's mouth — the one she had always hated — with a black eyeliner pencil.

"There," Oksana had said with satisfaction. "Just like Marilyn Monroe. Tré won't know what hit him, *ti cheri.*"

The others had awoken early in the afternoon to dress in their own finery. Well... all of them except Snag, anyway. Della still had a hard time thinking of herself as fitting in with a group of such attractive beings, but even she had to admit, after seeing herself decked out in the antique full-length mirror in the bedroom, that she looked *good*.

Which, she reflected, was just as well, since she would be on the arm of a tall, dark, handsomely brooding vampire wearing a white tie and black tailcoat with a sash in the traditional colors of Mardi Gras, and a mask matching hers.

Now, she just had to keep the mental picture of how she was supposed to look firmly in mind when they arrived wherever they were going and she transformed back into human form. She'd been practicing for days, so she sincerely hoped to avoid a repeat of her first hideously embarrassing transformation, in which she had reappeared wearing only her bra, panties, and one sock... which had a hole in the toe.

Yeah. The less said about that particular performance, the better.

Below them, the crowds were growing thicker as they approached the French Quarter. The owl could hear the sounds of teeming life on the ground beneath them, and Della felt her newborn hunting instincts rise. Some-day, she knew, she might feed from one of the countless thousands of humans celebrating the last days before Lent. But she was not yet ready to chance such a thing — content, for now, to seek nourishment from Tré when her hunger grew.

She was young yet — so very young, compared to the others — and she would not risk doing irreparable harm to some poor innocent, should her thirst for blood exceed her self-control. When she had explained all this to Tré and haltingly apologized to him for being a bur-den, he had made a sound deep in his chest that she couldn't readily identify, and drawn her into his arms, holding her tight and burying his face in her hair.

Now, Tré's owl was circling, honing in on a particu-lar building below them. Owls looked at the world differently than either humans or vampires, but based on the crowds and their proximity to the river, Della was fairly sure this was St. Charles Avenue. They were close to Canal Street — only a few blocks away from it, she thought.

A curl of amusement rose, though she had no way to really express it while in bird form. It would have been a nightmare trying to reach this area from ground level. Impossible by car or public transit with the parade in full swing, and grueling on foot, through the dense crowds. Instead, they would both glide in on silent wings, with almost no one the wiser.

She followed Tré toward the huge balcony of the extravagant townhouse that was apparently to be their destination. People milled on the balustrade, talking, laughing, and sipping drinks. The soft strains of a piano emerged from within the house. As they approached,

Della became aware of several familiar presences among the partygoers.

Eris. Duchess. Oksana. Xander. And another familiar aura that she couldn't quite place. But now, she needed to concentrate. Tré came in for a smooth landing on the balustrade, hidden from the people on the balcony by a row of lush, six-foot tall potted plants. The owl hopped down from the railing and Tré landed lightly on his feet in vampire form.

Della wasn't quite that skilled yet, so she aimed for the railing and steadied her balance with flapping wings for a moment before jumping down to the floor of the balcony while still in owl form. She thought very hard about all the clothing and small items she'd brought with her, and fixed a firm picture of her reflection in the mirror in her mind's eye.

Clothing. Hair. Makeup. Shoes. Jewelry. Mask.

She shifted into vampire form, accepting Tré's hand on her arm for support. She looked down — still dressed. She lifted a hand to her hair — still coiffed.

"Do I look all right?" she asked, just to be sure.

"Perfect as ever," Tré said, smiling down at her.

She smiled back. The soulful strains of Randy Newman's ballad, "Louisiana," filtered out from the piano inside. Xander appeared in front of them with a flute of champagne in each hand, which he tipped unceremoniously into the nearest plant pot. He handed them each one of the empty glasses and fished around for a flask inside his tailcoat.

"Took you long enough to get here," he said. "Here, have something to take the edge off."

He poured them both a generous draft from the flask and recapped it.

Tré glanced at the red liquid. "Do I want to know what this is, or where it came from?"

"Nope and nope," Xander said cheerfully. "Bottoms up."

Tré shook his head ruefully, but downed the glass all the same. With a shrug, Della did the same. The alcohol-spiked blood burned down her throat, warm and sharp.

"You're a hopeless degenerate, Xander," she accused fondly. The drink went straight to her head, leaving a pleasant buzz in its wake.

"At your service," Xander acknowledged with a smirk, and toasted them with the flask before making it disappear inside an interior pocket.

Della looked around, moving to the railing and craning to see up and down the street. "What is this place, anyway?" she asked, trying to orient herself. "And are we crashing this party, or are we invited?"

Eris joined them, with Oksana on his arm—both resplendent in their fine clothes and masks.

"We're invited," Eris said. "Xander *knows people*, apparently—as perplexing as that concept might be."

"Hey!" Xander protested. "People *like me*. I'm *charming*. You should try it some time."

Oksana swatted Eris on the arm with the fan she was carrying, no real ire behind the movement.

"Be nice to the person who got us private balcony access to Bacchus," she said, before turning to Della excitedly. "You'll never guess where we are, Della. You know the Cailey Townhouse, just downriver of Julia Street?"

Della's eyes went wide. "Nooo..." she said. "Seriously?"

"Yep!" Oksana said cheerfully. "Welcome to Mardi Gras Party Central, courtesy of a really rich guy who wanted a restored mansion where he could watch the parades go by with a hundred of his closest friends. And—apparently—with Xander."

Xander mock-glared at her. "See if I take you nice places again. Ungrateful sods, the lot of you."

Della was still in shock—she'd ridden past this place almost daily on the way to and from work. The tramline was just on the far side of the narrow street. The house was nicely restored on the outside, situated next to an apartment building called The Abbott, and across the street from a little bakery. But the place showed up frequently in human interest stories online or in the newspaper. The owner had picked it up for a song when it was a run-down tenement house, and spent a cool couple of million turning it into a residence fit for a king.

It was a hangout for rich people. Famous people. Not... *people like her.* Not receptionists from New Jersey. It was as though she'd gone to sleep and woken up inside a fairy tale.

Cinderella, you shall go to the ball.

She darted forward and kissed Xander on the cheek, startling him.

"Thank you for taking us nice places, Xander," she said, unable to stop the smile that was lighting up her face like a beacon.

Xander cleared his throat. "Well," he said, recovering, "at least *someone* appreciates my efforts."

"Your efforts are always appreciated, old friend," Tré said solemnly.

A smile quirked one corner of Xander's full lips, even as he struggled to regain his usual devil-may-care facade. "There, now. See how easy that was, Eris? *That's* more like it."

Eris huffed a breath of quiet amusement.

"You *have* to see the inside, Della," Oksana enthused. "Come on. This is the third story balcony. The second story one will be a better vantage point for the floats."

Della clasped Tré's hand and pulled him inside, following Oksana's lead. The house was amazing. Every available surface was finished with polished hardwood or solid marble, and decorated for Mardi Gras with streamers and beads. Even the statues were decked out with Carnival masks and jester hats. A grand staircase led down to the lower levels, where more party guests mingled and sipped drinks.

Looking down at the ground floor atrium, Della saw that it opened out into a ballroom, the floor a checkerboard of dark and white polished marble. Her breath caught.

"Do you dance, Tré?" she asked, looking up at him hopefully.

His mouth twitched beneath the mask. "Of course I dance, *draga*. One does not live five hundred years without learning a passable waltz. Come, then, if you are so eager for a turn around the floor. They're playing Tchaikovsky now, and it will be some time before the Krewe of Bacchus arrives."

The four of them made their way down to the dance floor, where Tré helped Della pin up the train of her dress so she wouldn't have to worry about stumbling over it.

"Where's Duchess, anyway?" Della asked.

"Sizing up the male contingent of guests, of course," Oksana said wryly. "We'll hook up with her outside on the balcony when the parade starts."

Della suspected that the male contingent had absolutely no clue what they were in for. Now, though, she let Tré take her in his arms and lost herself to the hypnotic *one*-two-three, *one*-two-three of the music, spinning slowly around the floor with her handsome lover gazing into her eyes.

Beside them, Xander danced with Oksana, despite their earlier teasing jabs at each other. With her floor-length gown, it was nearly impossible to tell that Oksana was wearing a prosthesis, unless one knew to listen for the telltale clack of spring-loaded metal against stone. Eris was quickly snapped up by a doe-eyed young human woman, whom he led gamely around the ballroom, genteel and reserved as ever.

Eventually, Della ended up dancing with all of the male vampires. She no longer felt the sense of intimidation she once had in Xander's or Eris' presence. Once, she thought, she would have been weak in the knees at the mere idea of dancing with two such strikingly handsome men. Now, while it was a pleasant enough diversion, it was Tré's eyes on her that warmed her core and made her heart beat faster.

He had, thankfully, gotten over his instinctive territorial protectiveness of her once she recovered from her turning and their mating bond settled—at least, to an extent, with the men he trusted like brothers.

But she still couldn't help it if the hint of a growl under his polite, "May I cut in?" made her heart swoop a bit as Eris handed her back to him.

This is where I want to be, she thought, settling into his arms. *Right here. Forever.*

They danced until the excited murmur of the other guests heralded the arrival of the first floats. Then, they hurried up to the second-story balcony, where they found Duchess waiting for them, wearing a cat-with-the-cream smile.

"Having fun?" she asked, taking them all in.

"This is *amazing*," Della enthused. "I still can't believe I'm actually here! What about you?"

"I always have fun," Duchess said, draping one arm over Oksana's shoulders, and the other over Xander's. "Xander, *mon chou*, please tell me your flask isn't empty? I'm *parched*."

"For you, Duchess, my flask is never empty," Xander said gallantly, and passed her the spiked blood.

Della basked in the happiness of being someplace so beautiful with the people who were quickly becoming family to her. She leaned back against Tré's broad chest and closed her eyes, drinking everything in. Again, she felt that strange brush of familiarity that did not belong to any of her fellow vampires, but before she could pursue it, a cheer from the street below announced the arrival of the first float.

The six of them pressed forward to get a spot by the railing, and she was aware of Xander shamelessly using his mental influence over the humans to clear a space for them. A sea of excited people milled a few feet below in the street, illuminated now by the strobing purple lights from the first float — Bacchus' chariot, adorned with gold trim and giant clusters of painted plaster grapes.

Della added her whoops and cheers to the crowd's as the masked and robed riders threw beads over the onlookers, then laughed in shocked glee when Duchess calmly unlaced her tight bodice and let her breasts spill out, the nipples artfully covered with a pair of tasseled purple pasties. A shower of beads and doubloons rained down on her. She grabbed several from the air and distributed them to Oksana and Della.

"Don't get any ideas, *draga*," Tré rumbled against the shell of Della's ear as he helped her arrange the cheap plastic necklaces, his fingers brushing her décolletage oh-so-casually as he did. "I'm not ready to share these perfect breasts with anyone else."

Della craned around to kiss him, her heart overflowing. "Don't worry," she said. "I have a theory that shamelessness is a side-effect of vampirism, but I don't think I've quite reached Duchess's levels of shamelessness yet."

Duchess smirked at her. "Ah, you're still young yet, *ma petite*. Give it a few hundred years."

They watched the gaudy floats go past one by one, their shoulders growing ever heavier with beads, thanks to Duchess' foolproof method of attracting the riders' attention. The head of the Bacchasaurus float had just passed by at eye level when Della's breath caught. That familiar presence was back, closer than ever, like cool spring water overflowing a stone basin.

"Ah. Francine," Xander said, turning to face the newcomer. "You're looking well. It's lovely to see you — our sincerest thanks for the invite."

Della's eyes flew to the wrinkled old woman with the coffee-colored skin, wearing African style clothing and a head wrap dyed in vibrant Mardi Gras green and purple. Her mouth fell open for a moment before she snapped it closed.

"*Laissez les bons temps rouler*, Xander, eh?" said the old woman. "Let the good times roll."

"Why, you've just encompassed my entire life philosophy in a nutshell, Madame," Xander replied, and kissed the knuckles of her extended hand in a courtly gesture.

"Wait," Della said, her brain trying to catch up with her mouth. "But... you're..."

"As I mentioned earlier," Eris murmured, "Xander *knows people*."

"Hello, Della," Francine said, looking at her with rheumy eyes. "Well, now. What have we here? I thought I sensed a change in the world, this past week."

"Hello again," Della said in a faint voice.

Madame Francine laughed gaily. "You needn't look quite so surprised, my dear. I like to know what's going on in my city, that's all."

Della swallowed, finally pulling herself together after her surprise. "Madame Francine. I need to thank you. If it weren't for what you said to me, I don't think I would have known what to do when the time came. You saved me, as much as Tré and the others did."

Francine's hazy eyes moved to Tré, who still had an arm around her shoulders. "Ha! Perhaps not *quite* as much as they did, child, but I'm pleased for you, nonetheless. So, you've thrown in your lot with theirs, then? Left your human life behind?"

Della nodded. "I have." A thought occurred. "Well... almost. I still have Jewel. My pet goldfish. Which probably isn't very vampire-ish of me."

She'd rescued the little fishbowl from her apartment once she'd recovered from her turning, and brought it to the plantation house. Perhaps it was her imagination, but the goldfish seemed a bit bewildered by events. Madame Francine made a soft sound of amusement, and Della had a sudden idea.

"I don't suppose your shop would benefit from a low-maintenance mascot to help greet visitors?" she asked. "We may be moving from place to place quite a bit, and it's not really practical to travel with a fish."

Francine smiled, the wrinkles on her face deepening. "I imagine that could be arranged, child. It's not every day that someone offers me a Jewel."

A small weight—one she hadn't even realized was there—lifted from Della's shoulders. "I'll come by on Ash Wednesday evening, in that case—as soon as it's dark enough. And... thank you again. I feel like what I did was the best choice, even though it means leaving my old life behind... fish and all."

Madame Francine lifted a wrinkled hand and brushed gnarled knuckles against Della's cheek. "Of course it was the best choice, Della. Look at you! You have become the very protection that you sought."

The idea circled through Della's thoughts for a moment before taking hold, sending tendrils of warmth through her heart. Tré's arm squeezed her tighter, holding her against him. She could feel his pride in her. His love.

"I can see that you still need to learn to listen to the unseen world around you, child," Francine continued gently. "Can't you hear it, now? The angel Israfael is weeping with joy."

And maybe... just maybe... Della *could* hear it, tickling at the edge of her mental awareness—a sound so pure and light that it made her heart swell.

She knew for certain, now. She had done the right thing.

258

EPILOGUE

Sevastopol, Crimean Peninsula. March 4th.

Bastian Kovac swore as he shook out his swollen and bloody knuckles. The Ukrainian agent who'd been sent to lure him into a fake money-laundering deal groaned up at him from his place lying on his back on the filthy floor of the dive bar. The man tried to lift his upper body into a sitting position, only to fall prone again, blood flowing freely from his broken nose.

"Come," Bastian told his current woman, who was still cowering in the corner, her eyes large and frightened. "We're leaving."

The bitch—*Sasha*—had been a recent acquisition of his, and one who was quickly outliving her novelty. She'd been a whore and a drug addict, and while her skill set did include having a tight ass and giving passable head, her drug habit was becoming increasingly expensive. Not to mention *irritating*.

Still, she was easy enough to keep in line with the occasional backhand to the face or threat of strangulation. And he could definitely use a good, hard fuck after this evening's epic shit-storm. A certain sniveling contact of his due for some serious payback after setting Bastian up with a *fucking narc*. A *Ukranian* narc, worse yet.

He gave Sasha a hard shove in the small of the back to get her moving toward the door, and she stumbled on the ridiculous stiletto heels she was wearing. She righted herself and seemed to hunch down, as though she were trying to appear smaller.

As if he was planning on expending any significant amount of his attention on her in the first place.

The bar was on the edge of the Kacha district of Sevastopol, home to an airbase and a lot of dingy gray tenement buildings housing railroad and dock workers. The central part of the city might have been a tourist destination, but out here, it was all brutalist Soviet architecture and the smell of quiet desperation.

Garbage lined the streets. This particular stretch of road smelled perpetually of piss and rat droppings. Bastian might have wished to deny it, but he felt strangely at home among the filth, human and otherwise. He'd grown up in just such a place, and while he had risen above it by doing things for money that weaker men weren't willing to do, business still seemed to drag him back down here to the gutters on a depressingly regular basis.

The room he was renting for the duration of his stay in Crimea was on the other side of the docks. The shipyards were deserted at this time of night, recent tensions between Russia and Ukraine having further eroded the already shaky economy of the area. Mud was creeping over the crumbling pavement of the road, as if trying to suck the manmade structures back into the earth.

Sasha slipped on a patch of the stuff, stumbling again and nearly falling.

"Keep moving," Bastian snapped, eager to get back to his flop, get himself off between those garishly painted red lips, and put this night behind him. "Watch where you're going, you stupid bitch."

She cringed again, hugging herself, eyes downcast.

Bastian shivered as a sudden blast of cold wind coming off the bay buffeted them. Even the fucking weather had it in for him tonight, it seemed. Sasha hugged herself tighter, her black miniskirt and halter-top doing nothing to protect her. Bastian shrugged his leather jacket a little higher around his shoulders and jammed his hands in the pockets.

The wind wailed past the abandoned cranes and through the broken windows of the warehouses, sounding almost like insane laughter. Bastian shook his head and frowned at the fanciful thought. A cold mist was rolling in as he watched, surrounding them like a muffling veil.

Sasha slowed. "I don't like this, baby," she said. "I c-can't see anything."

"Just follow the damned road," he growled, even as his own feet came to a halt, as if of their own accord.

The cold laughter came again, nearer this time. With no warning, Bastian was flat on his back, the wind knocked out of him, a suffocating weight crushing his chest as he was dragged off the pavement by an unseen presence and pressed into the cold muck. He flailed his fists, but there was nothing to hit—only the bone-deep chill and a feeling of tiny insect legs crawling over his skin.

He heard Sasha scream and caught a flash in his peripheral vision as she turned to run, hampered by her ridiculous shoes. Then, he was dragged over the edge of a pit in the ground and slammed into the sucking mud at the bottom. He fought to get free, but there was still nothing to fight against. The laughter tickled the shell of his ear this time; a sound of pure evil.

There is no escape from me, Bastian Kovac, said the unseen presence. *You will be mine, and together, we will bring this world to its knees.*

Bastian stopped fighting, his chest heaving like a bellows. "Who… are you?" he gasped.

I am your Master, said the voice. *And you will be my hunting dog. The teeth for my trap.*

"What do I get out of it?" Bastian asked, trembling as the cold filth he was lying in leached his body heat.

The laughter this time was maniacal. *You will get power, dog. More power than you could possibly imagine.*

Bastian licked his lips, contemplating the kind of power that an unearthly being like this might possess.

"… all right," he said eventually. "I accept."

A cold, slimy touch caressed his cheek, the gesture almost tender. *Oh, my arrogant dog… I was not asking your permission…*

Something reached inside of Bastian and *pulled*. His fingers scrabbled at the mud coating the sides of the pit, and he screamed in agony as his very essence was torn apart. It seemed to go on forever, an eternity of his own private hell.

Without realizing it, Bastian managed to claw his way out of the suffocating hole in the ground. He was *ravenous*. His insides had been torn out, and he needed to fill the empty space more than he had ever needed anything in his life.

A whiff of warmth and life pierced the veil of death surrounding him. He breathed it in, *thirsting* for that life. He had to have it. He had to have it *right now*.

The scent of sweat and cheap perfume called to him like a magnet called to steel. He plunged after it, abused muscles propelling him forward with inhuman speed. In what felt like no time at all, he was tackling the woman — the *whore* — to the ground, where she continued to scream and kick at him as he pinned her in place.

"Oh, my God! God have mercy on me!" she shrieked, the sound hurting his sensitive ears. "Get away from me, you son of a bitch! Don't hurt me, please, *don't hurt me!*"

The words meant nothing. Not when he could hear her pounding heart pumping blood beneath the fragile barrier of her skin. His Master's maniacal laughter split the night sky as Bastian surged forward and sank his teeth into the column of the woman's throat, ripping and tearing even as her body bucked and seized beneath his.

Blood and life force flooded his mouth like nectar, and he drank deep, pulling more and more into himself until her struggles subsided into twitches, and then, to nothing. He drained her dry, and let the empty husk fall back on the muddy pavement with a dull, lifeless *thump*.

Power coursed through him, until he felt that it would burst from his eyes like lightning. He reared up, his hoarse laughter joining his new Master's, until it seemed the darkness itself would burst open and unleash the denizens of hell upon the unsuspecting world above.

Bastian Kovac had spent his entire life seeking power. Now, power had finally sought him out in return.

The future was going to be *brilliant*.

End of Book One

Circle of Blood, Book Two

Lover's Awakening

R. A. Steffan & Jaelynn Woolf

ONE

"My life would be so much more difficult if people actually paid attention to what was going on around them," Trynn muttered as she slipped into a vacant back office.

She was illegally and unashamedly trespassing inside the main branch of the Hellenic Bank of Cyprus, near the city center in Nicosia, though you wouldn't have known it based on the reactions of the employees she'd met so far. After pulling her laptop out of its bag, she sat in a dusty office chair and laid it on an old desk that looked like it had been stashed out of sight to hide the graffiti etched on its surface.

With a few quick taps to her keyboard, Trynn opened a program and started her attack on the bank's intranet security, feeling the familiar swoop of adrenaline in the pit of her stomach.

Footsteps sounded outside the hall and Trynn paused, waiting to see if anyone would ask her for credentials. A lone bank employee walked by the open door, giving her a curious look before turning back to the stack of papers in his hands. Trynn shook her head.

If you act like you belong somewhere, no one even bothers to find out if it's true or not.

As far as Trynn was concerned, she had the best career in the entire world. As a professional hacker for Trajan Security, it was her job to try to infiltrate high-level security systems that would be prime targets for hackers with malicious intent. After her attempt, she would report back to her employers with her findings. They, in turn, would communicate with the companies and advise them on security improvements that would prevent future problems.

So, here she was at the Hellenic Bank of Cyprus, trying to access the accounts of several wealthy bank customers. Though in reality, her assault had begun as soon as she walked in the door.

As an uncommonly tall woman, Trynn knew she stood out in a crowd — something that she often used to her advantage. Usually, the best way for her to start her mission was to ensure that she was noticed immediately upon entering a business or company's front door.

Indeed, shortly after she had stepped inside the bank, one of the tellers approached her and asked if she needed any assistance.

"Your manager called about an hour ago," she told the woman. "He said there was something going on with the internet in his office? A glitch or something?"

The bank teller had looked momentarily confused and said, "I wasn't aware of any issues going on in the building." Her Mediterranean accent was thick, forcing Trynn to concentrate on what she was saying; making sure that she didn't miss any details.

"Well, he sounded like he was in a rush, so he didn't give too many particulars." Trynn tapped her fingers on her leg, telegraphing mild impatience.

"Yes, he's often like that." The woman's words were professional enough, but Trynn could detect a slight edge to her voice.

"Look — he sounded like he was getting angry, so I should probably get started before he takes out his frustration on anyone else," Trynn said apologetically, fumbling with her bag and keys as she started moving towards the hallway.

"Yes, all right. His office is just down this hallway on the left," The teller said, sounding relieved.

Trynn gave her a wave of thanks and walked confidently down the hallway. She casually glanced back, pretending to examine the various pictures hung artfully on the walls, but in reality she was making sure that no one was watching her. She passed right by the bank manager's office and turned left as soon as she could, traveling deeper into the building, where there were fewer offices and more storage closets.

It took a bit of searching to find the room housing the bank's router, but once she did, it took only a few seconds to check the sticker on the bottom and memorize the router key and Wi-Fi password. Afterward, she found the empty office that held a few desks and the one chair she was currently occupying.

As soon as her computer was connected to the supposedly secure Wi-Fi, she located the company intranet—available to all employees, but allegedly protected against outside agents.

Using a Trojan horse, she was able to bypass their firewall and enter the system.

The entire hack job took her less than twelve minutes. She made a note of that on her computer, as well as comments about the entrance and how easily she was able to access the private areas of the building unhindered.

"Too easy," she said in a quiet voice, bent low over her laptop. "*Way* too easy."

"Hey, what are you doing in here?" A voice asked in Cypriot Greek, interrupting her thinking. Trynn looked up and found an older gentleman who looked like he could work for the maintenance crew standing in the doorway. She expected him to look suspicious, but found that his eyes raked up and down her legs, which were crossed in front of her.

Trynn leaned forward seductively and said, "Can I tell you a secret?"

The older man straightened up, his wrinkled face going pink as he switched to English. "Yes, of course."

"I'm new here on the executive staff, and I'm not quite used to the noise out in the lobby yet," she said, pitching her voice low. "I've been sneaking back here to do some online training. It's much quieter, you see."

"Oh!" The man said with a bright smile. "Yes. *Um.* Welcome to Hellenic. I'm surprised I haven't seen you around more."

Trynn gave an airy wave of her hand. "I'm afraid I've been stuck in meetings for the most part, or trying to do this training. I haven't really had a chance to meet everyone yet."

"Well, watch out for the other guy on my crew, yes? He's a real prankster," the old man said with a twinkle in his eye. He glanced down at Trynn's legs again before looking back into her face. "I was just checking, since no one ever uses this office. Now I know to keep an eye out for you hiding back here."

"Just as long as you don't give away my secret, or everyone else will follow me back here to talk, too," she said with a sly wink.

"Your secret is safe with me," he said genially, and placed a hand over his heart in a theatrical gesture before lifting one finger to his lips in a shushing motion. He left the room without another word, pulling the door mostly closed behind him.

Trynn let out the breath she had been holding as the man left. Of course, she had a *get-out-of-jail-free* card in her pocket, of sorts, along with her identification—but she really didn't want to have to use it. Partly because she could think of better things to do with her time than explain her job over and over again to the authorities, and partly because she had a reputation to uphold. She was the only current employee at Trajan who had never been detained by a client, and she intended to keep it that way.

Trynn told her co-workers that it was her devilish smile that disarmed people and encouraged trust, but secretly she thought she was just better than most at reading people—as she had done with the janitor, just now.

He might have had a roving eye, but at heart he was the fatherly type, wanting to keep an eye out for others' best interests.

Taking advantage of the nature of the people she came across was what made her one of the top hackers at Trajan. Many of the other employees were world-class computer experts, but could barely interact with people at a level deeper than awkward stares and delayed blinking.

"The best of both worlds, that's me," Trynn murmured to the empty office.

No one bothered her for the remainder of her attack on the bank's security system. Several other people walked by, but they were either too preoccupied with their own business to bother with her, or else the janitor had instructed them to leave her alone.

She wasn't hiding, by any means. The light in the room was on and she made no effort to keep her noises to a minimum as she worked steadily through the firewalls and protective systems around the most lucrative accounts.

Trynn embedded a marker in the deepest lines of computer code in the entire system, which would serve as a beacon to her company as proof of her penetration into the program. The beacon would self-eliminate within 30 days, so she wasn't worried about it disrupting any of their systems.

"Well, that's a wrap," she said as she logged off her computer. Standing up, Trynn adjusted her tailored pants suit and slipped her trusty computer back into her shoulder bag.

As she slipped out of the partially open door, Trynn shut the light off and walked back towards the lobby, brazen as anything. Guessing that she would run into the woman who had let her into the building, she pulled her phone out, ready to fake an urgent conversation with a non-existent supervisor.

As she rounded the corner back to the main hallway, a cacophony of sounds met her ears. There were screams and cries, but they sounded as if they were fading in the distance.

What on earth was going on?

Trynn strained her ears, trying to make sense of the disturbance — completely bewildered. She slowed her pace and looked around, apprehension rising like a cold tide. There seemed to be no one in the lobby, although the revolving door was still turning.

A crazed shriek pierced the uneasy silence of the lobby.

As if in slow motion, Trynn's eyes swiveled. She saw a man rushing towards her, covered head to toe in black, from his scuffed leather boots to his balaclava.

Thump. Thump. Thump.

Her heart rate seemed to slow as the man approached her, waving some kind of device, like an old remote control, in his hand. Trynn watched the man's mouth move, but she couldn't hear any words coming out.

He gestured angrily to one side with his free hand. Still in slow motion, Trynn looked over and saw a small group of people huddled on the floor opposite the front door, a few meters to the left of the hallway she had just come from.

"What the *fuck* are you doing? I told everyone to get down! Get your fucking ass over there with the rest of them!" the man yelled in Greek.

It seemed as if his words were sped up, pitched higher than she would have expected and twice as fast as normal speech. Yet, his motions appeared sluggish, as if she were seeing things at half speed.

"Get your ass over there *now!*" he insisted, jerking his hand with the remote control towards her.

For a moment, Trynn's rebellious nature tried to rear its head, urging her to refuse to cooperate with this asshole. Out of the corner of her eye, though, she saw a man huddled by the wall wrap his arm protectively around the woman next to him, who was quaking in fear.

I can't refuse this guy, Trynn thought, practicality returning. *What if I set him off and he kills all these innocent people?*

There was nothing for it. She would have to resist the urge to fight back and just do what the man said... for the moment, at least.

Trynn took a step forward and nearly stumbled, her feet evidently still rooted in shock. As the man turned more fully towards her, Trynn's eyes were drawn to the vest that was wrapped around his shoulders and waist.

It was a bomb. She'd seen enough photos in the news to recognize a suicide vest when she saw one.

The fear that should probably have come earlier chose that moment to body slam her. She gasped and tried to back away from the man, but he lunged forward and grabbed her arm.

"Oh, no, you don't," he growled. "You get over there right now, bitch, and get on your fucking knees just like them! I swear to God I will blow us all sky-high if you don't fucking well do what I say!"

Terror clawed its way up Trynn's back, overpowering her desire to fight as she realized that the man was clearly insane.

He jabbed her in the back with something. A weapon? His fist? The sharp pain over her kidney forced Trynn to take a few faltering steps towards the small group of people being held hostage. Fighting the paralysis of fear that was wrapping itself inexorably around her limbs, Trynn sank to the ground next to a woman with curly brown hair who was shivering where she knelt.

The madman surveyed them, looming over them. "Keep your mouths shut—I don't want to hear a word from any of you!"

Breathe, just breathe, she told herself. *You're going to have to think, Trynn. Think your way out of this.*

But it was useless. The only thing that happened when she took several fast, deep breaths was that a sharp pain crept up her throat and she felt the world spin around her. Knowing that she was in danger of hyperventilating, Trynn forced herself to take slower breaths until the spinning slowed, and eventually stopped.

The suicide bomber was shouting again, but Trynn was concentrating too much on regaining control of herself to translate his words in her mind. When her ears finally caught up with the rest of her, Trynn realized that the man was making demands.

"Don't you *get it*? There's nothing anyone can say to talk me out of this! I want a *fucking* helicopter to land on the roof in the next thirty minutes. I've got to get out of here. The government is watching our every move and I can't take it anymore! No, you *shut up*!"

By the end of his tirade, the man was screaming and clutching his head. Trynn looked around, bewildered, since everyone in the group around her had remained completely silent. She'd thought maybe he was talking to someone on a cell phone, but it appeared that he was having a conversation entirely with himself.

"*Syria, Syria, Syria, Syria*," he muttered under his breath as he stalked back and forth, scratching his head with his left hand, still grasping the remote in his right.

Trynn wanted to ask him what exactly needed to happen for them to be let go, but her throat had gone completely dry and she didn't think she could manage to get a word out.

"I want you all to lie down! Yeah — on the ground. Now!" the bomber hissed, glancing around wildly at the large glass panes in front of the bank. Slowly, not daring to take her eyes off the bomber's hands, Trynn lowered herself onto the hard floor, turning her face to the side so that she could continue to monitor the man as he paced back and forth.

"No!" he shouted a moment later, backing away from the group with a terrified expression. "No! That's not right! Get up! All of you, get the fuck up and kneel with your fucking hands behind your heads. *Do it, now!*"

Trynn pushed herself up, just as slowly as she had dropped down, and laced her fingers behind her head.

The bomber stared at the group and, once satisfied that everyone was following his directives, he stalked away and started rifling through a desk hidden behind a half wall. Occasionally, he threw looks at them as if checking to make sure they hadn't moved, but he did not speak to them again.

"What does he want?" Trynn breathed to the woman next to her, barely moving her lips. She didn't want to draw attention to herself and have the man wearing the bomb come back towards them. "He said something about a helicopter?"

"That's right. A helicopter and a million Euros," the woman whispered back in heavily accented English. "Kept saying that the government is watching him."

Trynn felt a little ironic laugh escape her throat. "Well, if they weren't before, they certainly will be now."

"Make sure that the helicopter can out-fly Syrian border patrol!" The man yelled without warning. The brown-haired woman flinched and did not speak again.

For nearly an hour, Trynn knelt on the hard tile inside the bank, praying for an end to the situation. Although there were no police directly outside the large bay windows, she could vaguely hear the sound of a helicopter hovering in the distance somewhere. Occasionally the flash of blue light would reflect off one of the windows outside the building, giving Trynn hope that help was here and they would be rescued.

As one hour stretched into two, that hope began to die in her heart. She was in agony, having held the same awkward kneeling position for so long. Every time the bomber would turn his back, she would drop one hand to ease the strain on her back and knees for a moment.

The woman next to her shook her head frantically every time Trynn did this, even though her dark eyes were watering with pain.

Every now and then, Trynn would hear a soft sniffle from one of the hostages, none of whom were speaking. The bomber continued to pace, occasionally screaming out a string of profanity, and at other times falling into a moody silence.

Jesus. He's absolutely batshit, Trynn thought. *I'm going to end up blown to bits in fucking Nicosia by a crazy man with a bomb strapped to his chest.*

The thought sent ice through Trynn's heart, and she tried in vain to keep her emotions in check. It was beyond difficult, as she fought the tears of despair threatening to fill her eyes.

Would this nightmare never end?

TWO

Eris stared down at the elegant chess set before him. It was laid out on an antique, carved wooden table, set near the floor-to-ceiling windows in the luxurious hotel room where he and his silent, uninvited chess partner were staying. The drapes were drawn to protect the two of them from the deadly rays of the Mediterranean sun, but he glanced through the heavy fabric for a few moments as the glowing orb sank ponderously below the jagged lines of Nicosia's cityscape.

He had chosen the Merit Lefkosa Hotel partly for its extravagant amenities, and partly because a brief conversation with the hotel manager had ended with a rather hefty amount of money changing hands in exchange for the assurance that Eris wouldn't be asked too many questions. Often, anonymity was the easiest way to proceed when dealing with mortals.

Now, however, he was engaged in a furious battle of strategy. Or, as furious as a battle could be when one's opponent had not moved or spoken in over an hour, at any rate.

His companion had shown no interest whatsoever over the last few weeks as Eris planned his trip to Cyprus, only to show up randomly—not to mention, uninvited—shortly after Eris checked into the hotel. He supposed that Snag had followed him across the Atlantic out of something like affection, though the others would doubtless argue that the ancient and powerful vampire was incapable of any such emotion.

He moved his attention away from the fading light of the sun and back to the chessboard, hoping that Snag would make a decision soon about his next move. Stimulating though the contest was, by now it had dragged on long enough that Eris just wanted it to be over. Snag, however, was a deeply serious player who would plan out at least twenty moves in advance for each possible move available to him at that moment. The only reason Eris had agreed to the game — and the inevitable, humiliating defeat it would eventually entail — was that he needed to pass a few hours before meeting with his art buyer during the nighttime hours to seal their deal.

Who am I kidding? I lost the game the moment I moved the first pawn, Eris thought irritably, scratching his brow and dragging his wandering mind back to the game.

Despite Snag's cold visage, his eyes were moving around the room, as though he were growing restless as evening approached. This was not an uncommon occurrence. Eris often got the sense that his companion struggled with his private demons more as the sun was setting.

After a few moments, Snag's gaze sharpened and returned to the board. Slowly, deliberately, he reached forward with skeletal fingers and moved his remaining knight.

Eris almost let out a groan of frustration. *All of that, for a move that accomplished nothing in the broader strategy?*

"You and I need to find a different game to play," he said.

Snag's deep-set eyes rose to meet his, the pupils blown permanently wide like an owl's. He did not speak, but Eris felt a faint thread of amusement pass between them. He had the distinct impression that Snag, although clearly still uneasy about something, was enjoying his mild irritation.

Eris turned back towards the board and glanced down at all the pieces strewn across the black and white squares. With a sigh, he tipped his king over and sat back, signaling defeat.

Snag sent a flicker of annoyance towards him through their mental connection.

"Snag, why do we keep doing this?" Eris asked.

Snag looked steadily at him, but made no move to communicate.

"We sit here, day after day, playing chess at a pace slower than the Earth circling around the sun. We would have turned to stone before this game ever finished." He huffed a sigh. "Speed chess. Have you ever heard of it? *You should look it up sometime.*"

Snag still did not move or speak.

Eris shook his head, clamping down ruthlessly on the smile that tried to tug at his lips. "Well," he said philosophically, "at least you're a good listener."

A wash of hunger not his own flowed across his awareness for only an instant before it was gone. He frowned.

"You need to feed soon," Eris said. "Unfortunately, that means *I* need to feed, first."

The sudden rush of shame and buried rage was not unexpected, but it stabbed at Eris' cold heart, regardless. Snag refused to feed from humans, from animals — from any source of blood other than Eris. Even then, he fought to hold his hunger at bay until he was already weakened, like some form of twisted self-punishment.

He knew that Snag was in need of a fresh supply of blood, and soon, but he would be better able to provide for his sad, tormented friend after feeding from a human victim to replenish his own strength.

Despite the fact that Snag had eschewed verbal communication for years now, Eris made it a point to converse normally with him, attempting each day to draw him out of his self-imposed silence. Over the last few centuries, he had only heard Snag speak a small handful of times, and never in the last fifty years. Eris often wondered if Snag even remembered how, or if his vocal cords would still work after going so long without use.

Feeling more animated now that the chess game no longer loomed, Eris stood and turned toward the window. He did not open the drapes, but instead raised his hand, palm out, to touch the curtain separating them from the last rays of the setting sun. He could feel the heat under his palm, but he sensed that the sun was nearly below the horizon. It would soon be safe to leave the shelter of the hotel room.

"It's almost dusk," Eris said aloud. He felt Snag stir behind him, and he could tell that the older vampire was oddly anxious for Eris to hunt.

When the sun was safely hidden, Eris excused himself and headed out onto the darkening streets on foot. Breathing in the smell of the city around him, he allowed his mind to wander back to his mortal life.

He had been a smuggler, of sorts; although that was not the name they used millennia ago. At the time, he had considered himself a collector of fabulous treasures. The money he made from artifacts that had come into his possession—by fair means, or foul—had eventually lifted him from humble beginnings to the halls of wealth and power. Over the centuries, much of his wealth had been retained, invested wisely in gold, platinum, stocks, and real estate.

Still, every now and then it became necessary to draw from his private collection to fund some project or another. Hence his presence here tonight, so many, many years after he had first left the beautiful island he called home. As he walked down the jarringly modern boulevard, memories assailed him from the shadows, and he felt a pang of old pain.

So many memories, so much suffering, he thought to himself. It was true. This city held a long and checkered history, and much of it still haunted him.

Not willing to allow himself to sink into listlessness, he turned his attention to the people milling around him on the street. Hunger surged as he idly imagined luring one of them into a dark alley.

Contrary to the stories mortals often told each other, it wasn't necessary for a vampire to kill a human to feed. Vampires could lean heavily on a human's consciousness and wipe all memories of the attack, which minimized the possible fallout from panicked victims running to the authorities to babble about supernatural beings drinking their blood. Aside from feeling a bit weakened from blood loss, they suffered no further adverse effects from becoming a vampire's lunch date.

Eris' gaze wandered over the crowd, looking for a likely female target who would not put up much of a struggle. Shaking his head at himself, he realized that he was acting like Duchess, who always hunted in a crowd of men. Though she also tended to seduce her victims, sleep with them, and then feed before wiping their memories and sending them on their way — generally with vacant, ridiculous smiles on their faces.

He wondered how worried he should be that he was apparently turning into his Duchess in his old age. Though he, at least, would limit himself to a single victim at a time.

See, he told Duchess, even though she was half a world away and couldn't possibly hear him. *I still have some standards.*

As he rounded the corner, he almost ran face first into a woman who was coming from the other direction.

"Oh!" she exclaimed, dropping her cell phone on the concrete as they steadied each other. "I'm so sorry! I wasn't paying any attention at all…"

Eris smiled at her and leaned down, picking up her phone. He dusted it off, checked the screen for damage, and held it out to her. "No, no," he said. "The fault was entirely mine. Thankfully, your phone doesn't seem to be damaged, so no harm was done."

He could tell that she was taking in his appearance, subtly looking him up and down. He was playing *rich tourist* for this trip, rather than a local—a bit scruffy, a bit mussed. Khakis and white button-down shirt rolled up to the elbows, dark hair a few inches longer than what was fashionable. Judging by the pink creeping into her cheeks, she liked what she saw.

Almost too easy, Eris thought.

"You know, it's far too lovely an evening to spend it rushing around corners, engrossed in the screen of a phone," he said.

The woman touched her throat with her fingertips and laughed—a light, fluttery noise that caused new hunger to course through Eris' body in anticipation of what was to come.

"Oh, I don't know," she said, "If it results in collisions with dark, handsome strangers, maybe I should try it more often."

The exchange was so clichéd, so *predictable* after all these long centuries that Eris had to stifle a sigh of boredom, despite his need for her blood.

"And what has you so distracted that you're posing a hazard to pedestrian traffic?" he asked, playing the game even though his heart wasn't in it.

"Nothing that I couldn't whole-heartedly abandon," she replied in a sly tone.

"Well, then—why don't you tell me all about it over drinks?" Eris suggested, holding his arm out to her.

She looked flattered and shrugged agreement, but before she could reach out and take his arm, a strange feeling passed through his body like a wave. An odd, shivering vibration, deep inside his fragmented soul. It resonated within him and he looked up, alarmed, stretching outward with all his senses.

His sensitive hearing picked up the sound of police cars wailing in the distance. He knew that the woman next to him, looking at him oddly as he stood frozen in place, would never be able to hear the distant noise. Something he couldn't explain compelled him to follow the sound. He was powerless to resist the pull, like a moth drawn to flame.

"Forgive me," he said, stepping back from the woman and turning in the direction of the pull. "I've just remembered something, and I'm afraid I'm going to have to take a rain check on those drinks."

Behind him, his would-be victim was saying something about phone numbers, but he was already hurrying away.

Eris could not explain, even to himself, why he felt so strongly about the situation. He jogged. Then he ran. Then, he ran *hard*, passing people on foot left and right. He could feel their stares following him, but he didn't dare slow down long enough to apologize for the jostling or to account for his actions.

Get there, get there, get there, a voice inside him chanted. He managed to control his instincts just enough to run at a speed that would not raise alarm with the humans flashing past him, but Eris could feel the strange compulsion to *be there now* eating away at him.

He rounded corners seemingly at random, drawn forward by intuition rather than by his senses. Before he had traveled five blocks, he found himself approaching a police barricade erected a few hundred paces ahead.

Not wanting to be seen running towards a large group of alarmed police officers, Eris sidestepped quickly into the dark shadows of a nearby building's recessed doorway. He could taste human fear and tension hanging in the air around him, and he wondered what had happened to cause such a response.

The attention of the officers down the street seemed to be focused on a large building with a glass paneled front. He thought that it could be a stock exchange or a bank of some kind, and tried to orient himself against his mental map of the city. The Hellenic Bank of Cyprus, maybe? That would make sense, given where he'd started from and how far he'd run.

While he was taking in his surroundings, three officers decked out in riot gear came around the corner from a nearby side street, talking swiftly to one another.

"He's got an unknown number of hostages located at the northeast corner of the lobby. As far as we can gather, there's only one perp, but the text messages being routed through JointComm are garbled," the first officer rattled off.

It sounded to Eris like he was updating his superior on the situation at hand.

"Garbled? From panic? Or maybe injury?" the second man asked.

"Unknown, sir. It's possible that the individual is sending text messages when the perp isn't looking."

"Hmm. Base command?"

"One hundred fifty meters to the north of the front door. They're working on establishing telephone contact with the lobby right now."

Their voices faded as they continued forward, approaching the barricade.

A hostage situation, then, Eris thought, wishing that he could see past the group of armed officers standing nearby with guns drawn, and into the building. *Curiouser and curiouser.*

Ducking into an alley that he guessed would span the entire block flanking the cordoned-off area, Eris passed silently around the officers monitoring the perimeter. Once he reached the back of the large building, where the police presence was minimal, he slipped quietly by an officer who was intent on the large, hand-held radio pressed to his ear.

Eris drew his power inward and shifted into mist, rising unnoticed through the evening darkness and swirling toward the building, brightly illuminated with police spotlights. He circled, following the contours of the rooftop until he saw a second-story office window cracked open to let in a breeze. His vaporous form flowed unimpeded through the screen covering the gap.

He materialized inside an office that was completely deserted. The lights were off, but his vampire senses were much more acute than a human's. He had no trouble navigating his way into the dark hallway. For a moment he stood completely still, allowing his awareness to expand outward. He could smell a faint trace of blood, the scent tainted by fear, creeping up from the floor below this one. He followed it until he found a staircase. It opened into a wide hallway, clearly a main thoroughfare through the offices. He moved forward along the passage, still listening intently and allowing the smell of human blood to fill his senses as it grew stronger.

Finally, Eris saw light ahead and knew that he was nearing the main lobby where the hostages were located. His footfalls were so quiet that even he could barely hear them. Nevertheless, he proceeded cautiously, not wanting to startle a potential gunman.

He reached the end of the hallway and glanced quickly around the corner, taking in as much of the scene in one brief look as he could.

Shifting quickly out of sight again, Eris considered what he had seen. A huddle of people crouched together at the northeast side of the lobby, clustered into a bunch as if frightened. One lone figure stood before them, pacing back and forth. Eris had not seen evidence of a gun.

So, how was he controlling them, if not with a gun?

Suddenly a shout rent the air, making Eris jerk in reaction as the unexpected noise assaulted his sensitive ears.

"I swear, if you start talking again I will blow this thing sky high! *I know you're all plotting against me!*"

Eris could practically feel the hostages trembling with fear. One female voice spoke up, as if trying to reason with the man. "No one said anything at all, we just want to get out of here."

"Shut *up!*"

Silence fell again, and Eris closed his eyes, thinking.

He's unstable, possibly hearing things. And he's got a bomb. Not a good combination. He could snap and kill these people any second.

It was clear what Eris needed to do. Blocking out the sounds of continuing shouts in the lobby, he reached down into the pit of his damaged soul and pulled forth the memory of a peace that he had not experienced in many years. Breathing deeply, he allowed the feeling to swell inside him, until it felt like it was going to overflow the bounds of his body.

These days, in his perpetual state of worry and ennui, such peace was a sham. A ruse — and one that he would pay for afterward, especially since his meal had been interrupted earlier. But it would serve.

Exhaling, Eris mentally pushed at the feeling until — with the sensation of a popping bubble — the force expanded past the boundaries of his skin. He thrust it outward until his power of suggestion was filling the lobby and the hallway all around him.

As each person was enveloped in the serenity that he was pressing outside of himself with all his will, Eris became aware of that individual's mind and swirling emotions. All of the hostages were terrified, almost to the point of collapse after being held so long at the mercy of an unpredictable madman.

The madman himself struggled wildly for a few moments against the mental sedation that Eris was forcing upon him, before relaxing into a state of blissful surrender.

Knowing that it was now safe to emerge, Eris stepped around the corner with his hands raised in the air. Although he was focusing all of his energy on maintaining pressure on the mind of the man before him, Eris knew that with enough effort, the bomber would be able to jerk himself out of the peaceful stupor and become violent again.

"Hello, my friend," he said in the most soothing voice he could muster. "I'm here to help you."

As everyone, including the captor, turned towards him, Eris' eyes fell on a device strapped to the man's chest.

Ah. A suicide vest. That made sense.

Eris walked calmly forward, keeping his gaze on the bomber, never breaking eye contact. The man blinked slowly at him, still looking unnaturally relaxed. Eris was struck, the strangest feeling overwhelming him in that moment. He knew on an instinctual level that the person before him was not a bad person, but rather someone who had become lost in the depths of an evil not of his making.

Another victim of the dark curse spreading across the world. Would he never be able to escape the dark cloud of Bael's expanding power, even here on the island of his birth?

Sudden sympathy for the damaged man in front of him coursed through him.

"What's your name?" Eris asked quietly.

The man seemed to consider the question for a moment before answering, "Ibrahim."

"Well, Ibrahim, what seems to be the problem?"

The man called Ibrahim looked around, confused. "I—I don't know. I need to go somewhere."

"Anywhere in particular?"

"I—" The man paused, swallowing hard as his eyes glittered. "I have to get away. They're coming after me! You don't understand. I need to get out of the country."

"All right. I hear you," Eris said slowly, trying to placate him. "Go on, I'm listening."

"They have eyes everywhere," the man said in a desperate whisper, leaning closer to Eris. Ibrahim's eyes were so wide that Eris could see the whites all around his irises, which were darting around as if looking for the imagined gazes on him.

"Easy, there. Let's just calm down for a minute, and we can talk about getting you out of here. Does that sound like a good plan?"

The man breathed heavily through his nose, staring at him without blinking. He nodded at Eris' words.

"Good," Eris said to the group at large, "Let's start by getting these people out of here safely, yeah?"

Ibrahim glanced down, seeming almost surprised to find the huddled group of people at his feet. Eris wondered if he had any real awareness of the night's events, or if his confused mind had erased or blocked all of those recollections.

Several of the hostages looked up hopefully, but most seemed too scared to look Ibrahim directly in the eye.

There was silence for several moments while Ibrahim considered the people at his feet. Eris continued to press heavily on the man's mind, surprised that Ibrahim was still able to resist with such force. *Shouldn't he be tiring by now?*

"Where are we?" Ibrahim finally asked a woman near the front of the group.

She swallowed hard, her dark hair cropped close to her ears. "The H-Hellenic Bank in Cyprus."

"Oh."

"Can we—I mean, do you think we could leave now?" The woman asked him, shivering as her hands closed around her own shoulders, hugging herself.

Ibrahim considered her through heavy-lidded eyes.

"I suppose so," he answered eventually. Glancing down at his chest, Ibrahim touched the hardware on the bomb. Everyone stiffened, watching him closely.

Eris, trembling now under the effort of keeping Ibrahim calm, interrupted the man's examination in a low voice. "Would you like to take that off?"

Ibrahim nodded and started to unzip the vest holding together the bomb.

"No, wait!" Eris said, reaching a hand out. The control he had over the mood in the room shifted, and Ibrahim narrowed his eyes in sudden suspicion.

"Please," Eris said more calmly, redoubling his efforts to press serenity over Ibrahim. "Let's… just… leave that alone for now. I know some people who would be willing to help get it off of you safely."

"Oh. Okay. That's a good idea," Ibrahim answered mechanically. He stood completely still, his hands dangling at his side.

"Well, then," Eris said, keeping his voice calm and quiet. "If everyone would please stand up, I think you can leave now."

A few of the people clambered uncertainly to their feet. Their eyes never left Ibrahim, who was standing obediently next to Eris.

The woman who told Ibrahim what bank they were in seemed too nervous to stand, despite the backwash from the serenity he was projecting. With an encouraging smile, Eris reached out, offering his hand to her. She glanced at it quickly, then up into his face.

Stretching a hand up, she twined her slender fingers through his.

At the touch of her skin, Eris nearly staggered under the force of an electric shock that surged through him like a lightning bolt. Dumbfounded, he abandoned his single-minded focus on calming the turmoil in Ibrahim's tortured mind.

Eris heard the woman's sharp intake of breath and knew that the impossible had happened. She'd felt the same connection between them that he had. In an instant, the peace Eris had been forcing outward into the room and around the bomber collapsed like a popped balloon. A scream erupted from the unstable bomber, who clutched at his head, scrabbling at his temple as if trying to dig something out of his skull.

Shit, I've lost him, Eris thought, a bit dazedly, all the while maintaining his electric grip on the woman's hand — afraid to let go lest she slip away into the madness and panic erupting around them.

THREE

The bomber jerked and cried out, his forearms coming up to clamp around the sides of his head. Pandemonium broke out as the hostages started running towards the door.

Ibrahim shouted a long string of garbled words in no language Eris recognized, his eyes crazed.

In slow motion, Eris watched as his thumb moved toward what appeared to be the trigger for the bomb.

Coiling his muscles to spring, Eris wrenched his hand free of the woman's and lunged toward Ibrahim. Their bodies collided with a dull thump. Eris wrapped his arms around the smaller man and brought him down hard, suppressing a cringe and a heartfelt curse as he landed on top of the bomb. Miraculously, it didn't go off.

"Yeah... I'm not going to get that lucky twice," Eris grunted. He pushed up enough to grab Ibrahim's wrists and wrench the detonator from his hand.

When he looked up, the woman with the dark hair was backing away, a look of fear on her face. The other hostages had already fled screaming from the building, leaving the three of them alone in the echoing lobby.

Ibrahim began to struggle, still pinned by Eris' tall frame.

"*Don't*," Eris commanded through gritted teeth.

He was still staring at the woman with whom he had felt such a strong connection. Her large eyes were wet with unshed tears as she chewed nervously on her lower lip. Beneath him, Ibrahim began to screech, sounding half-strangled by the weight of the bomb vest tangled around his torso.

Eris looked down at him, trying to decide what to do next, caught between competing crises. A faint swish of noise caught his divided attention, but when he turned his head to look, it was as if the dark-haired beauty whose touch had ignited fire in his cold heart had never been.

He nearly roared in frustration, feeling his fangs lengthen and his eyes glow gold. Ibrahim's struggles grew stronger, more frantic, and Eris was already weakened from hunger and the strain of projecting mental control over a roomful of desperate people.

Saliva welled up in his mouth, and with no witnesses remaining to constrain his actions, he struck—sinking his fangs into the tender flesh of Ibrahim's neck and drawing hard at the blood exploding over his tongue.

His stunned victim twitched beneath him, a gurgle escaping his mouth. His blood tasted sickly sweet—the taste of evil and decay. Eris nearly gagged on it. The smell of Ibrahim's stale sweat rising around them mirrored the tainted taste. Eris suddenly wished that he could just leave the madman where he'd fallen and vanish from the situation.

But he couldn't... no matter how much he might want to be chasing after his mystery woman right now, rather than dealing with one of the demon Bael's sad, pathetic victims.

With the restorative power of Ibrahim's—admittedly rather disgusting—blood pouring into him, Eris found it easier to press against the man's mind, forcing him into submission. When Ibrahim lay limp in his iron hold, Eris released his neck and looked down.

Ibrahim wasn't dead, simply weakened by blood loss and sedated by the mental pressure Eris was exerting on him.

Disgusted by the whole situation, Eris swiped a smear of blood from his chin with his forearm and rolled away from his victim, staring up at the ceiling for a moment, trying to slow his thundering heart. Oddly, his anxiety had almost nothing to do with the insane man lying strapped into a bomb vest next to him, and everything to do with the woman who seemed to have disappeared like smoke.

The lobby was empty now, except for Eris and his unlucky victim.

Scrubbing a hand roughly over his face, Eris rolled onto his knees and crawled closer to the man on the ground, staring at the vest—now plainly exposed.

Fuck me, it's been a while since I've had to do this, Eris thought darkly, rubbing his brow. He'd never been a weapons or explosive expert, *per se*, but he had picked up a thing or two in the last few decades, mostly by virtue of being in the wrong place at the wrong time.

Story of my painfully long life.

He carefully examined the trigger lying on the ground next to Ibrahim, who made no effort to retrieve it. To his surprise, he found that the trigger had malfunctioned—a connection had come loose, possibly as they'd struggled. If the thing were going to trigger the vest, it would have done so when it broke. Which... wasn't to say the vest was *safe*, unfortunately.

With a sigh, he examined the zipper, which seemed to have no physical connection to the explosives strapped to the vest. That was good news, since the devices were often wired to explode if removed, once they had been put on a suicide bomber. It was clear that Ibrahim, even in his crazed state, had at some level intended on getting out of the vest without detonating himself.

"Good choice on that, mate," Eris said to the unresponsive man. With steady fingers, he unzipped the vest and carefully guided Ibrahim's unresisting arms through the holes, rolling him first one way and then the other.

"There you go," Eris finally told him. Ibrahim's bloodshot eyes darted to his face as he continued, "No harm done, eh? Now, let's get you up off this thing. I don't want any funny business, though. Are we clear?"

Ibrahim stared at him vacantly, not answering. Eris chose to interpret this as assent.

"So," he said as he helped Ibrahim to his feet and guided him away from the device. "That was fun. We'll have to do it again sometime. Only, y'know, without the terrified hostages and the deadly danger, preferably."

"What did you do to me? *They're going to get me now*," Ibrahim whispered. His eyes were no longer manic, but rather lost, as tears welled and leaked out of the corners.

"Who? Who's going to get you?" Eris asked, looking at him closely.

Ibrahim didn't respond, merely shook his head. He looked as if he had aged two decades in the last few minutes, and lived a lifetime of misery. His dirty blond hair flopped against his head as he noisily wiped his nose on the sleeve of his shirt.

Eris tugged on Ibrahim's arm, trying to get him to move towards the door, but the other man resisted. He made a pathetic groaning noise, almost a whimper of panic.

"It's all right," Eris assured him. "You're not armed, and you're going to surrender. Just make sure you explain to them about the people who are after you, and how you decided to let the hostages go because it was the right thing to do."

Eris felt no fear of exposure by this man. Ibrahim would never be able to trace the serenity that Eris was forcing into his mind back and truly understand what had happened to him. Besides, Eris had no intention of letting him leave this building with his memories intact.

It wouldn't do to have him babbling about vampires and blood-drinking and hypnotism once he was in custody. He'd be packing his bags for the loony bin immediately.

Of course, as it was, he would probably be headed that direction regardless.

"Just try to stay calm for me, will you? I'm hoping this evening might end with a little less drama than it started," Eris requested.

Still trying to maintain control of the situation, he guided the stumbling man towards the front doors where he knew that the police would be waiting, guns no doubt trained on the building.

Before they emerged, however, Eris reached up and touched Ibrahim's temple. He could feel the man's consciousness wavering under his fingers as shock began to set in. With practiced effort, Eris searched through Ibrahim's mind and found all the memories pertaining to their interactions. He pushed them down deep into Ibrahim's subconscious; so deep that he would never be able to recall Eris biting him and drawing blood from the wound on his neck—a wound that had already closed under the healing power of vampire saliva.

When only one darkened door separated them from the SWAT team waiting outside, Eris turned towards Ibrahim and looked him squarely in the eye. "Go through the door with your hands raised. Walk slowly and steadily. When the police tell you to lie face down on the ground, do it."

Ibrahim stared back at him, looking like a lost and frightened child. Eris hoped that the police would find it in the kindness of their hearts to make sure that he got the help he so clearly needed.

He could *smell* Bael's hand in this, and the idea that the demon had returned to his beloved island home raised gooseflesh across his back. Especially after his encounter with *the woman*.

"Go," Eris whispered, pushing the man forward. He maintained the gentle pressure on Ibrahim's mind, keeping him at peace and holding his fear at bay.

When Ibrahim turned towards the door and started to pass through it, Eris transformed himself into mist once more, drawing all of his life force to his center until he could dissipate and flow unnoticed through the door.

He could hear the barked orders and shouts from members of the police force as he floated away into the night, his mind already intent on finding the woman who had caused him such a shock.

He was so preoccupied with the thought of her that he didn't even register the sound of a single gunshot far behind, followed by pandemonium.

-o-o-o-

Several hours later, gliding over the city in the form of an owl, Eris felt dawn approaching as he turned back towards the hotel room he was sharing with Snag.

It had been immeasurably frustrating, flying low over the area around the city center, trying to find the dark-haired female hostage who had fled from the scene after bringing Eris' world crashing to the ground like falling icicles.

He'd had no luck whatsoever. It was with bitter disappointment that he landed on the windowsill of their hotel room and scratched at the glass to be let in.

As he sensed Snag moving towards the window, Eris swiveled his head, giving the city one last sweep with his amber eyes.

The glass popped open behind him and with one swift flap of powerful wings, Eris swept inside. He pushed his energy outwards from his center, concentrating on his human form. In mid-flight, he transformed, landing gracefully on his feet and dropping his arms to his sides.

Snag remained where he was, standing by the open window. Eris turned towards his friend and studied the intent look on the ancient being's skeletal features.

Eris felt a question brush on the edges of his mind, as if Snag were raising a mental eyebrow at him.

"I've had a rough night, all right? Let's just leave it at that for now."

Nothing changed in Snag's expression, and he remained completely silent. Eris leaned heavily against the arm of the sofa set against the wall of the living area, and let his chin drop to his chest. Weariness pressed down on him as the sun prepared to breach the horizon beyond the window. Yet, tired as he was, he still felt a mounting pressure to charge from the room and find the woman as quickly as possible.

Which was both absurd and impractical, of course, given that daylight was nearly upon them.

From the corner of his eye, Eris saw Snag move noiselessly across the room. Eris turned and watched with a raised eyebrow as he pulled the chair out by the table where they had been seated before, and lowered his thin frame into it.

The older vampire laced his fingers together and rested his chin on top of his joined hands. With a quick dart of his eyes, he told Eris very clearly to take a seat across from him at the table.

Eris sighed at him darkly. "You know, for a functional mute, you can be incredibly bossy."

Snag didn't respond to the jab, but only continued to level that timeless, disconcerting stare at him.

"All right, *fine*," Eris snarled as he dropped into the chair. "What do you want to know?"

An answering burst of irritation pulsed through their mental connection. *What do you think? Don't be dim*, it said quite clearly.

Eris blinked. It was highly unusual for Snag to communicate so directly, even across mental spheres. It made Eris wonder what Snag was picking up from him that would rock the older vampire so thoroughly.

"I went to go hunt for us," Eris answered aloud. "I'd just found a likely candidate when I felt something... *strange*... happening nearby."

Snag's head cocked to one side by approximately half a millimeter.

"I think it was something across a subconscious mental channel, because I suddenly had the overwhelming sense that I was... needed somewhere else. *Desperately.*"

Eris lifted his gaze from his hands, which were clasped together tightly on the table, and stared at his companion. Snag regarded him closely, but did not communicate further.

He felt another flicker of annoyance. He was having the crisis of the millennium, and here he was, talking to a vampire as old as the hills who had all the emotional range of a wilted turnip. Eris scowled at the impassive face across from him.

Snag made a nearly undetectable motion with his finger—a movement that nonetheless managed to convey the word, *continue*.

Eris sighed again. "I followed the mental pull, and found that a suicide bomber had taken a group of people hostage at a bank. He was clearly insane—he kept yelling at nothing and was obviously experiencing paranoia and hallucinations of some kind. I used mental pressure on him to calm him down, and set about getting the hostages out of the situation. Or... I started to, at least."

Eris paused, trying to gather his thoughts into something a bit less tangled.

"Everything seemed to be under control, more or less, so I reached down and gave one of the hostages a hand up—a woman who had been crouched on the floor nearby. When our skin touched, it was like being struck by lightning." He swallowed hard. "Snag, it was

Phaidra. I met the reincarnation of my soulmate to-night."

Snag, who had not moved or made any sign during the speech, gave Eris a look that plainly said, "No, really?"

A perfect replay of Eris' reaction the moment his hand had touched the woman's was shoved squarely into his consciousness, every bit as shocking now as it had been the first time. The only difference was the faint hint of someone else's asperity lurking beneath the memory.

Oh, Eris realized, with a hint of sheepishness. *I guess I must have been projecting my thoughts... just a bit. Oops.*

At which point, something occurred to him, and he frowned.

"Wait. You sensed all that and *didn't come to my aid*?" he asked, nettled. Snag simply looked back at him, blinking slowly.

Eris raised his eyebrows, trying to prompt him into speech, but—shock of shocks—nothing happened.

"Stubborn bastard," he finally muttered under his breath, before continuing in a louder voice. "Anyway, she ran off in the confusion. I tried to find her afterward, but had no luck."

Snag rose and crossed to the open, west-facing window, still in the shadow of the building as night gave way to morning. He closed it with a single, precise movement and gazed out across the city, tapping the glass thoughtfully with his finger. Putting aside his earlier irritation, Eris joined him, and the two of them stood silently side-by-side as the city outside woke.

Despite his best efforts, Eris found himself grateful that the other vampire was here. For reasons that were fairly obvious, Snag was an excellent listener, for all that his skills as a purveyor of emotional support left something to be desired. And, despite his lack of action the previous evening, his immense power made him invaluable in a crisis. If he had not raced to Eris' side, it was clearly because he believed that Eris could handle the situation without help or interference.

Eris supposed he should be flattered. Or something. But still —

"I don't know what to do now, Snag," he murmured, his breath fogging up the glass. "I have to find her before Bael does. He's coming. I can feel it."

Snag twitched restlessly. His bony ribcage expanded and contracted in a sigh.

"What?" Eris demanded. "Damn it, Snag. *What?*"

Danger. The word floated across his mind's eye, borne along the mental link that connected the two of them. *For both of you.*

Eris knew that Snag was thinking about the connection between Tré and Della, which had nearly caused such catastrophic consequences for both of them. For them all.

"It won't be like that," he said, not sure which of them he was trying to convince. "This is completely different. We know what we're facing now."

Snag gave him a look. The memory of Tré with an iron dagger lodged in his heart flashed before his eyes.

Eris sighed in exasperation. "*It's different,*" he insisted mulishly. "Things will be fine. I just have to *find her.*"

But, deep in his divided soul, Eris knew better. The vortex of chaos was already surrounding his beloved, and Bael's forces would not be far behind.

"Do you think that Bael's out there, right now?" Eris asked, jerking his chin toward the window, and the city beyond.

Snag didn't answer as he closed his eyes and breathed out deeply. All at once, Eris felt the ancient vampire's power wash over him, crashing through his mind and past him like a wave, expanding in all directions.

Though he probably shouldn't have been, Eris was staggered by the force he could feel surrounding him, penetrating him, filling him up. It was as though Snag's mind had pressed outward, encompassing the entire city like a storm cloud.

Eris stayed perfectly still and silent, aware that his every thought and movement would assault Snag's senses as he scanned the area around them. He could feel the power ebbing and flowing in his mind, at times a low thrum, and at others a blazing heat. Taken unawares by a particularly powerful wave, he swallowed a gasp, trying to stay upright under the immense pressure he could feel pressing down on him.

With a sensation like a sharp wind pulling the breath from his lungs, Snag's power receded, leaving Eris feeling shaky and disoriented in its wake. A sense of foreboding, deep and wide as the ocean, brushed his mind, and he knew that Snag had sensed Bael's power nearby.

Unable to speak, Eris turned away. Turned his thoughts inward. Tried to organize the facts he knew into something coherent and actionable.

Fact. This woman is my soul mate. Phaidra, reborn. He felt that this was a solid point. Unassailable.

A vortex of Bael's evil is already forming around her. It wasn't random that she was caught up in a madman's hostage standoff. This, also, seemed a solid truth.

It will only get worse. And if Della's experience was any indication, it will do so quickly.

How could he reach her before Bael did? She'd seemed to vanish off the face of the Earth in the moment between one breath and the next. How could he protect her and explain things to her, when he understood so little himself?

These pressing questions—all without good answers—circled through Eris' mind as the sun rose, bathing Nicosia in a golden glow beyond the shelter of the shadowed hotel room. His skin prickled, and he let the heavy drapes fall back, obscuring the light.

FOUR

Holed up in her low-end hotel room, Trynn spent what was left of the night downloading information from the miniaturized recording equipment that she had worn to the bank. A small pin at her collar, which matched the color of her blouse, was specifically chosen as the means of concealing a camera. The tiny lens looked like a small stone inlaid within the design.

Trynn had not yet been able to wrap her brain around exactly what had happened to her that evening. The entire chain of events was foggy and unfocused. It seemed strange and befuddling, as if it had happened to someone else who had simply described it to her. Her reason tried valiantly to catch up with her impressions, but try as she might, she was unable to reconcile what she knew must have happened logically with what her shocked heart insisted had happened.

All she knew for sure was that the man who had rescued them — the Hot Hypnotist, as she had taken to calling him in her mind — had touched her hand, and something amazing had happened. Even though she'd been terrified and exhausted at the time, Trynn had experienced a swooping sensation in her stomach just as a soul-deep jolt electrified her. For a brief moment, then, her panic had completely faded, and she could think of nothing else but her rescuer.

It was as though her heart was screaming a message about the man, but her mind couldn't interpret it. By the astonished look on his face, she thought he might have felt something similar. Or, Trynn thought wryly, he could have simply been reacting to her hand jerking in his. It was hard to tell.

Well, what you don't understand, you research, Trynn thought. She had never yet been stumped by a mystery, and she was not about to start dabbling in failure now.

She had already pulled a picture of the Hot Hypnotist off the camera pin, and was currently running it through facial recognition software that she had hacked from a government agency in the US, as a part of a security recon mission she'd been assigned. Of course, it was strictly illegal that she had kept the program after the job was over, but she felt that it was the least the Americans could do after she discovered the huge flaw in their security system.

It's like a payment, she justified to herself. *A tip for excellent service. Besides, it's not as though I use it for evil purposes. I'm simply trying to track down the man that saved me. Us. That saved us.*

Unfortunately, the program had failed her so far. But Trynn wasn't giving up. Not by a long shot. There were hundreds of thousands, perhaps millions of faces to trawl through. Dredging up his identity was not a task her small laptop could manage in just a few minutes.

Not unless I can narrow the search parameters, anyway, she thought. *That would cut down the possibilities by thousands of people. But how? What criteria would I need to impose?*

Her fingers hovered over her keyboard for a moment while she thought to herself. It felt like her brain, which was so usually sharp and quick-thinking, was trying to dredge through an oily sludge of exhaustion that had filled her up after the attack at the bank.

No time for that. Come on, come on, think!

With a sigh, Trynn got up and went into the pathetic little bathroom. She splashed some cool water on her face, trying to dispel the anxiety that had her heart thrumming in her ribcage. She dabbed her skin dry with a towel before hiding her face in the scratchy fabric for a few moments.

The threadbare excuse for a towel was one of the handful of *amenities* this shithole had to offer, yet she was grateful for the place. The employees had accepted her reservation without even checking her ID, which, of course, was fake anyway. It was still nice to know that they were turning a blind eye.

Through her company, which had sanctioned clearance with all the top government agencies, she was issued a letter giving permission to use fake identification. So far, though, her ID had never been questioned, which was pure luck —

Trynn nearly dropped the towel in shock. Travel! *That* was the answer to her question. She could find the man's identity by searching through recent travel logs and comparing his face to security footage at the major carriers.

Hurrying back to her computer, Trynn flopped down in the rickety chair facing her desk and began to type.

I must be out of it, if I didn't think of that before. Based on the rich tourist chic *thing he had going on, he wasn't from around here. He probably flew in recently. Maybe from Greece.*

Shaking her head at her own slowness, Trynn organized the search data to scan through security footage and passport images first, then resume its scanning of the entire database. Once the computer was again rifling through thousands of gigabytes of data, Trynn sat back in her chair, swinging one foot petulantly back and forth as she considered her options.

His eyes itched and stung with exhaustion. She knew that she needed to sleep, and very soon. Her mind was racing out of control, both from the trauma of what had happened a few hours ago, and, she suspected, from lack of sleep.

After efficiently preparing for bed, Trynn crawled under the covers and settled against the flattened pillows. Through the darkness in her room, she could see a flickering glow as her computer continued to scan through documents. The clock on the bedside table read 4:45am.

Groaning, Trynn closed her eyes and tried to sleep. She struggled for what felt like an eternity, because every time she started to drift off, her body would jerk her awake to resume reliving the horrid memories or begin contemplating her mystery man.

When she finally slipped into a fitful doze, Trynn dreamt of sand and the sound of soft waves crashing on a nearby shore.

-o-o-o-

In the dream, her surroundings materialized around her from a gray haze, and she found that she was on a beach at night. Though part of her was surprised, another part of her was happy. Excited, even. She laughed joyously and stared upward towards the bright moon that bathed her in its pale light.

A hand slipped into hers and she looked to her left, where a tall figure loomed in the darkness. The man lifted his face, and she recognized his handsome features in the silver light of the moon. For a moment, she couldn't remember where she had seen him before, but her confusion didn't last long as he grinned at her and spoke.

"Victory is ours at last, my love," he said. "Flavian agreed to the shipping contract without altering a single one of the terms. We're well and truly rich now, and we won't ever have to worry again."

Trynn swung around so that her arms were draped around the man's neck and shoulders. She drew him into a deep kiss, her skin tingling and heating with excitement as he returned it with obvious enthusiasm.

As his hands smoothed over her shoulders, she realized that she was dressed oddly, her body draped artfully in an elaborate toga. Part of her accepted this without question, but again, a part of her was confused. It was uncomfortable, as though she were being pulled into two pieces, one part clearly belonging in this world, and the other that was equally out of place and bewildered by it.

The man picked her up and swung her around in glee, her feet flying out behind her. Giggling madly, the two collapsed into the sand, which felt cool underneath her. Wrapped in his arms, Trynn grinned as he rolled himself on top of her, settling between her legs. Her dress was wrapped around them, keeping their bodies pressed closely together.

She could feel the sea washing up against her feet, soaking the bottom of her skirts. Neither part of her cared, however — both of her separate halves were too enthralled by the sensation of the long, lean body pressed against hers.

-o-o-o-

His touch was intoxicating, and she wanted to bask in the sensation even as her consciousness began to slip away from the dream world and rise back toward wakefulness. She groaned in discontent as her mind pulled her out of fantasy and into reality. A reality of musty sheets, mashed, lumpy pillows, and a dark, dreary hotel room that was distinctly unwelcoming after the delightful warmth and sea breeze within the dream.

Trynn jerked upright, swearing under her breath, feeling the unpleasant tackiness of the cooling sweat that drenched her entire body like seawater.

FIVE

Clouds of Turkish cigarette smoke hung in the air. The clink of glasses crashing together or being smacked heavily down on tables seemed unnaturally loud and irritating to the man sitting at the far end of the bar, shrouded in shadows. He was wearing a long, heavy coat with the collar pulled up, the folds of thick fabric hiding the well-tailored lines of the black suit that clung to his muscular frame.

With a sigh, he swiveled a glass of top-shelf whiskey under his hand, ignoring the suspicious looks the bartender kept throwing him. A babble of voices in several languages surrounded him like the buzzing of insects, tiresome and meaningless. This shithole bar in the ass-end of Damascus was well placed to host unscrupulous meetings, situated off the beaten path as it was.

"You need another?" The bartender grunted, glancing down at Bastian Kovac's nearly empty glass.

In reply, Bastian rapped his knuckles on the top of the counter without looking up. He was wearing reflective sunglasses despite the dim lighting inside the bar. He knew that secrecy would be his greatest challenge on this mission. Maintaining a shroud of mystery around his identity would keep his contact off balance during the negotiations.

Bastian was a master of using fear and hopelessness against people, and this pathetic arms dealer from Stalingrad would be no different.

Information he had received from a faithful contact told him that this man, Matvei Timur, was highly placed in the Russian mob. Timur was renowned for his brutality, destructiveness, and, perhaps more importantly, his untouchability. Neither his fellow mobsters nor the Russian government had ever been able to lay a finger on him.

Bastian let a smirk curl one corner of his lips. There was no power on this earth that could contend with the darkness now descending on the weak and subservient humans… at least, no power *created by man*. Other than his temporary usefulness, this arms dealer was no different from any of the other pitiful beings crawling around in the mud of this world. Bastian would twist him and bend him to his will as though he were made of soft putty.

A glass slid across the counter towards him and he grabbed it. As he lifted it to his lips and swiftly tipped it back, a form moved next to him in the semi-darkness, taking the chair immediately on Bastian's left.

Bastian held back a flicker of annoyance as a man laid his elbows on the counter, taking up more space than he needed to as he requested a drink.

"Are you Kovac?" The man asked, once the bartender had taken his order. His Russian accent was thick and heavy, leaving no doubt in Bastian's mind with whom he was dealing. He nodded once, not even bothering to look up from the dregs of his whisky, wanting to make it evident to the man that he, and he alone, held the power in this transaction.

Timur seemed to be waiting for Bastian to speak for several long moments. When Bastian did not oblige, he shifted uncomfortably.

"I have heard," he finally said, "that you are in the market."

Bastian lifted an eyebrow and let it drop, neither confirming nor denying the man's inquiry. Timur watched Bastian for several more moments before saying, "I may have what you are seeking, but you will have to pay a fair price for it."

Taking his time in answering, Bastian pressed out, expanding the malevolent aura that he knew surrounded him, reveling in the involuntary shudder that Timur attempted to hide.

"Where are your men?" Bastian asked, his voice a low growl that nonetheless carried straight to Timur.

"My men?" the mobster replied. "What men?"

"You did not come alone and probably have someone planted in this bar. I will not ask you again, where are your men?"

Timur swallowed hard, but his expression was angry. "I don't see how that is—"

With lightening quick reflexes, Bastian slapped his hand down on Timur's arm. He did not press or hold, but kept the contact between them as he forced his power into Timur's arm, deep into his bones.

The man began to struggle as the taint of Bastian's evil traveled up through his elbow and into his shoulder. Bastian watched with sick enjoyment as it became ever more intense... watched Timur squirm and attempt to pull away, beads of sweat breaking out on his head. From the corner of his eye, Bastian saw a man lounging against the wall twitch, his hand wandering toward an inner pocket. Another man seated at a table nearby straightened almost imperceptibly—the answer to his question about Timur's guards.

"You will cooperate with me, or this deal is off. Have I made myself clear?" Bastian said, the words barely audible over the voices and rowdy laughter from elsewhere in the bar.

The Russian tried to pull away, but was unable to sever the connection between them. Bastian saw the moment the fight went out of him. He slumped and nodded frantically, a burst of air escaping his lungs in relief when he was released. Immediately, he grasped his arm and wrapped it close against his stomach.

"You are either very brave or very foolish," Timur snarled, looking furious now that he was free, but also afraid. "Perhaps I will change my mind about this deal and withdraw it. You sit here smelling like a cheap cologne factory and making demands of me! Threatening me! You—you have a very inflated opinion of yourself if you think you can control Matvei Timur!"

Bastian did not reply to the man's tirade, but simply returned to his drink. He knew, just as Timur knew, that the deal would proceed. It was too beneficial for the Russian mob for them to back out at the eleventh hour.

"Let's not hear of such talk so early in the conversation," he said silkily. "I harbor no ill will, Timur. Perhaps you would be interested in hearing my other proposition before you make your final decision?"

Timur remained silent and wary, but did not rise to leave.

Bastian didn't allow the smile to reach his lips as he continued, "I operate a... business, of sorts, in Belarus. It might be of interest to you."

"Interest to me?" Timur demanded in a sullen voice. "You speak in circles. It was interest in your business that landed me here in the first place."

Bastian let a slow grin develop. "This would be more along the lines of leisure time for you and your men, rather than being *strictly* about profit margins. Consider it a token of my gratitude. Something I will add to sweeten the deal, if you will."

Timur raised a heavy eyebrow, looking intrigued almost despite himself.

Bastian took another drink, raking his eyes over Timur for a long moment. "I can give you all you need to indulge your more... animalistic instincts. Everything necessary to fulfill the wildest fantasies of your most perverted men." He lingered over the words, savoring them.

Timur's face cleared with understanding. "Ah, yes. I see. Women?"

Bastian nodded coldly. "Women. Men. Boys. Girls. Whatever you need. They have long ago learned the price of disobedience; you will have no problem controlling them."

Timur's face flushed and his eyes grew hungry, the eager light in them plain, even through the darkness.

"Girls?" he asked, leaning forward and dropping his voice.

"Their beauty and innocence is incomparable. I only take the best."

The Russian sat back, stroking his graying beard and surveying Bastian thoughtfully. "You are a difficult man to understand, Mr. Kovac. You prey upon pain and pleasure in the same meeting? What am I to understand from this?"

Bastian allowed inhuman intensity to fill his voice, making it smooth as oil and dark as night. "What are you to understand? That you have *no idea* who you are dealing with."

The sentence hung heavily in the air between them as Timur continued to stare at Bastian, clearly apprehensive.

"What are you proposing? Precisely?" he finally asked Bastian. "What type of... *merchandise*... do you need? Your initial messages were oddly unspecific on that point."

"That is because I needed first to discover whether you were a trustworthy man," Bastian replied easily. "I need something very specific. Something sophisticated, uncommon, and easily transported."

"Biochemical?"

Bastian's eyes narrowed. "Am I a cut-rate terrorist looking to give his enemies a stomach ache? Think bigger, Timur. What could I want from the Russian mob that I could not get more easily elsewhere?"

Timur cocked his head for a moment before his expression cleared in understanding. Avarice lit his eyes. "Ah. Now I understand you, I think. Yes. I have access to what you need. Six devices that can be carried in a backpack by any relatively fit man."

It was Bastian's turn to look hungry. "That," he said, "is *exactly* what I need."

"It will cost you," Timur warned.

Bastian waved a careless hand. "Money is no object. I will provide you and your men access to my... *business* in Belarus, and pay you ten million American dollars for each device."

Timur looked as if he were going to argue for a moment, but decided better of it. "Those had better be some truly exquisite girls, Kovac."

"You will not be disappointed."

They shook hands warily—Timur cringing a bit at the cold clamminess of Bastian's skin—and agreed to meet again the following day to make arrangements for the devices to be transferred. Bastian departed feeling triumphant.

As he passed out of a side door to the alley running beside the dilapidated bar, he felt a shadow loom over him. Within moments, it settled into a dense cloud that surrounded him, smothering him in cold, clinging vapor.

He fell to his knees, opening his palms skyward and waited. The power infusing itself into his surroundings pulsed and throbbed, going from cold to hot, heating Bastian from his core. The cologne that he wore to disguise the putrid smell of rotting flesh steamed away as the demon Bael entered his body, coiling through his awareness to read the thoughts of his best lieutenant, his servant, his greatest creation.

You have done well, my faithful one, a voice murmured in his ear. Bastian could feel the demon's breath sliding like black oil down his neck and back. He reveled in it, wallowing blissfully in the strength and awesome power of evil.

"Yes, my master."

Death surrounded him. He could sense the reek of it rising up from earth, centuries of filth and decay filtering up through the cracked pavement of the alley, swirling around them as Bael lavished praise upon his head.

You will use those tools to usher in my kingdom, and bring back the darkness from which we have been cast.

Bastian breathed in the stench, allowing it to fill him and burn like glowing lava inside his empty frame.

"Yes." He exhaled, feeling clarity settling over him. "I will destroy the humans and bring terror and chaos where there was once love and light. You will be avenged, and I will sit at your right hand forever — your most devoted servant."

Bring about my reign, dog. Nothing else matters to you, Bael commanded harshly. *Seek not your own glory or dominion, for I am your creator, and you will always bow to me. You are but a speck of dirt on the ground, animated only by my power.*

Bastian dipped his head, feeling a horrible weight press down on him. "Yes, my master."

The weight lifted incrementally. *Before my final triumph can come to fruition, dog, I have sensed a great danger which we must face, and soon.*

"Master?"

Another of the failed six is approaching his fated mate. They must not be allowed to come together.

Bastian remained silent, sensing his master's discontent. He had learned the hard way the price of interrupting Bael. After several moments of silence, however, Bastian tentatively spoke. "How do you wish me to proceed, master? Should I find the bitch?"

Bael did not answer, but Bastian could still sense his looming presence.

"I could destroy her for you," he whispered, shivering with pleasure at the thought. His knees were pressing hard into the cracked and filthy pavement, growing damp with the sickly dew that had descended all around him. "I could break her mind and body under torture, and demolish every last memory of the vampire she so foolishly loved."

No, Bael said, so sharply that Bastian jerked in surprise. *No, we shall wait. She is near. And she will draw one of the abominations straight to us.*

"To us?"

Her mate will come, but we will be waiting. When the vampire is in our trap, we will find out what he knows, and destroy him. His cursed half-life will collapse around him like a house of cards.

Bastian nodded submissively and touched his fingers to his forehead. "It will be as you say it will be."

Yes. It shall. Go now, dog, and bring forth my kingdom.

SIX

Trynn sat up slowly in bed, wiping her brow with trembling fingers. The dream had been so vivid, it was as though she had stepped through a doorway leading back in time, to a different life that was every bit as much *hers* as this dingy hotel room.

Rather than try to make sense of something so fundamentally nonsensical, she shook herself awake and turned her attention to the single greatest comfort in her life. *Work.*

Padding across the room in her socks, Trynn sat down at the desk and rubbed her finger over her computer's track pad to wake it from power-saving mode. She looked at the screen and sucked in a breath. While she'd slept, it appeared that the facial recognition software had found a match.

"What happened to my notification alert, damn it?" Trynn murmured, since the buzzer had failed to wake her out of the seductive darkness of her dreams. She could tell that it had gone off, though, as the alert was still showing on her computer.

Sighing in frustration, Trynn reviewed the search results. It seemed that her Hot Hypnotist had indeed arrived in Cyprus via plane a few days ago. The date stamp on the security footage noted that he had arrived at approximately eleven o' clock at night, three days previously. Curiously, there was no security footage from the city of Cyprus during the day. His face was only captured after dark, under the glare of a streetlight near the exclusive Merit Lefkosa Hotel.

He could be staying there, she thought. *I wish I could find a more definite picture of him either entering or leaving, though. Seems like this guy is a bit of a recluse and a night owl, when he's not busy swooping in to save the day like some kind of mild-mannered, khaki-wearing superhero.*

Still, Trynn wasn't overly bothered by this. She, too, felt more comfortable moving around outside after nightfall. The bright sun had always hurt her eyes and made her feel overly hot in her pantsuits and sleek, tailored dresses.

She knew with complete certainty that she wasn't going to be able to let this rest without digging further. With a sigh, she picked up her cell phone. Her boss was on speed dial, and she tapped the button with a feeling of trepidation.

"Mandy?" Trynn asked in a quiet voice as soon as she heard the bark of the bossy voice on the other end. "Yeah, it's Trynn. Look, I finished up my job at the Hellenic Bank here in Nicosia, but there was, uh… an *incident.*"

There was a pause on the other end of the line *"Wait. You had an incident? Tell me you didn't break your record of not having to talk your way out of a security detainment. I had a bet down that you'd last another six months!"*

"Er, not exactly…" Trynn replied, the words emerging with uncharacteristic hesitation. Despite her determination to stay collected and professional during the call to her boss, Trynn felt unwanted emotion well up as she remembered the hours of terror she had endured in the bank lobby.

Apparently her silence communicated more than her words because Mandy spoke in an anxious voice. *"Trynn. What happened? Talk to me."*

Trynn swallowed several times, trying to keep her voice steady. "I went into the bank, launched my cyber-attack, tagged the target accounts, and got out of the system clean. There was nothing triggered by my hacking.

As I was trying to leave, though, I walked out into the lobby right into the middle of a... of a fucking *hostage situation.*"

"*A what?*" Mandy's voice rose in pitch.

"Yeah, you heard me right. Some guy was standing there with a bomb strapped to his chest. He was completely out of his mind and he grabbed me before I could get out the door."

"*Oh my God, Trynn! Are you okay?*"

Trynn paused again. She was not sure there was a word that described the horrible sensation clawing its way up her chest or the swirl of emotions that was making it feel like she couldn't breathe.

"Yeah, um. Not great, I guess," she finally admitted. "I mean, I'm not really hurt or anything, but—"

She could tell Mandy had fallen effortlessly into Awesome Boss Crisis Mode.

"*What do you need?*" the older woman asked. "*How did you get away? Did the police catch the guy? Do you need me to fly out there?*"

Trynn's head was spinning under the barrage of questions. She sat down heavily on the bed, dropping her head into her hand as she pressed the phone to her ear. "No, look. I'm fine, really Mandy."

"*Is that right? Because you sound like hell.*"

Trynn rubbed her brow, unable to hold back a weak snort of amusement. "Okay, okay. I'm not my best, but I don't need you to come flying out here or anything. I just need..."

Her voice trailed away again. What did she need? Sleep? Alcohol?

The last option sounded pretty appealing at the moment, but she wasn't about to tell her boss that she wanted to go on a major binge-drinking episode. And anyway, that really wasn't her style. She'd probably pass out from exhaustion after the third shot of tequila and get hauled off to the drunk tank.

Finally, she settled on a thought. "I think I just need some time off."

Mandy didn't even hesitate. *"Done. I'll smooth it over with the higher-ups due to the traumatic situation. Do you need to talk about it with someone? You probably should, you know. We have an employee assistance program you can access, if you need it."*

She took a deep breath and let it out, feeling her clamoring nerves start to quiet a bit. "I think I'm okay. Honestly, right now I'm trying to track down the man who saved us. I need to talk to him."

"How did you get out of there, anyway?" Mandy asked.

Trynn really didn't feel like going into detail, but she knew she owed Mandy at least a basic explanation. "A guy came in and convinced the suicide bomber to give up, which gave us all time to escape. I don't know what happened after that—I ran straight out the door and didn't look back."

She heard Mandy blow out a breath. *"Did you give your statement to the police?"*

"No, I ran through the barricade. Someone tried to stop me, I think, but I shook him off. I guess they had other things to worry about at the time."

Trynn could tell by Mandy's hesitation that she did not approve, but didn't want to push the issue, either.

"Under the circumstances, they probably understood," she assured Trynn in a quiet voice. *"Look, Trynn. Please don't hesitate to call if you need something. Take as much time as you need."*

A lump rose in Trynn's throat, but she swallowed it. "Thank you, Mandy. I think I'll be okay with just a few days."

"Good luck with the search for your rescuer," Mandy said kindly. *"If you need any help with that, I'd be glad to lend a hand."*

Trynn smiled, feeling better now than she had a few minutes ago. She was truly grateful, at times like these, to have such a wonderful boss. "All right. I'll let you know how it goes."

She ended the phone call and set her cell phone down on the bed next to her. Leaning back on her hands, she stared blankly at the ceiling, lost in thought for several moments.

I have to talk to him. I might be crazy, but I have to try to understand what happened when our hands touched.

Straightening abruptly, Trynn climbed to her feet and marched to the tiny bathroom, shedding clothes along the way. In the shower, she tried to wash away the memories of the traumatic events, scrubbing at her skin, which was tight and itchy with dried sweat. Afterward, she toweled her hair dry and applied enough make-up to hide the bags under her eyes and the pale cast of her face. Stepping back out into her room, she surveyed her supplies carefully, trying to take stock of what she had available.

She threw on a nice outfit and packed her bag with her laptop and several electrical devices that were basically props. They looked impressive to the untrained eye, but she never actually used them.

Outside, the sun beat down on her head. As it always did, her body grew uncomfortably warm within minutes. Normally, she hated the overheated feeling, but today she felt like it was thawing out a part of her that had gone icy and cold while trapped in the lobby of the bank.

Banishing that thought, she turned her attention to the unofficial infiltration mission before her. A short cab ride later, Trynn was standing outside the grand entrance of the Merit Lefkosa hotel. She checked her reflection in the dark glass before stepping confidently into the building, nodding politely to the bellhop.

"Can I help you, miss?" a young man with wavy black hair asked from his station behind the massive front desk. His suit and tie were crisp, and his nametag read *Adrien*.

"Yes, I got a call about a server problem?" Trynn replied in a tone caught somewhere between boredom and professionalism.

Adrien's face wrinkled in confusion. "Miss?"

She let silence hang for a beat. "A server? You know, that thing that you log into on your computer," she answered with a faint note of derision, trying to put the young man on edge. To further illustrate her point, she gestured towards his computer. "I'm here to fix it."

The kid — *was he even twenty?* — looked down at the screen, then back up at Trynn. "I'm showing no errors with the computer, miss, and I can't let you past the lobby with our new security protocol."

Trynn sighed aloud. "It's only a partial outage. I need to assess the locations to figure out why your bosses are suddenly looking at kill screens and their RAM is being depleted, which, in turn, is bogging down the entire operating system."

Her voice was laced with annoyance, and she spoke slowly, as if addressing a small child. It was clear to her that this individual knew very little about computers, as his face flushed and he looked uncomfortable.

"I have clear instructions..." he said into the growing awkwardness.

"Fine," Trynn snapped, spinning on her heel. "Look, I don't get paid enough to deal with this kind of bureaucratic miscommunication and incompetence. If you're not going to let me look at the server, then why did you call me all the way out here for nothing? I'll just leave, and let you deal with the fallout. If this turns into a system-wide problem, it's likely everything will crash. Good luck dealing with your *security protocols* when all the electronic locks on the room doors suddenly pop open at once."

She made it about ten paces before the desk clerk caught up with her.

"Wait!" he said breathlessly. "Wait, I'll let you see our operations room, just let me get a copy of your ID first, please."

Trynn turned back with a put-upon sigh and passed him her fake identification. They returned to the desk, and she tapped her fingernails on the top of the marble counter in a bored rhythm as he copied the ID and scanned it into the system.

"Sorry about the confusion," the hotel clerk muttered, sliding her card back across the counter to her. "We've just been under a lot of pressure about security, what with all the crazy things going on recently."

"Yeah, sure. I understand," Trynn said, giving him a half smile. She readjusted her computer bag over her shoulder and followed him down a short hallway and into a room where the hub of the technology in the hotel was located.

"Please let me know if you need anything further," he said, looking eager to get away from her.

Trynn nodded and made a humming noise, but didn't speak, pretending to look closely at the status screen on a nearby computer.

As soon as the clerk left, Trynn sat down and pulled out her laptop, placing it on the desk in front of her. She connected her computer to the network, and immediately started hacking her way into the guest list.

Overall, she was impressed with the hotel's security system. She really had to pull out all the stops to get in, not a state of affairs that she ran into very often. When she was finally able to access the list and all the IDs that the guests had provided to the front desk, she searched through the hundreds of current hotel customers.

Trynn felt fairly certain she would recognize her rescuer as soon as she saw him, but she couldn't be totally sure. After all, she had been under a significant amount of stress at the bank, not to mention the fact that ID photos were notoriously awful and unflattering.

After roughly ten minutes, though, Trynn found him. His dark hair and five o' clock shadow gave him the look of a scruffy male model, and his eyes, which seemed to meet hers directly through the computer screen, were a startlingly deep chocolate brown.

A fluttering feeling climbed up her chest, and Trynn worked hard to quiet her rapid breathing. He was... *beautiful*. Truly gorgeous. And he had saved her life.

As unlucky as it was to be involved in that situation, she thought, *at least my rescuer was hot as hell.*

Scanning through his file, Trynn discovered that he had checked into the hotel alone a few days previously. His name was Nico Pavlaveous. For some reason, that surprised her. Trynn tried it aloud, and decided that it did not really suit him at all. At the very bottom of the page, she located his room number and committed it to memory.

Without leaving a trace of the breach, Trynn backed carefully out of the system. Logging off required her to enter a new set of credentials, which took time to override.

"God, they've really got this stuff figured out," Trynn muttered. She considered submitting the place for future consultation with her company to ensure they were continuing to maintain the highest level of security. Honestly, it would make a great model for other businesses.

When she was finally able to disconnect her computer without setting off any virtual alarm klaxons, she slipped all of her supplies back into her bag. Thanks to the beleaguered clerk, she had already passed the security checkpoint and simply needed to find room 706 in the west tower.

After searching for a few short minutes, Trynn finally followed a middle-aged woman with salt-and-pepper hair onto an elevator. She smelled like chlorine — the hotel obviously had a pool somewhere. Or possibly several, given the general level of opulence she'd seen so far. Trynn rode the elevator up to the seventh floor, pretending to be busy on her phone rather than having to make small talk with the woman standing next to her.

As soon as the doors slid open, she passed through them and turned quickly down the hall. She felt excitement growing, and the adrenaline rush drove away any vestiges of the horrors from the previous evening. It left a warm glow in her stomach, which wasn't tempered in the least by rational thoughts about the fact that she was going to bang on a complete stranger's hotel room at ten o' clock in the morning and demand that he explain to her why touching his hand had felt like touching a live wire.

Pushing all that aside, Trynn located the correct room and stood outside for a moment. Really, there was nothing stopping her from simply loitering nearby to see if he came out of the room on his own. She shook her head, too impatient to consider waiting, and stepped forward.

I've come this far. I won't back out now.

She rapped her knuckles briskly on the door a few times and stood back, waiting as the moments ticked past.

It's ten o'clock. He's probably out for the day. Damn, maybe I've missed him.

Just as she was starting to turn away, she heard the lock slide back, and the door opened.

There he stood. Her beautiful, gorgeous, brave rescuer, wearing nothing but a pair of pajama bottoms and

the confused, squint-eyed expression of the unexpectedly awakened.

He had clearly been sleeping—his mop of black,
wavy hair was plastered all over his head. This soft, disheveled version of her Hot Hypnotist was a dazzling
sight to behold, and she stared at him, running her eyes
over sleek muscles and smooth skin, words forgotten.

His eyes sharpened and raked over her. She saw
them widen in shock and his mouth fell open. It took a
while for anything to come out. A few moments passed,
and he cleared his throat significantly. When he spoke,
there was a low, gravelly quality to his voice, clearly
from having just woken up.

"What? How?" The stammered monosyllables were
the polar opposite of the glib words he'd used to calm
the bomber the previous night.

Without thinking or hesitating, Trynn lifted a hand
up to his chest and pushed him forcefully backwards
into the room. When the palm of her hand met his skin,
a flash of electricity exploded across her nerves, bouncing from her hand all the way down her body. Hot
pleasure coursed through her veins at the sensation. As
it faded, leaving goose bumps behind, Trynn stepped
closer to him. She had expected him to resist the manhandling, but he was still staring at her, open-mouthed.

"*Who are you*?" she demanded. "I'm not leaving until I get some answers."

-o-o-o-

Eris gaped at the slender, willowy woman with cropped
black hair standing before him. Her brown eyes were
staring at him intently, as if she could pull the truth directly from his fragmented soul.

Suddenly and acutely aware that Snag had been sitting in the chair across the room when he'd opened the
door, Eris moved a step to the side to interrupt her line

of sight. Foreboding rose in his chest at the thought of this woman unexpectedly seeing his companion, whose appearance was so distinctly inhuman.

He threw a quick glance over his shoulder, only to find that the room was now deserted. His relief lasted only an instant before he realized that Snag had abandoned him to have this incredibly awkward conversation without any sort of backup or moral support—*the bastard*. Eris decided then and there that he would give his so-called friend a few extremely choice words when he returned.

His unexpected visitor was still glaring at him, waiting for answers he had no idea how to give. What the hell was he supposed to say to her? How did you even *begin* that kind of conversation?

Eris wished with sudden urgency that he had taken more time to talk to Tré and find out how he broke the news to Della about the events in her past life. Because, face it—there was simply no good way to ease into something like that.

While he was standing, staring at the woman with his mouth partially open, she had stepped back, putting some distance between the two of them.

Suddenly, Eris found that he wanted nothing more than to have her hand back on his chest. He wanted to feel every fiber of his being singing under her touch. He wanted to feel the hair on the back of his neck stand up, to smell the sweet scent of her perfume on his skin.

"I—" he began before breaking off. It was useless, though. How could he possibly explain things to her?

The woman crossed her arms, glaring at him. Without consciously deciding to do so, Eris reached out with his senses and brushed the edges of her mind. He thought that he had used a light enough touch that she wouldn't notice, but she seemed to flinch involuntarily.

"Have you been having strange dreams lately?" he blurted, trying to distract her from the sensation that had stroked across her mind. *Yes, because that's a totally natural conversation starter.*

"Why?" she shot back, looking suspicious.

Eris paused, at a loss as to how to proceed. On the one hand, he didn't want her to think he was crazy. On the other hand, it seemed prudent to start with something that she could relate to. And it was clear by her demanding tone that, yes, she had been having odd dreams. The question was, how could he steer the conversation from dreams to events in real life?

"Have they been about me?" Eris asked cautiously, drawing back into the comforting shadows of the hotel room. *Brilliant. Not strange or creepy at all, Casanova. Maybe it's just as well Snag's not around to witness this masterful performance.*

It was the woman's turn to hesitate. She bit her bottom lip, her gaze sliding uneasily down to her feet. "What does that matter?" she said, obviously having to force her eyes to meet his again. "We were just involved in a major crime. It would only make sense that I dreamed about it."

Eris could tell by the tone of her voice that her dreams—like his—had nothing to do with the incident at the bank.

The woman seemed to think she owed him some kind of further explanation, because she suddenly said, "Look—I came here to thank you for saving my life. My name is Trynn."

"Trynn?" Eris repeated, the name oddly sweet as it fell from his lips. He blinked, trying to center himself. "My name is... Nico."

He held out his hand to her but she did not take it. Instead, she studied him closely, as if appraising him.

"Is that your real name?" she asked. Her voice held no hint of judgment, simply curiosity.

A smile tugged at the corner of his mouth. "No, it's not."

She gave a brief nod. "I didn't think it was. Pity, I was really impressed by the hotel's security earlier."

"You didn't think my name was Nico?" Eris asked, intrigued. "Why is that?"

Trynn considered him for a moment. "I can't put my finger on it, but it doesn't seem to fit you, somehow."

Can't argue with that, can I? He cleared his throat. "Well, you're right. My name is Eris."

"Eris what?" she asked.

"Just Eris."

Trynn resumed her intense scrutiny of his face, her eyes darting back and forth over his features.

"That seems much more like you," she said quietly.

"I'm glad you approve," he retorted, amused. "Is Trynn your real name?"

"Maybe," Trynn said.

"Trynn what?" he asked.

"Just Trynn," she replied.

He huffed a breath of amusement. "Fair enough. So, are you really here just to say thank you?"

Trynn paused. "Yes. Well… among other things."

Ah. Now they were getting somewhere. He hoped. "What other things?"

She took a deep breath as if steeling herself. "I have questions I want answered. The first and most important I already asked you. Who are you?"

Eris frowned. "I already told you, my name is —"

She waved him away impatiently.

"No," she said. "Who *are* you, really? Who are you to me and why do I feel like I've known you my entire life?"

Eris caught his breath and tried to decide how best to proceed with this conversation. Surely *not* with her still standing in the doorway to a room in a very public hotel.

"Please, come inside," he said quietly. "We do need to talk, but I would prefer not to do it with the door open."

A flicker of something like alarm passed across Trynn's face, and he silently cursed himself.

"Sorry, that made me sound like some kind of creeper, didn't it. You don't have to come inside if you're worried about it," Eris said, "but I assure you, I mean you no harm."

"Yeah, I guess you wouldn't, since you already saved my life once," Trynn replied, looking a bit sheepish.

Eris gestured her further inside and offered her the chair that Snag had recently vacated. Trynn sat primly, leaning forward to stare at Eris with an intent gaze. He became suddenly and acutely aware that his chest was bare and his hair was standing on end from having rolled out of bed so suddenly. *Brilliant. Way to make an impression.*

"Will you excuse me for a moment?" he asked, jerking his head towards the bathroom.

Trynn waved him on and curled up in the chair to wait. Eris hurried toward the bathroom, ducking into the sleeping alcove on the way to grab a shirt and trousers from his suitcase.

Once in the bathroom, he splashed some water on his face, still trying to decide how to break the news to this woman that they had been lovers in a previous life, he had become a vampire and killed her, and now her destiny was most likely tangled with his in a complicated and dangerous battle between the forces of good and ill.

Oh yeah, there was no doubt about it. This was going to go down *really well*.

After freshening up and making himself presentable, Eris walked back out into the hotel room to find that Trynn had not moved a muscle.

328

Patient, I like that, he found himself thinking. *Just like Phaidra.*

As his eyes met hers, he felt his heart swell with longing. At that moment, he wanted nothing more than to take her in his arms and kiss her until neither of them cared about the past or the future. He wanted her to feel his devotion, which had started as a spark when their hands touched in the bank lobby, and exploded into flame when she showed up at his door, demanding answers.

Sitting down in the chair across from her, Eris noticed that her eyes followed his every move and her pupils were blown wide. Gods above, this conversation was going to kill him, he was sure. He cleared his throat, and tried to find a place to begin.

"Do you ever feel like you don't really belong in this world?" he asked, echoing something he had heard Della say a few weeks previously.

Trynn's eyebrows drew together, and her eyes narrowed in suspicion. "What is that even supposed to mean? Doesn't everybody feel like that sometimes?"

Eris shrugged and continued, "Maybe so... but do you ever feel specifically like you don't belong here. Like you were made for... someplace else?"

Something like shock flashed across Trynn's face, but she covered it quickly. "That's preposterous, where else would I be?"

"I don't know," Eris answered. He didn't want to dump too many details on her at once, but she had definitely reacted to his words. "Perhaps... not so much another place as another time?"

Trynn was silent for a moment, digesting his words.

"Well... my grandmother always told me I have the soul of a gypsy," she offered, "but I don't know about that."

"You find it hard to stay in one place?"

She nodded. "Yes, that's why I have my current job. I can move from place to place, country to country, and no one even knows my real name."

Eris cocked his head. "Ah. So Trynn *isn't* your real name."

She simply looked at him, poker-faced. They stared at each other for several long minutes before Eris conceded defeat. Intriguing as it was, he knew the little contest of wills was a distraction from his attempt to explain the situation.

"I think I know why you feel that way about traveling," he said.

She continued to look at him, not speaking — making him do the heavy lifting in the conversation. The tactician in him admired her skill at it.

"I think it's possible that you do come from a different time."

Her eyebrows were traveling up her forehead in surprise. "What do you mean by that?"

"Do you believe in reincarnation?" Eris asked, looking at her intently.

Trynn frowned at him, clearly thrown off by the change of subject.

"I—" she stammered. "I... don't really know. It seems to make sense in some ways, I guess, but I'm not particularly religious so I've never given it much thought."

"In what ways does it make sense?"

"Just... my life, you know? Sometimes, I have these incredibly vivid dreams about times long ago. They seem so real," Trynn replied, in the smallest of voices. Something about her tough exterior seemed to have cracked, allowing a small truth — the tiniest admission — to seep out.

He latched onto it. "That's because they're not dreams, Trynn. They're memories. Those things you dream about — when you dream about me — it's *real*."

Her mouth opened and closed a couple of times before words came out. "No. That's impossible. Scientifically, inarguably impossible."

Eris didn't answer; he merely looked into her eyes. He imagined he could see something like the truth dawning there.

"It can't be true," she whispered.

"It can, and it is," he said urgently. "We were both born in the second century A.D. My name was Eris, and your name was Phaidra."

"Phaidra?"

"Yes."

Trynn's head bowed and she stared down at her hands for a moment.

"We were... *collectors*, of sorts," he continued. "We gathered fabulous treasures, sometimes by theft, sometimes by purchase, and we gained immense wealth from doing so. Until—"

Trynn lifted her head, and Eris could sense her quickening heart rate, as if memories were falling into place in her mind. His own heart beat faster in sympathy.

"Until?" she asked, barely a whisper.

"We were... torn apart," Eris said quietly. "Separated by a force of unimaginable evil. You died sacrificing yourself for me, and were reborn—who knows how many times across the millennia. We are soulmates, Trynn, destined to be together."

Eris felt like he was doing a very poor job explaining things, as his words weren't very informational. He grappled with the instinct to touch Trynn, to reaffirm their connection through physical contact, but something told him to remain where he was. Trynn was looking down at her feet again, sitting very quiet and still.

After what felt like an eternity, she looked up and Eris' heart fell at the expression on her face. It was a mixture of horror, skepticism, and open hostility.

"I can't believe I wasted my time trying to find you," she ground out in a low voice. "I thought you were some sort of—I don't know—*hypnotist*, or maybe a shrink or something, the way you were able to calm down that bomber. I thought you were a real hero. Yet here I am, alone with another complete lunatic, wasting precious hours of my life listening to you spin fairy tales about fate and destiny—"

"Trynn," Eris began.

"Shut up!" she interrupted. "*Shut up.* I don't want to hear any more of your lies."

"*I'm not lying.*" Eris could hear the desperation creeping into his voice, and hated it.

"This is completely nuts!" Trynn exploded, sounding angry now. "Reincarnation? Soulmates? The *second century*? You could've at least tried to come up with something believable!"

Frustration surged in Eris' chest and his lips curled back, his eyes glowing gold. "Believable?" he snarled. "This *emptiness* has been my life for two thousand years!"

Trynn scrambled to her feet, horror flooding her face. She backed away from him slowly, heaving unsteady breaths, and he hated himself for the fear he'd awakened in her.

"*I am not lying to you,*" Eris said in a dark, powerful voice. "In all our time together, I never once told you a falsehood. *You are Phaidra, and I am Eris.*"

The words seemed to shake Trynn to her core, and she turned, rushing for the entrance. With speed and reflexes that surprised him, she ripped open the hotel room door and fled down the hallway before Eris could even begin to stop her.

Knowing that it was full daylight outside, Eris had no choice but to let her leave. He could not follow her in any form without risking catastrophic injury under the sun's unforgiving rays.

Fury licked at his damaged soul, and he let out a snarl of frustration as he slammed the door behind her, throwing the hotel room back into semi-darkness. His sensitive eyes, however, picked out every object and color in the room.

As he turned back towards the sleeping alcove, a movement in the shadows caught his attention. Snag stood there impassively, staring at him with deep-set eyes.

"*Back so soon*? Thanks for that. You were a *huge* help," Eris snapped.

Snag did not move or speak. He simply regarded Eris with a thoughtful gaze.

"Why did you abandon me like that?" Eris exploded, feeling his temper pressing outward like a dark cloud. Snag did not flinch in the face of Eris' fury, but remained standing, solid as stone.

"Nothing to say for yourself?" Eris demanded. "Speak, silent one! Now, of all times, would be the perfect chance for you to dispense your *great wisdom*."

Eris allowed a terrible, cutting sarcasm to permeate the words, heedless of the consequences, in the heat of his anger at himself for failing to keep Trynn by his side.

Still, Snag did not reply.

"Fine," Eris snapped. "*Fine!* Don't speak. I have been here for you through thick and thin, I have stayed by your side and forced you to feed when your life was nearly spent. You would be a petrified *husk* right now if it weren't for me. And I have *never* asked anything of you in return, other than your friendship. Today, for the first time ever, I am asking for your help in understanding this mess. Yet you *refuse* to share your thoughts."

Snag merely allowed Eris to rant, pacing back and forth in the generous suite. When it was clear that no sort of response would come from that quarter anytime soon, Eris stormed back over to the bed, ripping his shirt off over his head and flopping down angrily onto the mattress. Without another word, he pulled the blankets up over his shoulder and turned so that he was facing away from Snag. He did not want to see the silent, unmoving outline of the ancient bloodsucker standing there in the dark, watching him.

Oddly, even though whirling thoughts and emotions were chasing themselves around Eris' head, he fell into a deep slumber within moments.

If he had been paying attention to anything other than his own distress, he might have noticed the way Snag was pressing serenity over his thoughts, banishing any painful dreams or recollections of the past. He might have noticed that Snag was giving Eris the peace that he needed to rest and recover from the day's events.

All the while Eris slept, Snag stayed nearby, keeping the darkness at bay and standing watch over his fellow vampire.

SEVEN

The sound of her fingers tapping against the keyboard soothed Trynn's frayed nerves better than anything else might have, as she lost herself in the lines and lines of code she was trying to sort through.

She was distracting herself with a job that had nothing to do with Trajan Security, or with a hot hypnotist who had turned out to be a freaking psycho rather than a hero. There had to be a way to break this encryption so that she could get a fix on her current target's server—there always was. And she needed a location to provide to her hacktivist organization so others could start working on the situation.

Trynn had been using her skills to assist online whistleblowers with locating and exposing dangerous individuals in the private sector for a couple of years now. Her expertise as a hacker had been vital in several projects, although no one in the group knew who she was in the real world. She used an alias and such a powerful, complicated system of encryption that it would take a technological genius to break through the multiple layers of defense with which she had shrouded herself.

Needing to clear her mind after her encounter at the Merit Lefkosa, Trynn had thrown herself into tracking down the identity of a man who was in Damascus attempting to purchase some seriously heavy-duty weaponry. She had intercepted the communications of a suspected Russian mob figure with someone requesting munitions for purchase, but the messages had been maddeningly vague as to exactly what kind of munitions. Her gut was telling her that this was a major deal that needed to be monitored, and she hadn't gotten this far by ignoring her instincts.

Now, though, she was having doubts. Perhaps it was nothing—just one of the hundreds of backroom deals that went on in parts of the world where law and order were more of a distant dream than a reality. Perhaps this transaction would never even come to fruition, or if it did, the weapons would never see the light of day.

Or, *perhaps* it was the situation with the man who called himself Eris that had completely unnerved her and was making her question herself. She scowled, her thoughts once more drawn back to their bizarre conversation despite her best efforts. Trynn had certainly been unable to banish the preposterous notions he'd fed her, wrapped in fantastical tales that were not remotely believable.

Shit like this just doesn't happen, Trynn told herself for the dozenth time, staring straight through her computer screen without seeing it. *A gorgeous man does not just randomly show up in your life, save you from a suicide bomber, and then announce casually that reincarnation is real and that you were once his soulmate centuries ago before you sacrificed your life for him like some sort of lovelorn Romeo and Juliet.*

Trynn shook her head in disgust, a bitter chuckle escaping her throat. *Yeah, right.*

"Insanity," she whispered aloud, trying to keep her mind focused on the task at hand.

It was useless. Eris, with his beautifully chiseled body and sculpted features, kept breaking into her thoughts without her volition.

His mussed hair. His striking eyes. His flat, sexy abs.

Trynn swallowed, feeling heat creeping down her spine. Yet, in one part of her mind, she could not banish the image of him drawing his lips back as his eyes glowed gold.

His fangs. His fucking *fangs*.

Maybe he wasn't the crazy one after all. Maybe *she* was.

There were two possibilities here. Either she hadn't seen what she thought she saw, or... she had. Was she hallucinating? She didn't feel like she was hallucinating. Though, she supposed that was sort of the point. If you knew you were seeing things, you'd know they weren't real. Right?

She knew what the pointed fangs and glowing eyes reminded her of. But... that was nuts.

Her thoughts had carried her down such a ridiculous path that she was staring blankly into space, her warm laptop heating the tops of her thighs as the processor hummed. She scolded herself sharply for even entertaining such nonsense.

He was obviously a delusional mental case who just so happened to also be into playing dress-up. Why else would he just randomly be wearing vampire teeth at ten o'clock in the morning during the middle of summer? And his eyes? Well, maybe the light had just hit them oddly for a moment. That was probably it. If there was one thing for certain, it was that such things didn't really exist in the world.

Feeling more at peace, Trynn settled back to work. Forty minutes later, she finally had a breakthrough in her hacking project. Letting out a heartfelt exclamation of victory, Trynn practically pounced on the keyboard. With the final access key in place, she was able to pull up the account information behind the intercepted message.

The user's name was B. Kovac and his originating IP address was based in Syria. Damascus, to be exact — just as she had suspected.

"Next time, choose a better VPN service, creep," she muttered.

Still, she experienced a twinge of disappointment. This was certainly an important step forward, and one she was going to share with the other hackers in her group, but she could have guessed all but the man's name from the info they already had. Feeling let down, Trynn tried to work backwards and find more information regarding the recent communications and movements of the seller involved in the illegal deal, rather than the buyer.

After another two hours of digging, Trynn confirmed that Kovac was attempting to purchase something from a known Russian mob figure. Trynn had originally recognized the man's name from an international crime bulletin that she received occasionally from one of her former clients. Now, she was sure it wasn't a mistake or a case of similar names. The mystery man, Kovac, was dealing with Matvei Timur, an infamous arms dealer who had access to some of the worst weapons humanity had to offer.

As she carefully translated the most recent email she'd plucked from his server, an uneasy sensation gripped her stomach. Trynn quickly hopped onto Internet Relay Chat — a hub for hackers trying to find something to do with their time. Trynn was a member of MASQUE; a group whose aims were largely to dismantle powerful trade rings within the black market, most of which were run by people that law enforcement would consider to be respectable and above reproach.

Hell, some of them *were* respectable — on the outside, at least. And some of them were power-hungry maniacs with no scruples or redeeming characteristics whatsoever.

Trynn wondered with some trepidation where B. Kovac fell on that spectrum.

Connected now, she typed out a quick message to relay what she had discovered about Kovac. She noted that she was going to continue working on intercepting messages between the two parties. Taking a deep breath, she outlined the contents of the last email and asked if it implied what she thought it implied.

Several other people chimed in, confirming her fears. After a few more exchanges, most of them encouraged Trynn to continue hunting this person in hopes of discovering what he was going to do next. One of the hackers who seemed to know what they were talking about when it came to the last email offered to take the information to the US government.

Trynn agreed and signed off. The sick feeling remained, though. These days, governments across the world were too busy trying to maintain basic order in the streets to follow up every unsubstantiated lead that came their way.

Exhaustion was pulling at her now, after the brief flush of excitement over what she'd found. It felt like her eyelids were being dragged closed and her fingers had minds of their own as they stumbled over the keyboard. After jerking herself awake twice from dozing off with her neck at an uncomfortable angle, Trynn gave up and shut down the system, wanting nothing more than the lumpy mattress on her rented bed.

She stood, stretching her back and looking at her reflection in the mirror over the beat-up dresser. Huge dark circles were smeared beneath her eyes, and she gazed at them in disgust.

Am I ever going to look and feel like myself again? Maybe it's a good thing that nothing happened with the hot, crazy guy—he'd've be frightened off as soon as he saw me without make-up. Christ.

Hoping that she just needed more sleep than she'd been getting, Trynn walked into the bathroom and washed her face. Feeling a bit more refreshed, she finished getting ready for bed and slipped out of the bathroom.

Even in a place as unfamiliar and uninspiring as this cheap hotel room, crawling into bed felt like being wrapped in a warm cocoon. Immediately, Trynn began to drift off, sinking effortlessly into a dream that both soothed her, and heated her flesh from the inside out.

-o-o-o-

A gentle hand caressed her face, and a fingertip traced over her lips. In a flash, she darted her tongue out of her mouth, tasting salt on callused skin and drawing it inside. A moan of longing reached her ears, and she smiled around the finger.

As she languidly opened her eyes, the world again seemed to solidify around her. The light was dim, with a reddish tint. She could see drapes and hangings all around the room, covering whitewashed stone. Eris' face swam before her vision, banked fire smoldering deep in his eyes. He was leaning over her, pressing her down into the deep bedding all around her.

Placing a hand down on the bed, Trynn pushed her fingers into the cool, soft fabric.

"Phaidra, my love," Eris' soft voice whispered in her ear, trailing the finger over her chin and down the tender column of her throat. "How is it that you grow more beautiful to me every day? When we are both old and gray, I will be unable to even look upon your face, for fear that your radiance will blind me."

She turned her gaze back to him, just in time for his mouth to capture hers in a passionate kiss. Her head spun and she could taste wine on his lips. As his hands found her waist, she could feel him press deeper and settle hotly between her legs.

Trynn arched her back, trying to get him closer. His hands moved to hers, their fingers intertwining. He slid their joined hands upwards, so that her arms were pinned above her head as he continued to plunder her lips with his own.

He was like a drowning man offered air, the way he seemed to drink in her moans and sighs. Desire so intense it drove out every other thought flooded her, and beads of sweat broke out across her skin. Eris mouthed his way down her neck and then kissed each of her collarbones before dragging his tongue up to recapture her mouth.

Murmuring his name on the back of a broken sigh, Trynn tried to free her hands so she could grab his hips and pull him into her, but Eris resisted the movement. They wrestled each other for a moment — an uneven contest if ever there was one — before Trynn gave up with a breathless laugh.

"You whisper sweet words in my ear one moment, only to torture and deprive me the next," she accused, her eyes twinkling.

The slow smile that tugged at his lips made new heat flood her belly. "You love it," he shot back, with a careless shrug of one shoulder. His confidence was infectious as he stared down at her — a playful, well-fed lion, toying with its prey.

The heat of their bodies warmed the furs and blanket around them. Just as Eris shifted both of her wrists to one hand, freeing the other to slide her long, draped skirts up her legs, Trynn felt her mind drifting. She could see him, his eyebrows furrowed in concentration, but she could also feel the scratchy sheets from her hotel bed.

-o-o-o-

No, no, I want to stay, she thought desperately.

It was no good. A moment later, she opened her eyes to darkness and solitude. Her heart was pounding hard and fast, and sweat beaded her brow. The complete silence was broken only by shuffling from someone moving around in the room above hers. Snapping back to reality, Trynn groaned and threw her arm across her forehead.

Great. She had just had a major sex dream about the crazy — and crazy-hot — weirdo who had rescued her, and then tried to scare her out of her mind with a bizarre fairy story and a set of plastic fangs. Wonderful. Perfect.

Damn it.

EIGHT

The next morning, *yet again*, Trynn awoke suddenly from a sound sleep, pleasure washing through her body like a warm tide. Again, it faded abruptly as the remnants of the dream slipped from her consciousness.

She sat up and rested her elbows on her knees, cradling her head in her hands.

"Right," she told the rumpled bedclothes. "This has got to stop. I can't keep having sexy dreams about this guy. I'm going to go insane."

The sheets remained unhelpfully silent. Something about the way they were tangled around her gave the impression that they'd had more fun last night than she had, waking repeatedly from dreams just before she got to the good parts. Right now, she kind of resented them for it.

No more sleep, she decided, flipping her legs over the edge of the bed.

With her pulse still thrumming through her and heat pooling between her legs, Trynn decided that a cold shower was in order to banish the last of the fantasy that had plagued her all night long.

Once under the icy spray, she found it easier to ignore her body's demand for release as she pondered her current situation. Trynn had never struggled with a lack of libido, but what she had experienced in the last several hours was far beyond anything she would consider reasonable or average. She had been involved in a fight for her life little more than a day ago, for Christ's sake.

Surely this should be a time for her mind to focus on something besides her raging sex drive.

Yet it very obviously wasn't. Sure, Trynn was deeply disturbed by what had happened at the bank, and she had thus far avoided watching the news or looking at much social media in an effort to escape frightening images and accounts of the incident. Yet, the more she thought about Eris, the more the experience seemed to fade into the background as her thoughts dwelt on him and him alone. Because, oh yeah, *that* was totally healthy.

But, *damn*. The dreams were enough to drive a person crazy.

Trynn washed her hair and body, trying to ignore the way her skin prickled under her fingers, as if longing for Eris' touch despite the chilly spray of the shower. If she'd thought it would help, Trynn would have scolded her body aloud for getting so caught up in a lunatic's twisted fairytale. *Down, girl! Have some respect for yourself!*

An hour later, Trynn was completely dressed and as ready for the day as she was likely to get, sitting at her computer and staring at a picture of Eris that she had pulled from the hotel's security system.

Why the hell did he have to be so handsome, Trynn thought, a bit sadly. *He should be married to a supermodel, churning out genetically superior babies. Not holed up alone in an expensive hotel room, celebrating Halloween three months early.*

Trynn scowled at the screen and tried to resist the temptation to look him up on a social media site.

She rarely bothered with social media herself, usually finding it to be too unreliable a source from which to gain useful information. Yet, in this case, Trynn *really* wanted to see what she could find.

Unfortunately, without knowing his real last name, the search for Eris yielded no definite results. There was nothing under the fake name he'd given her at first, either.

I'll just have to go back to his hotel and talk to him again, she thought savagely. *He at least owes me that much.*

It was that certainty which drove Trynn forward through her morning. She forced down some food—even though food had seemed completely unappealing since her run-in with the bomber—and dressed in comfortable clothes for walking.

It didn't seem to matter that she was only intending to return to the Merit Lefkosa so she could confront Eris about his crazy story and weird behavior—she still couldn't help worrying about her appearance. Glancing critically in the mirror, she stared at the dark green canvas pants that she wore with a plain white V-neck t-shirt. She could pass as a tourist, she decided, with her simple tennis shoes on.

She had decided to walk back to his hotel rather than taking a cab, in hopes that the Mediterranean sunshine would do something for her ghastly pale skin. Her short, dark hair was spiked lightly and she pushed sunglasses onto her face to cover the bags under her eyes.

It sort of disgusted her that she was so worried about her looks when she going to meet a man who was plainly as crazy as a box of frogs, but on the other hand, she still felt the eerie connection—not to mention, attraction—to him.

I'm the one who's freaking crazy. What the hell am I doing stressing out about this?

It was true—Trynn was completely unaccustomed to feeling uneasy around a man. In the past, when she'd had casual relationships, she'd found it easy to be cool and aloof. She'd never been one to settle down in one place, or with one guy. For many men, it made her the perfect girlfriend—in other words, not a real girlfriend at all.

Now, though, she felt butterflies stirring in her stomach, and a sheen of sweat breaking out across her brow.

I just need to get moving, Trynn thought as she slung her handbag over one shoulder. *It will be better when I don't feel so idle.*

Walking helped manage her nervousness, and before she knew it, Trynn reached Eris' hotel. Hoping that the same young man was not working the front desk, Trynn kept her sunglasses on as she stepped into the large lobby.

To her relief, she did not recognize anyone from her last visit. Suppressing a sigh, she pushed her sunglasses up on her head and strolled confidently towards the elevators. No one stopped her, confirming her earlier suspicion that the security was not as foolproof as she had originally hoped.

When she approached the seventh-floor room for the second time, she did not hesitate to knock. This time, when Eris answered, he looked like he had been awake for a while.

"You came back," was his tense greeting. The curtains were drawn inside the room so that the light was dim, making it hard for her to parse the expression on his face as she stood under the bright glare of the hallway outside.

"I need to talk to you again," she said, girding herself as if for battle. "You owe me a better explanation than that crap you spouted last time."

Eris only nodded and moved aside, gesturing for her to come in. She stepped inside and looked around suspiciously for a moment. She'd had the oddest sensation—a cold chill, almost as though something had brushed against her arm as she moved into the room. As she glanced around the dimly lit space, however, she saw nothing.

They sat across from one another in the same chairs as last time, awkward and uncomfortable.

"So, you wanted to talk to me," Eris said after a moment, his voice heavy and resigned.

Thank you, Captain Obvious, Trynn thought, but she quashed the impulse to be a complete bitch to him. She needed to keep her wits about her so she could make sure all of her questions were answered.

"Yes," she said, trying to find words to describe her thoughts. "I need to know what happened the last time I was here."

"What do you mean?" Eris asked, looking at her steadily.

Trynn considered him. He looked genuinely unsure as to what she meant, which surprised her.

"I—" she started before falling silent. How could she tell him that she spent half the night practically humping the mattress in her sleep because of crazy dreams of fucking him silly? There was seriously *no good way* to provide that information.

"I had some intense dreams last night about you. I know that you must have some sort of…ability to influence others, because of how you handled that guy at the bank."

Trynn stopped speaking, hoping that Eris would simply confirm or deny her suspicions. He, however, seemed to be in a less than helpful mood.

"Um… okay?" he replied, obviously waiting for her to elaborate.

"Well," she said in a slow voice, "I wondered if you had done the same thing to me. You know, if you put… like… a mind-whammy on me or something?"

He blinked. "A mind *what*?"

Trynn felt her face go red. God, she sounded like a complete idiot. "I don't really have a good word for it," she snapped. "But I'm also not accustomed to having sex dreams about complete strangers that keep me up half the god-damned night."

Oh, shit. She'd said that last part aloud, hadn't she?

Eris started to chuckle, but smothered it when she glared at him. He shook his head. "No, I didn't put a *mind-whammy* on you."

She continued to glare. "How do I know that for sure?"

Eris slowly brought his eyes up to meet hers, his expression intense.

"Because if I had put a *mind-whammy* on you," he said, sketching air quotes around the ridiculous words, "it would have felt like this."

Eris' eyes glowed with that eerie inner light, and a strange, overwhelming sensation flowed through Trynn's mind. He was looking directly at her, those unearthly eyes fixed on her face without blinking or turning away. It made her feel like a mouse frozen under a cobra's cold regard.

Her heart stuttered once and pounded against the walls of her chest, all the blood in her body rushing abruptly south. She gasped and gripped the arms of the chair. Desire surged through her so powerfully that it took every last bit of her self-control not to fling herself forward across the space separating them and crawl into his lap, rutting like a bitch in heat. She could feel her restraint slipping more with every heartbeat as she twitched with longing, trying to keep her disobedient limbs under control.

She was panting, open-mouthed, so hot she was surprised clouds of steam weren't rising from her skin. Images raced through her mind of Eris plunging himself into her depths... gripping her hair... bringing his lips to her neck. They were so real that she could almost feel the ghost of his teeth against her throat, the dart of his tongue against her sweaty skin.

The ache of raw need between her legs was unbearable, and she wrapped her arms around herself, trying to stop the onslaught of sensations. Finally, Trynn could take it no longer. She scrambled out of the chair, stumbling towards him on rubbery legs. Her hot palms gripped his arms as she tried to mold her body against his, desperate for contact, for release.

Without warning, everything vanished. The heavy, drugged feeling in her mind dissipated and Trynn could breathe easily again. Although her heart rate remained high, she could feel her body calming as the glow dimmed from Eris' eyes. He maintained his steady grip on her and Trynn realized, with horror, that he was restraining her, holding her back from climbing his body like a tree.

She gaped at him, aware that he had just reached out with his mind somehow and tampered with her thoughts. Embarrassment and horror coursed through her, making her face burn with shame. It took a moment to lock her knees and get her feet back under her, but then she jerked back so quickly that the contact between them was broken.

Without the burning, ravenous desire for Eris or the electric feeling that raced through her every time their skin came into contact, Trynn found that she felt rather empty and cold.

Fortunately, anger came to her defense an instant later.

"You *jackass!*" Trynn yelled, setting herself before smashing her fist squarely against his jaw in a vicious roundhouse punch.

To her consternation, the blow barely seemed to register with him. His head snapped to the side, but he merely shook it off and looked at her in shock. Her fist, on the other hand, exploded into agony. She drew it against her stomach, cradling it and gritting her teeth.

She couldn't suppress the hiss of pain that escaped her lips.

Out of the corner of her eye, she saw movement to her left. As she whirled to see what it was, she caught Eris making a sharp gesture with his hand, though he didn't speak.

Every single rational thought fled from her mind as her eyes fell on a ghastly creature stepping out of the shadows. Although it was roughly human-shaped, its features were so distinctly inhuman that Trynn immediately knew she was in the presence of a monster.

A monster. A vampire. Jesus Christ, she hadn't been delusional before after all. Vampires were *real*. A pitiful squeak rose in her throat as she backed away in sudden terror, her eyes jerking towards the door.

"Please," Eris murmured, "*Trynn*. It's all right. You're not in danger. Don't run away again. He's a friend."

Trynn looked back and forth between the two otherworldly figures, fear and indecision writ large on her face.

Every bit of common sense she possessed demanded that she flee before she was killed. She *knew* that the creature before her was powerful. *Deadly*. Its empty, cold eyes were pitiless and frozen. A chill seemed to emanate from it, infecting her, freezing her soul.

"A *friend*?" she whispered, looking at Eris, the tone clearly saying that he had lost his *freaking mind*.

"Yes," Eris answered, glancing quickly at the monster. "A friend. This is Snag."

Trynn forced her gaze back to the... *creature*, and studied him more closely, still poised to flee if he made any sudden moves. "*Snag*? What kind of name is that?"

The creature—*Snag*—turned his head a fraction in response, but did not speak. Trynn frowned, her frantic heartbeat slowing gradually as her panic ebbed.

"Yeah, well, it's nice to meet you, too. I guess. You're... not human." Still, the creature did not reply.

Eris sighed and said, "Actually, he's every bit as human as I am."

There were two ways that statement could be taken, and Trynn could guess which one he meant. She felt her stomach clench and a cold sensation pass through her yet again. How was it possible that this was happening? She'd wanted answers, but she hadn't wanted *this* answer.

"What *are* you?" she asked, hugging herself. The knuckles of her right hand still ached and throbbed from hitting him. "How can this be *happening*?"

"Please, Trynn," Eris said, sounding tired, "sit down. I'd like the chance to try and explain things better than last time."

That was what she'd come for, wasn't it? And neither one of the pair had made any move to hurt her—not even when she'd punched Eris in the face. Trynn found her way back to her seat and crossed her arms defensively, still feeling uneasy under Snag's impassive stare. Now that her panic had faded to manageable levels, she shamelessly studied the gaunt creature on the other side of the room.

His skin was grey and papery, covered in scars. Some looked like claw marks. Some were in the shapes of complex symbols. Some appeared to be from burn marks. He was completely bald, without eyebrows, but his eyelashes were thick and dark. They framed deep-set eyes so black that she couldn't see the boundary between pupil and iris. Trynn shivered as he regarded her silently, his face completely expressionless.

Eris looked over to him and shook his head. "I know we've had this conversation many times, old friend, but you *really* need to work on your people skills."

Snag did not answer, but swiveled his gaze towards Eris, the dark depths of his eyes never flickering.

"You were going to answer my question," Trynn reminded him. She wanted answers, and she wasn't willing to wait another minute.

Eris nodded and cleared his throat. "You'll have to forgive my awkwardness. Your presence is… unnerving."

"You hang out with *this* guy, and you think *my* presence is unnerving?" Trynn asked, incredulous.

"It is, though. I never expected to find my lost soulmate," he said. "When we found Della, I thought it was a fluke. A happy accident."

Della? Trynn filed the name away to ask about later. "And you're sure I'm this lost soulmate, are you?"

Eris huffed a breath that could have been amusement or frustration. "Without a doubt. Even ignoring the spark between us whenever our skin touches… I've been having dreams, as well."

"Wait. You mean we're having the *same* dreams?" Trynn demanded, taken aback by this piece of information—though maybe she shouldn't have been.

Eris flickered an eyebrow. "Yes, Trynn. I mean that we're having the same dreams."

Silence followed his statement, and Trynn forced out a hollow laugh. "Yeah, right. Sure we are. Look! We can't be having the same dreams—that's impossible. If they're similar, it's probably just a coincidence."

"It's not. I am a vampire, and you are human, yet our souls are connected. We experience certain aspects of our lives together, especially when we revisit old memories."

"But none of this makes any *sense!*" Trynn exploded.

"I can't explain it any better than that to you," Eris said. "But, I can tell you that reincarnation is real. For example, feelings of *déjà vu* are nothing more than the mind struggling with an old memory from a past life."

"*Déjà vu* is supposed to be a trick that your mind is playing on you," Trynn said dismissively. "How do I know you're not tricking me, too?"

"You don't," Eris replied in a serious voice, "but I'm not."

Trynn studied him carefully for a moment. "Then explain more."

Eris sat back. He was silent for several moments before speaking. "It starts at the beginning of time."

"Okay, maybe not quite that much," she said. She might have wanted answers, but she had no desire for a lesson on the entire history of the universe.

"I'll try to be concise," Eris said, his tone growing mildly annoyed.

"Fine," she said with a resigned sigh. "Do please continue."

"The universe was formed around the forces of good and evil. These forces are the source of most religions. All of them believe in the struggle between good and bad, love and hate. Well, the struggle is real. There are angels and there are demons. Or, at least, there are beings that may as well be angels and demons. One demon in particular, Bael, is the force of evil incarnate on this planet."

"Like the devil?" Trynn asked, trying to remember all she could from the world religions elective she was forced to take in college. Mostly, she remembered how much she'd hated the damned class.

"In a sense," Eris said. "Not exactly. He has the power to rend souls and destroy lives. Everything bad that happens on this planet has something to do with him. He is the bringer of darkness, pain, and desolation. The harbinger of filth, disease, and rot."

Trynn shuddered at Eris' words, but she did not interrupt him.

"Bael has one great weakness, however. He has no ability to understand the unconquerable power of love. There's a saying in the Christian Bible that he seems to have forgotten."

"What's that?" Trynn asked.

"Perfect love casts out all fear."

"What does that *mean*, though?" Trynn asked, drawn in despite herself.

"For him? It means that when he decided to destroy my soul and the souls of my friends, he made one mistake that all of our soulmates exploited."

Trynn held completely still, listening. Her eyes never left Eris'.

"Their love for us protected us from utter annihilation. Instead of becoming Bael's undead puppets, we were reborn as vampires, our souls split into two pieces, the Light and the Dark—both contained in one body."

Trynn blinked once, confused.

"But in saving us, their lives were sacrificed. You were Phaidra, and you died millennia ago. Apparently, I've been waiting for your return all these endless years, and never even knew it until I found you."

"How do you know for sure it's me, though?" Trynn asked, her voice a bare whisper. "You said you knew without a doubt, but how?"

Eris stretched out his hand and touched her skin. And, yes, there was that same electric current of energy passing between the two of them, making Trynn's heart race and the hair on her neck stand up in anticipation.

"*That...* is how I know," Eris said. "We have already located the reincarnated soulmate of another of my friends. We have a bit better idea what to expect, now."

"And they had the same zap between them? Like we have?"

Eris nodded. "Exactly the same."

Trynn wasn't really sure how to argue with that. Or even, her traitorous heart pointed out helpfully, if she *wanted* to argue it.

"What does this mean, exactly?" she asked instead. "For me, for you, for this struggle between good and evil that you say is taking place around us?"

Eris scratched his head and threw a long look at Snag, who had not moved throughout the entire explanation. "I'm not certain right now. There's a lot more to the story, but that's the basic version. The important thing to know is that Bael will be trying to track you down. He doesn't want us to reunite because he fears it will fulfill a prophecy. So, he's going to try and kill you to prevent it."

Okay, then. Suddenly, her presence at the bank just when a crazy bomber showed up to take hostages took on a more sinister cast.

"What type of danger am I in right now?" she asked, her hand coming up to the base of her throat.

"The serious kind. Chaos is closing in around you, and it will only get worse. Riots, shootings, bombings, terrorism—"

"What?" Trynn yelped, her eyes going wide.

"I'm sorry," Eris answered, and he truly did look it. "I know you never asked for any of this. I am *so sorry* that your life is in danger yet again, because of your connection to me. This was never your battle, but now you'll have to fight it nonetheless."

"No, no, that's not what I meant," Trynn answered quickly, shaking her head. "You said terrorism. You said bombs!"

Her blood ran cold, her thoughts turning toward MASQUE and the intel she had intercepted about the arms dealer and his mysterious client. It seemed like way too much of a coincidence to think that Eris was warning her about chaos and terrorism while a major weapons deal that could potentially cost tens or hundreds of thousands of lives was going down at the same time.

Eris looked confused. "Yes, among other things. What—"

"Eris, I'm a member of MASQUE. I'm tracking a man right now who's trying to buy suitcase nukes from the Russian mafia. You're talking about terrorism? I... think that probably qualifies."

NINE

The ominous words settled over Eris like a pall and he realized, with a stab of dread, that he was too late. The vortex of chaos and evil was already firmly established around his mate. First the bomber at the bank, and now... *this*. He had hoped that by arming Trynn with information early on, he could spare her the same sorts of horrors that Della had experienced. It seemed, however, that he had failed — and that failure made his stomach drop sickeningly.

"When did you find out about this? Have you passed on the information to the authorities?" he asked sharply. Trynn's face blanched under his intensity.

"About the nukes? I found out last night," she answered in a small voice, looking suddenly young and scared. "I picked up his trail some weeks ago, and several of us have been monitoring the deal's progress as best we could. I informed the group of my findings right after I translated his last email. One of them is supposed to pass it on to the US government, but you can guess exactly how much good that's likely to do."

"And you don't know what sort of timeline he's operating on?"

She shook her head. "No."

"How did you find him? What do you mean about tracking him?" Eris demanded, something cold and bitter clawing its way up from the depths of his gut. It might have been fear.

Trynn ran a shaking hand through her dark, spiky hair and said, "I'm a member of a group of hackers that exposes these types of deals. We call it hactivism. Some of what we deal with is governments abusing their citizens, but sometimes it's black market crime rings and weapons deals. We monitor these kinds of exchanges and post our findings anonymously to the group. When we can, we disrupt them."

Eris stared at her. *Of course* his Phaidra couldn't be content with a quiet life somewhere. *Of course* she would be in the thick of things, chasing excitement and danger. How very like her that was.

"That... sounds like a rather hazardous hobby," he said eventually.

"Not as much as you'd think," Trynn replied with a shrug. "We never really have contact with the people we track, and they don't know our identity. Most of the time everything is going on half a world away."

Eris scowled at her. "They could find out who you are and target you."

A wan smile flickered across Trynn's face, and was gone. "I doubt that. They'd have to be a better hacker than I was."

Somehow, this wasn't comforting to Eris. Something of his thoughts must have shown on his face, because she frowned at him again.

"Oh, come on," she said, a bit of irritation creeping into her tone. "I'm fighting bad guys in the best way I know how."

"I don't want you drawn into the middle of this evil," Eris murmured, rubbing his chin in exasperation.

"Says the man who defuses hostage situations on his nights off." Her tone was still sharp.

He started to say *that's different*, but thought better of it. "Can you at least tell me more details about this deal?"

"Look—I'll tell you what I can," she said, more calmly. "Though I don't know what you could possibly do with the information that would help. A few months ago, we started seeing mentions of this mysterious guy in the European underworld. He was a new player, and was gathering all manner of black market assets. Drugs, weapons, human trafficking rings."

A prickling of foreboding played across the back of Eris' neck, and he glanced at Snag before motioning for Trynn to continue her story.

She took a deep breath. "He's become hugely wealthy in a very short span of time. Then, over the past few weeks, I've been snooping around this arms deal. I only got a name for the buyer yesterday — B. Kovac. And I only made the connection that he was our mysterious underworld figure when I realized what kind of weapons they were discussing. Very few private individuals are in a position to pay for something like that, but he's definitely one of them."

"What do we know about these weapons? Are we talking nuclear suicide bombs, here? Stroll in someplace, push the button, and take out half a city?" He wasn't sure he really wanted to know the answer.

Trynn chewed on her lower lip in thought. "Possibly. More likely something that could be smuggled into a strategic location, and then blown up by remote."

"And there's no way of knowing exactly how powerful they are?" he asked.

"No," she said. "Not unless they start blabbing about it by email, anyway."

Eris dropped his head into his hands and scrubbed at his face, trying to clear his thoughts. Right now, all he could focus on was Trynn. *Of course* his mate would be wrapped up in this mess. That was just so fucking typical —

"Eris?" Trynn asked, clearly worried.

He did not answer right away. He needed a moment to think, to consider his options and how he was going to proceed. Maybe he could convince Trynn to withdraw from the situation? *Yeah, right*. Like that was likely to happen.

Besides, as much as it was at the top of his current priority list, it didn't really help the situation. For all he knew, this *B. Kovac* could be targeting Nicosia with one of the bombs. He could convince Trynn to let the situation go, only for her to be blown to kingdom come the following week.

Straightening his spine, he looked back at Trynn. "So. What's his next move?"

"He's been making contact with a well-known figure in the Russian mob and forging business ties with him," Trynn said. "They had a big meeting in Damascus, and it's very possible he was finally able to secure what he was after."

Gods above, Damascus was a paltry three hundred kilometers away from here. Practically on their doorstep. "And where would he be likely to use these bombs, assuming he plans on detonating them?" he asked.

Trynn considered the matter. "We can't really know. I guess it depends on what his aims were."

Eris could easily guess what his aims were. "And if he wanted to cause the maximum amount of chaos and carnage?" he asked, already knowing the answer.

Trynn's voice went very quiet. "Then he'd set them off in places like Jerusalem. Ankara. Beirut. Cairo. Cities where any major attack would immediately start proxy wars."

Eris was bombarded unexpectedly by a brief but powerful flash of emotion from Snag. He flinched in surprise, his eyes seeking the other vampire. His expression betrayed no hint of what he had just broadcast accidentally, but Eris knew that Snag was originally from somewhere south of Cairo. He'd never told them where, exactly… but they were discussing the potential destruction of his ancient friend's home, too.

"What is it?" Trynn asked, glancing between them. Snag gave Eris a calculating look, but the mental channel fell silent. Eris continued to lock gazes with Snag for a long moment, before turning back to Trynn and nodding for her to continue.

"It's nothing. Please go on. If you had to guess, what sort of timeline do you think we're looking at?"

"Probably soon," she said, grim. "Once he gets the bombs, why wait?"

Why, indeed? Eris sat back, leaning against one of the arms of his seat. He rested his chin on his fingers, deep in thought.

This could all just be a huge coincidence. Perhaps this black market deal was completely unrelated to Trynn, and she was in no more danger than any other human was, these days. This transaction might be no different than any of the other dozens of cases she'd doubtless worked on as part of this group of hers. He longed to be able to believe that, certainly.

Trynn echoed his thoughts and said, "This could all just be nothing, though. We've had intelligence reports like this before and they've never amounted to anything."

Eris watched her closely before taking a deep breath and turning back to Snag.

"Do you sense Bael's hand in this?" he asked.

Snag remained silent across their mental connection, but Eris could sense his uneasiness. His companion was obviously weighing the words carefully.

After a short pause, a sense of corruption and rot permeating the sunlit paradise around them teased Eris' mind, and was gone. Snag dipped his chin the tiniest fraction, sketching a nod.

Eris nodded as well. "I feel it, too. It's as I feared. Do you think there's any chance at all that we're *not* already caught up in the vortex of Bael's evil?"

Eris sensed the answer in Snag's silence. It was an answer he'd already known in his bones; desperate though he was for Snag to refute it.

Snag's bony chest lifted and lowered as he breathed out silently. Eris felt the ancient being's power flickering around him, as if Snag's life force was surrounding him and filling him up. Eris closed his eyes, letting it in, feeling a huge increase in his own strength and awareness. As his friend's life force mingled with his own, Eris could sense evil pulsing all around them. He could feel it, like a malignant, oily cloud hanging in the air. He shuddered and shook his head, trying to free himself from the stench.

But he knew he would not be able to escape it until they'd fought the battle ahead and won. And Snag must have been aware of that the whole time.

No wonder you were so antsy, Eris communicated. *His presence is horrible, and it's covering this entire region. I felt something similar to this in New Orleans. I didn't stop to think how much worse it must have been for you.*

He shivered, feeling a flash of pity for Snag's powerful awareness.

We need to stop this, Eris thought with iron resolve. *The idea of Bael controlling someone with access to nuclear bombs is too horrible to contemplate.*

Snag did not reply, but Eris could sense his agreement. Also, his unutterable weariness.

"Something tells me you two are having a conversation without me," Trynn said, and Eris realized that she had been quiet for an unusually long stretch, watching them intently.

Eris felt Snag's power recede back into the bounds that normally encompassed it. Yet he could still sense Bael's presence, looming over them like a shadow. Snag had given him that gift, if you could really call it such a thing.

"Sorry about that," he finally said, throwing a quick glance in Snag's direction. "I didn't intend to be rude, but as you may have gathered, he's not much of a talker. I just needed a bit of help from him to see the bigger picture."

Trynn's eyebrows drew together, and Eris' attention was drawn to the small crease of discontent like iron filings drawn to a magnet. "I don't know what that's supposed to mean, in this context," she said.

Eris huffed a sigh. "It's a bit complicated to explain. Snag is very powerful. He can sense things that I can't. The demon I told you about is nearby. His evil is permeating this whole situation. Guiding it. Shaping it."

"Okay," she answered slowly. "So what are we going to do about it? How do we stop him?"

Eris stood up and started pacing, unable to stay still. He could feel both Trynn's and Snag's eyes on him.

"First and foremost," he said, "we need to ensure your safety, Trynn. I really think that you should stay here with us, where it's safer."

Something flashed across Trynn's face so quickly that Eris couldn't parse it. "Stay here?" she echoed. "With you?"

"Yes," Eris replied. "The two of us can protect you more effectively here."

She looked decidedly flummoxed, and he realized that while she wasn't actively disputing his claims anymore, she hadn't truly taken this new reality on board.

"No," she said, "I can't do that. I'm scheduled to return home soon. And I need to get back to work."

Eris shook his head. "You don't understand the amount of danger you're in. Trynn, you're being hunted by a powerful demon from the underworld. He has nearly limitless resources available to find you and follow you. Leaving this city would only end up bringing catastrophe down on your home. More importantly,

Snag and I are *here*, and we're the best allies you could hope for right now."

Trynn hesitated an instant before shaking her head again. "No, this whole thing is preposterous. You don't even know for sure that this *demon* is after me—"

"We've been over this," Eris said, suddenly, viscerally aware of his growing weariness. If he could just get a few hours of sleep—and maybe some blood—Eris knew that he would be able to think and plan more effectively. Now, exhaustion pulled at him with the same relentless intensity as the sun beating down on the window outside, beyond the heavy drapes.

"Bael is after revenge," he continued. "You—or Phaidra, if you prefer—saved my life by sacrificing your own. You *defied* him. Vampires are Bael's greatest failures, and he will see you destroyed, if he can. He'll do whatever is within his power to prevent you becoming part of the Council."

"The... what?" Trynn asked, clearly overwhelmed by the day's events.

Eris sighed and massaged his temples with his fingers. "It's complicated, and we aren't even sure of all the details. But I've been studying an ancient text. It states that Bael will fall when the Council of Thirteen unites against him. At that time, the angel Israfael's power will be restored and balance will come back into the world."

"God help me. That's the short version?" Trynn asked dryly. Her eyes narrowed, and she looked at Eris closely. "Tell me something, Eris—and don't lie. When was the last time you got a decent stretch of sleep?"

Eris swayed where he stood and shook his head. "It doesn't matter. What matters right now is keeping you safe. Please, Trynn, you have to stay with us."

Trynn's eyes moved to Snag for a moment before she looked back at Eris. "What if I just got a room here instead? I mean... I barely know you, after all."

Eris raised an eyebrow. "We've been in a hostage situation together, I've mind-whammied you, and you've punched me in the jaw. Surely, all that counts for something? Trynn, I don't want to have to worry about getting to you in time if something happens. I think the best option is for you to stay here in this room."

Trynn sighed in exasperation. "Look. It's not that I don't appreciate what you're offering, even if I don't fully understand what's going on. But I have a life! I have a job! Bills I need to pay! I can't just put everything on hold to play hide-and-seek with a vengeful demon."

"I would think you could contact your employer and get some kind of trauma leave, after the incident at the bank," Eris pointed out.

Trynn looked decidedly cagey for a moment, and appeared to be trying to think of another way around his suggestion. He was struck with the oddest sense of *déjà vu* for a moment, before he realized it was because he had seen that exact expression on Phaidra's face more times than he could count.

"*Trynn*," he said, coming up to her chair and crouching down so that he was at eye level with her. "I promise you, we're here to protect you. We mean you no harm. I wouldn't ask this of you if it wasn't a life or death situation for both of us. I would never ask you to walk away from something that you love on a whim, but you've *got to understand*. If you step out of those doors, there's a very real chance you could die. You might die, and there would be nothing I could do to stop it. Don't ask me to live through that again."

Eris poured as much intensity into his gaze as he could, allowing his senses to expand until they gently brushed her mind. He could sense that her resolve was crumbling; that his sincerity was winning out over her innate independence and skepticism.

He knew that he could use his power on her, to tip her over to his way of thinking. But he knew just as surely that doing so in this moment would destroy the fragile beginnings of trust they'd built.

Please, Trynn, Eris urged silently. *Please, just agree to stay here, where we can watch over you. I can't lose you again. I wouldn't survive it a second time.*

Eris tried to hold back anguished memories of cradling her lifeless frame in his arms, but the image was burned into his mind like a brand. Over the centuries, he'd become a master at the fine art of denial when it came to coping with haunting memories that would not fade, but the deep ache never really seemed to abate.

Now that he had found his Phaidra against all odds, he never wanted to let her out of his sight again. He was desperate to protect her, to spare her the horror that surely lay in wait for both of them like a crouched tiger. His hatred for Bael rose like bile in his throat and he swallowed it back down, fighting to stay calm.

"All right," Trynn said at last, a note of defeat in her voice. "Fine. I'll stay, but I need to get my stuff first. Especially my laptop."

"You can use mine," Eris offered, relief nearly overwhelming him.

Trynn gave him a horrified look. "Are you kidding? That's the equivalent of using someone else's *toothbrush*. No, no—I need my computer."

Perplexed by her vehemence, Eris made a noncommittal noise. "After dark, perhaps, when we can go with you," he countered. "Deal?"

She looked unhappy, but nodded. Relieved to have things settled—for the time being, at least—Eris crossed to the desk in the corner and sat down. After a few moments' deliberation, he composed a terse email to Tré, explaining the situation as best he could in a few words.

Tré would understand if anyone would, Eris knew. After their experience with finding Della, Eris was confident that he and the others would drop whatever they were doing and come to his assistance. And in the meantime, he had Snag.

With his most immediate worries resolved, Eris let his gaze stray over the top of the bulky laptop and back to Trynn, who had moved from the chair to the couch. She wasn't looking at him. Instead, she was frowning, leaning forward in her seat to rest her chin on her hands, the way she used to all those centuries ago—clearly lost in thought. His gaze raked over her like a starving man's, taking in every svelte curve and tantalizing angle. She was tall—her body slender and coltish where Phaidra had been all softness. He longed to explore the differences.

Eris swallowed hard and looked away, trying to get a grip on himself.

He stood from the desk rather abruptly and walked past Trynn, who lifted her eyes to shoot him a challenging look. Snag, on the other hand, followed his path towards the en-suite bedroom with his customary impassive gaze.

Exhaustion still nagged at Eris, and his vision spun in ponderous circles as he flopped down onto the bed without even pulling back the covers. With a touch as light as air, Eris felt Snag brush against his thoughts a moment later, a question hanging between them.

"Please keep an eye on her for me," Eris murmured. Snag's gaze turned back towards Trynn.

Worries and plans spun endlessly through Eris' mind, making sleep impossible as thoughts of the coming darkness consumed him. In the space of a day, he'd come to appreciate what Tré must have experienced when Della emerged from the shadows and walked into his life. Eris hoped that he would have a chance to apologize for some of the impatience he'd expressed during the trying time before Della's turning. He could understand fully now why Tré had felt so protective of his mate.

A peace that came from outside him settled over Eris, and he shuddered as the tension he'd been carrying flowed out of his muscles without warning. *Damn.* He must have been projecting his thoughts more loudly than he realized. Snag had apparently had enough of listening to his internal monologue, and had decided to take action.

Eris reached out mentally. *We can't let this escalate into a nuclear war, Snag,* he said. *It will take the others time to get here, but I could go ahead to Damascus and scout around. See what's happening. We'll need some reconnaissance before we go in en masse, so we'll know what we're facing. We've got to neutralize this threat.*

In response, Eris received a surge of disagreement and disapproval. With his brow furrowed in a deep frown, Eris allowed his displeasure to radiate across the mental connection.

What the hell else am I supposed to do? he asked. *We need to move on this. We can't sit around hoping the bombs don't off before the others can get here.*

Another wave of opposition.

Wait. The single word was emphatic.

We don't have time to wait! Eris shot back, his frustration growing. *This has to be resolved before it turns into a disaster! But we also can't risk leaving Trynn unguarded. You need to stay here and protect her. I'll go ahead to Damascus and see what I can do on my own about the situation. You know how important Trynn is —*

Eris felt a flare of irritation along the connection, but ignored it.

— and we sure as hell aren't taking her along. We'd be delivering her straight into Bael's hands, he continued doggedly.

Then I will go. You will stay.

It was Eris' turn to be angry. Why was Snag making this so difficult? The logic was simple — plain as day.

Don't be ridiculous, he shot back. *You're more power-ful than I am. I need you here, with Trynn, protecting her. Please, Snag, just do this for me.*

Snag did not respond but Eris felt a chill of power emanating from him. Snag's anger seemed to be grow-ing, filling the entire suite. Eris could tell that Snag thought he was being an idiot.

It's pragmatic, and you can't stop me from going unless you plan on fighting me outright, Eris pointed out. *I'll find out exactly what we're facing in Damascus, so that we can stop whatever Bael is intending with these bombs.*

He took a deep breath and pulled out his trump card. *And I swear on my life, Snag, if you abandon Trynn or allow anything to happen to her while I'm gone, I will pur-posely lose every game of chess we ever play from this day forward in ten moves or less.*

There was a very pronounced silence following his words. Eris could tell Snag was musing over the threat, trying to decide if it was legitimate.

Apparently, he realized that it was. After the space of several heartbeats, Snag relented. Eris could tell by the way the tight bond of energy between the two of them relaxed. Snag was clearly still unhappy, but Eris had—somewhat to his own surprise—won the argu-ment.

And anyway, it wasn't as though Snag was *ever* particularly happy.

Good. Now that it's decided, I'm going to sleep, Eris sent, pulling a pillow toward his chest. He settled deeper into the soft mattress, and allowed his mind to drift.

Several hours later, he awoke with a start. His dreams had been confused, a swirl of memories and worry about the current situation that left him disori-ented in the wake of his slumber. Shaking his head, Eris stretched out his senses and found that the sun was set-ting.

That was a relief; it would be easier to embark on his mission without having to worry about the possibility of being burned by its rays if he wasn't flying fast enough across the narrow stretch of the Levantine Sea that separated Cyprus from Syria. After his unexpectedly restorative sleep, Eris felt he could wait no longer to start his self-imposed mission.

As he stretched his awareness outward, he found that Snag was gone. For a moment, this concerned him, but then he sensed the familiar presence outside, hovering in the deepening shadows. He had merely left the room when Eris started to stir, apparently to give Eris and Trynn some privacy.

Eris pushed wordless gratitude across their mental connection as he climbed from the bed and walked back into the living area of the generous suite.

He found Trynn fast asleep on the couch, one arm draped across her forehead, the other wrapped protectively around his laptop.

He stared at the computer for a beat, blinking in confusion. Hadn't he locked the screen earlier?

Fascinated by her sleeping form, Eris walked over to her and knelt down next to the couch where she was slouched. He stared at her face, drinking in the unfamiliar lines, unable to stop himself from falling back into memories of their life together, all those centuries ago. She was just as captivating now as she had been then. Even though her features were different, his heart clearly recognized its other half and rejoiced at their reunion.

I will protect you, he vowed. *I won't let anything bad happen to you. Not again. Never again.*

Trynn's breathing, which had been slow and soft, deepened as she stretched, coming awake. With her free hand, she rubbed her eyes and looked around, blinking.

Her eyes landed on Eris, kneeling next to the couch, and she pushed up on her elbows. "Where's the other guy?"

Eris hesitated, unsure how much to tell her. Trynn didn't know yet about the alternate forms that vampires could take, and he wasn't sure now was the moment to enlighten her. While part of him longed to tell her everything, all at once, the more cautious part warned that she was still struggling with the things she'd learned earlier that day.

"He stepped out for a few minutes," he said. "He's not far away, though."

Trynn relaxed back. "Oh."

"I see you made yourself right at home," Eris teased, gesturing at the laptop that had slipped down between Trynn's leg and the back of the couch when she woke.

Completely unabashed, Trynn gave him an appraising stare. "I was doing research on you while you slept."

"And?"

"You're an art thief," she accused, narrowing her eyes. "I hacked into your laptop."

Eris snorted. "I guess I should've seen that coming, huh? Though I prefer the term *collector*."

Trynn didn't respond to his attempt at humor. "That's not all I found out. I..." She swallowed. "I was an art thief, too, wasn't I?"

Eris raised his eyebrows, surprised at her revelation.

"How —" he began.

"I dreamed it just now." she said faintly. "I dreamed the past."

He caught his breath. "You dreamed it? You dreamed... us?"

TEN

Trynn stared up at Eris' beautifully sculpted features. The remnants of her dream shrouded everything in a hazy, comforting cloud. She could still feel his hands on her, untying laces, slipping through lengths of soft fabric, dragging clothing up and off. Her heart pounded in her ears as the echo of sensation sang along her nerves.

Eris' eyes darkened, his pupils growing large as he gazed down at her.

Can he sense my arousal? Trynn wondered. She pressed her knees together, trying to restrain the urge to leap on him then and there.

If I don't get up and get some space between us, this is going to end very badly. Or possibly very well... depending on how you look at it, she thought, a bit wildly.

The dreams had been so vivid—so real that she could no longer hold onto her doubts about the validity of Eris' claims. How could her mind *possibly* formulate such vivid images and sensations based on nothing but the random synaptic firings that supposedly made up dreams? How could a dream encompass another entirely separate life?

Trynn was no idiot. She understood that there were things in the world that she didn't understand. Was the existence of angels and demons and vampires and soulmates really so far-fetched? Was it so impossible that reincarnation existed? Right now, Trynn didn't think it was.

Of course, all of these musings basically meant that her wild dreams of carefree and uninhibited sex surrounded by a room full of beautiful treasures were more than likely real.

"We were… happy once," she whispered. "Weren't we?"

His voice was hoarse. "Yes. We were."

"Maybe we could be happy again?" Trynn asked in a soft voice, watching him.

Eris swallowed hard, clearly struggling with some powerful emotion. His breathing quickened as Trynn searched his face for answers.

She laid her hand on his arm and traced her fingers up perfect skin, smooth and unblemished. She could feel the electric pulse between them… feel the goose bumps erupting beneath her touch—tiny, dark hairs standing at attention. She knew—without knowing *how* she knew—that he loved soft, ghost-like touches. She also knew that he liked the scratch of fingernails across his back, and the sensation of her legs locking around his hips, pulling him in deep.

They had spent only a few hours in each other's company, yet her familiarity with him was absolute.

She trailed her nails down his arm, pressing harder so that they dragged across his skin. He reached out with his free hand, quick as a snake, and caught her wrist in a tight grip. Trynn felt a thrill of excitement pass through her body.

He lifted her trapped wrist up to his nose, smelling her skin and rubbing its sensitive underside against his stubble.

"Your scent," he said, his eyes falling closed. "Like jasmine and musk on a summer night. How can it be *exactly the same*, after so long?"

Trynn rolled up, propping herself on her left arm so they were eye level with each other. He let her wrist slide free from his grip, his eyes flickering down to her mouth and back up. Her tongue darted out instinctively to moisten her lips.

A callused, long-fingered hand cupped her cheek, as though she were something precious. The electricity between them crackled with renewed tension.

"Phaidra…" Eris breathed, framing her face in both hands. His expression was lost. Dazed. The expression of a man staring at an oasis in the desert, expecting it to melt into a mirage and disappear as soon as he reached for it.

Something about that look pierced Trynn's heart like a blade. She couldn't bear it, and she would do anything it took to remove it. She grabbed Eris' sleep-rumpled collar in her fist, jerking him forward until their lips crashed together.

As though a dam inside him burst, Eris responded, pressing Trynn down into the soft cushions of the couch as he plundered her mouth. She kept her vice-like grip on his abused shirt as insurance he would not pull away, and moaned into the kiss as one of his hands raked over her stomach, searching for bare skin.

The first brush of his fingertips against the burning flesh of her belly was like a lightning bolt. They both gasped in reaction, and Eris pulled away from the kiss. Trynn stared deeply into his gold-flecked eyes, desire for him radiating outward from her center until she thought it must surely be pouring from her skin like a beam of light, illuminating her from within.

Slowly, his fingers slid further underneath her shirt. Trynn arched into the contact and smiled in satisfaction when his palm pressed greedily against her skin, no longer teasing. He spread his fingers, his large hand possessively spanning her flat stomach, and Trynn felt the burn of fresh desire between her legs, as the air around them seemed to heat.

Eris angled his upper body over hers as they resumed the kiss. His hand was fully underneath her shirt now, working steadily upward toward her aching breast. Trynn's legs fell open of their own accord, as if inviting Eris to cradle his body between them. The small movement did not go unnoticed, and a low growl rumbled in the back of his throat.

His tongue and teeth traced the edge of Trynn's jaw line until his lips met the soft skin of her throat. She shivered with pleasure, the sensation sending waves of hot and cold down the length of her body. She could feel the tip of his tongue teasing her skin before his lips and teeth closed over the same spot, worrying at it. He kept at it, utterly single-minded until he had driven her into a frenzied state of nearly animalistic need.

She was only vaguely aware of his rapid breathing, and the fine tremor that had taken up residence in his sleek, athletic frame. It was only when he pulled back rather abruptly and dropped down to sit on his heels next to the couch that she truly took in the wild look in his dark eyes.

That look called to her own wildness, and Trynn tried to pull him forward again to resume her exploration of his mouth. He resisted the movement.

"No," he said in a rough voice and covered her hand with his. Clearing his throat, he continued, "I'm sorry, Trynn. If we keep going, I don't think I could... stop myself."

Trynn's desire-muddled brain tried to make sense of that statement, and failed. Wasn't it the point of sex not to stop? Her confusion must have been evident on her face. Eris leaned forward to place his lips over her jugular, and kissed her there twice, very softly, the points of his teeth rasping against the thin, delicate skin.

The rush of understanding made Trynn suck in a breath, her body suspended on the knife-edge separating horror and dark, forbidden lust. The image of those sharp fangs sinking into the flesh of her neck during the throes of passion was simultaneously terrifying, and the single hottest thing she'd ever imagined.

Before she could act on the insane idea of trying to test Eris' resolve, he pulled away again and stood up, turning away from the couch and running one hand over his face as if to clear away cobwebs.

"*Gods*," he muttered—hair mussed, shirt rumpled, and still breathing heavily.

Trynn's answering groan was *not* one of pleasure. More a combination of fear, dark excitement, and a truly staggering degree of sexual frustration.

Great. He's the hottest thing I've seen on three separate continents. I've never been so fucking turned on in my life. Aaaand… now he's walking away from me. Maybe the forces of Satan really are *controlling my life.*

Before she could do anything too humiliating—like begging, or, y'know, jumping up from the couch and rutting against his leg—Trynn scrambled to her feet and awkwardly excused herself to the bathroom.

Standing before the mirror, she glared at her own reflection, roundly cursing would-be suicide bombers, ancient demons, the Russian mafia, and hot vampires with their goddamned oral fixations.

"Fuck, fuck, fuck, fuck, *fuck*!" she grated, still feeling like one giant ball of aching *need*.

She took a deep, slow breath. And another. And another.

It didn't help.

She looked around. The bathroom in this place was goddamned *epic*; she'd noticed it when she'd ducked in that afternoon to use the toilet. She'd lived in flats that were smaller, for one thing. In addition to the marble vanity with two sinks, there was a giant walk-in shower enclosed in glass, with four showerheads arrayed around the top. The entire far end of the room was devoted to a sunken, jetted tub large enough to accommodate two people who didn't even particularly like each other.

No, Trynn, stop right there. Do not *think about two people in the freaking jet powered mega-tub! Not. Helping.*

A line of bottles containing bubbles and bath oils stood along one edge like colorful soldiers. Fluffy towels hung on warming racks. A pristine white bathrobe hung on the inside of the bathroom door.

Making an abrupt executive decision, Trynn crossed to the tub and turned on the tap, adjusting it until steam billowed up from the depths. She examined the bottles and poured in the contents of a couple that appealed to her, then stripped out of her clothing and stepped in.

If I'm staying here, then I'll damned well make myself at home, she thought bitterly, as the water churned up mountains of fragrant blue bubbles, rising to cover her body. When the water was lapping over her collarbones, the bubbles tickling her chin, she turned off the tap and sank back with a sigh.

Good God. Trust me to find the only smoking hot vampire on the planet with a conscience.

Intellectually, she knew she should have been terrified by what had almost happened. She also knew that she had some pretty deep-seated issues centered around thrill-seeking and recklessness. If he hadn't stopped, could he have killed her accidentally? A dream image flashed across her mind for a bare instant, too quickly for her to grab hold of it. A shiver wracked her despite the warm water cocooning her body, but she dismissed it.

Eris would not have hurt her.

The phantom touch of fangs on skin made her tremble again, but for a different reason. He would not have hurt her in any way she wouldn't have thoroughly enjoyed, she amended.

The thought was too much for her overwrought libido, which rose up and demanded satisfaction after the last hour of slow torture followed by sexual frustration.

She closed her eyes, letting memories of Eris' touch play across her mind's eye.

He would have continued teasing her vulnerable throat until she finally growled, and rolled him off the couch to wrestle for dominance on the thick, luxurious carpet. Although she would give him a good fight, he would win, pinning her on her back with her wrists above her head, held firmly in one of his large hands.

With the other, he'd peel off her clothing, baring her to his gaze. Rather than take the time to undress himself, he would merely unfasten his fly, pulling his erection free. Would he be dripping precome for her? Her mouth watered, and she decided that, oh yes, he *definitely* would.

Her fingers slid down her belly, missing the electric tingle that his touch always spread along her nerves.

They would both be too impatient for further foreplay. He would pin her down and cover her body with his, lining himself up and thrusting into her hard enough to make them both gasp.

Her fingers slid along the folds of tender flesh between her legs and slipped inside, her passage slick with excitement despite the bathwater.

He wouldn't be gentle, and neither would she, dragging fingernails roughly across his back and urging him deeper with her heels pressed into his tight, perfect ass. He would pound into her until she screamed, and when they were both about to come, he would drag her head to the side and sink his teeth into her neck, sending them both over the edge.

Trynn pressed the heel of her hand hard against her clit and rocked, biting her lip to hold in the cry as her long-denied orgasm crashed over her. When her shudders finally quieted and she sank back against the edge of the tub, exhausted, she realized that her teeth had drawn blood.

-o-o-o-

Half an hour later, she stepped out of the steamy bathroom, feeling much better disposed toward the world even though things were probably going to be awkward as hell now. Trynn glanced around the suite, looking for Eris. Instead, she saw Snag standing looking thoughtfully out of the suite's large picture window into the darkness beyond.

Wrapping her robe more securely around herself, she cleared her throat.

With a painfully slow movement, Snag turned and stared at her with his large, dark eyes. He rarely seemed to need to blink, and considered her silently for so long that she became unnerved.

"Where's Eris?" she asked.

Snag did not answer.

Right. Either he really hates me for some reason, or he actually can't speak, Trynn decided as Snag continued to regard her solemnly. *Let's just assume option number two, until proven otherwise.*

"Okay, never mind," she amended. "I'll just go to bed now, and get out of your hair." Her eyes lifted to his bald head, and she flushed in embarrassment. "If you, erm, had any hair, which obviously you... don't. Sorry about that."

Just as she started to turn and slink away in shame toward the sleeping alcove, Snag lifted a skeletal hand and pointed at a piece of paper on the desk.

A note? Trynn kept her eyes warily on the ancient being in front of her and walked towards the desk. Still not looking away from him, she fumbled until she felt the piece of paper under her fingers. Grabbing it, she took several slow steps backwards.

He considered her for a moment longer before turning back towards the window.

Trynn felt the breath exit her lungs once those cold eyes were no longer pinning her like a captured butterfly. She took the paper into the alcove where Eris had slept that afternoon and sat down on the edge of the bed. Breathing in his smell all around her, she read the short note.

Trynn,

I am truly sorry about earlier. I know I was abrupt, but I don't believe I could have stopped myself from getting carried away. Your presence is intoxicating and I think I would have lost myself in instinctual desires. I'm in no way willing to take that chance with your safety.

I'm going out to get a bite to eat (ha!) and will return shortly. I asked Snag to watch over things while I'm away. If you happen to play chess, you could probably convince him to start a game. He's an elite Grandmaster with a rating of 2800, so he's very good, to put it mildly.

I've added you as a guest in the suite and cleared you to order anything you would like from room service, so please don't hesitate to get food if you're hungry or anything else you may need. Expense is no object, so if there is something you would like, order it.

Sincerely yours,

Eris

Her stomach grumbled. Trynn realized with a start that she was absolutely famished, and had not eaten anything all day long.

Oddly, she felt more comfortable with Snag, knowing now that he did something as ordinary as play chess, so she walked casually back towards the desk and picked up the room service menu.

Running her finger down the list of dishes, Trynn thought that she was hungry enough to eat every single one of them.

When was the last time she'd had a really good meal? Thinking back over the last few days only presented her with confusing memories that all seemed to run together. She could not remember what the hell she'd eaten, or if she'd eaten much of anything at all.

Resisting the temptation to order a bottle of wine, Trynn requested the most expensive dish on the menu be delivered to the room as soon as possible.

After wolfing down the food—delicious, but extremely spicy—Trynn found herself feeling full and sleepy again. She didn't really want to go to bed until Eris had returned, so she sat in the living room watching Snag out of the corner of her eye. He remained standing at the window, staring out into the night with a fixed expression on his gaunt features. She didn't think he'd moved or made a single sound since he'd pointed out the note from Eris.

"Snag?" she asked tentatively, eager to break the silence. "How long have you known Eris?"

The older vampire turned his head towards her but did not speak. He did not look angry or challenging, he simply gazed at her with a neutral expression.

She raised her eyebrows at him as if to encourage him to speak, but he remained unmoved.

She cleared her throat. "Look, I understand if you don't really like me, but I'm getting the impression that we're going to be stuck here together for a while. It would probably be easier if we could get along and interact, you know."

Snag remained completely silent and still. He didn't appear to even be breathing, which... yeah. Was a bit unnerving.

Thinking about Eris' note, she walked over to the table where a chessboard was set up, ready and waiting. She'd played chess for years online in various tournaments and considered herself to be decent. Of course, if Snag was as good as Eris said he was, she was no match for him. But it was still something to do.

Sitting down, Trynn considered the board for a moment before looking up at the silent specter and jerking her head towards the seat across from her.

"Do you want to play?" she asked, fully expecting him to remain like a statue by the window, regardless of what Eris had said.

To her surprise, however, Snag immediately walked over and lowered himself into the chair. He moved with an easy grace that she would not have expected, as if his feet were as light as air. He barely made a sound or caused the cushions in the chair to rustle as he sank down across from her.

She chose white, which always went first in a match.

They started to play at an easy pace. She did not press Snag to talk again, respecting his desire for silence even as the game became more heated.

Within ten moves, she was beaten, and tipped her king in defeat. Without a word, she put the pieces back in place, and they played again. She was able to hold out for thirteen moves in the second game. By the third, she had lasted fourteen moves.

Eris hadn't been joking. In fact, Trynn was willing to bet that he'd been going easy on her to extend the games.

The contest went some way toward thawing the ice between the two of them, and she studied Snag closely across the table. Even though he was a terrifying, spectral creature with nearly translucent skin covered in scars, no hair, and large, dark eyes that almost seemed to glow from within, Trynn could sense a kind of sadness in him. She wondered if he, too, had lost someone dear to him in the distant past.

When their eyes met briefly over the chessboard, she felt for a moment that she was seeing past the icy exterior, into the heart beneath. Though she couldn't have said why, she got the impression, before Snag's shutters fell shut again, that he was consumed with worry over Eris.

Again, she wondered how long the pair had known each other. If he was to be believed, Eris was nearly two thousand years old, and compared to him, Snag looked *ancient*. How old *was* he? What had he seen across all those countless centuries?

If Snag did have a heart buried under that impassive exterior, you wouldn't have known it by his style of play, which was highly aggressive, brutal, and unforgiving. His motions were sharp and each time he captured one of her pieces, he knocked it off the board with a tightly controlled vehemence that suggested it had done him a personal wrong. His gaze was intense, a scowl fighting to slide over his features every so often, only to be carefully suppressed before it could fully surface.

He was an enigma, and she could barely read him at all. Educational though the chess games had been, she wished that Eris would return to break the tension. They were in a lull between games, and Snag was currently sitting in the chair across from her with his eyes closed meditatively. Trynn wondered if he were thinking, or listening carefully to the sounds of life around them. Every now and then, she could detect the muffled slam of a door down the hallway, and knew that people were coming and going from their rooms, despite the lateness of the hour. It was a bit comforting, really—evidence that she hadn't truly fallen down the rabbit hole.

Beyond the door, life continued as normal.

Exhaustion was once more creeping up on her, but she knew that sleep wouldn't come until Eris returned. Indeed, she had no idea where she was even supposed to sleep. Even though she and Eris had started to act on the overwhelming desire possessing them, it still seemed foolish to assume she would be sharing his bed that night—especially after what had happened earlier.

Of course, if he *was* a vampire, maybe he wouldn't sleep at night anyway? She'd seen him sleeping—or just awoken—during the day on three separate occasions now. Perhaps they could switch off with the bed. Still, it seemed rude to assume.

Maybe she would just go grab a pillow and blanket and curl up on the couch. It had been comfortable enough when she'd fallen asleep on it earlier.

Giving up on her musings for the moment, Trynn retrieved Eris' ancient laptop and sat back down to scan the web. She needed more information to give to Eris, who clearly intended to do something about the situation with the arms dealer and their mystery man, Kovac. Though she had no idea what action he could reasonably take.

Without her own computer, she could not access the MASQUE portal, although she was able to see the public information forum and know that several of her fellow hackers were intent on following the lead she'd provided.

Wishing she could go back to her hotel and get her stuff, Trynn finally succumbed to the combination of boredom and curiosity, and broke through the light security on Eris' email account. Knowing that she was pushing her luck with a man she had barely known for twenty-four hours, Trynn scanned through his recent emails. Her eyes were drawn to the subject line— charmingly titled *'Don't be an idiot'*—of personal correspondence from someone called Tré. She opened it.

Eris,

We're headed your way, but travel from the US to Cyprus is very limited right now, so soon after the coordinated pipe bomb attacks at JFK and La Guardia. We're attempting to get something out of LAX instead, but it will delay us for an additional day or so. With luck, we'll be able to get a flight out of here sometime late tomorrow. Please don't do anything stupid before we get there.

Tré

A sense of foreboding settled over Trynn like a blanket, smothering her.

"Snag, come look at this," she said quietly.

She heard no noise of approach, but looked up to find Snag's pale face looming over her shoulder, his dark eyes staring unblinkingly at the computer screen. Something in his features seemed to harden as he skimmed over the message, confirming her fears.

"He's done something stupid, hasn't he?" she whispered.

Trynn stared up at her guard, willing him to speak. It was in vain, however, as Snag made no comment, but only straightened and returned to his place by the window.

Trynn leaned back in her chair, weariness making her limbs feel heavy.

He's out there somewhere, all by himself. How do I know he's safe?

An instant later, another thought rose up. *What does it matter? I barely know this guy. Why should I be obsessed with his safety? He can probably take care of himself, anyway.*

The internal arguments chased each other around her overtired brain. She felt dizzy, and knew that she needed sleep more than anything in that moment.

I want to stay awake and make sure he gets back all right.

Don't be stupid. He's nothing to you. Get some sleep while you can. Besides, he'll wake you when he gets back.

Pressing her fingers against her pounding temples, Trynn let out a little growl of frustration before getting up and stumbling towards the sleeping alcove. She no longer cared if it was proper or weird. She no longer cared if Eris showed up later and wanted to speak with her. Trynn's body was demanding sleep, and she could do nothing more to fight it tonight.

Trynn threw herself gracelessly onto the foot of the California King-sized bed. She crawled up towards the headboard and managed to pull down the covers so she could crawl under them. It was soft and warm, and the sheets smelled of Eris as she buried her face into his pillow. With a heavy sigh, Trynn immediately dropped off to sleep.

This time, however, instead of a room full of priceless artifacts and a man who loved her, Trynn fell into restless dreams full of impenetrable darkness and distant screaming carried on the wind.

ELEVEN

Bastian kicked aside a broken pallet and lowered himself onto a dusty couch with large slashes across the cushions. He brushed dust off his dark suit and tilted his head first to one side, then the other, feeling the satisfying crack of his neck.

Looking up, he found that he was being watched dutifully by a hoard of his men, their blank, dead eyes glittering in the semi-darkness.

"It is nearly time, my friends," he crooned. None of them responded to the words, or even blinked. In most cases, he had made sure to utterly annihilate their individuality, plunging them into the darkness and evil that flowed through the fabric of the world. Bastian had chosen each one carefully from humanity's dregs—the desperate and the destitute—and they had not resisted his call. Now, their souls were forever trapped, and their bodies were vessels for his master's will.

"Soon, we will take delivery of our precious cargo. Then begins a reign of destruction that will transform this world into our master's kingdom." Bastian could not keep the growing exultation from his voice. It was his dream to stand beside his master and rule at his right hand. He would be the most honored servant. Beloved. Held more dearly than a son.

Bloodlust rushed into his fevered brain as he thought of what they could do, once the world was theirs. It was a wonderful feeling, and his excitement threatened to spill over. Sensing the growing storm within him, his slaves grew restless. The mental energy he was using to ensure they did his bidding grew frenetic, and their limbs twitched under its pull.

Calm yourself, dog.

Bael's command echoed through his being, sending a shiver down his spine. He immediately clamped down on his frenzied emotions, forcing the undead in the room back under control. Keeping his mania bottled up was difficult. Bastian felt crazed, and longed to take it out on some helpless living thing. He knew, however, that his master would be displeased if he disobeyed a direct order.

To stay focused, he pulled out the itinerary that the Russian, Timur, had provided for delivery of the bombs. Bastian was expecting five individually wrapped and sealed crates containing the portable nuclear devices. He had agents standing by, ready to transport them to various cities around the region for simultaneous detonation.

The sixth device would be delivered separately to his agent in central Damascus. There was little point in bringing it out here to the war-damaged neighborhoods east of the city, just so they could turn around and take it back to the government district a day later. It would be detonated outside of the Parliament building for the Syrian People's Council. The resulting deaths would produce the maximum possible destabilizing effect in a country already torn by conflict and fighting.

Wild giddiness threatened to overpower him once more as he felt Bael's power pulse around him. It was nearly their moment. Nearly their time to rule.

The plan for six simultaneous terrorist attacks against large, soft targets in major Middle Eastern and North African cities would produce catastrophic results. It was a stroke of genius.

Thousands of lives would be lost right away. More importantly, though, every nation in the world would be thrown into disarray, pointing fingers at each other and trying to find someone to blame for the atrocity. Christians would blame Muslims. Capitalists would blame communists. The West would blame the East, and vice versa. Markets would crash, security would be increased a hundred-fold.

And all the while these petty, pathetic little countries would become more and more divided, more suspicious of one another, until someone's finger slipped and pressed a button, bringing down Armageddon. It was a masterstroke for engineering the fall of the world to Bael's power, and Bastian would be squarely at the heart of the transformation.

He and the undead had already been turned by Bael, so they had nothing to fear from the coming nuclear fallout. They could enter the hot zone and find trapped victims. It would be easy to turn them into more undead soldiers for the great army of the apocalypse. Their chances of detection would be minimal under the cloud of chaos that would descend across the planet in the wake of the attacks.

And the families of those lost would never question the lack of a body to bury.

Bastian could barely keep his energy leashed. He stood and walked over to a broken window, staring out across the ruined landscape of bombed-out buildings in the watery moonlight. A sea of bleached and crumbled concrete stretched before him, with blank windows staring into the night like empty sockets in a skull.

The bleak vista extended as far as the eye could see. Despite the torpid summer night, a chill wind gusted through the room. Dust and filth swirled around Bastian, an appropriate shroud for the power that he was about to unleash.

"What targets do you anticipate will be taken out, sir?" a voice said from behind Bastian.

He recognized the voice as belonging to one of his top men—a leader, of sorts, among the undead, who still retained a shred of personality and will. Bastian did not turn to answer him. He continued facing toward the window with his hands clasped behind his back.

Breathing in, he replied with satisfaction. "Many targets will fall, here in Damascus. Several media outlets and various government buildings will be totally destroyed in the blast. We must make sure that we surround the area before the local authorities arrive on the scene to begin rescue and recovery operations. It won't be difficult. They will hesitate to approach too near the center of the blast, due to the radiation."

Feeling euphoric, Bastian smiled, still looking out across the city towards the western horizon, where he could just make out the silhouette of the skyline denoting his future hunting ground.

I am coming for your deaths. Your utter destruction, he thought with something like glee. A shiver traveled down his spine, and his mouth began to water at the thought of all the blood that would be spilled. It would be his moment to avenge himself against humanity. Humanity had never done anything for him except toss him in the gutter and grind his face into the filth. Humanity had made him what he was, and now it would reap what it had sown.

As he stood gazing out of the window, the softest brush of something grazed against the edges of his mind. The sensation was so faint and fleeting that, for a moment, he thought he'd imagined it.

But, no. He went completely still, like a dog on the hunt. His patience was rewarded long minutes later, when he felt the presence again, closer than before.

The presence both drew and repelled; it was like him, yet not.

Turning slowly on the spot, Bastian stared around the room. Several of the undead looked up as his eyes settled on them, but again, none of them spoke. As he approached the window on the adjacent wall, he finally turned away from his suspicious examination of those with him and looked out the window again.

Could one of Bael's six abominations truly be approaching alone? Could they be so lucky on this auspicious day?

He felt certain that there was only a single vampire, but he was hesitant to stretch out with his mind and reveal himself without knowing more about the situation.

As the breeze from outside swirled through the broken widow, bringing the smells of the night with it, Bastian inhaled deeply. He caught the faintest hint of a vampire's scent on the air — sweet and metallic. A single male, approaching from the southwest. His presence was light as air, and Bastian caught the whiff of something animal. Something large, feathered, and predatory.

A wide smile split Bastian's face as he scanned the dark sky around the abandoned building. He couldn't see the abomination yet, but he knew it was close by. The strange feeling of being simultaneously drawn and repulsed grew stronger, like an approaching beacon. Bael was no longer present after his brief appearance earlier, but Bastian knew that his master must be warned of the abomination's approach.

He consciously relaxed his body and called for his master. Moments later, Bael descended like a malevolent aura around the bombed-out complex. The demon's eagerness was infectious as he, too, sensed the approach of one of his failures.

Find him, Bael commanded, triumphant. *Question him. Break him.*

"Yes, master," Bastian vowed. He could hear shuffling around him as the undead sensed Bael's excitement. The prospect of catching and torturing a vampire — one of his failed creations — seemed to fill Bael with the same frenzy that had possessed Bastian earlier as he contemplated the coming nuclear war.

Discover all that he knows about me, about the prophecy, and about the Council of Thirteen. Show him the meaning of pain.

"It will be as you say, my master," Bastian assured as he moved towards the door.

-o-o-o-

Swirling through the air over the two hundred kilometer stretch of open water near Damascus in the form of fast-moving mist, Eris allowed his thoughts to wander back to Nicosia. He knew that Snag was going to have his head once he returned, and Tré would probably tear apart whatever was left. Both had urged him, quite sensibly, to wait until the others arrived before setting off to confront whatever awaited them in Damascus.

Eris had disregarded their advice with good reason, though. He could not ignore the feeling of impending doom that had settled over his senses like a pall. His awareness of Bael's power had seemed to grow tenfold, even in the short time since he convinced Trynn to stay with them at the hotel. It was impossible for him to ignore. Soon, the demon's power would grow so strong that Eris would be unable to protect his mate.

Her kiss lingered like a phantom on his lips, and even in mist form, he could still feel the brush of her skin against his. He wanted to revel in the sensation, but needed to remain focused on his destination. He could not allow himself to become distracted now. It was important that he be on guard.

Would Bael become aware of his presence? Eris was taking care to shield his thoughts, but he knew he would have to proceed carefully in order to scope out the base where Bael's servant was holed up. If he were detected, the consequences could be catastrophic.

Though they'd have to catch me first, he thought grimly.

Eris thought back to Trynn's words about a simultaneous nuclear attack in multiple cities. This was no longer just about saving her life, even if that *had* been his primary motivator for running out on Snag. No, this was about saving all of humanity.

As vampires, fate had arrayed the six of them—seven, now—against Bael's vile power. Fighting him any way they could was, at this point, their only reason for existing. They would never surrender in their effort to prevent the complete desolation of the Light and rise of the Darkness.

In the distance, Eris thought he could make out the shore. Twinkling light from the port city of Beirut glinted off the water, and Damascus lay barely a hundred kilometers beyond. Eris sped up as his goal approached.

He would not allow Bael to destroy his mate—his *life*—again.

Stay focused, he reminded himself. He needed to remain aware of his surroundings. He could not afford the smallest lapse in concentration.

Thanks to Snag's transfer of power earlier, he now had a mental fix on the beacon blazing from Damascus like a sickly green flame in the darkness. Indeed, now that his eyes had been opened, so to speak, he could scarcely banish the nauseating awareness of it.

This is a living hell, no wonder Snag never speaks, he thought wryly.

The evil miasma smothering him like a thick cloud was both familiar... and *wrong* on every level. He could tell that the life force behind the beacon was an undead soul, twisted and mutilated by Bael, but the power emanating from it was shocking. It was much stronger than anything he had sensed before from the undead—even when he and the others had been elbow-deep in the things' entrails, fighting to protect Della and Tré.

No. This was something different. Something new.

As Eris ate up the distance separating him from his goal and passed into the city, he tried to devise a strategy to assess this new and unknown threat. The force drawing him like a moth to flame was centered to the east, away from the bustling central hub of life within the war-torn city.

He approached the source of the taint and circled, trying to get his bearings. He could tell he was very near his goal. Pulling in his life force, he transformed into a great, dark owl. Borne aloft on powerful wings, he glided gracefully through the darkness, barely flapping, approaching in total silence. One building in the bombed out area he was circling held the flickering, insubstantial light of a lit fire. He zeroed in on the structure, focusing all his senses on the interior, and the faint signs of life coming from inside.

He could see a figure standing, outlined by a blazing brazier behind him, gazing through a blown out window. Their eyes met, and dread that he could not explain gripped his mind like a vice. A moment later, the figure vanished.

Before Eris could do more than register his disappearance, a freezing cold mist surrounded him. The particles were like ice against his feathers, weighing him down, dragging him towards the earth.

The owl flapped wildly, letting out a piercing screech of anger as Eris fought to free himself from the all-encompassing icy vapor. Like quicksand, though, the more he struggled, the more he became ensnared by the trap, which closed tightly around him.

In desperation, Eris tried to push his life force out and explode into mist to escape the situation, but his power met a hard, invisible wall that surrounded him and kept him in his avian form.

Trapped as an owl, unable to fly and plummeting towards the earth, Eris let out a mental cry towards the heavens, hoping beyond hope that someone, anyone, would hear him.

If I survive, I am never, ever going to live this down, he thought as his body smashed into the windshield of an abandoned car with a deafening crash of breaking glass.

Agony shot through his left wing, which had taken the brunt of the impact. Eris felt muscles tear and heard a telltale crack as it was crushed beneath him, totally useless. His body bounced once, sliding across the hood to land on the cracked pavement.

Even on the ground, the cold mist continued to press down on him, flattening his lungs and crushing his damaged wing even more. Unable to draw breath, Eris stared up at the starry sky as the world faded into darkness.

-o-o-o-

Back in Nicosia, in the dark hotel room where Trynn slept restlessly in Eris' bed, Snag sat in a chair by the window, silent and unmoving. His head was bowed, his fingertips pressed together as if in meditation, as his consciousness expanded out into the night.

He was breathing deeply, listening to the night sounds of the hotel and world around him, gauging the growing strength of the cloud of malevolence emanating from the mainland across the Levantine Sea.

All was silent and still. But it was not the still of peace. It was the still of waiting.

From nowhere, a distant cry of pain and rage rent the stillness — terrible in its familiarity.

The ancient vampire's head snapped up; his eyes flew open.

If Trynn had been awake, she would have seen the deep-set orbs glowing white, like a cold, furious fire.

TWELVE

Trynn blinked awake to find the pale light of morning glowing from behind the curtains. *Thank god for that,* she thought as she sat up in the rumpled bed. The night had seemed to drag on forever. She had woken often, frightened and restless from half-remembered dream images.

It was a relief to finally rise and face the day.

Padding her way to the bathroom, she showered quickly and brushed her teeth with a disposable complimentary toothbrush from the hotel. As she wandered out into the suite's living area, she found Snag sitting by the window, staring at the heavy curtain as though he could see through it, miles away. His face held none of the stony neutrality it had the previous day. Instead, it was set in gaunt lines of cold rage.

She glanced around, searching for Eris, a sinking feeling growing in her stomach. After a moment, it became clear to her that he had not returned from his night's travels.

Spinning on her heel, Trynn rounded on Snag. "Where is he? Why didn't he return?"

Snag, who barely seemed to have moved since the previous evening, turned his head towards her but did not answer. His eyes glowed, deep in their sockets, and she had to cover a flinch.

"*Where. Is. He.*" She took a step towards Snag, her fists clenching. "*Tell me!*"

He remained completely silent, still staring at her with those glowing eyes. It quickly became obvious that she would get nowhere by demanding his help.

Where could Eris have gone? He couldn't still be hunting during the day, could he? Could real vampires go out in daylight? Eris had made it sound like they couldn't.

Trynn realized that she didn't really know anything about these creatures. How often did they need to hunt? How long did it normally take them?

With an uncomfortable squirming feeling in her stomach, Trynn wondered if they killed their prey. Could Eris be a murderer, too? Had she been fetishizing murder last night when she fantasized about letting him bite her?

Suddenly, agreeing to remain with them in their hotel room seemed downright reckless. What the hell had she been thinking? How did she know that she wasn't their next meal?

The memory of Eris' lips against her own and the way his mouth had grazed so lightly across her neck made her shiver, her body caught once again in that intoxicating no man's land between fear and arousal.

But… no. She didn't really think he'd been keeping her around for an easy meal.

He had been too solicitous. Too concerned for her safety. It had been as though he was terrified she would vanish in the blink of an eye.

But… if he was so worried about her, *why wasn't he here*?

Remembering the private email she'd read the previous day, Trynn recalled that the person called Tré had cautioned Eris against doing anything stupid. *Don't be an idiot*, the subject line said.

What did that mean? Was Eris likely to make a rash decision and put himself in danger?

It seemed more and more likely, the more she thought about it. Combined with Snag's taut and angry visage, Trynn felt certain that Eris must have had left against their advice and set out on his own.

"He went after the terrorist, didn't he?" Trynn asked after a moment. Her voice emerged faint and wavering.

Although Snag did not answer in words, there was a sharp edge to his expression which all but confirmed Trynn's suspicions. Eris, wherever he was, whatever he was doing, had gone after the man that Trynn had been tracking. He was alone, without any form of support or backup.

The panic that welled up inside her took her by surprise. She felt breathless, as if her muscles were tightening around her joints, trying to make her curl up in a ball.

Anger followed a bare moment later.

How could he do this to me? How could he just leave?

She had to do something. She had to *move*. She didn't know exactly what she could do, but getting back to her laptop and trying to find new information about what was going on in Damascus seemed like a logical first step.

Glancing around frantically, Trynn crossed to the table, snatched up her bag, and headed for the door. Before she could even get a hand on the doorknob, a lean figure blocked her path. Trynn looked up into Snag's set face, blinking at him in the room's dim light.

Standing so close to the spectral creature made the hair on Trynn's neck stand up. A deadly chill poured off of him in waves.

A sudden, inexplicable sleepiness drifted over her. Exhaustion seemed to settle in her bones, and she swayed, eyelids drooping. Trynn shook her head, fighting hard against the sudden feeling of sedation. *What the hell?*

She banished the fog with an effort of will, breathing deeply in an attempt to flood her body with oxygen as she stared at Snag's face. Perhaps it was her imagination, but she thought she saw a flicker of something like consternation pass across his harsh features.

The heavy weight lifted as suddenly as it came, and Trynn guessed that, somehow, Snag had tried to put her into a sleep.

Yeah, no. Not happening, Sunshine.

Deciding in a flash that she wasn't going to bow to his mind games, Trynn reached around him and grasped the doorknob. With her other arm, she tried to use her elbow to drive Snag backwards, away from the door.

Initially, Trynn thought this would be an easy move. Snag, after all, was a rail thin wisp of a creature who looked as if a stiff breeze would knock him down.

To her surprise, Trynn realized that Snag must be made of stronger stuff. He didn't flinch or move a muscle, even when she drove the point of her elbow deep into his ribs. No grunt of pain or whoosh of breath suggested to her that he even noticed her attempt at making him move, and his feet did not waver an inch from where they were planted in front of the door.

Stymied, she glared at him. "Get out of my way!" she growled. "You can't keep me here!"

Her voice rose in anger until she was nearly shouting. Snag blinked once, then pressed one bony fingertip against her forehead. This time when the woozy feeling assaulted her, she thought she'd be ready for it. But she was in no way prepared for the direct onslaught of his will as he sliced effortlessly through her mental defenses.

"No..." she moaned, her voice trailing away.

Trynn was distantly aware of the way her body listed to one side, her shoulder bumping against the wall by the door. Her head spun. Numbness spread down her body, into her fingers and toes.

Darkness was descending over her vision, no matter how hard she fought it. Within seconds, she could no longer resist the overwhelming exhaustion pressing down on her mind. She slumped forward, caught by wiry arms that supported her weight without effort as she fell into a deep sleep.

-o-o-o-

Eris came back into awareness slowly, feeling like his thoughts were trudging through the much-reviled swamp mud that surrounded the old plantation house he and the others had stayed in outside New Orleans. Oh, how he'd hated that damned swamp.

The first sound he became aware of was that of quick, excited breathing.

Right. Yes. Damascus. Suitcase nukes. Bael. Focus, Eris.

He realized in a rush that he was flat on his back, bound to whatever hard surface he was lying on by thick ropes and straps of leather. He tested the restraints, jerking against the bindings, only to feel blinding pain erupt in his shoulder. That was also roughly the same point at which he realized he was naked.

A soft chuckle echoed through the room.

"I wouldn't do that, if I were you," a voice said.

Eris tried to open his eyes but found that they were gummed together against his lids with something that felt like glue.

"Thanks for the advice," he croaked. His throat was parched and raw, as if he had been screaming. He swallowed, trying to moisten it before he continued. "Bit much for a first date, though. Don't you think?"

He made a vague waggling motion with the hand of his uninjured arm, indicating the bondage, and the being naked, and... well... *all of it*, actually. He had a feeling that Snag was going to be really, *really* cross with him at some point in the very near future.

There was no answer from his captor, but Eris heard the unmistakable sound of metal being dragged across metal. The noise made the hair on the back of his neck stand up; it sounded like two sword blades being pulled slowly across one another.

With a sinking sensation in the pit of his stomach, Eris thought, *Damn, if Snag doesn't kill me, Tré will. This is really not shaping up to be my finest hour.*

For some reason, mental focus seemed much harder to achieve than it normally was. He had a vague recollection of crashing through a car windshield and then being suffocated… which, yes, okay, probably had something to do with it. Feeling dizzy, he tried to breathe deeply, but found that this only made the spinning worse. Also, his ribs hurt rather a lot whenever he inhaled.

"You are probably feeling quite weak right now, but don't be alarmed. I did that on purpose."

"Wait… did what?" Eris slurred, trying again to concentrate. "What did you do to me?"

"When you flew so unwittingly into my clutches, I decided to drain your blood to weaken your life force."

"Drained… me?" Eris ground out, trying to get his brain to sync up with his mouth.

"Yes, that's right," the man said with a low chuckle. "I prefer more…compliant victims, shall we say?"

Lovely.

Eris struggled again, but his efforts only seemed to sap him of more energy.

His captor clicked his tongue disapprovingly. "Now, now, lie still and be a good boy."

Slumping back against the hard surface of the table, Eris blew a derisive breath through his lips. "Sod off. I was never *good* even when I *was* a boy. And you need to work on your people skills. I've got a friend — the two of you could start a self-help group."

"Perhaps it's past time someone taught you a lesson."

The relish in the man's voice was obvious, but Eris allowed no trace of alarm pass across his face.

"Oh, good," he said, mock cheerful even though his voice was still gravelly. "A sadist. This is going to be fun, I can tell already."

His nonchalance seemed to aggravate the man, who began pacing in circles around the table to which he was bound. Eris sort of wished he could pry his eyelids open… but, then again, there was something to be said for not getting an eyeful of the torture instruments before they were put to use, he supposed.

"You will learn some manners before this day is done," his captor snarled.

"Many have tried —" Eris began, only to be cut off when the man swooped down on him silently and gripped his hair in an unforgiving fist.

Jerking Eris' head back painfully, he brought his face close to Eris' exposed throat. He was mere inches away, and Eris could smell the man's putrid breath on his face. It was all he could do not to gag.

So, he thought as the sadist ran a ragged fingernail down the thin skin over his jugular, *I guess this is how the other half lives. At least I have the good manners to hypnotize them first.*

Suddenly, the earth underneath them shook, and the grip on Eris' hair disappeared.

"Yes, my master," the man breathed. "What is your bidding?"

Eris strained to open his eyes, even just a sliver. Finally, he managed to rip one of them apart a slit, feeling as if several of his eyelashes had parted company with his skin during the process. He was able to see a small portion of the room through the tiny gap, though it was blurrier than he thought it probably should have been.

"What was that about?" he asked mildly. "Got new marching orders, have you?"

The sadist didn't answer, but Eris could sense him moving away.

"What's the matter? Cat got your tongue?" Eris called after him. "And I thought we were getting along so well!"

Something about goading his captor seemed to be pouring life back into him. Perhaps it was merely the small act of resistance that fueled his surge of energy. He knew it would not sustain him forever, though. After that, the mental image of Trynn would be his talisman against the tempting darkness swirling at the edges of his mind, whispering of sweet oblivion.

Out of the crack in his eyelids, Eris saw movement and tried to flinch away, but his reactions were far too slow. A streak of stinging pain opened along the length of his cheek. He hissed, feeling hot blood trickle down his face. Blood that he probably couldn't afford to lose.

"My master grows weary of your impertinence. If you do not hold your tongue, I will slice you to shreds with this knife," the man threatened.

Well, that certainly escalated quickly.

Eris breathed heavily through his nose, forcing his reaction to the fresh pain under control.

Stay focused. Think. Concentrate.

Reaching out with his consciousness, Eris discovered that he and his captor were alone in the large bunker-like room in which he had awoken. There were other presences nearby, but not so close that he could shout out for help and expect to get it. And even if they had been, the presences felt... *off*. More than likely, he was surrounded by Bael's mindless puppets, which certainly didn't make things look any brighter.

"Now that I have your attention," his captor said in a softer voice, "I want you to know how this is going to work."

Even without decent eyesight, Eris could tell that the man was pacing around him again. They'd barely gotten started, and he was already finding the habit intensely irritating.

"I'm going to ask you a question—"

The man's voice was interrupted again by the sound of metal sliding across metal.

"—and you are going to answer the question, completely and truthfully. Do you understand me?"

"Not really."

"What do I need to clarify?" his captor replied in a dangerous voice.

"Oh, nothing. I just don't really get why you think that's going to happen. It seems pretty unlikely."

The sadist laughed. "Ha! I hardly think so. I will break you under my ministrations. Slowly. Deliberately."

The evil that poured out of the man while he spoke made Eris feel as if black oil were coursing over his body and face.

"People skills," he reiterated. "Just saying."

Without warning, a fist slammed into his face, breaking his nose and making blood spray everywhere. Despite his attempts to remain stoic, Eris let out a grunt when he was struck and felt his eyes immediately begin to swell.

Well, fuck. So much for being able to see.

"Do you know who Bael is?" the sadist asked, looming over him.

Eris spit blood out of his mouth, only to have it dribble down his chin. "A loser."

"Want to rethink your answer?"

"Not so you'd notice." The words made it sound like his sinuses were clogged, which felt somewhat less than dignified.

This time the unexpected blow was to his diaphragm, knocking the air out of him. He couldn't seem to drag it back in, his mouth gaping open like a fish. Being a vampire, he could almost certainly go without for a bit if he had to, but that didn't make it any more pleasant.

"I will ask you again, do you know who Bael is?" the sadist demanded, this time pacing back and forth on his left.

"A demon," Eris choked out, when he was finally able to breathe again.

"Very good. That wasn't so hard, now, was it?"

The man leaned over the table, his clammy hand pressed against Eris' exposed leg. Eris shuddered and tried to pull away, but the ropes around his ankles were too tight.

"I don't think you give my master enough credit," the man said conversationally.

As he spoke, Eris felt the tip of a knife press into his leg. He held his breath as the man slowly pressed harder and harder, until the blade pierced his skin.

Eris gritted his teeth together, struggling not to cry out as the knife was forced downward, towards the table, slicing through his skin.

"And you are a vampire, correct?"

"Correct," Eris gasped, squeezing his swollen eyelids together as pain streaked through him in sharp bursts. "As you're well aware."

"One of the thirteen?"

Eris hesitated. Even if he had been in his right mind rather than strapped to a table being tortured, it was too complicated a question to answer.

There was so much that they still needed to learn regarding the prophecy. So much they didn't understand.

"I've no idea," he said truthfully.

The man withdrew and could be heard rummaging some distance away.

"You will find," he said, his voice echoing around the chamber, "that I was fully prepared for you to refuse to cooperate. Tell me, which part of your body do you value most?"

"My brain, I suppose," he said.

"We'll need that for a bit longer yet, I'm afraid," the sadist said, coming closer as he spoke. "Such as it is."

Without warning, Eris' skin erupted into fiery agony. It was unbearable, unendurable, and Eris arched his back, struggling wildly against his bonds despite his shattered arm.

He let out a deafening scream as the sun's rays blistered his exposed skin. Behind his swollen eyes, glowing red seemed to grow out of the darkness, as though he were being consumed by the undying inferno at the heart of a star.

Eris lost track of himself, of his surroundings, of what was being done to his body under the pain and agony of direct sunlight. He could no longer hear himself screaming at the top of his lungs or feel the cool metal table underneath him. He was trapped in the scorching flames, unable to escape.

Quite as suddenly as the torture had begun, the flames were extinguished. The sun's rays were blocked, plunging him back into blessed, cool shadow. He lay limp in his bonds, his strength spent after mere moments under the unforgiving glare.

I will not. I will not. I will not.

He was still in pain from his blistered skin, yet it was so much better than being in direct sunlight that he thought he could withstand it eternally, if it meant never undergoing that unbearable agony again.

He started to shiver, his body slipping into shock after the abuse it had sustained over the last few hours.

"Are you one of the thirteen?" The man repeated.

Eris' teeth were chattering so much that his answer was barely understandable. "I d-don't kn-know. W-we s-s-still have m-much to learn about-t the p-prophecy."

"Hmm… yes," his captor said thoughtfully. "It is a bit of an enigma, is it not?"

Eris did not reply. It was taking all of his strength and determination to remain conscious; he was not going to give the man what he was seeking.

"How many are there in your coven?"

And so the true test began. Eris tried to turn his face away in refusal. He would not betray his friends. He would not make them a target for this madman. He would die before giving away their secrets.

"So be it," his captor said in a resigned voice. He stood again and moved off towards Eris' feet.

Eris could hear a drawer sliding in and out and then the man returned to his side.

"It didn't have to be this way, you know," he said in a condescending tone.

Eris felt a metal rod being pressed against the worst of his burns. For a moment he was confused. Then, the cold hit him.

Iron. Second only to living wood when it came to damaging vampire flesh.

Against his blistered skin, the iron rod felt like a block of ice. Rather than the cold penetrating only the top few layers of his skin, though, it seemed to seep through his muscles and right into his bones, further draining his life force.

With a groan of pain, he tried for what seemed like the hundredth time to yank his flesh away, to protect himself. Yet to no avail. He was trapped in the clutches of this minion of Bael with a taste for cruelty and torture. His skin started to crystallize under the rod, only to have Bael's servant move it to more and more sensitive areas on his body.

Eris abandoned all pretense and screamed as loudly as he could, desperate to draw attention to himself, for someone, anyone, to come to his aid.

"You can scream all you want. The ones outside obey only *my* command," the man said maliciously.

Removing the rod, he left Eris lying on the table, panting and soaked in icy sweat. He was completely spent, his body desperately weakened. He convulsed; his muscles jerked and spasmed, completely outside of his control.

"I want you to tell me all you know about the Council of Thirteen," the undead man demanded, coming close to Eris' face again.

Eris, who was bordering on delirium, giggled feebly. Breathing in heavy gasps, he tilted his face blindly toward his captor and mumbled, "Can you guys smell each other? 'Cause, I'm sorry, but... you really smell bad. Even with... that cheap cologne thing... you've got going on."

Despite his numbed brain, Eris could hear how slurred the words sounded. Despite all the pain he'd experienced, he was still resolutely set against giving this man any information about Trynn, the council, or his friends, though. He would protect them at all costs.

He began to understand that this struggle, this battle, could and probably would claim his existence. He had no idea how long he could hold out without being pitched into insanity. His best bet would quite likely be to goad his captor into destroying him before he accidentally revealed anything important.

But how long would this man tolerate his defiance? Would Bael himself come down to finish the job he'd started millennia ago?

I will never get to see Trynn again, he realized, his chest aching from more than the screams. Grief welled up, and he struggled for a moment with the impulse to drop into the darkness pressing all around him. He was so very tired—his reserves spent from who knew how many hours of torment.

"Tell me who you are," Eris demanded.

He wondered idly if the sadist would answer, or just start torturing him again.

"My name is Bastian Kovac," the man growled, "and I am my master's greatest creation. His *success*. I am the embodiment of his victory."

"Sounds very gratifying for you," Eris rasped.

Bastian gripped Eris' face with alarmingly strong fingers. Sharp fingernails pressed into Eris' skin.

"You are the failure! Vampires are the perversion of my master's power, useless and weak! Your frailty makes me sick. You, who cannot tolerate a weak ray of sun on your skin—"

He paused for a moment and Eris imagined he was shaking his head. "You can be destroyed by a stake through your heart."

To emphasize his words, it seemed, Bastian pressed the rod against Eris' bare chest, directly above his heart.

Eris arched and bucked as Bastian laughed, the sound cruel.

After several moments, Eris was released from the icy agony. With no warning, his mental connection with Snag exploded into life within his mind, and he groaned. Apparently, the threat of iron so close to his vulnerable heart had broken through the mental shields he'd erected to keep Bael from sensing his thoughts.

The connection surged, strong and vibrant. Eris could feel Snag's fury at him for landing himself in danger, just as he felt Bastian's consciousness probe at his vulnerable mind.

In response to the oily touch of Bael's servant, Eris felt Snag wrap a mental shield around him, forcing Bastian out and away. A low growl sounded in Eris' mind, and he knew that Snag's rage was about to spill out of control. The usually silent, sedate, and impassive vampire's power was building. He was drawing, it seemed, from the very earth itself.

Bastian let out a snarl of anger at being forced away. His self-control appeared to snap, and blows rained down on Eris' body, seemingly at random. Eris felt a couple of ribs shatter, and sank back into his mind, allowing Snag's strength to cradle his fading consciousness. The pain grew duller and he lay completely lifeless, unable to fight any more.

Meanwhile, Snag's anger mounted, and the air around Eris seemed to crackle like an immense weapon charging, ready to rain down destruction.

As he began to slip into unconsciousness, Eris heard Snag's voice, low in his ear.

You deceived me. You forced me to remain behind and protect her, and all the while you intended to sacrifice yourself.

Eris could not reply. Could not defend his actions by stating the truth, that he'd been a fool and underestimated Kovac's power, probably at the cost of his own life. He couldn't muster the energy necessary to do anything more than send a single plea.

Keep... her... safe...

There was a long pause.

I made you a vow. I will not break it.

Comforted by the promise, Eris slipped gratefully into darkness. He did not hear Snag's final words.

I will keep you both safe.

-o-o-o-

Trynn groaned as consciousness returned. Every inch of her body felt heavy and painful, as if she'd endured some tortuous full-body workout that pressed her muscles far beyond their endurance.

Her eyes cracked open—even her damned *eyelids* hurt—and the world around her spun momentarily before coming into focus. She was lying on her right side on the comfortable couch, facing the partially open window. Hazy, sodium-yellow light filtered through, adding to the indistinct glow illuminating the room.

Pushing herself into a sitting position, Trynn squinted and peered around, trying to remember what the hell had happened. She stared blankly through the window for several moments, and saw that the yellow glow was from the roof light on the building across from the hotel.

It was pitch black outside.

Shit. *Shit.*

"Snag!" she yelled, furious, scrambling upright on shaky legs. She staggered forward a few steps towards the door and nearly collided with the pale vampire, who seemed to have appeared from nowhere.

"*You!*" she accused, pointing her finger into his chest. "You knocked me out!"

Snag did not respond to her accusation—*surprise, surprise.* Instead, he simply stood there, staring down at her. Perhaps it was the low light, but his features seemed even more sunken and spectral than usual.

"How dare you?" she railed, too angry to even try to calm down. "You had no right to do that to me! I am *not your hostage.* I can leave whenever I damn well please—*you are not in charge of me!*"

Again, Snag remained infuriatingly silent in the face of her tirade. He blinked at her once, the moment stretching between them.

Desperation sang through Trynn's veins, her desire to storm from the hotel growing stronger every moment. *She had to find Eris. She had to make sure that he was safe.*

She let out a wordless yell of rage and spun on her heel, pacing back and forth along the length of the couch she had just vacated. Running her hands through her hair, Trynn considered her options. How could she find Eris when the only clue she had was a vague suspicion that he'd gone after Kovac?

On her next pass, her eyes fell again on Snag. Something about the look on his face made her think he was well aware of what was going on, and where she could find Eris. She knew he wouldn't answer if she asked him directly where Eris was, but maybe she could provoke him into speaking some other way?

Trynn knew she could be a manipulative bitch when she put her mind to it. And she was *damn* well going to put her mind to it right now.

"You're a terrible friend," she snarled, staying just out of reach in case he got any ideas about putting her to sleep again. "How can you stand there blinking at me like a simpleton when Eris is out there, somewhere, in god-knows-what kind of danger? *How can you just sit by and let it happen?*"

Snag didn't move an inch, nor did his expression change. His lack of response didn't surprise Trynn in the slightest. She hadn't expected him to give over the information that easily. But that was fine. Trynn was not, in the end, a particularly nice person. And she had plenty more ammunition where that had come from.

"Do you even care about him at all?" she demanded, narrowing her eyes. "Maybe you were relieved when he headed off into danger, so you could stay here, safe and sound. Maybe all you care about is your own sorry, pathetic hide."

Snag did not react outwardly, yet something made the hair on the back of Trynn's neck stand on end. The atmosphere of the room filled with electricity—like the instant of eerie stillness in a storm just before lightning struck.

But if there was one thing Trynn had never learned how to do, it was *stop*.

"*What did he ever do to you*?" she hissed. "He's been nothing but a friend to you, and for how long? How many centuries? Yet you betray him like it's *nothing*."

A muscle at the corner of Snag's jaw contracted. As Trynn watched with a sudden surge of trepidation, he raised his right hand to his temple and closed his eyes.

Without warning, images exploded into life in front of her mind's eye. They were vivid. All-encompassing. She was still in the hotel room, but it was daylight, and the viewpoint had changed. Instead of standing by the couch, she was seated in Snag's preferred chair by the window. She could sense that Eris was lying in the bed within the walled-off area of the sleeping alcove, though she couldn't see him from her spot by the window.

We don't have time to wait!

That was Eris, speaking without speaking. Trynn could hear his rich tones as clear as day, though he was still in the other room.

This has to be resolved before it turns into a disaster! But we also can't risk leaving Trynn unguarded. You need to stay here and protect her. I'll go ahead to Damascus and see what I can do own my own about the situation. You know how important Trynn is—

Trynn felt Snag's flare of irritation at his friend's words.

—and we sure as hell aren't taking her along. We'd be delivering her straight into Bael's hands, Eris continued doggedly.

Then I will go. You will stay.

Snag's mental voice was deep and commanding. But now Trynn could feel Eris' anger, as well.

Don't be ridiculous. You're more powerful than I am. I need you here, with Trynn, protecting her. Please, Snag, just do this for me.

Snag did not respond, but Trynn felt a chill of power emanating from him. His anger was growing, filling the entire suite just as it had moments ago in the real world, when she had goaded him.

It's pragmatic, Eris pointed out, and you can't stop me from going unless you plan on fighting me outright. I'll find out exactly what we're facing, so that we can stop whatever Bael is intending with these bombs.

The image before her shifted and changed between one breath and the next. They were someplace unfamiliar. She could see a dark chamber with a light above a table where a lone figure lay.

Immediately, she recognized the man as Eris, yet he looked completely different from when she'd last seen him. His face was bloody, bruised, and swollen—his eyes crusted over with some sort of black sludge.

"Eris! *Eris!*" Trynn cried, but her voice was lost before it ever reached her lips. No matter how hard she tried, no sound escaped.

She could see burn marks upon his marble white skin, and large swatches of purple flesh where he had clearly been badly beaten. She tried to reach out and touch him, but her hand was as insubstantial as smoke.

He was barely breathing, and his skin was covered in a sheen of sweat.

Trynn felt a presence beside her, and looked up to find Snag standing next to her, staring down at Eris' broken form. He looked up slowly and met her eyes. As their gazes locked, she felt what he felt—Eris' agonizing pain and terrible weakness, the strain on the fragile thread binding his soul to his ruined body.

An instant later, Trynn was back in the real world, crouched on her hands and knees in the hotel room, trying in vain to throw up her fucking *toenails* onto the soft rug beneath her. After retching for what felt like hours and bringing up only stomach acid, she clumsily tried to push herself upright—only to fall to the side, leaning against the front of the couch.

"Oh, God," she croaked, shaking in reaction like a leaf in the wind.

She looked up at Snag through tear-blurred eyes. He was still standing in front of the doorway. As she watched, he lowered his hand from his temple and let it hang limply at his side.

Trynn swallowed several times, choking on bile, and tried to speak again. "W-we have to stop this. We have to help him! Snag, *please!*"

She was begging by the end, staring up into Snag's dark, pain-filled eyes.

He didn't answer, and hope began to die in her heart. Just as the first sob of wretched grief tried to rise and jerk free of her chest, a strange rushing sound filled the room.

Trynn looked around wildly, trying to find the source. A cool mist was swirling through the open window—something that was clearly impossible on such a sultry Mediterranean night. The cloud of vapor filled the whole room, wrapping around the two of them like a soothing caress.

Snag closed his eyes, his chin dipping, and breathed out in a slow sigh.

THIRTEEN

The swirling mist seemed to suck the air directly out of Trynn's lungs. She jerked back, her shoulders banging against the couch.

"What the hell?" she rasped, looking up at Snag. The ancient vampire still had not moved.

Trynn blinked, trying to clear the tears from her eyes. When she opened them again, the cloud of mist had disappeared, and five people stood in the center of the room—three women, and two men. She remained frozen, kneeling next to an acrid puddle of bile as she stared at the mysterious intruders.

What? How – ?

"We caught most of that, Snag," a tall man with dark hair said. His tone was that of someone who was used to being obeyed. His unnaturally light grey eyes flashed toward Trynn, who remained in the unflattering position she had been in before their arrival. "Do you know where Eris is? Can you track him?"

Snag did not speak, but the newcomer nodded as if he had.

Trynn looked over the remaining members of the group with wide eyes. Next to the leader stood a short, curvy woman with long, honey-colored hair and a mole on her face, like some old Hollywood movie actress. She returned Trynn's gaze with a look of sympathy and re-assurance.

"We should go after him right away," the second man said. He had brown hair and striking green eyes that seemed to see right through her. There was an air of easy charisma about him that permeated the room as he spoke. Trynn had the distinct feeling that whatever he wanted, he generally got.

The two women standing closest to the window were also watching Trynn with poorly veiled interest. One was a haughty vision of beauty, with porcelain skin and pale blond hair flowing around her shoulders. Intelligence blazed from her bright blue eyes, but so did cynicism.

The other had mocha skin and large, soft brown eyes. She was also a picture of loveliness, her perfection marred only by a state-of-the-art prosthesis where her left ankle and foot should have been. She looked friendly, where her companion was aloof, and Trynn was instantly drawn to her. She bestowed a quick, tense smile on Trynn before she turned back towards their leader, who was speaking.

"I don't like it much, but we'll have to split up." His silver eyes turned back towards Trynn, regarding her thoughtfully. "Snag, you've fulfilled your vow. Go. Della and I will remain behind and guard Phaidra."

Trynn felt a flash of annoyance at the mistake, though she knew it was petty.

Before she could even draw breath, Snag dissipated into a vaporous cloud right before her eyes, and hurtled out through the window. The blond woman and the dark woman were right on his tail, followed an instant later by the brown-haired man. The eerie sound of rushing wind echoed behind them for a moment, and then all was still once more.

Trynn abruptly realized that she was still crouched on the floor by a puddle of her own sick, and scrambled to her feet.

"My name's not Phaidra, it's Trynn," she said, happy when her voice barely quivered.

The Hollywood pinup girl stepped forward and steadied Trynn with a hand on her shoulder when her balance threatened to desert her.

"Of course it is," she said. "You'll have to excuse the lapse. It used to make me crazy whenever one of them slipped up and called me Irina, so believe me, I understand. My name's Della, short for Delaney, and this is Tré."

"Uh... hi," Trynn said automatically, still completely bewildered.

"Now," Della said in a no-nonsense tone. "You look like you've been through the wringer. Come on, you need to freshen up. I expect we'll be stuck here waiting for a while."

Before Trynn could protest, Della was herding her towards the bathroom with surprising effectiveness given her petite frame.

They were halfway across the suite before Trynn recovered her wits enough to put the brakes on. "I don't need to freshen up, I need answers!" she snapped.

Della looked at her sympathetically. "You'll get answers, don't worry, but first you really do need to get cleaned up. No offense, Trynn, but vampire noses are sensitive, and not to put too fine a point on it, you smell."

She wanted to be affronted by the gently delivered insult, but when she drew in breath to say something sharp, an unpleasant smell assaulted her. With a sinking feeling, she pulled her shirt up to her nose and sniffed.

Dear God. Okay – a shower was definitely necessary.

"Trynn, look. We aren't going to hear anything for a while," Della said. "You might as well take care of yourself first."

There was a certain logic to that, even if Trynn didn't much like it. She took a damned shower.

Fifteen minutes later, she stepped out of the bathroom wrapped in a fluffy robe, her wet hair plastered to her forehead. She found Della and Tré seated at the table, speaking quietly. When she came around the corner, they both looked up and Della smiled, though it was strained.

"Feeling better?" she asked.

"Yes and no," Trynn answered cautiously. "No longer stinky. Still need answers."

"Please, join us," Tré said.

Della pushed the third chair out and gestured for Trynn to take it.

Sitting down, Trynn wrapped her hands around the steaming mug that had been placed on the table in anticipation of her return. It was tea. She sipped it and looked at the two vampires expectantly.

"Xander always says that Americans drink too much coffee and not enough tea," Della said. "So we try to humor him—even though tea-drinking isn't our natural instinct, so to speak."

"Natural instinct?" Trynn echoed, confused. Then it dawned on her that these two were vampires, and probably preferred blood to bergamot. "Oh! Right... vampires. Uh, sorry. This has all been a bit much, to put it mildly."

Della waved her off. "Don't apologize. It takes a lot of getting used to."

"So, what can you tell me?" Trynn asked, looking back and forth between the pair.

Della and Tré exchanged a look.

"We were actually about to ask you that question," Della said.

"*Me*? Why?"

"We know what we overheard from Snag's mind as we were arriving. But we don't know everything," Tré said. "We need you to tell us more about what's been going on."

Trynn swallowed and scrubbed a hand through her damp hair, gathering her scattered thoughts. "Um, yeah.

Well—I'm a member of an online hacktivist group. We uncover and disseminate secret information when we feel it will have beneficial humanitarian effects."

Della and Tré listened intently, letting her explain at her own pace.

"I don't know as much as I'd like to about what's going on, honestly," Trynn said after a moment of awkward silence. "Just what I've been able to gather from emails I've been intercepting."

"What kind of emails?" Tré asked, leaning forward and folding his hands on the table.

Trynn swallowed. "There's an Eastern European underworld figure who has been amassing power and wealth at an astonishing rate. We have a few guesses about where he came from and how he's doing it, but no one can really confirm any of it. We think he gained the vast majority of his wealth from illegal trafficking of weapons, drugs, and humans, all of which can be extremely lucrative."

"Go on," Tré prompted.

"Recently, it appears he's been amassing his own private stockpile of weaponry and not reselling it." She took a deep breath. "Our latest information suggests he's planning a simultaneous attack with suitcase nukes in several cities around the region. The closest I've gotten to details was finding out about a scheduled meeting between this guy and a powerful Russian mafia kingpin in Damascus a few days ago."

"Okay, *that* is legitimately terrifying," Della said, her brown eyes growing wide.

Tré's already pale skin went a bit paler, though his eyes grew sharp. "And your information is good? How certain are you about the details of this plan?"

Trynn hesitated. "We usually have excellent intel, since we hack it all ourselves. Most of these criminals assume that their information is safe behind firewalls and security devices. I can't say that we're right a hundred percent of the time, but I am absolutely confident that this guy, B. Kovac by name, met with someone who has access to nukes and bartered a deal. I saw an email with my own eyes—one arranging transport of the weapons."

Tré swore under his breath in a language Trynn didn't recognize, and ran his hands through his dark hair.

"This reeks of Bael," Della observed quietly.

"Bael? The demon thing?" Trynn asked. "Yeah, that's what Eris thought. He seemed pretty convinced of it."

Della shivered visibly. "So, we think Bael has got this Kovac guy trying to destroy the world?"

"It seems quite likely," Tré answered. "I'm not at all certain we have enough muscle to manage this."

"Muscle? What do you mean?" Trynn asked.

Tré looked grim and angry. He pushed away from the table, rising to pace a few steps across the room. "I mean that four vampires may not be enough to avert this disaster—even when one of those vampires is Snag. I can't guarantee they'll be able to stop this attack and rescue Eris at the same time."

Trynn's stomach clenched. What was he saying? That they wouldn't even try to save Eris? Selfish anger rose. Yes, the thousands of possible victims in this act of violence mattered. Yes, it would be a devastating blow to the world if the radioactive fallout killed or injured thousands of others. The course of humanity would be irrevocably changed.

Yet, panic welled up at the thought of losing Eris. Didn't his life matter, too? These people were his friends! Shouldn't they be doing everything in their power to rescue him?

Trynn thought back to the malicious words she'd hurled at Snag. The accusations she'd made. At the time, she'd only been interested in goading him into speech. Now, she felt sickened by the exchange.

She'd goaded him, all right, and he'd ended up communicating far more than she had expected or intended. It was obvious that he cared for Eris deeply. After what she had seen in his mind, she would have known that even if he hadn't hurtled off without a moment's hesitation to rescue his friend, the instant he was released from his vow to protect Trynn.

Surely he, at least, would not abandon Eris to his fate.

Christ. She needed to apologize to Snag when he got back—probably on hands and knees.

Even that thought was chilling, though. With powerful demons and evil men wielding nuclear weapons arrayed all around them, how could she be sure that Snag *or* Eris would return? She didn't know if she would ever see either one of them again.

The growing sense of helplessness ballooned inside her chest, constricting her heart, nearly overwhelming her.

Della was looking at her as if she could see right into Trynn's thoughts. Hell, maybe she could.

Now was not the time to be selfish. She had to focus on all of the lives that could be lost to these attacks. She needed to be thinking up a plan to help, not blubbering in the corner like some kind of damsel in distress. She needed to figure out a way to *stop this.*

Trynn took a deep breath and searched desperately for some way to resolve the bomb crisis and save Eris at the same time. She dropped her head into her hands, staring at the darkness behind her closed eyelids. She squeezed them shut so hard that lights flared like red starbursts. Before the whirling patterns had fully faded, an idea came to her, springing from her subconscious fully formed.

Trynn jerked upright. "*Shit*! I know what we can do!"

Della had jumped in surprise at Trynn's outburst, and Tré spun around, his intense silver stare pinning her in place.

"Okay—you're not going to like this part," Trynn said quickly, "but I have to get back to my hotel room across town and pick up my computer."

"If Bael is after you, that's ridiculously dangerous—" Della said, but Trynn interrupted her.

"You don't understand! I *have* to, Della—untold human lives depend on this information! *Eris'* life depends on this information!"

The two vampires stared at her intently, then at each other. With a flash of irritation, Trynn realized that they were conversing silently—discussing her as though she weren't sitting right in front of them.

"I'm serious," she said through gritted teeth, shoving her chair back from the table and jumping to her feet. "I'm not crazy. *I have an idea.*"

"All right," Della said unhappily, standing up as well. "We'll take you, but we have to go now, while it's still nighttime."

"I'll get dressed." Trynn nearly sprinted the length of the suite. Her shirt was ruined, but her sensible trousers were wearable. After a bare moment of hesitation, she rummaged through Eris' luggage for one of his casual button-down shirts and rushed into the bathroom to change. She emerged moments later with his sleeves rolled up to her elbows, the hem of the shirt hanging to the top of her thighs. She snatched her handbag and threw it over her shoulder as she headed towards the door, where Della and Tré were standing, ready to depart.

They passed out of the palatial hotel peacefully enough—most of the inhabitants were fast asleep at this hour. Trynn felt an unnatural stillness press against her as soon as they stepped outside. No breath of wind was stirring, and the air felt heavy with a coming storm. Sirens wailed in the distance.

"It's already starting," Della said. "I can feel it. We'll need to hurry."

The normally sleepy city seemed to be holding its breath, waiting for something. Trynn's hair stood on end, gooseflesh erupting across her arms even though the street in which they were standing was calm and no sign of disturbance reached them from the nearby buildings. Trynn glanced towards the west, and saw a flickering, insubstantial glow of orange reflecting off the distant buildings.

Fire.

"It's normally not like this," Trynn whispered, hesitant to even lift her voice enough to penetrate the darkness. She swallowed hard, feeling as though a shadowy presence was closely watching her every move.

"It's part of the vortex forming around you," Tré said grimly, his eyes scanning the shadows. "You are the eye of the storm."

Trynn shifted uncomfortably for a moment before taking a steadying breath and heading in the direction of her hotel. An agonized scream rent the air a few blocks away, and she flinched hard, nearly stumbling over her own feet.

"All of this can't really… be because of me, can it?" she whispered.

Della steadied Trynn with a hand on her back. "In a manner of speaking, yes," she said. "The same thing happened to me, you see."

Trynn stared down at the shorter woman, dumbstruck. "What do you mean, it happened to you?"

"I used to be just like you, Trynn," Della said. "I was living in New Orleans and working in an *insurance office*, for god's sake. One day, everything was fine, and then... all these terrible things started happening in the city."

Della's voice trailed off. They walked silently for several moments, as Trynn waited for Della to continue.

"So many lives were lost," she finally said, her voice brittle with bitterness and old pain. "I didn't realize that it was all my fault until I met Tré and the others."

"It wasn't your fault, *draga mea*. There is only one being at fault for the pain and death... and his name is Bael," Tré interjected. Della shook her head, frowning. Trynn could tell they'd had this argument before, perhaps many times.

"But it was like it is here?" Trynn asked, suddenly breathless. "There were fires, and shootings, and suicide bombers, and other horrible things?" Her eyes lingered on the orange glow, shining more brightly now as they made their way further into the city. Heavy, acrid smoke hung in the air. Sirens screamed in the distance, but everything around them was completely quiet as they moved along the deserted street. It was eerie, in a way that chilled Trynn to the bone.

"Yes," Della confirmed. "Just like here."

"But *why*?" Trynn asked. "I haven't *done* anything!"

Della and Tré met each other's eyes, communicating silently again. Trynn felt an unexpected stab of jealousy at the obvious bond between the two, even amidst all the chaos and uncertainty. Trynn felt like her whole world was a breath away from falling apart, and the two of them were busy making doe eyes at each other.

"Sorry," Della said a moment later, tearing herself away from her lover's gaze. "Inside joke. I said pretty much exactly the same thing—on more than one occasion, as I recall."

"To answer your question, we have some theories on that," Tré said quietly. "We think Bael becomes aware of the reincarnated souls of our mates when we wander close enough to them for the bond between us to reconnect. Once he finds them, he pursues them to wherever they are staying. For you, it was here. You got too close to Eris and Bael discovered your presence in Nicosia. His greatest power is in turmoil and violence, so he unleashes the full weight of it and uses it to revenge himself on his enemies."

Trynn scratched her neck, thinking. "Why am I his enemy, though? Why should he care whether Eris and I are reunited or not?"

Della huffed in sympathy. "That's what I wondered, too. What you don't understand is that your existence is a threat to him. You are the one the few people who has ever defeated him."

Her footsteps stuttered to a halt as she turned to looked at Della. "I… *what*?"

"You don't remember?" Della asked, frowning. "You haven't dreamed about it?"

Trynn tried to force down the flush that tried to stain her cheeks at the mention of dreams. But—

"No," she said. "I… uh… I know we were together. In someplace that looked like… Ancient Greece, I guess? We seemed really happy."

"It was ancient Cyprus," Tré said, his voice low. "You're walking the streets of your ancestral home as we speak."

A dull spike of shock pierced her, but something about his words also seemed *right*, like a puzzle piece slotting into place.

"Oh," she said.

Della's words were gentle. "Trynn, for whatever reason, Bael singled out Eris and attempted to turn him. Bael tried to make Eris into his servant, a shell completely immersed in darkness, who would do his bidding without hesitation or conscience."

"Turn him?" Trynn asked, as the three resumed their progress towards her hotel. "How?"

Tré shivered and looked away, making Trynn wonder.

It was Della who answered. "He attempted to tear Eris' soul into two halves, the Light and the Dark. If he had been able to complete the turning, Bael would have drawn the Light out of Eris and cast it forever into the pit of Hell, leaving only Darkness behind."

Trynn gripped her hand to her chest, picturing it. "And I stopped that? How?"

"Only you and Eris know for sure," Della said, "but certain ancient texts tell us that only the willing sacrifice of true love can protect someone from Bael's destructive power."

"Sacrifice?" Trynn echoed, her mind whirling. *Jesus.* She'd wanted answers, but…

Gathering herself, she spoke again. "So he survived and I—what? Died?"

Tré and Della's silence was all the answer that she needed. It was an odd feeling, knowing that she had been so in love with Eris at one point that she had willingly sacrificed her life for him. Now, she was tortured by the idea of something bad happening to him, but she hadn't really worked out how she felt about Eris, or what their next steps would be.

Assuming he survived. Assuming *she* did.

The uncertainty was unpleasant for Trynn, who was used to being able to confidently take control of a situation; who always knew what she wanted from life.

The past few days had thrown her into a tailspin, unable to grasp what was happening around her. Trynn's life had burst out of its seams, unraveling before her eyes. Demons? Vampires? Reincarnation? A great war of good versus evil?

What could possibly be next?

Yet, it was all real. She'd been thrown into a nightmare from which there was no waking up, no blessed relief that it had all been in her head. She was walking down a darkened, silent street next to two vampires, being smothered by stifling smoke that hung in the air as the city of Nicosia burned around them. They were standing in the terrifying eye of a vicious storm, praying that they could pass through and come out the other side alive.

It felt like the entire city was teetering on the edge of a chasm, about to slide into chaos and utter destruction. Tension crackled in the air, waiting to explode into violence.

"We need to hurry," Trynn said, quickening her steps as they rounded the corner and her hotel came into view. Next to the grandeur of the Merit Lefkosa, the place appeared dilapidated and worn down. Shabby bushes flanked the front door, through which the three companions entered warily.

The sleepy attendant cracked open a wary eye before tipping further back in his chair, his feet propped up on the desk as they passed by.

Down the hall, Trynn unlocked her hotel room door and walked inside, flipping on lights.

To her relief, nothing had been disturbed. Seeing her laptop still sitting on the desk where she left it, Trynn pounced on the device like a cat on an unlucky mouse.

With frenzied clicks, she logged into her computer and began working as fast as she could, praying that her plan would work.

Della sat on the edge of Trynn's bed, watching her without speaking.

"What are you doing?" Tré asked, wandering around behind her and looking over her shoulder. "What does this plan of yours entail?"

"I'm sending an email," Trynn answered, the words clipped and terse as she worked, focusing on her screen as though Eris' life depended on it.

Because, *oh, yeah…*

It did.

FOURTEEN

Silence met Trynn's simple words, and even though her eyes never left her computer screen, she could tell that Della and Tré were communicating telepathically again.

They probably thought she'd lost her damned mind.

"Trynn," Della said hesitantly, "how will that help?"

A vicious smile spread across Trynn's face as her fingers flew over the keyboard. "I'm about to turn the tide against our friend, Mr. Kovac. He's going to fucking well learn what happens when he tries to attack the world on *my* watch."

Despite the tension in the cramped room, Tré let out a snort of laughter at her assertion. "Yes, you're Eris' mate, all right. Now, take a breath and *explain*."

"Hold on just a second," Trynn murmured, clicking between several screens as she tried to ensure she had all the relevant information available to her, while composing a message in Russian in her head.

After several moments, she spoke. "Okay, so we intercepted this information in the form of emails, right?"

"Right," Della said, and Tré shrugged agreement.

"But we don't know the true identity of the guy purchasing the suitcase nukes. Nothing beyond the name B. Kovac, which could be any one of hundreds of people—maybe thousands," Trynn continued. "He always sent these encrypted emails through a series of different servers to hide any identifying information."

Trynn could feel herself falling into teaching mode as she explained her theory. "Now, we've been trying for months to discover who this guy is and where he came from, but maybe we were going about things all the wrong way? We didn't know until recently if this information was even legitimate, so we've been trying all the while to establish whether this guy is truly a threat. Well, we're past that point now. He's obviously a huge threat."

"Obviously," Tré agreed, frowning at her—clearly not getting it.

"We haven't paid much attention to the suppliers because we know who they are. That part wasn't a mystery, since there are databases used by the US government and Interpol that track all the active members of each criminal organization. We already knew their part in the plan, so we never really dug deeper than that."

"And that's what you intend to do now?" Tré asked.

"No. I'm not acting as a spy in this war anymore," Trynn corrected. "Fuck that. I'm picking up a gun and changing the course of the battle."

"But *how*?" Della asked, looking just as confused as Tré.

"I told you, we already know all about Kovac's supplier," Trynn said in measured tones. "So... what do you think would happen if the Russian mafia suddenly received correspondence from Mr. B. Kovac, stating that he wasn't going to uphold his part of the deal? For example, something stating that he wouldn't be making the full payment?"

Neither Della nor Tré answered, but slow smiles spread across their faces. For the first time, Trynn could believe that they were predators—she'd seen just such a smug expression once on the face of a cat, contemplating a bird with a wounded wing.

"I don't think they'd be very pleased, do you?" Trynn finished blandly.

"They probably wouldn't, at that," Tré replied.

"I imagine they'd be a bit cross, yes," Della put in.

"Plus," Trynn added, "they're not really known for their patient and forgiving natures. If a major deal like this went south at the last second…"

Her voice faded away as she threw them a wide-eyed, innocent look. "Who *knows* how they might respond?"

Turning her attention back to the email, Trynn scanned through what she had written one last time and sent the message.

Once it was away, she pulled up Twitter and focused on finding the users she was looking for. She'd noted several of the more outspoken players in the Russian mafia over the years, and searched now for their handles on the social media website.

Where are they? C'mon, c'mon, don't leave me hanging, here, she thought, scrolling through the fast-moving feed. Trynn knew that many members of the Russian mafia communicated through Twitter. She was hoping to see evidence of a sudden shock within their criminal organization as word spread of Kovac's betrayal. Trynn turned back towards the two vampires.

"Is there a way for you to communicate with the others?" she asked grimly.

"The other vampires who are going after Eris?" Tré asked.

Trynn nodded.

"There's a growing distance between us, but Snag is incredibly powerful. I think I can reach him from here."

Tré fell silent and cocked his head, as if trying to listen to an elusive sound. After a few moments of quiet, he nodded. "Yes, he can hear me. What should I tell him?"

Trynn ran through the details of her plan in her mind again, wanting to keep her message short.

"Tell him that we are trying to disrupt the arms shipment and that the Russians are likely to retaliate against Kovac."

Tré nodded. "Della—*draga mea*, lend me some of your power for a moment." He closed his eyes, and Della did, too. Trynn watched in fascination as Tré took several deep breaths, as if to center his thoughts.

Finally, they both opened their eyes and Tré nodded, which Trynn took to mean that the message had been successfully delivered. A combination of excitement and apprehension flooded her stomach as she stared back at the screen, contemplating the events she'd just set into motion.

A memory of her childhood in Canada popped inexplicably into her mind.

"Snow angels, Mummy!"

"Yes, darling. Yours are beautiful, just like you!" Her mother replied, her pink cheeks visible over the scarf wrapped around her chin. Bright eyes followed Trynn's progress as she knelt carefully in the snow next to the head of the snow angel she had just created.

Trynn reached out a gloved hand and carefully drew a smiling face into the snow.

"My snow angel is really a superhero in disguise, Mummy. She's going to save the world," Trynn called in a high voice. Her dark hair fell over her shoulders, tied back by the headband covering her small ears.

"You think so, darling?"

"Yes, of course. That's what good angels do. They save the world!"

She'd been young then, in that bright and happy time before everything had gone bad—her father's death. Her mother's second marriage. Breaking glass and quiet crying, the snap of a leather belt, the dull thump of fists hitting flesh.

Trynn had run away at fourteen, leaving the smiling angels behind. At twenty-seven, perhaps she'd finally found them again.

She blinked several times, jerking herself back to the present.

"Trynn?" Della asked, concern in her voice.

"Sorry," Trynn murmured. "It's nothing. Just thinking about snow angels."

Della looked bewildered, but Trynn just waved her off. She turned her attention back to the Twitter feed as the first confused messages started to fly back and forth.

"*Oh, yeah,*" she said, voice fierce. "*That's* what I'm talking about. Shit, meet fan."

Trynn snapped her laptop shut and scooped it and the power cord into her bag. Taking only a moment to stuff a handful of clean clothes in her bag, she returned to the two vampires, and all three of them hurried for the door.

-o-o-o-

"You are my life and soul, beloved… I give mine willingly for you. I will be in the very air you breathe, now and forever. Every time your heart beats, I will be there, my love," Phaidra's *soft, breathy voice whispered in his ear.*

Shrouded in darkness, Eris twisted his head back and forth restlessly, trying to find the source of the voice, and the delicious warmth emanating from it. Confused and disoriented, he could not understand what was happening. The evil that had possessed his spirit was receding. He felt more like himself, yet something was different. His senses were sharper, and he felt a terrible chill stealing through his soul. There was empty space within him, where before there had been light and happiness.

He moaned, feeling himself being pulled awake against his will. The nightmare of his turning gave way to the nightmare of the present. He knew he was too weak to withstand any more torture, yet his body betrayed him by dragging him back into wakefulness.

The world spun, and Eris felt certain that the table on which he was still bound was tilting, a hairsbreadth away from crashing to the floor. Even though his equilibrium was screaming in alarm, Eris made no effort to fight his bonds.

He turned inward, trying to slip away into sleep again, in hopes of finding a kinder dream this time, and felt his consciousness start to drift. At the edge of his awareness, Eris thought he could sense Snag's presence. Yet, it was so elusive that it, too, might have been a dream.

Losing himself felt like sinking into swirling water, being buffeted by deep currents. His breathing grew more and more labored, as though a great weight were pressing on his chest. His heart rate sped up, fast and thready as his body tried to compensate.

Without warning, Eris felt his senses sharpen and his awareness expand beyond his shattered physical form.

He could sense Snag again. It wasn't a dream. This time, his presence was as plain as day. To his horror, he realized the presence was nearby, drawing ever closer. *Snag had abandoned Trynn to come after him.*

He let out a weak groan of denial, hoping against hope that the sound had not attracted the attention of his captors. He had not been able to restrain the small noise of anger and betrayal.

No! Snag... goddamn you! You promised me... you would... keep her safe...

Even his thoughts sounded breathless. The strain of communicating telepathically with Snag drained him of the paltry amount of energy and life force he had left.

For a moment, sickly flashes of light wavered across the blackness before his eyes and he could do nothing but lie there, feeling giddy and sick.

Well, that's gratitude for you, another familiar voice said in his mind.

Xander?

Who else?

But — Eris tried to blink his eyes open. One cracked open partway, only to be dazzled by a powerful spotlight above him, drowning out the darkness beyond, making it impossible to see anything beyond the ring of light. *But — how?*

We're flying to you, genius. What did you think? Shit, they really have done a number on you, haven't they? Even you aren't usually this dense.

Eris could sense others pressing close to the mental link, but he didn't have the strength left to tune them in. It was like staring into the bright light above him and trying to discern the shadows beyond its edges. The more he strained, the less he could make out, and the more it made his skull ache.

His confused thoughts turned back to Trynn, who must even now be in grave danger without Snag's protection. What the hell did Snag and Xander think they were doing, trying to rescue him? *She* was the one who needed their help!

He had clearly been left alone here, the gritty dryness in his mouth proclaiming that he had been unconscious for several hours, at the least. It was likely that in the absence of any useful information from him, his captor had abandoned his broken body to petrify, slowly but surely hardening into stone as his life force leached away.

Their experience led them to believe that vampires could not die natural deaths from illness, starvation, or age. If the old texts were to be believed, there were only a few ways to truly kill a vampire. But in the absence of the animating force they drew from human or vampire blood, they would eventually enter a petrified, husk-like state that was not truly life, either. He'd seen that firsthand; Snag had been nearly in that state when Eris had stumbled upon his tomb, millennia ago.

A snort of disgust echoed across the mental bond. Clearly Eris had been unable to shield his thoughts from the others in a weakened state.

Sounds deeply unpleasant, Xander observed. *You had to know we weren't just going to leave you to that fate.*

It would have taken a very long time, Eris retorted, feeling distinctly waspish and wishing more than ever that he could just go to sleep. *Trynn needs protecting right now.*

Merde, another familiar voice scolded. *She's well protected, you idiot. Tré and Della are guarding her. For once, could you worry about yourself right now?*

Oh, good, Eris thought. *Duchess is here, too. My day is now complete.*

I heard that.

Well done, mate, Xander congratulated. *Way to insult the rescue party.*

Leave him alone, both of you! We're coming, Eris, all right? Just hang on a little longer.

That was definitely Oksana, whose mental voice sounded decidedly strained. She and Snag seemed more aware than the others of the extent of Eris' highly weakened state. Or perhaps the other two were simply dealing with it in the way they knew best, namely through sarcasm and bitchiness.

Pain was sweeping through his body in horrible, sharp waves; growing worse the longer he remained conscious. He tried to shift himself to the right to ease the pull on his shattered arm... but no luck there. He was tied fast, and, if he were being honest, so weak he probably couldn't have moved anyway.

How the hell did the four idiots think they were going to get him out of here, anyway?

Snag growled at him across the link.

As plans went, *blind rage* left something to be desired, in Eris' opinion.

He squeezed his eyes shut against the light. He'd always hated winging it.

You didn't exactly leave us much choice, Xander observed. *Since you went off half-cocked without any sort of a back-up plan. Or any sort of original plan, from the looks of it.*

I had a plan, you ass, he managed. *It just happened to be one that failed. It happens, all right?*

He was honestly too worn down to feel much in the way of shame or embarrassment, which was probably just as well. The fact of the matter was, he'd been stupid. He'd underestimated the enemy, when the enemy was a demon who could rend souls and rain down chaos.

He'd acted rashly, and now he was reaping the consequences. It had been desperation to protect Trynn that had driven him straight into the arms of Kovac. The truly fucked-up part was, he'd probably do it again under the same circumstances.

Fog settled over his thoughts. He was vaguely aware of the mental voices jabbering at him, but he couldn't make out what any of them were saying over the fast beating of his heart and the sound of his labored breathing.

Maybe he'd finally be able to pass out again now.

Eris, no! Stay with us! Oksana commanded. The urgency in her voice jerked him out of his twilight state, and he moaned in displeasure.

We need you to show us where you are, Xander said. *What do you remember about your arrival?*

East of the city center, I think.

Not the most specific directions you could have offered, Duchess retorted, her irritation bleeding through the link.

Call to me. Snag's wordless command brooked no argument.

Eris sighed heavily, exhaustion pulling at him. *I'll try.*

Yet he found it hard to remain conscious with the tantalizing promise of painless sleep hovering over him like a cloud. He struggled against it, but his surroundings dimmed as warm darkness wrapped around his thoughts.

A savage mental blow buffeted his mind — an image of Bael wrapping sharp, bloody claws around Trynn forced itself in front of his mind's eye. He exploded into motion, struggling against the chains as a roar of rage tore free from his throat.

Fuck's sake, Snag, Xander cursed. *Are you trying to kill him? Eris? Best stay awake, mate, or I'm not sure we can keep him from doing that again.*

Adrenaline coursed through Eris, like fire burning through his sluggish veins. He yelled again in rage, but still could not free himself.

As his awareness sharpened and all thoughts of sleep were forcefully driven from his mind, Snag surged forward and melded their minds more fully than he had done in years. His awareness of the older vampire was so strong that he could actually see the world through Snag's eyes.

The group was circling over the ruins, drawn by his life force towards what looked to be an abandoned warehouse. Parts of the roof had caved in and almost every single window had been blown out. Streaks of sooty blackness caked along the roofline and above the windows told Eris that there had been a vicious fire in the building.

Snag's powerful nose was able to pick up the faint whiff of smoke and burned flesh. Eris recoiled at the smell, but Snag did not let him break the connection.

He swallowed against his rising gorge and focused his waning strength on a message of warning. *Undead nearby. Don't know how many.*

He felt Snag's acknowledgement as he and the others swirled downward.

As one, the four vampires streaked as mist through the closest of the blasted out windows and took human form in the corner of the warehouse. Standing back to back, they scanned the area with eyesight much more acute than a human's. Large containers and crates of supplies loomed in the darkness, creating a confusing labyrinth in the enormous building.

"Which way?" Oksana whispered, her voice so low that no human would be able to hear it.

Snag shut his eyes, cutting off Eris' telepathic view of his surroundings.

Instead, he felt Snag's mind expand with a cold, white light. The ancient vampire pressed outward, filling the entire space with his life force. Through it, Eris could sense the other vampires more fully.

He could tell that Oksana needed to feed on human blood. Her last meal had been Bon Bons, which she was now regretting in light of the coming battle.

Xander was fighting a vicious hangover—so in other words, he was perfectly normal.

Duchess was the picture of health and vitality.

An oily sensation with the stench of decay slid across Snag's awareness—a large group of undead soldiers about one hundred meters to their west. It seemed to both Snag and Eris that they were standing guard over something, possibly an entrance to the basement beneath the factory building.

Snag projected the impression to the others and gestured in the direction they needed to go.

Brilliant, Xander projected with false cheer. *This is going to be shed loads of fun, I can just tell.*

Eris gritted his teeth, frantically yanking his good arm against the ropes, hoping to free himself and help with the fight. It was useless, of course.

A cold sweat broke out over his body and bile rose in his throat as Eris sensed the group of vampires creep forward towards the unsuspecting undead. Snag's power pulsed through the building.

Bael's minions must have been completely mindless to not realize something powerful was approaching. But where was Kovac? Eris wriggled his less-injured wrist, which was now soaked with sweat. To his delight, he was finally able to drag his hand out of the loop of coarse rope wrapped around it.

He closed his eyes and sank fully into Snag's consciousness.

Snag was peering around a large metal container, looking at a light source he could make out through the damaged door.

"It looks like a lantern or small fire," Xander murmured under his breath.

"How many creeps are there?" Duchess asked, cool and unruffled as a spring morning.

Snag reached out and slid his consciousness over the undead in the other room. A few of them looked around in confusion at the sensation, but there was no sense of alarm. Clearly, the unfortunate creatures had been so thoroughly immersed in evil that they could no longer even recognize the presence of the Light.

Oksana was concentrating on the mental link. "Nine behind the door, which leads to a passage down to the basement — probably where they're holding Eris. There are more underground."

"Then let's get this party started," Xander answered, his eyes lit with green flame. His lips curled back, baring his fangs.

The four of them fanned out, approaching the door. Snag gave Xander a significant look, and the younger vampire moved forward, ready to burst through the door and lead the charge into the midst of the oblivious group of undead.

Just as his fingers were about to grip the handle, the door was pulled open from within. One of the undead stepped out, staring at the ground before bumping stupidly into Xander's chest.

"Well, hello there," Xander greeted as the thing's head snapped upward and its mouth fell open in shock.

Through Snag's eyes, Eris could see that its teeth were rotted and green. He smelled the pungent, suffocating stench filtering through the doorway.

Before he could even draw breath to yell for help, Xander slammed his knuckles into the zombie's face, its head flying backwards under the force of the punch.

The incapacitated foot soldier stumbled backwards and fell into the room, knocking over the lantern that was sitting in the middle of the floor. Its fellows leapt to their feet with snarls of surprise and fury.

A vicious fight ensued. Although these undead were no more capable of independent thought than those the vampires had fought in New Orleans, they were clearly trained to fight, and battled relentlessly.

Several more poured out of the door before the vampires had a chance to respond. The new arrivals waded in, battling ferociously.

Duchess was locked in hand-to-hand combat with a man nearly twice her size, and although her centuries of experience at fighting kept her one step ahead of the monster, she was unable to finish him. Instead, she danced lightly in a circle, evading blow after blow aimed at her head.

Eris felt Snag draw his mental power into a hot ball in the center of his chest. Every time one of the undead approached him, he simply forced the creature back with a blast of his life force. The Light penetrated the Darkness inside the undead, making them stumble, recoil, and fall to the floor. Yet, with each burst of power, Snag weakened his own reserves.

Unfortunately, the others were faring about the same. Xander was wrestling with a man roughly the same size and strength he was, and, following Duchess' example, Oksana was using her light frame to evade, rather than deal a deathblow.

Snag snarled in impatience and sent another undead soldier flying backward.

"Doing the best we can here, mate," Xander gasped. His opponent had managed to get him in a headlock, and he wrestled to free himself.

Snag sprung forward and struck the zombie in the temple with his elbow, causing the creature to lurch away, stunned by the blow.

Xander gasped and clutched his throat, dragging air back into his lungs.

Snag pressed his hand against the zombie's head and forced sleep into its mind. The creature struggled for a moment, and then went completely limp as his animating force drained away into nothingness.

Oksana let out a cry of victory as she finally knocked her opponent backwards onto the floor with a burst of strength. The thing's chest was impaled on the sharp end of a broken metal pipe cemented into the ground. It shuddered once, and went limp.

Her victory was short-lived, however, as more of the undead leapt through the door, ready to take their fallen comrades' place in the battle.

"This is meant to delay us!" Xander called, and Eris felt Snag's agreement, echoed a moment later by Oksana and Duchess.

As one, they pulled their life force inward and dissolved into a swirl of mist that circled the group of bewildered undead and plunged through the open door. Experiencing the flight through Snag's senses made Eris feel sick and dizzy.

He pulled his mind back and opened his eyes, back in his own body. He could sense that Snag was close now. He'd managed to pull his right wrist free earlier, but the effort had cost him. He was too weak to do more than lie there and drag in one shallow, rasping breath after another as the bright light pointed at his face stabbed into his slitted eyelids.

Groaning, Eris fought the sudden urge to give up completely as he saw Bastian Kovac stride into the room, hatred etched in every feature.

"Oh, yes, I am aware that your little ragtag band of rescuers is close, but make no mistake, nightcrawler. You will not leave this place alive. I will not allow them to take my prize from me."

Hopelessness washed over Eris, and he had no strength to fight it. He could sense a huge, billowing darkness building within Kovac. Bael was coming to aid his servant, and Eris' poor judgment had drawn his friends into a trap.

Even if the others got to him, it seemed unlikely they would ever be able to fight their way back out.

There was only one small glimmer of hope. None of them had ever seen Snag's power fully unleashed. Eris knew him to be one of the strongest creatures in existence. Idly, he wondered if that power would stand against this bastion of the Dark.

Heh. Bastion... *Bastian*. The ridiculous thought suddenly seemed inappropriately amusing...

Eris jerked, realizing that his consciousness had started to slip away at the worst possible time. He could sense that Snag and the others were right outside the door. They were held up by another battalion of the undead, and struggling to repel the Dark force emanating from Kovac.

Finally, with a massive effort, the four vampires burst through the door at the far side of the cavernous room in which Eris was being held. Oksana slammed it behind her and turned the lock with a loud *click*.

The four vampires stood in the shadows facing Kovac, who stood in front of the metal table, blocking their access to Eris.

"You have made a grave mistake, coming here tonight," Kovac said darkly.

None of the vampires answered, but Snag took one step forward. As his foot touched the ground, the concrete under it buckled and cracked.

A shudder ran through the building. Dust fell onto Eris' face and he knew that the ceiling had been compromised somewhere above them.

Kovac had not moved a muscle as the concrete around them cracked and shifted. Completely impassive, he regarded the vampires who were slowly spreading out to surround him with a sneer. His attention caught and held on Snag.

Oksana took the opportunity to slip behind a pile of boxes, making her way closer to Eris on the table.

Tension filled the air as Snag and Kovac stared each other down. They were completely silent, but he could tell that Snag was straining against Eris' captor, grappling with him mentally, seeking to wound or to control.

While Kovac's attention was fully occupied, Oksana continued to skirt around the room in the darkness, making her way towards Eris' head.

Kovac whirled in place with no warning, a black cloud swirling out from around him and spreading in all directions. Everything that the cloud touched exploded or was hurled aside. Xander and Duchess flung themselves on the ground as the disk of darkness passed over their heads.

Oksana crouched behind the table on which Eris was being held and the dark force passed inches over their heads.

Snag had not moved, but as the darkness rushed towards him, he threw a hand up, palm out, and exhaled in a rush.

Light exploded from every part of his body, even brighter than the spotlight above Eris' head—blinding him with its intensity. The mushroom of light expanded toward Kovac, and the swirling darkness still pouring from him blasted apart as the two forces met.

Extreme heat filled the room and Eris felt Oksana's cool hands on his face.

"Let's get you out of here, *ti frere*," she whispered.

Eris blinked. Both Xander and Duchess had appeared at his side as well.

He twisted his head to better see the battle raging between Snag and Kovac.

Just when he thought that Kovac must surely fall under the intensity of the Light, Bael's servant raised his arms and a great wind picked up in the underground chamber.

Papers flew everywhere. Old crates skidded across the floor and crashed into one another. The wind became so intense that the vampires struggling to free Eris were forced to cling to the table to stop themselves from being hurled against the wall.

Eris could see Xander's mouth moving, but his words were lost in the deafening howl of sound that had filled the entire room. Snag's aura was receding, being pressed back into his body.

The ancient vampire was sliding backwards, his feet dragging across the crumbling floor as he struggled to remain upright. Finally, he swung his arm around, almost as if he were going to throw a right hook at Kovac. Fire exploded in a ring around Eris' tormenter. It raged higher and higher, consuming everything around him.

Despite his weakness and complete exhaustion, despite the fact that almost every ounce of his lifeblood had been drained from his body in the hours he had been held in this desolate bunker and tortured, Eris was overcome by a sense of awe at the sight.

Snag's power, his absolute fury, the waves of destruction that were pouring off of him should have annihilated anyone foolish enough to cross his path. Yet the battle between the two beings seemed even. Neither was able to deal a fatal blow; they were merely holding their own against each other.

The spectacle was so incredible that Eris momentarily forgot he should be trying to help free himself from the table.

Oksana's impatient voice brought him back to reality. "Eris, come on—help us out here. We've got to get you out of here."

"Wait," Xander said, going abruptly still. "Do you hear something?"

Over the crackling of power from Snag and Kovac, not to mention the sound of parts of the building collapsing under the force of the battle, the four vampires could make out the sounds of a dull, growing rumble.

"Earthquake?" Duchess suggested through gritted teeth. "Because, you know, that would be the *perfect* denouement to this day." She was tugging on the restraints at Eris' left wrist, finally freeing his fractured arm.

"No, I don't think so. I think..." Xander's voice trailed away. With a gasp of understanding, he began working more frantically, finding weak points in the leather and metal to pull against, exerting all of his considerable strength.

"We seriously need to get out of here," he said urgently.

"Why? What's happening?" Eris asked, his words slurring as his injured body protested the manhandling.

"It's about to get very crowded," Xander said unhelpfully.

Finally, with a snap of parting rope, Eris was free. Oksana and Xander tried to pull him to his feet, but he was too weak to stand. He crumpled backwards onto the table with a harsh cry.

This seemed to attract Snag's attention. He looked at the ceiling, taking in the growing rumble of approaching vehicles. Understanding flashed across his face.

Go! The mental command echoed across their mental connection with such force that Oksana, Duchess, and Xander knew better than to question him or argue.

They stepped backwards quickly and transformed into mist. Before Eris could draw breath, all three had vanished into the darkness.

"Your friends have abandoned you," Kovac taunted Snag. "Soon, my master will descend and crush you. But, before you die, Ancient One, I will make you watch as I consume this one's flesh, one slow strip at a time."

With a roar of fury, Snag threw himself forward. Eris watched in horror as he and Kovac were entangled in an ever-shifting web of Light and Dark. The power locking the two great beings together made the hair on Eris' head stand on end. The electricity in the air was so strong that sparks zapped Eris' skin where it made contact with the metal of the table. A buzzing whine grew louder and louder until it completely drowned out the roar of engines outside and the shouts of men coming their way.

For Eris, time slowed to a standstill. Everything was frozen except his eyes, which rolled weakly as he tried to focus on the battle. The web locking the two beings together pulsed with power, an angry, actinic glow. Eris' heart beat sluggishly, loud in his ears as he waited for something, *anything*, to happen.

A colossal noise ripped through the static-filled air, a combination of an explosion and the crack of a lightning strike. Indeed, a bolt of electricity flashed down between Snag and Kovac, throwing both of them in opposite directions as the web shattered. Kovac's body smashed backwards through the door, which was blown off its hinges under the impact. He crumpled in the hallway, insensible, glass and concrete raining down around him.

Snag staggered backwards toward the table, but he remained on his feet, victorious at last.

Men in black combat gear poured into the passage outside, shouting to each other in Russian. One pointed a Kalashnikov at Kovac's crumpled form and fired at least two-dozen rounds into him. Eris blinked rapidly, trying to clear the sweat and blood from his eyes. When he opened them again, he was staring down the barrels of several automatic weapons pointed at him.

In an instant, Snag was there, throwing his wiry body over Eris' as gunfire erupted around them in a deafening *rat-a-tat-tat*. The retorts and the echoes from the concrete walls mixed together, a tangled din that made Eris' head pound in agony.

At the same time, he felt his life force being pressed inward by a strength not his own, and both he and Snag dissolved into mist as the high-caliber bullets riddled the place where they had been.

Eris did not have enough power left to move or even hold this form, but Snag enveloped him, supporting him and pulling his insubstantial cloud of vapor through the building—now swarming with mafia foot soldiers. The pair burst into the open air, and Eris huddled further into Snag's protection as he became aware of the deadly sun slipping above the eastern horizon.

His body, even as mist, screamed in agony, protesting both the movement, and the terrible heat and light. Snag gathered him close and raced through the fickle morning shadows, fleeing for safety with no thought given to anything but speed.

Eris wanted, with every fiber of his being, to black out so he could finally escape the pain and slip into blissful nothingness, but it seemed that Snag's power was strong enough to not only transport him, but to also keep him tethered to life and consciousness.

The elder vampire seemed to be following some internal beacon as he wound expertly through bombed out, half-collapsed buildings.

Deep in the heart of the war-torn neighborhood, Eris could see a large structure that appeared to be mostly intact. At one time, it must have been some sort of government building or courthouse. The stone was cracked and burned, but still held strong. Most of the windows on the front were blown out, but Snag whisked Eris inside one of them and raced down a dark hallway towards the interior of the building, blessedly sheltered from the early morning light outside.

The smell of sweet wood smoke wafted through the air, coming from deeper inside the building. Eris felt Snag pressing his life force outward, materializing both of them into their human forms. Eris landed on his feet but immediately collapsed, unable to stand. With inhuman reflexes, Snag caught him before his body could hit the cold floor.

Although Snag's physique was frail and seemingly fragile, he lowered Eris carefully to lie propped against him, seemingly without effort.

His mental call echoed through the bond, making Eris' ears ring. He winced, but continued to lie still in Snag's embrace, limp and spent. A door nearby was thrown open and Oksana appeared, looking chalky pale despite her dark complexion.

"How is he?" she asked, fear evident in her melodic voice. "And you? Snag, you're burned."

Snag did not answer, but rose with Eris still in his arms, carrying him as if he weighed nothing. Eris' let his eyes slip closed, trying to resist the nausea clawing up his throat from the sudden change in elevation.

He was lowered gently onto a pallet of dusty couch cushions that had clearly been scavenged from elsewhere in the building. It was covered with old blankets scrounged from the rubble and one small, faded pillow.

Eris gasped in distress as his broken bones ground against each other. Once separated from Snag's life force, he immediately started to drift away into the darkness beckoning at the edges of his mind.

Hazy voices passed back and forth above him, discussing their next move. Eris could take no part in the conversation. He was beyond the point of caring. All he wanted was to slip into the quiet warmth of oblivion.

"He's far too weak to be moved," Duchess said, laying a hand on Eris' forehead. "I can barely feel his life force."

"He'll need to heal for days before we can return to Cyprus," Xander said from close by. "What do we think? Are we safe enough staying here?"

"We're a couple of kilometers away from the site of the battle," Duchess observed. "They could still find us fairly easily if they came looking... but will they bother?"

Snag shared the images from their last moments in the basement of the warehouse.

"Sustained automatic weapons fire will probably have destroyed most of the undead, or at least made it hard for them to travel any sort of distance. And the Russians have no reason to come looking for us. Why would they?" Oksana said. "Come on. We should build a bigger fire in the grate. We need to keep him warm while his body recuperates."

The others moved away and Eris continued to float, confused, just below the surface of consciousness. On some level, he understood their words, but it seemed to take a long time for his mind to catch up with what was being said.

Something brushed across his lips, leaving a salty, metallic smear behind.

Eris knew that he needed the offering of healing blood desperately, yet he could not make his jaw move or his throat swallow. He was too tired —*far* too tired —

to think of feeding at the moment. All he wanted was to see Trynn one more time, and then...

You will feed.

The words were a command, implacable and unassailable. Skeletal fingers pried his jaw open with surprising gentleness. A moment later, blood dripped into his mouth and slid down his throat, even as his consciousness finally slipped away.

FIFTEEN

Trynn sat curled up on the couch in Eris' hotel suite, her laptop perched on the arm of the sofa. After a brief discussion back in Trynn's hotel room, Tré had decreed that the more defensible location on the seventh floor of the Merit Lefkosa hotel was worth the added risk of going back outside. Trynn agreed, and so did Della. It wouldn't take much for rioters to burst into her ground floor room at the no-name hotel in the bad part of town.

The trip back had been far more fraught than the trip out, but apparently the presence of two vampires was sufficient to intimidate the gangs of young men with bandanas pulled over their faces who were roaming the streets, breaking shop windows and setting fire to cars. She wasn't sure whether it was the eerie, glowing eyes, or whether the mind-whammy was in play. Either way, she wasn't complaining.

Trynn was sporting a fresh bruise on her temple where one of them had clipped her with a thrown bottle, but she'd also gained a new appreciation of the benefits of being a vampire when, an instant later, her assailant was being pinned against the nearest wall by five-foot-nothing of curvy Hollywood starlet. Della hissed up at him with bared fangs and gold eyes. The kid staggered off a few moments later looking docile and confused.

Back in Eris' hotel room, Trynn was burning holes through her laptop screen, following the constantly updating Twitter feed, hoping for some news from the Russians regarding the raid they planned against Kovac.

She felt a huge sense of accomplishment, knowing that she had instigated the attack, but also a mounting sense of trepidation.

The worst part was, there was *nothing* online. Not one single word, since the initial flurry of Tweets when the news spread. Not a solitary mention of the events that had happened over the course of the past few hours.

The higher-ups must have ordered radio silence, Trynn thought.

With a huff, she set her chin in the palm of her hand, her eyes drifting out of focus. Dawn had risen and the morning passed without any word from the other vampires.

Tré had told her that his connection with Snag had been severed as the group approached Damascus.

"Why? What happened?" Trynn had demanded.

"It takes concentration to maintain that kind of connection over a great distance. My guess is Snag had other things to worry about besides keeping us in the loop on what's going on."

She'd known he was right, of course, but the hours of hearing nothing were wearing at her.

"I'm going to go mad at this rate!" Trynn exclaimed, straightening and shifting restlessly. "I have to know what's going on!"

"No news is good news," Tré said with that same infuriating calm. "If there'd been a detonation, we'd have heard about it by now."

He was right about that, too, damn him. There was no mention on the news, nor any intelligence coming in from MASQUE, that indicated an attack had occurred. They were stuck waiting, relying on some kind of contact from the others to tell them what was happening.

If they were still alive.

Feeling an overwhelming surge of exhaustion, Trynn tipped her head back against the couch and closed her eyes. What she wouldn't give for even one night of uninterrupted sleep. Looking back, she couldn't remember the last time she'd slept undisturbed. At least, not without having first been hypnotized by a skeletal creep who she was totally going to *strangle* if he didn't hurry up and *let them know what was going on.*

Della sat on the other end of the sofa, scanning through news channels on the huge, flat screen TV, trying to find any information that might give them a clue about what was occurring in Damascus. She clicked the remote so quickly that Trynn wondered if there was any way she could even see what was flashing across the screen before the channel was changed.

Tré, who sat at the desk staring unblinkingly at Eris' computer, had not moved or spoken in over an hour. Occasionally his finger would scroll down on the mouse he was holding, but otherwise he might as well have been made of stone.

Suddenly he inhaled sharply. Even though the sound was barely audible, Trynn jumped to her feet, nearly sending her computer crashing to the floor.

"What? What is it? What's happening?" she snapped.

Tré held up a hand for silence, and she thought she'd have a breakdown right there and then.

"It's over," Tré murmured eventually, his hand dropping back to the desk.

"The battle?" Trynn clarified.

"Yes."

"What about Eris? Are the others okay? What's going on? When are they coming back?" Trynn knew she was firing off questions without giving him a chance to answer, but she couldn't seem to stop herself.

Della stood and moved behind Tré, her hands closing on his shoulders. The picture made Trynn's heart—which already felt like it was lodged somewhere in her throat—ache with longing.

"Eris is badly injured," Tré answered in a faraway voice. His eyes were glowing with that eerie silver light.

"How badly?" Della whispered.

"Badly. Snag is trying to help him, but he was severely weakened in the battle, as well. Apparently it was pretty much a cluster—" His voice trailed away as his eyes flickered toward Trynn and away again. "Well, let's just say it wasn't the smoothest rescue mission ever conducted."

In her mind, Trynn recalled the agony that Snag had shared with her, the result of hours of torture that Eris had been subjected to. She swallowed hard, and made a decision.

Taking a deep breath, she squared her shoulders and lifted her chin. "I *have* to get to him now. I don't care how dangerous it is."

Tré opened his mouth—to argue, she was sure—but Trynn saw Della squeeze his shoulders.

He craned around to look up at her, his brow furrowed, and they communicated silently for a moment before Tré relented.

"I understand, Trynn," he said. "Just as *you* need to understand that Della and I have vowed to keep you safe. But… let me see what I can do."

Trynn nodded tightly and hugged herself, trying to stay calm while she waited for Tré to do whatever it was he was doing.

After a quick consultation with Della, he pulled out his phone and started placing calls. He seemed to be arguing with whoever was on the other end, trading sharp words in a Baltic language Trynn couldn't quite place.

"Don't worry," Della said, sitting next to her and curling a leg under herself like a contented cat. "I've been exactly where you are right now. We'll get you to him. I've never seen Tré fail yet."

Tré was apparently multi-tasking, because he paused in the sharp exchange long enough to cover the phone's speaker with his hand and quip, "Your lack of faith wounds me, *draga*. Failed *yet*, she says..."

In the end, his cockiness was not completely misplaced. All in all, it took Tré about an hour and a half to secure transportation to Damascus for them.

"We'll have to wait for nightfall," Tré told her when everything was settled. "I'm sorry, but there's no way around it if you want to arrive with living bodyguards at the end of the journey, rather than matching piles of ashes."

Trynn shivered. Almost two days had passed, and Eris had been the prisoner of a vicious sadist for much of that time. Had he suffered the effects of the sun's rays? She let out a growl of frustration at the idea of waiting, and pressed her fingers against her temples.

"You should try to get some rest," Della suggested. "No offense, sweetheart, but you look like hell."

"Fine," she replied in clipped tones, and more or less stormed off to the bathroom.

Trynn couldn't really argue with Della's blunt assessment as she gazed at her reflection in the bathroom mirror. Dark circles were smeared beneath her eyes like smudged mascara. She looked raw and edgy, as if she were on the verge of crawling out of her own skin.

After cleaning up, Trynn collapsed face down onto the bed. Maybe she'd overestimated her own endurance, because she immediately fell into a deep, blessedly dreamless sleep.

What seemed like seconds later, Della was shaking her insistently awake.

"Come on, Trynn, you need to get up. We've got a flight to catch. *Trynn*."

Della obviously wasn't taking no for an answer, and Trynn tried to reboot her groggy brain. "Huh?" she asked, sitting up suddenly and pulling her arm away.

"We need to leave," Della said, slowly and clearly. "We have a flight to catch."

That brought everything back in a rush.

"Shit!" Trynn immediately sprang from the bed, straightening her rumpled, borrowed shirt and rummaging around for her things. "I'm up. How long have I been asleep?"

"Hours," Della answered with a shrug. "You were really out of it; I could barely wake you. I don't doubt you needed it, but now we have to move."

Trynn tossed all of her scattered possessions into the duffle bag she had brought from her own hotel room. When she had everything—and there wasn't much, really—she threw the bag over her shoulder. "I'm ready. Let's go."

Tré and Della had clearly not been idle while she slept. All of Eris' and Snag's belongings had been packed and were now waiting by the door.

To her relief, she realized that they would not be returning. That suited her fine. She didn't know how much more of being solicitously guarded and confined to this room she could stand. It might have been gilded, but it still felt like a cage.

Della hailed a cab, and the three of them rode through the restless streets of Nicosia. Trynn was more than a little shocked to see the extent of the damage in parts of the city. The fires had damaged or destroyed whole blocks, and many of the roads were impassable.

Eventually, they made it out and into the suburbs beyond. Their destination, it turned out, was a small, private airstrip just north of the city.

"How did you manage this, anyway?" Trynn wondered aloud as they pulled up to the small facility.

"Persuasion," Tré retorted in a dark voice.

"And by *persuasion*, he means *money*," Della added wryly.

Trynn peered at them in the dim light of the cab's dashboard. "So you're rich, then?"

"Long-term investments become simpler given our... unusual circumstances," Tré said, still grim. "But no one said I used my own money. Actually, I used Eris'. It only seems fair under the circumstances, and I daresay he can spare it."

She'd known, intellectually, that Eris was well off. That much was obvious from the hotel room and his own thoughtless, casual elegance. Plus... *art thief.* So maybe it shouldn't have come as a surprise. She just hadn't quite made the connection between *staying at the Merit Lefkosa* kind of money, and *chartered flights from a private airfield on short notice* kind of money.

Movement caught her attention through the back window, and she tensed as a private security team approached the car on foot, guns drawn. Their cabbie began making frightened spluttering noises and put his hands in the air.

"Our apologies, my friend. Please relax — you're in no danger," Tré assured the man. Trynn wondered if there was a bit of vampiric suggestion behind the words, because the cabbie seemed to grow very relaxed, very quickly under the circumstances.

Handy, she thought, *as long as it's not being aimed at me.*

Tré stepped out of the vehicle with his hands raised at shoulder height in a token of non-aggression.

"Peace, my friends," he said in the same arresting tone of voice.

To Trynn's astonishment, the men, who had been walking towards them quickly and with purpose, slowed. Their steps faltered and they stumbled to a stop, standing under the glow of a streetlight and looking vacantly at Tré.

"Who are they? And what did he do to them?" Trynn whispered to Della as they pulled their bags from the trunk of the car.

"I imagine they're airfield security, and were coming over to check our documentation," Della said, keeping an eye on the men but not seeming overly concerned. "He just temporarily stunned them. They'll be perfectly fine in a little bit."

Trynn nodded knowingly. "Ah. The mind-whammy. Right."

Della let out a bark of surprised laughter, and quickly covered her mouth with one hand. "Oh my god," she said from behind her muffling fingers. "You call it that, too? You should have seen the look Tré gave me the first time I said it…"

Luggage in hand, they walked around a low building to where Trynn could hear the sounds of a helicopter's engines starting up. The unmistakable *thwack thwack thwack* carried across the small airfield.

Within moments, they were approaching the nervous-looking man standing just outside of the zone of turbulence created by the chopper's blades.

"You have the cash?" he demanded in a low voice, throwing a look over his shoulder as though he expected someone to be spying on them.

Tré pulled out a thick wad of Euros folded into a money clip, and held it up for the man to see. Immediately, the pilot's hand snaked out and grabbed it, flicking through it to make sure that he was not being shorted.

"It's all there. Let's get moving — we have a long journey ahead of us." Tré seemed mildly irritated by the delay as the man rubbed one of the bills between his fingers as if to ensure it wasn't counterfeit… though he hadn't batted an eye at the outrageous cost of the flight.

"Yes, yes, let's go," the man said in a heavy Greek accent as he turned towards the chopper.

Trynn followed the others to the sleek aircraft, keeping her head ducked to minimize the turbulence from the spinning blades. Having never been on a helicopter, she didn't know exactly what to expect. She found a headset with earphones and a mic sitting on a seat across from Della and Tré, so she picked it up and slid into the seat, adjusting it over her ears.

"Buckle up," the pilot's voice barked over the radio, and she hastened to obey.

All in all, the flight itself wasn't too bad. The takeoff off made her stomach drop uncomfortably, but the rest of the time they simply hurtled through the dark night towards their goal across the narrow stretch of sea.

It was a testament to how exhausted she was that she dozed off halfway through the flight, only to jerk awake when a hand fell on her arm.

"The pilot says that the place where we need to go is too badly bombed out for him to land and take off," Tré told her. "He's going to land in a vacant area close to the airport, so we can avoid having to answer awkward questions. We should be able to find someone willing to rent us a car from there, though we may also have to travel some distance on foot. Snag indicated that the roads around the building where they're staying are blocked by rubble."

Trynn nodded, but did not speak.

She wondered how much Tré had told the pilot about their journey, and guessed that the man actually knew very little, other than their destination.

Behold, the power of large wads of cash.

By the time they touched down in Damascus, Trynn was beginning to feel a jittery sense of anticipation. She needed to see Eris with her own two eyes before she would believe that he was still alive. She *needed* to, like she needed air and water and food.

"Della," she whispered as they stood waiting for Tré to finish haggling with a man about the price to rent his battered four-door Skoda. The pilot had taken off practically the instant they'd disembarked and moved out of the landing zone, which made Trynn wonder what threats or coercion Tré had used to get him to take the job in the first place.

"Yes?" Della replied.

Trynn swallowed. "Did you ever question whether or not you really were one of these...*fated mates* of a vampire?"

"There were times that I did, at first," Della recalled. "The whole story was so crazy and out-there that it seemed insane."

"I hear you on that," Trynn muttered.

Della snorted, then grew thoughtful. "And yet... I had these dreams. It's like my heart was saying *yes*, but my mind just couldn't accept the reality. It's a tough place to be, especially since I didn't really believe in the paranormal beforehand. But... the more I was involved with Tré, the more distant those doubts became."

"Really?" Trynn's voice was wistful as she thought about how little time she'd truly had with Eris, to try and figure things out.

"Yes, really. It will be the same for you, I'm sure of it. You and Eris have barely begun getting to know each other again. Soon, you'll be sharing memories, and when you're together you'll realize that you've just been half a person without him."

Trynn raised her eyebrows at the flowery proclamation, unable to help herself. She'd just never been a hearts-and-flowers kind of girl.

"Don't look at me like that," Della chided. "I'm serious! You'll see. You'll be amazed what you find once you have a chance to truly be alone together and talk."

"Maybe," Trynn replied evasively. "Honestly, I think I'm still in shock."

The driver stopped arguing with Tré and reluctantly handed over the keys just as Della leaned closer, bumping shoulders with her.

"Yeah, that's pretty normal," she said. "If there even is a *normal* for this situation. It's a lot to take in all at once."

"I don't think I'll ever get used to it," Trynn admitted as Tré took the keys and handed over another, smaller wad of cash.

"Of course you will," Della retorted. "I feel now like I was always meant for this life. Kind of like I spent all those years as a mortal hurtling forward towards the moment when I met Tré and then was made a vampire a few short days later."

Trynn had been trying really hard not to think about the *being turned into a vampire* part, but—

"Did it… hurt?"

Della didn't answer for a moment, but dropped their small bags into the trunk of the car before sliding into the front seat next to Tré. Trynn got in behind her and sat in the back, staring out of the window at the lights of Damascus.

It seemed like a very long time before Della answered.

"It did," she admitted. "It was physically and psychically painful, it's true… but I don't really remember it."

"You don't?"

"No, not really. It faded in the face of what came after. Trust me… the joy and all the amazing feelings of being with the one you were meant for more than make up for it. *That's* what I remember."

They fell into silence, each consumed by their own thoughts. Trynn was assailed by a sudden image of Eris screaming in the moonlight, flailing in the sand, his fingers curled toward her like claws.

She caught her breath, her heart beating faster. The memory was startling, especially since Trynn didn't know where it came from or how it got into her head.

"Do you know exactly how Eris was turned?" Trynn asked, breathless.

"No, we weren't there," Tré answered. "Except for Snag, Eris is the oldest of any of us, by quite a stretch."

"*You* were the only one that was there," Della reminded Trynn. "In a manner of speaking, anyway."

Even though neither of the vampires in the front seat could see her, Trynn nodded, trying to follow the memory further.

There was a confusing rush of sounds and darkness. Even in these odd dream-memories, Trynn could feel a pounding sensation in the back of her head that made her think she'd either been struck by something, or had fallen to the ground and hit her head.

Trynn could remember stumbling blindly into the swirling darkness, choking on the horrible stench that filled her nostrils. She'd fought her way towards Eris, feeling as if she were battling a cloud of stinging insects that scrabbled against her exposed skin.

Screaming filled Trynn's ears and with a rush of surprise, she realized that it was her own voice raised high, shrieking to the heavens. The dark cloud solidified around Eris, making an impenetrable barrier that kept them apart. Trynn flung her body forward over and over again, unable to get through and reach her beloved.

Refusing to give up, she lunged forward the final fraction, and was able to touch him.

"Trynn?" Della's voice broke through the memories in which she had become lost. "You still with us, there?"

She blinked. "What? Uh... yeah. Sorry. I... think I'm starting to remember more details about the night Phaidra died, is all."

Saying it matter-of-factly like that helped Trynn feel more in control, despite her fluttering heart and the clammy sweat breaking out on her skin. It felt like she could bring it into reach and understand it better if she owned it, rather than hiding from her past.

Della only nodded, a sad smile pulling at one corner of her full lips before the expression collapsed into sympathy

"How much further?" Trynn asked, trying to focus on the present.

"I don't really know," Tré answered. "Though we're definitely going to have to walk to our final destination."

"Then we'll walk," Trynn replied, brooking no argument. She was not going to let a little rough terrain stop her from reaching Eris tonight.

About an hour later, Trynn, Tré, and Della reached the end of the road. Quite literally, in fact. There was a makeshift roadblock in front of them, illuminated by the headlights. Behind the roadblock the pavement appeared to be gone, leaving only a pile of twisted rubble.

"I think this is our best bet," Tré murmured, getting out of the car. "They're directly ahead of us, and I doubt we'll get any closer via a different road."

Della and Trynn got out without a word and grabbed their bags from the trunk of the car. Tré hefted the bag containing Eris and Snag's belongings and peered into the darkness before them.

"This could be a rough journey," he warned. "Especially with human levels of night vision."

"It's fine," Trynn said. "Let's go." She couldn't understand why they were standing around talking when they could be making their way towards Eris. When the two vampires started their trek, she hurried ahead, clambering over large embankments of concrete that had been ripped up.

After reaching the top of a portion of the street that had buckled around a bomb crater, Trynn looked down into the pitch black hole beneath her. The lights from the occupied part of the city no longer reached this far, and the rest of their path was cast into shadow.

"I should've brought a headlamp or something," Trynn muttered as Della and Tré joined her at the top.

They peered towards the bottom and Trynn wondered if their superior eyesight could see through the darkness.

"That would've made things easier," Tré agreed. "But on the positive side, I don't believe there are any of the undead around."

"*Undead*?" Trynn echoed. "Jesus Christ. Do I even want to know?"

Della sounded distinctly uncomfortable when she replied, "Yeah, you probably don't. Think zombies with attitude and you're not far off."

Okay, then. Frankly, Trynn's brain was operating just about at capacity at the moment, so she decided maybe she'd just pretend she hadn't heard that particular nugget of horror.

"Can you see the bottom?" she asked instead.

Tré squinted downward. "Mostly. It's very dark back here, but I think that the drop will be onto concrete, just like how we climbed up here."

She nodded. "Okay, I guess I'll try to slide down on my feet."

Tré made a noise of protest. "Or you could let me go first, so there's someone to catch you if you fall."

"This is really no time to get into a feminist debate with you, but you can go first if you want," Trynn said between clenched teeth. "As long as *someone* goes."

Tré stepped over the edge and slid down into the darkness with a controlled grace that did nothing for Trynn's irritation.

A moment later the scraping noise stopped and Tré called up to them, "It's not too bad. You should be able to make it down if you're careful."

"Arrogant son of a…" Trynn muttered, hopefully too low to be overheard. She and Della followed him down one at a time. Trynn got a small spot of road-rash on the palm of her hand, but was otherwise unhurt.

They walked onward, Trynn stumbling repeatedly in the dark despite the weak light of her cell phone's flashlight app. She really hoped that Tré or Della had some sense of where the hell they were going, because she was hopelessly lost in the twists and turns they took to avoid significant damage and debris in the road.

Finally, Tré pointed to a dark silhouette in the distance. There was no light visible from within, only a denser darkness that told Trynn they were approaching a large structure. It took them another good half hour to get to it, but finally they reached a relatively undamaged stretch of pavement in front of the place.

"Looks like it used to be a government building of some kind," Della murmured, staring through the gloom. Evidently, vampire eyesight was, in fact, strong enough to pierce the darkness.

"Xander says we're going to have to reach a second story window to get inside." Tré said.

"Great, climbing up a building in the pitch dark," Trynn grumbled. "What could *possibly* go wrong? Why can't we just go in the front door? Or the back door? Or the *side* door?"

"Everything is boarded shut," called a voice from high above them.

"Duchess!" Della called back. "It's good to see you!"

"Snag thought you might need a little help getting into the building, so he had me hunt down some rope," said the other vampire, the hint of a French accent coloring her words.

"Brilliant!" Della exclaimed. "I wasn't sure if we were going to have to make Trynn scale the side of a building or not."

"Will you be able to climb up to the second story with a rope?" Tré asked her.

From the window above, something was tossed and landed on the ground with a dull *flump*.

"I guess we're about to find out," Trynn said skeptically.

"We'll carry your luggage," Della offered.

"Any chance you could carry me?" she countered.

"Unfortunately, Snag is the only one of us strong enough to fly with a human," Tré said. "And I'm afraid he's otherwise engaged at the moment, tending to Eris."

Trynn felt her way forward and tested the strength of the rope. She could tell that it was tied fast to something solid. Examining the wall of the building, she found that the stone was not smooth, but had uneven edges and recesses where she could place her hands and feet.

In the end, the task was done—though she hoped never to have to repeat it. Trynn used the rope to pull herself up over parts of the wall that she could not scale without assistance. Della stood below her calling up encouragement, while Tré hovered nearby in case she fell.

After pulling herself clumsily through the window and toppling onto the floor, Trynn heard a rush of sound and found that Della, Tré, and their luggage were standing next to her as she pulled herself to her feet.

"That's a handy parlor trick," she grumbled, trying to dust herself off.

"Come on, this way," Duchess insisted, sounding impatient with her griping. She led them swiftly down a dim passage. The moon emerged from behind the clouds, a faint glow reflecting through the smashed windows on the west-facing side of the building. According to her phone, it was nearly dawn, and Trynn knew they needed to remain under shelter for the vampires' sakes.

Duchess stopped before a closed door. Flickering light crept out from the gap underneath. Glancing back towards Trynn curiously, she pushed it open and led the way inside, closely followed by the other three.

Trynn pushed her way forward, and her eyes fell on a horrible scene. On a pallet of soft blankets and cushions, Trynn could see Eris. His face was bruised, swollen, and bloody. He seemed to barely be conscious, stirring fretfully under the threadbare blanket covering him. He moaned unhappily as Snag pressed a bony wrist to his mouth, and tried to turn his head away.

The dark-skinned woman was crouched on his other side, running a soothing hand through his hair. "Come on, Eris, you need to feed again. Please."

"Oh, Eris…" Della said, her voice fading away.

Trynn walked forward on numb legs, anger and shock welling up inside her.

Why would anyone do this to him? Surely, not because of me?

She couldn't voice the thoughts aloud, but Snag, who seemed to have been listening, turned towards her with rheumy, sunken eyes. He looked exhausted and even paler than usual. Blisters and angry red marks peppered his exposed skin.

"*Snag,*" Tré said. "When was the last time you fed?"

The ancient vampire didn't answer. He merely turned his gaze back towards Eris.

"You can't feed him alone," Tré insisted. "Not when you're this weak. Let one of us take over for a while."

His voice seemed to startle Eris, who jerked and turned his head towards the door. Through the slit in his swollen eyes, Trynn could see the glitter of his dark gaze, staring straight at her.

"Trynn," he whispered, his voice cracking.

Her name was all it took. Restraint breaking, Trynn ran forward and threw herself at Eris, who didn't even raise his arms. She collapsed against his chest, crying silently, her fingers hovering over his injured face, afraid to even stroke him. His breath rasped beneath her cheek after the strain of speaking. After a few moments, he took a deep breath and exhaled slowly.

After a long moment, Trynn sat up and looked around, though she still leaned over Eris protectively. "What's going on? What did you mean, Tré? Shouldn't we try to get him to a hospital?"

"A hospital can't help him. That's the last place an injured vampire should go," Tré said. "Eris needs to feed from another vampire. By sharing their blood and life force, he'll be able to heal himself. There's only one problem."

"Which is what?" Trynn demanded, looking around the room at the others. If that was what he needed, why were they all standing around? Why had it looked like Eris was trying to refuse Snag's blood when they first entered?

"Snag is insisting that he has the strongest life force and therefore he should be the one to feed Eris—" Tré explained.

"Okay," Trynn interrupted.

"—but Snag is severely weakened. He's just battled one of the most powerful beings we've ever come across, and hasn't given himself time to feed and recuperate."

"Not only that," the pretty black vampire added, "but he won't even feed from one of us to replenish his strength."

"It's fine," Eris choked out, his voice slurring. "I'm fine."

Some of the anger that Trynn had been holding inside for days snapped and started pouring out of her. "No, you're not *fine*! Have you looked in a mirror recently, Eris? Because it's not a pretty sight! Goddamnit, how could you possibly think of running off like that? Tré told you to wait. *Snag* told you to wait, but you just had to go and take matters into your own hands!"

"I had...to keep you...safe," Eris whispered. It sounded as if every word cost him a great effort.

"How did this keep me safe? Besides, I didn't *need* to be safe," Trynn shot back, tears springing to her eyes again. "I needed *you*, to help me figure out this craziness! Just you!"

Before she could stop them, sobs choked their way from her throat, despite her efforts to hold them back. "How c-could you even th-think of l-leaving me?"

Eris' eyes slipped closed — as if he could not bear to see Trynn's tears.

"I'm sorry," he whispered. "I realize now that I played right into Kovac's hands."

"*You think?*" Trynn fired back angrily, trying in vain to wipe her streaming eyes and nose.

"Can you forgive me for being so pig-headed?"

Trynn looked at him and found that his swollen eyes were staring unblinkingly at her. It was unnerving, seeing him like this — his face was so damaged that he was not immediately recognizable as the devilishly handsome man who left the hotel a few days previously.

She wanted to stay angry with him. She wanted that rather desperately, in fact. But, try as she might, she couldn't do it. She knew he'd just been doing what he thought would help stop something terrible from happening. He'd been playing the hero, yes — but only to keep her safe. Her, and the untold thousands of other people who might have become Kovac's victims.

"I forgive you, you bastard," she whispered. "Just don't ever fucking do it again, all right?"

Eris seemed to slump in relief. "Good," he breathed.

She could feel him weakening under her hands. His body sank into the makeshift bed of cushions, and his breathing grew sluggish. There was no time. He needed help, and the one trying to give it was in no condition to help anyone right now.

Trynn wasn't quite sure what game the old vampire was playing by refusing to feed from any of the others, but she had an inkling—there was an obvious solution that no one had broached yet. The consequences for her were life changing... but Trynn had already spent half a lifetime leaping before she looked. Why should now be any different?

"Snag?" Trynn asked, seriousness etched in every word. "Could you feed from me?"

He didn't respond, she had not expected him to. Instead, she turned towards Della and Tré, the look on her face stubborn and set. She stood up and folded her arms, ready to take on any challenge.

"He could," Tré finally answered. "But, to my knowledge, Snag hasn't fed from anyone but Eris in centuries. He doesn't hunt humans."

Surprise threaded through her haze of worry. She looked at the old vampire and saw him in a new light. Good god, no wonder he and Eris were so close. She took a deep breath.

"You wouldn't be hunting me. I'm offering. Eris and I are bound together somehow. Whatever bond you have with him that makes you willing to drink his blood extends to me, too. You can feed from me to restore your strength, so you can help Eris. I'm asking you to turn me, Snag," Trynn told him.

Blank shock followed her words and no one in the room spoke for a moment.

"Don't you want to think about that for a minute before—" the man called Xander began.

Trynn didn't let him finish his question. "No."

"Trynn, this is a really big—" Della started.

Trynn turned and gazed at her new friend, her expression hard and determined. "No. This is right. I can feel it in my bones. This is what I need to do. I am where I've always been meant to be."

She looked down at Eris. "By his side."

No one spoke or dared argue with her.

The tense atmosphere in the room had roused Eris back to consciousness, it seemed.

"Ph-Phaidra? Are you sure?" he asked, his voice wavering. "Are you completely sure?"

Trynn slid her fingers through his tangled hair. "My name is Trynn. And I'm more sure than I've been about anything in my life. Eris…"

Her voice trailed away, and her eyes moved to the vampires scattered around the dark room. They were all regarding her solemnly as she spoke.

"The seven of you are fighting the most evil being on this planet. This war… this *horrible* war will continue to tear people apart and destroy all the good that we've been trying to build in the world. Humanity will be consumed unless we do something to stop it."

She turned back to Eris. "I may not truly understand it, but I'm connected to you. That makes me part of this battle, whether we like it or not. I didn't ask for this, but I'm in it now, and I'm not going to hide in the shadows and wait for this *evil* to snap me up."

Eris looked up at her, anguished. It was clear that he was undergoing some painful internal struggle.

"Eris," she said, forestalling his words, "I know. I get it. You don't want to see me turned. It's all right, though. I love you. I am in love with you and I want to be together for all eternity. I think… maybe… this is fate."

He searched her eyes. They stared at one another for a long moment, but Trynn did not break the silence.

Finally, he said, "I could never refuse you anything. Never."

His voice was feeble, as though the decision had taken every last ounce of his strength.

Despite Trynn's assurance that she had no second thoughts, sudden nervousness crept over her as she turned her eyes towards Snag.

How did vampires feed from humans? Della had warned her it would hurt…

The only point of reference she had to go on were old movies she'd watched as a kid. In each of those films, a tall, dark figure had trapped a helpless, screaming woman in an alley or abandoned house and sunk his fangs deep into her throat.

Still kneeling on the ground, Trynn turned to face Snag. He was looking at her with keen interest, as if he had never seen anything like her in his long life.

With careful movements, Trynn dragged her shirt away from her neck. She turned her head so that soft skin was exposed and she shut her eyes. She might have made her decision, but she didn't really want to watch it happen.

Somebody in the room made a faint, strangled noise, but she didn't open her eyes to investigate the source. A soft swish of movement told her that Snag had lowered himself to his knees in front of her. A rush of adrenaline flooded her body, trying to throw her into fight-or-flight mode. She breathed through it, her heart pounding like a drum.

It was going to happen any second now. She was going to become a vampire.

An icy hand touched her arm, making her jump. Her eyes flew open and she looked around, despite herself. Snag was indeed kneeling, but well back from her, having to lean forward to touch her arm.

She watched as he cradled her wrist in his hands and raised her arm towards his mouth. Their eyes remained locked on one another the entire time, as if Snag was testing her resolve. She stared back without blinking. Could he see her fear? Sense the way she was frozen under his gaze like an unlucky mouse before a cobra? He paused, his head tilting to one side.

Trynn let out a shaky breath and inhaled again, hoping that the pain would be minimal but having nothing with which to compare it. *Do it*, she urged, knowing that he'd be able to hear her if he was listening.

She felt Eris' hand slip into her free one. She could only imagine the effort it cost him as he tangled their fingers together and squeezed.

Snag's lips touched the inside of her wrist, and a shiver ran up her spine. In some ways, it was a shockingly intimate sensation, and a red flush of embarrassment crept up her neck. Suddenly, she was very glad he'd ignored her neck when she offered it. His lips drew back, and Trynn saw his brilliantly white fangs press against the smooth part of her skin.

She only had an instant to notice that one of them was crooked — *snaggle-toothed, oh, I get it now* — before a flash of movement and a spurt of red, red blood made her gasp. Snag's fangs sunk deep into her arm. It was surprisingly painless. He shuddered, his eyes slipping closed, and began to drink.

Oh. This isn't so bad, I guess, Trynn thought, as the world around her grew increasingly hazy and distant. She could feel him drawing blood out of the vein in her wrist. She could see the stain of red coloring his lips.

Warmth crept through her, and sleep played at the edges of her mind, making everything drift. Trynn fought to keep herself from sinking into slumber. *Why was it getting so hot in here?*

The prickly sensation of heat increased, and sweat broke out across Trynn's forehead. She frowned, her eyes wandering aimlessly around the room. The other vampires stood, resolute, watching Snag drain her blood. Trynn's eyes moved back towards Snag, and she opened her mouth to say something. Was it supposed to feel like this? Had he taken enough blood yet?

Before she could, the smoldering heat flared, igniting her flesh from the inside out. She was on fire, burning up, consumed by invisible flames. A searing pain wrenched her chest as her soul started to pull apart at the seams.

"What's happening?" Trynn cried, consumed by agony. The vampires looked on with expressions of empathy, but no one spoke.

Her balance deserted her, and she collapsed sideways onto the floor near Eris' bed, rolling onto her back and shaking like a seizure victim. Dimly, Trynn was aware that Eris rolled onto his side to face her, groaning with the effort of doing so. He reached out and stroked her hair off her sweaty forehead, shaking nearly as badly as she was. He murmured words of comfort that Trynn could not understand.

The tearing sensation grew exponentially, and blackness flooded her mind. The void expanded, bringing ice and Darkness where there was once life and Light. Yet, the Light had not vanished. Not completely. Trynn could sense it, pulsing angrily near her heart, where it had been ripped free and tossed aside.

She screamed at the sensation, terrible shrieks that scraped her throat raw and stabbed like tiny knives at her lungs. As she thrashed, Trynn felt a cold, bony hand clutching at her shoulder, restraining her flailing body. Someone was trying to calm her, pressing peace into her mind from an outside source — the sensation causing a harsh dissonance when it touched the horror of her rent soul.

Tears streaming down her face, Trynn's grip on the world started to slip away.

"Hold on, Trynn. I will if you will," Eris whispered in her ear. "I'll see you on the other side."

With one last whimper, Trynn surrendered herself to the darkness.

-o-o-o-

It was odd, hearing the sound of waves. Damascus was a dry place, wasn't it?

But, no. She could hear the ocean. She could smell it — a salty tang in the air. Where was she?

She opened her eyes and found herself standing in darkness, the pale light of the moon splashed across her face like wan silver mist. She brushed sand away from her hands and arms. Had she been lying on the beach? The grains clung to her legs as well.

Salt water teased her feet and ankles, white foam clinging to her skin as the tide ebbed and flowed around her. The sea breeze lifted her hair off her neck and filled her nose with the smell of salt.

"Come dance with me," a voice whispered in her ear.

She looked to her right and saw Eris standing beside her in the darkness, the light of the moon reflecting in his merry eyes.

Giddiness stole over her and she laughed, smiling up at him. "Of course, my love."

Eris pulled her into his arms and led her in a rollicking dance, twirling her around and around until she shrieked with glee, dizzy and flushed. When he put her down, she stretched up to kiss him, grinning against his lips.

With a mischievous smile, she grabbed his hand and dragged him back into the surf with her, the two of them laughing as they crashed through the waves. Her long dress floated up around her legs, as soft as silk against her skin.

"This is our victory!" Eris proclaimed to the heavens. He threw his arms wide, sweeping them towards the small town situated at the ocean's edge. The hearth fires burning inside the huts and cottages were visible through the darkness, promising warmth and light. "Now that the shipping deal with Flavian is sealed, this island will be our kingdom! We'll never want for anything. We'll never have to steal and scrounge and hide in the shadows again!"

She framed his face with her hands. "You will be my King, and I, your Queen."

"Nothing can stop us from having the life we always wanted, Phaidra," Eris declared, covering her hands with his as he laughed, clear and happy. "Not now."

His simple, toga-like chiton was soaked from their dip in the ocean, and his hair dripped from the spray.

Phaidra smiled, happier than she'd ever been in her life, and pressed her lips against his... just as the wind around them changed.

Pulling away, she shivered and looked around in confusion as a cold breeze wafted over her damp skin. Shaking off a brief flutter of unease, she smiled again. "Come out of the water, my love – the evening is growing chill. Help me find some seashells! I'll make us two necklaces so we might remember this night always."

Eris beamed at her and lifted her slight frame into his arms, spinning her around in a circle as he had done earlier. "Anything for you, my sweet."

He bent and kissed her neck before setting her on her feet and leading the way back up the beach. They gathered all the shells they could find. Phaidra tucked them in the folds of her toga, where they clinked together when she walked.

As they searched, they spoke of their newly acquired wealth in reverent tones. Thieves they might have been once, but now their quest to become honest traders had finally reached fruition. With the Roman shipping contract in place, they would soon have enough money to purchase all the land around them. Eventually, they would control this entire part of the coastline.

The chilly breeze grew positively frigid. Phaidra straightened and looked around in alarm.

"Is a storm coming?" she asked, turning towards Eris.

Eris checked the sky, his eyes drifting out over the darkened ocean. "No... there are no clouds on the horizon, only millions of brilliant stars."

A gust of wind nearly knocked Phaidra off her feet. She staggered into Eris' arms. They turned towards the town of Lapethos, only to find that the flicker of fires they had been able to see earlier had disappeared. A dense, clammy fog was descending on them as they crowded together.

"I don't like this," Phaidra whispered, feeling fear climb up her throat. "This is no natural wind. It's the work of the gods; it must be."

An explosion of sound echoed around them. The two lovers clutched their ears and fell onto their knees. Phaidra screamed—she could no longer see the sky, the moon, or even the vast expanse of the ocean. She was lost in the black fog, and her grip on Eris' strong arm was the only thing holding her to reality.

"No!" Eris shouted, pressing her behind his solid form. "*No!* Begone, demon!"

"What?" Phaidra asked, confused. She could see nothing but impenetrable blackness.

Suddenly, a deep, cruel laugh reverberated around them. It was so powerful that it seemed to shake the foundations of the earth itself, making the sand swirl and shift beneath her. She sank as if into mud, until her hands and legs became trapped in the quaking surface beneath her.

"You have grown powerful, little mortal." The disembodied voice rolled around them like thunder. *"For that, you will now pay the price. You have become...* useful *to me, and now I will turn you into my creature."*

Phaidra stared at Eris, who gazed upward with a look of horror on his face.

"Your soul is mine," the voice continued. *"I will rend and devour it, until your flesh is nothing but an empty shell, ready to be filled up with my will. You will be consummated by my evil."*

Even as he gasped for air in the smothering cloud of darkness, Eris straightened his spine in defiance, though his hand on her arm was trembling. "My soul is not yours to take! It belongs to another. It is for her and her alone that I sought power and wealth. I will not serve you, filth!"

The evil laughter echoed around them once more. Sudden agony burned Phaidra's skin, as if the black mist had turned to vitriol. She screamed, jerking violently in an attempt to get away.

The mist receded, the pain disappearing as quickly as it had come. With shaking arms, Phaidra managed to pull herself free of the sucking sand, which had grown still now that the demon appeared to have focused its attention on Eris.

Eris! She looked to her left and saw the dense darkness swirling around him. She could just make out the outline of his body, lying face up in the sand. His back arched in torment, yet he made no sound. The beach had gone completely silent, as if the heavens themselves paused to listen.

"*Eris, no,*" Phaidra whispered, petrified with fear. Her lover did not respond. Unnatural green lightning, the likes of which she had never seen before, crackled across the beach.

The central mass of fog coalesced into a monstrous, twisted figure. It was huge—larger than life. The creature bent menacingly and gripped Eris with slimy, bloody claws. The reek surrounding it made Phaidra's stomach churn.

The thing's attention turned towards Phaidra, and she recoiled in disgust. It had the body of a man, but the head of a toad. The head gulped wetly, its long tongue shooting out to lick one eyeball. The wide, slack mouth looked as if it could swallow Eris whole.

"*No!*" Phaidra shrieked, struggling forward to try and reach Eris through the cloud surrounding man and beast. The urge to flee was nearly overwhelming, but she would *not* leave Eris at the demon's mercy. She threw herself forward, over and over, but the mist surrounding the two figures had grown thick as treacle. Finally, she lunged forward a final fraction, and was able to reach him. Her fingers found the edge of his toga, soaked now with sweat and blood as well as seawater.

Even pulling with all her might, Phaidra was barely able to move his writhing body a finger's width. The creature was clearly amused by her attempts. It cackled with glee, and the hair on the back of Phaidra's neck stood on end at the horrible sound.

It was evil. Pure evil.

"*You cannot save him, insect. You are nothing more than a worthless whore. A warm place for him to stick his cock. He is mine now,*" the toad said.

Phaidra swallowed a sob and shook her head, trying to draw on the defiance that Eris had shown earlier, even though she was still too petrified to speak or look directly into those horrible eyes.

"*His inner Light will be cast into the underworld and tortured for all eternity,*" the beast continued. "*I will make him my slave until this world crumbles to nothing. He will serve me loyally, feasting on blood and skin and sinew.*"

Phaidra recoiled in revulsion at its words, and tried again to pull her lover's body out from under the suffocating cloud surrounding him. Still, her meager strength was insufficient to free Eris from the demon's clutches.

"M-my life for his." Phaidra forced the words through chattering teeth.

The black miasma swirled around her, flooding her nose and mouth, making her sputter and cough for air.

"*You would give your pathetic life to save his?*"

The terrible voice crooned the words in her ear like a lover. She shuddered in disgust as the toad's tongue traced up her neck.

"*My life for his.*" She repeated the words with more force this time.

Her love for Eris burned brightly in her chest, filling Phaidra with a strength she had not known she possessed. Will overcame fear as she looked up at the demon and stubbornly set her chin. "You will take my life, offered freely, and spare his in turn."

Phaidra glanced down to find a faint golden glow emanating from her skin, luminescent in the swirling darkness surrounding her—the light of her love, stark against the demon's dark power.

The creature's face twisted and changed. Instead of a toad, she was staring into the eyes of a rabid cat. Anger laced its next words like poison. *"I will destroy you, insolent mortal. By the time I am through with you, you will curse the day you were born."*

Phaidra took a steadying breath and jerked backward as hard as she could. The cloud shifted with her, following her, partially freeing Eris' body.

The sound of skittering insect legs assaulted her ears. She clenched her teeth, trying to stop her body from shaking and jerking. It felt as though fire ants were crawling up her legs, eating her flesh from the outside in.

Her cries were lost in the rushing noise that surrounded her, but despite the intolerable sensation of insects creeping over her skin, one small part of her mind held onto sanity and awareness of her surroundings. Immortals were dangerous and capricious, but they could be bargained with, if one knew what drove them.

"A wager, then!" she cried, trying to make her voice heard over the rush of noise. "You call me his whore, but I know the truth of our bond! I will wager that our love is stronger than your evil! If I'm wrong... if I lose... you will have everything you want. You will get to watch as my heart shatters with grief, and afterward he will be your creature."

There was a pregnant beat of silence. Encouraged, she continued. "But if I'm right, you will spare his life. He will be forever protected by the sacrifice of true and unconditional love."

As Phaidra spoke, she struggled to unsteady feet and took one stumbling step backward, pretending that her trembling legs could not hold her weight. The creature paced her, and the movement completely freed Eris from the dark cloud surrounding the demonic being.

The silence stretched longer, and she held her breath.

"If he is so important to you, human, it will be as you say it is. You are but a mindless beast, in the end. Your fear will overcome your sickening nobility the moment you see the truth of what I have done to him."

The air escaped her lungs in a whoosh. "You're wrong. He is worth everything to me," she said. "And that is what I am offering you as my part of the wager. Everything."

There were no more words. The demon did not speak again. Its power coalesced above her like a heavy stone, crushing her. She fell beneath its weight.

As her body dropped to the ground, her gaze flickered and came to rest on Eris, covered in blood, twitching weakly on the sand a few paces away. As she watched, he curled onto his side, facing her. His eyes glowed red, and his handsome face twisted into a mask of animal hunger. There was no recognition in his ravenous gaze.

With a sinking feeling, she wondered if her beloved was already gone forever, his soul sacrificed to a demon's lust for power. But... no. The creature had agreed to her wager. Her love could still redeem him. She had to believe that. She *had* to.

What the demon didn't understand, was that she couldn't bear the thought of living in a world without Eris. She had no fear of what might happen to her, because it couldn't possibly be worse than losing him.

Eris was struggling onto all fours, now, stalking toward her like a predator. She felt the demon retreat, leaving her prostrate and helpless in the sand as it fell back to watch. She could feel its bloodthirsty glee.

Her beloved was close enough now that she could read the anguish behind that blood-red gaze. The *need*. He hungered, and her eyes fell to the full-lipped mouth that had brought her so much pleasure over the years.

He had *fangs*.

The demon's words returned to her. *He will serve me loyally, feasting on blood and skin and sinew. Your fear will overcome your sickening nobility the moment you see the truth of him.*

That fear tried to rise now. She didn't let it.

Eris crawled up the length of her body, caging her with his arms and legs. Looking down at her. A drip of saliva fell from one of his fangs, to land warm and wet on her throat.

She swallowed. "Eris, my love," she said hoarsely, "I know you can't see anything but the Darkness right now. And that's all right. I will be the Light for both of us. I offer you everything I have to give, and ask only this in return. *Don't let this creature win.*" Her voice fell to a whisper as Eris wrenched her head back by the hair, and lowered his mouth to her neck in a sick parody of a lovers' embrace. "I love you. Through death and life —"

Eris snarled, and sharp pain pierced the sensitive flesh of her throat. She cried out, blood gurgling. As her soul was dragged forcibly from her body, a single thought flickered before her awareness slipped away into nothingness.

But now, I'll never know if I won the wager…

-o-o-o-

Trynn shivered violently. The air against her back felt icy, but there was warmth beneath her. Was she still in the dream? She *hungered*, as Eris had hungered on that beach in the distant past. A feast lay a mere hairsbreadth from her lips. She could feel it. She could *smell* it. All she had to do was —

Her teeth buried themselves in salty flesh, and warm nectar flowed over her lips. She lapped weakly at it, and some slipped down her parched throat. It should have been horrific, but she knew it couldn't actually be real. She was still sleeping, no doubt, her brain concocting some kind of fantasy dream-revenge on dream-Eris for biting her earlier.

That was all.

A hand cradled the back of her head, holding her steady. "That's it, beloved." The hoarse voice sounded relieved beyond measure. "Drink from me. Everything will be all right, now."

She suckled like a hungry newborn, completely on instinct. The warmth inside her grew, driving back the icy chill. Exhausted, she slipped into sleep.

-o-o-o-

Trynn still couldn't open her eyes. They were too heavy. Her aching body weighed a ton; her fingers might as well have been made of wood for all the feeling in them.

What — ? Where — ?

Indistinct voices murmured above her, the words unintelligible as she drifted in and out of sleep. Trynn tried again to open her eyes. The lids parted reluctantly, only to slide closed again as the world around her spun.

She moaned, and wrenched a numb, heavy hand up to her head, pressing the heel clumsily against her temple.

"Easy," a voice whispered. Strong arms held her against a warm, naked chest. "Rest now, Trynn."

She nodded, past the point of caring what she was agreeing to or with whom she was agreeing. She knew that voice. She trusted that voice. That was all that mattered.

Trynn drifted vaguely for what seemed like a long time, resting with the warm body on the soft pile of pillows. Someone pulled a dusty blanket up over her shoulders and she relaxed further, concentrating only on the feeling of blood pumping through her veins and arteries. It was strange, hearing the soft, rhythmic *shush-shush* so clearly, though she couldn't have said *why* it was strange.

Some time later, she became aware of an odd chasm inside her chest that had not been there before. She didn't like it. Something about it made her feel lopsided. Off-balance.

Don't be stupid, she thought. *You're lying down. How can you be off-balance when you're lying down?*

Realization struck.

Oh. Right. Snag had ripped her soul in two earlier. She probably should have remembered that part sooner. It was kind of important. Did that mean she was going to hell now? Which... yeah. Apparently hell was a real place, so...

I certainly hope not, a voice murmured inside her head. *For one thing, that would require dying first. But if you do, gods forbid, I will be by your side the whole way down — my word on it.*

She was so startled by the mental intrusion that she physically jerked in surprise. A warm hand settled on her arm, rubbing soothingly.

"It's all right," the voice said aloud. "Sorry about that. Don't worry, that's normal."

Trynn's tension bled out when she recognized the person lying next to her as Eris. Warmth enveloped her, knowing that he was with her and standing guard over her while she recovered.

Still too exhausted to speak, Trynn wondered if she could communicate with Eris mentally. It was worth a try, she supposed.

Am I a vampire now? she thought as hard as she could, hoping that Eris would be able to hear her.

"Yes, and there's no need to shout at me," Eris responded wryly.

"Shout?" The word emerged a bare rasp of sound.

"You were projecting very loudly. I don't doubt that every vampire in the vicinity could hear you."

Oh. Whoops. Trynn tried again to open her eyes and found that the world was still swirling. The longer she held them open, however, the more the view righted itself. She was curled up in a familiar, run-down room with bare stone walls and floors.

A cheerful fire burned in a dilapidated, crumbling fireplace, warming the air around them. The other vampires were lounging comfortably in chairs and on the floor, all dressed for survival and combat.

Trynn's eyes fell on Della, who was studying her with a worried expression.

"How do you feel, Trynn?" Della asked, coming closer to the bed where Trynn and Eris were lying and crouching next to them.

Trynn cleared her throat, though the terrible dryness persisted.

"Tired," she finally managed to croak.

Della nodded. "I bet. You've been through a lot this week."

Eris squeezed her shoulder in comfort as she nodded, still fighting sleep.

"She'll bounce back," Eris assured the room. "Her life force has already grown stronger since the turning, and it's only been a few hours."

"Hours?" Trynn murmured, allowing her eyes to fall closed again. "God. It feels like days."

Eris brushed her short hair away from her forehead. "I don't doubt it. You'll feel much better after you've fed again."

At his words, Trynn felt bone-deep thirst flare inside her, followed closely by repulsion at the idea of drinking blood.

"Can we take that part slowly?" Trynn asked, a note of apprehension in her voice.

"Of course," he replied. "It won't be as bad as you think. You've done it once already, though you may not remember it. Honestly, though, it's perfectly natural for us."

And I'll help you, he whispered in her mind.

Relieved, Trynn nodded again. Her head fell back against Eris' strong shoulder, and she slipped into a light sleep.

What seemed like mere moments later, a hand on her shoulder shook her gently awake.

"Huh?" she slurred, cracking her eyes open. "Wha's wrong?"

"Trynn, you've slept too long. It's time to feed now." Eris' voice was quiet, but insistent. She could feel him spooning her back—his body wrapped around hers protectively.

"I can't," Trynn whispered, unable to gather enough breath to raise her voice any more.

"You have to," Eris said. "Trust me, it will help."

Trynn ran her swollen, dry tongue over her teeth and discovered that her canines had lengthened into fangs. She shivered. Clearly, her body knew what she needed, even if her stomach clenched at the idea of preying on a human.

Eris seemed to know what was troubling her. "Not yet, beloved. Not until you gain enough control not to hurt them accidentally. There's no need. Feed from me, for now."

With her eyes still closed, Trynn felt his wrist touch her lips. Before she could stop herself, instinct took over and she bit down hard on his exposed flesh. Blood gushed into her mouth, tasting like the sweetest gift from the heavens.

Eris groaned as her teeth sank deeper into his skin—not from pain, but from longing. She could feel it, through the tenuous mental link joining them. His breathing grew rough and uneven in her ear as she sucked hard, drawing his lifeblood into her body. She felt energized, even as the evidence of his growing desire pressed against her from behind. As she continued to feed, he lowered his mouth to her exposed neck and nibbled playfully along the sensitive skin. He pressed the entire front of his body against her, as if trying to meld them into a single being. His breath hissed out sharply against the side of her throat, and goose bumps erupted along her arms.

"You are the most perfect thing I have ever seen," he said in a husky voice. "Absolutely flawless."

She did not answer, too focused on the feel of his body against hers and his blood flowing across her tongue. The heat of it filled her up, sending ecstasy coursing through her. As his life force passed to her, she felt their souls connecting and intertwining. What had been the pain of a broken soul became completion, the likes of which she had never known before.

This was what it meant to be truly alive. And to think, she'd only had to die to achieve it.

Eris chuckled, still breathless behind her. "Well stated. I can tell you still have the same sense of humor. Twisted... just the way I like it." He kissed the back of her neck. "You are mine, Trynn, and I am yours forever."

Finally sated, Trynn lowered his arm from her mouth and let him wrap it around her waist. She rolled over to face him, feeling whole and complete for perhaps the first time in her life as she buried her face in his neck.

Exhausted from their recent trials, Trynn and Eris slipped into a deep, easy sleep, resting peacefully in each other's arms.

SIXTEEN

Wakefulness crept up on her slowly, many hours later. She stretched, feeling completely refreshed and healthy—somewhat to her surprise, it must be said.

Opening her eyes, Trynn saw they were still in the same room as before. The fire next to them had burned low, only a few embers still glowing red. Eris was obviously already awake, and he stroked gentle fingers through her close-cropped hair.

"Hello," he said, his voice raspy.

Trynn turned towards him, studying him as the events of the past couple of days finally started to sort themselves out in her memory. Surprise and relief swelled as she took in his handsome features. "Hey! You look great."

Eris laughed, a deep rumble. "Uh... thanks? As opposed to before, you mean? Yes, I'm feeling much stronger, mostly because of Snag's generosity. There's something to be said for getting a top-off from the most powerful vampire in existence. His blood has me pretty much healed, I think."

To demonstrate, Eris lifted his arm. Where there had been cuts, deep bruises, and broken bones from hours of torture at Kovac's hands, there were now only faint pink lines. The wounds were almost completely knitted back together. Many had already faded, revealing new, tender skin underneath.

"Will I heal like that now?" Trynn asked in awe, glancing at Eris' face.

"Yes, I expect so. You've got Snag's blood running through your veins now, too—even if it was filtered through me first." His gaze narrowed. "However, that is *not* an invitation for you to go out and do something dangerous."

"Of course not... *Dad*," Trynn answered with an eye roll. She strongly suspected that even though she was functionally immortal now, Eris would still worry about her safety.

Remembering the others, Trynn looked around and realized that the room was empty except for the two of them. "Where is everyone?" she asked.

Eris jerked his chin toward the door, and the corridor beyond. "They're in another room down the hall. They got tired of waiting for you to wake up, and went out to explore the building. It's daylight, so there's not much else to do at the moment. I gather Tré and Xander are unearthing a partially destroyed piano right now, trying to figure out if it still works."

Trynn stared at him. "Okay. Why?"

One dark eyebrow quirked. "Now that you have an immensely long life, you'll find that there's time to dedicate to those types of pursuits."

She continued to stare. "Pursuits like abandoned and destroyed pianos?"

He snorted. "That... or old vehicles, like Xander. It just depends, honestly. Oksana is obsessed with human junk food and wine, of all things. She considers herself a *connoisseur*. I love to read, and Duchess spends more than an hour a day putting on her make-up. She claims that it's for the purposes of disguise, but I suspect it's actually a vanity project." One muscled shoulder lifted in a shrug. "You just... find things to occupy your time."

"Like Snag and his chess, I suppose. What about Della and Tré?" Trynn asked, genuinely curious.

Eris wagged his eyebrows suggestively. "Oh, I'm pretty certain they're still in their honeymoon phase."

"Ah," Trynn replied as understanding dawned — followed by amusement. "Since when?"

"It hasn't been long since we found Della, and she was turned. Only a few months. I don't think the novelty of near-constant sex has worn off yet. We haven't seen much of them during that time, to be honest."

And that brought to mind another question. The seven of them were obviously close, but—

"So, how does this work? Are you neighbors with the other vampires or… ?"

Eris shook his head. "We all live together, usually. It's safer that way, with Bael's power growing stronger, day-by-day. Every now and then, one or more of us will go off on our own, as Snag and I did when we traveled to Cyprus. But we are a family. We always return to the nest eventually."

"And where is this *nest*? Someplace in America, right?" Trynn asked, fascinated. No doubt she should have thought more about things like that before she was turned, but she still couldn't bring herself to regret it.

Eris scrubbed a hand through his tangled mop of dark hair, mussing it further. "Most recently we lived in New Orleans. An old plantation house that we've been working on fixing up. It's on the market right now, and I think we've just about got a buyer lined up. While the others were closing the deal, I came here to sell a Greek artifact that I've kept over the centuries."

Trynn gave him a sidelong look. "Part of our ill-gotten gains?"

Eris paused, his eyes crinkling at the corners, as if he were reveling in her use of the word *our*. "Yes. Just so. I still have a store of artifacts and exotic pieces. I sell them off one by one, as needed. I didn't see much point in keeping them—too many memories attached."

Trynn nodded thoughtfully and said, "I'm surprised you held onto them for this long. Why not sell all of them immediately and get the cash?"

"Too dangerous. I don't want to flood the market. It might raise suspicion. Besides, in the normal course of things, we're hardly short of money," Eris answered with an indifferent shrug. "Xander's the businessman. He's got his fingers in everything. My little contributions are a mere drop in the bucket."

Trynn settled back against him, thinking.

"Also," Eris continued, as an afterthought, "I'll admit to feeling a pang whenever I sell one. It feels too much like losing another little part of you."

Her chest tightened. "I can understand that," she said quietly. "It was something we did together."

Eris nodded, his dark eyes tracing her features like a caress. "I still keep half-expecting to wake up, and find that these last few days have a been a dream. We've studied ancient texts about the so-called Council of Thirteen for centuries, but we'd assumed it referred to existing vampires we simply hadn't found yet."

"And now you think it's us?" Trynn asked, fascinated. "People like Della and me, I mean?"

He gave her a small, helpless shrug. "I think it must be. Until Tré found Della, none of us had ever come across the reincarnations of our soulmates. We were beginning to assume the whole thing about the Council was nonsense—a myth. I certainly did. And I'd long ago given up hope of ever finding love again."

Saddened and touched, Trynn wrapped her arms around his neck and clung. "I'm sorry I made you wait."

Eris huffed. "Don't be daft. You had no control over that." He nuzzled into the crook of Trynn's neck and took a deep breath, as if inhaling her scent before pulling back and continuing, "I'll never hold that against you, Trynn; I'm just glad you're here now. I can barely remember my life before you walked back into it, even though it was only a few days ago."

"That's how I feel," Trynn said, wonder coloring the words. "It's like... I can remember things that happened, but they feel foggy and disconnected, almost like a story someone else told me."

"Maybe you are a different person now, in a way," Eris suggested. "Tré thinks that we are completely reborn as vampires, just as you were reborn from Phaidra into Trynn—and who knows how many lives in between."

Trynn considered this possibility, readjusting her body against Eris'. "I don't think so. I still feel like *me*, but it's like... I've woken up now. Like, my life before you was all a dream, and everything after has become so much more real to me."

"The fog has been lifted," Eris concluded.

She snorted. "Yeah, I guess." Silence reigned for a moment before she continued. "So, if you're selling this plantation house, where will we go next?" she asked, still curious about their living arrangements. "I guess I'll have to call my boss and give her my notice. Pity. I liked that job. But this way, I'll have more time for MASQUE... and that's more important, by far."

He nodded. "I don't know yet what we'll do now," he replied thoughtfully. "I suppose we'll have to see where the next vortex of chaos forms. We think that's the best way to try to locate the others like you and Della."

"Seems impossible that one place could even stand out, when pretty much the entire world is mired in violence," Trynn murmured.

Eris shrugged agreement. "I know what you mean. Though I'm starting to wonder if it's more a case of the chaos finding us, rather than the other way around."

They lay quietly for a few more moments before Trynn got up and stretched out her arms and legs. Eris rolled into a sitting position to watch. She could feel the new strength in her muscles, unlike anything she'd felt before. It was intoxicating.

Eris followed the path of her thoughts effortlessly. "You have many new powers now," he said. "We'll teach you how to use them over the coming days and weeks."

"*Powers*?" Trynn echoed. She narrowed her eyes playfully, suddenly intrigued. "*Do tell*. Powers like what?"

Catching onto her mood, Eris grinned, slow and dangerous. Something in her belly tightened.

"Well," he began airily, "Let's see. You have an owl form, now. That's always an interesting experience — being able to fly."

Trynn took a step closer, reaching down to touch Eris' cheek. "What else?"

He swallowed and looked up, his pupils blown wide as he continued to play the game with her. "Hmm. Oh, yes — you can also transform into mist. I believe you've seen that trick already, haven't you?"

She nodded. "So I have. What else?"

"You can press impressions into another person's mind," he murmured, his voice going husky. "You've seen that one, too. I still have the imprint of your knuckles on my jaw to prove it."

"Show me again," Trynn breathed. "I probably won't hit you this time."

Eris nodded and shut his eyes. As he took several slow breaths, Trynn felt something heavy and sweet creeping over her. Heat radiated outward from her core, but it was not the same kind of consuming fire that she had experienced while being turned. This fire warmed, rather than burning her. It settled in her belly, turning liquid.

"Oh. Is that all?" she asked, reaching for affected nonchalance as the sensation lifted.

Eris raised an eyebrow at her. "I believe you called it a *mind-whammy*, back in Nicosia. You seemed... rather affected, at the time."

Trynn laughed. "All right... *guilty*. And you're obviously never letting me live it down. So, as a vampire, I can make horniness into a mind-whammy. That's, uh, useful, I guess?"

"Do *try* to get your mind out of the gutter, Trynn." His voice was smug as he sent another wave of desire rolling through her body. "You can transmit any emotion. Anything."

Trynn gasped and ran her hand down her stomach, trying in vain to hold herself together. "And... how would I go about doing that? Exactly?"

Eris sprawled back on the bed of cushions they'd recently vacated, and let his legs fall open. He was wearing only the pair of well-worn, low slung pajama pants she'd first seen him in at the hotel, and Trynn thought he had absolutely no business making them look as good as he did. For fuck's sake, he looked good enough to *eat*.

Her mouth watered.

"Take the feeling you want to pass on," he said, "and force it into a ball inside you, like crumpling up a wad of paper. Turn it into something you can grasp. Then, pick it up."

Trynn nodded and concentrated on bundling up the hot, liquid feeling in her gut.

"Now," Eris whispered, "pass it along to me, just like when we were speaking telepathically."

In her eagerness, Trynn shoved her arousal towards him hard, unsure if she would be able to separate it from herself... or if she even needed to.

To her surprise, it passed easily along the mental connection they shared, but at the unwonted force of her attempt, Eris cried out in surprise and arched, his hips flexing. "Too much, *too much*!" he protested, the words caught between laughter and sexual agony.

With an evil smile, Trynn shook her head, remembering the second time she'd come to his hotel room for answers. "*Oh, no.* That's just a taste of what I'm going to give you. It's payback time!"

"Immortal or not, you're going to be the death of me, woman," Eris said around a chuckle, flopping back with his legs akimbo. His grin turned as devilish as hers. A golden light glowed behind his eyes. "But don't mind little old me. Do *please* continue."

She tried, but now the connection on his end was shielded, somehow.

"You're cheating!" she accused.

"I'm sure I have no idea what you mean," he said, right before he hooked an ankle around hers, taking her feet out from under her and sending her sprawling on top of him. He caught her in his arms, breaking her fall, and suddenly she was nose to nose with him, her mouth open in a round *oh* of surprise.

She met his golden eyes and tried again to regain the upper hand, scowling when her mental attempt slid away from the edges of his mind like droplets of water on an orange peel. "You're blocking me somehow."

Eris' look of faux-innocence wouldn't have fooled the most credulous of onlookers. One moment, she was lying on top of him, taking a mental measure of the *very* promising bulge nestled against the crease of her hip. A heartbeat later, she was pinned beneath him on the pile of cushions, held effortlessly in place by a careful strength that far outstripped hers, even now that she'd been turned.

Trynn didn't really need a mind-whammy of horniness at this point; her body had that angle taken care of, all on its own. She wriggled in his grip, not yet ready to throw in the towel in whatever game they were playing.

Right. *Shit.* So, maybe she didn't *need* the mind-whammy... but it looked like she was getting it again, ready or not. A wave of hot lust swept over her and ebbed, dragging an undignified noise from her throat.

Somehow, Eris was still able to press desire into *her* mind, even though he was blocking her from doing the same to him.

"*Definitely* not fair," she groaned, her head falling back against the cushions as the next wave came.

"Nonsense," he said, though the hint of gravel under his voice betrayed his own dwindling control. "There ought to be *some* advantage to being as old and experienced as I am. It's *perfectly* fair."

She writhed, wanting to feel that strength holding her in place... loving the way it ratcheted her raging desire even higher than before. Trynn redoubled her efforts to shove the molten ball of lust back across the link, and was rewarded by a sharp intake of breath as he thrust against her hip. The one-way shield strengthened a moment later, and he made a tisking noise.

Trynn felt like a volcano about to erupt, all pent up, with nowhere to go.

"*Touch me,* damn it," she demanded. "God! You're driving me mad, Eris!"

He smirked. "I *am* touching you," he said, squeezing her wrists and thrusting against her hip again to demonstrate.

She groaned aloud. "*Argh*! Not like that. *Touch. Me.*"

He still looked inordinately smug. "Hmm... not yet, I don't think. For one thing, I'm quite enjoying you like this." He rolled his hips, and she bit off a frustrated curse — which he ignored. "And for another, I don't think we've really explored the *mind-whammy* in sufficient depth, yet. I did promise to educate you in the use of our powers, after all."

Trynn made a desperate noise as the tide of *want* rose even *higher*, building impossibly within her with no outlet for release. Sex had always been a casual game for her in the past — a harmless amusement. It was a game she was used to winning. She had always been a *champion* at getting what she wanted in the bedroom.

Right now, she was definitely *not* getting what she wanted. She had a suspicion, though, that by the end of the night, she was going to get exactly what she *needed*. A new wash of lust washed over her, stealing her breath. Her body shuddered as she tried to hang onto control, but it lasted for only a moment before the thread snapped.

She went limp and heavy, surrendering to the overwhelming feelings coursing through her. Satisfaction rumbled through Eris' chest, her mild-mannered lover transforming into a growling, possessive panther before her eyes.

"So beautiful," he said, releasing her wrists to run his thumb over the seam of her lips. "And *mine*."

The touch ignited every nerve as she lay beneath him, pliant and waiting. "Please," she whispered against his callused fingertip. "Eris, *please*."

His thumb slid past her lips, the skin tasting of salt and musk as he pressed in deep. Her body balanced on the knife-edge of orgasm, aching and untouched.

"Yes," he said. "You're so close, aren't you? I want to feel you come merely from the touch of my mind against yours."

She whimpered around him. He stroked over her tongue and pressed an image into her thoughts of his cock sliding inside her with a single smooth thrust. Trynn cried out around the flesh in her mouth and came hard—still fully dressed, and without him having come within six inches of her clit, or even her breasts.

"Jesus *fuck*," she whispered after he slid his thumb free, and the aftershocks had died down to tremors. "I can see already that I'm going to have to up my game in the bedroom."

He stroked the backs of his knuckles over her cheek tenderly. "Your game is magnificent," he said, his tone sounding nearly reverent. "But, right now, I think it would be even more magnificent if you were naked."

Coming untouched might sound like serious fantasy material, but the reality was that it only left her wanting more, with a deep, empty ache that longed — no, *demanded* — to be filled.

"Naked is absolutely a plan I can get behind," she agreed. "As long as it's mutual, anyway."

"Very, very mutual," he said, sliding the soft cotton pajama bottoms he was wearing down and off without ceremony.

And... *yup*. The bulge had not lied, earlier. He was hung. And she was staring, to his evident amusement.

"No wonder you and Phaidra fucked constantly," she said. The words emerged sounding a bit faint.

That startled a bark of unrestrained laughter from him. "Should I even ask?"

She shook her head, trying to clear it. "Uh... I may or may not have had a whole series of extremely raunchy sex dreams about us in the past, those first few nights after we met."

His expression grew far away, and she ached for him in a new way as he looked down, breaking eye contact for a moment before peering through the tangle of his messy hair at her.

"I have tried for a long time... not to think about that part of the past," he said, all hints of teasing gone.

She smiled up at him sadly, and lifted a hand to stroke his jaw. Mirroring his earlier action, she brushed her thumb over his full lower lip. He grasped her wrist, holding her in place as he pressed a kiss to the pad.

"The time for sadness is past," she said. "I'm here. You're here. There's no reason to be sad any more, is there?"

His eyes closed, and she felt a fine tremor run through his body. When he opened them again, they were wet, but gold glowed behind his gaze.

"Trynn," he whispered hoarsely.

She smiled, and reached down to grasp the hem of her shirt so she could pull it off. She watched him watching her as she removed the rest of her clothing, piece by piece. She knew her body was fit, but not classically beautiful — she was a bit angular, a bit boyish.

But one glance was enough to tell her that in Eris' eyes, she was perfect. Part of her wondered if she resembled Phaidra physically. She guessed not, since he hadn't seemed to recognize her when they first met. Apparently, it didn't matter to him in the least. He was watching her avidly, hunger in his golden gaze.

"No more games," she breathed.

"No more games," he agreed. And then, he was stalking up the length of her body, pressing closed-mouth kisses along her inner thigh.

Oh, thank god, she thought, as he nuzzled between her legs and breathed in, rubbing his stubbled cheek against her, openly wallowing in her scent. Watching him like this... it was... *fuck*... it was the sexiest damn thing she'd ever seen in her life.

She could feel arousal not her own resonating along their bond again as his tongue darted out to taste her folds. This time, though, it wasn't a tease or a contest of wills, she knew. He just couldn't stop himself. Somehow, that realization made it even sweeter. Trynn felt the echo of desire flow freely back and forth, growing as they fed off each other's lust.

There was no reason to hold back.

It took almost no time at all for the touch of his mind and his delving tongue to bring her to the edge and push her over. She came, gasping, feeling him struggle not to follow her down into release.

A torrent of deliciously filthy images flashed in front of her mind's eye, a movie reel of her dreams and fantasies from the past few days. She very clearly saw herself masturbating in the Merit Lefkosa's decadent bathtub, to thoughts of Eris sinking his fangs into her neck.

Just as clearly, she felt Eris go still between her thighs, shock and uncertainty echoing through the connection. It took a minute for her to gather her wits after her orgasm. When she did, Eris was looking up the length of her body, his brow furrowed.

"What?" she asked.

He blinked. "You... want such a thing? After what I *did* to you, all those centuries ago?"

Understanding dawned, and the breath left her lungs in a slow exhale. "Oh, *Eris*." She swallowed. "Not everything has to be about the past, does it?"

He was still watching her intently. "The past defines us."

She shook her head. "Only if we let it," she argued. "Is it so difficult to accept that maybe, just maybe, I have an untapped vampire fetish that doesn't have deep, dark implications from millennia in the past? Especially given the fact that *I'm a vampire now*."

The crease between his brows deepened. "But—"

"But nothing," she insisted. "It was just a passing thought. I'm not asking you to do anything you don't want to do. I trust you, though. I trust you with that completely. And I *want* that kind of bond with you. It's the same bond you share with the others, isn't it? The bond of blood?"

His expression softened into desperate longing, but she was relieved to see a hint of humor underneath. "Well," he said, pressing a kiss to her mons, "perhaps not *quite* the same."

She laughed, breathless. He kissed his way further up her body until he was poised above her. When his mouth closed over hers, she tasted herself, and moaned into the kiss. Her legs circled his hips, urging him forward. His hard length slid into her, stretching her passage deliciously. Filling her to perfection.

She gathered him close to her body and held him tight as they rocked together. She might have expected urgency from him during this, their first coupling. Instead, it was sweet beyond measure... slow and tender. Exquisite.

The world fell away, and for the first time she understood what he had said about having *time*. There was no hurry. They had forever.

She could feel what he felt; he could feel what she felt. It was the same. It was love.

When the sharp slide of his fangs pierced her neck, it was painless — the most natural thing in the world. When the deep pulling sensation as he drank from her joined the feel of him moving inside of her, a profound, all-consuming release washed through her body. He followed, filling her up even as he drew from her, the connection between them whiting out with ecstasy.

When he was finished, he kissed the fast-healing twin wounds left by his fangs, and buried his face against her neck. She felt the warm wetness of his silent tears, and held him close, cradling him to her.

"So long," he whispered against her skin, his arms clutching her. "It's been so long, beloved."

"I know, my heart," she soothed, stroking his messy hair. Feeling wise and strong. Cherished and protected. "I know. It's all right, now."

-o-o-o-

Some considerable time later, Trynn pushed open the door and the two of them emerged, turning left down the darkening hallway. Eris led the way, moving expertly through the maze-like corridors, and Trynn understood that he must be receiving directions from another vampire.

His large hand clasped her slender one. She could feel the power pulsing between them as their life force intermingled, tangled together after the hours of love-making. Adoration swelled in Trynn's chest, filling up the unpleasant empty place in her soul that had plagued her after her turning, until it overflowed. It seemed that being reunited with her mate bridged the gap between the Light and the Dark within her. She wondered if it had done the same for Eris, but she wasn't sure how to ask.

Apparently, they had reached their destination. He gestured towards a door and ushered her inside.

Trynn had a sneaky suspicion that she'd spent the last couple of hours projecting ecstasy to every vampire within mental listening distance. In the dwindling light of the room, she felt a hot blush creep over her cheeks as the others looked up. Della smiled, having pity on her.

"Yeah, I'm afraid you did, a bit," the other woman said, her eyes crinkling. "Don't worry, though. Anyone who didn't want to hear it shielded their minds against you. You'll get used to it, and it'll be easier to control next time."

Della's gaze flickered involuntarily to Tré, and Trynn spared a brief moment of embarrassed curiosity over the idea that certain people might *not* have shielded. She cleared her throat to cover it. *Yup... none of her business.*

"Yes," Xander said. "You, uh, really might want to work on that. Before *some of us* have to leave the country for some peace and quiet."

Trynn blushed harder, and Eris gave Xander a look that was *thoroughly* unimpressed.

"Hey!" Xander raised his hands defensively. "Don't give me that glare. You don't understand how it is, being celibate while having to listen to the *happy couples* sneaking around."

"Goodness. Celibate *and* sober at the same time?" Eris asked. "The horror."

"Well... sober-*ish*," Xander clarified, making a waggling, half-and-half motion with one hand.

"My heart bleeds for you," Eris said, dry as dust. "Oh! Wait. No, I was wrong. I think it was just a moment of indigestion."

Xander slapped a palm over his chest, playing at being wounded. "*Ouch.* I feel like you're not fully appreciating my suffering, here."

"From the hangover, you mean?" Eris mused. "Or the existential angst?"

"As entertaining as this is," Duchess interrupted, "I think everyone is looking forward to leaving this rundown shithole as soon as it can be arranged."

"Yes, the whole *bombed out war zone* thing is getting kind of old," Oksana agreed. Her gaze settled on Eris. "Also, the whole *people I care about nearly getting themselves killed* thing."

Eris had the grace to at least look regretful. "I'm sorry, Oksana. Not least because my misjudgment put the rest of you in jeopardy. But there were nuclear bombs involved, and an unknown timeline regarding when they might detonate. You weren't here, and I had to leave Snag behind to guard Trynn. I regret the way it turned out, but I'm very much afraid that under the same circumstances, I'd do it again."

The others were quiet. A lump rose in Trynn's throat, but she swallowed it down. "And would you lie to me again, about what you were doing?" she asked, remembering the way he'd looked when she'd first arrived here with Tré and Della. Broken. Half dead.

Eris' face softened. "No. No, I wouldn't lie. Tré told me what you did, with the email to the Russians. If I'd talked to you first, the whole thing might have been avoided."

Honesty compelled her to say, "I don't know. Maybe not. I only came up with the plan because I was so desperate to save you after Snag showed me what that fucking bastard Kovac had done to you."

Tré had been silent, but he spoke up at that. "At least now we know the truth about Bastian Kovac. We know what kind of power we're facing. A power almost equal to Snag's, even though Kovac was turned only a short time ago."

Trynn looked towards Snag, who was standing still and silent in the corner of the room. As she gazed at him, she felt a surge of affection stir in her heart. Perhaps it was because they were connected now — bound by blood. Maybe it was due to that newly fledged bond, or maybe becoming a vampire had adjusted her eyesight, but he appeared less like a spectral monster to her now. His burns were healed, and his face seemed less gaunt than before. She could detect a hint of warmth in his pale skin, and light in his eyes, which moved to rest on her.

As their gazes connected, Trynn felt the corner of her mouth lift up in a smile.

Thank you, she sent. She felt fairly sure that she'd managed to keep that message for him alone.

Snag tipped his head towards her in a tiny gesture of acknowledgement, before turning his gaze back towards the window.

"So. Where should we go next?" Oksana asked, brushing dust off her dark trousers.

"I need a vacation after this," Xander answered, looking aggrieved. "This has been one gigantic clusterfuck from start to finish."

"Yeah, it has, at that," Eris agreed, abandoning their earlier sniping. "Let's just be happy that it's over and —"

Without warning, the entire building rocked on its foundation. Trynn and Della staggered and fell to their knees. A wall of sound crashed against their ears, and dust rained down on their heads as beams and chunks of plaster fell from the ceiling.

Trynn felt herself being dragged sideways just as something heavy smashed where she had been crouching. Eris flung his body across hers and shielded their heads with his arms.

As more debris rained down, Trynn heard a scream from somewhere to her right. It sounded like Della.

With a final quake, the building grew still. The only sound was the clatter of falling masonry. Trynn coughed and pushed Eris off of her.

"I'm all right," she croaked. "Is everyone else okay? What the *hell* just happened?"

The others stirred, pushing debris aside, seemingly unhurt.

"I've no idea," Eris said, wiping dust from his face. "Anyone?"

Listen. The silent order echoed across the mental connection between the vampires, and after a moment's confusion, Trynn realized it came from Snag.

"Listen to *what*?" Tré demanded. Through the gloom, Trynn could see him helping Della to her feet. They both looked shaken.

Snag was the only one of them who had remained standing through the shock wave. He stood before the window, clutching the windowsill with tension radiating through his slender body.

"*Mon dieu.*" It was Duchess. She had gone pale, her china blue eyes wide and unseeing. "*Merde.* The screaming. Can't you hear it? It's coming from the city…"

Trynn couldn't, and looking at Duchess' expression, she was immeasurably glad of that fact.

All of them rushed to join Snag at the window. They crowded around, in time to see a mushroom-shaped fireball of brilliant orange, yellow, and red slowly lifting into the sky a few miles away.

"Oh my *god*," Della exclaimed, horrified. "No, it can't be. It *can't* be! Not after all that!"

Trynn's heart sank, even as nausea rose. Dear god. She hadn't stopped it. *She hadn't stopped it.*

"This is a nightmare," Xander whispered, running a shaking hand through his hair.

Tré broke free of his paralysis. "Satellite phone," he said. "We can try to get a signal on the cell phones, but the system is likely to be down. Xander, who can we call to find out what's happening elsewhere? We need to know if this was the only detonation, and how the world's governments are responding."

Xander took a deep breath, visibly gathering himself. "I'll try some of my business contacts in the UK. They have dealings with the government there, and should have some idea of what's going on."

-o-o-o-

It took well over an hour for Xander to reach someone and get news. Trynn *itched* for a data connection — Twitter… IRC… *anything* that would let her put a finger on the pulse of the outside world. Tré had been right, though. Those parts of the cellular network that hadn't been destroyed by the blast were overloaded with everyone trying to use their phones at once.

Finally, Xander put the satellite phone aside and scrubbed a hand over his face. "This was the only explosion. It's touch and go, but it looks like the western governments and Russia are tentatively willing to view it as an isolated act of terrorism, not the beginning of all-out nuclear war. There will be boots on the ground and drones in the sky within hours. Every country with a suspected terrorist presence is about to become a hot zone — including this one. But the world's nuclear warheads are still in their silos. That tiny thread of sanity appears — somewhat shockingly — to have prevailed."

Trynn thought she should probably feel more relieved than this, at the knowledge that the world was not about to end in a rain of fiery ICBM-fueled terror from the skies. But she wasn't relieved. She was numb.

"What do we do now?" she asked, turning towards Eris.

He seemed to be at a loss for words as he stared out the window at the aftermath of destruction.

"I'm… not sure there's anything we *can* do," he replied slowly.

"But we're immortal, right?" Trynn demanded, turning towards the other vampires. "*Right?*"

"Yes," Oksana said hesitantly.

"*Then let's go help,*" Trynn said, tugging on Eris' hand.

She felt a sudden urgency to rush to the aid of the people of Damascus. Her heart broke, knowing that she was witnessing the slow, painful death of thousands — perhaps tens of thousands — of men, women, and children.

"You're suggesting that we rush into a fire-riddled, radioactive pile of rubble to help a bunch of humans who will probably die anyway?" Duchess challenged, her voice brittle.

"Yes!" Trynn said, staring the other woman in the eye. Not backing down.

Their gaze locked for a long moment before Duchess shrugged, feigning indifference. "All right, then," she said. "That's what we'll do. Just clarifying."

"Can the radiation hurt us?" Della asked, looking at Tré.

"No," Xander answered, his tone clipped.

They all looked at him.

"And you know that… how, exactly?" Tré asked, brow furrowed.

Xander shifted on his feet. He took a deep breath "There was an incident in the nineteen-fifties… and… I, uh, just happened to be at the scene during a leak at an experimental nuclear reactor…"

He trailed off, looking pained. "You know what—never mind. Suffice to say, there shouldn't be any lasting effects on us. Probably."

Tré's eyes lingered on Xander for a long moment before he blinked and dragged his gaze away.

"Are we all in agreement, then?" he asked, his piercing silver eyes meeting each of his fellow vampires' in turn. They nodded in response.

"Do we have any supplies that would be useful?" Eris asked, looking around at the destruction surrounding them.

Tré shook his head. "I don't think there's anything we can really get on short notice that will help much. This... is going to be terrible."

Trynn saw Eris' chest rise and fall. He took her hand, lacing their fingers together and lifting her knuckles to his lips. "Not the honeymoon I'd envisioned, beloved," he murmured.

She felt tears threaten. "It doesn't matter," she managed. "We're together. Not just you and I, but all of us." Her gaze took in the others—battered... shell-shocked... and poised to fly straight into the heart of hell, in hopes that they could make some small difference in the face of horror. "We're together, and we're going to do what's right. Demons and madmen be damned."

"Hear, hear," Xander said quietly.

Eris squeezed her hand. "Yes. We're together. I will never leave you again, Trynn. Never. We'll face whatever the future throws at us, shoulder to shoulder—my beloved."

She looked up at him, a single tear slipping free to slide down her cheek. "*Beloved*," she whispered, echoing the endearment. "Come on, then. Let's do this."

Surrounded by her strange, unexpected new family, Trynn turned toward the fiery night sky in the distance, and the others turned with her. She felt Snag gather her under the cloak of his power, guiding her first transformation into cool mist.

The others transformed, swirling around her, and the eight of them plunged forward into the unknown.

EPILOGUE

Bastian Kovac limped awkwardly through the rubble that covered every street and sidewalk in what used to be central Damascus. As he listened, he could still hear parts of buildings crumbling, sounding like heavy rain on a crashing ocean.

He breathed, smelling the heavy sent of burned flesh and decay.

It had been two days since the bomb had detonated in the heart of the city, and while the single point of destruction had not been exactly on the scale he had originally planned, it was effective as far as it went. With so much death to feast on, Bastian had recovered quickly enough from the Russian bullets that had ripped through his body.

However, the punishment from Bael for his failure was not so easy to shake off.

As he drew the radioactive air into his lungs, Bastian sucked in the dark power of his master, thrumming through the scene of devastation like a current.

This was their time. Their victory. Their chance at dominion over this twisted, pathetic world. Evil swirled through the air around him, palpable as a cold wind.

As Bastian's dark hair whipped around his face, the reek of death penetrated straight to his still, cold heart, calling like to like. His dead eyes surveyed the darkness around him, easily able to discern the lifeless bodies hidden under the rubble, away from the sight of men and vampires.

Oh yes—the abominations had been here, picking at the edges of the kill zone like vultures in search of the living. He'd watched from the shadows as they plucked injured men, women, and children from half-collapsed buildings under cover of darkness. Bastian had shielded his presence carefully, knowing that he was too weak to risk another confrontation with them so soon.

Around him, Bael's power swelled.

"Bring forth my army, to rule over all." The deep voice resonated through the earth, making it tremble.

Bastian climbed to the top of a mound of debris near a demolished building. Even though his left leg was mangled and bloody, he pulled himself upright and stood, spine straight, looking out over their kingdom.

"My master, your wisdom is as endless as the seas. I will build your empire with the help of your new servants, who now await your command," he proclaimed.

As he lifted his voice to the demon, Bastian held out his hands in front of him, palms facing downwards. He could feel power vibrating between his body and the earth as Bael's force grew and solidified.

"I will build your sovereign nation," he whispered, closing his eyes and allowing the darkness to flow through him.

A black bubble formed in the center of the zone of destruction, and expanded outward. Evil spread like an oil slick, coating everything it touched. The power balance between the Light and the Dark strained, and burst its bonds.

With a sudden, deafening *crack*, the bubble of power exploded, forcing animation into every frail, broken body in the city.

"Let your will be done!" Bastian cried, cold sweat pouring down his face as he concentrated on maintaining his connection with the earth. He would not fail his master now.

All around, he could hear the sound of feeble limbs scraping at the dirt, cracked fingernails scrabbling over broken concrete and twisted metal as the undead pulled themselves free of their unmarked tombs.

Bastian opened his eyes and looked around, surveying his new creations in wonder and ecstasy. Unbridled joy flooded him. He closed his hands into fists and threw his head back, uttering a roar of victory.

An army of the dead was rising from the ashes of Damascus, patiently awaiting their creator's command.

End of Book Two

CIRCLE OF BLOOD BOOK THREE:

LOVER'S SACRIFICE

R. A. STEFFAN & JAELYNN WOOLF

ONE

This really wasn't how Mason had expected to spend his Friday morning.

Endless piles of paperwork? Definitely. Arguing over the phone about continued funding for the clinic? Probably. Counseling sessions with some of the children under his care? Yep.

Staring down the barrel of an automatic weapon wielded by a twelve-year-old? Not so much.

The black muzzle of the AK-47 never wavered as it pointed at Mason's chest, held securely in the hands of a wild-eyed Haitian boy. The child appeared dwarfed by the high-powered assault rifle cradled against his scrawny shoulder, but Mason knew all too well how deadly he could be.

The MP escorting a small group of newly liberated child soldiers to Mason's rehabilitation clinic had turned his back for less than a second before the boy struck like a snake—yanking the weapon from his slackened grip and turning it on the people he no doubt saw as enemy captors.

Both Mason and the MP stood frozen in place. The MP's mouth was hanging open in surprise. No doubt the man had thought himself lucky to draw such a cushy posting in Port-au-Prince, guarding adolescents instead of fighting in the rebel-held villages out in the hinterlands.

More fool him.

As the physician in charge of the ragtag, underfunded *Center for the Rehabilitation of Underage Conscripts*, Mason knew exactly how hazardous the duty they were performing here could be. And if he survived the next few minutes, he would bloody well find out who had failed to adequately brief the hapless soldier standing next to him. At which point, he would rip that person a new orifice, Hippocratic Oath or no.

It was fairly obvious that the MP was going to be little help in defusing the situation, though Mason supposed it would have been worse if he'd decided to go all Rambo on the kid and do something fatally stupid.

Mason stood perfectly still, his hands hanging loose at his sides, trying to breathe calmly through the massive adrenaline dump coursing through his body. He recognized the hallmarks of the body's fight-or-flight response, though his detailed medical knowledge of the process did little to curb the wash of instinct that was trying to shut down his logical thinking ability just when he *seriously fucking needed it.*

His senses were heightened, strained to their utmost, taking in the oddly jarring sounds in the background of the tense scene. The happy shouts of children playing. The creak of palm trees swaying in the sea breeze. The smell of salt clinging to the air, buried beneath vehicle exhaust and decomposing garbage.

The way the matte black finish of the automatic weapon's barrel seemed to swallow the daylight.

Mason mentally shook himself, trying to force his focus back to the boy — to his body language and facial expression. Remaining calm was the key. Panic would only get him — and possibly a lot of other people in the immediate area — killed.

There was no cover to speak of in front of the clinic, and few options for outside assistance. Even if the wide-eyed child holding the rifle felt like letting Mason stroll around the corner for a moment to place a leisurely phone call on his mobile, calling the coppers in Port-au-Prince these days was about as effective a method of summoning help as picking up a random tin can from the street and shouting into it.

Face it, mate, he thought. *It's up to you to keep this thing from going tits-up.*

He took a slow, measured breath and let it out before speaking.

"Okay, let's just take a minute to calm down and talk," he began, his Aussie accent becoming more pronounced than usual, as it always seemed to when he was under stress. "You're in charge... you've got the gun. I promise you, you're perfectly safe here—"

The boy lifted the gun a fraction, his aim moving from Mason's chest to his head. "I might be safe, *blan,*" he said, eyeing Mason's pale skin and obviously foreign mode of dress, "but *you* aren't. Have this soldier take me an' the others back where you found us, or I'll kill you." He bared white teeth. "Maybe I'll just kill you anyway, eh? What d'you think of that?"

Movement in the corner of his eye drew Mason's attention, and a face appeared at the screen door of the building next to him. *Bugger.*

"Joni," he said in a calm voice, speaking to the young nurse who was little more than a teenager herself, "why don't you take the rest of the children out the back way and go down to the beach for a bit?"

Their eyes locked, and he saw the same fear he was holding at bay reflected in her face. He forced a reassuring smile and jerked his head toward the back of the structure, silently imploring her to get herself and the other children to safety. With a clipped nod, she backed away from the door, and he could hear her issuing quiet instructions to the kids who had gathered at the front of the clinic for their mid-morning medications.

He turned his full attention back to the boy and steeled himself to try something that would either improve the situation... or escalate it.

"It's me you need to talk to," he said in the same conversational tone. "I'm the one in charge, here. Let's have a chat, just you and I." He flicked his eyes to the MP. "You—take our other guests inside, please, and help Joni."

The soldier looked at Mason like he was bent in the head. He might've even had a valid point about that. Still, Mason nodded toward the door, insistent.

He met the eyes of the half-dozen other children who had arrived with this group. "Go on—please make yourselves at home. There are bottles of Coke chilling on ice in the corner of the front room. Help yourselves."

The other boys looked uncertainly at each other, but after a few moments of indecision, two of them wandered toward the door and peeked inside. Upon seeing the large red cooler sitting in the corner as promised, they went inside. The others followed.

"Go on," Mason told the MP, praying like hell that he wasn't making a deadly mistake.

With a final, uncertain nod, the man backed cautiously away until his hand brushed the doorknob. He opened the door and slipped through, closing it silently behind him. The AK-47 did not erupt into a deafening hail of gunfire, though its muzzle did begin to tremble almost imperceptibly.

Well, that's everyone except me out of harm's way, at least.

Letting the air flow silently from his lungs, Mason turned back towards the boy in front of him and tried to give him the same friendly smile he'd used to reassure Joni. It felt like the muscles in his face had frozen, though, and he didn't think he'd really pulled it off.

The child staring at him with bloodshot eyes did not react, simply gazing back with a sort of dull, distant anger. The only move he made was to readjust his grip on the powerful AK-47 clutched in his small hands. He shifted on his feet, standing in front of Mason in baggy cargo shorts and nothing else, save for the soiled green bandana tied around his head.

Mason didn't want to make any move that might startle or upset the boy, but, at the same time, this stalemate needed to end. The longer they stood out here, staring at each other with a high-powered weapon between them, the greater the likelihood that Mason would end up riddled with bullet wounds.

Moving slowly, Mason lowered himself into a crouch so that he was below eye level with the scared and angry boy. At the same time, he did a quick visual inspection, cataloging the child's condition with the eye of a physician.

Short, brittle hair. Bloodshot eyes, flat affect, dilated pupils. Probably under the influence of some sort of stimulant. Discharge from the eyes and nose. Chapped lips with sores in the corners of his mouth. Thin frame. Bloated belly. Multiple scars and marks from badly healed wounds. Partially healed gunshot wound to the upper right arm, from approximately six weeks ago. Cracked feet showing signs of advanced fungal infection.

"How old are you?" Mason asked, looking up at the boy.

The question seemed to startle him. He blinked several times, and a look of confusion crossed his features before they hardened back into flat anger. "I'm fifteen, *blan*. What do you care?"

Stunted growth due to emaciation.

"I bet you're a hell of a soldier," Mason said in lieu of an answer. "You overpowered that MP like it was nothing."

"I'm the best in my unit," the youth bragged, tipping his chin up as if daring Mason to dispute it. "That's why you're gonna send me straight back, and the others, too."

"Okay, let's discuss that," Mason said easily. "My name's Dr. Walker, by the way. What's yours?"

There was a tiny hesitation. "They call me *San Silans*."

Silent Blood? Christ on a crutch.

For the thousandth time since arriving here, Mason mentally shook his head in disbelief over what was being done to Haiti's children during this long and bloody civil war.

"Sorry, San—my Creole is shit, as you can probably guess," he said, not completely truthfully. "What's your real name?"

He'd seen this before, many times, from other child soldiers receiving treatment at the clinic. Their captors would take them from their families—sometimes dragging them straight from the arms of screaming or dying relatives—and erase their pasts. They would brainwash the children, ranging in age from those who were barely more than toddlers to those in their teens, using a combination of drugs, intimidation, and rudimentary psychological techniques.

After a few weeks or months, the victims were utterly convinced that their loved ones had been killed and desecrated by "the enemy," and that to avenge them, they were honor bound to kill any government soldier who came into their sights without hesitation. The rebel unit was their new family, and the penalty for disloyal behavior was death at the hands of their fellow child soldiers.

The boy hesitated at Mason's question about his real name, a flash of something like unease crossing his features. "*My name is San Silans.*"

"It's just that *San Silans* is an unusual name," Mason pressed carefully. "Maybe there was something else you were called before people started calling you that?"

The kid pursed his lips together in a tight line, his knuckles tightening around the stock of the rifle. He stared hard at Mason, as if sizing him up—or perhaps trying to understand him. Mason returned the boy's gaze without blinking, purposely keeping his energy low and calm.

The moment stretched out like taffy, before Mason's captor dropped his eyes to the side, giving a bit of ground. Though he maintained his firm grip on the weapon, a fraction of the tension bled out of his shoulders.

"I used to be called Eniel," he muttered.

"Eniel," Mason repeated. "That's a traditional name in the south, isn't it? A good name. Strong, like you."

"Yes." Eniel still wasn't meeting his eyes.

"Well, Eniel, since you're here at the clinic, what can I do to help you?"

Eniel's eyes hardened. "I already told you, *blan*. You can send me back where I belong. I need to report to my commander. I won't stay here with you government scum."

Mason spread his hands in a gesture indicating harmlessness. "Eniel, mate—I'm Australian. I'm not a rebel *or* a government lackey. I'm just here to help pick up the pieces."

Eniel lifted the gun and jerked his chin toward it. "The stupid *kochon* I grabbed this from is government scum. You could smell it on him."

"And you ran him right off, so no need to worry about him right now," Mason said. "Eniel, we can't send you back to your commander. Your commander's the one who sent you here in the first place."

"Lies!" Eniel snapped, his voice rising.

Actually, that much was the complete truth. Mason and his contacts had been negotiating the release of child soldiers from rebel forces for months now. Public image was enough of a concern for the insurgents that they were willing to give up some of their low-value fighters in exchange for the goodwill it would garner.

Especially the ones who were already on the verge of physical or mental breakdown... though it would probably be better for Eniel not to hear about that part, just now.

"I'm afraid it's the truth," Mason countered. "Your commander was worried about you. He sent you here for medical help. That's a gunshot wound on your arm. It must be bothering you, even though you're such a good soldier that you hide it well. I could help you with that."

As if on cue, Eniel's body began to quiver. He sniffed hard, wiping mucus from his nose with the back of one arm. It smeared and glistened across his face as his eyes glittered in the bright sunlight. "He said I had to get in the truck with the others. He didn't say what would happen or where we were going."

Mason nodded in understanding. "And what did you think about that?"

Eniel raised and lowered one shoulder. The shaking in his body intensified, and he scowled at Mason, almost as if another personality had consumed him. "I thought maybe it was a test, or a mission." He pointed to the clinic building. "They are from the government; they are the people responsible for killing my family! I thought, maybe, this is a way for my commander to infiltrate the enemy, by sending me here to kill them!"

Mason knew better than to argue with him. He'd heard the same story many times before. It was common practice to tell young, impressionable children that the government had been the ones to kill their families. The rebel leaders instilled that hatred among their young soldiers early on to ensure total obedience. It would take them months, if not years, to undo the brainwashing most of these boys had sustained.

"Like I said," Mason began, "I'm not a part of your war. I just want to help you, like your commander intended when he ordered you to come here. So, when was the last time you ate? Are you hungry?"

At the mention of food, Eniel's gaze seemed to tighten on Mason's face. What had been dirty looks and constant scanning before, suddenly became almost dog-like hunger, focused and unmoving.

"Come on," Mason coaxed, keeping his tone calm and matter-of-fact. "We'll get you a meal and you can tell me a bit more about yourself."

The boy stayed completely still for several moments, staring at Mason's face.

Shite, I'm getting too old for this. My legs are going completely numb, Mason thought, as he tried to slowly shift positions to allow the blood flow to return to his tingling right foot.

Eniel's shoulders sagged and his grip softened on the AK-47. He grimaced, as if in physical pain. "You should be afraid of me. I have... done things. Terrible things."

Mason felt his heart ache, as it always did when the children at his clinic spoke about their past. All of them had been turned into monsters by the rebel kidnappers that forced them into the war, giving them weapons and brainwashing them until everything they used to believe was forgotten. Many of them had killed hundreds of people, mowed down opposing forces, or even killed other child soldiers in different militia units during the night for scraps of blanket or morsels of food.

It was likely that Eniel was no different, standing here in the bright sunlight with snot smeared across his face, pointing a high-powered weapon unerringly at Mason while looking so weak and malnourished that it was amazing he could even stand up.

Most people would look at Eniel and see a murderer. But Mason knew that he was merely seeing a weapon, fashioned and honed by adults who placed more value on winning a war than on the sanctity of childhood.

Ironically, the phrase "it's not your fault" was one of the surest ways to enrage a child soldier. They hated hearing it, because it chipped away at their tenuous sense of control over their own lives. And yet, it was true. One did not blame a grenade for exploding and killing people. One blamed the person who pulled the pin and threw it.

Eniel was not to blame for the lives he had taken. Every day, Mason told himself that the rebel command-ers at whose feet those deaths truly rested would pay eventually. At times like this, he almost wished he could personally extract that payment—but he knew that his place was here, healing the broken bodies and damaged souls of these, the most vulnerable victims of Haiti's re-lentless war against itself.

"Eniel," he said after a quiet moment, "lots of the young people here have done bad things. I still want to help you."

"Why?"

Mason had to gather himself for a moment before answering, "Because in this clinic, we don't leave any-one behind."

Eniel cocked his head at that, fidgeting, his thin fin-gers trembling around the stock of the gun. He shrugged one shoulder towards his ear several times, as if to dis-place an irksome fly. Shifting his weight back and forth, his gaze turned towards a gap between the buildings, where only a few palm trees blocked the view of the beach and stunning blue ocean.

Finally, Eniel looked at Mason and parted his chapped, raw lips. "I... I..."

Mason didn't move, just remained frozen in his po-sition, a look of quiet expectation across his face.

"I left people behind," Eniel said in a rush. Wetness glistened in the corners of his eyes. "My friends..."

In a very soft voice, Mason replied, "Why don't you put the gun on the ground and tell me more about that."

Eniel gripped the gun harder for a second, pulling it towards his chest. A wild fear seemed to grip him, making him look eerily like a cornered animal. Mason remained still, his calm expression never wavering.

After a long moment, Eniel relaxed. Never taking his eyes off Mason, he lowered the gun slowly towards the ground. As soon as it was resting on the dirt path in front of the clinic, Mason carefully rose to his feet and gestured Eniel towards the steps.

Thank God for crisis intervention training.

The boy stood still and watched suspiciously as Mason crossed to the steps and sat down, his legs and feet still numb from his awkward, crouched position.

To further put the boy at ease, Mason made quite a show of removing one of his shoes and massaging life back into his foot. He guessed that Eniel would feel more comfortable moving nearer if he wasn't faced with uninterrupted eye contact.

To Mason's relief, the boy took a few faltering steps towards the stairs and lowered himself down against the railing, as far away from Mason as possible.

"Thank you, Eniel," Mason said. Out of the corner of his eye, he saw the boy chew on his lower lip thoughtfully. The gun lay abandoned in the dirt in front of them.

"Now… you were telling me about your friends?" he prompted, pulling his sock back on and brushing the sand and dirt off the fabric.

Eniel was silent for several moments before he spoke, watching Mason carefully adjust his shoe and retie the laces.

"We camped at night in a line, a long line of men and boys. Some had guns, some did not," Eniel began in a hoarse whisper. "My place was near the middle of the line."

Mason nodded to show he was listening, though he looked out through the palm trees dotting the landscape in front of the clinic. His fingers mindlessly found a stone stuck in the crack of the wooden stairs, and he pried at it with a fingernail just to give himself something to do while Eniel spoke.

"I could not sleep, so I stayed awake and watched the stars. The fire in the camp flickered, throwing many shadows. There was no noise except the wind in the grass and trees. Then, I heard screams from the far end of camp. I ran to them, but they were already gone. I raised the alarm, but it was too late. They disappeared."

"Other soldiers?"

"Other boys. Their sleeping places were empty, and their shoes left behind. This happened many times while we traveled, and even though we searched, we could never find them afterward. Never. They are gone... lost in the hills."

Mason breathed out slowly through his nose. *Must have been the government forces taking the boys in secret*, he mused. *But that doesn't make a lot of sense. If they were all sleeping except for a handful of lookouts, why not just capture the entire band of rebels, or kill them? Why just take a few?*

He shook his head, trying to clear his thoughts. He would never understand the ways of the military, and he knew better than to start raising questions that might embarrass the people who held the fate of his clinic in their hands.

Turning his attention back to Eniel, Mason tried to regain the thread of the conversation.

"It sounds like you did everything you could though, right? You kept watch, and you raised the alarm when you knew something had happened."

Eniel stared at his hands, which were cracked, scabbed, and dirty. He nodded, but a frown still marred his features. "James was lost," he said quietly.

"Who was James?" Mason asked.

The frown grew deeper. "My friend. We were together from the very beginning. He was very tall, so his place was near the end of the line. He was taken during the night and I never saw him again."

Eniel's shoulders trembled and he wiped his nose on his arm once more.

"I'm sorry Eniel, I lost a friend not so long ago myself," Mason said. It was true—one of his friends from uni had recently been killed in a suicide bombing in Sydney. Admittedly, the two of them hadn't been terribly close in the years since they'd both graduated and had gone on to different medical schools. Still, Mason knew that he needed to establish a rapport with Eniel, and this was one way to do that.

Eniel turned towards him with glittering eyes. "You did?"

"Yes, and it hurts me very much." Also not a lie. Bess had been like the sister he'd never had growing up. Thinking of her brilliant spark being extinguished during a pointless act of terror made him ache, even months later.

Eniel nodded and set his head down on his arms, which were propped up on his knees. "I am tired of fighting. So tired."

"You fought bravely for a long time. You deserve to rest now," Mason told him. "Think of it as military leave, if that helps."

Eniel snorted. "I was traded by my commander to the government, and they sent me here." He muttered something under his breath that Mason didn't understand, but by the tone of his voice, Mason guessed it was expletives.

"Yeah, I hear you, mate," he said. "It sucks balls when you're told what to do and have to obey sometimes."

"I am a *soldier*, not a child!"

Mason blinked at the sudden rage and anguish that filled Eniel's face, but he didn't back down. "You are both of those things. And soldiers are no strangers to obeying orders, as I imagine you know very well." He reached down and plucked a long strand of the pampas grass stubbornly clinging to life next to the steps. Absently, he weaved the grass leaf through his fingers.

The motion mesmerized Eniel, who watched with wide, unblinking eyes.

"Can I tell you what I want right now, and you tell me what you want?" Mason asked in a soft voice, still toying with the grass.

Eniel's lips parted, and it looked like exhaustion was crashing over him. Even so, he rallied enough to nod at Mason's request.

Mason nodded back. "Good. I want for you and I to go inside together, and check you out medically. We need to make sure you're okay; then you can eat and rest. Now, what do you want?"

Eniel jerked, as if taken by surprise. He glanced into Mason's face and then back towards the ground. "To forget."

Mason sighed quietly. "I'm afraid it's not quite that simple, Eniel — but I can promise you that the bad memories will start to fade, and things will get better with time."

For a second, Mason thought he could make out a tear trickling down the side of Eniel's face. It was wiped away so quickly that he couldn't be sure, though. He stood up slowly and watched as Eniel flinched, recoiling from him.

"It's okay," Mason said, "I'm just going to make this gun safe — that's all."

Eniel did not respond, but continued to watch with wary eyes as Mason carefully disarmed the weapon and pulled the strap over his shoulder, letting the rifle rest against his back. With the chamber empty and the magazine held securely in one hand, Mason walked past Eniel and pulled open the rickety screen door, which creaked loudly. He held the door open for the boy, who remained sitting on the front steps.

Eniel's gaze flickered back and forth between the packed dirt of the street and the front door several times, as if he was trying to make up his mind about something. Finally, he rose to his feet, his back straight, and walked into the clinic.

-o-o-o-

Many long, exhausting hours later, Mason sat down heavily at his desk, pushing aside the clutter of folders until he could power up the laptop he'd brought with him to Haiti. With the way things were in the capital these days, they didn't have the option of reliable cable or DSL internet service. Thankfully, Doctors Without Borders had provided him a satellite uplink to ensure he could remain connected to their agency and the outside world.

After carefully documenting the events of the day and sending an incident report to headquarters, Mason checked his watch.

He frowned at it. Where had the time gone? Christ... his brother Jack would be calling any minute.

Sure enough, within a matter of moments, an alert popped up on his screen that he had an incoming FaceTime request. He accepted it and smiled into the camera, his mood lightening immediately.

"Sitting at home on a Friday night again? You're getting old, Jack," he quipped.

"Greetings from Singapore, brother mine," Jack responded with a matching grin. "Age has its compensations, you know — we can't all dwell in the youth of our twenties forever."

Jackson Walker was only four years older than Mason was, in reality, but the disparity was still a running joke between them. He and Mason both shared their father's piercing blue eyes and light brown hair. At six-foot-two, Mason had a few inches on his brother, and he had been a bit more dedicated when it came to staying in shape after years of playing rugby.

"No, I suppose we can't," Mason agreed.

At twenty-nine, there were some days that he still felt invincible and on top of the world, but more and more of his nights were turning weary. Even if he had been living in a trendy first-world city somewhere, rather than the outskirts of the impoverished capital in civil-war-torn Haiti, he was beginning to feel like he wouldn't have been able to keep up much of a social life after the toll his job took on him.

He'd seen too much in the past few months. It felt sometimes as though he'd aged far beyond his years. These days, even the most studious of his peers were starting to seem shallow and vain to him, with their successful careers, posh houses, and expensive BMWs. Meanwhile, the horrors Mason had witnessed while volunteering in war-torn areas would be forever branded on his memories — and today, staring down the barrel of a gun held by a child who should have been playing ball in a schoolyard somewhere, was one of the days he was unlikely to forget.

Apparently, enough of this showed on his face to be obvious even over a pixelated video chat, because Jack sobered.

"Something happened, didn't it?" Jack asked, perceptive as ever. "Want to tell me what?"

Mason sighed. *Where to even begin?*

"Right, little brother. I don't like that expression *at all*. Start at the beginning," Jack said, as if reading his mind.

Mason shook his head and relayed a concise version of the day's events. "… and then I finally convinced him to come inside, where I got a nurse to help me with an examination. Let me tell you, *that* was a huge battle, all on its own. I don't know if this kid has ever seen a doctor before, but there were times he screamed hysterically at us about spirits and curses—all sorts of superstitious craziness. He's seriously emaciated, and he needed antibiotics for an infection in his lungs, but he fought like a madman when I tried to put in the IV."

Jack swore. "I don't know how you do it, Mason. I'd tear my hair out if I had to deal with things like that."

Mason cocked an eyebrow, dredging up a brief smile. "No shit. That's why you're an engineer."

"Exactly my point," Jack agreed. "I fix things that other people mess up, and design stuff that, ultimately, some crappy builder somewhere is going to end up changing without my permission so the whole system will fail to work. *You* deal with snotty noses, messed-up children, and having high-powered rifles pulled on you every other day. *I* deal with infuriating clients and impossible deadlines. Though I guess, when you look at it like that… it's practically the same thing, right?"

Mason snorted. "You always were the funny one."

"Damn right. The funny one… the good-looking one…"

"The modest one," Mason put in, still smiling. He sighed, sobering. "Really, though, they're *not* bad kids, Jack. This little guy isn't some spoiled brat. He's deeply traumatized, starving, hopped up on drugs, and brainwashed."

The humor drained from Jack's expression as well. "Jesus. I still can't wrap my brain around the idea of stealing kids to fight in a war. It's just… *sick*. I mean, how do they get them?"

"Depends on the kid," Mason answered, rubbing his tired eyes for a moment. "Depends on the family.

Sometimes it's revenge kidnapping; sometimes they come in after a battle and take the survivors away. Sometimes it's just opportunity. They'll grab a kid who's walking alone."

Jack was uncharacteristically quiet for a moment. "Then they go to war and—"

His voice trailed away. Mason did not break the silence for a moment but eventually took a breath and said, "And they're soldiers. They carry out their orders and kill dozens, if not hundreds, of people over their years of captivity."

"And then they come to you."

Mason laughed—an ugly sound. "And then they come to me. The government realized that this was a tactic the rebels were using not long after the practice started. Whenever it's feasible, the youngest children in the rebel forces are captured by the government soldiers, rather than being killed. They're taken and matched with missing children reports, when possible."

"How often does that happen, though?"

"Rarely," Mason admitted. "Haiti is being torn apart at the seams. Any information from the smaller villages being held by the rebels is old, often inaccurate, or contains nothing useful. The rebels intercept most unencrypted messages, and they don't want the government to realize just how many children they're holding hostage."

Jack whistled behind his teeth and shook his head. "This is fucking depressing, Mason."

"You think?" Mason didn't even try to keep the bitterness from his voice.

"These kids are coming to you so messed up that they'll pull a gun on you and nearly kill you?"

Mason shook his head. "If you'd asked me a month ago, I would have scoffed and said it wasn't that bad. That sort of thing never used to happen. Don't get me wrong—these kids have problems. They're sick, half-starved, full of parasites, and emotionally traumatized. We have all the problems you would associate with that kind of thing—fighting, bad behavior, nightmares, and so forth. For the most part, though, once we get them weaned off the drugs, they're sweet and scared."

"If I'd asked you a month ago?" Jack echoed. "What changed in the last month?"

Darkness settled over Mason's heart like a pall, and a shudder rolled down his spine. He couldn't bring himself to look at the screen and see the concern in his brother's face. Nor could he banish the sense of evil that seemed to be creeping over him like black oil. In his mind's eye, he could see the same darkness covering all of Haiti, inciting bloodlust and insanity everywhere it went. It was like a heavy plume, billowing outwards across the land, blocking out all the beauty and light from the sky. A superstitious chill pierced his heart.

"Mason?" Jack pressed, concern in his voice. "What's changed?"

Mason looked directly into the camera at the top of his computer, his mouth dry and his voice hoarse. "Everything."

TWO

"Wait," Xander said, looking down at Oksana as though he wasn't sure he'd heard correctly. "You're telling me they pour perfectly good alcohol onto the *ground*? And they do this *on purpose*?"

Oksana blinked at him, even as Duchess let out a rather indelicate snort from her other side as the three of them walked down the street in Port-au-Prince.

"Xander," Oksana said, meeting his scandalized green gaze, "we're in the middle of a war-torn nation struggling under a yoke of poverty and corruption. I've just explained about the ceremony we're about to witness so that I can ask the vodou spirits—"

"The loa, yes," he interjected. "See, I was listening."

"So that I can ask the vodou loa for assistance in finding Bael's next vortex of chaos," she continued patiently. "And *this* is the part you're worried about?"

"When one is stuck in a war-torn, poverty-stricken land, one *drinks* the booze, Oksana. One does *not*," Xander said very slowly and clearly, "spill it onto the dirt. Now, I have as much cause as anyone to respect the vodou gods—"

"Sure he does. Just ask Madame Francine," Duchess interrupted dryly.

A smile of amusement tugged at the corners of Oksana's lips, almost despite herself. She and Duchess had both heard the account of Xander's rather humiliating run-in with the elderly New Orleans mambo in the days before he and Tré had called the rest of them to the Big Easy.

Xander raised a finger, leaning around Oksana to point it at Duchess without slowing his stride. "Excuse me," he began, "but you know full well that we do *not* speak of that incident. *Ever*. Now, as I was saying, Oksana, I have every reason to respect these loa you worship, but the booze thing is just plain wasteful. Shockingly so. You can't possibly expect me to approve of such a practice."

She rolled her eyes. "If the priest or priestess doesn't offer the loa food and drink, they won't come. Which would rather defeat the purpose of the exercise, don't you agree? If it makes you feel better, there will probably be people smoking ganja, and maybe taking mushrooms. Just... do please try to be discrete? This is my home, after all."

Duchess snorted again. "Xander is always discrete, *ma chérie*. Well, except for that one time in Tokyo. And the one in Brisbane. Oh, and Montreal. We mustn't forget Montreal..."

"Duchess," Xander said, "you know I adore you. But I'm not sure you're the one to throw stones when it comes to the quality of discretion. Does the term *glass houses* ring a bell?" He scowled. "And I still have no memory of anything noteworthy ever happening in Brisbane."

"Yeah, you probably wouldn't," Oksana murmured under her breath, and smiled sweetly when his scowl turned on her. "Anyway, like I said, if you're hungry, you shouldn't have trouble finding someone suitable after the ceremony begins to wind down."

Honestly, it was no surprise that Xander was in search of a bit of chemically mediated oblivion — short-lived though it would be, given his vampire metabolism. Haiti was no holiday destination these days, but even compared to Port-au-Prince, all three of them had spent the last couple of months in hell.

In fact, their friends were still back in that abyss of suffering, where they had all spent the first days after the detonation of the suitcase nuke in Damascus pulling survivors from the rubble under cover of darkness. After that, rescue had turned to recovery, only for them to find that someone — or *something* — had been there before them.

The undead were rising *en masse* from the wreckage, spreading outward across Syria and into neighboring countries, to the accompaniment of growing hysteria from the human population. Tré, Snag, Eris, Della, and Trynn had stayed behind to monitor the situation and step in whenever doing so might make a difference without getting them all killed in the process.

Oksana had spoken to Eris after experiencing several odd dreams during the stolen hours of sleep she was able to catch here and there as they worked. Communications in the region were spotty at best, but the nightmares had started after she'd heard a snippet of a BBC newscast about reports of war crimes and a humanitarian crisis related to Haiti's current round of rebel insurrection.

Eris encouraged her to follow the strange pull that seemed to be drawing her back to her homeland, pointing out that, with as little as they truly understood about the war Bael was waging on the world, her dreamlike visions were as a valid an avenue for investigation as any other.

Tré listened to them both and agreed almost immediately, though he insisted she not go alone. Duchess had volunteered, and Xander had shrugged in easy agreement when Tré asked him to go along as well.

The cynical part of her — a part she tried to keep buried lest it swallow her whole — couldn't help noticing that their trio comprised three of the four of them who had not yet found their reincarnated mates. Given that Snag pretty much did whatever he wanted to do, no matter what Tré or anyone else said about it, it seemed fairly apparent that there had been some behind-the-scenes discussion between Tré and Eris about sending her, Xander, and Duchess away, specifically.

The rational corner of her mind knew that it made a sort of sense. Eris had found his mate Trynn during the disaster in Damascus, and it seemed highly unlikely that another of their reincarnated mates would just happen to be located in the same area. If she, Duchess, and Xander were traveling, moving around, it was more likely that they would stumble across one of the strange vortices of chaos that formed when a vampire drew close to his or her mate. It was simple statistics.

Unfortunately, the *less* rational part of Oksana's mind tended to shut down completely whenever she contemplated the idea of finding her beloved Augustin, reborn. In the most abstract sense, she understood that it was a thing that might happen someday.

In a more concrete sense, she couldn't really come to terms with what it would mean if she suddenly had to confront that part of her past. She knew the others thought of her as *the nice one*. The sweet one. Youngest, except for Xander. Well—also Della and Trynn, now that they'd been turned. She didn't think the rest of them understood that if she presented a lighter, happier demeanor to the outside world, it was only because she had cut free large swathes of her past and let them drift away, as a form of self defense against the memories.

Or, perhaps it would be more accurate to say that she'd buried those memories. There was an almost painful irony to that metaphor. She choked back a snort of bitter laughter that had nothing to do with humor.

Buried, indeed.

The scrape of her state-of-the-art Flex-Foot Cheetah prosthetic foot replacement against the gravel beneath her was the only sound for a few minutes as she and the others walked companionably down the road. The smell of the sea grew more pronounced as they entered an impoverished area of Port-au-Prince near the coastline, where former factory and warehouse sites had given way to slums, as the island's shaky economy grew ever weaker.

"You really believe this might help us learn something useful?" Xander asked.

She shrugged. "I don't know. Eris thinks it's worth a try. The older I get, the more I've come to believe that all religions hold facets and reflections of the truth of the Light and the Darkness. Haitians are closer to the spirit world than most; we always have been. And, once upon a time, the spirits seemed to favor me."

"Fair enough," Xander said. His eyes crinkled at the corners briefly as he added, "though I still think we should try to rescue some of that wasted alcohol."

Her laughter this time did not hold the same tinge of bitterness, so she let it come. She looped her arms through her companions', glad beyond measure that they were here with her.

-o-o-o-

The trio continued their journey toward the coast. The smell of salt water, fish, and garbage grew more pronounced as the breeze from the ocean stirred the dust around them. The houses became smaller and smaller until they were surrounded by mud-walled shanties with tin roofs. As the last light of evening gave way to night, children came running along dirt paths through the grass, shouting and laughing as they waved goodbye to each other and returned to their families. Women walked briskly along the road, carrying large pails and jugs of water after their last trip of the day to a nearby pump.

As they came to a crossroads that led down towards the ocean, Oksana jerked her thumb and gestured them on towards the right, following the mental map she carried in her memories.

"You really know your way around here," Xander murmured, the words escaping into the deepening darkness.

"It's my home," Oksana said simply. "Don't tell me you couldn't navigate London's twisting roads and alleys just as easily."

"Maybe so." Xander gave her another flicker of a smile and turned to Duchess. "Still, it's a good thing we have our own personal GPS unit to walk around with us. Who needs modern technology, eh?"

Duchess jerked her head around to look at him, as if he had startled her. "Hmm? Oh... yes. Quite right."

Her eyes wandered back to a small girl in a dirty pink dress who was crouched outside of a dilapidated shanty, staring at them with wide, hungry eyes. Duchess had practically made a life's work out of hiding her soft underbelly, but Oksana knew that the weeks spent dragging injured and dead children from radioactive wreckage in Damascus had left her friend raw and aching in a way that the rest of them could not fully appreciate.

They all had their particular demons to slay. And not *just* the real life demon that wanted them dead.

The sound of drums beating reached Oksana's sensitive ears. "We're getting close now," she said, hoping to draw her friend back to the present.

A couple of minutes later, they rounded a corner and the peristil came into view. It was a rough structure, mostly open on the sides, with a roof of mismatched lengths of tin supplemented with tattered blue plastic tarps.

She gestured. "Here we are."

Duchess stared at the unprepossessing ceremonial hall. "Are you sure this is the place?" she asked. "For some reason, I expected something a bit more... grand."

Oksana shrugged. "Yes, this is it."

"Your Catholic roots are showing, Duchess," Xander chided. "Religion isn't all cathedral spires and gold crucifixes, you know."

Duchess glowered at him, but then she appeared to shake herself free from her earlier distraction, giving Oksana's shoulder an apologetic squeeze. "I'm sorry, *ma petite*. That was crass of me. What can be found inside such a place is far more important than the roof and walls."

Oksana covered her hand to show she wasn't angry. "It's all right. For what it's worth, we have Catholic churches here, too. Though I imagine the gold has mostly been looted by now."

She led the others into the peristil, ignoring the suspicious looks thrown their way as people stared at her companions' pale skin. The three took up inconspicuous positions along the structure's only wall, next to the handful of wooden benches occupied by worshipers. The rough concrete blocks were cool at her back, in contrast to the stifling heat of so many human bodies packed close together in the humid Haitian night.

A group of men and women knelt in a circle around a flickering fire at the center of the peristil. A man with smooth skin the shade of burnished teak stood inside the circle, pacing back and forth, eyes closed, as he murmured unintelligible words under his breath.

The darkness outside had fallen fully over the city, and the only light in the peristil came from the ceremonial fire and the multitude of candles burning on the various altars set up to the loa. Some held food, some held bottles of drink, some held money, while others held more obscure items like cosmetics or jewelry. The scent of incense hung in the air.

Each spirit demanded a different offering, in accordance with their individual persona and eccentricities. Without the offering, they would not deign to enter the peristil and inhabit the body of one of the people present. The vodou religion was steeped in tradition, and while the sight of possessed worshipers might appear chaotic to an outsider, the beginning of a ceremony never deviated from established ritual.

The man at the center of the circle wore a flowing white shirt and loose trousers, with a vest covered in intricate beadwork of the African style. His hat, too, was covered in patterned beads, with a small plume of white feathers attached at the front.

He held a large beaded rattle with a bell attached at the bottom, which he shook in time with the drumbeats. The men and women in the circle started to chant, their voices rising and falling to the beat.

"That's the houngan," Oksana whispered, confident that her vampire companions would be able to hear. "He'll lead the ceremony, even though there may be several other priests and priestesses in the circle. The calabash rattle is called an asson. It's the mark of his station, and contains snake bones."

Her audience of two looked on with interest.

"I can feel it," Duchess said, keeping her voice low. "There's power in it, though I can't tell where it's coming from."

"Everything in the ceremony is meant to intensify the houngan's connection with the spirit world," Oksana replied. "That's the source of a houngan or mambo's power. Often, such a ceremony would take place outside, under the stars and near a focus of power such as an ancient tree. They must not want to attract attention tonight."

"After the reports we've heard of attacks on vodou practitioners in the city, you can't really blame them," Xander said, all his earlier flippancy gone without a trace.

"No," Oksana agreed. "It still troubles me, though. I've never known any houngan to be afraid of the night."

Sadly, the backlash against the old religion was not unexpected. Nor was it the first time it had happened. It seemed those Haitians who claimed to be the most progressive were often the most superstitious, at heart. Whenever strife came to the island, violence against vodou practitioners followed close on its heels as frightened people blamed vodou curses for their woes.

It was a running joke that Haiti was seventy percent Catholic, thirty percent Protestant, and one hundred percent vodou. The Christian population might dismiss the existence of the loa publicly — but privately, they believed in the spirits' power over their lives.

The ceremony continued, with those chanting in the circle calling on Papa Legba to open the gates to the spirit world so the loa could pass through. Afterward, each spirit was summoned individually with the proper form. Oksana heard Xander's quiet noise of disgust when the houngan laid out a geometric pattern on the dirt floor with cornmeal and poured a bottle of vodka over it.

When the bottle was empty, he straightened and raised his arms. His body began to shake and twitch, the drums intensifying as if to keep time with the movements of his body.

Without warning, memory rose up and drew Oksana into the past.

-o-o-o-

Standing in the bright sunlight, Oksana clutched her mother's hand as they approached the houngan. He sat in the dust at the side of the road, eyes closed — still as a statue.

Their master had sent Manman and the other women into town to gather supplies for a feast later that night. They were returning now, with heavy baskets and slings full of food tied to their backs. Even though Oksana could only count seven years, she was laden like all the others.

"This is how we used to do it in Africa, child," her mother always whispered to her as she tied on the burden.

Another woman in their group had spotted the houngan and insisted they stop to speak to him for a few moments. Oksana pressed closer to her mother in fear. She had never been to Africa, but she thought the man looked wild.

He's a lion-man, she thought, remembering the stories of the great maned beasts with their fangs and claws.

"Tamara," Oksana's mother called to the woman approaching the houngan, "there's no time. We need to get back."

"No one will ever know we stopped," Tamara replied, brushing off her concerns.

"Time," the houngan said in a low, slow voice, "makes fools of us all."

Tamara knelt in front of the seated man like a child before a teacher. "What can you tell us from the spirits?" she asked, her voice low and respectful.

The houngan did not answer, but closed his eyes and tilted his face towards the sun. A breeze whipped around them, stirring the dust and dirt into spirals on each side of the man. Oksana watched with wide eyes, mesmerized by the sight of the wind and the earth dancing together.

I want to fly someday, she mused, her eyes following the path of a leaf of dried grass floating back to the earth.

"Come to me, my pale-skinned child." The houngan commanded, ignoring Tamara.

Oksana jumped in surprise and turned towards the man, only to find him looking straight at her with eyes so dark they almost seemed black. A great stillness seemed to settle over the group, and Oksana tightened her hold on her mother's hand.

She hated being different — even though Manman's friends made much of her lighter skin, telling her she was beautiful and special because of it. She'd heard them whisper many times about Manman and the master, though she didn't understand exactly what they meant. Her skin did not look like the master's, which was pale pink, like all the other white people she'd seen.

Of course, Oksana's skin didn't look like her mother's, either. Her mother's skin was beautiful — dark as ebony.

"Do not be afraid, child," the houngan insisted, motioning again for her to come closer.

Oksana felt her mother release her hand and nudge her forward. She looked up into Manman's face and received a reassuring smile in return.

Several tentative steps brought her within a few feet of the man. She was still wary of getting too close. The houngan sat up straighter. He reached out a wrinkled hand and pressed his forefinger gently to the center of Oksana's forehead.

She felt a strange force pass through her, as if a chill wave had rolled over her body. She shivered and took a hasty step back, breaking contact with the houngan.

"You ask the wrong questions," the houngan said in a strange tone, his gaze flickering to Tamara for a moment.

"I'm sorry?" Tamara asked, confusion evident in her voice.

"You ask the wrong questions," he repeated, settling himself back. He rested his elbows on his knees and clasped his hands together in front of him.

"I still don't understand what you mean," she said.

"Just a moment ago," he replied after a lengthy pause, "you asked me 'what can you tell us from the spirits?'"

The houngan paused again, his head tilted to one side as he considered Oksana.

"The wrong question," he murmured.

The group of slaves stood in total silence as Oksana shifted her feet uncomfortably back and forth. She didn't like being the center of his focus as he stared at her in thoughtful contemplation.

"You should ask 'whom have the spirits sent to us?'"

As Oksana looked around at the adults standing in the sun, each and every set of eyes turned towards her. Their gazes felt heavier than the pack of food strapped to her back. The weight of their eyes might as well have been the weight of the world settling across her young shoulders.

-o-o-o-

A touch on her arm startled her. Duchess was looking at her with mild concern. "Are you still with us, *mon chou*? Something is happening inside the circle."

Oksana blinked and focused back on the houngan before her, instead of the one wrapped in ancient and hazy memory. He was being supported by two of the women. His eyes closed and his face transported as his body continued to shake.

"The spirits are here," she said quietly.

Other people were rising from the benches now, chanting along with the group in the circle, their bodies moving and swaying with the beat of the drums.

"They're possessing people?" Xander asked, looking around in interest.

"Yes," Oksana confirmed. She closed her eyes, reaching out to take in her surroundings, and then shook her head in frustration. "I can't feel them at all, though — only see their effects. I'd hoped, maybe…" The words trailed off.

"You'd hoped… what?" Xander asked, his attention firmly back on her.

She blew out a disappointed breath. "Ever since I was turned, the loa ignore me. My soul was too badly damaged, I think. I'd hoped, perhaps… with Bael drawing nearer… with our soulmates reappearing… that might have changed."

Duchess spoke, ever practical. "Maybe it's for the best. I'm not in any particular hurry to see you possessed, *ma chere*. If you have questions for these spirits,

548

just ask one of *them*." She tilted her chin to indicate the houngan and several others who appeared to be lost in possession.

Oksana squared her shoulders. "Yes," she said, pushing away the old bitterness that threatened to rise. "You're right, of course."

The priest straightened away from the hands supporting him. He reeled for a moment as if he'd forgotten how to use his legs, but then his equilibrium returned.

"Two great realms are crushed together," he proclaimed. "They will bring chaos as the barriers crumble. The beast grows hungry. Upheaval will follow!"

Xander sharpened like a hawk sensing prey.

"Will it indeed?" Duchess asked, her perfect brows drawing together.

Oksana was already on the move, pressing through the dancing, chanting crowd, using her mental influence to clear a path for herself. She felt the others right behind her as she slipped through the last few people to reach the houngan.

"Please, you must tell us," she said, hoping that whichever loa currently inhabited the man was a sympathetic one, and not a trickster. "Is Bael coming here? What should we do?"

The houngan's eyes seemed to burn as he looked down at her from his advantage in height. His lips curled, and his voice was oddly deep and resonant as he replied with two words.

"*Get. Out.*"

THREE

Oksana only became aware that she'd staggered back a step when Duchess and Xander steadied her. The jolt of shock and pain at being ordered away from a peristil by a priest stole her voice for a moment.

She felt a prickle of power from her left as Xander bristled and stepped forward, standing half in front of her.

"Now just a *bleedin' minute*, mate—" he began, his tone low and menacing.

He was interrupted when two things happened simultaneously. A low rumble tickled at the edges of Oksana's awareness, and the houngan turned, addressing the crowd at large as he bellowed, "*Get. Out!*"

Duchess' hand clenched around Oksana's shoulder. "Can you feel that?" she asked; then she raised her voice, as well. "Earthquake! Everyone get outside!"

"*Shit,*" Xander cursed, barely audible. He and Oksana added their voices to the call, ordering people outside in French and Creole.

To their credit, the people of Haiti were well acquainted with earthquakes. Despite the revelry of the dancing and drumming, it took only moments for the crowd to heed the cry and hurry into the street outside. The rumble grew into full-scale trembling just as the three vampires followed the last of the people from the peristil into the open.

Oksana steadied herself as the earth bucked and rolled in waves, relying on vampirically enhanced balance to overcome the disadvantage posed by her prosthesis. The pulses of energy as the earth's crust slipped against itself jarred her preternatural senses, making her clench her jaw against a wave of nausea.

Around her, people cried out in fear, more of Port-au-Prince's residents spilling onto the road rather than risk staying under a roof that might fall on their heads. The quaking went on for a little over a minute before subsiding, leaving Oksana feeling like she needed a moment to get her land-legs back.

She swallowed and looked around, her night vision allowing her to see her surroundings despite the lack of light. Many of the mud and plaster walls on the buildings around them were cracked, but none appeared demolished. Some of the mismatched tin from the peristil roof had come partially free from the rafters and was hanging over the edge of the roof. A couple of the wooden posts that supported the open-air structure were off-kilter, but had not snapped.

"It wasn't a bad one," she said aloud.

"Bad enough," Duchess replied. "It doesn't look like anyone here is hurt beyond cuts and grazes from falling down, though."

Xander's mouth was a grim line. "I need to get access to a data link. Find out if there's a tsunami warning for the area."

He pulled out a mobile and flicked the screen-lock. Oksana and Duchess followed suit.

"Nothing," Oksana said, unsurprised.

"The satellite phone is back at the hotel," Xander said. "But we're too close to the beach for comfort here."

"Right," Oksana agreed, and switched back to Creole. "Everyone! Get your families, grab whatever you need, and head for higher ground in case a big wave comes! Don't risk yourselves by staying here. Spend the night in the highest place you can find and come back when it's safe!"

There was muttering as the frightened people around them debated the merits of leaving their homes unprotected overnight, but several other people lifted their voices in support.

"She's right! Don't risk it…"

"Be quick and we'll all go together."

"Yes, let's do it."

Convinced that most of them, at least, would do the smart thing, Oksana gestured for her companions to follow her into the shadows where they could transform unseen into mist, and fly back to the hotel rather than waste time walking. As she turned to go, however, running footsteps approached.

The smell of sweat, antiseptic, and human fear teased Oksana's nostrils. The sound of a pounding heart driving blood through arteries in a frantic rush reached her ears an instant later. A young woman with dark skin and close-cropped black curls burst into their midst. As she clutched a stitch in her side with one hand, she began pointing urgently back up the road down which she had just come with the other.

"What is it?" Xander asked in French, moving forward to stand in front of her.

"Help us!" she gasped, taking huge, deep breaths. "Hurry, please! A roof collapsed and children are trapped inside!"

Duchess was off in the direction the girl had come from before the echo of the final word faded. Xander shot Oksana a dark look. They followed, keeping pace with the young woman, who ran as fast as she could even though she was still gasping for air and clutching her aching side.

Oksana took care on the uneven footing of the pockmarked dirt road, feeling the compressed power of her flexible Cheetah foot propel her effortlessly forward with every stride. She judged that their destination couldn't be far, given how quickly the girl had arrived after the trembler subsided. They were re-entering the area of abandoned warehouses and factories, some of which had obviously been turned to other purposes since the economic downturn.

One of those buildings had a collapsed wall, with the heavy roof lying over it in a twisted pile of wood and metal. Adults in medical scrubs scrambled over the scene with flashlights and kerosene lanterns, prying up pieces of tin and pulling bloody, crying children form the rubble.

"What can we do?" Duchess called, grabbing the arm of a woman trying to rush past with an armful of towels.

"The roof collapsed before we could get everyone out! We've got about fourteen children trapped inside," she snapped in reply, already pulling free to continue toward the building.

"We've got recent experience with search and rescue. We can help you get them out," Xander told her, as they followed her to the collapsed section.

Too right we've got recent experience, Oksana thought grimly. *I'm still finding bits of radioactive rubble in odd places after Damascus.*

They hurried after the woman, to a side of the building where the wall was leaning over. Soft whimpers could clearly be heard, coming from the dark gap beyond.

"Hello? Can you hear me?" Oksana called into the hole, which looked big enough for her to fit through. *Just.*

A strangled cry of fear emerged in response.

"Eniel!" A strong male voice came from behind Oksana, woven through with an Australian accent. "Hang on, Eniel. We can hear you. You're going to be all right!"

Oksana turned to see a man perhaps an inch or two taller than Xander, with intense blue eyes and tousled, light brown hair. He, too, was wearing scrubs, though they were dirt-smeared and bloodstained.

"We need to get him out quickly. I don't know how stable this section is," the man said in a low tone, not blinking at the sudden appearance of three strangers at the scene. It was obvious that his entire focus was on rescuing the trapped children, and everything else was secondary. "I was just trying to find some rope in hopes of feeding it through the gap to him and pulling him out," he continued, "but everything remotely useful seems to be buried."

Oksana felt an odd little jolt in her belly at the man's single-minded focus on the boy's safety. "Well," she told him, "it's a good thing you have someone small enough to squeeze through the gap, in that case."

Duchess' bright eyes landed on her, and the other vampire's brow furrowed. "Are you sure, *ma petite*? You and small spaces are not the best of friends. I might be able to fit."

Oksana looked at the gap again. Duchess was all voluptuous curves where Oksana was slender lines, and frankly, she doubted it would work. Before she could say so, the Australian spoke again.

"You're claustrophobic?" he asked. "If so, you shouldn't go. We'll find somebody else. Joni could probably get in. She's around here somewhere, I think —"

"No," Oksana said, cutting him off. "It's fine. I can handle it. Though I may need someone to help pull us out afterward if it's too tight for me to turn around inside."

And I may also need someone to give me a mental smack if my brain decides to go stupid on me — since I am, in fact, claustrophobic, she added silently.

On it, Xander assured.

Of course, said Duchess, adding, *Be careful, petite soeur.*

"Okay. I've got this," Oksana said. "Oh—and in case it's not self-evident," she added, glancing at the Aussie's arresting blue eyes, "Don't pull on the left foot when it comes time to drag me back out. It comes off."

The barest hint of humor touched the man's face, transforming it into something beautiful in the light of the sputtering lanterns before it settled once more into worried lines.

"Don't worry," he said, "I'll make sure to leave you a leg to stand on. You can trust me—I'm a doctor."

The last was added with a wink so quick she wasn't sure she'd actually seen it. Then his focus was back on the hole, his flashlight directed inside.

"Eniel," he called, "someone's coming in to get you. She'll be with you in just a minute. Don't be afraid!"

He glanced at Oksana and she was caught yet again by the intensity behind his stormy eyes. Tearing herself away, she crouched down and eased onto her stomach, wincing a bit as rocks and pieces of debris poked at her through her thin black t-shirt.

She took a deep breath, purposely not focusing on exactly what she was about to do, and army-crawled through the tiny gap under the roof. The cries of fear from within had subsided to muffled sobs, as if Eniel was trying desperately not to let the sound of his weeping be heard.

Oksana took a couple of steadying breaths and used her knees and elbows to propel herself forward. The dirt beneath her collected against her shirt as she scooted further into the gap, some of it getting inside the low scoop of the shirt's neckline, where it made her skin itch.

She coughed, eyes watering as dust swirled in her face. "I'm almost there," she croaked, hearing the boy's racing pulse only a few feet ahead. "Talk to me so I can find you more easily."

Of course, to her enhanced senses his heartbeat, thrumming blood, and warm body were like a beacon in the low light, but he didn't need to know that. Talking would—hopefully—keep him calmer and listening to him would—hopefully—keep her attention on the here-and-now rather than on a part of the distant past better left buried.

Buried. *Ha.*

"Please," a small voice begged in Creole. "Please, hurry..."

Of course, that was the moment when the spring-loaded epoxy arch of her prosthesis managed to get hooked around something, halting her forward progress. As soon as she felt the constriction of her left leg, coupled with the darkness and sensation of walls all around her, her thoughts crashed down around her like falling icicles.

She was trapped... trapped underground... her foot... what had they done to her foot?

Oksana! Her name was a sharp bark inside her mind, piercing through the momentary confusion.

It was Xander. She blinked rapidly, trying to reorient herself in the present. She was in Haiti, yes, but this small, dark space was a collapsed building, not a—

She cut the thought off harshly.

Focus, mon chou, Duchess said in her mind.

I'm all right, she sent back to them. *My Cheetah just got hooked on something.* She backed up a couple of inches and twisted her leg until she felt the prosthesis come free from whatever it had been stuck on. *I'm free now.*

"Where are you?" called Eniel. "I can hear you but I can't see you!"

There was a movement in the darkness ahead of her. She reached out with all her senses, and the darker shadow coalesced into a child. Male. Young. She could smell his blood in the air and knew that he was injured.

"It's all right. I can see you now," she told him. To the others, she called, "I see him! He's hurt—I'm not sure how badly."

"Can you get him out?" The Australian doctor's voice came back immediately.

Of course, there was no way to know until she got a better idea of the boy's circumstances, but she hadn't crawled in here just to fail. "I'll get him," she replied with certainty.

She crawled forward the last couple of feet, the space ahead of her opening into something a little less confining. She reached out, feeling around the debris and broken glass until her fingers grazed warm skin. The boy caught his breath in surprise at her touch.

"There you are," she said, keeping her voice calm and friendly. "Your name is Eniel, right? I'm Oksana."

Hesitation followed her question, the silence stretching between them. Finally, a small voice answered, "Call me San."

Her brow furrowed in surprise. San, as in the Creole word for blood? She shook off the moment of confusion. It was hardly relevant in their current circumstances.

"Sure thing, San," she said. "Now, what do you say we get out of here? I don't know about you, but I wouldn't mind seeing the sky right about now."

"I can't see anything," the boy said. "I don't know how to get out."

Oksana silently cursed herself for not having brought a flashlight. She might not need it, but it would have been reassuring for Eniel—or San, as he apparently preferred.

"That's okay," she said, "I can see a bit. I know the way out. Can you crawl toward me while I crawl backwards toward the gap?"

Another pause, and Oksana worried that perhaps the boy was pinned by a fallen beam or something. When he answered, his words took her by surprise.

"You... won't hurt me?"

Oksana caught her breath, half from her own reaction to the unexpected question, and half at Duchess', who had obviously been eavesdropping through their link.

Why would he think you would hurt him? Duchess's words were low and dangerous.

Rescue now. Questions later. That was Xander, and when *Xander* was acting as the voice of reason, it was definitely time to regroup.

I heard that, came his mental growl.

She ignored him in favor of reassuring the frightened boy. "No, I won't hurt you, San," she said, putting a bit of will behind the words to calm him into compliance. "Let's you and I get out of here. Can you crawl?"

The pause this time was shorter. "Yes."

"Follow me, then," she instructed, and started to shimmy backward, his small hand grasped in hers. To her relief, he followed.

She continued to push herself the way she came with an awkward hitching motion, feeling claustrophobia threaten once more in the suffocating stillness of the tight space. She focused on the boy whose hand she clasped; the last thing he needed was for the stranger helping him to lose her shit and start gibbering about being trapped.

Hang in there. Xander again. *We can almost reach you — just a little further and I'll help pull you out.*

"We're getting close," she told the boy. Light from outside filtered through the hole behind her, illuminating his frightened face. He had a gash on his forehead that was bleeding freely, but he seemed otherwise unhurt. He did not meet her eyes even though there was enough light now for him to see, his gaze darting around the tunnel instead.

Hands grabbed her right ankle and she gasped, even though she'd had ample warning.

Easy, ma petite, Duchess reassured her.

"Okay," Oksana said, "They're going to pull me out, and I'll pull you. Just hold on, San."

He nodded, wide-eyed, just as Xander tugged her backward. She gripped his hand harder and pulled him after her as they passed through the gap and into the gloriously fresh air.

Well... maybe not *fresh*. The air actually still smelled like garbage and fish, but compared to the stifling, dusty atmosphere inside the collapsed building, it was heavenly.

Once the child was free of the building, Oksana rolled into a sitting position and coughed, rubbing at the dirt on her face.

"Hmm, that's actually not a half bad look for you," Xander said, gaining his moment of revenge for her quip earlier. He, of course, looked enviably unruffled even after having dragged her out of the rubble.

"Thanks for that," she grouched, still trying to brush herself off. And — yes — there was, in fact, gravel inside her sports bra now. *Brilliant*.

Duchess knelt on the ground next to her and reached out a hand to help Eniel sit up. He recoiled from her and looked around with wide eyes.

"Let me take a look at the cut on your head," Duchess said in a gentle voice. "I won't touch it, just let me see."

His red-rimmed eyes glared out from a tear-streaked face, but he turned his head toward her grudgingly. Xander fished his phone out of his pocket and shined the light on the boy's forehead. The blue-eyed doctor leaned in and examined the injury under the light. The tension in his broad athlete's shoulders eased slightly.

"I think you're in luck, my young friend," he said in a light voice, "this just needs cleaned and a couple of butterfly stitches."

"Not lucky," Eniel said in a low voice.

The man sighed and nodded. "Yeah, okay, maybe *lucky* isn't the word. But the reality is, it could have been a lot worse." He gestured for the woman who had been carrying the towels earlier to come over. "Natacha? Would you get Eniel here an antiseptic wipe and some butterfly strips for his head?"

The nurse nodded and hustled Eniel away, the boy casting glances over his shoulder as they left. Duchess rose smoothly to her feet, waving off the hand the doctor offered her. He lifted an eyebrow and met Oksana's eyes, reaching for her hand instead. She smiled and took it, only to practically leap to her feet when a jolt of electricity sizzled from the point of contact straight to the base of her spine, lifting the hair at the back of her neck as it passed. She slammed her mental shields down so quickly that both Duchess and Xander gave her a questioning look.

The man — *oh, god, the man* — jerked his hand back in surprise, his blue eyes wide. He blinked in confusion, and then seemed to shake off the odd moment. "Best move away from the rubble," he said. "There, uh, must be some exposed electrical wires here..."

Of course, that was complete rubbish, since a glance showed that the power was out in the entire area. And both Xander and Duchess were still staring at her, damn it.

"Oksana?" Duchess prompted.

Not. Now. Her mental reply was unnecessarily harsh, but she could feel cold sweat popping out on her forehead, and the same claustrophobic feeling that had swept over her inside the collapsed building was returning. She tightened her shields further, trying not to succumb to sudden, irrational panic.

Xander's green gaze pinned her for a moment longer before he turned his attention to the doctor. He held out his hand. "Sorry — I didn't catch your name, sir."

For the briefest of instants, the Australian hesitated, but then he grasped Xander's hand in a firm grip.

"Dr. Mason Walker, of Doctors Without Borders," he said as they shook.

"A pleasure to meet you, the unfortunate circumstances notwithstanding. My name is Xander. This is Duchess, and our pint-sized search and rescue expert here is Oksana," Xander said gesturing to his companions in turn.

"I'm more than pleased to make your acquaintance," Mason replied, making no comment about their unusual names. "Not many people would have offered to help strangers in such a way."

He shook Duchess' hand next and lowered his proffered arm awkwardly when Oksana gave him a small, painfully self-conscious wave of her fingers instead of offering to shake.

"Hi," she said, relieved when the word didn't emerge as a ridiculous, high-pitched squeak.

"Hi to you, too," he replied, looking at her curiously. Her skin tingled where his eyes moved over it.

Spirits have mercy on her.

It took Mason a moment to tear his attention away, and she almost sagged in relief when he did.

"The clinic building isn't safe," he said as he turned towards a group of nurses nearby. They were all tending to children that had been pulled from the rubble. "We need to come up with some sort of alternative place to shelter."

"What sort of clinic is this?" Duchess asked, clearly thinking about Eniel's obvious fear of them.

"My colleagues and I help with the rehabilitation of child soldiers," Mason said. "It's a serious problem in Haiti these days."

Duchess made a noise of pain. "Child soldiers? *Mon Dieu*. There is truly no end to the depths to which humanity will sink."

"We all do what we can, where we can," Mason said, sounding like a man who had lately spent too much time plumbing those dark depths.

Oksana could sympathize. With a flush, she realized she was still staring at Mason like a slack-jawed crazy woman. She snapped her mouth shut and looked away before he could notice.

From the corner of her eye, she saw him gesture them to follow in the same direction the nurse had taken Eniel. A group of children was sitting on the ground in an area that was relatively free of rubble. Some were crying quietly; others seemed to be in a complete daze.

Right now, she felt a certain kinship with the latter group, to be perfectly honest.

Nurses were moving from child to child, reassuring them and tending to their injuries. Mason joined them, leaning down to speak with each child as he inquired about their wellbeing. Again, Oksana'a gaze was drawn to him without her conscious volition, following his every movement. She was so engrossed that she jumped a bit when Duchess appeared at her shoulder.

"Talk to me," her friend said in a voice so low that none of the people around them except Xander would be able to hear. "Are you all right?"

Was she all right? Oksana had to swallow back a laugh that would have emerged sounding more than a little hysterical.

"No," she managed. "*All right* is not the description that comes immediately to mind."

FOUR

Duchess nodded, as if that much had been obvious. "Is there anything I can do?" she asked instead.

Oksana thought about it for a second and sighed. "No, I just need to think. I don't want to talk about it right now. It's not the time."

Indeed, as if to underline the words, a small aftershock rocked them. Cries from the terrified children rose into the night sky. Oksana looked up for a moment — after crawling through the wrecked building, the view above was stunning, unimpeded by clouds or haze. Stars winked peacefully down on the scene of fear, pain, and chaos below.

After a last unhappy look at Oksana, Duchess turned her attention to practicalities. "What are the options for temporary shelter?" she asked Mason.

He looked up from the boy he was examining. "There are a couple of possibilities. I've got Joni working on it now. First things first, though. We need to get a head count and make sure everyone is accounted for, then search if anyone is still missing."

Xander spoke up. "We aren't very far from the beach here. It's not safe. My friends and I were just going to try and find out if there's risk of a tsunami when your nurse found us."

Mason nodded. "I sent Evens to watch the tide as soon as the trembling stopped. Our radio got flattened under that section of collapsed roof, so we'll have to keep tabs the old-fashioned way. If the water recedes, he'll report back and tell us, so we can make a run for it before it washes back in. As soon as these injuries are treated I'll send the children to higher ground as a precaution, but I'm not leaving anyone behind unless it's life or death."

Of course, Oksana thought. *Of course he had to be competent and handsome and compassionate… and oh dear god, what am I supposed to do now?*

Her traitorous undead heart stuttered as Mason rose and turned to her. She tried to tear her gaze away from his, but it felt like her eyes were glued to the man now pulling out a notepad and pen from a pocket in his scrubs.

"Here," he said, holding them out to her. "Would you mind taking down every child's and staff member's name? I've got a couple of people I still need to treat here. It shouldn't take more than a few minutes, though."

"Of course," Oksana managed, taking the offered items. She was careful not to let their skin touch as their fingers came close to one another.

She worked her way through the group of people, putting a mark on everyone's left hand as soon as she recorded their names. After several minutes of walking around, she had a full count of every child and adult.

As she worked, she could intermittently feel Mason's intrigued gaze resting on her. Doing her best to ignore him, Oksana checked in with one of the nurses.

"How many of the children are injured?" she asked, poised to take notes.

"Just over half," the young Haitian man said, "but all except a few are minor injuries. Mostly cuts, a few sprained wrists or ankles, and a couple of possible fractures. Nothing more than that, thankfully. We were lucky."

She jotted down the final notes, tallied the number of children and staff, and managed to paste on an encouraging smile for the young man.

"I'm glad to hear it wasn't worse," she said.

Dreading it, she crossed the impromptu triage area and approached Mason. He was watching her, a thoughtful expression clouding his attractive features. Before he could speak, Oksana held out the notepad.

"I think this is everyone. They pulled another child out of the rubble a few minutes ago. Mostly minor injuries, thankfully."

A crease formed between his eyebrows in response to her clipped tone. Oksana couldn't help it; there was no room left in her mind for friendliness or an upbeat demeanor in the face of the darkness surrounding her. It pressed in on her as surely as the confining tunnel under the rubble had pressed in on her earlier.

Basic politeness was about all she'd be able to muster until she'd had a chance to get away for a bit and think. She had to keep her distance from this dangerously alluring doctor until she could sort things out in her mind and deal with the emotions that were threatening to swallow her whole.

As if on cue, Xander swooped in on the conversation. "So, everyone's accounted for, then?"

"Yes, thank heavens," Mason said in clear relief, glancing over the notepad.

"Good news," said Xander. "What's the plan now, Oz? Where can we take this lot to keep them safe tonight?"

Mason's eyes lingered on Oksana for a moment before he turned towards Xander and spoke. "Joni managed to get a mobile signal out, and we've arranged for them to be temporarily housed with the American Red Cross. They're setting up tents near the city center."

"Americans?" Xander asked without enthusiasm. "Well, I suppose needs must. Is it far from here?"

"It's a little over two kilometers away. Most of the roads are closed, so we'll have to walk, but the distance isn't what I'm worried about."

Duchess had joined them in time to hear that last exchange. "And what *are* you worried about?" she asked.

"Port-au-Prince is dangerous after dark," Mason said grimly. "The city has been experiencing an upswing in violence recently. No one really knows what's going on, but we suspect that some soldiers from the rebel movement have penetrated the center of the city and are causing havoc to de-stabilize the area."

Xander's knowing green eyes flicked to Duchess, and then Oksana.

"Yes. Well," he said, his tone mild, "we do seem to live in interesting times these days, and I mean that very much in the *Chinese curse* sense. I imagine that the addition of looters and opportunists after the quake won't improve the situation, but we can't exactly stay here."

"And we'll be traveling in a large group," Duchess added. "That should help."

Mason's eyes took the three of them in. "You're willing to assist us in getting the children relocated, then? You've already been an immense help tonight. I can't reasonably ask you for more of your time, but — "

Duchess waved him off. "Some of these young ones have sprained ankles and other injuries that will prevent them from walking. You need all the help you can get."

Mason's reply was heartfelt and utterly without artifice. "That I most certainly do, Madame. I'm in your debt — all of you."

Oksana swallowed around a hard lump that either wanted to be a laugh or a sob — she wasn't sure which. *In our debt, indeed. Would you still feel that way if you knew the truth, I wonder?*

"Right," Mason said, oblivious. "Let's get this parade underway." He put his fingers to his lips and let out a loud whistle. Silence fell as all faces turned towards him.

"Here's what we're going to do," he called in a commanding tone. The sound of his voice sent a shiver down Oksana's spine, and she cursed herself for it. Mason continued, "We have a shelter available in the center of the city. Unfortunately, we don't have access to any vehicles right now. We'll have to walk."

A few of the boys nearby made disparaging noises as they clutched injuries to their feet and ankles.

Hearing them, Mason turned and gave them a reassuring smile. "Don't worry, mates, we'll make sure you get there in one piece. We have some wonderful volunteers who helped us get people out of the wreckage of the clinic. They have agreed to stay and help us tonight. Anyone who needs a lift, raise your hand. Don't be shy!"

The group started clambering to their feet, nurses helping those who could hobble on one leg. Xander walked over to a small boy who was crying silently on the ground with his hand raised, clutching a swollen and bandaged ankle with the other hand.

"Looks like you could use a ride, huh?" Oksana heard Xander ask. The boy nodded as he continued to cry.

Xander gently scooped him into his arms and turned to Mason.

"This lad barely weighs anything, Oz," Xander observed.

"Maybe right now he doesn't. He had some health challenges to overcome when he arrived, but we're going to build him up," Mason said. "Isn't that right, Cristofer?"

"Yes, Dr. Walker," the boy answered in a tremulous voice.

Mason picked up another boy, and the male nurse Oksana had spoken with earlier took a third. After a brief mental exchange, Oksana pulled a dagger from the hidden sheath at the small of her back, while Duchess pulled one from her boot. The two of them took point, while Xander dropped back to take rear guard. He still carried Cristofer and did not draw a weapon, but with his keener senses and vampire reflexes, he would be able to alert them to anyone approaching from behind long before any of the humans noticed.

Mason came to an abrupt halt upon seeing the lethal dagger held in Oksana's hand. Had she been human, she would have flushed under his disbelieving regard—and once again, she was immediately angry with herself for her subconscious reaction.

"Is there a problem, *Docteur*?" Duchess asked coolly. "I believe you were the one concerned about the children's safety, given the increase in violence in the city, *non*?"

Mason blinked, his eyes flicking from Oksana to Duchess, and back again. She got the feeling that he was assessing them, trying to determine if they actually knew how to use the weapons in their hands. After a moment, he purposely relaxed his shoulders.

"No bloodshed, please, unless it's absolutely necessary to defend the group," he said, speaking English—presumably to avoid frightening the children.

Duchess smiled dangerously, not *quite* wide enough to expose her fangs. Oksana sent her a quelling look, but she only raised a perfectly plucked brow in response. "Really, *Docteur*. Whatever do you take us for?" she asked, all innocence.

Mason stared at her for a moment longer before breaking his gaze away. He addressed the group, giving them the directions to the Red Cross camp where they were heading. *Smart*, noted an objective part of Oksana's mind. *That way, if anyone gets separated, they'll know where to head for safety.*

The group got underway, and after speaking quietly to several of the nurses near the front, Mason dropped back to walk near the rear of the group. *Keeping an eye out to make sure no one wandered off?* It would make sense, given what she'd seen of his protective nature.

Oksana forcibly refocused on their surroundings, watching the eight o'clock to twelve o'clock sweep of their flank, while Duchess took twelve o'clock to four o'clock, and Xander, four to eight.

With one small part of her attention, Oksana listened to the conversation behind her. Much to her chagrin—if not her surprise—Xander seemed to have taken a great interest in Mason and was asking him for more information about the Doctors without Borders mission.

"We were called here after receiving reports of rebel child soldiers being captured by the government," Mason explained.

"A repulsive practice," Xander observed, "but not a terribly surprising one under the circumstances, I suppose."

The doctor nodded. "Sadly not. Things like this have been going on elsewhere in the world for decades. The rebel commanders go into these small, rural villages, murdering the adults and capturing the children. The boys, they make into soldiers, and the girls… well, I'm sure you can imagine," Mason said, sounding tired and bitter.

Oksana's stomach clenched.

"We've had some success bartering the release of the boys who are in poor health, or seem close to a mental breakdown," Mason continued. "We've had little to no success freeing any of the girls, but we won't stop trying. Anyway, once we have them, it's our job to medically stabilize them and start the rehabilitative process."

"That sounds like quite a challenging undertaking," Xander observed. "How much success have you seen in rehabilitating them?"

Oksana glanced back in time to see Mason run a gentle hand over the back of the boy in his arms, who appeared to have drifted into exhausted sleep. He turned a sad, kind smile on the youngster cradled in Xander's sure grip.

"Oh, quite a bit. Wouldn't you say so, Cristofer?"

Dear lord, he has a beautiful smile, Oksana realized, as if it were some sort of divine revelation. She couldn't help but watch the way the young doctor interacted so smoothly and effortlessly with both the children and adults around him.

Cristofer smiled back and nodded. "You help."

"Cristofer was one of the first children ever treated at the clinic. He's been with us for almost a year now and does an excellent job every day," Mason explained.

The boy ducked his head under the praise, but couldn't hide the grin on his face. "I want to be a doctor, too."

"Oh, yes?" Xander asked, glancing down at the boy. "That's quite a good thing to be."

Cristofer nodded with clear enthusiasm. "Dr. Walker shows me all his instruments and lets me listen to his heart sometimes."

Mason chuckled as he gestured the group to turn down a side street. "So far, I've been diagnosed with scurvy, the sniffles, and a broken heart."

Oksana's own traitorous heart lurched, as if in sympathy.

"Well, you don't have a girlfriend," Cristofer said accusingly. "That's why you're sad sometimes."

Mason gave a genial huff and raised an eyebrow at Xander. "We're still working on refining our medical diagnoses, as you may have gathered."

Anything Xander might have said was interrupted when the sound of nearby gunfire rent the night air.

"Get under cover!" Oksana shouted.

The children and clinic workers flattened them-selves against the wall of the nearest building. A few of the children cowered and covered their ears with their hands.

A yell of rage and terror caused Oksana and the others to turn toward the middle of the group. Two of the nurses were wrestling with Eniel, the child Oksana had pulled from the rubble. The one who had told her to call him San—the Creole word for blood. She hurried forward and dropped to her knees in front of the boy, who was being forcibly restrained by both arms.

"Let go! Let go!" he raged, tears streaming down his face. He kicked out wildly, temporarily suspended in mid-air by the adults' firm grasp. "Free me, *now!*"

"Eniel," Oksana said in a low voice, trying to catch his eye. "*Hey.* Eniel, look at me."

Eniel closed his eyes firmly and continued to fight, thrashing his head back and forth.

"*Eniel,*" Oksana said, more softly. The boy did not respond, but continued to struggle. With a sigh, Oksana reached out very gently with her mental power and touched his mind. She caught a small glimpse of the boy's pain and rage, the out-of-control emotions cours-ing through his body like acid.

Oksana could sense that he was completely disen-gaged from their surroundings. Attempting to reason with him would be useless. He was lost in the memories conjured by the gunfire still erupting sporadically from a couple of streets over.

Taking a deep, calming breath, Oksana layered a soft mental blanket of peace over Eniel's awareness. She did not force it upon him—simply offered it to him. For a moment, nothing seemed to change. Eniel continued to exert all his energy on escape, while the nurses re-strained his flailing limbs.

Eventually, though, his movements grew less fran-tic, and stilled. Oksana breathed in and out, allowing her life force to flow around the two of them. She could sense Xander and Duchess' life forces swirling and combining with hers, bolstering her, adding to the tranquility hanging gently in the air.

"There, now," she said. "That's better. That noise certainly was a bit unexpected, wasn't it?"

Eniel breathed in time with her, his thin chest rising and falling like a bellows. He nodded slowly, as if dazed. She could feel that he was clinging to her projection of calm as his anger and anxiety drained away. She made brief eye contact with the nurses, who released his arms and stepped back a bit, giving him space. The boy didn't move, but stood there breathing heavily and staring around, his eyes glittering.

"Are you ready to keep going?" Oksana asked.

"Yes," Eniel answered.

"Okay, good. The shooters are some distance away, but there may be more gunfire as we're walking. We're going to keep moving towards safety unless it gets closer to us, though. Can you do that?"

"Yes." The word was soft, but steady.

Oksana nodded that they were ready. The group continued on, but this time Eniel stayed close to Oksana. He did not speak and flinched anytime the *pop-pop-pop* of automatic gunfire sounded nearby.

Mason appeared beside Oksana and murmured, "Thank you."

"It was nothing," she replied, trying hard not to let her gaze linger on him.

"Bollocks. That was frankly amazing to watch," Mason said conversationally. "Have you worked with kids for long?"

He's trying to start a conversation, Oksana. Don't shut him down, Xander sent, obviously eavesdropping even though he was several meters behind them.

Could you maybe mind your own business? Oksana grumbled silently. *This is bad enough with only me in my head.*

Xander sent the mental equivalent of a shrug. *Hey, if you're so worried about privacy, you should be shielding better.*

She gritted her teeth. *We're trying to herd more than two-dozen adults and children through streets riddled with gunfire and rattled by aftershocks! I appear to be just a tiny bit distracted, for some strange reason.*

So... get un-distracted? She could picture his raised eyebrow as clearly as if she'd seen it.

Oksana groaned aloud in irritation and slammed her mental shields down on him.

"Er... did I say something wrong?" Mason asked.

She swallowed a sigh. "No, of course not. Sorry. I was just thinking. To answer your question, I don't work with kids, but I do enjoy interacting with them."

"Oh?" Mason responded, looking surprised. "What do you do, then?"

Oksana paused, caught out. Wait—hadn't her plan been to avoid him until she could figure out what to do?

"Um, it's a little complicated to explain."

If anything, that seemed to make him *more* curious. "Try me," he said.

Brilliant. How could she possibly explain anything to him when she was still reeling from discovering he existed? This entire situation was a nightmare. What a fool she'd been, to assume this wouldn't happen to her—that she'd have time. Time to come to terms with the reality of what finding her lost love Augustin would mean.

She was rescued from her predicament when they turned a corner, getting a view of a large plaza a block or so away.

"Doctor," the nurse named Joni called. "That's it, right?"

Mason smiled in relief. "So it is. Looks like we made it, everyone."

The open area was near the city center, and they were far enough from the ocean now to be safe from any waves that might come their way after the moderately powerful quake. There were several tents set up, where people in civilian clothing were talking to aides with the American Red Cross symbol emblazoned on their shirts.

As Oksana watched, workers scurried about, intent upon their business. Large floodlights illuminated the area, casting dark shadows around bushes and tents.

"Well," Xander said, looking around. "They certainly mobilize quickly. The earthquake was only a couple of hours ago."

"Oh—they were already here," Mason explained. "They've been trying to help with relief efforts following the violence and civil war. We just negotiated an informal agreement where they're temporarily going to house us as well, now."

"Dr. Walker?" a voice called through the crowd.

Oksana looked up and saw an older white man moving towards them, a weary look on his face.

"Yes?" Mason replied.

The man held out a hand, and Mason shook it. "I'm Jeff Sentry, I spoke on the phone to one of your people earlier."

"Of course," Mason said. "How are you?"

Jeff rubbed tired eyes. "Making it. Are these all of the children?"

Xander moved closer to Oksana, still holding Cristofer in his arms.

Mason nodded and gestured to the group. "Yes, this is everyone."

Jeff nodded and motioned for the cluster of people to follow him. He led them through the crowd, which was finally beginning to thin, heading towards a cluster of tents that were positioned off to the side of the operation, as if they had been erected as an afterthought.

"When were you able to get these set up?" Oksana asked.

"About thirty minutes ago. We didn't manage to get the bedding sorted out, but there are stacks of cots, pillows, and blankets inside. It's the best we could do on such short notice. We're running low on supplies at the moment, but we should still be able to feed everyone, at least for a few days."

Oksana used the cover of the children being directed towards tents to move away from Mason. She could tell that he was still watching her as if fascinated, but she tried her best to keep all her focus onto the task at hand.

"Eniel, which tent would you like to sleep in tonight?" she asked him.

The young boy had trailed behind her for the entire walk through the city. He glanced back and forth, and then looked at her with a lost expression.

"Hey," she said, squeezing his shoulder. His gaze flickered first to her hand, and then back to her face, as if he was surprised she'd touched him. "Listen," she continued, "I know this is really hard, okay? It's perfectly understandable for you to be a little freaked out, but I think these are good people that are going to take care of you, now."

Eniel's lips tightened, and he looked slightly angry. "I'm not a child."

She raised an eyebrow. "Eniel—child or adult, *everyone* needs help sometimes. Let these people do their job, all right?"

He sighed at her words and looked around again. His eyes settled on Mason for a moment, as if considering his options. "Yeah. All right."

"Very good," Oksana answered. She helped Eniel and several of the other less injured boys get their cots set up. They spoke very little, but instead yawned widely. After getting everyone into bed, Oksana ducked out of the tent and found several of the clinic staff huddled in a group a short distance away.

"Everyone settled in?" one of the nurses asked as Oksana approached.

She nodded. "Yes, finally. They were all so tired they could barely pull the blankets over themselves."

A conversation from a short distance away floated to her ears.

"... and I know this operation has been going on for quite a while now, but I think we need more help," Mason said.

Oksana peered around the nurse and saw that Duchess and Xander were deep in conversation with the Aussie doctor. She hesitated for a moment before moving in their direction. Still caught between an unmistakable draw and the desire to be far, far away, Oksana shuffled her steps until she was standing close to Duchess.

"Why is that? Too many children?" Duchess was asking.

Mason's face grew dark and drawn. "No, not exactly."

"So what's the problem, then?" Xander asked.

Mason rubbed a hand against his forehead and looked over at Oksana. Their eyes met for a moment before she blinked and looked down.

"I..." Mason began, but then his voice trailed away for a moment. "Look... I know this will sound crazy, but I've been hearing strange reports from some of the outlying villages. Anytime I try to bring it up with people in my agency, though, I get brushed off."

"Go on," Xander pressed.

Mason took a deep breath and let it out. "There are mutterings from the front lines of the fighting. Villagers have seen what they call *the lifeless*. Child soldiers who blindly obey orders, seem to have no emotion, and are incredibly destructive. Some people are saying that the vodou are preying on the people of Haiti, and have started claiming the island's children, turning them into something like... zombies, I guess, as ridiculous as that sounds."

Duchess made a soft, strangled noise in her throat, matching the feeling of stifling dread that settled in Oksana's chest at the words. She looked over at her friend in time to see all the color draining from Duchess' face. Duchess turned wild eyes on Oksana and Xander.

No. Her mental voice was harsh with denial. *Mère de Dieu – no. Does this evil know no bounds?*

"It's a frightening prospect—I agree," Mason said, clearly misinterpreting her emotion. "I'm sure there's an explanation, though. My guess is that it's a drug cocktail we've never seen before. A lot of these kids come to us high on cocaine—Eniel, for one. But this? I don't know... I can't imagine what it could be, to produce such effects."

The three vampires' eyes met and locked, a single word resonating through the mental link joining them.

Bael.

FIVE

A fierce, red flame of rage encompassed Duchess' aura. In the other's minds, she grew bright, and the light she bathed them in was hot, like fire. *This will not stand,* she swore. *By my life, this demon will pay for his crimes!*

Oksana needed to be away from this place, *now* — the urge to flee growing more difficult to ignore with each passing moment. *Not here, Duchess,* she sent, some of that desperation leaking through. *Not now.*

"*Fuck,* I need a drink," Xander muttered, almost too low to hear. In a more normal tone, he said. "All right, Oz. Here's the deal. It's almost dawn, and we have some business today that can't really be rescheduled. But — " He lifted a finger when Mason drew breath to speak, cutting him off. " — we want to talk with you more about this. Will you still be here tonight, say half an hour after dusk?"

Mason appeared surprised that they were taking him seriously. He nodded. "Yes, I'll be around. I'll try to meet you where we are now, but if I'm not here, just ask for me — I'll be inside one of the tents."

Xander clapped him on the shoulder. "There's a good chap. We'll see you then. Not to worry — we'll figure out a way to get to the bottom of your strange reports."

Still taken aback, the doctor nodded. "That's... *thank you.* That's just about the first good news I've had all day. I'll see the three of you tonight."

"Until then," Xander said, and Oksana thanked him silently for taking the lead. Duchess was still fuming, her anger no less incandescent than it had been earlier, and she herself was moments away from losing her shit completely and making a thoroughly undignified run for it.

She didn't *actually* run as Xander gave a final wave and headed for the shadows behind the row of tents, but it was a close thing. It was a huge relief to transform into mist with the other two and swirl away into the night air—a far safer option than traveling as owls in a city wracked by random gunfire.

If only she could leave the crushing weight of her past behind as easily as the weight of her corporeal form.

-o-o-o-

Thankfully, the Royal Oasis hotel in the nearby Pétion-ville suburb did not appear to have sustained any serious damage. Power was out in the area, but the building's generator was running, and lights glowed from the windows of the occupied rooms.

Oksana was no less of a hot mess now than she had been earlier, and it was a relief when Xander waved them into his suite and closed the door, pointing imperi-ously at the white leather sofa.

"Sit," he said.

Oksana flopped down on the comfortable cushions and pinched the bridge of her nose; Duchess ignored his command and paced.

Xander turned to rummage in his luggage for a moment and came up with a flask. Duchess waved him off in irritation. He shot her a side-eyed look, but con-ceded that particular battle in favor of standing before Oksana and thrusting the shiny metal container under her nose, instead.

"You," he said, with uncharacteristic firmness. "Drink. Now."

Oksana swiped the flask out of his grip and tipped it up, nearly choking on the liquid it contained. The stuff was lightly aged B-negative—her favorite type, usually—but it had a blood alcohol content so high it was a wonder the donor hadn't succumbed to ethanol poisoning and expired on the spot. How the *hell* did Xander manage to get things like this through customs?

"By hypnotizing the customs officials, obviously," he said, as if she'd spoken aloud. "Don't be a lightweight, Oksana. Bottoms up."

She glared at him as she drained the spiked blood, which had approximately the same delicate bouquet as paint stripper. When she was done, she capped the flask and tossed it in his general direction. He snatched it neatly out of the air.

Within moments, warmth spread from her stomach outward—not an entirely pleasant sensation given that it was paired with an uncomfortable twist of queasiness. Nonetheless, some of the tension bled out of her shoulders, and she leaned forward, resting her elbows on her knees and her head in her hands.

She heard Xander put the flask back into his luggage and settle against the corner of the heavy dresser on the other side of the room. Duchess fetched up near the east-facing window, where the first gray light of dawn would just be starting to peek in through gaps in the heavy curtains.

A small aftershock rattled the building, but everything in the room that was in danger of falling over had already done so before they got here, so Oksana ignored it.

"Right, then," Xander said, matter-of-factly. "It appears we have two competing crises. Somebody pick one to start with."

Oksana made an ugly grating noise in her throat and pressed the heels of her hands more tightly against her eye sockets.

"Dr. Oz it is," he said, and she flipped him a rude hand gesture, not bothering to lift her head. He ignored it. "So. Talk, Oksana. I'd've thought this was an occasion for congratulations, not a reason for me to have to give away my entire stash of liquid courage in one go."

She raised her head to stare at him through narrowed eyes. A glance in Duchess' direction showed that her friend was also watching her with interest, some of her earlier anger having finally drained away.

Oksana didn't much like being the center of attention like this. "And if it had been one of your soulmates we'd stumbled on, you'd have skipped merrily into the sunrise humming *It's a Small World After All*?" she asked pointedly.

"No," Xander said without hesitation. "But that's because I'm a dirty rat bastard who deserves a second chance about as much as Bobby Brown deserved Whitney Houston, and Duchess is a dangerous man-eater. Whereas *you're* a nice person who just happens to have fangs and a bad case of photosensitivity. It's a completely different situation."

Spirits above. She stared down at her hands as if they belonged to someone else. They were shaking. When they didn't stop, she clenched them into fists and stuffed them between her knees.

"You have no idea what you're talking about," she said.

"If he doesn't, *ma petite*, it's only because you never talk about what happened to you when Bael turned you," Duchess said.

"None of us ever talks about what happened when Bael turned us," she muttered.

"No," Duchess said. "We don't. Because it was horrific, and each one of us killed the very people we should have died to protect—or else we wouldn't be here. But that didn't stop Tré from finding Della. It didn't stop Eris from finding Trynn. And now you have found the one *you* lost."

"The one I murdered, you mean," she whispered.

"The one who willingly sacrificed himself to save you," Duchess corrected, "and whose death lies squarely at Bael's feet—no one else's. So, why is it that you look as though you'd rather lose another limb than even trade a handful of words with this man? A man who seems kind and brave, and who risks himself to save lost children?"

The feeling of being trapped—of being hemmed in on all sides with no light, no air, and no hope of escape—returned.

"I don't want to talk about this," she said.

"Oh, well," said Xander, laying the sarcasm on with a trowel. "Problem solved, then. Because I'm *certain* that if you ignore this situation, it will simply go away."

And why not? she thought, a bit desperately. If she could just steer clear of Mason until they left Haiti...

The sofa dipped as Duchess sat next to her. "*Petite soeur,*" she began, and Oksana *hated* the careful quality in her friend's normally haughty voice. "We can see that something about this is hurting you terribly, even if you will not tell us what it is. But you cannot ignore the prophecy. Not after what we have all seen over the past months."

"Watch me," she said, knowing as soon as the words passed her lips that they were a lie.

The Council of Thirteen. It was like a taunt echoing in her mind.

An assemblage of thirteen of Bael's greatest failures, and the only force that could hope to stand against him. With the addition of Della and Trynn to their ranks, Eris was more convinced than ever that prophecy referred to vampires.

So... not only was Oksana supposed to relive the night that had turned her into this sad and broken thing every single time she looked in Mason's eyes; she was also supposed to condemn the soul of the man she loved to that same sentence of almost-death. The invisible walls closed in a fraction tighter around her.

"I'm not having this discussion right now," she said again. "End of debate. Move on to crisis number two."

Silence stretched, broken only by Duchess' unhappy huff of breath.

"Fair enough," Xander said eventually. "So. Undead children. We're stopping this — how, exactly?"

If Oksana allowed herself to examine the fact that she was relieved to be discussing this new subject, she would probably break down weeping on the spot.

Duchess had no such compunctions. "It seems likely that Bael has a human or undead agent here on the island. Find that agent and reduce him to his constituent molecules. Problem solved."

"Direct and to the point," Xander stated. "Next problem — how do we find him?"

"Talk to the same villagers *le docteur* spoke with," Duchess said immediately. "The ones who originally tipped him off to the presence of the undead."

Xander nodded, thoughtful. "And, of course, the quickest way to find those villagers is —"

" — to have *le docteur* take us to them and perform introductions," Duchess finished.

Oksana's stomach dropped. "Mason?" she asked incredulously. "You're joking, right? This is just a really bad joke?"

"Of course we're not joking," Xander said, rubbing the back of his neck in thought. "It's not a terrible idea, you know."

"Uh... yeah, it kind of *is*," Oksana insisted, anger flooding in to fill the hollow left by shock. "You're trying to force us together — both of you are! I already told you, *I can't do this.*"

Duchess stood rather abruptly and Oksana rose to match her, standing toe to toe. Well... toe to prosthesis, at any rate.

Duchess' blue eyes flashed. "*I'm* trying to rescue innocents from Bael," she said in a cold tone. "It's not immediately obvious what *you're* trying to do, beyond having an existential crisis while elsewhere, children are being condemned to a fate worse than death!"

Taken by surprise, Oksana reeled back a step, the words more painful than a slap across the face would have been. Hands closed on her shoulders from behind, steadying her. She hadn't even seen Xander move from his spot across the room.

"A little more tact, perhaps, Duchess?" he suggested, sounding tired.

Duchess' eyes still snapped fire. "Tact will not save lives. The truth will."

Shame flooded Oksana, tears stinging ridiculously against the backs of her eyes.

"Shit," she said, her voice thick. She pulled away from Xander's support and practically threw herself at Duchess, who caught her and held her tight. "Shit, I'm sorry, *cheri mwen.* I'm so sorry — I can't think, everything's just this big, dark blur and I don't know what to do. But we have to save these children. Of course we do."

Duchess spoke into her hair. "We can't help you if you won't talk to us, *mon amie,*" she murmured.

Oksana pulled back and wiped surreptitiously at her eyes, turning her face away from both of them. "No, I'm... I'm all right. I've got it under control," she said, pushing everything down and back, into the dark space behind her ribcage.

"You won't thank me for this, Oksana," Xander said, "but it's fairly clear that it hasn't occurred to you yet. Whether you're ready to deal with Mason or not, you coming into contact with him means that a vortex of evil and chaos will be closing in around him over the coming days. Like it or not, the safest place for good old Dr. Oz will be with us."

Ice crept down her spine at Xander's words. She barely made it back to the couch before her knees gave out, as visions of everything that could happen to an unsuspecting human in a war-torn country with undead on the loose played like a movie reel behind her unfocused eyes.

The panic that gripped her as she pictured it drove out any delusions she might have harbored about being able to walk away from him and never look back.

"If he is with all three of us, we can protect him," Duchess said.

"All right." The words emerged as a hoarse whisper. The thought of having to stare into the face of the past she had hidden away was terrifying. But the thought of something happening to the fiercely protective doctor who housed the soul of the man she'd once loved more than life itself? That was worse.

"Well, thank goodness for that," Xander said with false lightness. "Now, I'm calling you room service. You need to eat, and I don't trust you to go out and do it on your own."

She sighed and scrubbed a hand over her face. "Fine. Have them send up whatever looks like it has the most sugar in it from the dessert menu, along with a bottle of merlot."

Duchess muttered something under her breath. Xander gave her that vaguely nauseated look that the others always flashed her when she said something like that. He shook it off abruptly and turned toward the room's phone.

"Whatever you say," he agreed. "But—as you're no doubt well aware—I was referring to the *hotel staff* when I said you need to eat."

She nodded, already resigned to the fact that she would need blood if they were about to plunge headlong into god-knew-what in the outlying villages. "Yes, fine. I'll be a *good girl* and eat my Brussels sprouts before I have dessert. Are you two going out for a bite later?"

Duchess waved a hand. "I fed before we left for the peristil last night."

"I'll hit the bar downstairs in a few hours," Xander said.

"When the serious alcoholics start drinking, you mean?" Oksana asked, unable to resist the jab.

Xander's smile was tight, as were his words. "Too fucking right, pet."

Oksana breathed out slowly through her nose and curled against the arm of the couch. Her gaze focused on a threadbare patch in her dark jeans, where rubble from the clinic had weakened the worn denim. In the background, she was vaguely aware of Xander phoning for room service, while Duchess started pacing restlessly once more.

Coping mechanisms, indeed.

-o-o-o-

Mason glanced at the late afternoon sky—a lovely cornflower blue vista that seemed at odds with the dingy surroundings of the overcrowded Red Cross camp. Still, it would have been churlish in the extreme not to appreciate his American colleagues' generosity in allowing the children's presence here after the loss of their clinic building.

The youngsters were safe—at least, as much as anyone was in Haiti these days. Their injuries had been tended, and none of them was life threatening. They'd been fed and had blankets to sleep under. So far, there hadn't even been any serious outbursts from the former child soldiers, whose behavior could be unpredictable, to put it mildly.

Things could have been worse. So much worse.

"Mason?" A familiar, gravelly female voice had him turning on the spot, craning to look over the heads of the people wandering around the camp.

"Gita!" he called, catching a glimpse of rapidly approaching silver hair piled up in a messy bun. "You're back safe! Thank heavens for that."

Dr. Gita Belawan, Mason's partner at the clinic, pushed through the refugees waiting in line for handouts of rice. She was a tiny woman—a stereotypical grandmotherly type whose head barely came up to his collarbone.

"Yes, we made it," she said by way of greeting. "Some of the roads were blocked by fallen trees, but we managed to get back around noon. Seeing the clinic roof collapsed gave me quite a shock, I have to say. Injuries?"

"Several," Mason replied grimly, "but nothing more serious than a simple fracture. Now that you're back with us, everyone's officially safe and accounted for."

Gita had been out in the field when the quake hit, trying to broker more meetings with the rebel military forces in hope of securing the release of more children. They had been taking turns with that duty since they'd arrived in Haiti, so that one of them was always available at the clinic to oversee their young patients.

"Any luck with the rebels?" Mason asked, already thinking ahead about how they might house any potential new arrivals after yesterday's disaster.

But Gita shook her head, her wrinkled face pulling into a frown. "None. They're spooked, and that was *before* the earthquake hit. Things seem worse in the rural areas than they were last time I went out, which is saying something. There's—I don't know—an *atmosphere* around the villages. Like something big is about to happen."

A chill settled in Mason's stomach.

"Anyway," Gita finished, "thanks for leaving that note about where to find you scrawled on the wall. I might've had a right panic otherwise."

"No worries, Gita," Mason said. "Now, why don't you grab something to eat? It's just rice, I'm afraid—they ran out of beans last night and it'll probably be another couple of days until the emergency shipments start getting through again."

Gita snorted. "*Please*. As if I didn't practically live on rice for the first sixteen years of my life, you spoiled Australian."

She gave his arm a quick squeeze, belying her teasing, and let him show her to the mess tent. By the time they made it through the line and emerged again, the sun had fallen below the horizon and the generators were kicking on. Floodlights glared into life, illuminating the camp as the natural light continued to fade.

Gita ate quickly before excusing herself to check on the children and let the staff know she was back safely. Mason lingered outside, curious to see if the three good Samaritans from last night would show up as they'd promised.

He was leaning toward *no*, but a part of him hoped he'd be wrong about that. He tried to put it down to excitement over the idea of someone—*anyone*—giving credence to his worries over the reports from the outlying areas about children being... *changed*. And that was true, as far as it went.

But it wasn't the *whole* truth. The strangers had been oddly magnetic, with an undeniable charisma that intrigued him. In particular, his contrary streak drew him to find out more about a woman who would fearlessly dive into the rubble of a collapsed building despite suffering from claustrophobia. A woman who wielded a dagger as if she'd been born with it in her hand one moment, and calmed a young boy's PTSD episode the next.

And—good lord—she had been *stunning*. Though, of course, she had also acted as though being within ten feet of him made her want to cringe.

Yep. Contrary, that was him.

The other two strangers had landed somewhere on the spectrum between businesslike and congenial. Which made him wonder why the petite, dark-eyed beauty with the Cheetah foot prosthesis had seemed like she wanted to sink down into the ground and disappear whenever she interacted with him.

He was ninety-five percent certain he hadn't said or done anything too terribly offensive. Well, unless you counted giving her an accidental shock when one of them had brushed against an exposed electrical wire in the rubble, or whatever it was that had caused that odd jolt when their skin touched.

So, yeah. He was curious. And possibly harboring a slight crush, because, well, *damn*. There was *attractive*, and then there was *saving a kid's life by risking your own* levels of attractive.

He wanted to hear her story, spoken in that honeyed Caribbean voice. How did she know the others? Her male companion was obviously a Pommy—that posh English accent wouldn't sound out of place reading the BBC news. The blonde woman had sounded French. But *she* hailed from right here in Haiti, he was sure of it. She'd spoken Creole like a native, and the accent clung to her impeccable English as well.

As if his thoughts had somehow conjured them, the trio appeared from the shadows, emerging into the central space adjacent to the tents that had been set up last night. *Bloody hell.* He certainly hadn't been mistaken about her. She was goddamned *gorgeous*.

She also still looked like she'd rather be pretty much anywhere but here. Which raised the question — if that was the case, why *was* she here? Even if her companions were curious enough to want to talk to Mason again, why would she accompany them if she didn't want to be here? Again, he wondered what their connection was with each other.

They came straight to him, as if they'd known just where to find him amongst the slowly dispersing crowd in the camp.

"You came back," he greeted. "I wasn't sure you would."

The blonde woman — Duchess, as he recalled — wasted no time on pleasantries. "You described some very alarming reports from the outlying villages," she said. "We wanted to follow up with you."

Mason nodded, falling into the same businesslike demeanor. "I appreciate that, believe me. You're the first people who've shown an interest. But, much as it pains me to say it, I've already told you pretty much everything I know — which isn't much."

The green-eyed Pom tilted his head. "So, you've not run across any of these children yourself, then? Just heard rumors?"

"No, I haven't. None of the boys who've come to the clinic have shown the kind of behavior the villagers describe," he said. "They've been brainwashed and hyped up on stimulants, true — but at the end of the day, they're just normal children who've undergone a terrible trauma."

A half-formed memory slipped into the front of his mind, and he went still, frowning.

"What is it?" Oksana, the dark beauty asked — the first words she'd spoken since she arrived.

He took a breath and held it for a moment before answering, new puzzle pieces coming together in his mind.

"Sorry—I was just remembering something Eniel said, shortly after he arrived at the clinic. He talked about some of his friends being spirited away from the rebel camp in the middle of the night—just... *disappearing*, never to be seen again."

"I'd imagine desertions and raids would be a normal occurrence under the circumstances," the man called Xander pointed out.

Mason shook his head, still putting things together. "I thought that at first, too. But Eniel said that they would find the boys' shoes left behind. If they were deserters, they would have put their shoes on before sneaking away. And if it were a case of night raids by government forces, why sneak away quietly with only a few children, when they could capture or massacre the entire group?"

"So, you're saying you believe these disappearances are tied to the appearance of the undead children?" the Frenchwoman asked sharply.

Mason raised an eyebrow, taken aback. "Undead? Let's be clear right up front—*The Serpent and the Rainbow* might've been an entertaining book, but zombies don't exist."

The blonde and the Pommy shared a flicker of a glance that Mason couldn't decipher. He put it aside and chewed his lower lip for a minute, trying to follow this new thread to its logical conclusion.

"Honestly, I don't know that Eniel's report makes any more sense than anything else," he concluded. "I mean, if the rebels are using some crazy new protocol on their child soldiers, why go to the trouble of sneaking them away under cover of darkness? Why not just march them off under orders in broad daylight?"

"Well," said the Englishman, "there's only one way to find out."

Mason's frown deepened. "And that is—?"

Xander smiled, showing very white, very even teeth. "Why, we go see for ourselves, obviously."

"Uh, go… where?" Mason asked, feeling like he was missing something obvious.

The French woman answered. "Go to whatever village you visited when you first heard the reports, of course. And, from there, to the source of the sightings."

Mason blinked, not having expected the strangers' vague interest to escalate into a proposed field trip to the front lines in the space of less than ten minutes.

"You're serious?" he asked cautiously.

"Very," said the blonde woman, sounding it.

"And we want you to come with us, to act as a guide," added the man, as if it was an afterthought.

Wait. They wanted *him* to go along with them? His knee-jerk reaction was to protest that he couldn't; that he was needed *here* with the boys under his care, especially now that they no longer had a clinic.

But Gita was back now. And while it was true that there were a lot of things that needed doing, it was also true that she and the rest of the clinic staff were eminently capable. In an operation like theirs, no single person was indispensable. They'd made certain of that. Stability was too important for these children to risk upheaval if something happened to one of them.

"We completely understand if you're too busy —" his mocha-skinned muse began.

So, she was still trying to get rid of him, then. At this point, burning curiosity about what he'd done to offend her was nearly killing him. Maybe she had something against Aussies? His stubborn streak spurred him to find out, but it was his worry over the alarming reports from the front lines that finally swayed him.

"I am busy, it's true," he said. "However, my partner at the clinic returned today, and I was scheduled to go out and meet with the rebels in a few days anyway. Given what's at stake, it only makes sense for me to head out early and see if anything can be done for these lost children."

"Perfect!" the man called Xander enthused. "You can help me balance out all the estrogen floating around."

Both women scowled at him, and Mason couldn't help wondering how wise it was to antagonize two people who apparently carried concealed knives on their persons at all times.

"Which I say with all the respect and admiration in the world for my two comrades, of course," Xander added, possibly coming to the same—if slightly belated—conclusion.

Their flat stares made Mason think that vengeance would likely be extracted at some unknown future date, but for now, they let it slide. Oksana's gaze met his for the barest instant before darting away. Without a word, she turned and walked back the way they'd come.

The other woman's china blue eyes followed her. She met Xander's eyes, a furrow between her perfectly plucked brows. "I'll talk to her," she muttered. "You get things set up with *le docteur*."

With that, she spun on her heel and followed her friend, disappearing into the darkness beyond the floodlights' pool of illumination. Mason gave Xander a questioning look.

"What was that about?" he asked, hoping for some clue as to Oksana's apparent aversion to him.

Xander flashed a quick smile that did not touch his eyes. "Nothing for you to worry about, mate," he said mildly. "Now, since we're apparently heading out into no-man's land, let's you and I talk logistics."

-o-o-o-

"I don't know how to feel about this," Oksana whispered into the darkness, feeling an unaccustomed need to unburden herself. "If Bael's minions are really taking children from the front lines, this is going to be complicated enough without him there."

"What is it, exactly, that you're worried about?" Duchess asked, moving alongside to walk at Oksana's shoulder.

"I don't know!" she snapped, her frustration spilling over. "Everything. Nothing."

Duchess sighed and tossed her wavy blonde hair over her shoulder. "That's helpful."

"Look," Oksana said, pulling Duchess to a stop in the shadows of the derelict buildings around them. "I can't deal with the fact that this is happening right now. There's too much going on. First Damascus, and now this mess with the children and the rebels—"

Duchess met her gaze squarely, blue eyes glowing. "You can't escape it, though. This is happening, whether you want it to or not."

Oksana frowned at her friend, who looked back with an uncompromising expression.

"I can see this is hard for you, *petite soeur*," Duchess continued, "but you're strong. You always have been. You can get through this like you've gotten through everything else. For, truly, what other choice is there in the end?"

With a heavy sigh, Oksana looked up into Duchess' face. "How on earth do I tell him the truth?"

"The truth? That you were the one who killed him?" Duchess asked.

"All of it." The words were a hoarse whisper. Their truth—the truth of Bael, and the evil that was nearly upon them—was knowledge she wouldn't wish on her worst enemy, much less a soul she'd once loved more than her own life.

"I don't know," Duchess admitted, "but perhaps that conversation can wait for another time. He doesn't need to know any of the specifics right now. Things will make more sense to him after he's been turned."

"What?" Oksana yelped, stepping back in shock.

"You haven't thought that far ahead?" Duchess said wryly. "Come, now, *ma petite*. You need to get your mind back in the game. Think about Tré and Eris. Both of their mates have been turned. With what we know about the prophecy, you need to expect that *le docteur* will be, too."

Oksana made a disgusted noise and pressed a hand to her forehead. "I can't think about that. Let's just see if we can find these missing children, and then go from there, all right?"

Duchess stared at her, but gave in. "You can't avoid this forever," she said pointedly.

Oksana spun on her heel and started walking again. "Watch me try."

SIX

A few hours before dawn, Mason finally sank onto a spare cot in the corner of one of the tents they borrowed from the American Red Cross. His eyes itched and burned with exhaustion, but he couldn't quiet his mind enough to fall asleep. Thoughts and plans chased themselves around his brain, keeping him alert when all he wanted to do was rest.

Knock it off, he told himself sternly. Forcing his eyes to close and his breathing to deepen, he tried to resurrect the talent for napping that had served him well in medical school and, later, as an overworked resident doctor. After lying completely still for what felt like over an hour, he finally gave up.

Bugger. Guess I'm pulling another all-nighter.

He rolled upright and pulled his laptop out of the rucksack full of stuff he'd been able to salvage from the wreckage of the clinic.

Luckily, the battery still had some life, and he was able to connect to the Red Cross Wi-Fi. Good on the Americans. He logged onto Skype and saw that his brother was online.

At least that was a lucky break. He quickly tapped out a greeting on the Instant Messaging app and hit send, hoping that he would catch Jack before he went to get dinner.

Mason: *You busy?*

Jack: *Just trying to finish up some work. Nothing important. How ya doing there, brah? Heard on the news you got shook up a couple of days ago.*

596

Mason paused, his fingers poised over the keyboard. There was so much that he wanted to tell his brother, but it felt like the words were stuck inside him, like there was a block between his brain and his fingers.

Before he could decide what to say, another message popped up.

Jack: *Isn't it like 4am there? Or am I off in my reckoning?*

Mason: *No, you're right.*

Jack: *What the bloody blazes are you doing up so early? Everything OK?*

Mason: *...I never went to sleep.*

As if to punctuate the statement, Mason yawned widely. He felt as if his jaw might crack open, and his eyes watered.

Jack: *What happened, eh? That's not like you.*

The gentle question seemed to unblock Mason's brain, and he knew where to start the story.

Mason: *It's been one hell of a couple of days. First, we were getting ready to do nighttime meds for the kids, and so everyone was up at the office. The earthquake struck just as we started passing out meds and the roof collapsed on top of us.*

Jack: *Oh my god, are you all right?! They said it wasn't a bad one!*

Mason: *Yeah, that makes it sound worse than it was, honestly. The office was made of some really shoddy materials, or it wouldn't have come down. Thankfully, there were no serious injuries. A few of the kids needed help getting out and we have some minor stuff, but nothing too bad.*

Jack: *Jesus, that's awful! I'm glad you're okay but damn, that's bad luck. Especially after the craziness with that kid who got hold of the gun.*

Mason: *Yeah, I hear you on that. I need some sanity, too. Because then? Things got REALLY crazy.*

Jack: *Something worse than an earthquake and a roof collapsing on top of you?*

Mason tapped his fingers over the keyboard, composing his thoughts.

Mason: *Three strangers ran up to the clinic to help us get the kids out. And one of them was this woman…*

Jack: *OMG that is so totally you.*

Mason: *What the hell is that supposed to mean?*

Jack: **snort* What do you think? Only you would pick up a woman in a disaster zone.*

Mason: *I DIDN'T PICK HER UP. I just… I don't know. She's gorgeous. Gorgeous, and brave, and great with the kids.*

Jack: *You totally picked her up.*

Mason: *Not hardly, mate.*

Jack: …

Mason: *… but I can't stop thinking about her now. It's like she's just hanging out in my head. She helped get the kids out and they worked with the staff to get everyone to safety. They spent all evening with us.*

Jack: *You've got it bad, brah. This sounds like a serious crush if you're that smitten after only a few hours. That's not like you, Mister Love-'Em-and-Leave-'Em.*

Mason: *Don't be an arse. Besides, she acts like she doesn't want to be within a hundred feet of me. It's probably all in my head, and it'll be gone after I've gotten some sleep.*

Jack: *Yeah, maybe. And since you brought it up, when WAS the last time you slept?*

Mason: *Uhhh, I got up at 5am yesterday. I think?*

Jack: *Jesus. Get some damn rest already!*

Mason: *I've been trying. I can't get my brain to turn off.*

Jack: *Uh-huh. Thinking about this woman?*

Mason: *Yeah, I guess. And some other things, too. So you know those weird stories that I've been telling you about? Where the kids go missing and then turn up on some sort of drug making them really screwed up and ultra-violent?*

Jack: *Yeah*

Mason: *Well, I finally have a plan to get to the bottom of those reports. These people — the ones who helped at the clinic — they want me to go with them to some of the remote villages and get a first-hand account.*

Jack: *Going in there to kick ass and take names, little brother?*

Mason: *Haha, yeah right LOL. No, we just want to get some information to see what we can find out.*

Jack: *And you're going with this mystery woman? What's her name?*

Mason: *Oksana, and yeah she's going.*

Jack: *OK, so here's what you have to do. 1) Don't fuck it up. 2) Send me a picture of her ASAP.*

Mason: *LOL all right, fine. I'll get with you once we come back.*

Jack: *You do that, brah. Be safe and let me know how things are.*

Mason: *You got it, J. ttyl.*

Mason turned the power off to conserve the battery and set the laptop on the floor next to the cot. He leaned back, finally feeling like he had siphoned off enough of his swirling restlessness to sleep. As soon as he got settled and pulled a blanket up over his shoulder, though, he heard some of the boys around him starting to stir.

Argh, no, please just go back to sleep, Mason thought, a bit desperately.

Unfortunately, his wishful thinking was not enough to quiet the boys, who were now clambering around and talking to one another.

"Dr. Walker," one of them whispered.

When Mason did not immediately respond, he felt a couple of jabs on his shoulder.

He let out a sigh and cracked open one eyelid. "This had better be an emergency."

"We're hungry," the boy said earnestly.

By the time he had scrounged up a meal for the boys and the other children who had started to wake up, he had long given up on the thought of sleep.

Maybe I can catch an hour or two this afternoon, he thought, stifling a yawn.

-o-o-o-

Oksana, Xander, and Duchess showed up as Mason was helping Gita settle the boys after the evening meal of rice. Mason had to wonder what business they had that kept them occupied during the day—he realized that he'd only ever seen them after the sun set.

Xander tossed him a sturdy rucksack.

"Here," he said. "We packed one for you."

Mason caught it and hefted it, testing the weight. He rifled through the contents and found a medical kit, satellite phone, several bottles of water, and some snacks.

"It should be enough for a day or so traveling light," Xander commented as he hefted his own rucksack over his shoulder.

"What are we doing for transportation?" Mason asked.

"I have some contacts," Oksana said, not looking at him. He watched her curiously as she stuffed several packages of pretzels into her bag.

"Closet pretzel aficionado, then?" Mason asked conversationally. He wanted to learn everything he could about the woman standing before him, and right now, he knew almost nothing. He felt inexplicably drawn to her, more so than he could ever remember feeling toward a woman. The instinct to reach out and touch her was nearly overwhelming—

Jesus, mate, get a grip, Mason thought, mentally shaking his head at himself. A pleasant buzz had seemed to creep over his entire body as he looked at her, but this was no time for fantasizing. There were kids' lives in the balance, for god's sake.

"Among other things," Oksana said, still not meeting his eyes.

Mason blinked in confusion, having completely lost the thread of their conversation. It took an awkward moment for his brain to catch up with her words.

"Oh," he finally said, remembering the snacks. "So you're a non-denominational snack food lover, then?"

"Oksana considers herself a connoisseur of all things that come in crinkly plastic packages," Duchess said.

Mason thought he saw Oksana elbow the other woman in the ribs, but it was so quick he couldn't be entirely certain. "Hmm. It's a trap, you see," he joked. "They get you hooked on one snack, and then it leads to another, and another, and another…"

Almost despite herself, she bestowed a quick smile on him that made his heart soar, before she abruptly turned back towards the others.

"Are we ready?" she asked. "I think I hear our ride approaching."

"Yes, I believe we're good to go," Xander said, after a quick glance around.

"Yeah, we're ready," Mason reiterated, eyeing the battered Land Cruiser that pulled up with some trepidation.

It was well founded, as it turned out. Any thought he had of sleeping on the ride was quickly dashed. Oksana's contact took them along back roads and rutted tracks. The potholes and damaged parts of the road pitched and tossed them like dinghies on a stormy sea.

The experience was not helped by the darkness, broken only by the crazily bouncing yellow beam of the single working headlight. By the time they finally arrived at their destination, many hours later, Mason felt mildly queasy. He rubbed his neck, which ached from being jerked around so much.

"Well. That was certainly unpleasant," he said as he stood and tried to stretch the kinks out of his spine.

Oksana looked sheepish, but surprisingly unruffled by the jouncing. "Sorry about that," she said. "I should've warned you that this gentleman has an aversion to driving the more well-traveled roads."

"What's the problem with at least using a gravel road?" Mason couldn't help asking. While this village was remote enough that there would have been at least some rough travel regardless, they could certainly have used the better roads to start with.

"He tries to avoid drawing too much attention," she answered, her tone evasive.

Mason raised a curious eyebrow at her retreating back before his attention settled on the sway of her hips. He blinked himself back into awareness of his surroundings and followed behind her, only to have his gaze caught by Xander's knowing eye.

"What are you staring at?" Mason asked, a bit defensively, feeling his face heat up despite his best efforts. *Good god above – what had gotten into him?*

"Nothing at all, Ozzie," Xander replied blandly. "Nothing at all."

Right, Mason thought. *So much for subtlety.*

"Look—" Mason began, but Xander interrupted him with a wave of his hand.

"Say no more. You've got nothing to explain to me, old chap," he said.

Mason scowled, trying to get a read on him, but he was distracted when he realized that Oksana and Duchess had led them past the center of the village and were heading towards a run-down building, barely visible in the starlight.

Mason increased his stride to catch up to Oksana. "Have you been here before?" he asked.

She didn't turn to look at him. "Yes. This is Mama Lovelie's place."

"Mama Lovelie? Who's that?"

She did meet his eyes, then—but only for an instant. "You'll see."

With that, she knocked twice. There was a short stretch of silence, but then a sharp command to enter issued from the back of the structure, despite the ungodliness of the hour. Oksana pushed the door open and stepped inside, not waiting for anyone to appear and let them in.

Still feeling confused and out of his depth, Mason followed Oksana inside, with Xander and Duchess right behind them.

"What are we doing here?" Mason asked, lack of sleep erasing the filter between his brain and his mouth. "When I was here before, I spoke to a man on the village council. Will this woman know anything about the missing children?"

Oksana was a black silhouette against the dark gray of the unlit room.

"Mama Lovelie is a mambo—a vodou priestess," she said. "If we're going to embark on such a mission as this, we should have the blessings of the vodou spirits— the loa—first. As a mambo, Mama Lovelie has a direct connection with them, and can appeal to them on our behalf."

Mason regarded her, willing his eyes to adjust to the darkness. "Do you really believe in spirits?" he asked, genuinely curious.

Oksana hesitated, throwing a look at her companions, who were still standing near the door.

"Yes," she said. "I do believe in spirits. I don't know if they are exactly as we Haitians believe them to be, but it certainly can't hurt to ask for some good fortune with our quest."

Could it hurt? No. But superstition wouldn't help them, either. Still, there was no reason for him to trample on anyone's beliefs, even if he *was* sleep deprived and impatient to get started with what they'd come for.

"I suppose that's true," he said neutrally.

A derisive snort came from across the room. They turned as one to see a small woman with dark skin leaning against a doorframe, holding a lit candle. She had short, iron gray braids covering her head, and there was an odd expression on her face.

"Mama Lovelie, I don't know if you remember me—" Oksana began, only to be abruptly cut off.

"I know who you are," Mama Lovelie said. "Or, rather, I know *what* you are."

Oksana blanched, her *cafe-au-lait* complexion going pale in the flickering candlelight.

Mason glanced towards the others in confusion, only to find that their features had gone cold and wary.

"I know what you are," Mama Lovelie repeated in a quieter tone. "Why have you come here? You see, at my age I don't have a lot of time for small talk. Not when there's work to be done!" She tipped her chin up, looking down her nose at them despite the fact that all of them, except Oksana, were several centimeters taller than she was. She lifted an imperious eyebrow. "I'm a very busy woman, you know."

"Uh…" Oksana began, clearly at a loss.

"Forgive our intrusion, but we need your help with a very important matter, Madame," Duchess interjected smoothly, coming to Oksana's aid.

A slow smile spread across Mama Lovelie's face, revealing white, square teeth. "That much," she said, "is painfully obvious."

Mason wasn't sure if he should feel amused or offended on the others' behalf. The expression on Oksana's face was so gobsmacked that it made him want to chuckle. He stifled it, not wanting to give her any more reason to feel uncomfortable around him. He definitely got the impression that she was second-guessing her decision to bring them here, though.

Oksana appeared to recover herself. "Mama Lovelie, we are here to investigate reports of children disappearing from this region, only to reappear later, but changed."

She indicated Mason with one hand. "This is Dr. Walker — a physician who specializes in helping traumatized children. He tells us that he's heard reports of these disappearances from families in the villages around here. I felt that it would be... *prudent*... to request blessings from the spirits before we venture further into this matter."

"Can't, luv. I'm far too busy," Mama Lovelie said dismissively, and bustled out of the room, taking the candle with her.

Mason couldn't see a damned thing, but the silence spoke volumes.

"Is she really too busy?" Mason asked, when it seemed no one else would break the stunned hush.

Another pause, before Oksana said, "No, I think she's just testing our resolve. Follow me."

Mason heard the rustle of clothing as the others moved to go with her. He could barely make out shapes in the dark, but followed cautiously after the sounds, feeling his way to avoid bumping into anything.

Oksana led them into a modest room at the back, lit with a kerosene lamp. Five small, circular mats were laid out on the floor, as if awaiting their arrival. Candles and incense burned on a low table in the corner.

One might almost think that Mama Lovelie had been expecting four visitors, though of course that was ridiculous. This village was in the middle of nowhere, and it was either ridiculously late or ridiculously early, depending on one's point of view.

Their eccentric hostess stood off to one side, preparing a tray with three cups on it. She looked up as they entered.

"Oh, you're still here?" she asked. "Well, I suppose you'd better sit down and have some *akasan*, in that case."

She finished stirring and handed one cup to Mason and one to Oksana before lifting the third to her own lips. Mason looked down at the milky, anise-scented drink, and back up at Mama Lovelie.

"Aren't you going to offer some to the others?" he asked, more than a little bewildered by the woman's actions.

She waved off his question with her free hand. "They don't want any."

His confused gaze moved to Xander and Duchess. Xander only shrugged. "As bodily fluids go, I can't say milk holds much appeal, no."

Oksana sank gracefully onto the nearest mat and looked up at the others with an expectant flicker of one dark eyebrow. Mason lowered himself down onto the mat next to her, careful not to spill the warm drink he was still holding.

The room seemed very still, as if he had just stepped, completely unprepared, into a church or holy site of some kind. He had never been a particularly religious man, and here he was, apparently right in the middle of a vodou ceremony designed to ask for the blessings of spirits he didn't remotely believe in.

Still, the only polite things to do were to sit down, shut up, and respect the beliefs of others. He only wished it wasn't costing them precious time.

Mama Lovelie finished her drink and set it aside. She knelt on the mat facing Oksana, her head tilting in curiosity like a bird's.

"Why do you come here seeking the blessings of the spirits, child?" she asked. "Surely you have the favor of the goddess?"

"That's... a little up in the air, I guess you could say," Oksana replied, looking more than a bit discomfited.

Mason knew he was missing the subtext, here, but there was nothing to be gleaned from either the mambo's cryptic remark or Oksana's vague answer.

"Why would you say that, child?" Mama Lovelie pressed. "Her light shines inside three of you, and the human has potential."

Mason blinked. The *human*? What on earth was this woman talking about? This conversation was veering straight past *odd* and into *surreal*.

If possible, Oksana looked even warier than before. "Perhaps, but... that's really not why we're here. We just need blessings from—" she began, only to be interrupted again.

"You," Mama Lovelie said in a sharp voice, jabbing a small stirring stick towards Oksana, "do not get to come into my house, asking for blessings from the loa, while you are so desperately trying to hide what you are. What you have become. The cosmos is moving around you and the prophecy will be fulfilled. You cannot flee from this. You cannot stop what has already been set in motion. Your cowardice will anger the spirits and drive them away."

Mason, unable to stay quiet any longer, cleared his throat. "Look, I'm sorry—but do you all know each other somehow? What is this about, exactly?"

Both women ignored him, still locked in a staredown.

"It's not cowardice," Oksana said, her voice burning with intensity. "*I'm trying to protect him.*"

"How is this protection? You *cannot* protect him," Mama Lovelie replied. "You know that."

Oksana *flinched*, a small, wordless noise torn from her throat. A flicker of sympathy crossed Mama Love-lie's face, replaced a moment later with determination.

"I'm sorry, child," she whispered, reaching out and patting Oksana's knee. "This, you cannot avoid."

"She's right, Oksana," Xander murmured, breaking the tense standoff. "It's time. It's *past* time, in fact."

"It's not!" Oksana insisted, her eyes going wide. "We don't even have confirmation that Bael is behind this—"

"*Petite soeur*," Duchess said gently, "of course he is."

"Right," Mason said. "Would someone *please* tell me what the hell you four are talking about?"

Xander closed his eyes, and when he opened them, they were blazing green with a bright, unnatural light. Mason's heart stuttered once and began to pound.

"What—" he choked out, his eyes caught fast by that otherworldly glow.

Xander smiled, his lips pulling back to reveal lethally pointed canines. "If you'll forgive the mis-quote—there are more things in heaven and earth, Ozzie, than are dreamt of in your philosophy."

SEVEN

Mason sat completely still, barely even breathing as he stared at the...*man? Creature?* At the *individual* in front of him. He thought he understood now what a rodent must feel like when staring into the face of a cobra poised to strike.

Hypnotic eyes, and the teeth of a dangerous predator.

Both set in the face of a charming Pom who'd chatted with Mason pleasantly and teased him for being from Australia. The implication of the fangs was obvious, but Mason... just... couldn't make his mind go there. He was a *doctor*, for fuck's sake. A man of science. Bad enough that he was wandering around in a war zone searching for zombie children—not that he believed in zombies, either.

The Englishman—who apparently wasn't a real Englishman—continued to gaze at Mason until the silence became stifling. Then, he blinked, and when he opened his eyes, they were once again a striking—but totally normal—shade of moss green. He frowned at Mason, as if perplexed.

"Okay... I'll admit I was expecting a bit more of a reaction that that," he said. Mason opened his gob, but no words came out when Xander leaned over and spoke out of the side of his mouth to Duchess. "Er... I didn't accidentally break him, did I?"

Mason closed his jaw with a snap and looked at Oksana, who seemed to be silently willing herself to sink straight through the dirt floor beneath her and disappear. Then, he looked down at the cup of *akasan* he'd set aside after taking a few sips.

"There was something in the drink, wasn't there?" he demanded, his eyes narrowing as he pinned Mama Lovelie with a suspicious glare. "What did you dose me with? Was it in all three cups, or just mine?"

The mambo snorted. "There were several things in the drink, *blan*. Milk. Corn flour. Sugar. Cinnamon and star anise. A pinch of salt. I'm sorry to say, I ran out of vanilla beans last week, however."

"You're not hallucinating," Oksana said hoarsely. Her eyes flashed angrily at Xander, and Mason was certain he saw a flare of violet light within their dark brown depths. "Xander, how *could* you?"

The look Xander gave her was almost pitying, but there was steel beneath it. "You'll thank me for it later."

Duchess snorted. "She'll *thump* you for it later, more likely," she muttered, before lifting a perfectly plucked eyebrow at Oksana. "But it still needed to be done, *chérie*."

Mason had surreptitiously taken his own pulse during the exchange and run himself through a short cognitive test. Everything seemed... *normal*. And now, he wasn't sure which idea was more upsetting—the idea that he was hallucinating the results of his quick and dirty self-diagnosis, or the idea that he *wasn't*, and the last couple of minutes had truly happened.

"You and I need to talk," he told Oksana, since this madness seemed to center around her, somehow, if their hostess was to be believed.

She still looked like she wanted nothing more than to vanish into thin air, but Mama Lovelie said, "Yes. You two talk. There is to be a ceremony tonight in the village center. I will use it to appeal to the loa for deliverance from the evil that has gripped our country. You may attend and ask for their blessings on your journey at the same time. If the spirits favor you, we will speak in more depth afterward."

Mason's attention was mostly for Oksana, but he was peripherally aware when Duchess rose gracefully from her mat and crossed to the small window in the far wall.

"It will be dawn soon," the blonde woman said. "Will you offer us sanctuary, Madame, or should we leave you in peace and find shelter elsewhere?"

"You may stay," Mama Lovelie said. "I require payment, though."

Xander reached into a trouser pocket. "That's not a problem. Do you prefer American dollars or Haitian gourdes?" he asked.

The mambo laughed—a clear, rich sound.

Xander quirked an eyebrow. "So... Euros, then?"

"Oh, nightwalker," said Mama Lovelie. "You are a sly one, aren't you? I have no use for your paper notes. What I require is far simpler—a few drops of blood from each of the three of you."

Oksana stiffened, her earlier reticence forgotten. "Why do you want it?" she demanded.

Duchess turned her gaze from the window, suddenly watchful. Xander deliberately lowered his eyebrow and pulled his hand from his pocket. "I'd be curious about the answer to that question, as well," he said in a deceptively mild voice.

Mason clambered upright, fighting an unexpected moment of vertigo as his body chose that moment to remind him that he'd barely slept in the last two days. He was so far out of his depth right now that the surface was merely a distant glimmer. Part of his exhaustion-fogged brain insisted that he was the butt of some kind of elaborate joke, and the punch line would come any minute now. The other part was babbling, *now the voodoo lady wants to take blood from the sodding vampires, are you fucking well kidding me?*

Mama Lovelie regarded Oksana with an inscrutable expression. "Why do I want it? Why do you think? There is power in blood."

Mason stepped up shoulder to shoulder with Oksana. "Yet you don't ask for mine. Just theirs."

Amusement was clear in the mambo's reply. "Some kinds of blood have more power than others, *blan*. Perhaps I will ask for yours another day."

Duchess pushed away from the window. "We can leave. There is still time to find someplace else to stay."

Oksana lifted a hand, her gaze not leaving Mama Lovelie's. "Give me your word that you don't intend to use our payment in a way that would bring harm to innocents."

"Oksana. Are you sure about this?" Xander asked, looking at her quizzically.

Mason couldn't stay quiet any longer. "This is mad." He rubbed at his eyes until he saw stars, trying to scrub away the fogginess. "Okay, so look. You're a vodou mambo. I get it. There are certain expectations from the villagers you need to meet, right? You have to display the trappings. But it's *just blood*. The only way it could be dangerous is if it contains disease vectors, or if you transfuse it into a person with the wrong blood type!"

There was a beat of silence, before Xander murmured, "Ozzie... oh, mate. You have *no idea*."

The mambo was still staring at Oksana and ignored his words. "If I am able to utilize it to bring harm to someone, child," she said, her tone flinty, "it most certainly won't be an innocent."

Oksana's shoulders tensed visibly. "So, you *do* know something about the children."

Mama Lovelie snorted. "Am I a fool? Of course I know what is happening on my own doorstep. I already told you—make your peace with the truth, and then, if the spirits favor you tonight, we will talk further."

After seeming to struggle with a moment of indecision, Oksana looked at Duchess and Xander. Her eyes moved to Mason next, but they slid over him like water across an orange peel — as if she found it physically painful to look at him.

"All right," she said. "Fine. We'll pay your price."

-o-o-o-

After Oksana, Duchess, and Xander had each sliced their palms with the knife Mama Lovelie provided and squeezed a few drops of blood into the three glass vials she indicated, the mambo carefully sealed the containers before giving the four of them a quick tour of the house where they would apparently be spending the day.

It was larger than most structures one would expect to find in a village such as this, with four modest rooms in total, plus a raised and covered sleeping porch built against the north wall. Xander and Duchess retired a short time later, giving Oksana what seemed to Mason to be rather pointed looks as they left to get some rest.

Oksana looked... *cornered.* Mason pondered the idea of giving her an out — pleading exhaustion and begging off to sleep for a few hours. But for one thing, he didn't think he *would* be able to sleep until he talked to her and got some kind of mental handle on this insanity, and for another, he thought the other two might well intervene if they thought she was in danger of weaseling out of the conversation.

There were more undercurrents swirling around than he could possibly hope to follow in his present befogged state, but it was painfully clear that they needed to talk. He followed her out onto the sleeping porch as the sky began to lighten with the coming dawn. The outdoor space was homey and welcoming, with a hammock hanging from two of the posts holding up the roof, and a mattress taking up one corner of the floor. A couple of rattan chairs with a low table set in between completed the setup.

Mason flopped down in a chair. Oksana moved to one of the posts supporting the hammock, her smooth, almost feline grace belying her missing lower limb. She leaned against the rough wooden pole at an angle that let her look out across the village, while keeping Mason in the corner of her eye.

The first hint of golden light appeared as the sun breached the horizon, and they watched it from the shadowed porch. Mason let the silence stretch until it became clear that she would not speak unprompted.

"You're uncomfortable around me," he observed, breaking the spell of the morning stillness. "Painfully so. Why?"

Her pause was long enough to make him wonder if she would refuse to speak at all. He let his gaze wander, taking in the low bank of slate-colored clouds hugging the western horizon, illuminated now by the morning sun. A flash of electricity crackled within the gray, swirling mass.

Was there a storm coming this morning? Well, now... how terribly apt.

Oksana sighed — a sound of capitulation.

"It's complicated," she said.

He looked away from the distant lightning in favor of examining her beautiful, melancholy features. "Try me."

Her eyes met his, that spark of glowing violet visible once more within their soulful depths. "You saw what we are, yet you don't believe the evidence of your own senses," she accused.

Mason regarded her steadily. "I'm sleep-deprived well past the point where hallucinations are common, and I still have no guarantee that I wasn't drugged with something in that drink," he said. "I wouldn't be much of a doctor if I immediately jumped to the *least* likely explanation for what I thought I saw, now would I? Occam's Razor cuts both ways."

She gave a frustrated shake of her head. "Then what is the point of us talking, if you won't believe anything I say?"

He frowned. "As you'll recall, I didn't ask you about Xander's teeth, or about that violet glow I've seen in the depths of your eyes. I asked you why you were uncomfortable around me, when I'm not aware of having done anything to make you react that way."

Her eyes flicked back from the view beyond the porch, settling on him properly for perhaps the first time since they'd arrived here.

"Because my presence here has drawn you into danger," she said. "The worst danger you've ever faced."

He snorted. "The worst danger I've ever faced? And you're sure of that, are you? I hate to disillusion you, Oksana, but three days ago I spent a good twenty minutes staring down the barrel of an AK-47 held by a frightened teenager who was hopped up on so much cocaine he could hardly see straight." He gestured at the sleepy village around them. "I assure you that I was in far more danger *then* than I am now — and I hadn't even met you at that point."

His intention might have been to reassure her, but his words appeared to have the opposite effect. Her expression grew devastated.

"The vortex," she whispered. "It's already forming around you."

Mason shook his head, trying to stay on top of the conversation.

"Look," he said. "Maybe you're right, and this isn't the best time to try and have this talk. Like I told you, I'm knackered. I'm guessing you can't be much better off. Why don't you let me bandage your hand, and then we can both get some rest and tackle this subject later today."

Her brows drew together in confusion. "Bandage my hand?"

He gestured at her left palm, which hung loosely by her side. "Yes, that's what I said. I'm a doctor, after all, and that looked like a wicked slice on your palm earlier when you offered up your little unplanned blood donation to Mama Lovelie." A noise of irritation escaped him. "I think our hostess must be the real vampire here."

After the barest hesitation, she pushed away from the post and crossed to stand in front of him, moving like she was caught between the desire to come closer and the desire to flee. She stretched out her hand, palm up, to reveal smooth, unbroken skin.

He stared at her unblemished palm stupidly, forcing his groggy brain to confirm that it had definitely been the left one she cut with Mama Lovelie's sharp little blade.

It was; he was certain of it.

"But... that's..." The words emerged slowly, and with no plan as to how the sentence would end.

He reached out and grasped her hand in his, intending to turn it more fully toward the light. Instead, he sucked in a sharp breath as the same shock he'd felt when he helped her up from the rubble of the clinic ricocheted up his arm and down the length of his spine like lightning.

His jaw hung open. The sane thing would have been to let go. To jerk back, breaking contact. Instead, his fingers tightened on hers. His eyes lifted to her face. She looked as though she wanted to weep — her expression one of the most exquisite pain.

The initial jolt would have been enough to put him straight on his arse if he hadn't already been sitting down. Now, though, the buzz of inexplicable power seemed to settle along his nerves like a comforting cloak, banishing his exhaustion… energizing him.

"What… *is that*?" he asked breathlessly, still not releasing her. There were no exposed wires here. Hell, he'd seen no indication that the village had electricity at all — no lines, no generators.

Oksana was still staring at him as though she were grieving for him, even though he was sitting right in front of her.

"It's the outward manifestation of a bond that draws the two of us together," she said. "A bond that has drawn you into danger — the likes of which you can't even begin to imagine."

After a few more moments, she drew her hand back. He fought a brief, confusing impulse not to let her go before rationality returned and he allowed her fingers to slip from his. As soon as the contact broke, a feeling of emptiness washed over him, exhaustion close on its heels. He blinked rapidly, trying to marshal his fragmented thoughts into some semblance of coherence.

"Your hand. The cut. It's completely healed," he said blankly. "Or am I hallucinating again?"

She shook her head. "It was only a small injury. It healed almost instantly."

"But… *how?*" he asked.

"Because I am a vampire," she said simply.

"No. Vampires *don't exist*." Even in his sleep-deprived state, he could hear the undertone of desperation behind his words.

Rather than answer directly, Oksana turned away. She walked across the porch and down the rickety steps. Pausing at the edge of the shadow cast by the porch roof, she stretched one hand out in front of her, the movement slow and cautious. Seconds later, she pulled it back and retraced her steps, tension coiling in her shoulders.

A teasing whiff of something unpleasant reached Mason's nose — the acrid scent of burned flesh. When she held her hand out for inspection — the same hand he had held only moments ago — his stomach churned. Skin that had been smooth and uninjured was now mottled red, with ugly blisters rising as he watched.

"Good god," he breathed, and rose from the chair to grasp her forearm. "Oksana, those are second- and third-degree burns! Come inside, I brought a medical kit—"

"Wait," she said, cutting him off. "Watch."

Her voice was tight with pain, but no less commanding for it. The words snapped him back from instinct to logic. She'd never left his line of sight. He'd *seen* her stretch her uninjured hand into the sunlight, and pull it back mere moments later, burned and blistered. This wasn't some easily explained medical condition, like porphyria.

Human skin simply did not react to the sun like that.

As he watched, the blisters gradually subsided. The mottled red burns turned shiny, pale new skin covering them like accelerated time-lapse photography. The skin smoothed and changed shade to her natural mocha tone. He blinked, and when his eyes opened, her hand was once again completely normal and unblemished.

His knees gave out, and he fell back into the chair.

"Tell me what you wanted to tell me," he said. "I'm listening."

The lines of tension in her shoulders eased. She pulled the second chair around to face him and sat in it, leaning forward intently.

"There's a war, Mason," she said. "A terrible, unimaginable war... and you're part of it now. You're part of it, *because of me.*"

She sounded so sad — so full of regret.

"There have always been wars, Oksana," he argued. "And I came here because I wanted to help pick up the pieces, not because I was somehow drawn here against my will."

She shook her head. "I don't mean *this* war. Though I suppose this war is part of it, given what we've learned. But it's not just Haiti. Not just Damascus."

"Damascus? The suitcase bomb? That was a terrorist attack," Mason pointed out. "A terrible one, certainly. Perhaps the worst in history, but—"

"No," she interrupted. "It was an opening salvo in the war that will make or break humanity. Only luck and a desperate last-minute ploy kept six nukes from going off in cities around the Mediterranean and Middle East, rather than just one. Can you imagine what would have happened if that had occurred?"

There had been no mention on the news of other nukes, or a broader plot. "That's the first I've heard of other bombs," he said cautiously. "What source did you hear that story from?"

She snorted. "I don't need a source. I was there, along with Duchess and Xander. Our other friends are still in the region, trying to track the movements of the man who orchestrated the attack—and the movements of the forces he unleashed in its aftermath."

He blinked stupidly at her. "You... were in... Damascus? When the bomb went off?"

Her eyes grew far away. "Yes. We were—close enough for the shockwave to drop part of a ceiling on our heads. Close enough to see the mushroom cloud rise... and to sense the screams of the dying victims."

Thinking of how close the sad-eyed woman before him had come to annihilation made something cold and heavy settle in Mason's chest.

"You told me to say what I needed to say to you," she continued. "There are forces in the universe, Mason. Powerful forces arrayed in opposition to each other. Good and evil. Light and dark. When they are balanced, they drive the patterns of nature. Of life and death. But the balance has shifted. My friends and I are victims of that power shift. So are the kidnapped children whose souls are being destroyed. And so, now, are you."

He wasn't ready to tackle all of that, with his thoughts muddled by exhaustion. Instead, he took a different tack.

"You called yourself a vampire," he said. "Help me understand that. The idea of vampires is a human construct, with roots in societal and religious history. It's a reflection of human insecurities and fears about life and death, not a description of a real condition. So… when you say *vampire*, tell me exactly what you mean."

"You've seen some of it," she pointed out.

He thought of glowing eyes, gleaming white fangs, and fresh skin growing over burns as he watched. "Tell me the rest."

Oksana regarded him for a long moment. "I don't know that you're ready to hear what I have to say quite yet," she said eventually. "I could tell you that I was born only a few kilometers from here, in the year 1769. I could tell you that I can change form—even prove it by vanishing into mist and reappearing behind you an instant later.

"I could even tell you that you just tipped over that little side table next to you because I planted the suggestion in your mind, and then told you to forget that I'd given you the command. But you won't believe a word of it."

Mason's eyebrows drew together in confusion. She looked pointedly to his left, and he followed her gaze to see the little table that had stood between the two chairs lying on its side. His hand rested on the edge. He stared down at the upended piece of furniture stupidly.

"I… don't—" he began.

"Yeah," she sighed, sounding suddenly tired. "I know you don't. It's all right. You should get some sleep. We can talk again later."

He was still eyeing the table. As she spoke, he righted it. He wanted to dispute her claims, but his brain felt like a saturated sponge that couldn't take on another drop of water.

"Maybe you're right," he said in a blank tone. He looked up at her. "Tell me one more thing, though. You keep talking about a bond—saying that you and I are being drawn together somehow. What makes you say that? How do you know?"

The slender hand that he had seen healing from second-degree burns lifted to smooth over his cheekbone and cup his jaw. He gasped, a jolt of raw power zapping from the point of contact straight down to the base of his spine where it coiled restlessly, sending heat pulsing through him.

He couldn't look away from the violet glow behind her burning eyes. The look of veiled torment was back on her face, and in that instant, he would have done *anything* to make it disappear.

"This is how I know," she whispered. Her hand slid away, leaving him shaking with reaction. Before he could recover himself enough to speak, she was gone, disappearing into the house.

EIGHT

It was a testament to the depths of his exhaustion that Mason was eventually able to fall asleep, fully clothed, on the mattress in the corner of the covered porch. The arrival of the rain pattering on the metal roof above him was oddly soothing—a natural lullaby.

He dreamed… shadowy, half-formed visions of Haiti as a lush paradise rather than a desolate wasteland of war, deforestation and over-farming. A faceless woman with mocha skin stood by his side, and even though he could not seem to glimpse her features, he knew that she was beautiful.

Beautiful, and *his*.

No one disturbed his rest, and he awoke many hours later to find that he'd nearly slept the day away.

As was often the case after recovering from an all-nighter, Mason almost felt worse after waking than he had before he'd gone to sleep. Still, he knew intellectually that he was better off now than he had been earlier. His thoughts were sharper, lending his conversation with Oksana that morning an almost fantastical, dream-like quality by comparison.

He needed food, something with caffeine, and—with luck—a basin of water to wash up in. As it turned out, the former and latter items were readily available. Coffee, on the other hand, was apparently in short supply in the village, with the fighting so close around them. He settled for more the goat milk *akasan*, a pitcher of which had been laid out next to a crock of

pumpkin soup and a bowl of rice with black mushrooms.

Xander wandered in as Mason was sitting down
with his simple meal. The collar of his spotless white
button-down was open, the sleeves rolled up to his elbows. His hands were thrust casually into the pockets of
his khakis. Tousle-haired and with a day's worth of
stubble shadowing his chin, he looked for all the world
like a stereotypical well-to-do British tourist abroad.

"Evening, Ozzie," he greeted. "I see you found the
nosh. Our charming hostess had to leave to get ready for
the ceremony. We're to follow her once the sun is all the
way down."

Mason swallowed his mouthful of soup, and gestured Xander over.

"Let me see your hand," he said. When Xander
raised a bemused eyebrow, he clarified, "The one you
sliced open last night. I want to see the cut."

Xander sighed. "Ugh, *scientists*. Tiresome sods, the
lot of you. But... where would the world be without you,
I suppose?" He extended his right hand, palm up, to
reveal skin marred only by old calluses. No wound.

Right. Mason lifted his eyes, meeting the other
man's quizzical green gaze. "Tell me where you were
before coming here to Haiti."

"Damascus," Xander said without hesitation. "Pulling survivors out of radioactive rubble." He raised a
pointed index finger. "And, for the record, there are two
things about your question that piss me right off. First, it
implies that you believe Oksana to be a liar, since you're
checking up on her story behind her back. Second, it implies that you think we're too stupid to coordinate our
stories amongst ourselves, if we *were* going to lie to you
about something."

Mason shrugged, not backing down. "Well, if you
get too brassed off at me, I suppose you can always
grow fangs and drink me to death. Assuming that's a

real thing? I'm afraid Oksana and I didn't quite get that far into the subject."

"You didn't? Funny," Xander said. "That's usually one of the first questions."

"The answer to which, is…?" Mason pressed.

"Short answer? Yes. I most certainly could grow fangs and drink you to death. Longer answer? Doing so would upset a very good friend of mine, so you're probably safe."

Mason nodded. "You do drink blood, then? From humans?"

"Cheerfully, and at frequent intervals." Xander tilted his head. "And to answer the question you're pointedly not asking—no, we don't kill humans to feed. A hint of mental suggestion, a modest blood donation, and off they pop afterwards, none the wiser."

"They're not alerted to something being wrong by the presence of fang marks the next morning?" Mason asked dryly, still caught up in a strange mental give and take—half of his mind sliding into this bizarre new reality, while the other half screamed at him to get a fucking grip and stop encouraging the delusional lunatics around him.

"Vampire blood and saliva have healing properties," Xander said.

Healing properties. Of course they did. Buggering fuck. Mason glanced around until he saw the knife Mama Lovelie had thrust on them that morning, to exact her payment for the lodgings. He reached over and picked it up, using it to open a shallow cut across the meat of his forearm—where it wouldn't be too much of a hindrance if he had to wait for it to heal naturally.

"Show me," he challenged, placing the injured arm flat on the table in front of him.

"We're not your lab rats," Xander observed mildly, making no move toward him. "And besides—what do you expect me to do? Come over there and drool on you?"

An irritable sigh sounded from the room's entrance. Duchess came in, brushing past Xander.

"Don't be more of a prick than usual, *mon chou*," she chided. Her blue eyes glowed in the room's dim light, and she curled her full lips back to reveal razor-sharp canines curving down. She scored her thumb on one fang and squeezed a couple of drops of crimson onto Mason's sluggishly bleeding cut.

The same part of him silently screaming for rationality knew exactly how stupid it was to let a virtual stranger's blood near an open wound like this. The rest of him was oddly unsurprised at the intense itching sensation which ensued almost immediately, his flesh knitting back together before his eyes. He licked his thumb and used it to swipe their mingled blood away, revealing a pink line that faded to nothing as he watched.

"Impressive," he said, meaning it.

"*Impressive*, he says," Xander muttered, tossing a sour look in his companion's direction. "When he has us stuffed into glass tubes with needles stuck in our veins, pumping the blood out of us for research purposes, I'll know exactly who to blame, Duchess."

"Why so worried?" Mason said blandly. "You could always hypnotize me and make me forget what I just saw, right?"

Xander only made a disgruntled noise and turned to leave the room. When he was gone, Duchess's china blue eyes pinned Mason with a speculative look.

"I wasn't sure about you, *Docteur*," she said, "but I believe you're starting to grow on me."

"Er... thanks?" Mason hazarded in response to the backhanded compliment. "Where's Oksana, anyway?"

"In one of the other rooms, pretending to sleep," Duchess said. "Your presence has her... decidedly rattled. I've never really seen her like this before—and I've known her for almost two hundred years."

Mason was getting better at letting the parts of a conversation that were *batshit insane* slide across the surface of his consciousness to be dealt with later. Practice made perfect, he supposed—even when it came to insanity.

"It was never my intention to upset her," he said truthfully. "In fact, I still haven't managed to pry the reason for her discomfort around me out of her. I mean, I get that she thinks we're linked together somehow — and to be fair, I've got no explanation to offer for that crazy electric jolt when our skin touches. But unless she's just really narked about being mysteriously bonded to some Aussie transplant she doesn't know from Adam—"

"I can't tell you that part of the story, *Docteur*," Duchess cut in. "It's not mine to tell."

He subsided with a sigh. "No. I suppose that's fair." His eyes wandered to the small window in the wall across from him. "Looks like it's almost dark out. I gather we need to leave for this ceremony we're supposed to attend?"

"Yes," Duchess agreed. "It's almost time."

"So, what are your thoughts on vodou rites?" he asked curiously. "Are you a believer in the power of spirits?"

"Indeed I am, *Docteur*," she said. "I only remain unconvinced about the desire of those spirits to assist the damned in a foolhardy quest."

Mason forced a smile. "Surely no one is more in need of help than the damned. If they're benevolent spirits, what better deed could there be?"

Duchess' answering smile was cold. "Benevolent? Whoever told you that these spirits were benevolent?"

With that, she pivoted on her heel and swept out. Mason stared after her for a moment before turning his attention back to his soup, mulling the conversation over as he ate.

-o-o-o-

Oksana reappeared just in time for them to leave. If Mason was any judge—which, as a doctor, he was—she'd barely slept. Admittedly, there were several assumptions involved in that statement. Did she even need to sleep? If so, how often and for how long?

Whatever the case, Oksana looked like hell. When her eyes met his before glancing away an instant later, Duchess' words floated through his mind.

I've known her for almost two hundred years.

For the first time, he could almost believe it. It took more than the twenty-odd years of age she appeared to be for someone to amass that much pain behind their eyes.

That pain... it ate at him. It made him want to cut his bleeding heart out of his chest and present it to her as an offering. It also terrified him, because he had never before in his life been prone to that sort of overwrought, romantic rot. *What the hell was she doing to him?*

Ever since that first jolting touch at the clinic, she had fascinated him. The second lingering touch this morning had drawn him completely into her thrall. He needed to get her to tell him more about this strange, otherworldly bond that they apparently shared.

He also wanted to feel it again. Preferably soon.

He followed the others out and shut Mama Lovelie's door behind them, before lengthening his strides to catch up to her. The others hung back, and he wondered if it was deliberate. When he reached her side, he slowed to match her pace. She didn't look at him, but when his hand brushed hers, she didn't pull away. Instead, somewhat to his surprise, she tangled their fingers together and held tightly. The small gesture made his heart lift all out of proportion with what it represented.

Holy hell, you've got it bad, mate, he thought.

Rather than risk breaking the fragile spell by pressing her for more personal information, he asked, "What will be expected of us at this ceremony tonight? I'm embarrassed to say that even after months here in Haiti, I don't know much about vodou beyond the clichéd crap from books and bad movies. Which, I assume, is mostly wrong."

She seemed to relax a bit. "Wes Craven has a lot to answer for, it's true," she allowed, the faintest hint of humor tingeing her voice. "To answer your question, though, nothing will be expected of you tonight. At least, nothing beyond being respectful and not interfering."

"Respectful, I can do," he promised. "I'm brilliant at respectful."

She snorted softly, the noise both unladylike and utterly, inescapably charming.

"See, it's like this," she continued. "Vodou is an African religion. At the risk of being politically incorrect, the loa will only visit those with African blood in their veins. Mine is only half, but when I was young, the spirits seemed to favor me. Right up until the night they didn't."

Mason digested this for a moment, weighing his next words. "Okay… on a scale of one to ten, how disrespectful would it be to point out that every single human being on the planet has African blood in their veins? We all originally came from there, after all."

She blinked up at him, surprise chasing the sadness from her eyes in the moonlight. He caught his breath, unable to look away.

"Not disrespectful at all," she decided. "Merely a bit vexing." She chewed her lower lip thoughtfully, drawing his trapped gaze down to her full, lush mouth.

"I'm not sure it's so much a matter of DNA, as of the shared race memory of slavery and conquest."

He nodded, trying to rein in his wandering gaze and his wandering thoughts. "Far be it from me to discount that," he said. "Australia has its own history of ugliness. It still stains the land and its people to this day."

She squeezed his hand briefly in acknowledgment.

"Yes," she agreed. "At any rate, tonight Mama Lovelie will invite the loa to visit the living and possess them. In the Christian tradition, possession is portrayed as something evil. Something to be feared. In vodou, it is our people's means of touching the divine. Many people will be possessed by spirits tonight, and that is considered neither frightening nor unusual."

Mason thought back to what their hostess had told them. "Mama Lovelie said that she would talk with us further *if the spirits favored you*. Does that mean you will seek to be possessed?"

"That may or may not be what she meant," Oksana said. "But, yes, I will invite the loa to enter me." She paused, the tension returning to her spine. "Unfortunately, the spirits haven't chosen me once during the two hundred twenty years since I was turned."

Mason frowned. "Turned. Meaning, into a... vampire?" It was still difficult to get the word out, his rational mind trying to throttle it, unspoken, despite what he'd seen in the last twenty-four hours.

"Yes."

Silence settled around them. He mulled over her words. If such possession — be it real or imagined — was an important aspect of her religion, he could see how its loss might affect her so strongly.

"Why do you think that is?" he asked, wanting to draw her out.

She was silent for another long moment.

"My soul was irreparably damaged," she said eventually, the words emerging so softly that he had to strain to hear them. "The human spirit contains both light and darkness. It's the balance between those forces that makes us who we are."

Mason looked down at her tiny frame. "I can understand that analogy," he said slowly. "But, having watched you risk your life to save a boy you'd never met, I can tell you with certainty that your soul is *not* irreparably damaged."

She waved off his words far too quickly to have properly taken them on board. "My life was never in danger the other night. I'm a vampire, Mason. A roof collapsing on me would hardly have slowed me down."

He continued to look down at her, unimpressed. "But you *are* claustrophobic?"

Oksana shrugged, and he could feel her closing off.

He tried a different tack. "Okay, so I'm apparently not going to win that argument. Why don't you help me understand what you think is wrong with you? With your... soul."

She flickered an eyebrow at him, in irritation... or perhaps in challenge. "A demon ripped it free of its moorings and tore it into two pieces," she said evenly. "But you don't believe in any of that."

No. That was true. He didn't.

"I believe that each of us chooses, every day, whether we act for good or evil," he said, picking the words carefully. "I believe that in the end, our actions are the only metric by which we can be judged. If we leave the world a better place than we found it, who would dare condemn us for the condition of some unseen vital force that supposedly resides inside of us?"

They were approaching the center of the village, and Oksana was spared from answering by the sound of drumming and chanting coming from the grassy open space ahead of them.

"We're here," she said, and slid her fingers free of his. Mason swallowed a sigh of frustration, knowing that further discussion would have to wait.

The scene was both primal and exotic. A large bonfire dominated the open space, throwing golden light over the figures of the village folk. Most were dressed in loose, white clothing. Many were dancing in a slow rhythm around the fire, while others sat on stools or on the ground, singing or beating small drums.

His eyes scanned the chaotic space until they settled on Mama Lovelie, wearing a beaded tunic and skirt decorated with a pattern in the African style. She was bent over a makeshift altar, holding a gourd rattle with a small silver bell attached to the bottom. Smoke from burning incense rose above the low table, curling into the night air.

When Mason dragged his attention back, Oksana had already slipped away. Xander stood in her place, and Mason suppressed a faint, instinctive shudder at the unnaturally silent way they both must have moved when he wasn't looking.

"The ladies went to join the dancing," Xander said. "Can't say I'm in too much of a hurry to join them. I'm guessing you're not, either. Do you have a grasp of what's happening here, out of curiosity?"

"Only in the broadest sense," Mason said cautiously.

Xander only nodded. "I'm afraid I'm barely qualified to offer commentary, but what the hell. Right now, the mambo is running through a very particular set of rituals to summon the loa. First, the one who's a sort of gatekeeper for all the rest, and then all the ones who they're hoping will show up to possess some poor, random sods and *ride them like horses*, as the natives put it."

He eyed Mason sideways before adding, "You might want to settle in. We're going to be here a while."

Mason lifted an eyebrow. "Not a true believer, then?"

Xander made a sharp noise that might conceivably be interpreted as laughter. "Me? Blimey. I'm not a *true believer* in anything, Ozzie."

Mason let his attention drift back to the dancers. Duchess' pale complexion was an anomaly among the swirling mass of dark skin. Oksana also stood out in her t-shirt and denim cut-offs. Mason's eyes followed her movements, graceful despite her high-tech prosthesis. Both of the women were welcomed into the crowd of revelers — *worshipers?* — despite their obvious differences. The sight made a smile tug at one corner of his lips.

"You two looked a bit cozy on the walk over here," Xander observed, his green eyes on Mason rather than the spectacle. "Did you chat about anything interesting?"

Mason bristled. "What's that supposed to mean?"

"Exactly what is sounded like," Xander said. "It's a fairly straightforward question, I'd've thought."

"I'm not sure our private conversation is any of your business, mate."

A spark of brighter green kindled behind Xander's gaze. "You'll probably want to rethink what you consider a private conversation, when you're within range of vampire ears, *mate*," he said. "But, as it happens, you're sniping at a potential ally. I had a talk with Oksana earlier today. Tried to convince her to relax a little and be more herself around you."

"Oh," Mason said, floundering a bit. "Er... thanks?"

Xander smiled, briefly flashing teeth that — while not pointy or elongated — were still disconcertingly straight and white.

"You're welcome, Ozzie. You see, both Duchess and I want Oksana to be happy. That's very important to us. Do you know why?"

Mason felt a frown furrow the skin of his forehead. "She's your friend."

"She is," Xander agreed. "But there are things you should probably know about us, before you spend more time with her. You see, Duchess and I are not good or nice people. We never have been. Oksana, by contrast... *is*."

The frown cleared as Mason's eyebrows tried to climb into his hairline instead. "Wait. Are you... am I seriously getting a shovel talk from a vampire during a vodou ritual?"

"Of course not," Xander said. "That would be ridiculous."

Mason relaxed his tense stance and drew in breath to apologize for jumping to conclusions, but Xander cut him off.

"This could hardly be construed as a *shovel talk*. Because if you hurt our girl, Ozzie, I promise you — *there won't be enough of you left to bury*."

There was a pause as the drums and chanting swelled behind them.

"O-*kay*, then," Mason said.

Xander patted him on the shoulder. "Good. I'm glad we could have this little chat." He seemed to lose interest an instant later, his attention turning back to the scene unfolding in the grassy lot. "Oh, look. The loa are possessing people already. Capital. Maybe we'll actually be able to get out of here before dawn comes and fries us all."

Mason did that thing again where he let the crazy roll off his back and moved on to whatever came next. Which, in this case, was apparently spiritual possession. And to think, a few days ago, he'd thought his life couldn't get any stranger than staring down the barrel of an assault rifle held by a child who only came up to the level of his chest.

He returned his gaze to the people around the bonfire. Oksana was still dancing, her head thrown back now; her eyes closed.

She was breathtaking. He didn't want to look away, but several other people were acting strangely, now. Some were shuddering in the supportive grip of other worshipers. Others lay on the ground, their backs arching like seizure victims. Mason's instinct was to go to them and check on their vitals—make sure they were all right—but a hand closed around his upper arm, holding him in place with a grip that hinted at inhuman strength.

"Best not," Xander said. "I'm told it's all perfectly normal."

Mason clenched his jaw, but stayed where he was. As he watched, some of the people on the ground rose and began to wander around. They wove their way among the crowd, some strutting, some using an odd, hitching gait, like actors playing some over-the-top role in a pantomime play.

As more people began to exhibit the strange behavior, which Mason presumed was associated with being possessed, the circle of dancers broke up. Those allegedly possessed by loa spoke with the other villagers, or embraced them, or made gestures of blessing over them.

Mason did a double take as he noticed Duchess. No… his first impression hadn't been mistaken. She really was tongue-kissing the hell out of a rather plain looking middle-aged Haitian woman.

Xander followed his gaze. A moment later, he let out a vaguely long-suffering sigh. "Stick your eyeballs back in their sockets, mate. Apparently that villager has been taken over by a male loa. Duchess said something about wanting to find out what the blood of someone possessed by a god tastes like. We find it's best to just let her have her way when she gets like this."

"And… when did she tell you this, exactly?" Mason asked, trying valiantly to get a handle on his *what-the-hell* expression.

"Just now," Xander said. "We can read each other's thoughts. Did Oksana not cover that part, either?"

Just let the crazy roll off like water, Mason reminded himself. *Deal with it later.*

"Oh, dear," Xander said. "Look over there—I do believe that Mama Lovelie has left the building. The lights are on, but somebody else is home."

The mambo's eyelids were fluttering, her head lolling back as she straightened away from the altar and lifted her arms over her head, spreading them wide.

Xander winced. "Ouch. That's a formidable one. Crikey, she's leaking power like a sieve. Can you feel that?"

Mason slanted a look at him. "Run-of-the-mill human over here, mate. I have literally no idea what you're asking me."

Xander's distracted grunt was his only reply.

A moment later, an inhuman shriek shook Mason so completely from his focus that he stumbled back a step. The unearthly wail was followed closely by more recognizably human cries of fear, and he cast around, looking for the source. Next to him, Xander had gone very still.

The hair on the back of Mason's neck stood on end as he saw a disturbance at the edge of the crowd. People were backing away, nearly falling over one another as they fled the terrifying sight in their midst.

It was a girl. A single, raggedly dressed girl, perhaps seven or eight years of age, shuffled into the circle of firelight. A putrid stench tickled Mason's nose as the girl turned dead, milky eyes towards the figure by the altar. In her right hand, she clasped a dagger—dark stains coating the blade.

"Oh, *hell* no," Xander murmured, barely audible over the confusion.

The child opened her mouth again, and the same hair-raising scream filled the night air. Several people shouted commands for her to leave, none of which were obeyed.

The people around the fire stood frozen, as if transfixed by her keening cry. No one moved except for Mama Lovelie, who took several slow deliberate steps forward.

The girl's blind gaze turned towards the approaching mambo. Lank, wet braids swung around her shoulders as the firelight flickered over her unnaturally gray skin. Everything about her seemed to have a cast of decay, including the rotten teeth visible through the rictus of her lips.

"Begone. I command you!" The mambo said, her voice sounding louder and more resonant than humanly possible for such a small woman. Mason struggled with the instinct to cover his ears as he watched with wide eyes, still paralyzed by the sight.

Faster than his eyes could follow, the girl moved. As she lunged toward Mama Lovelie, Mason felt Xander tense beside him and leap forward. In the space of time it took him to blink, all three of the vampires were hurtling towards the girl with inhuman swiftness. The child had the dagger raised, ready to plunge it into the mambo's heart.

Mason tried to rush after them, but his limbs were hopelessly sluggish in comparison to the lightning speed of the events unfolding around him.

The dagger slashed downward in a shining arc.

NINE

Oksana sprang forward, aware of the other vampires doing the same. Knowing even as she flung her body toward the pair by the altar that they would be too late. A small part of her — quickly subdued — felt dismay at the idea of attacking a child, but she knew in her heart that the spirit of the young girl was long gone. Only her body remained, a puppet of Bael's will. For all intents and purposes, she was dead already.

An animalistic snarl ripped from the child's throat, and Oksana's fangs elongated in instinctive reaction. The need to protect Mama Lovelie rushed through her veins like ice water.

Oksana had good reason for being protective of any priestess that she happened to meet. As a youngster, a local mambo had guided her in her journey to open her soul to communication with the loa — a kindness she had never forgotten.

On rainy days, which came often during the stormy season, Oksana would sneak away from the plantation where she and her mother were slaves. She would sit with the mambo, an old woman who lived in a hut not far from their owner's property.

Oksana was a mere girl, and far below the old woman in station. Yet the mambo had schooled her, always treating her with respect and kindness.

"You will be very powerful, Oksana. I can already sense it. Far more powerful than I am." The old woman spoke quietly, brushing Oksana's braids back from her forehead.

"But that's not possible," Oksana answered in her clear, girlish voice. "No one is as powerful as you!" Even so, she preened a bit under the praise of the woman whom she had begun to see as both grandmother and guide.

"We all have our time, child, and yours is just beginning. If you continue with your studying and your prayers, you will become a favorite of the loa."

Oksana stood and hugged the woman around the middle.

"My goodness! You are getting big," the woman observed, patting Oksana's shoulder. "How old are you now?"

"I've seen nine summers," Oksana answered looking up at the woman with adoration.

"Nine, eh? Well, now! May you see many more, little one."

The memory flashed through Oksana's consciousness in the space of a single heartbeat. She and Duchess had been about the same distance from Mama Lovelie when the undead child attacked; Xander was a bit further away. Had the girl been human, they might have had a chance of stopping her in time.

But she wasn't.

An instant before the tip of the knife would have sunk into her chest, the mambo raised a hand, palm out. A wave of power exploded from her, and Oksana felt as though she had flung herself head first into a pile of pillows. The very air around her absorbed her momentum and she fell to the ground, unable to move any closer.

"What the—" Xander hissed. She could sense that he and Duchess had both met the same impenetrable force.

Oksana stared at the tableau in front of her, wide-eyed. The girl stood frozen, the knife halted mid-arc.

"Oh, child. You have been gone for some time now, haven't you?" There was compassion in the voice emerging from Mama Lovelie's mouth—but it was not the voice of the mambo. It was the voice of the powerful loa who now possessed her. "It is time for your soul to rest."

Oksana heard her start to mutter in tongues. The undead child who had been standing before her, still as a statue, crumpled to the ground. Her unseeing eyes rolled up, and she lay unmoving. In the distance, a plaintive wail of despair rose and fell on the wind before trailing off to nothing.

Some of the people who had been standing near the fire moved forward to examine the body, wearing expressions of the deepest disgust.

"Sprinkle the corpse with bitter herbs and wrap it up, but be careful not to touch it," the possessed mambo instructed. "Also, the knife is coated with poison. Throw it in the fire."

With that, Mama Lovelie's body sagged. The power holding Oksana and the others back disappeared at the same instant, and Oksana scrambled upright. Only the mambo remained, now. The loa who had possessed her and saved her life was gone.

Mason jogged up to Oksana. Electricity crackled between them as he took her upper arm. He gave her a quick once-over before turning his attention to the girl. Two men were already rolling the small body up in a blanket.

"Wait, I'm a doctor," he said. "I should check on her first—"

Oksana shook her head, lifting a hand to catch his and hold him back. "There's nothing to check, Mason. Believe me. Let them deal with her."

He resisted for a moment, but a glance at the girl's milky eyes and decomposing flesh before the blanket covered her face seemed to stop him. She felt a faint shudder travel through his body.

Xander had recovered himself enough to approach Mama Lovelie, who still appeared disoriented.

"Are you well, Madame?" he asked, a hand hovering near her elbow. "The knife didn't break your skin?"

She waved his offer of support away, shaking off her moment of weakness. "Of course not. Erzulie Fréda Dahomey would never allow her servant to be harmed in such a way. As the spirit of love, she is far stronger than a single child tainted by darkness."

"Why was the girl sent?" Oksana asked. "This was hardly a random attack."

Mama Lovelie raised an eyebrow. "I expect she was meant as a message."

Mason was still watching, with sick fascination, as the child was taken away, but now his attention turned back to the mambo. "A message? From whom?"

Bael? Oksana thought to the others. *But... that doesn't really make sense, does it?*

No, I agree, Duchess replied silently. *Bael prefers grand gestures. If this had been his doing, that poor* enfant *would have been strapped into a bomb vest, or something equally horrendous.*

Mama Lovelie's dark eyes played over them, as though she were somehow aware of their silent exchange. "There is a powerful bokor in the village west of here. He is a twisted thing of pure evil, who has committed heinous crimes in the name of money and power. This was his doing, I am certain."

"And he is the one you planned to speak with us about tonight... if the spirits favored us?" Xander asked, his voice level.

"Just so," Mama Lovelie confirmed. "Come. I must complete the ceremony to close the door between our world and the spirit world. When that is done, we will talk."

-o-o-o-

It was not yet midnight when the five of them returned to Mama Lovelie's home. Their hostess waved them into the main room before collapsing rather abruptly into a rickety chair by the table.

Is she all right? Both concern and curiosity colored Xander's silent question.

Oksana gave the mambo a quick once-over before sitting across from her. *I think she's just drained from the ceremony,* she replied. *I've seen similar things before.*

That was a lot of power she was hosting, Duchess put in.

Mason, meanwhile, had been poking around until he found a pitcher of water and a cup. He set the drink before the mambo, who shot him a glance of thanks.

"You're certain you weren't injured at all?" he asked her.

Oksana felt the now-familiar ache take up residence in her heart again. Why did Mason have to be so kind? So earnest? So intelligent?

So damned handsome?

Mama Lovelie waved him off, though not as brusquely as she might have done the previous day. "Of course I wasn't, *blan*. Don't fuss."

"You said there was a... what was it? A bokor?" Xander asked, getting them back on track. "Forgive my ignorance, but what exactly is that?"

"A sorcerer for hire," Oksana said. "Someone with both power and a lack of scruples, who is willing to perform dark magic for money."

"Don't tar all bokor with the same brush, child," Mama Lovelie said severely. "Nothin' wrong with taking handouts in exchange for a bit of spirit work. Lots of bokor out here, you know, and not all of them are Dark."

Oksana had definite opinions about anyone who charged money for what the loa would willingly give for free, but airing them would only derail the conversation.

"This one is Dark, though?" Duchess prompted.

Mama Lovelie's lip curled. "This one is twisted. He has committed heinous crimes without fear of reprisal."

"Crimes like what we saw tonight?" Xander asked, looking vaguely ill.

"Just so. Rumors are circulating that he is hunting at night, plucking children out of war-torn areas and destroying their souls."

"Destroying their souls? How is that even possible?" Mason asked, and Oksana could sense him struggling to reconcile what he'd seen with what he believed about science and medicine. "How could that girl have been walking and holding a knife, when her body was obviously undergoing the decay of death?"

The mambo looked at him with an expression of pity.

"The soul, while in some ways a discrete entity, is also two-fold, *blan*. The two parts are known as *gros-bon-ange*, which controls the body, and *ti-bon-ange*, which is the personality. While they are united, the person exists in balance, with the body's base needs held in check by the conscience."

"Two parts? That sounds familiar," Mason said, turning his eyes towards Oksana, who nodded.

"Yes," she said. "The Light and the Dark."

Mama Lovelie shook her head. "It's not that simple, child. *Ti-bon-ange* and *gros-bon-ange* are not good and evil. They just *are*."

Mason frowned. "So, again, what exactly happened to this child?"

Mama Lovelie sat back in her chair, regarding him. "Through dark sorcery, a powerful bokor can divide the soul, literally ripping out the ti-bon-ange and leaving simply a body that moves and functions without a will. There is no moral compass to moderate behavior. The victim becomes extremely impressionable. This is what is happening to the children of our villages."

"Their souls are being ripped in two and the ti-... ti—" Mason stopped, as if trying to remember the word.

"Ti-bon-ange," Xander offered helpfully.

"Yes, that. The ti-bon-ange is just... gone? Forever?"

A troubled expression filled the mambo's face. "Gone forever? I believe so, yes. There are still some practitioners who believe a person can be reunited with their missing ti-bon-ange, but I have never seen this. I do not know how it is done."

Mason sighed and rubbed the heel of his hand over his forehead. "Okay. Let's say that I believe this. You're basically talking about turning children into... *zombies*."

He looked like he wanted to choke the word back as soon as it passed his lips, but Mama Lovelie only nodded.

"Yes. It is slavery in its worst form. Our people knew slavery for many centuries, but nothing the whites did to us was any more horrific than this."

"And these children are being bought and sold?" Oksana asked, aware that if the man they were after was a bokor, there must be money involved. Already, this seemed like a much more organized venture than simply creating child zombies and turning them loose on a war-torn country.

"Oh, yes," said the mambo. "Some of the children, he sells to the military commanders and militia men. They do their superiors' bidding better than regular child soldiers because they have no emotional needs."

Mason's face had gone pale, Oksana noticed, and she knew he must have been thinking of the battered and damaged children in his care back in Port-Au-Prince.

"You can't help these children, Mason," she said quietly "The best we can do for them is stop this bokor before he adds to their ranks any further."

"That's true," Mama Lovelie agreed. "There is nothing a foreign doctor like you can do to save the *gros-bon-ange* from their fate. All they need is burying."

The words were innocent, but Oksana couldn't help the faint shudder that snaked along her spine. She was aware of Duchess shooting her a concerned look, but she ignored it.

Xander cocked his head. "I notice you said that only *some* of the children were being sold to the military. What about the others? What happens to them?"

The mambo sighed. "Therein lies a strange tale, nightwalker. Some, he sells to the soldiers. But others are packed onto boats and shipped away. People say he is sending them across the ocean; selling them in faraway lands."

A chill went through Oksana—one that had nothing to do with the temperature. This sounded frighteningly familiar.

"Selling? To whom?" Duchess asked, her usually mellifluous voice sounding strangled. She was staring hard at the mambo, blue eyes unblinking.

"There is talk of some rich European man who seems to be a—" the mambo paused as if considering her words. "—collector."

"*Bastian Kovac.*" Xander's words emerged as a hate-filled growl. "It has to be."

The noose closed a little tighter around Oksana's neck, as the full weight of the danger she'd put Mason in became apparent.

"Who's Bastian Kovac?" Mason asked, frowning.

"A rat bastard in serious need of burning, staking, beheading, and anything else I can come up with before the next time we meet," Xander grated.

"The man behind the attack in Damascus," Oksana said simply.

Mason's eyes widened. "Wait. You're saying that the three of you had a run-in with this bloke in Damascus, and then you randomly came to Haiti only to find that he's somehow involved here as well?"

Xander cocked an eyebrow. "We didn't randomly come to Haiti."

Mason's gaze moved to him. "Okay. So why did you come here?"

"Because you're here, Ozzie," Xander said. "We followed Oksana's bond with you."

Oksana leveled a glare at him. *Shut up, Xander,* she sent, her eyes burning holes in him. *Seriously. Not. Another. Word.*

In her peripheral vision, she saw a faintly glazed look come into Mason's gaze for a moment before he appeared to shake it off.

"Let the crazy roll right off your back, mate," he murmured, low enough that a human wouldn't have been able to hear it. He cleared his throat. "Okay, then. So we've got this bokor arsehole trafficking children, both locally and internationally. But... how is he getting away with it? I mean... that girl was..."

"A walking corpse?" Xander supplied helpfully. "Not all of them are like that. Not... the newer ones."

Mama Lovelie nodded. "That little girl had been gone for ages. A fresh gros-bon-ange might look pale or sickly, but not dead."

Mason ground the heel of his hand against his left eye socket. "This whole thing is..." He trailed off and shook his head.

"Horrific," Duchess agreed quietly. "And we're stopping it."

There was silence for a moment before Mama Lovelie levered herself out of her chair and nodded.

"Let me think on things for a while," said the mambo. "This bokor. This *man*—if he even can be called that anymore—he is a very formidable practitioner. I am drained now. I must rest and figure out what to do. We will talk again later."

Without another word, she turned and walked slowly toward the back room.

Silence settled over the group once more, after her footsteps had faded. Oksana tapped her fingers against the worn surface of the table — a thoughtful rhythm.

"Should we call the others here?" she asked eventually.

Xander and Duchess shared a look, but it was Mason who spoke first.

"The others, meaning your friends who stayed behind in Damascus?"

She nodded. "Yes. I'm sure they would come to our aid without hesitation, but with the state of things in the Middle East, it might still take some considerable time for them to book travel and get here."

"Not to mention the fact that what they're doing is important," Xander said. "Bastian Kovac is obviously a big part of this puzzle, and they're already trying to track him down."

Duchess's blue eyes flashed. "We can't wait. How many more children will be defiled and subjugated while Tré and Eris are trying to arrange connecting flights?"

"Agreed," Oksana said, fighting another shiver of unease. "We can't just rush in blindly, though. You saw tonight what kind of power a talented bokor might wield. We'll need an edge of some sort."

Xander leaned back in his chair and crossed is arms, looking unhappy.

"Yes, I for one am well aware of the capabilities of vodou practitioners," he said, and Oksana knew he was once more thinking of Madame Francine, his eccentric acquaintance in New Orleans. "We'll just have to wait for our mambo friend to recharge her batteries and come up with something for us. Best if we get some rest, too, I suppose."

Oksana's mouth tilted down. *And how many more children will be defiled while we nap here, safe and comfortable?* she wondered, echoing Duchess's sentiment.

Of course, neither of the others could offer an answer.

Mason looked around the table, taking in their expressions. "Xander's right. It won't do these children or anyone else any good for us to go blundering in and get ourselves captured or killed by this bloody wanker, whoever he is. We'll come up with better plans when we're rested."

Duchess pushed back from the table abruptly and stalked off toward the back of the house. Xander rose as well, but spared Oksana a tight smile first.

She's just upset about the children, he sent.

I know, she replied. *We all are.*

A moment later, Oksana found herself alone with the man who was the reincarnation of her dead soulmate. The bond between them, which she had been trying all evening to ignore, tugged painfully at her heart.

Over the decades and centuries, she had grown used to being alone, even when surrounded by her friends. She carried the guilt over what had happened all those years ago walled up inside her damaged soul, jealously guarding it as though it were some kind of sick treasure. By pushing that pain down deep inside, she was able to continue.

In some ways, she prided herself on being a happy person—at least, to all outward appearances. Cheerful Oksana. Eccentric Oksana. The vampire who dined on Crackerjacks, Twinkies, and pinot noir, with only an occasional blood chaser as required. Yet, after a scant couple of days spent in Mason's presence, she had already turned into a sharp-tempered emotional wreck.

No wonder Duchess and Xander were worried.

And now, here was her soulmate, sitting only a few feet away from her. Hale, hearty, and whole… and still with that old, unconquerable drive to help those less fortunate than himself. No doubt about it—Oksana was completely doomed.

Mason sat back, regarding her with interest. "So. Rescuing people from collapsed buildings. Stopping evil witch doctors and battling knife-wielding zombie children. Is this just a typical day for you lot, or what?"

There was a hint of despair behind the choked-off bark of laughter that slipped past her control. "It's starting to feel like it, I'm afraid. Though… it wasn't always like this. For many years, it was just the six of us— wandering around, pursuing our various interests, and occasionally trying to make a little excitement for ourselves to relieve the boredom."

"That sounds all right," Mason said. "Did you work, or—?"

"Xander's the entrepreneur among us," she replied. "Though the rest of us do have money, of course. Honestly, it's hard *not* to amass wealth when you live for hundreds of years. Invest a few dollars here and a few dollars there, and it just sort of happens while you're not paying attention."

Mason snorted. "I'll admit, I can't really relate to that sentiment. I know doctors are supposed to be loaded, but in my experience it's all scrounging for grants and wondering where the money for the next truckload of medical supplies will come from."

He regarded her, tilting his head. "Though I must say, I have a difficult time picturing any of you clocking in at a nine-to-five gig."

Her laugh this time was a bit more genuine. "Yeah, I suppose I'm more of a night shift girl, myself." She shook her head at herself before sobering. "We don't age. And after a few years of not changing appearance, people start to talk. We tend to move around a lot."

"But always as a group?" Mason asked, clearly fascinated.

"Not always," she said. "Lately, though, it's safer if none of us are alone. We've learned that the hard way."

"Because of this war you've been trying to tell me about."

"Yes," she whispered. "Because of Bael."

A furrow formed between Mason's eyebrows. "All right. I'll bite. Who or what is Bael?"

Oksana took a deep breath and let it out slowly, trying to ignore the thundering of her pulse as the conversation veered in precisely the direction she didn't want to go.

"Bael is the name of the demon who turned me. Who turned all six of us—the six original vampires, I mean. He is the Darkness. The force that seeks the destruction and desecration of the world and those who live in it."

To his credit, Mason did not immediately denigrate her words, but sat mulling them for a long moment.

"I'm not sure what to say to that," he replied eventually. "I've always found that humanity was perfectly capable of manufacturing its own evil, without the need for gods and devils pulling strings in the background."

Right. He wasn't quite there yet. And that wasn't surprising, she supposed.

"I sincerely hope that you don't end up with firsthand proof of Bael's existence," she told him, knowing deep down what a futile hope that was. "Humanity is a microcosm of universal forces, it's true. Humans choose every day whether to act for good or ill. But the true horror of Bael is his ability to take away that choice and steal a person's free will. Do you think that child tonight chose to act in the way she did?"

"No," Mason said, very quietly, "but I also work with brainwashed children every single day. Their agency wasn't taken away by a demon. It was taken away by ruthless men with access to illegal drugs and a basic knowledge of psychology. I don't know exactly what happened to the girl tonight, Oksana. But I do know we need to stop it. For now, we're agreed on that, and it will have to be enough."

She studied him, noting the pall of exhaustion that still seemed to hang over him. A pang of guilt at yet again keeping him from his rest accosted her. It was followed by a traitorous sense of curiosity about what it would feel like to sneak into bed with him while he was sleeping. Would he sense her nearness and roll over, still half asleep, to curl around her? Would his strong arms feel the same as Augustin's had, so many long years ago?

She shut down the unwanted train of thought, appalled at herself.

"You should… get some rest," she said tightly. "You look dead on your feet, and it's going to be a long couple of days."

He nodded and yawned, not protesting the change of subject. "Yeah, I could definitely use some more sleep."

"Go on, then," she said. "One of us will come and wake you up whenever Mama Lovelie decides to talk to us again."

Mason nodded, stifling another yawn. "Okay. Goodnight, Oksana."

"Goodnight," Oksana answered. She turned to go to the back room where the others were resting. Still, she couldn't help glancing over her shoulder as Mason headed for the sleeping porch, an unaccountable feeling of longing pulling at her divided soul.

TEN

Oksana didn't fall asleep until just after dawn, thoughts and worries chasing themselves around and around inside her head like a dog chasing its own tail. It seemed only moments later when a familiar voice intruded on her thoughts.

Are you awake, ma petite? Duchess asked, the words flowing along the mental connection that wove a gossamer web across the three vampires' awareness.

Oksana startled into awareness, rousing from a restless doze. She glanced at her watch and found that it was just after eleven-thirty in the morning. Sunlight streamed from underneath the worn curtains drawn firmly across the window.

"I am now," she replied dryly, glancing up at the figure hovering in the doorway.

"My apologies," Duchess said with the barest hint of contrition. "But it's growing late, and Xander left a few minutes ago to see if Mama Lovelie was ready to speak with us. I thought I'd take the opportunity to talk to you, while he talks to her. We're worried about you, *mon chou*."

Oksana frowned at her friend. "I'm all right."

"Are you, now? I'm pleased to hear it," Duchess said tartly. She flopped down on the end of Oksana's bed and crossed her arms. "So. You've found your mate. Now what?"

Oksana groaned and pulled the dusty pillow over her head. It smelled vaguely of mildew. "Can we not do this thirty seconds after I've woken up?" she asked, the words muffled.

"Why not? It seems like a perfectly good time to me," Duchess retorted. "We need to have a plan, *n'est-ce pas*?"

Oksana pulled the pillow away in disgust. "Yes, fine. We need a plan. But I think our *plan* should focus on disrupting Bael's hold on Haiti, stopping the flow of undead children to Bastian Kovac, and helping the government re-establish peaceful talks with the rebels. Not on my..." She paused before finishing, "... predicament."

Duchess raised a graceful eyebrow. "I disagree. You said yourself that we needed the mambo's help for those other problems. Your predicament, as you so charmingly put it, is the *only* thing we can deal with at the moment. So. Talk to me, Oksana."

Oksana swallowed a growl and threw the disgusting pillow against the wall. "I can't, though!" she insisted, struggling to keep her voice low enough not to be heard by everyone inside the thin-walled house. "That's not what's most important right now."

Duchess's sky-blue gaze was almost pitying. "You're what's important to me right now, *petite soeur*."

Her friend's soft words took Oksana by surprise. Duchess might be inclined toward pet names and fleeting caresses, but she was not frequently given to flights of genuine tenderness.

Oksana opened her mouth to say... something, but no words came.

"You can stop putting everyone else's needs before your own just this one time," Duchess continued. "It's all right to think about *yourself* in this situation, because this situation is undeniably overwhelming. It's also terrible timing."

Oksana laughed bleakly, covering her face with her hand. "Yeah, it's definitely terrible timing. Though I'm not sure what would constitute *good* timing."

"You know what will happen, *non*?" Duchess's tone was uncompromising. "It's obvious that you fascinate him. A blind woman could see it. He wants you. After all, you're the other half of his soul."

"That's the part I can't afford to think about," Oksana murmured, still hiding her face in her hand.

"Why ever not?"

Oksana sighed, and felt the ridiculous burn of tears behind her eyes. She was glad that her face was covered, but that, too, was ridiculous. The pain in her heart was beyond shielding; Duchess would have been able to feel it from a mile away—much less an arm's length.

"I can't let myself get my hopes up," Oksana admitted. "Think about it, Duchess. Both Eris and Tré are far older and more powerful than I am, but it was all they could do to keep Della and Trynn from falling into Bael's clutches. What if I'm not strong enough to keep Mason safe?"

"It's not just you, though, is it?" Duchess said. "Don't you know that Xander and I would give our lives to protect you and yours?"

Oksana swallowed hard, the ache in her chest growing sharper. "I don't *want* you to give your lives protecting me and mine," she said, very quietly. "I don't want you to give your lives for anything, period. Please, don't make me talk about this any more."

She felt the mattress shift as Duchess leaned forward to squeeze her knee in sympathy. "Very well, then. We'll leave it for now. I just wanted to make certain you were all right."

The laugh Oksana let out was not a pleasant noise. "Yeah… no. I lied earlier. I'm not remotely all right. But thanks, all the same."

"Well, then. In that case, you'd better get your *derriere* off that mattress, you layabout. We've got things we need to do," Duchess said briskly, reaching down next to the bed and tossing Oksana her prosthetic leg.

"Supportive friend to drill sergeant in the space of two seconds," Oksana muttered. "Why am I not surprised in the least?"

With a sigh, she tried in vain to smooth her hair into something presentable. Maybe she would get it done in braids again one of these days, to make it easier to deal with. She'd been sleeping in nothing but a camisole and her underwear, so she pulled on a fresh shirt and her cutoffs from the previous night. When she was dressed, she stuck her left leg, which ended in an ugly stump below the knee, into the padded plastic sleeve of the Cheetah foot and stood up.

Oksana brushed past Duchess to get to the ewer and basin in the corner.

When did I get so dependent on hot showers? Oksana wondered, as she splashed lukewarm water on her face and neck.

About five minutes after they were invented, if you're anything like me, Duchess replied wryly. *Now, hurry up.*

Oksana snorted and busied herself buttoning the white shirt over her camisole top as she and Duchess exited the room. They found Xander waiting in the hallway.

"Is Mama Lovelie ready to talk to us?" Oksana asked.

"In a few minutes. Do you want to wake Mason?" Xander asked.

Oksana stood irresolute for a moment. She wanted nothing more than to slip silently into Mason's room and find him sleeping quietly. It would be a perfect opportunity to sneak into the bed next to him, curl up, and rest for a few minutes listening to his strong heartbeat and the gentle sound of his breathing. She could wake him up by running her hands over his soft, warm skin and —

A soft whistle like a birdcall dragged her attention once more to Xander, who was waving a hand back and forth in front of her unfocused eyes. "Oksana?" he prompted. "You still with us?"

She blinked "Oh. Yes. Sorry, I was... uh... just worrying about what the bokor is doing to those poor kids."

The lie wouldn't have convinced a total stranger, much less someone who'd known her for more than a century. She was thankful, though, that her dark complexion hid the hint of a blush rising up her neck.

"Right," Xander said, drawing out the word. "Well, if you think you can keep your hands off your pet Aussie for longer than five seconds, you should probably go get him up. I mean... *wake* him up."

She threw him a dirty look over her shoulder as she wheeled and walked to the door leading onto the sleeping porch.

Oksana raised her hand, hesitating, and glanced back again. She could practically feel her companions' interested gazes burning holes in her back.

"A little privacy, maybe?" she suggested, a hint of a growl behind the words.

Neither of them replied, but she could sense Xander's wash of amusement as he allowed Duchess to herd him further into the house.

With a sigh of relief, Oksana knocked on the door and waited. No sound came from the porch beyond. Oksana stretched out her awareness, hesitantly probing the space on the other side of the door for a moment or two before she sensed Mason's presence. He was still sleeping.

She knocked again, louder this time, and felt him jerk into wakefulness. Drawing her senses back inside herself, Oksana took a step back as soft footfalls approached the door.

Mason opened it just a crack, and one sleepy eye appeared. Oksana could see that his hair was tousled and messy from sleep. A small, traitorous part of her wondered how it would feel to run her fingers through it, straightening the tangled strands. It looked so soft...

An unexpected revelation hit her.

Good god. She could... *actually have that*, she realized, as if the thought were truly penetrating for the first time. If she reached out — right here, right now — he wouldn't stop her. She could have him. Have someone again, for the first time in over two hundred years.

Only... she didn't dare. Once she took that step, she'd be lost. And if she were lost, he would be, too. Lost to Bael, if she was too distracted — or too weak — to protect him when the moment came. And it *would* come. Of that, she had no doubt.

She had to stay strong. She couldn't let herself fall into the past. Not the good parts. Not the bad parts. She had to stay grounded in the here and now.

"Hey," she said, pleased when her voice reflected none of these troubling thoughts, all of which had tumbled through her mind in the space of a second or two. "It, uh, sounds like we're about to be granted another audience with our hostess. I assume you'll want to be there?"

Mason opened the door wider, blinking at her owlishly. "Yeah," he said, his voice gruff with sleep. He scrubbed his hands over his face, trying to rouse himself further. "Give me a couple of minutes and I'll be right out."

"Take your time."

Relieved that nothing further was required of her, Oksana escaped back into the depths of the house.

-o-o-o-

Mason wandered into the sitting room a few minutes later, yawning and stretching the kinks out of his back. Xander pinned him with a look, lifting an eyebrow at his less than put-together appearance.

"Thought you humans were supposed to sleep at night and stay awake during the day," the vampire observed.

"And I thought vampires were supposed to be nocturnal," Mason shot back. "You seem pretty chipper for midday."

"He's always like this," Duchess said. "At least, he's like this when he's not hung-over."

"Yes, it's true," Xander agreed readily. "The level of sobriety I've been suffering lately has become truly vexing."

Let it roll off, Mason reminded himself. Rather than risk being drawn further into the exchange, he moved to stand next to Oksana, who tensed at his approach. He was really, really starting to dislike seeing that reaction from her.

"Good morning, again," he said quietly, taking in her rather brittle and red-eyed appearance. "How did you sleep?"

"Oh, you know…" she said vaguely. "Not bad. You?"

Mason would lay money on that being a bald-faced lie. He let it pass, however, and replied, "Better than I expected, actually. Of course, that's probably down to me having been up for almost thirty-nine hours straight before we arrived here."

"Hmm. I guess that'd do it," she said, relaxing a bit.

"Suppose so. I had some crazy dreams, though," he mused. "Wish I could either skip those completely, or at least remember them properly when I wake up. I don't usually dream like that."

Oksana stiffened again at his words, but the exchange was interrupted by Mama Lovelie's arrival. She was dressed in a loose white caftan and looked much better than when they'd returned here last night after the interrupted ceremony. The mambo gestured them to sit on the mismatched chairs scattered around the room before pulling up her own seat and facing them.

"So," she began, "you four intend to confront this bokor, despite the strength of his magical abilities."

"Yes," Duchess said. "We won't allow this destruction of young lives to continue. Not when we have any chance at all of stopping it."

Their hostess leaned back and tapped her chin thoughtfully. "Then I must commend you for both your commitment and your energy in pursuing it." She quirked a dark eyebrow. "Ah, to be young again."

Duchess let out a derisive snort. "I'm far older than you, Madame. As I suspect you are well aware."

"Yet you still fight the battles of the young," the mambo retorted.

The two women locked eyes, sizing each other up. There was a beat before Xander replied, "When necessary, you bet we do. The question is, can you help us?"

"The bokor is very dangerous, as I told you last night," said Mama Lovelie. "He is far more powerful than I am."

"How did he become so powerful?" Oksana asked.

The mambo sighed and shook her head. "It's a sad tale. That any man should feel such greed and lust for power is a sickness within humanity, a cancer that cannot be cured."

Silence reigned for a long moment; nothing could be heard but the sighing of the wind through the open window. The curtains were drawn against the sun to protect the vampires from its direct rays, but the summery smells of light and life still wafted through the sitting area.

"He was born a man, just like any other," Mama Lovelie continued, "and raised in a village west of here.

As he grew up, he learned the ways of our people, the traditions that drive us, and the deep spirituality we share. He was sensitive to the loas' presence, and often feasted at their table. Over time, he became immensely powerful by anyone's standards, and acquired considerable wealth through bartering and trading.

"Exactly what happened next is a mystery, but the people around here say that one night, he went into the forest, drawn there by the darkness. He engaged with the most sinister of the loa, some of who were jealous of his successes. They enticed him, promising him greater influence and a position of vast power in exchange for pieces of his soul. He accepted. The more of it he bartered away over the years, the more blackness has been woven into his blighted spirit."

She fell silent and shook her head again. "I dare not challenge him directly."

Mason watched Oksana cross her arms, a stubborn expression stealing across her lovely features. "There must be something you can do. You can't just stand by while this evil perpetuates itself, practically under your nose!"

The mambo gave her a fixed look. "You should learn to listen better, child. I said, I dare not challenge him *directly*."

Mama Lovelie rose abruptly and walked around the room, looking at each of them in turn, as if appraising their possibilities. When she reached Oksana, the mambo stretched out a hand and touched her temple. Mason felt it more than saw it as Oksana shivered, her dark eyes sparking with brilliant violet.

"I might be able to weave a spell around one of you, drawing on the darkness that resides within you," the mambo mused, returning to her seat. The crease between her eyebrows was the only thing that communicated her displeasure with the idea.

"And that would make us strong enough to destroy the bokor?" Xander asked. Mason could make out the glint of battle shining in his eyes, brightening their natural moss-green color. The mambo scowled at him.

"I do not know if it would be enough or not," she replied. "But I do know it would weaken the spell-bearer, perhaps permanently."

"Wait. It wouldn't be reversible?" Mason asked, suddenly not liking the direction the conversation was going, even though he told himself firmly that he didn't believe in any of this fanciful witchcraft rot. But, even still… "I thought vampires healed really fast?"

"Yes, we heal. Much faster and more completely than humans, at least in some respects," Duchess replied immediately.

"You speak of the physical," said Mama Lovelie. "Whereas I speak of the spiritual."

"I'll do it," Oksana said.

"No," Duchess snapped. "I'm the oldest. If something like this is to be done, it should be me."

"Oksana," Xander said, lifting his hand in a suppressing gesture. "Look, it's not that we don't think you're a total badass and everything, but you're really tiny and you've only got one leg—"

"Your point, Xander?" Oksana asked, glaring at him.

"—So I don't think you're the best candidate for a major spiritual warfare knock-down-drag-out, if you know what I mean," he finished.

Oksana bristled. "You really have no idea what you're talking about. This isn't a matter of physical size or strength. A deep connection with the loa and an understanding of the spirit world is going to be of more importance than how vertically challenged I happen to be!"

Before Mason could open his mouth and join Xander's side of the argument, Mama Lovelie interrupted.

660

"Oksana is correct," she said. "You must remember that she is a daughter of Haiti. None of the rest of you can claim that heritage."

Mason felt a muscle in his jaw twitch. "This is crazy. Not that I necessarily believe in this stuff, but we need a plan that doesn't hinge on someone being permanently injured, physically or... otherwise."

"Mason," Oksana said, laying a hand on his arm. "I appreciate the concern, but this may well be the best way... if not the *only* way."

His skin tingled under her light touch. "Why?" he demanded, turning to meet her eyes. "Why is this the best way?"

For once, she didn't look away. "Because I have a connection to this land. I was born here; this is my birthright. These are *my* spirits, *my* loa, and maybe this is what will convince them to finally welcome me home. If any one of us has a chance of drawing enough power from them to defeat this evil man, it's me."

Their eyes remained locked, Oksana's hand still burning with that strange energy against his skin. Despite himself, Mason felt his heart stutter and beat faster. He opened his mouth to speak, but Oksana forestalled him.

"I'm right, aren't I, Mama Lovelie?" she asked, turning everyone's attention back towards the mambo.

"You are, child," the mambo answered. "I believe you alone will be able to challenge the bokor, but only if the loa choose to bless you and take your side."

"I still don't like it," Duchess said, brushing her blonde hair away from her face with an impatient gesture.

"Seconded," Xander said tightly.

"Thirded," Mason agreed.

"Too bad, since I don't see that we have much of a choice right now," Oksana answered with a sigh. "I do realize this isn't ideal." Ignoring their unhappy looks, she turned back towards the mambo. "We still need an actual *plan*, though. This is too vague."

The mambo nodded her agreement. Xander pressed his thumb and forefinger to the bridge of his nose.

"All right," he said. "Let's suspend rationality for just a moment and say that we all agree to this. You're just going to waltz in there, battle the bokor while we sit twiddling our thumbs, and then we take the kids away to… where, exactly?"

"Bring them back here first, and then try to reunite as many as possible with their families. Take the ones who need additional care on to Mason's clinic," Oksana replied promptly, and Mason forced himself to move beyond the crazy vodou trappings of the plan and focus on logistics instead.

"The clinic that was destroyed in an earthquake, you mean?" Xander asked.

Mason waved the question off. "I'm sure that the Red Cross and Doctors Without Borders are working on finding us an alternative location, even as we speak," he said. "They're very resourceful, and they have a lot of contacts on the ground in Haiti. That part of the plan is sound enough. Though I don't know what, exactly, we're going to be able to do with children whose souls have been partially destroyed once we get them back. There's no research or treatment regimen in place for something like this."

Duchess frowned, her attention turning back to the mambo. "You said there might be a way to reunite the two parts of their souls?"

Mama Lovelie shook her head. "I said some people believe there is, but that I've never seen evidence of any such thing. For one thing, the bokor is the one holding the children's stolen ti-bon-ange. And I can't imagine he'd give them up willingly."

Mason could barely suppress a shudder at the thought of being responsible for the wellbeing of a group of corpselike children without any will or self-awareness. Nausea washed over him as he envisioned them all trapped in the bokor's village, held captive in a pit or something, bumping around blindly in the darkness. And the others expected him to take them away and fix them? If they were like the girl with the knife, how the hell was he going to do that? Even their resident expert seemed to think it was impossible.

"Maybe they'll be turned already, and maybe they won't," Oksana said grimly. "We'll just have to see once we find them."

Please, Mason thought, *let them still be whole.* As a physician, he was equipped to deal with trauma. But not with the living dead.

Duchess looked as ill as he felt. "We need to find them as soon as possible," she said. "He mustn't be allowed to destroy any more innocents than he already has."

"Right, so how about this?" Xander asked, after a moment of thoughtful silence. "We send in Oksana to battle the bokor, armed with Mama Lovelie's spell to make her more powerful. He's so busy dealing with her that he doesn't notice the rest of us getting the kids out. Then, Duchess and I go back once the children are safe, and help Oksana finish him off. That way, if he has guards with him in the village, they won't have time to hide or move the children once they realize they're under attack."

"That's a slightly better sounding plan," Mason said, thinking that at least Oksana would have some backup. He had to admit, he was unable to summon any real remorse about the idea of seeing bloody revenge meted out on this twisted bastard, despite the Hippocratic Oath he'd taken.

"Yes. The sounds reasonable," Duchess said. "We'll leave the children with you, *Docteur*—hidden close by, but out of sight. You're best qualified to care for their medical needs, if they have any."

Again, the sense of being in over his head accosted him. Would he be able to do anything at all for these kids, if the worst-case scenario came to pass and they were all like the girl from the ceremony? Still, if it came to that, he knew he would have to try.

"Some of the children who've ended up at our clinic have been in bad shape," he said grimly. "Many of them are extremely emaciated or hopped up on drugs, so I'm used to seeing that. But whatever is ultimately to be done for these youngsters, I won't be able to do much of anything out here in the bush. I don't have the supplies or the staff."

"Do you think you could reach anyone at your clinic who might be able to get out here and help us?" Oksana asked.

"We can't really spare anyone," Mason replied. "The kids that are there already need all the help they can get, especially after the quake. And even if I could get other people, it would take time to get a message back, and more time for someone to travel here and join us."

"*Docteur*," Duchess said calmly, "we all realize this isn't ideal, but we still have to do our best get these children to safety, given the circumstances. You understand that, I know."

"Of course I do," he snapped. He took a deep breath, knowing that they were short on options, and the clock was ticking. "Look. I'll go along with this plan, but I want you all to know that I strongly protest the parts of it that put Oksana in danger."

"Duly noted," Xander said, not sounding much happier than Mason felt. "So, the tentative plan is for the mambo to put a spell on Oksana, who will hopefully gain enough power from the loa to challenge and distract the bokor in a fight. Duchess and I will rescue the kids and bring them to Mason, who will keep them hidden and care for them as best he can, given the obvious limitations. Then, Duchess and I will join Oksana, in case she hasn't finished the bastard off yet. Afterward, we can share our power with her to counteract any lingering effects of either the spell or the fight."

"Do you believe this can work?" Oksana asked, turning towards the mambo.

The woman gazed at each one of them again, her deep-set eyes troubled as she silently appraised the determined group.

"I think it will be possible for the four of you to save at least some of the children," she said heavily, "but at what cost, I do not know."

No one had anything to say in reply.

ELEVEN

That afternoon, while Mama Lovelie prepared what she would need to complete the spell, Oksana slept under the shade of the covered porch.

-o-o-o-

You deserve a better life than slavery, Oksana," Augustin whispered against her temple, his arm shifting to cradle her more closely against his chest. Oksana blinked up at the waving branches of the tree above them, patches of blue sky shifting and appearing between the ever-moving leaves.

"No one deserves slavery, Augustin," she said quietly. "Unrest is spreading across the island, even now. There will soon come a day when those who have been trodden down will rise up and demand their freedom."

They were propped against the old tree's thick, knobby trunk, hiding away from the prying eyes of the household. For months now, the two of them had been sneaking away to catch private moments with each other — stolen kisses, soft words, fleeting caresses.

"I know," Augustin said, his voice heavy with foreboding. "And you're right, on both counts. Your mother certainly didn't deserve the treatment she received at your father's hands. In fact, I wake every morning asking myself how you can even bear my touch, after what she endured."

"That was different," Oksana said quickly, pushing away from his chest so she could look at him. "Don't you ever compare yourself to... that man!"

Oksana's father had been a white French slave owner, and her mother had been his property. So had Oksana, until the Frenchman had sold her to Augustin's father at the age of ten. Augustin had been only a year older than she was, in fact. As children, they'd had little direct contact, though Oksana occasionally caught Augustin watching her with interest as she went about her duties.

Shortly after he turned seventeen, Augustin's father had died of a fever, leaving him in charge of the plantation and all its slaves. Three years later, Augustin had kissed Oksana for the first time, setting her heart alight and altering the shape of her world in the space of a heartbeat.

He was her owner, and she was his property. Just as Oksana's mother had been her father's property. But there, the resemblance ended.

Augustin had never forced Oksana, only wooed her. He had never exerted his power over her to gain what he wanted. He had only ever shown her his love, and she loved him in return.

Now, her beloved gazed up at her with soulful blue-gray eyes and an earnest expression. "How can I fail to compare myself to him?" he asked. "Until now, I've been no better than he. But that changes, today."

She stared at him in incomprehension. "What are you saying, Augustin?"

"Today, I am asking you to become my wife."

Oksana blinked several times in rapid succession, certain that she had heard him incorrectly. "Wh-what?"

"I want you to be my wife," he repeated. "A free woman of color. In fact, I intend to free all my father's slaves and offer them honest, paid employment instead."

Augustin's lips widened into a hopeful smile as Oksana stared at him, completely dumbfounded. "Please say yes, Oksana."

"Yes!" she blurted. "But... what will the other slave owners say?"

"Why should I care?" he countered. "I have never allowed the words of others to influence how I manage my own affairs."

Oksana opened her mouth and closed it again, unable to think of any reply to that.

Augustin lifted her hand and brushed his lips across her knuckles, setting her skin tingling.

"I care nothing for what they say, Oksana," he continued. "I want you. I want you now and forever. You are irresistible, intoxicating, and blazingly intelligent. I would be proud to stand next to you and support you as we flourish together."

Leaning forward, Oksana grabbed the front of his shirt and brought their lips together in a searing kiss.

-o-o-o-

She woke with a start, breathing heavily as she tried to orient herself. Looking around with wild eyes, she found that she was reclining in the shadows of a sleeping porch overlooking a small, flourishing garden. Birds chirped in the distance, and the same sweet-smelling flowers bloomed that had been blooming in Haiti for hundreds of years.

"I thought I heard noises," a concerned voice said. "Nightmare?"

Oksana rolled into a sitting position and whipped her head around. Mason stood in the doorway. Unbidden, tears rose to her eyes and overflowed at the sight of him. His expression morphed into shock, and he was kneeling at her side in an instant, his fingers tilting her chin so he could look at her more closely. Energy rippled between them at his touch.

"Oksana," he breathed. "*Christ.* Your eyes—"

She swiped at her cheeks, unaccountably embarrassed by the watery, rust-colored streaks that she knew would be there.

"Sorry," she said wetly. "Sorry, it's nothing. I'm not sick or hurt—the blood in my tears is just a vampire thing. I'm fine."

Mason's face lost its panicked edge, but he didn't let her go. "You're not bloody fine. You're crying."

Yeah... bloody crying, she thought, a bit hysterically. *Bloody tears...*

God. He needed to stop touching her like that, before she —

"Please don't cry," he murmured. "Whatever it is, we can —"

She surged forward and kissed him.

For a moment, he froze, and so did she — appalled by what she was doing. Then, he made a low noise into the kiss. Before she knew what was happening, gentle, unassuming Mason — physician to Haiti's hurt and frightened children — had his hands tangled in her hair and was taking possession of her mouth as though he would die without the feeling of her breath mingling with his.

Oksana's undead heart slammed against her ribcage, the ragged rhythm echoing the word *home... home... home...* along every fiber of her body. The spark of energy between them flared almost painfully, before settling, warm and intense, along her nerves. She changed the angle of their mouths, lips slanting against his as the kiss deepened.

And just like that, she was no longer kissing a man she'd met only days ago — she was kissing Augustin. The sense of completion — of utter, incontrovertible *rightness* — flooded her until she thought she would overflow with it.

"Oksana..." he murmured into their shared air. "*God...*"

Their foreheads rested together for the space of a handful of heartbeats, and then he was delving into her mouth again, his tongue tangling with hers. She didn't realize that she'd climbed onto his lap until the brush of her breasts against the hard muscles of his chest sent a wash of heat rushing through her to settle low in her belly.

The sudden clench of need in a part of her that had been cold and dead for so long was beyond shocking. Her body was still trying to get closer, closer, *closer* to his, as if she could somehow climb inside of him and disappear. As if merging their bodies might finally knit the torn parts of her soul back together.

Someone was making a high-pitched, needy noise. At first, she didn't even recognize the whimpering sound as having come from her. One of Augustin's hands had abandoned her hair in favor of sliding down to rest low on the small of her back, pressing her hips to his where she straddled him. His hard heat ground against her liquid warmth through two layers of clothing, and with no further warning she was gone — completely lost in the past.

Instead of straddling Mason on a shabby mattress, she straddled Augustin in a huge four-poster bed, curtained by gauzy white material that turned it into a cozy love nest, hidden away from the outside world.

Augustin cradled her face tenderly, pressing his lips gently to her cheeks, her forehead, her eyelids — teasing her until she caught his mouth with hers for a proper kiss. She pulled away after a few moments, meeting his hazel eyes, her expression sobering.

"Augustin, I want to, but we can't right now. I have to leave before dark, so I can perform the ceremony."

Augustin tucked some of her braids behind her ear and regarded her seriously. "You believe one of your spirits will descend tonight, to tell you the best place and time for the slaves to rise up?"

"I hope they will," Oksana said. "Lately, it feels as though the loa are pulling away. It frightens me. I don't know what I've done to offend them."

He stroked his knuckles over the curve of her cheek, and she closed her eyes, savoring the caress.

"Do you think it's because of me?" he asked after a short pause. "Because you married an outsider?"

She drank in his handsome European features, troubled by his words. "You've done as much for our people as anyone, Augustin. Supporting the slaves behind the scenes. Talking to the slave owners and trying to sway them toward emancipation. Why should the loa punish me for loving you?"

Augustin's lips twitched in a brief smile. "Why do supernatural beings do anything?" he asked. "If you think it would help, I'll come along tonight and offer a sacrifice. There's a bottle of fine rum in the cellar, and I daresay we can spare a cockerel or two in pursuit of a good cause."

Oksana smiled brilliantly and kissed him again. "You're a horrible Catholic, my love," she said. "Has anyone ever told you that?"

He snorted. "So many times I've lost count, starting when I was six and asked the local priest why he was wearing a dress instead of trousers. I have a poor track record with deities and their earthly representatives, I fear. Now, shall I come tonight? Even if my offering doesn't sway the spirits, you know how much I adore watching you dance."

Love swelled in Oksana's heart until she thought it might burst. "Yes. Come along with your rum and your cockerel. Who knows? It certainly can't hurt."

The tiny part of her mind that still maintained some awareness of the present quailed. *No, no, no,* it chanted. *Don't come along… please, no, you mustn't!*

But it was too late. She and Augustin were no longer in the cozy, gauze-curtained bed. Instead, they were outside, and it was dark.

No, no, please, no…

The ceremony was a small one. Large gatherings risked too much attention these days, with tensions running as high as they currently were between the slaves and the foreign plantation owners.

About a dozen people gathered around the trunk of an ancient mapou tree, chanting and offering sacrifices to Papa Legba—the gatekeeper of the spirit world. Oksana felt unaccountably off-balance. The energy tonight felt... wrong. She wasn't alone in the feeling, she could tell—several of the older slaves were busy setting out geometric markings of protection on the ground around the group, while others hung trinkets in the branches to appease the angry spirits.

Oksana raised her voice in rhythmic song, calling for the protective spirits to come down and join them. She was aware of Augustin seated on a blanket nearby, watching the proceedings with the same fascination he always did. At first, his presence had made the others nervous, but his respectful demeanor and the offering of one black cockerel and one white cockerel in addition to the bottle of good rum had quickly appeased them.

Now, if only it would appease the loa.

It frightened Oksana on a deep level to feel the way the spirits seemed to be avoiding her lately. Since her childhood, they had been as much a part of her life as any earthly presence. But now, when she needed them most, they floated just out of reach.

She felt vulnerable. Unprotected. When the oldest of the hounci present in the circle cried out, "The loa do not favor us tonight! We must close the portal to the spirits before evil enters," it came as no surprise. Several other voices rose in agreement, breaking the chant.

In the very next moment, freezing black fog descended from the mapou tree's branches. She heard Augustin shout something, fear in his normally steady voice. Before she could call back, though, the fog surrounded her, filling her mouth and nose like foul, oily water.

Oh, my child, crooned a chilling voice, *you thought opening yourself to these foolish folk spirits would make you strong. Instead, they only opened the way for me.*

Oksana flailed, panic overtaking her. She tried to flee, to escape the suffocating mist. But she couldn't even breathe without drawing the darkness deeper inside herself, and jagged flashes of light started to flash behind her tightly closed eyelids as her lungs burned.

Begone, she thought desperately. *Begone, evil spirit, begone!*

The dark voice laughed, a grating sound that scraped against her skin like sandpaper. *Witless girl,* it taunted. *You think yourself more powerful than me? You have much to learn.*

A terrible weight drove Oksana to the ground, crushing her until she felt ribs snapping like sticks. She opened her mouth to scream, but the greasy black fog rushed in, choking her before she could emit so much as a squeak.

You are mine. I will do to you whatever I please. Take from you whatever I please. And what pleases me tonight is to take your soul.

A horrible tearing feeling in her chest brought tears to her eyes. At first, she thought her broken bones must be slicing into her organs, but it was even worse than that. Fire erupted inside her, burning up every bit of moisture in her body. An agony worse than anything she had ever known overtook her. Her last thought, before thought became impossible, was a plea for the spirits to protect her — to protect Augustin and the others from this terrible evil.

There was no reply.

-o-o-o-

Thirst beyond bearing brought her back to something that might have been called awareness. She was empty, so very empty, and if she didn't fill herself up *right now*, the madness swirling at the edges of her mind would consume her.

"Oksana!" The hoarse shout was audible now through the clearing darkness. The fog disappeared, sinking into the ground she was lying on. "Oksana—dear God, no!"

Hands were grasping her, lifting her, cradling her against something warm that thrummed with the nourishment she craved. She *had to have* that warmth, that life, that sweet liquid rushing under the tender barrier of skin. She had to have it *now*.

Nothing else mattered. Her terrible injuries didn't matter. The cries of fear and alarm echoing around them didn't matter. Only the gaping emptiness mattered. Only the succulent, rushing fount of life hovering over her was real.

"*Loup garou!*" other voices were crying. "Hurry, hurry! Get nets and weapons!"

Hands tried to drag the thrumming source of life away from her, but it only held her more tightly, growling, "Get away from us—get your hands off! *I'm not leaving her!*"

She groaned, the sound scraping along her parched throat like broken glass.

Gentle fingers tilted her face upward, until her lips and teeth were only inches from throbbing veins hidden under thin, breakable skin. A blue-gray gaze looked down at her, wide and frightened.

"Oksana, my dearest love," The voice choked. "Mother of God, your eyes! What has happened to you? What can I do?"

Another voice answered. "You can do nothing for her, *blan*. Evil has stolen her soul! You must get away from her, before she kills you and uses your blood to strengthen herself!"

The hands holding her tightened again, and Oksana's lips pressed against the salty flesh — all that stood between her and what she needed to fill up the emptiness. Her canines lengthened and sharpened, scraping at the inside of her cheeks.

"Wait," the voice above her said, oblivious to the threat she posed. "She looks so pale. You say my blood can... help her, somehow? Can strengthen her? I've seen your people give blood offerings to the loa before —"

"No, fool! You mustn't!" The other voice cried, even as her fangs sank into the delectable banquet before her.

Her victim gasped, shuddering in her grip as her fingers dug into him like talons. "Oksana," he croaked, "It's all right, beloved... if this will save you —" An ugly gurgling noise erupted under the choked words. "All I have is... yours... it always has been..."

The sweet lifeblood flowed over her tongue, bringing relief from the agony of thirst and longing. She shook her head back and forth savagely — a mindless attempt to get *more, more, more* until the spurts slowed to a trickle, and then, to nothing.

She wailed in frustration, giving the bloodless corpse a final shake and letting it drop. More warm bodies approached from behind her. She whirled, ready to pounce, but a heavy rope net enveloped her before she could spring at them. The wail rose to a shriek as she tore at the tangled ropes confining her.

"Is he dead?" frantic voices babbled. "Did she kill him?"

Something about the words penetrated the haze of bloodlust in her mind, and a new kind of emptiness replaced the aching thirst. Her thoughts were still mired in animal rage at the net trapping her, though, and she could not concentrate on the slow-growing feeling of dread hiding beneath the panic.

"Is she cursed? What should we do with her?" the onlookers asked, and the commanding voice replied,

"Bring a coffin, and someone go find me an iron spike and a mallet."

Oksana roared, her body twisting and rippling. Feathers erupted from her blood-soaked skin, her limbs trying to contort into new shapes and failing.

"Look. Her human soul is gone," the commanding voice intoned. "She is *loup garou* now. She is cursed, and her spirit has merged with an animal's. Give me one of the poisoned darts."

A moment later, something sharp pierced her neck and lodged there. She tried to scrabble at it with her hands, but they were hopelessly tangled in the ropes. She struggled and spat and screamed and snarled, but the dart remained lodged in place.

Numbness stole across her senses by degrees, radiating outward from the stinging point embedded in her neck. Her feverish thrashing grew slower. Less coordinated. Gradually, her body went limp. Her open eyes stared upward. She was aware of what was happening, but unable to move or make a noise.

She was aware of the net being removed.

She was aware of Augustin's broken body lying nearby like a child's discarded rag doll, when the jostling as she was moved made her head loll in that direction.

She was aware of being lowered into a simple wood coffin, and of the fierce agony as they nailed her left foot to the bottom with the iron spike, to keep her from wandering free of her grave.

She was aware of the lid closing, and the coffin being lowered into a hastily dug hole.

She was aware of the dirt raining down on top of her, burying her and muffling the sounds from above until there was nothing but the noise of her sluggish heartbeat reflected back at her.

She was aware of the air growing stale. A board in the coffin lid cracked under the weight of the earth above. When a trickle of fine dirt started raining down onto her face, she couldn't even move enough to close her eyes or roll her head out of the way. Blind panic swallowed her, sending her into the blessed relief of darkness.

When her consciousness returned, the paralysis had lifted. She flailed, trying to get away from the soil covering her eyes, nose, and mouth. Her arms hit the side of the coffin and her forehead impacted the lid, which lay only inches above her face. At the same moment, her left foot exploded in icy agony as it jerked against the iron spike nailing it in place.

Unaccustomed strength flooded her limbs. She went mad, tearing at wood until she could reach her left leg, then tearing at flesh, sinew, and bone with the single-mindedness of a trapped animal set on escaping its prison at *that very instant*, or else dying in the attempt.

There was a horrible cracking noise, followed by a ripping, tearing sensation, and she was free of the icy burn of the iron that had pierced her. The coffin lay in splinters around her, dirt sliding and shifting in to take its place. She turned her attention to the wet weight of it pressing down on her from above, clawing at it with bloody fingers.

-o-o-o-

Escape was the only thought in Oksana's mind as she scrambled backward, away from arms that tried to hold onto her for only an instant before letting go. Someone was saying something—sharp words of worry. Questions. She couldn't understand any of it. Nearby, the sun burned in a sky hazy with low clouds. She fled its terrifying heat, seeking shelter in the darkest place she could find, aware that she was half-stumbling, thumping into walls and using her hands to pull herself along.

When she could go no further, she put her back against an unyielding surface and curled up into a ball, rocking. Her eyes were unfocused; her mind blank as it tried to reject the horror of what had been done to her. Of what she had done to herself.

Of what she had done to the man she loved.

Time passed; she could not have said how much. A silhouette filled the doorway, its shape familiar. Oksana blinked, and the silhouette resolved into Xander, bleary-eyed and disheveled from interrupted sleep. He paused, looked at her intently for a long moment, and then wandered further into the room, giving her a wide berth. A moment later, he fetched up against a bare stretch of wall next to a low altar lit with candles, and slid down to sit across from her, still regarding her with a steady green gaze.

"Did I wake you?" Oksana asked faintly. She looked around at the space Mama Lovelie used for ceremonies, taking it in, along with her position jammed into one corner. "Sorry—I didn't realize I wasn't shielding. I don't... quite know what just happened." She scrubbed at her eyes. They were wet.

Xander drew his knees up and rested his chin on them, searching her face. "No, Oksana. You didn't wake me," he said, with studied casualness. "Your cute doctor did. Said you, and I quote, 'demonstrated several symptoms typical of a PTSD episode,' and I should come check on you. You want me to go get Duchess for you instead? I'm afraid I'm no one's idea of emotional support."

Oksana shook her head. "No, let her sleep. Again, I'm sorry about that. I don't know why Mason woke you rather than just coming after me himself."

A smirk tugged briefly at one corner of Xander's mouth, making the years fall away from his handsome face. "Ah. Well. About that. I might or might not have given him the shovel talk the other day, you see."

Oksana blinked, her eyes going wide, some of her earlier horror draining away to be replaced by shock. "Xander. You didn't."

Xander shrugged, still watching her. "I might've done. So, talk to me. What happened? Do Duchess and I need to start scouting places to dispose of a body?"

Oksana shivered and looked away. "Don't even joke."

But Xander wouldn't let it go so easily. "Oksana. Did he do something to upset you?"

She scowled at him. "No, he didn't. Don't be ridiculous."

"Then, what?"

Another tremor wracked her, and she hugged her knees. "We were... sitting together on the veranda. It was nice, at first. But then, I started remembering the night I killed him. The night Bael tried to take me." She met Xander's eyes again. "Did you know my foot is still buried here on the island somewhere, in an unmarked grave outside the capital?"

His brows drew together. "I'd always wondered why it didn't just grow back. Jesus, Oksana." He took a slow breath and let it out. "You know, the others almost seem to delight in wallowing in the horrific natures of their pasts. But you and me—we're different. We really... don't. And I'm starting to think... maybe... we're not doing ourselves any favors by pretending that horror never happened to us."

"I can't go back there, Xander," Oksana said. "I can't. If being with him means reliving it like this, I don't know what I'm going to do."

Duchess chose that moment to enter the room, silently crossing to curl up at Oksana's side and pull her into a one-armed embrace. "It will work out somehow, *ma chérie.*"

To Oksana's surprise, Xander rose and crossed to crouch in front of her, pressing a chaste kiss to the top of her head. He stroked a callused, long-fingered hand over her hair before settling back to sit on his heels.

"It will, you know," he agreed. "If His Royal Broodiness and the Emotionally Constipated Bookworm can make it work for them, I have no doubt you can do it as well. You're probably the most deserving of any of us. Right now, though, I'm honestly more worried about this vodou spell. Are you absolutely sure you won't let me confront the bokor instead?"

"Or better yet, let me do it," Duchess said. "As I said earlier, I'm the oldest, and the most powerful. Xander's a mere babe in arms by comparison — barely past his hundredth birthday."

Oksana shook her head. "No, it won't work right. The loa are African folk spirits. You two don't have the same connection with them that I do. Let's save Xander's youth and your power for putting me back together afterward, in case it all goes wrong, shall we?" She looked down at her prosthesis, and her voice turned wry. "Well, the parts of me you can find, at any rate."

Duchess pulled her in close and pressed a sisterly kiss to the top of her head in the same place Xander's lips had brushed earlier. "Always, *petite soeur*. You know we'll never let you fall apart."

TWELVE

Mason paced up and down the short hallway in front of the door where Oksana had disappeared after fleeing his embrace. His hair was mussed from running his hands through it, and his emotions felt just as messy right now.

She'd kissed him. And what a kiss it had been, until—

The door opened, and Oksana emerged, still looking pale. Her friends flanked her on either side, and she looked up at each of them in turn, as if for support. Duchess squeezed an arm around her shoulders before letting it slide away, while Xander placed a hand on her back in a brief, supportive gesture. Then, they peeled away and left her alone with Mason. Xander's disconcerting green gaze pinned his for a long moment as he walked past, heading toward the sitting room.

When the others were gone, Mason looked at Oksana, trying to quiet the muddle of worry, attraction, and existential dread currently clamoring for supremacy.

"You've been assaulted in the past, haven't you," he said, not even making it a question. "I've seen that kind of reaction before. It was a PTSD flashback. I won't ask you to tell me details unless you want to, but please tell me how I triggered you, and how I can avoid it in the future."

If anything, she paled further. "You already know how I was assaulted," she said, and her voice was steady even if her hands were shaking. "A demon violated me and tore my soul into pieces. He left no part of me un-touched." She bit her lip, worrying at it for a long moment. "But... when I told you about that before, I didn't tell you about the worst part."

He frowned. "You don't have to —"

She interrupted him. "In the mindless bloodlust that followed, I ripped out my husband's throat with my teeth and drank his blood until he died."

Mason's stomach lurched, as he tried to reconcile what he knew of the woman before him with the words she'd just spoken. If she hadn't stated it so calmly, so matter-of-factly, he might have been able to convince himself that it was part of some delusion or bizarre cop-ing mechanism her mind had come up with to deal with past trauma. But...

"Several people witnessed it," she continued in the same flat voice, "and men from the village brought a heavy net to trap me. There was a hounci present. He knew the secret of preparing poisons laced with magic. I was still weak, and the villagers managed to subdue me with the poison long enough to seal me in a coffin. They nailed my left foot to the bottom to keep me there. Then, they buried me alive. As soon as the poison wore off, I broke my own leg and ripped it free of my body to get loose. Once that was done, I clawed my way up from the grave. They'd left a teenage boy behind to keep watch over me for the first few nights. I killed him, too. I didn't regain anything approaching sanity until days later, when I found myself crawling aimlessly around a cane field in the dark, dragging the bloody stump of my left leg behind me."

Mason felt blindly for the wall behind him and half-slid, half-fell into a seated position against it. "And... this is what you flashed back to, when we kissed?" he asked, his voice a hoarse whisper.

She nodded slowly, still looking a bit distant. A bit untethered. "It's because of Augustin. My husband.

You're hi—" She paused, as if reconsidering her words in mid-sentence. "You… remind me of him."

He looked up at her dark, angelically beautiful features, lost for words.

"We should go after the others," she continued, as if they'd been discussing lunch plans rather than murder, vivisepulture, and violent self-dismemberment. "Mama Lovelie will be wanting to perform the spell on me soon."

She reached a hand down to him and he took it without thought. The contact tingled, and the strength that lifted him to his feet was—

Inhuman. Her strength was inhuman. Her balance as she hefted his larger frame upright didn't waver a millimeter, despite the prosthesis on her left leg. A few more chunks in the foundation of his rational belief system crumbled, leaving him off-balance, even if *she* wasn't.

"I want to talk more about this," he said, hearing his voice as though it were echoing through a tunnel.

She nodded, the movement small and hesitant. "After we rescue the children, though," she said. "We need to stay focused on them right now."

"All right," he replied after a beat, not sure if waiting would make the conversation easier or harder.

They followed the path the others had taken, back to the room with the mismatched chairs. Inside, in addition to Duchess and Xander, Mama Lovelie awaited them with three young women in their late teens or early twenties. The newcomers appeared nervous but determined.

Mason looked at the mambo in confusion, wondering if these three were supposed to be part of this spell ceremony… thing, and if so, in what capacity. Xander pinned Oksana with a stern look, and Mason caught her brief grimace in response.

"Our hostess ordered in for us," Xander said mildly. "No need to go out for takeaway tonight. We might've had a rocky beginning, but I'm starting to warm to her."

It took a moment for Mason to manage a vampire-to-English translation, and when he did, he blanched. Xander couldn't mean —

"Hello," Oksana said quietly in Creole. "Do you understand why Mama Lovelie brought you here?"

One of the girls seemed a bit braver than the other two, and she stepped forward, her chin jutting out.

"Yes," she said in the same tongue. "You're night-walkers, and you're going after the missing children." She gestured to the young woman next to her. "Our brother was taken." She jerked her chin toward the third girl. "So was her little sister. The mambo says you need blood to bolster your strength before you go off to fight the bokor. You can have ours."

"I'm fairly sure this marks the first time I've ever had someone volunteer," Xander mused. "It's a bit odd, honestly."

"The first time?" Duchess muttered. "Really? I'll introduce you to some Goth clubs I frequent in Los Angeles one of these days."

Mason felt Oksana sigh more than he heard it.

"You're certain?" she asked the girls, and all three of them nodded. "Very well, then. Do you want to forget afterward that it happened?"

"No," said the young woman who had spoken up earlier. "This makes me feel like I'm doing something to help."

Her sister nodded agreement, but the other girl raised her hand in a tentative motion, like a student in a classroom. "I'd... rather not remember. I don't like blood."

"Of course," Oksana said, her demeanor softening. "Come here, *pitit mwen*. Thank you for your gift — you are very brave. I promise you won't feel a thing, or remember it happening."

The girl swallowed and shot a look at Mama Lovelie, who smiled and nodded encouragement. "Go on, child. I'll make sure nothing bad befalls you."

She squared her shoulders and came forward, taking Oksana's hand when she raised it invitingly. Oksana glanced in Mason's direction for a bare instant before her eyes slid away, as though she were embarrassed at the idea of him watching.

For Mason's part, his thoughts were still whirling so badly that he didn't know how to react. Again, the part of him that was a doctor cried a silent warning about the dangers of bite wounds, infection, and bloodborne illness. His inner scientist anticipated the next few minutes with detached fascination. And the man in him ached for the woman he was so quickly growing to care about.

Unsure what to say, and feeling every inch the outsider that he was, he kept quiet.

Duchess flickered an eyebrow at him that seemed almost challenging. "No words to offer, *Docteur*?" she asked blandly.

Mason met her gaze and then Xander's, but his eyes were on Oksana as he spoke. "I trust you wouldn't be doing this if there was any danger to you, or to these young people. Given that, I'm not really in a position to speak on the subject, beyond wondering why none of you approached me if you needed blood."

"It seemed rude to ask, under the circumstances," Xander said, "and, besides, I don't particularly relish the idea of going into a dangerous situation with a human suffering from a temporary iron deficiency."

Oksana's eyes flickered to Mason's and away again, then she seemed to steel herself, her attention solely for the girl in front of her. "Don't mind them, *ti chou*. Look at me for a moment. That's it…"

He watched as the girl met Oksana's glowing violet gaze, her plain features going through a complicated series of expressions before growing slack. Her eyes drifted closed, and a hint of a smile played at her full lips.

"There, now," Oksana said, brushing her knuckles over the girl's cheek. "Nothing to worry about."

The young woman made a noise of sleepy contentment and did not resist when Oksana lifted her left arm, cradling her wrist. Oksana paused, tension visible in her shoulders, her eyes darting to Mason's yet again. Sensing that he was the one causing her distress, Mason took a deep breath and tore his eyes away.

Across the room, Xander, too, held his—*victim's? Donor's?*—arm, lifting her wrist to his mouth. Duchess was not so coy, and had slipped behind the oldest, most outspoken of the girls and tipped her head to one side, baring her neck. The vampire's eyes glowed vibrant blue as her fangs sank into the young woman's dark flesh.

Mason stared, unable to help it—both captivated and repelled. There was something undeniably sensual about the act. Even drinking from a person's wrist, as Xander was, it looked as much like a seduction as an attack. He fought not to let his eyes return to Oksana, to watch her lips caressing the third girl's skin, but his reaction to what he was seeing was wrong on so many fucking levels—

The process was quick. Much quicker than he would have expected. Before he'd decided on the right words to mentally chastise himself for his decidedly unscientific reaction, it was over. Duchess wiped a tiny trickle of blood from her donor's neck and popped the finger in her mouth, sucking it clean.

Xander flipped the other girl's arm over and dropped a courtly kiss to her knuckles. "All right, poppet?" he asked politely.

The girl blinked, seeming to come back to herself. "Y-yes, nightwalker. I barely felt a thing."

Mason finally lost the battle not to look at Oksana. She was steadying the youngest girl, who looked a bit confused.

"What happened?" she asked, no alarm in her voice, only curiosity. "Mama Lovelie, I—"

The mambo waved her off. "Don't worry, child. You came with the others to offer a blood sacrifice, which was very courageous of you. It wasn't needed after all, though. The nightwalkers will leave soon to look for your sister and the others, and we will tell you when there is news."

"Oh." The girl blinked large brown eyes up at Oksana. "Thank you, nightwalker." She stiffened her spine, lifting her chin. "If you need my blood when you return, you only have to ask."

Oksana smiled, though her eyes were sad. "Thank you, Beatrice. Your offer honors us."

Mason was quite sure that the girl had not told Oksana her name.

With difficulty, he dragged his mind back to practicalities. "You're feeling all right?" he asked, directing the question mostly to the other two villagers, though he watched Beatrice from the corner of his eye. "Not dizzy or weak?"

"A little tired," said the older one. "It's fine though."

"Do have a bit of faith, Ozzie," Xander said, mild irritation crossing his features. "We're not going to impose unduly on people who made such a generous offer. What exactly do you take us for?"

Mason ignored him in favor of addressing the young women again. "Eat something, and drink plenty of fluids tonight. Fruit juice if you have it, or *akasan*. Something sweet."

"Something sweet? That sounds brilliant, actually," Oksana muttered, so low Mason barely caught it.

"Please, just get our siblings back," the oldest girl said solemnly. "No matter what it takes."

-o-o-o-

After the young women left, snacking on the honey cakes Mama Lovelie had given them when they went, Xander turned to Duchess and Oksana.

"That was rather strange," he said, crossing his arms and leaning back against a convenient section of wall. "I wasn't joking when I said no one had ever offered me their blood freely before. Well... no *human*, I mean." He scowled. "At least, not since..." The words trailed off, his eyes growing distant for a moment before he shook it off. "Anyway. It felt different. Unless it's just me?"

"Not just you," Oksana said, her eyes fixed on the floor.

Duchess shrugged. "As I said earlier, there are rare places and situations where humans will offer their blood, though not with a true understanding of what they are doing. I suppose it adds a certain piquancy to the meal."

Mason looked from one of them to the other. "Why would that matter? Blood is blood. Nothing about its composition changes based on the donor's mood. Unless there's something about the stress hormones —?"

Xander waved an irritated hand. "Ozzie. *Ozzie.* We're vampires. We don't live on the chemical composition and nutrients in blood. We live on the life force of the people we drink it from."

Mason tried to let the bizarre assertion roll off his back like all the rest, but he'd apparently reached capacity when it came to crazy proofing himself.

"*Life force*?" he echoed. "All right... seriously. What does that even mean? I'm a doctor. I've seen more people die than I care to remember. Life is nothing more than a collection of chemical and electrical processes. When those processes break down—*poof*. No more life. It's not some magical force that you can take from another person like drinking through a bloody straw!"

Mama Lovelie snorted. "Oh, *blan*. How little you understand, for all your fancy book learning. As certain as you sound, you'd better hope you're wrong... since that's exactly what your pretty *kòkòt* will try to do to our enemy tonight."

He shut his mouth, taken aback.

"Is it time, then?" Oksana asked. "Are you ready to cast the spell?"

"Yes," the mambo answered. "Come, let us go to the altar room."

She herded them back to the room where Oksana had fled earlier, after their kiss. Once there, Mama Lovelie turned to her. "Tell me, child. How do you travel?"

"As mist, or as an owl," Oksana said without hesitation.

The mambo nodded. "Hmm. In that case... hair, feather, blood, I should think."

"More blood?" Xander asked dryly. "No wonder you topped us off first."

Oksana ignored him, twining her fingers through a few strands of hair and tugging sharply, then handing the little tuft to Mama Lovelie. She submitted to another bloodletting without complaint, and Mason watched as the cut healed in seconds.

What happened next, though...

Reality twisted, and where Oksana had stood a moment before, there was now a dark owl with white flecks decorating its wing feathers. It perched on one leg, the other curled protectively against its body, terminating in a stump.

"What — ?" Mason asked in a faint voice.

"Need to sit down for a minute, mate?" Xander asked. "Owl got your tongue, perhaps?"

Duchess held out an arm, and the bird flapped up to perch on it, fluttering its wings daintily for balance before refolding them. Even Mama Lovelie took a moment to admire the striking transformation.

"The goddess is present in you three, no doubt about it," she said softly, before becoming businesslike once more. She plucked a small flight feather from the owl's wing and made a tisking noise when the creature pecked at her in retaliation. "Cheeky…"

The owl spread its wings, and Duchess gave it a little boost as it flapped away. Oksana dropped lightly to the ground an instant later.

Mason's jaw was open. He snapped it shut. "But… that… that's…"

"Hmm… I do believe the realization train has finally arrived at the station," Xander observed. "About time."

"*That's impossible*," Mason finally got out. "And you just did it anyway, right in front of my eyes."

Oksana shrugged, not looking at him directly.

"Everybody out. You're distracting me," Mama Lovelie commanded in a no-nonsense tone. "Leave me be for a few minutes. I'll call for you when I'm done."

They filed out. Mason turned on Oksana. "You're an owl," he said stupidly.

She met his eyes and scowled at him, which was such an improvement over her earlier looks of discomfort and embarrassment that he nearly smiled.

"Well, not all the time, obviously," he amended. "But… how do you make your clothing disappear and reappear? And your prosthesis?"

"Centuries of practice," Oksana growled.

A snort, quickly stifled, came from Xander's position behind him.

"Just wait until she disappears into mist on you at an unexpected moment," Duchess said.

"Okay... look," Mason said, scrubbing a hand over his face. "Either I have, in fact, gone completely troppo, or else I'm here at a vodou priestess's house with a bunch of vampires who can transform into birds, and absorb humans' life force by drinking their blood. Since we're apparently about to go hunting a sorcerer who's turning children into undead zombies, I'm willing to work on the second assumption until the men with white coats and butterfly nets show up for me. Deal?"

"Deal," Oksana said softly.

"Fine by me," Duchess put in. "As it happens, some of my closest friends are clinically insane."

"You do realize that the men with white coats stopped carrying butterfly nets in the nineteen-fifties?" Xander added helpfully.

"Case in point," Duchess murmured.

They were silent for a bit, Mason mulling over what he'd seen, and the others apparently content to let him stew. After what felt like half an hour or so, Mama Lovelie called them back in. She held out a blackened dagger balanced across her open hand. A small cloth pouch was fastened to the base of the hilt with twine.

Duchess looked at the blade curiously. "Isn't that..."

The mambo nodded. "The knife the child tried to use on me, yes."

Mason looked at the soot-covered weapon more closely. "But the fire will have destroyed the poison on the blade," he said. "That's why you had it thrown into the flames, wasn't it?"

She shrugged. "That wasn't me; it was the Maîtresse Dahomey, possessing me. But the poison is of no use to us, *blan*, though the bokor may well try to employ magic-laced poison against Oksana during the battle," she said. "No, it was the knife itself that I needed. It carries the imprint of both the bokor and one of his gros-bon-ange creations. Now it carries Oksana's imprint as well."

Oksana took the weapon, testing its weight and balance. "This will kill him?"

"It will drain him. If your strength is greater than his strength, it will destroy him," Mama Lovelie explained. "You need only break his skin—even a tiny cut will release the magic."

"And if his strength is greater than Oksana's?" Mason asked.

"Then it will destroy her."

"This is utter and complete madness," Mason stated baldly.

"This is warfare," the mambo retorted. "And warfare always brings madness in its wake."

-o-o-o-

Minutes later, the sound of a sputtering engine outside broke the early evening peace. The vampires had been discussing last minute plans and contingencies, but they looked up at the approaching racket.

"Ah, good," Mama Lovelie said. "He came."

"Who came?" Mason asked, angling a glance out the window, where an ancient Ford truck with a generous flatbed was coming to a halt in front of the house, its brakes squealing in protest.

"Beatrice's grandfather used to be the village healer before his oldest daughter—Beatrice's aunt—took over. Their family is one of only three in the village to still have a working vehicle with fuel in it. I asked the girl to tell her grandfather what was happening and request his assistance. I fear that you may have need of additional help."

Mason took that in for a moment. "He was a healer, you say? A medical man? What kind of training does he have—do you know?"

Mama Lovelie shrugged. "The same as any village healer, though I believe he also went to the city to learn from some American missionary doctors for a few weeks when he was younger."

Mason met the others' eyes. "Better than nothing," he said. "If he's willing to risk the danger, this bloke really could be helpful to us."

A stoop-shouldered man with wiry gray curls exited the truck and walked up to knock on the door.

"Come in, Anel!" the mambo called.

The door creaked on its hinges, admitting the newcomer.

"Evening, Esther," he greeted, his voice hoarse with age and cigarettes. "Heard you've got some folks heading out to do something brave and stupid."

"It's almost like he's known us for years," Xander quipped, reaching out to shake his hand. He cast an admiring glance out the window, taking in the ancient vehicle outside. "Love the truck, by the way. Nineteen-fifty-eight F-500?"

Anel gave Xander the same sort of once-over Xander had given the truck. "Fifty-nine, in fact. When they introduced the four-wheel-drive option."

"Ah, brilliant!" Xander enthused. "Though it does sound like your engine timing is a bit off. I could take a peek under the hood for you when we get back."

The old man shrugged, a hint of wry amusement lurking behind his dark eyes. "If you like, friend. Though there's only so much to be done for an aging inline six-cylinder engine with no access to either parts or machine tools."

"Even so," Xander said, "I could still have a look."

Both Duchess and Oksana were staring rather pointedly at their fellow vampire, Mason noticed. A moment later, Xander cleared his throat and backed off a bit.

Mason came forward to take his place and offered his hand. "Dr. Mason Walker. Pleased to meet you. Mama Lovelie said you were a medical man as well, and might be willing to help us?"

"Well met, Mason," the man said, shaking his hand with a firm grip that belied his obvious age. "Call me Anel—everybody else does. If you're going after these poor children, I'll help you as much as I'm able. Though I'm sure you know there's not much to be done for the ones like that girl they buried today."

"Even the use of your truck would be immensely helpful," Oksana said. "We can't ask you to risk yourself by coming—"

Anel made a scoffing noise. "Nonsense. First off, I'm one of very few people who can sweet-talk that old junk heap into running for more than ten minutes at a stretch. And second, one of the few benefits of being elderly and decrepit is that you can take foolish chances, knowing you don't have all that much left to lose."

"Well then," Xander said cheerfully, "welcome aboard. The evening express to Crazytown is about to embark."

"I don't suppose you have any medical supplies with you?" Mason asked. "I know they're scarce these days, but we're not sure what we're likely to find if we do get these kids out."

"I brought along whatever I could scrounge," Anel told him. "Nothing fancy, but I've at least got some clean bandages and herbs for a sedating tea."

Duchess cocked her head. "And did your *petite-fille* Beatrice tell you about the three of us?"

Anel raised a bushy eyebrow. "She did, night-walker. But I mostly leave that sort of thing to Esther, here." He indicated Mama Lovelie with a small wave of his hand. "So, are we ready to go?"

With a deep breath, Mason looked around the group. "As we'll ever be, I imagine. Assuming we know *where* we're going, of course. Do we?"

The mambo answered. "The most recent gossip says that the bokor is holed up in the village of Savaneaux, about ten miles from here."

Anel nodded. "Hmm. Makes sense. The war's already been through there. Not too much left of the place, I imagine. The people who weren't killed will have fled to other villages, most likely."

"In that case, let's get underway," Xander said. "Moonlight's burning."

Anel shrugged. "Fine by me. I can fit two of you in the cab, but the other two will have to ride in the back."

"That's not necessary," Oksana said. "Mason can ride with you, but we'll fly."

"Yes, better to get a view from above," Duchess agreed. "We'll have more of an idea of what we're up against."

"Whatever you say," Anel told them. "Like I said, I try to leave those sorts of things to other people."

-o-o-o-

An hour or so later, the truck was creaking and jouncing along a disused road leading into the abandoned village of Savaneaux. Mason had climbed into the cab of the old vehicle, and when he'd turned back, Oksana and the others had disappeared.

Occasionally, the flash of a feathered wing would appear in the illumination of the ancient headlamps, only to disappear an instant later. Anel kept up a steady stream of conversation, asking Mason about what he was doing back in Port-au-Prince with the child soldiers, and telling stories about the odd and amusing things he'd seen over the years as a village healer.

Distances could be deceiving in Haiti with the rough, pothole-riddled roads, but Mason thought they must be getting close. His suspicions were confirmed a few minutes later when a familiar dark-haired figure appeared in the middle of the road in front of them and lifted a hand, palm out.

"*Merde!*" Anel cursed, hitting the brakes and causing the truck to judder to a stop. "Give an old man a heart attack before we even get to the village, why don't you!"

Flapping wings descended on either side of Oksana, and an instant later, Xander and Duchess were flanking her. She came around to Anel's side of the cab.

"There's no cover to speak of ahead," she said. "We should leave the truck here and go the rest of the way on foot. The engine noise and headlights will draw too much attention. Savaneaux is a little less than a kilometer away, just over the next hill. Anel, you should probably stay here with the truck."

Anel snorted. "Don't be ridiculous. I may be old, but I can still walk. And if you need my help with the children, you'll need it in Savaneaux, not here."

"It will be dangerous, Anel," Mason warned.

"Really?" Anel said dryly. "A rogue bokor tearing children's souls apart and you think it might be dangerous? Not only can I still walk, Mason, but I'm also *not an idiot.*"

As much as he hated the idea of putting the old man in harm's way any more than they already had, Mason knew that they needed his help.

"Then I guess we'd better get going," he said. "We'll take the most vital of the medical supplies with us and leave the rest in the truck. Hopefully the fact that the fighting has already been here and moved on means the supplies — and the truck, for that matter — will still be here when we get back."

"Give me the dagger," Oksana said. "I'll approach with you on foot, while Duchess and Xander fly in and start searching for the children."

Mason rummaged in his pack and came up with the blackened knife, wrapped securely in sackcloth. Something about it sent a shiver up his spine as he handed it over to Oksana. She took it, being careful not to let their fingers brush as she did.

Another faint shock passed through Mason as Xander and Duchess took to the skies—not as owls, this time, but as pale swirls of mist. He'd been warned, of course, but even so…

"Come on," Oksana said, watching them as they disappeared into the night air above. "Let's go."

The approach to the village was indeed exposed. Deforestation was rampant on the island, most of the trees around populated areas having long ago been harvested for building materials and cooking fires. The overworked soil meant that only low tufts of grass and weeds hugged the ground around Savaneaux, offering no cover.

As they grew close, it became apparent that the village was, in fact, deserted. No lamps or hearths lit the falling-down buildings, and the quiet was absolute. So absolute that Mason had sudden doubts as to whether their objective was even here. They were operating on rumor and hearsay, so there were surely no guarantees.

"What happens if we don't find him? Or the children?" Mason whispered.

"He's here," Oksana replied in the same low voice. "I can feel him, and the others have just located the place where he's keeping the children. At least some of them are still whole."

"How can you know that?" Mason asked.

"Duchess told me," she said. "We can communicate mentally across moderate distances, as long as we aren't shielding our thoughts."

Telepathy. That's right, the vampires had fucking *telepathy*. Xander had alluded to something of the sort, but Mason had mostly discounted it. A hundred new questions jostled to join the thousand he already had, but this was not the time. He'd seen enough by this point that his first reaction wasn't to assume she was delusional, though a few days ago it probably would have been.

"All right," he said, quashing any other words that might have tried to slip free.

"Look," Anel said, pointing at a relatively large structure illuminated by the weak moonlight. "The peristil is still mostly intact."

He was right—one corner of the roof had collapsed, but the rest of the open-air building appeared undamaged.

"That seems like a good place for the others to bring the children once they're free," he said. "Can you convey that to them?"

"Agreed, and yes, I'll tell them," said Oksana. "There's no one nearby. Let's go in."

The shadows under the peristil roof were so deep as to be almost impenetrable, even though the structure only had two walls. Anel flicked the wheel of an old metal cigarette lighter, and the tiny flame lit the area around them sufficiently to show that everything of value had been cleared out during the looting.

"This will do," Oksana confirmed, and set to pulling items from Mason's knapsack.

He'd assumed the bottle of spirits inside had been intended for disinfecting wounds or instruments, and the flour, for preparing food if they were forced to stay in the bush with the children for any extended length of time. So he was surprised when she opened both and began sprinkling them onto the dirt floor.

"What are you doing?" he asked.

Anel answered. "She's laying out protective markings, to keep the bokor's power from gaining entrance to this place."

"And here I thought you didn't deal with the spirit world," Oksana chided. "Though I should warn you, if the loa don't favor me, they may not come, and the protection won't work." She straightened, frowning at the bottle and the bag of flour. "In fact, maybe you should be doing this."

Anel waved the words away. "I wouldn't have the first idea about it, nightwalker. Besides, I've never been able to draw anything more artistic than stick figures. *Bad* stick figures, at that. We'll be safer leaving it to you."

Oksana looked unhappy, but she resumed laying out the complex geometric patterns around the edge of the usable space in the damaged building. Anel's lighter flickered out a few moments later, but Mason could still hear her moving around. By the time she was done, his eyes had adjusted enough to make out the other two as darker shadows against the gray.

When Oksana approached him, he lifted a hand, aiming for her shoulder, but finding the graceful sweep of her neck instead. She shivered at the touch, but it didn't feel like a negative reaction, so he let his fingers slide down to grasp her upper arm.

"I'm going now," she said. "Stay quiet and stay inside the markings I laid down. With luck, this won't take long and the others will get the children to you shortly. They're waiting to make their move until I can distract the bokor."

"Can you tell where he is? Will the others know where to find you afterward?" Mason asked, his misgivings growing as she prepared to leave.

"There's a lone person moving around near the square at the center of the village," Oksana told him. "That's where I'm headed."

She started to pull away, but he tightened his grip on her arm.

"Be careful," he said.

"I'm a vampire. We're hard to kill," she replied. "Don't worry about me; worry about the kids."

He took a deep breath. "We need to talk, afterward — once the children are settled. Promise me, Oksana."

That odd sense of foreboding — of dread, almost — was still swelling in the pit of his stomach.

"I—" she began, only to cut herself off. She seemed to waver for a moment, and then a small hand was cupping his cheek, guiding him down to her level. Soft, full lips pressed against his, and his fingers squeezed her arm convulsively.

"I promise," she whispered, after pulling back with every indication of reluctance. An instant later, she slipped away, leaving him with his hand still poised in midair, grasping nothing.

He stood there for several moments, fighting the sick feeling churning in his gut.

"Well, well, Dr. Mason Walker," Anel said. "That's a hard path you've chosen."

His hand fell. "What do you mean?"

The old healer made a scoffing noise. "Loving a nightwalker? Such creatures aren't of our world."

"It's not really something I chose," Mason said. "It just sort of… happened."

He crossed his arms, tucking his hands under his armpits as a sudden chill swept over him despite the balmy island night. What was causing this awful sense of impending disaster? Everything was going smoothly so far. Going exactly to plan, in fact. He started to pace, feeling as if he had to move or he'd crawl right out of his skin.

"You want to follow her, don't you?" Anel said. "You sense that something is wrong."

Mason swallowed the growl of frustration that tried to rise from his chest, and continued pacing. "I can't follow her. I need to stay here and help the children when they arrive."

Silence stretched, broken only by the sound of feral dogs yipping in the distance.

"You should go," Anel said eventually, his voice quiet in the darkness. "I'll stay. I may not have fancy letters behind my name, but I can bandage cuts and calm frightened children—I've been doing those things longer than you've been alive, son. Your heart knows something your mind doesn't about what is going to happen. Best listen to it."

Mason's instincts pounced on the offer, demanding that he accept it and go now before it was too late. He clenched his jaw.

"Are you sure?"

"I'm not in the habit of saying things I'm not sure of, Mason. The village square is in that direction." Anel took Mason's shoulders and pointed him the right way. "Go. *Hurry.*"

Mason took a deep breath and went.

THIRTEEN

Torches burst into flame around the village square, illuminating it as Oksana approached with the dagger held ready in her hand. It was clear that the bokor was making no effort to conceal his presence, for all that he was still hidden from her view.

A laugh echoed around the open space, harsh and chilling.

"Well now, little nightcrawler," a deep voice boomed, "look at you! Neither *loup garou* nor *gros-bon-ange*... whatever am I to make of you?"

She did not respond, knowing the sound of her own voice would make it more difficult to pinpoint the small noises that might alert her to the man's location — the rustle of fabric, the beating of a heart. Oksana looked around carefully. Several of the rough buildings around the edge of the common area were badly damaged, as if by mortars. But a couple on the northwest corner had escaped the fighting relatively unscathed.

She lifted her chin, scanning the shadows with sharp eyes. The darkness under the cover of a front porch was broken by a white slash of teeth bared in a cruel grin.

"Come out. Face me," she called.

The bokor stepped from the shadow of the building, still grinning. His expression reminded her of a shark's.

He was powerfully built, and darkly handsome. The loa had not been miserly in their gifts when they aided him, but the nature of the deal he had struck was visible within his cold, flat eyes. It was apparent from that blank abyss the loa had not been stingy when extracting their payment, either.

I have him, she sent to Xander and Duchess. *Get the children. Hurry.*

"Why would you do this?" she asked the bokor, hoping to draw him out while the others worked. "Why *children*?"

Her enemy titled his head, as if considering her. "The path of least resistance is always the best path," he said. "The spirits require payment in souls—more and more, every year. Children are easy prey. Simple to acquire and to control."

Oksana's stomach churned with disgust, but she forced herself to stay calm and in control. "And when you can no longer make the payments your masters require? What then?"

He laughed, short and harsh. "I will ensure that day never comes. The world's appetite for corrupted innocence is endless. As long as human sheep continue to breed, there will always be children. And there are powerful men in the world who will always pay well for compliant slaves."

Bile rose, hot and sharp. "*Bastian Kovac*," she spit.

The bokor's brows drew together as if she had surprised him, but she was distracted at the same moment by twin flashes of horror flaring through the telepathic link.

Christ! Xander's mental voice was equal parts revulsion and dismay. *Oksana—some of these kids are okay, but a bunch of them have been turned. He's armed them, and—damn it! Look out, Duchess!* There was a moment of confusion across the bond. *—And they're fighting back.*

Oksana nearly clutched at her chest as she felt the sharp stab of Duchess's distress over whatever they were seeing.

Ma petite, her friend said, *this won't be as quick or simple as we'd hoped. Please be careful!*

"Problem?" the bokor asked solicitously, that slow shark's smile spreading across his features again.

Fangs lengthened into lethal points behind Oksana's lips, and she felt her eyes burning with a predatory light. "Oh, yes. You and I have a definite problem. Don't worry, though. If I have anything to say about it, it will only be a temporary one," she said, and sprang at him.

He met her in a clash of bodies, his movements faster than a human's. Shockingly fast, in fact. She dodged and ducked, gauging his strength—also inhuman. She only needed to get in the quickest slash, the tiniest cut, but he was larger, and had a longer reach than she did. Every move she made, he blocked.

She swirled into mist, trying to get behind him, but in the instant it took her to rematerialize, he was always ready and waiting to meet her next feint. The fight became a brutal dance, whirling ever faster as they angled for advantage.

The mental link, which had been quiet as the three vampires focused on their individual fights, flared with agony, the unexpected pain bursting through her shields.

Son of a bitch! Xander cursed, before he tamped down on the unintentional broadcast.

Oksana spun away, staggering back a few steps to gain distance as she recovered from the distraction. In the space of a heartbeat, the bokor pulled a small wooden tube from his belt and raised it to his lips.

A sharp sting embedded itself in the base of Oksana's neck, cold numbness spreading outward from the tip of the poisoned dart. Her eyes went wide, panic clawing at her mind as the past rose up. She stumbled sideways, her muscles growing weak and unresponsive. The view of the village square faded, replaced by the echo of darkness and the memory of wet earth trickling down onto her face through the gap in a coffin lid.

Oksana screamed.

-o-o-o-

Mason made his way cautiously through the silent village, knowing that he'd help no one by running headfirst into the bokor, or anyone he might have here assisting him. The village was small enough that once he was clear of the peristil, he'd been able to see a faint, flickering glow emanating from the direction in which Anel had indicated the central square lay.

He kept to the shadows of the burned and damaged buildings, wincing whenever his feet accidentally kicked against bits of debris. The sounds he made seemed far louder than they probably were, but he couldn't help pausing each time — waiting to see if he'd been detected by anyone, human or inhuman.

With his own hearing strained to the utmost, he could make out indistinct voices coming from the lit space ahead, though not what they were saying. He tried to move faster, but still without drawing attention to himself.

Then, the scream came.

Every nerve in his body jolted into shrieking life, straining toward the sound of *Oksana in danger*. He sprinted forward, all thoughts of stealth forgotten between one heartbeat and the next. Teeth gritted, arms and legs pumping, he rounded the last building blocking his view.

In the center of the open space, Oksana was down, bracing herself on one hand and one knee, the fingers of her other hand scrabbling feebly at something in the side of her neck. The spelled dagger lay forgotten on the ground at her feet. Her eyes were open, wide and unseeing.

A tall, muscular man circled her, grinning down at her with gleaming teeth, his dark face set in lines of cruel glee. Mason didn't stop, didn't think. He just charged — his years as a rugby fullback propelling him toward his target. Dark eyes looked up, flashing with inhuman power, but the bokor had registered his approach an instant too late. Energy crackled around the man's body, but Mason hunched, slamming into him low, under his opponent's center of balance.

It felt like hitting a goddamned brick wall, but at least it was a brick wall that toppled under the on-slaught. Mason's lungs seized, the breath knocked out of him, but he knew he couldn't afford time to recover. He rolled free and lunged toward Oksana, whose eyes had snapped back to the present, blazing violet in the torch-light.

Mason dove for the dagger, his hand closing on the scorched hilt at the same moment Oksana shouted, "*No!*" The word was hoarse and choked with agony, and she scrabbled forward clumsily toward him, her move-ments slow and uncoordinated.

He'd meant to grab the knife and immediately lunge toward the bokor, who was already rolling smoothly to his feet a couple of meters away. All it needed was a cut, supposedly — he just had to break the man's skin anywhere he could.

But as the knife settled in his hand, a strange, terri-fying sensation flooded his body. The blade was pulling at something inside him, drawing the energy from his muscles and the will from his mind. He staggered up-right by virtue of sheer stubbornness, but made it only a couple of steps before he crashed back to his knees, the impact jarring his teeth.

"Mason!" Oksana cried, "Let it go; *let it go!*"

She tried to reach him, but fell flat on her belly, her fingers tangling in the fabric of his loose trousers. His mind was reeling from the sudden weakness. Let *what* go? Did she mean the knife? Was it still in his hand? He couldn't tell... dizziness was clawing at his awareness, trying to drag him down.

"It's draining your life force," Oksana whispered, "trying to add it to mine and fight the poison. But you're human—you're not strong enough! Please let it go!"

Mason toppled onto his side. If he was still clutching the blade, he couldn't feel it... couldn't unclench the muscles of his fingers to release it. Gray fog swirled around the edges of his vision.

A cold laugh came from above them. He rolled his head in the direction of the noise, his heart laboring as it tried to pound faster, while at the same time, all the energy drained out of his body.

"Oh," said the bokor, "this is priceless. Do I have that crusty old bitch Esther Lovelie to thank for this entertainment? It positively reeks of her pathetic powers."

He kicked a booted foot into Mason's side, rolling him onto his back and ignoring Oksana's feral snarl of rage. In his peripheral vision, Mason saw her try to claw at the man's leg, but her movement was slow and he merely stepped out of the way, still laughing.

"Touch him again and I'll torture you until you beg for death," Oksana grated, but Mason could hear the undercurrent of fear behind the threat.

The bokor snorted. "Will you now, nightcrawler? Or will you lie there, helpless, watching while I slit this one's throat before I drive a stake through your rotting heart?"

He strode away, wavering in and out of focus as Mason's vision swam. Drawing breath was becoming a struggle—he had to concentrate very carefully to make his diaphragm pull air into his lungs and push it back out.

Mason saw the bastard walk over to a half-collapsed porch and grasp a thin length of broken board that had once been part of the railing. He jerked at it sharply, and a piece of the wood snapped off in his hand. It was about the length of his forearm and ended in a jagged point where the thin board had cracked and split. He turned and approached again, his other hand pulling a curved blade from a sheath at his waist.

"No," Oksana moaned, her fingers still clenching at Mason's clothing as she tried and failed to rise. "No, no, no…"

Fear had drained away along with everything else inside Mason, but now a single thought crystallized with diamond-edged clarity.

Oksana was a vampire. She was practically helpless — poisoned — and this fucker was coming at her with a sharpened wooden stake in his hand.

The bokor walked casually up to them, his lips twisted in a sadistic smirk. Mason hated that smirk with more passion than he'd ever hated any goddamned thing in his entire life. The fucker used the pointed end of the stake to shove Oksana onto her back and placed the tip casually between her breasts.

"What does it feel like to watch someone with whom you share a soul-bond bleed out onto the dirt, nightcrawler?" he asked, examining the gleaming blade of the hunting knife held in his other hand with casual interest.

Oksana growled and tried to push upright, as though she would impale herself without thought if that was what it took to get to the man standing over them. At the prospect of seeing that stake slide into Oksana's chest and pierce her heart, a massive adrenaline dump flooded through Mason, his body's last-ditch effort to combat the effects of whatever was happening to him.

Was he still holding the dagger? Fuck, he couldn't even tell. This was his only chance, though — *their* only chance. Using the last terror-fueled bit of strength in his body, Mason half-rolled, using the resulting momentum to help swing his heavy, unresponsive arm in an arc toward the outside of the bokor's knee.

His vision clouded over with gray fog, but the bokor cursed and cried out, staggering backward. For an instant, everything went silent... or perhaps Mason's hearing had gone now, as well as his vision. But, no. That theory was shot down a moment later, when the bokor began to howl with agony.

Oh, good, Mason thought, right before the drain on his energy accelerated into a whirling, sucking maelstrom, dragging him toward darkness. The last thing he heard before his senses shut down was Oksana's piercing shriek of rage and denial joining the bokor's.

-o-o-o-

Oksana screamed for help with the desperation of the freshly damned. Her cries echoed through the abandoned village, and also along the mental connection with her fellow vampires.

A few steps away, the bokor's shouts of pain faded into choking noises as his strength failed under the combined essence of her life force and Mason's. His body crumpled to the ground, collapsing into itself until only a pile of dust remained. And still Oksana screamed.

Any satisfaction she might have hoped to gain from the defeat of their enemy was as nothing compared to the sight of Mason's body sagging, the muscles of his chest going soft and lax with a single, slow exhalation. The poison spreading through her bloodstream was the same thrice-damned poison that had paralyzed her on the night she was turned. She could feel it combining with the drain of having Mason's essence siphoned through hers by the knife's spell, the dual forces trying to freeze her limbs into immobility.

But she was no longer a newly turned vampire, weakened from shock and terrible injury. She had been growing in strength for more than two hundred *fucking* years since then, and she would *not* lie here, powerless, while the man she loved breathed his last a mere arm's length away.

Oksana moved, dragging herself forward, forcing her body to comply. Her hands fell on Mason's unresponsive form, her senses questing outward, seeking the spark, the tiny, precious flame that glowed at the heart of every living being.

No, no, no... she chanted, feeling that tiny light flickering like a candle in a hurricane. Feeling the sluggish way Mason's heart stuttered and paused, stuttered and paused.

Desperation lengthened Oksana's fangs and made her eyes glow with inner light. There was only one way Mason could survive the next few minutes. Or rather, there was only one way he could *fail* to survive — but still come back afterward. Even as she plunged razor sharp teeth into his defenseless jugular, the knowledge that her poisoned blood would ultimately be his death sentence burned through her like acid.

She could take from him, rending his soul as hers had been rent, but the willing sacrifice of her poisoned blood afterward would not save him, as Augustin's sacrifice two hundred years ago had saved her.

No. It would only doom him.

And, yet, what else could she do? Turning him was their only chance — even if it was, in reality, no chance at all.

Bloody tears streamed down her face as she pulled his sweetly intoxicating blood into herself, wrapping her decimated strength around the flickering remnants of his life force while praying ceaselessly to spirits who had abandoned her centuries ago.

Please, she beseeched. *Please, help me save him! Somebody... anybody —*

Oksana felt Mason's soul rip free from its moorings, torn by the force of her assault on his blood. But she could not give him back the blood she'd taken—now mingled with hers—without poisoning his weakened body. Instead, she used the remaining strength she had stolen from him to gather up his fractured spirit, trying to keep it from leaking away into the night like water held in cupped hands.

She cradled him close and prayed for a miracle from the only source left to her. Long moments later, the sound of potential salvation reached her ears.

"*Oksana!*" Xander's voice was hoarse with pain. He staggered into the circle of torchlight, covered in blood and clutching one hand against a horrific slash in his side, as if worried about what might fall out if he didn't hold everything in. He stumbled to his knees beside her. "Dear *Christ*—"

Oksana knew how she must look, crouched over Mason's deathly still form with his blood staining her lips and running down her chin. Wild-eyed and tear-streaked.

"Help me!" she begged, frantic. "Xander, oh, god, please! I have to turn him, but I'm poisoned—my blood will kill him!"

In all the decades she'd known him, Oksana had never seen Xander look as shell-shocked as he did now, like he'd been peering into hell and seen things too awful to live with. Some small and distant part of her quailed at the thought of what could have caused that dull, haunted flatness now hiding behind his normally sharp green eyes.

That paled before her terror for Mason, however. Xander blinked, as if trying to recall himself from whatever abyss threatened to claim him. Without hesitation, he tore his fangs into the wrist that wasn't pressed against the open gash in his side. Blood only dripped from the fresh wound rather than spurting, but he pressed it to Mason's slack mouth.

"Make him swallow," he croaked, swaying a bit as he clenched and released his fist, trying to squeeze more blood through his depleted veins.

Oksana forced numb fingers to work, panic lending her strength as she massaged Mason's throat muscles, willing him to swallow even as she strove to keep his shattered spirit from floating away.

"Mason," she whispered, "please don't leave me... *please*, I'm so sorry... I'm *so sorry*."

"Duchess is with the unturned children," Xander whispered, sounding frighteningly weak. "The turned ones collapsed into dust as we were trying to subdue them."

"Mason killed the bokor," Oksana said in a faint voice. "The undeads' existence must have been tied to his life force in some way." She felt the soul cradled by hers flutter weakly. "Xander, I can barely feel him. It's not working!"

Xander swayed again and shook his head as if to clear it. He lifted his wrist to his teeth and tore the wound open wider before lowering it back to Mason's lips. "Keep trying. Don't give up on him, Oksana. You mustn't—you're all that's keeping him here."

FOURTEEN

"*Mon Dieu –* " came a new voice from the edge of the square.

That heartfelt curse was quite possibly the sweetest sound Oksana had ever heard. Duchess slid to her knees next to Xander, blood streaking down her upper body from a bullet graze in the side of her neck, and a thicker trail dripping from a hole blown through her hip.

"Oksana's blood is poisoned, and I'm running on empty," Xander grated. "How much do you have?"

Duchess's china blue eyes hardened. "Whatever it takes, that's how much I have," she said grimly. She eased Xander aside, and he flopped onto his back nearby, grunting.

"Bloody, buggering *shite*," he groaned, still clamping a hand over his side. After a moment, he seemed to get a handle on the pain. "Duchess... the children?"

"With Anel," Duchess replied shortly. She spared only an instant to cup Oksana's tear-stained face in one palm before she set to work, opening her wrist and letting the blood drip into Mason's mouth.

"We should have waited," Oksana whispered. "We should have called the others."

"Doctor *Hero* here should've stayed the hell back and followed the damned plan," Xander retorted in a tight voice, not moving from his spot on his back.

"If he had, the bokor would have staked me while I was weakened by the poison, and then gone after the rest of you," Oksana said, new tears threatening.

"Jesus fuck," Xander growled, and Duchess's expression hardened into granite.

"We were shielding our minds," Duchess said. "Trying not to distract you with what was happening on our end. We didn't know, *petite soeur*."

Her friend's complexion had been porcelain and cream to begin with, but it was already paling to chalk as she drained the contents of her veins into Mason's mouth. Even weakened by gunshots and blood loss, though, Oksana could feel Duchess's power bolstering hers, helping her contain Mason's spirit between them. Xander reached out clumsily, a hand grasping Oksana's right ankle. His younger, badly depleted life force twined with theirs, as well.

She held her breath, waiting. Still praying to any power that might listen. Mama Lovelie had said on two occasions that the goddess — the Angel Israfael — was with her, but Oksana had spent hundreds of years blaming the angel for her trials. If Israfael had not weakened, if she had not ceded the cosmic battle of Light and Dark to Bael, how much suffering could have been avoided?

Please, Angel of Light, Goddess of Love... grant me this one thing and I will dedicate my life to your will, she bargained. *Just this one thing — this one, tiny thing.*

For long moments, nothing happened. Even Duchess's formidable strength was fading, and Xander had nothing left to give except the unspoken support of his presence. Mason's life force dimmed, then flared brighter, flickering in fits and starts.

"Mason," she whispered, "please come back to me. *Please*. Don't leave me alone in the dark again."

That energy sputtered, but then blazed higher. Mason's jaw moved, his throat working weakly under Oksana's numb fingers. Duchess sucked in a sharp breath, and Mason's shaky hand lifted to grasp her forearm, holding it to his mouth.

"That's it, *Docteur*," Duchess said, relief loosening the tight line of her shoulders. "Have it all. Take everything you can pull from me — I'll get more later."

He drank with single-minded focus until Duchess wavered, and finally slumped against Oksana's side. Mason still seemed dangerously weak as well. He did not open his eyes or move again once Duchess's arm fell away from his lips.

But he was *alive*... albeit, sentenced forever to the same shadowy half-life the rest of them were. Oksana held Duchess with one clumsy, heavily weighted arm, and Mason with the other. Xander's weak grip still clasped loosely around her leg.

"Thank you," she murmured to the dark sky above her, and the vampires at her side. Tears shook free of her body, her chest hitching, but she didn't fight to stop them. "Thank you so much..."

They lay together, exhausted, the first indigo wash of predawn prickling against Oksana's back.

"Dawn's coming soon," she rasped. "We'll have to get under cover."

There was a beat of silence.

"That... may actually be a bit of an issue," Xander said.

She tried to drag her tattered composure together enough to take stock. "You and Duchess could still feed from me. Would poisoned blood be better than no blood?"

"Perhaps," Duchess whispered weakly, "but if we're all poisoned, there's no one to feed Mason when he wakes."

"There's no one to feed him *now*," Oksana pointed out with growing worry. "You're both bone dry."

"Anel's still here, looking after the children," Xander said.

As if on cue, an engine coughed into life in the distance. Moments later, the sound changed, growing further and further away until it faded to nothingness.

"Ah," Xander corrected himself. "Anel is *not* still here with the children. Because that would be too easy, apparently."

"He's probably gone to get help," Duchess murmured.

Oksana forced her mind back into gear, knowing decisions had to be made. "Xander, drink from me. My body is already fighting the poison. Between us, we'll get the others under cover, somehow. With luck, Mason will sleep through the daylight hours, anyway. And if no one has come by dusk, we'll... I don't know. Look for some animals for Duchess to drink from, I guess. I heard dogs barking in the distance earlier."

"Dog blood? Be still my undead heart," Duchess mumbled. "I can hardly wait."

"I'm open to alternative suggestions," she replied pointedly.

Since there were none, Oksana eased Duchess and Mason to lie flat, then scooted around to offer Xander her wrist. He took it, and a moment later, she felt the puncture of fangs and the deep, drawing sensation as he drank. When he was done, he dragged the back of his hand across his mouth. She could see that the torn flesh of his wrist was already starting to close over.

"*Ugh*. No offense, luv," he said, as he carefully eased into a sitting position, "but that shit in your blood is truly foul." He went quiet for a moment, as if listening to his body. "Although... on the positive side, now I can barely feel my guts trying to fall out. Of course, I can barely feel my hands and feet, either. Or, you know, my face." His brows drew together thoughtfully. "Actually, I withdraw the *foul* comment. This concoction is kind of growing on me. I don't suppose you have the recipe?"

"Talk to Mama Lovelie," Oksana said, her voice tight. "Just keep it the hell away from me, unless you want a very small, very pissed-off amputee going medieval on your Pommy arse."

"Message received and understood," he replied, and cautiously pulled his blood-soaked hand away from his side to check it. "All right, let's move this circus sideshow indoors before someone here ends up with a bad case of sunburn."

Both of them reeled like drunkards from the poison, barely able to grasp anything with their clumsy fingers. Their legs were weak and uncoordinated.

Oh, how the mighty have fallen, Oksana couldn't help thinking as she and Xander dragged first Mason, and then Duchess, across the dusty square, all thoughts of dignity abandoned in favor of practicality as the sun's rays lightened the eastern horizon.

They made it inside with about five minutes to spare, collapsing in a looted hut that had miraculously escaped mortar fire. There was very little of use left inside, but the roof was intact, which was the most important thing as the sun rose. Flies buzzed around them, drawn by all the blood.

"Well, this is certainly cozy," Xander said, faux cheerful. He nudged a discarded bottle out of the way with his foot. It sloshed as it rolled over, still about halfway full, to reveal a Rhum Barbancourt label. "Oh, you have got to be joking. They looted the place, and left *rum* behind? Now that's just cruel and unusual punishment, that is."

Despite decades spent in the pursuit of rampant alcoholism, as a vampire, without a human's blood to filter it through first, the rum was useless to Xander.

"You could always offer it to the loa in exchange for a conveniently timed rescue party," Duchess muttered.

"Give it here," Oksana said, stretching across, careful to avoid jostling Mason's head in her lap. She made a couple of unsuccessful attempts to unscrew the cap with uncooperative fingers before growling in frustration and breaking the glass neck against the edge of the cook stove next to her.

Xander stared at her as she tipped it up, ignoring the sharp edges of the glass against her lips as she downed the contents. The rum burned in her stomach like acid as her body rejected and neutralized it.

"I won't bother to ask how the hell you can stand to do that, because you never answer with anything more than a shrug," he said finally.

She let the bottle fall to the dirt floor with a hollow clank. "I never answer because you're asking the wrong question," she muttered.

He pondered that for a long moment. "You're right. Forget the how. *Why* do you do that?"

She thought of all the human food and drink she'd forced into her aching gut over the decades—the brief moment of pleasure as her taste buds activated, followed by the discomfort or outright pain as her stomach refused it and her body broke it down into useless waste that offered no sustenance.

"Because Bael cursed me to drink only blood, but he won't stop me from swallowing whatever food and drink I damn well please," she said.

"Even if it hurts like the devil afterward," Xander finished, looking at her with new understanding.

"Even so."

They were quiet after that, huddled in a corner of the hut that would not lie in the path of the sunlight streaming through the structure's small windows. Mason was as still as death, but Oksana could feel the faint, reassuring thrum of the life force hidden beneath his pale skin. If no one came, though... if she or Xander weren't recovered enough to fly for help, what would the evening bring? They needed blood—untainted blood—and she wasn't at all sure an animal's blood would suffice.

-o-o-o-

It was midday, and Oksana was trying not to succumb to the lethargy caused by daylight combined with the magic-laced cocktail of poison slowly working its way out of her veins. She'd been keeping watch while the others—who were in far worse shape than she was—dozed.

The rattle of an aging combustion engine split the peace of the deserted village, growing louder as it approached.

"Xander," she hissed, knowing he was the only one who would be able to muster any sort of useful defense with her if the approaching vehicle carried foes rather than friends.

"I hear it," he mumbled. "It's the same truck, isn't it? Anel's Ford?"

"I think so," she agreed.

Which doesn't mean rebels or someone else didn't hijack it, Duchess sent along the mental link, rather than expend the energy needed to speak aloud.

"What've we got for weapons? Just in case?" Oksana asked, drawing her personal dagger—*not* the spelled one Mama Lovelie had given her—from its sheath.

"Four blades, and a pistol I took from one of the chil-" Xander cut himself off, his jaw clenching. "From one of the undead."

Assuming whoever was approaching was human, there wasn't much they'd be able to do to a group of vampires, unless they'd come prepared for an afternoon of staking or decapitation. Which did not, of course, mean that things wouldn't become very unpleasant, very quickly, depending on how heavily they were armed.

Even weakened, she and Xander could *probably* overpower a truckload of humans using mental influence, unless they burst in with automatic weapons already blazing. The bigger worry, though, was Mason. Oksana honestly had no idea how vulnerable he might be right now. He was alive—turned—but he hadn't drunk his fill from Duchess before her blood ran out. Would he awake as a ravenous berserker, or would he be weak and susceptible to injury or death?

Oksana held her breath as the vehicle rattled into the square outside their shelter. Its rusted doors creaked open, and she heard unfamiliar male voices speaking. She tensed and met Xander's eyes, clutching her dagger in fingers that still tingled with numbness.

The truck doors slammed shut, and the voices quieted. After a tense moment, a new voice carried to them.

"The bokor is dead," Mama Lovelie proclaimed. "I can no longer sense his power here. Ah—it appears the loa have claimed their debt—these ashes are all that remain of him."

Oksana nearly sagged in relief, and Xander slumped back against the wall he'd been using for support. "Oh, good," he said. "The mambo-led cavalry is here. And it sounds like she's brought along some carry out for dinner."

FIFTEEN

Mason's nightmares were all the worse because they felt so frighteningly real. He saw Oksana. His beloved. His wife—her eyes glowing from within as she ripped into the flesh of his throat like a wild animal. Pain tore at his awareness. His lifeblood spurted... pulsed... then slowed to a trickle as his heart stopped and his consciousness succumbed to the darkness.

Now, the same bloodlust flooded him, drawing him toward warm bodies with pounding pulses that sounded like beacons. The emptiness inside him was insatiable, as cold and bleak as the vacuum of space, and if he didn't fill it with that tempting warmth, he would go mad.

Each time he tried to rise, hands held him down—how were they so strong? *Nothing* should be able to keep him from reaching what he needed! But, still, they restrained him, and instead of warm flesh, his fangs—good Christ, his *fangs?*—sank into pale, cool skin. The sweet nectar that flowed through the wounds soothed the ache of icy, burning hunger, and sent tendrils of power coiling through his body, but it still wasn't... *right*. It wasn't the nourishment he craved most.

Blessed darkness claimed him, and when he dreamed again, it was of a woman sitting next to his bedside, weeping silently, her face hidden in one hand. The sun was low in the sky, slanting through a small window to paint the wall across from him with a square of light that hurt to look at.

"Oksana?" he rasped, and the scrape of his voice against his aching throat made him realize that he was awake, and this part, at least, was real.

Her head whipped up, and he was struck again by the rusty brown streaks of her tears. This time, though, the jolt of shock hit him low, in his stomach, making it cramp and rumble.

"Mason?" she asked. "You're awake? Do you know where you are?"

He tried to gather his scattered thoughts into something coherent. "Yes, I'm awake, I think. And... sorry, no idea. What's wrong? What's happened?"

Her expression started to crumple, though she fought against it valiantly. Bits of memory began to trickle in.

Telling her and the others about the missing youngsters.

Mama Lovelie. Anel. The scorched dagger. The—

The bokor.

"Oh, god—Mason," Oksana choked. "I'm so sorry."

The bottom fell out of his aching stomach. "Sorry? For what? You don't mean... the children...?" A new memory slotted into place. He'd done something—he'd left Anel alone, ignored the plan—

She shook her head. "Duchess and Xander were able to save about two dozen of them." Her voice was hoarse. "The others had already been turned."

He digested that for a moment. *Some of them had been saved.* That was the part they needed to focus on. "So, there are two dozen children who are safe, and who wouldn't have been without our help."

She nodded and tried to swipe away the bloody tear tracks on her face, but more spilled over even as she was trying to hide them.

"You're not just crying for the lost children," he realized. "Oksana. Tell me what's wrong."

She stared at him with bloodshot eyes, her chest shaking with emotion for several moments before she mastered it. "I killed you," she whispered. "*Again*. Oh, god, Mason..."

He reached out, grasping her wrist when she would have covered her face again. "Oksana, sweetheart—I'm right here. It might feel like someone used me for punt practice, but I'm sure I'll be right as rain in a day or two."

She gazed down at him, and Mason had never seen anyone look so sad in his life.

"No," she said quietly. "No, Mason—you won't be. You've been turned. You're like me now."

Stark denial stiffened his shoulders and drew his expression into tense lines. "Don't be ridiculous," he said reflexively. "I remember... I tackled that arsehole who was trying to kill you, right? I must've gotten clocked in the head, or something. Maybe I've been out for a while, but I'm fine now—"

She only continued to look at him with that awful expression.

"No. Stop looking at me like that. This is crazy," he said, and cautiously swung into a sitting position. He still felt like someone had squeezed him through his great-granny's laundry wringer, but there was strength in his limbs despite his aches and pain. He pushed past Oksana and stood, glancing around the room until his gaze settled on the small rectangle of sunlight against the wall. It made his eyes water, but he strode over to it, intent on putting a stop to this nonsense right the hell now.

"Look, I don't remember exactly what happened last night, it's true," he said, and stuck his hand into the too-bright light. "But you can see I'm not—"

Agony erupted in his hand, smoke and steam rising from the skin as it blistered. "*Sweet bleeding Christ!*" he gasped, staggering backward. He clutched his wrist, wide eyes flying to Oksana.

She was still in the chair, one hand clenched in the bedclothes, her eyes twin pools of agony every bit as intense as the fiery pain in his hand.

"I'm so sorry," she said again, and fled the room.

-o-o-o-

Mason sat on the edge of the bed, staring at his hand. The pain of the second-degree burns was enough to take his breath away, but as he watched, the blisters started to subside. Intense itching spread across the ruined skin. He could not have said how much time passed, but it was surely only minutes as, right before his eyes, delicate pink skin grew across the damaged area.

At the same time, the ache in his stomach that had formed a sort of somatic background noise intensified. It grew harder and harder to dismiss, though a part of him was trying valiantly to do so.

No, the rational part of his mind insisted. *It's just the power of subconscious suggestion. This is all some kind of huge mistake, or maybe it's just another dream. It sure as hell doesn't mean that you're actually a vampi* —

As though merely *thinking* the word somehow gave it physical power, a stomach cramp doubled Mason over, flooding his mind with thoughts of *hunger violence blood.* Everything around him suddenly seemed terribly loud. There were no warm bodies *inside* the building, but *outside*...

The sun had slipped behind the horizon while he was busy staring at his miraculously healing hand. Between one breath and the next, he was lunging toward the window, and the tempting heartbeats that lay beyond it.

A small figure appeared between him and his objective as if by magic, one hand splayed across his chest to halt his progress. Unthinking rage flickered at his awareness like flame, trying to send his rational thought up in a fiery conflagration.

"*Stop.*" The single word echoed in both his ears and his mind, ringing like a French-accented bell and interrupting the spiral of unthinking, furious need.

He doubled over again, clutching his stomach. Panic overtook anger. "Duchess? Oh, god... what's—what's wrong with me?"

"Nothing is wrong." The hand closed on his upper arm and manhandled him back to the bed with far more strength than it should have had. "Well, nothing like what you're thinking, at least. You're hungry, and you need to feed."

Feed. Not *eat.* Mason shuddered, coming back to himself a bit more. He looked up, taking the blonde vampire in properly for the first time since she'd come in. She looked like hell. He got the impression that wasn't a normal state of affairs for her, to put it mildly.

"Where did Oksana go?" he asked, fighting the growing compulsion to launch himself at the nearest vein he could reach.

"To deal with her issues in private," Duchess said.

While Duchess had never been warm with him during their short acquaintance, Mason was struck by her flat tone and her flat eyes, their usual brilliant blue now looking more like the color of ice.

"Something's happened," he forced out through gritted teeth, clutching at the ravenous pit that was his stomach. The desire to *rend tear consume* rose again. Images from his nightmares flashed through his memory, and a horrible, heart-stopping thought assailed him. "Oh, god—I didn't..." He swallowed bile. "Duchess, did I hurt anyone?"

The children? The unspoken words hung in the air.

She tilted her head, as if assessing him. "No, *Docteur.* You didn't hurt anyone except the bokor." There was a faint pause. "Well, to be accurate, you *did* actually get a decent strike in on Xander while he was helping to restrain you this morning. But the rest of us generally work on the assumption that Xander deserves it whenever someone punches him. Even if he hasn't done anything recently, it's a fair bet that someone, somewhere owes him one."

Mason winced, but his combined relief and mortification disappeared under a new onslaught of hunger.

"Drink," Duchess commanded, thrusting her wrist at him. "And now that you're past the worst of the blood frenzy, concentrate on not doing more damage than necessary. Also, you should try stopping before you're completely full."

"I don't want to hurt you—" he managed, between rounds of painful cramping. To his horror, he felt his canines lengthening into points, prodding at the inside of his lips.

Duchess snorted. "I'm a four-hundred-year-old vampire, *Docteur*. While I may not be quite up to full strength yet, I assure you that nothing you can do to me with your little baby fangs will result in any serious damage."

She might have been several inches shorter than him, with dark circles under her hollow blue eyes and a half-healed furrow the side of her neck that looked like nothing so much as a bullet graze, but something deep in the same part of him that longed for blood recognized the aura of power that surrounded her. Nothing human in him controlled his instinctive grab for that proffered arm, or the way his razor-sharp canines sank into the cool flesh of her wrist. Yet the part of him that sensed her power kept a veneer of control for the first time, drinking without turning it into an attack.

"Better," she approved, when he dragged himself away, feeling deeply discomfited by what he'd just done... yet undeniably sated, at the same time.

He sat back, running a shaking hand over his face.

"I can't... do this," he said, overcome by a sense of *wrongness* that he couldn't escape. "For god's sake, I'm a *doctor*."

"You are doing this," Duchess said, still in a flat tone. "It will be better for you, once one of us can knock some sense into Oksana."

Longing filled him upon hearing Oksana's name, rising with a strength that he didn't understand. He tried to call on logic... to focus on learning more facts about what had happened. About what was happening around him.

"You're injured," he said, examining the furrow in her neck more closely. "Why are you the one feeding me when you've got a half-healed bullet wound and you look like hell?"

"Two half-healed bullet wounds, to be precise," she corrected. "They'll disappear eventually. In the normal course of things, I would feed from one of the others to heal my injuries more quickly. But Oksana was poisoned during the fight. Do you remember that?"

He remembered hearing her scream, finding her on the ground, nearly unable to move. "I saw the symptoms, but I could only guess at the cause. She's all right now, though?" She'd *seemed* all right—if very upset— when he woke up earlier. "And what about Xander?"

"Oksana is largely recovered from the effects, but it still lingers in her bloodstream. Xander was badly injured, and he fed from her even though she was poisoned. It was the only way the two of them could recover enough strength to move us under shelter and defend against possible threats. I did not drink from her, to ensure there would be someone untainted left to feed you."

He remembered Duchess squeezing a few drops of her blood over the cut he'd carved into his arm as a test, mere days ago. "So vampire blood heals other vampires as well as humans?"

"Our blood and saliva do, yes," she said, and then seemed to hesitate. "By rights, Oksana should have been the one to feed you, but we weren't sure how the poison might affect a newly fledged vampire. None of us were willing to take the chance."

His new instincts rose up, as if to cry, *damn right I should have had Oksana's blood*, but he still asked, "Why should she have been the one to feed me?"

"Because you are her mate," Duchess said.

He resisted the urge to tell her that someone might want to inform Oksana of that fact, since she seemed more interested in running away from him than talking to him. Instead, he focused once more on Duchess's words, trying to piece everything together.

"How were you and Xander injured? Did the bokor have guards watching the children?"

Duchess's body went very, very still.

"In a manner of speaking, he did," she said in a flat, deliberate tone. "Ten of the children had already been turned. They were armed with firearms and blades. Xander and I foolishly tried to overpower them without... damaging them any more than necessary. In doing so, we nearly left Oksana to her death—and you, as well."

Mason closed his eyes against the mental image of the two vampires trying to rescue the living without injuring the already dead. "Your opponents looked like kids, even if they weren't, any more," he said. "Of course you'd try not to hurt them."

Her expression didn't waver. "An ill-advised waste of energy and effort. As soon as the force controlling them was destroyed, they crumbled to ash in front of our eyes." She looked at the small window, but he didn't think she really saw the late-evening dusk beyond.

"If you've had your fill of blood," she continued, "then I will leave you now. The humans know to stay out of this building until you gain better control over your impulses. Feel free to move around, but remain inside. When the hunger pangs return, tell one of us immediately."

She left without a sound. Mason sat on the edge of the bed, staring at nothing and feeling his life slowly unravel around him. He was a doctor whose veins apparently ran with a miracle drug, but he couldn't go out during daylight. And at the moment, he couldn't get near a human being without risking descent into a frenzy of bloodlust.

With a fresh pang, he thought about Jackson.

His brother. What in god's name would he tell Jackson? What would he tell Gita?

And why did Oksana continue to flee from his presence, when every newly raised instinct he possessed screamed that they should be by each other's sides? Yet, the touch of his lips on hers—the very *sight* of him, it seemed—sent her into an emotional breakdown. She'd been trying to get away from him since practically the very first moment they'd met.

The idea of facing this new reality, even with her standing steadfast at his side, was daunting. The idea of doing it alone was...

He hurled himself off the bed and started pacing before he could finish the thought. He needed distraction. After casting his mind about for a few moments, he settled on the only one of the three vampires he hadn't seen since he'd regained his senses.

Apparently, he'd slugged Xander a good one at some point while he was out of his skull—and done so while the other man was already injured *and* poisoned. Plus, he'd sent Oksana running off in tears on not one, but two occasions since being on the receiving end of Xander's less-than-subtle shovel talk.

However you looked at it, Mason almost certainly owed him an apology. Of course, he had no way of knowing whether Xander was more likely to punch him in the face in retaliation, or start quietly searching for likely places to stash a dismembered body. But either way, he supposed it would be an effective distraction from the clusterfuck that was apparently his life now.

He found the other vampire at the back of the building, sitting on the sill of a large window with one foot propped up against its side. The glass — if the window ever had any in the first place — was missing, and Xander stared out across the desolate area that might have housed a garden, once. A bottle of something alcoholic looking hung loosely from his right hand.

"Feeling better now, Ozzie?" he asked, without looking away from the darkness beyond the window.

Mason wasn't sure which he was coming to dislike more — Oksana's open anguish, or the others' flat, exhausted monotones.

"Yes," he said cautiously, approaching until he could look out past Xander and into the night. "And no."

The vampire grunted, the sound offering neither encouragement nor censure.

"Do you mind, mate?" Mason asked, taking the bottle of cheap vodka from Xander's slack grip. "God knows, I could use a drink right now that doesn't contain platelets."

He opened it, and Xander finally turned from his study of the barren ground outside to fix Mason with dull green eyes. The smell coming from the bottle was foul, but alcohol was alcohol, and right now he wasn't in a mood to be picky. Xander watched him throw it back… only to collapse into choking and coughing after the very first swallow. He glared at the bottle, hurling it away as if it was a snake that might bite him if he kept touching it.

"Yeah," Xander said. "I could've warned you about that."

"What the—" Mason managed to wheeze. "What the *fuck* is that shit?"

"Vodka, just like the label says." Xander quirked a sardonic eyebrow. "Apparently, something about being on this island makes people want to dump it on the ground. I still haven't really figured that whole thing out."

Mason stared at him. "That. Was *not*. Vodka."

He swiped a hand across his mouth in disgust, the smell nearly overpowering him. The tiny bit that had made it down his esophagus settled in his gut like a hot brand, curling and twisting angrily.

Xander shrugged and went back to looking out the window. "You're a vampire now, Ozzie. If you want vodka, you're going to need to convince a human to drink it for you first. Either that or follow Oksana's example and learn to live with your body throwing a fit over it."

Mason digested this for a few moments.

"Look," he said, when the silence threatened to stretch too long, "I, uh, just came to apologize for slugging you earlier. I was completely off my head the first few times I woke up... but I gather I've got you and the others to thank for keeping me from turning some poor, random sod from the village into an all-you-can-drink buffet while I was troppo."

Xander lifted a shoulder again, and let it drop. "Don't mention it. It's been a decade or twelve since it happened to me, but I remember how it is... right afterward."

Mason regarded him. "How did it happen to you?"

"How was I turned, you mean?" Xander didn't move to look at him as he spoke. "The same way as Duchess and Oksana. I attracted the wrong kind of attention from the wrong kind of evil power, and someone close to me was stupid enough to sacrifice their life in exchange for my worthless arse."

The words were delivered in the same flat monotone Mason was growing to hate, though the bitterness behind them was clear.

"Was it this... demon, then? Bael?" he asked.

Xander snorted, no humor in the sound. "It still twists you up inside to even say things like that, doesn't it, Ozzie? Yes, it was Bael." He paused, and then continued in a quieter tone, as if musing over the words. "It's starting to frighten me, the level of hatred I feel for that filthy stain on the universe. All day, every day, I'm filled with it. It's in the air around me... I breathe it in; it flows through my veins. I spend half my time plotting new ways to hold it at bay for an hour or two. Sex. Drugs. Alcohol. But it always comes *right* back afterward. Seeing those undead children yesterday..."

He trailed off and shook his head.

"This war you've all talked about," Mason said, just as quietly. "Can we win it?"

"Win it?" Xander's eyes flicked back to meet his. "Mate, I have absolutely no idea."

SIXTEEN

Two days later, the others apparently decided that Mason was no longer a danger to anything warm-blooded that came within his reach. Mama Lovelie entered the building where they'd been sheltering, and plans for returning to the village they'd come from got underway.

Duchess had tasted a few drops of Xander's blood and declared it clear of the poison, before drinking from him to heal the remains of her wounds. Oksana was like a ghost, hovering on the edges of conversations, and disappearing the moment Mason started trying to think of a way to talk to her privately. The cloud of guilt surrounding her was a nearly palpable thing.

In some ways, it was a relief to get back to the comfortable house where Mama Lovelie had first sat them down, fed them sweet *akasan*, and calmly demanded payment in vampire blood for their room and board. In other ways, being here was decidedly uncomfortable since it brought Mason one step closer to the inevitable task of dealing with the toppled ruins of his former life.

The satellite phone on the table next to him had been taunting him for hours now. It sat there, as if daring him to pick it up and dial Jackson's number.

He was on the sleeping porch, where Oksana had kissed him four days ago and turned his life upside down. Odd, he supposed, that he marked the upheaval as starting on that day, and not the day when he'd been turned into a vampire.

Steeling himself, he reached for the damned phone. With a sigh, he pulled out the satellite antenna and checked the battery levels — low, but enough for a call. A flick of the power button called up the menu, and he chose the +65 country code for Singapore before entering Jackson's number from memory. Nerves made his foot jitter against the rough boards of the porch, and he stilled it, irritated.

The cheerful GlobalCom tone let him know the call was being connected. It rang twice, three times, four times… and on the fifth ring, a familiar, gruff voice answered.

"Yes? Who is this?"

"Hello, Jack," Mason said quietly.

"Mason! Sorry — I didn't recognize the number. Are you all right, little brother? I was starting to worry, after what we talked about last time, and then not hearing from you for several days."

Mason opened his mouth, but his brain was stuck fast. *Why the hell hadn't he figured out ahead of time what to say?*

"Mace?" Jackson prompted, real worry entering his voice. *"You still there? Hello?"*

He shook himself free of the momentary vocal paralysis. "Yeah. Sorry. I'm here, Jack. It's just… it's been a rough few days."

"Yeah." His brother's heavy tone seemed out of place, but he continued before Mason could question it. *"So, uh, did you find any new information about those missing kids?"*

"We did. And then we found the kids themselves."

"No shit!" Jackson exclaimed. *"Were they okay? Did you get them back?"*

Mason swallowed. "We got… some of them back."

There was a pause, before his brother said, *"Oh, Mason."*

"No. It's good though," Mason said. "There are twenty-two children who can get the help they need now, and hopefully go back to their families if they have any. Only…"

Another pause.

"Little brother – the way you sound right now, you are seriously scaring the ever-loving shit out of me. Something else happened. Talk to me. Please."

He couldn't tell Jackson about what he'd become over a tinny satellite connection. He just… *couldn't*. But if he didn't unburden some of the weight that was pressing down on him like a boulder, he'd go mad.

"I don't really know where to start, Jack," he said. "The children who didn't make it back… what had been done to them… it was so much worse than what I'd imagined. They weren't… *human*… anymore. This man who took them – he stole everything that they were."

"Jesus. You don't mean –"

"What?" Mason prompted.

"You make them sound like those reports coming out of Syria," Jackson said, and even over the poor connection, Mason could hear the same heavy, shell-shocked tone he'd noted earlier.

"What reports out of Syria?" he asked cautiously.

The beat of silence was enough for Mason's stomach to sink.

"Mason… haven't you seen a news broadcast in the past few days?"

The sinking feeling grew worse. "Jack, I'm in the middle of nowhere, in a war torn, third world country that just had its infrastructure shaken by an earthquake."

"Oh, my god. You really haven't heard."

"Heard *what*?" Dread sharpened his tone. "Jackson –"

"They're trying to pass it off as some kind of disease; maybe something to do with radiation exposure after that terrorist nuke went off," Jackson said. *"People acting crazy –*

just mindless and violent, and they keep coming even when the police or military shoot them. Like what they used to say about PCP users going into a berserker rage."

"Oh, dear god... no," Mason whispered.

"I mean, it's obvious the news outlets are trying to downplay it," Jackson continued, *"but, Mason, no matter how they spin it, people are starting to freak out, and I can't exactly blame them. This is some serious next-level, horror movie sounding shit."*

It could be nothing, Mason tried to tell himself. Bad reporting, or news organizations looking for ratings. But every fiber in his being told him that this was real, and he'd just been plunged into it, headfirst.

"Jackson," he said, "I can't prove it, of course, but... I think what we ran into with these kids may be connected somehow with what you're describing. Tell me — have there been any reports like this in Singapore, or elsewhere in your region?"

"No, nothing like that around here," his brother said, and Mason's shoulders sagged in relief. *"Just the same bomb threats and killing sprees as always."*

As if that wasn't bad enough.

"Okay," he said. "Good. That's good. But... do me a favor, Jack. Even if what I'm saying sounds a little crazy. Keep your head down. And if reports like that start popping up near you, grab Yi Ling and the girls and just... *go*. Go on vacation, or something. Go anywhere that those reports *aren't*."

Mason could make out Jack's deep breath before he answered. *"This has really got you freaked, doesn't it."*

Mason closed his eyes for a moment, rubbing at them. "Yeah. It does. If you'd seen what I've seen in the past few days..."

"Okay, little brother," Jackson said quietly. *"Rest easy. I've got no desire to get sucked into playing a bit part in a bad horror movie. Don't worry about us. We're fine. So's Mum.*

You worry about you, especially since it sounds like you're the one living in Zombie Central right now."

He relaxed a bit, mollified. "Thanks. Yeah, I will. Hopefully I'm just jumping at shadows, and all this will turn out to be nothing." A beep sounded in his ear, indicating a low battery. "Um, look—I had to borrow a satellite phone to call you, and I think it's about out of juice."

"Sure, no problem. Just look after yourself, Mace. Oh, and before you go—how are things going with your disaster zone girlfriend?"

Mason grimaced. *Oh, y'know, not so bad,* he thought. *First she kissed me, then she immediately had a panic attack, and the next day she turned me into a vampire.*

"She still runs for the hills whenever I get within a hundred feet of her, thanks for asking," he replied instead.

Jackson snorted. *"Sorry—I'm having a real hard time picturing that for some reason. I don't suppose you've actually—oh, I don't know—told her how you feel? Just a thought."*

"Well, of course I—" Mason began, only to halt mid-sentence. He thought for a moment. "Oh. Shit."

"Uh-huh," Jackson said patiently. *"Look, Mace. The world's going to hell around us. Listen to your big brother on this one. If we're destined to be sucked into a bad zombie movie, you'll want a kick-arse sheila who loves you at your side. Life was already too short, even before the inmates started taking over the asylum. So get off the damned phone and go tell her you want to be with her."*

Mason was quiet for a long moment, the phone beeping its critical battery warning in the background.

"Yeah. Okay." He squared his shoulders. "Thanks, Jack. We'll talk again soon. Hug Yi Ling and the kids for me."

"Sure. Oh, and don't forget—I'm still waiting on that photo of your mystery woman. Goodbye, little brother."

-o-o-o-

Mason was fully intending to take his brother's advice, and just lay all his cards on the table with Oksana. He would do that... just as soon as he could figure out the best time. And the best place. And the best words to use.

It wasn't the sort of thing you rushed into, he told himself. He only had one shot at this, so he needed to make sure everything was right. That was all.

Then, of course, Mama Lovelie informed them there would be a celebratory feast that evening, to mark the defeat of the bokor and the return of the surviving children. Mason didn't get the impression that the other vampires felt any more like celebrating than he did, but turning down the invitation would be beyond churlish.

The village was decked out with as much of a festive air as could be expected in the middle of nowhere during a war. The food, while not rich, was plentiful — even if the smell of it threatened to turn Mason's stomach whenever he let himself focus on it too closely. The dancing and singing dragged long into the night.

Mason made himself take part. In a way, it was a sort of test, to wander among so many humans and interact with them as *people*, rather than as walking ready-meals. Of course, he'd made a point of topping himself off — courtesy of Duchess, as per usual — before heading outside. Though her injuries had faded soon after she'd been able to drink from Xander and utilize the healing properties of his blood, she still looked haggard — as did Xander.

Mason made a point of speaking at length with Anel and his daughter Emily, who had taken over from him as the village healer. Anel apologized profusely for having fled Savaneaux with the children, rather than coming to Mason and Oksana's aid.

Doing so had been a totally rational decision on the old man's part, though, and Mason hastened to tell him that. Mason had left him alone, and Oksana had screamed shortly afterward. When Duchess brought the surviving children to the peristil and hurried off to help the others, Anel had no way whatsoever of knowing which way the battle would go.

Better to leave with the children than risk the bokor surviving the vampires' attack and coming after them. And he'd sent help back for them as soon as he could, after all.

Since then, Anel and Emily had been caring for the children as best they were able. Mason hated the fact that he'd been in no condition to assist with that. But the last thing a bunch of traumatized children needed was for Mason to lose his composure and terrify them with bared fangs or an unearthly, glowing stare.

Because his eyes, as he had discovered with one of Mama Lovelie's mirrors, now burned with an eerie cobalt-blue light when his hunger was roused. That had been more of a shock than it probably should have, given everything else he'd seen and experienced in the past few days. He supposed he was lucky that he still had a reflection at all.

Tonight, though, he let Anel and Emily take him around to meet the children they had rescued. He wanted to assess their condition for himself, even if he couldn't be as heavily involved in their care as he would have wished. Mama Lovelie and others with clout in the local area were already busy trying to track down the kids' relatives. Those with no family left, he planned to transfer to Port-au-Prince once he had a chance to speak with Gita.

And, oh, yeah—*that* was another conversation Mason wasn't much looking forward to. He suspected there would be several such conversations in his near future.

When the crowd started to feel overwhelming with its warm bodies and pumping blood, he sought out a quieter area. His newly uncanny night vision caught a glimpse of someone seated in the shadows of a mapou tree, leaning back against the trunk. An instant later, his senses said *vampire*. A closer look revealed it to be Xander.

Mason wandered over and draped an arm over one of the low, thick branches, looking down at him.

"Lots of drunk people out there," he said by way of greeting. "Also a group having a choof around the back of the peristil. I've gotta say, mate, you're really not living up to your party animal reputation."

Xander peered up at him. "*Having a choof?* Good god, man, are you even speaking English right now?"

"Smoking marijuana," Mason clarified. "You know… weed? Ganga? Grass? Come on, Xander. I was told you were a man of the world."

Xander just raised a sardonic brow. "I hope you'll understand that I mean this in the most respectful way possible, Ozzie, but unless you've got something to say, please fuck off."

"All right, then," Mason said. "I'll be blunt. You and Duchess think I don't get it. But I do."

"Do you, now." Xander's voice was flat.

"About what you saw in Savaneaux? Yeah. I do. I'm a pediatric doctor who specializes in deprogramming adolescents, and I volunteer in war zones. I'll let you take a moment and do the math on that."

Silence was his only response, so Mason continued, "You tried to save innocent children. You gave it your all—everything you had inside you—but it wasn't enough. And then you watched them die right in front of your eyes. Been there. Done that. It's tattooed into my flesh so deep that I'll never be free of it. Is any of this starting to sound familiar?"

"Surprisingly enough, yeah," Xander muttered.

"So, is there anything I can do to help?" Mason asked.

"Not really. Duchess will do what she always does—go have sex with a bunch of pretty boys until she's able to stop thinking about it for a bit. And I'll do what I always do—drown my sorrows in the most exotic cocktail of drugs I can find contaminating a human bloodstream." He sighed, tilting his head back to look at the branches waving above them. "Maybe I'll go home for a bit. Just slip away by myself for a week or two."

"Is that wise, with the new reports coming out of Syria?" Mason asked, thinking of Oksana's comment about them staying together recently for safety.

Mason had immediately passed on what Jackson told him over the phone, but none of the vampires had been surprised. They'd been there, after all.

Xander only shrugged.

"On the positive side, Bael's low-level minions can't fly, and they're also painfully stupid." His tone darkened. "It's the higher-level ones you have to watch out for."

Mason pondered that, but let it go for now. "So, where's home for you, then? London?"

"Yeah." They were silent for a bit, though it was a surprisingly companionable silence. Eventually, Xander added, "Actually, there is something you can do for me."

"What's that?" Mason asked.

"You can tell me why the hell you're standing here like an idiot, talking to me, instead of talking to Oksana like you should be."

Mason sighed and firmed his jaw. "Touché, mate. All right. I'm going."

"About bloody time," Xander muttered under his breath as Mason turned around and headed back toward the festivities.

SEVENTEEN

Oksana stared at the plate of honey cakes set on the table in front of her, not truly seeing them. Once, for a little slave girl living on a cane plantation, honey cake had been a coveted treasure. Later, Augustin had indulged her sweet tooth to her heart's desire.

Now, the cakes might as well have been fashioned out of sawdust.

The sounds of late-night revelry drifted in through the windows of Mama Lovelie's house, teasing her sensitive ears as she sat alone in the dark, with only her misery for company. She knew she needed to snap out of it. All of them were suffering in their various ways — holed up here in this little village, licking their wounds.

Realistically, though, they couldn't hide here in the mambo's house forever. Xander had left a terse voicemail for Tré before the battery on their satellite phone completely gave up the ghost. She knew they would travel back to Port-au-Prince soon, so they could communicate more easily with the outside world.

As much as she dreaded it, Oksana needed rather desperately to talk to Eris. He was the one with the most knowledge about the prophecy. Because of her, a ninth vampire had been called into being — but, spirits above! How could she have fucked things up so badly? Had she ruined everything?

Thirteen vampires were supposed to come together, forming a council that could stand against Bael's power. For that, they would need to be united, surely. But if Mason didn't hate them already, he most certainly would once he'd had time to come to terms with what she'd *done* to him without his knowledge or permission.

He would hate her, at the very least. It only remained to be seen whether his hatred would be able to eclipse the burning hatred she felt for herself right now.

A soft noise penetrated her accelerating spiral of self-loathing. Someone had entered the house. Her life force recognized Mason's in the space of a single heartbeat, as though her guilt had somehow called him here to further torment her with her own failures. She pushed away from the table, poised to flee, but it was already too late. He was standing in the doorway, blocking her escape unless she wanted to shove right past him.

He was getting better at moving quickly and silently, it seemed.

"I was just—" she began.

"Oksana," he interrupted. "I've been dreaming, these past few days. I've seen... things. I've seen your husband, Augustin. The man you loved. The man you killed. *I'm not him.*"

Her knees gave way, and she fell back into the chair.

"You are, though," she said. "And I stole your life a few days ago, as surely as I stole it then. I murdered your humanity and condemned you to a life of darkness without your consent."

Mason dragged a chair over to sit in front of her and lowered himself onto it deliberately. His storm-blue eyes met hers, holding them as he spoke. "I told you that I dreamed. And, all right, maybe I am somehow connected to this man from the past. I guess it wouldn't be the maddest thing I've seen or experienced over the past week. But I'm still not him. I'm me, and you need to have this conversation with *me*. Not with a man who's been dead for more than two hundred years."

He was right, of course. She owed him that much. She nodded, not speaking.

"Good," he said. "So. First things first. Do you know what happens when someone on a battlefield or in a disaster zone needs emergency medical care? Let's say... someone's trapped under debris. He's unconscious, and his legs are crushed under tons of concrete."

She stared at him, not sure where he was going with this.

"Without help, that person will die in fairly short order," Mason continued. "But the only way to save him is to amputate his trapped limbs, which will alter his life irrevocably. He's unconscious; he can't give informed consent, and there's no time to try to track down someone with power of attorney. So who decides?"

"It's not the same thing —" she protested.

He cut her off with a shake of his head. "The doctors decide. Two doctors can agree that emergency amputation is the only viable response, and if they do, the patient's consent is unnecessary. Doing nothing would be fatal, so doing *something* is the best available option."

His eyes bored into hers. "If you and the others hadn't turned me, would I be dead now? Yes or no."

"Yes," she said, pain wracking her.

"Then by human reckoning, you did nothing wrong," he said.

She stared into his eyes with the same intensity. "And by your reckoning?"

"By my reckoning? I'm not dead. I'm still here. As far as I can see, that's a win."

A new question clawed its way up her throat. "Why did you come after me when I went to fight the bokor?" she asked. "Why did you leave the peristil, when you *knew* how dangerous it was?"

"Because somehow, I knew you needed me," he said simply.

Mason reached out, covering her hand with one of his. She caught her breath at the low thrum of power emanating outward from the contact — deeper and more insistent than ever, now that he'd left his mortal life behind.

"I came because of *this*," he continued. "You're the one who told me there's an unbreakable bond between us. Looks like you were right."

She was trapped like a fly in amber between his stormy eyes and the magnetic pull of his touch.

"But, Mason," she breathed, "I've done almost nothing but try to push you away."

"True. But I know now that you thought you were doing it to protect me," he said. "And I realized something else, though it took two different people calling me an idiot for it to really penetrate. Gotta say, I've been called a lot of things over the years, but not that."

"You aren't an idiot, Mason," Oksana said. "Far from it."

"On the contrary," Mason insisted, "they were both absolutely right. I've been a Grade A, bone-headed fool."

She shook her head in bewilderment. "Why would you say such a thing?"

A rueful smile tugged at one corner of his lips. "I'm a certified halfwit, because I haven't done this again."

His free hand came up to cradle the side of her face, and he leaned forward, drawing her toward him until his lips brushed hers — soft as the finest silk. She choked down the sob that wanted to rise and reached for him. Oksana could no sooner have stopped herself than she could stop the tide. His tongue teased the seam of her lips, and he made a noise of want that shattered any misconceptions she might still have had about his feelings toward her.

His fangs lengthened, new instincts not yet under his control. The kiss deepened, and one of those razor-sharp points pierced her lower lip with a bright flash of pleasure-pain. Blood welled up — thankfully purged of the bokor's poison now. Mason groaned, low and filthy, as he sucked the coppery drops into his mouth and rolled them over his tongue before swallowing.

He tore himself away from her mouth, breathing hard. "*God*," he said. "Please, Oksana... please, I n-need—" He closed his eyes, which were glowing with a desire and bloodlust that called to her like siren song. "I need more. Nothing Duchess or Xander gave me felt right. It's *your* blood I crave—"

She felt her own fangs lengthen in response and knew her eyes were glowing with violet light. In a flash, she was straddling him on the chair, pressed against him from pelvis to chest, pulling his head down to her throat.

The feral growl he released when his lips and fangs brushed the side of her neck went straight to her sex. When he pierced her skin, she gasped like a drowning woman and rolled her hips against his growing hardness, needing to feel him like this so badly, it hurt.

The sensation as he drew the first mouthful from her vein was completely different from any of the other hundreds of times another vampire had fed from her. It made her freeze in surprise, only to melt against him in ecstasy a moment later. He made low, male noises of pleasure, each swallow echoed by a twitch of the thick length she was mindlessly rocking against.

The mental link between them, which lay nascent until now, flared into life as their essences mixed and swirled together.

Finally... finally... so good... so beautiful and perfect...

His nearly mindless chant as he drank from her neck chased away any lingering doubts about the sincerity of his feelings. When he finished and reluctantly pulled away, she had to fight the wash of disappointment at the loss. He rested his forehead on her shoulder, panting.

"Oksana," he said hoarsely. "I need all of you. Please say yes..."

It was all she could do not to start rending the fabric of his clothing with inhuman strength, right there in Mama Lovelie's sitting room. But... he needed to know what he'd already gotten a glimpse of, the first time they'd kissed.

Mason, she sent along the bond. *You have to know first that something inside me is broken. You saw before, when I lost myself to the past after I kissed you. The feelings you stir in me... they're all tangled up with what Bael did to me, and what I did to you. Or rather, what I did to Augustin.*

Mason straightened so that he could meet her eyes, and she could feel through the link as he dragged his need under control.

"You're not broken," he said aloud, "and did I happen to mention that I'm a doctor who specializes in helping people move beyond traumatic experiences?"

His crooked smile, along with the feel of his emotions through the mental connection, robbed the words of any sting they might have had beyond gentle teasing.

She found an answering smile for him, though it was tremulous. Her voice was wry when she said, "I imagine none of your previous patients have been nursing their post-traumatic stress disorder for more than two centuries."

He raised an eyebrow. "Maybe not. But that only means you already have some pretty damned good coping mechanisms in place." He regarded her for a moment, his eyes fading back to their normal ocean blue. "You're claustrophobic, but moments after I met you, you were crawling through a collapsed building. How did you do that?"

Humiliation rose to her cheeks. "No great feat of psychology there, I'm afraid. I told Xander and Duchess to give me a mental smack upside the head if they felt me start to lose my shit."

He snorted in amusement, but the feeling leaking through the bond was respect. "An elegant and no-

nonsense solution," he said, succinctly. "Why am I not surprised in the least?"

He lifted a hand to smooth her hair back, his thumb brushing her temple. "Okay, next question. Do you trust me to listen through the mental link while we make love? I probably still suck at using it, I'm afraid. Duchess tried to show me, but it was only just now that I really started to feel it properly."

Mason, she sent, *if I didn't trust you, I'd be shielding. Being able to sense you like this is one of the most incredible things I've ever felt in my life.*

He made another one of those low noises that played havoc with her senses. *Then let me look after you. Because I have an idea about that.*

His communication was a little clumsy... a little louder than it needed to be. It also made her want to burrow into his aura of protective warmth and never see the light of day again. Could she do this? Could she let go and trust Mason to keep her from falling?

Please, she said. *Help me stay here in the present. With you. I can't do it alone.*

Saying it so bluntly along the bond almost felt... *freeing*. She was still straddling him, but now she was the one burying her face in the crook of his neck, as his muscular arms wrapped around her back and held her close. Utilizing the new strength that came with vampirism, he moved one hand down to cradle her hip and stood up, still holding her against him.

"Does the door on the guest room lock?" he asked, with the barest hint of humor. "I can't really say I'm in the mood to give our hostess—or anyone else—a free show."

"Sorry. You won't find locking doors in a place like this," she said, wrapping her legs around his hips carefully, so as not to accidentally stab him with the Cheetah's epoxy arch. "But the others won't be back for hours yet."

I'm going to hold you to that prediction, he sent, his mental voice already gaining confidence. His tone of delicious promise sent a clench of desire through her belly.

The small guest room only held a single, narrow bed. While it was far from grand; compared to the slave shack in which she'd grown up, it was a palace. And given a choice between being back at the Royal Oasis in Pétionville, or here with Mason—feeling fragile tendrils of hope for the future unfurl behind her ribs—she would choose this simple house in rural Haiti any day of the week.

I'm right there with you, sweetheart, Mason said, setting her down with infinite care. *Luxurious trappings are overrated. Though I'll admit I'm relieved as well—I did warn you I was a poor doctor, not a rich one.*

The mattress was soft beneath her back. She smiled up at him, a feeling growing inside her that she tentatively identified as… *joy.*

"Here's what's going to happen next," he said, his fingers caressing the contours of her face. "I'm going to taste every single square inch of your body."

Her eyes flared as he straightened away from the bed and began matter-of-factly unbuttoning his shirt.

"And the instant I sense that you're starting to drift away from me," he continued, "I'm going to do something to remind you just exactly where you are and who you're with. I'm going to bite you, and I'm going to drink from you."

A rush of heat swept over her cool flesh from the roots of her hair to the toes of her right foot. "*Yes…*" she breathed.

The shirt slid to the ground, and Mason pulled off the black tee he wore underneath. His were not the sculpted muscles of a gym rat, but rather the hard muscles of real use—hauling crates of medical supplies, trekking from village to village to meet with rebel leaders, swinging a hammer to fix and maintain substandard facilities.

He toed off his shoes, his hands dropping to the fastening of his trousers as he went on. "Then, when you're crying out my name, begging me to take you, I'm going to sink my fangs and my cock so deep inside you that all you'll be able to feel is *me*."

Trousers and boxers slid down together. A lust far different than the sweet and tender excitement she'd felt as a girl in Augustin's arms surged up. It was the lust of one dark creature for another—the part of herself that Oksana had spent centuries denying, controlling, and subsuming.

Now… it wanted *out*.

She scrabbled at her top, dragging it off. After a mere moment's frustration with her sports bra, she ripped it down the middle—not really having intended to do so, but not particularly worried about it either. Meanwhile, Mason had crawled onto the foot of the bed, and was now prowling up her body to drag off her shorts and panties.

When he pulled them down to her knees and then paused, it was as though someone had thrown a bucket of ice water on her. He was looking at her prosthesis. Her breath caught in her throat, but Mason only threw her a gently chiding look, and paused in his removal of her shorts to ease her leg free of the Cheetah's molded sleeve.

He set it aside on the floor near the bed, and pulled everything else off, leaving her bare. Despite her best efforts, her mind hummed with uncertainty.

Well, now, sweetheart. Mason's mental tone was wry, but there was a hint of sadness in it, as well. *I think that solves my dilemma of where to start first.*

She watched in amazement—in near disbelief—as he cradled her left leg and pressed an open-mouthed kiss below her knee, only inches above where the limb

750

terminated in an ugly stump. It was such an odd feeling, that gentle press of lips. With the exception of the occasional lucky blow by an opponent during a fight, no one had touched her there since—

Since… well… *ever*.

How could he stand to *do* that? It was such a hideous deformity, with the puckered scars and the muscles atrophied—the visual distillation of her monstrous nature. Of the unnatural *thing* she'd become, in those moments when she'd awoken underground and started tearing at the boards of the coffin… at her own flesh and bone…

Fangs sank into her leg, and the twin flashes of pain followed by a deep, drawing heat jerked her back to the present with a gasp.

I did warn you, Mason sent.

He drew another mouthful of her blood from the wound, and the wash of carnal pleasure that flooded the bond from both directions blasted away the unwanted memories under its force.

"M-Mason," she moaned, and received an answering rumble as he pulled out, lapping at the wounds until they closed.

He resumed kissing his way up her leg, awakening every nerve as he passed. It had been *so long*. So long since she'd felt anything more intimate than a chaste kiss on the cheek or a sisterly embrace. And when she had felt something like this, all those long years ago, Augustin had always started at her breasts, cupping and teasing them. Not running his tongue up the inside of her leg, teasing his way slowly upward—

I told you, said the voice twining inside her mind, *I'm not him.*

Fangs slid into the sensitive flesh high on the inside of her thigh, and she cried out, writhing, hands clawing at the bedclothes as he drank again. The dark lust from earlier surged back, swamping thought and leaving only need behind.

Mason pulled his fangs out and caught her wrists, pinning them by her hips when she reached for him. *Fuck, yes,* he thought, *That's it — I don't want you thinking, Oksana. I want you feeling.*

And, oh, was she feeling. She felt every wrinkle in the blanket beneath her as she twisted restlessly against the bed. She felt the addictive jolt of pleasure through the bond as Mason's hips flexed unconsciously against the mattress upon seeing her give herself up to sensation — give herself up to *him.*

She felt the ache of delicious frustration as he continued to kiss up her body, bypassing the place that burned for his touch, in favor of sucking marks onto her belly that faded almost as fast as he could make new ones.

She didn't slide into the past again. Yet he still pierced her with his fangs and drank, over and over, because they were vampires and they both wanted it, and why shouldn't he?

At some point, he released her wrists. By the time he finally kissed his way up her neck to her lips, she was growling and digging furrows into his back with her fingernails. She quieted when his mouth slanted over hers, demanding entrance, teasing her tongue out to duel with his. He coaxed her to invade his mouth in return, sucking on her tongue as his fangs scraped deliciously against her tender flesh.

Her sex throbbed, aching and wet, though he'd barely so much as brushed it with his lips on his way up her body. She tore her mouth away from the kiss, tasting blood, though she wasn't sure whose.

"Take me, damn it!" she nearly snarled. "Take me right now, Mason, or I swear I'll drink you dry, just so I can feed you our mingled blood and then do it all over again!"

Some tiny, quiet part of herself was completely shocked by both the threat, and how very much she meant it. But Mason was a vampire now. She couldn't hurt him by feeding from him. Nothing she could do to him with her fangs would damage him permanently. Quite the opposite. The wall of lust that slammed into her from his side of the mental link proved that if she did get the upper hand on him in such a way, he would go down happy and come back looking forward to the next round.

We might need to work on your begging skills just a bit, sweetheart, he sent, even his mental voice sounding breathless. *But in the mean time, far be it from me to argue.*

A strong thigh forced her legs apart, and teeth sank into her neck, pinning her in place as his cock, large and blunt, slid along the folds of her sex, further enflaming her. She canted her hips, lining him up, and keened as he thrust inside her tight passage.

After so long untouched, the sudden penetration was savage, punishing, and perfect. It was everything she needed, and nothing like *anything* she'd ever had before. It was exactly what her inner darkness craved. She didn't want time to adjust to his girth piercing her. She didn't want tenderness and sweet nothings whispered in her ear. She wanted her mate, all at once, here, now, with nothing held back.

Her fingernails raked down Mason's back and dug into the hard globes of his arse, dragging him into her body over and over as they sweated and writhed together. Her head started to swim as he drained her blood, the room growing dim and hazy around her. Oksana's perception narrowed, all the unimportant things falling away, one by one, until everything was focused on those two incandescent points of contact between them.

She reveled in the feeling of their life force twining together. In the way his pleasure grew and grew, until he jerked his head away from her neck, red liquid dripping down his chin and pleasure coiling at the base of his spine, ready to explode.

She surged up, fangs tearing into his neck, swallowing great mouthfuls of their combined blood as he cried out. He jerked into her, arms holding her tightly to him as his blood and seed filled her at the same time, flooding her with their mingled power. Ecstasy shook free from her center, spreading outward through her awareness in great, rolling waves until she was certain her body would not be able to contain it all.

When the blood red haze across her vision finally faded, it revealed that she and Mason had collapsed into a tangled heap on the narrow bed. He'd rolled to the side just enough not to crush her, but her legs around his hips meant that his length was still nestled intimately inside her.

"Bloody *Christ*," he mumbled against her neck. "Oksana…"

She held him in a tight embrace, something like awe blanketing her mind.

I guess I was a bit overdue when it comes to accepting what I am now, she thought, a bit sheepishly.

A puff of cool breath against her collarbone accompanied the Mason's flash of exhausted amusement. *Well, whenever you need a reminder…*

I know exactly where to come, she agreed.

He lifted his head enough to look at her with eyes still lit from within with sparks of cobalt. She smiled, bringing a finger up to swipe a thin trail of red from his lips before sucking it clean. Despite the shattering climax they'd just shared, his cock twitched inside her at the sight. They both shivered in reaction, oversensitive, and she reluctantly let him slip free.

"I don't know how I could possibly have gotten this lucky," she said, the words barely more than a whisper.

His mouth twitched. "Funny, I was thinking very nearly the same thing." He rolled them into a more comfortable position in the cramped space, her head resting on his chest, one arm and one leg flung over him.

"I can't say that I'm not terrified by what's coming," he said truthfully. "But it would still be coming whether we'd found each other or not, Oksana. This way, we have someone to lean on, when times get hard. I'm so glad that we stumbled into each others' lives."

Tears clogged Oksana's throat, and she didn't fight them. Unlike all the bitter ones that had choked her over the past days, these felt cleansing. Freeing.

Mason must have sensed that, because he only held her tighter against him as she let them run their course.

"I was lost," she said, once they'd passed. "I've been lost for *so long*, Mason. But you've showed me the way home."

They kissed, with none of the urgency of lust, and none of the bitterness of the painful past. When Oksana finally pulled away, she settled back against him and traced her fingers over the hard lines of his chest.

"What will you do about the clinic?" she asked, knowing that she would do anything in her power to support whatever he decided.

"I don't know yet. I plan to talk to Gita—she's my partner there." Mason met her eyes, his expression serious. "I intend to tell her the truth, Oksana. I trust her with my life, and something inside me says that it's time for us to stop living in the shadows."

A week ago, Oksana might have protested. But she had felt the same thing in the last few days. "I'll speak with the others," she promised. "But I think you may be right about that. It feels as though something is changing. Something fundamental."

He nodded.

"What about family?" she asked. "Do you have any?"

"My mother is in Australia, at a nursing home in Sydney. She has early-onset Alzheimer's. I'd like to visit her, but it's unlikely she'll recognize me," he said, and she could feel the old pain leaking through the link. "I have a brother, though. In Singapore. His name's Jackson. We're as close as two people can be, who live on opposite sides of the world. So that's another difficult conversation I need to have."

"Then we'll go to Singapore together, if that's what you want," she said.

He smiled. "I'd like that. He's going to go head over heels for you, you know. I bet his wife and their kids will, too."

A faintly sheepish look came over his face, and Oksana looked at him questioningly. "What is it?" she asked.

"As it happens, you've got Jack to thank for us being here right now," he said. "He's one of the two people who called me an idiot."

That strange, unfamiliar feeling of joy crept over Oksana once more. "In that case, I'm even more excited about meeting him. Though he was still wrong."

"You two can argue that one without me," he said with a smile. He paused and gave a short laugh. "Oh. You know what? That just reminded me of something. Stay here for a tick."

He eased out of bed and rummaged through the pockets of his discarded trousers in the dark. When he came back, he held a mobile phone. Oksana looked at him curiously, but didn't protest as he got back into bed and arranged the blanket over them, pulling her back to rest against his chest when they were settled.

"That's not a sat-phone," she pointed out. "You won't be able to get a signal out here."

"I know," he said. "The battery's about dead, anyway. But Jack has been after me since the day you and I met to send him a picture. I assume since I still have a reflection, that means I can take a photo?"

Oksana nodded, amused.

Mason unlocked the screen and pulled up the camera app, before holding the phone out at arm's length and angling it toward their faces. "I think this one will convey all the relevant information, don't you?"

She laughed softly. "I guess it will, at that."

His chest moved beneath her cheek as he chuckled. "Smile for the camera…"

She did, not blinking as the flash went off. He brought the phone down and tapped the screen, bringing the photo up for her to see.

He'd been absolutely right. His incandescent look of happiness, combined her satisfied, cat-with-the-cream smile, would tell anyone who saw it *exactly* what they needed to know.

No question about it.

EPILOGUE

London, two weeks later

Xander's mobile phone buzzed in his trouser pocket, and he ignored it. Like clockwork, some thirty seconds later, it vibrated again to indicate a new voicemail. After debating with himself for the space of a few heartbeats while the pounding bass of the club's music system throbbed through his chest, he pulled it out.

Under the strobing blacklight, his pale skin looked even paler than usual. His hand felt pleasantly and ever so slightly disconnected from the rest of him, after the blood he'd just drunk from a random junkie who'd been skulking around the hallway in the back. He flicked a thumb across the screen lock, unsurprised to see Tré's number at the top of the notification list.

Tré's smooth, Eastern European accent competed with the deep house track rumbling through the club, only vampire hearing allowing Xander to untangle his words from the din around him.

"Xander. Pick up your damned phone. Disappearing like this is foolhardy under the present circumstances, as you well know." A pause. *"Oksana is concerned for you, tovarăș."*

Xander ground his jaw for a moment before opening up a text window.

Fuck off, Tré. You can give me a damned week without breathing down my neck every fifteen minutes.

The reply came almost instantly.

Are you in London?

Of course I'm in bloody London. Now. Fuck. Off.

He powered the phone off and slipped it carelessly back in his pocket. Already, his pleasant buzz was wearing off, his undead metabolism breaking down the drugs in minutes. Just another one of the many, many shitty things about vampirism.

The atmosphere of *Club Cirque* wrapped around him like barbed wire dipped in anesthetic. Hidden under the rails not far off Lambeth Road, the only public access was through an unmarked railway arch that looked like nothing so much as a simple garage.

Lambeth at large had a reputation—not undeserved—of being home to gangs, drugs, and murderers. *Club Cirque* had a reputation of being home to freaks—also, not undeserved. Dressed in a burgundy button-down, black tailored trousers, and polished Berluti Scritto shoes, Xander's only real concession to the unofficial dress code had been to undo a couple of buttons at the top of his shirt, baring a triangle of pale chest and collarbone.

By rights, this should have made him stand out like a sore thumb among the sea of tattoos, piercings, whips, chains, leather, and dyed hair. That was the thing about freaks, though—they always recognized their own.

His black mood settled firmly back around his shoulders, and he scanned the crowd. Alcoholics weren't going to do it for him tonight. Where was a heroin addict when you really needed one?

A small commotion erupted at the entrance to the hallway where Xander had partaken of his second-hand coke hit a little while ago. It was a woman, maybe thirty years of age with waist-length black hair and a light brown complexion with olive undertones. Her dark eyes were wide, and more than a little frantic looking. Like him, she was not decked out for a place like this—indeed, the look she was sporting could best be described as *newly homeless*. Yet something about her made his intuition tingle.

She was stopping people, talking to them urgently, but they brushed her off. She cast around, saw Xander looking, and closed the distance between them. Something odd teased his nose, but it was impossible to place it within the potent cloud of perfume, smoke, and human body odor that choked the atmosphere of the underground venue.

"Please, I need help," she said, a faint accent coloring the words. Indian—probably from the Kashmir region or thereabouts.

He leaned against the bar, regarding her from his advantage of height. "Sorry, luv. I'm off the clock tonight. The bartender can call 999 for you if it's an emergency."

She shook her head. "No, you don't understand. It's my sister. Some… *thing* attacked us in the alley, and she got in front of me. She's hurt—I can't wake her up."

Xander stopped himself before he could say, *A mugging in Lambeth? How shocking*, because there was being brusque, and then there was being unnecessarily arsehole-ish.

"Emergency services can send an ambulance around," he said instead, and started to raise a hand to get the barman's attention.

"But the thing that attacked us!" she said, her voice rising. "It wasn't human!"

He lowered his hand.

Don't get involved, counseled the truncated and badly atrophied remnants of his good sense. *You need this kind of shit right now like you need eight hours inside a full-spectrum tanning booth.*

"What do you mean, not human?" he asked, sounding tired even to his own ears.

"It was a child," she said, her wide brown eyes begging him to believe her. "But he had these eerie, glowing eyes, and he moved so fast he seemed to blur. Right before he leapt at my sister, he sort of snarled at us, and I swear I saw these long, sharp teeth—like fangs!"

Xander's brain crashed to a standstill, thoughts piling up like derailed train cars.

"What." His tone was utterly flat.

"Please—I'm not crazy! I know what I saw!" She gestured the way she'd come. "Just come back with me and help me with my sister... her neck's all torn up and I'm afraid by the time an ambulance gets here it will be too late!"

Had he said *heroin addict*? After this, he'd need to bypass heroin altogether, and go straight for meth. He pushed away from the bar. If nothing else, he could at least open a vein and heal the poor girl's neck, assuming she wasn't already dead.

"Come on, then," he said, "show me." The implications, if this woman had actually seen what she described...

But, no. Implications could wait until he saw the victim and the scene for himself. His companion broke into a run, and he jogged alongside her to keep up. The tradesmen's entrance to the club consisted of a flight of stairs next to a rickety lift designed to ferry freight up and down to street level. They took the stairs two at a time, and the woman pushed through the double doors leading to the dingy alley running behind the railway arches.

"She's just up here," the woman said breathlessly, gesturing toward a darker stretch of shadows that ended in a solid brick wall.

Xander opened his mouth to ask what the hell two women had been doing walking through a dark, dead-end alley at four in the morning, but then the stench of the place assailed him and he snapped it shut again, grimacing. Piss, vomit, rotting garbage, animal droppings, and—

"Over here." She waved him toward a gap between a dumpster and some discarded truck tires.

—and wet dog.

He whirled back toward the mouth of the alley, in time to see around a dozen feral looking men and women melt out of the shadow, blocking the exit. His erstwhile damsel in distress turned and darted past him to join the group. He let her go.

"Oh, you have *got* to be shitting me," Xander said, wondering for a bare instant which god he'd managed to piss off this time, and how big of a charitable donation it would take to get back on that deity's good side.

"Sorry," the dark-haired woman told him, sounding genuinely sheepish. She jerked her chin at the man next to her, who was decked out in chains and ripped camo like some sort of cut-rate Mad Max reject. "He didn't think you'd come if you knew what we really were, vampire."

"Smarter than he looks, then," Xander said blandly. "Good to know."

The man's answering smile was thin and cruel. "You'd be amazed." He cocked his head. "No doubt you're getting ready to fly away home, little vamp, but you should hear what I have to tell you first. I've got something you want."

"You think so?" Xander asked. "What is it? Fleas? Kibbles? A squeaky toy? Maybe a nice, meaty bone?"

That cruel smile never wavered. "I've got that little baby vamp Manisha described to you, all chained up in iron shackles so he can't get away. Interested, now?"

"God, I fucking hate werewolves," Xander told him, tone still conversational. "Have I mentioned that yet?"

"Oh, well. Off you flap, then," the leader said, making a shooing motion with one hand. "Nothing stopping you, is there? Not unless you want us to take you to see Junior first…"

Xander gritted his teeth, wanting nothing more at that moment than the human ability to crawl into a bottle, get blind, falling-down drunk, and never crawl back out.

"Fine, Fluffy," he grated. "You win. Take me to see this alleged vampire, and I won't brandish the rolled-up newspaper."

Fluffy's flat, hard eyes were starting to make Xander's skin crawl, quite honestly. But he held back any further insults as Fluffy shrugged a brawny shoulder.

"That's real magnanimous of you, mate," said the werewolf. "Best follow us, in that case. Dawn's coming soon. You wouldn't want to get a terminal case of sunburn, now would you?"

Actually, mate, Xander thought sourly, *you might be surprised. Lately, that prospect has been growing more appealing by the day.*

finis

The *Circle of Blood* series continues in *Book Four: Lover's Absolution.*

To get the free prequel to the *Circle of Blood* series sent directly to your inbox, visit www.rasteffan.com/circle

37511425R10422

Made in the USA
Lexington, KY
27 April 2019